DIVA

DIVA

a novel

CAROL KANE

HarperCollins*Publishers*

FIRST EDITION

Designed by Cassandra J. Pappas

Library of Congress Cataloging-in-Publication Data

Kane, Carol J.
   Diva / Carol Kane.
     p.   cm.
   ISBN 0–06–016319–4
   I. Title.
 PS3561.A467D58   1990
 813'.52—dc20   89–46570

90 91 92 93 94   WB/HC   10 9 8 7 6 5 4 3 2 1

To Tom Miller,
my editor and best audience

"If music be the food of love, play on."

—WILLIAM SHAKESPEARE,
Twelfth Night

CHAPTER 1

*T*he Capetown courtroom was hot. Even the six spindly ceiling fans did nothing to provide relief, although they kept churning doggedly, high above the heads of the perspiring spectators. The atmosphere was so tense in that crowded room, nobody was even remarking upon the temperature. They had more crucial matters on their minds.

"Mrs. Devereux," whispered her husband's lawyer, "the bailiff tells me Pat's about to be brought in for the sentencing."

Young Maeve glanced nervously at the two grown-ups, her mother and the lawyer. Their faces were nearly the same color—dead white despite all the heat. It couldn't be a good sign. Her mother looked as if she were about to faint, and Moira Devereux had never been known to faint in her life. Maeve was terrified.

"There are an awful lot of soldiers here today," Maeve observed suddenly, taking in the khaki crowd ringing the courtroom. "Outside the building too. Do you suppose the Brits expect some trouble?"

"They'll surely get it if they hand down the wrong sentence," Moira snapped, rallying a little.

"Watch it, Moira," cautioned the lawyer, a Jack Sanders. "None of that, or all hell will break loose. These bastards will arrest half the people here. And you first of all."

Moira flashed him a look of contempt and proceeded to fan herself with the square bit of printed parchment on an ebony stick distributed by a local funeral parlor. "We try to ease your sorrow," claimed the message below a sentimental scene of fluffy sheep in a dark valley. Maeve supposed it had to do with a few psalms, mixed together for maximum effect. It wasn't easing *their* sorrow.

Sanders noticed how alike the two women were, as if he were seeing them for the first time. Seated next to them in the stifling courtroom, he observed their nearly matching profiles, very refined, very delicate. They resembled each other even more than most mothers and daughters, despite the difference of their beautiful hair. Moira's was black and glossy, Maeve's a gleaming shade of mahogany. Both wore elegant white linen shirtwaists and the new trumpet skirt. Both sat on the courtroom's rickety wooden chairs as if they were perched on gilded red velvet seats at Windsor Castle. They certainly had an air. Sanders dreaded their reactions.

"Remember," stated the lawyer, choosing his words carefully, "the judge is under pressure himself to make an example of Pat. If there's any kind of protest, it will make things even worse for him."

Maeve's large blue eyes sought his. "How many years do you reckon?" How could they take her father away from her and her mother?

"Hard to predict. But I'm inclined to suspect the maximum. Remember, Pat was an administrator in the colonial civil service. He committed treason."

"Oh God," murmured Moira. "Here they come!"

Hearts pounding, Maeve Devereux and her mother rose with the rest of the spectators as the British judge entered the courtroom and strode majestically to the bench, his white wig and black robe comically out of place in this African torpor. Maeve peered intently at his fat, florid face: ugly old man. Trying to detect a trace of kindness on that Yorkshire pudding of a face, she failed entirely.

"Bring in the prisoner."

Other things were said, other commands given, but "Bring in the prisoner" was all Maeve and Moira heard. Shortly afterward, a tall, sandy-haired man in handcuffs was escorted into the room by six British troopers.

Ah, the bastards, thought Moira, filled with rage as she clutched the stem of her fan. Handcuffed! Are they so afraid of him, then? She tried unsuccessfully to catch her husband's eye, to let him know she was with him. He looked haggard, as if he hadn't slept in days. She began anxiously to search his face for any trace of a beating, suspecting his captors of the worst.

Maeve felt her insides turn to ice as she clung to her mother's hand. The shock of seeing her father like this—a prisoner in handcuffs—was so great, she began to have difficulty breathing. Heat and fear were making her light-headed. She felt herself floating on a cloud of sheer hysteria. Moira stared straight ahead, fixing the judge with a look of pure animal hatred.

The lawyer was beginning to sweat in earnest now. There were too many soldiers, enough to put down a small rebellion if they had to. These troopers had already fixed bayonets. What the hell did *that* mean?

As the bewigged judge began his address to the prisoner, upbraiding him for the crime he had committed in time of war—aiding and abetting the rebels—Maeve suddenly knew why the soldiers were there.

"Prisoner at the bar, the sentence of the court upon you is that you be taken from hence to the place from which you came and thence to a place of execution, and you be there hanged by the neck until you be dead and your body buried in the precincts of the prison in which you shall last have been confined, and may the Lord have mercy on your soul."

A stunned gasp greeted the sentence, quickly followed by pandemonium. Pat turned chalky white, then became crimson as he roared something at the judge. At a furious gesture from His Lordship, the soldiers surrounded the prisoner to haul him out of the room, but not before Moira had rushed from her seat and thrown her arms around Pat's neck.

"Order in the court!"

It was a madhouse. Men were shouting, women sobbing, soldiers barking orders all at once. Screams of outrage filled the air on one side, cries for order on the other. Maeve looked on in stunned disbelief at the finality of the sentence. Then she saw the soldiers forcibly tearing Moira from her husband as they dragged him away, Pat shouting in protest at the court's decision. It couldn't be true, Maeve thought. She was dreaming this.

"Maeve!" he cried out as he fought with his escorts at the door, "I . . ." But whatever words he intended to leave her with were drowned out in all the uproar and he was gone, hustled half off his feet by the troopers.

Moira was nearly out of her mind with fury. Fighting with the lawyer as he sought to restrain her, she knocked him off balance and took hold of one of the rickety chairs. While the rest of the spectators created their own ruckus, beautiful Moira Devereux locked eyes with the astonished presiding judge and hurled two chairs straight at his head. His Lordship sensibly ducked, but not before Maeve had followed her mother's example and let fly with an inkwell plucked from a nearby table. When the judge rose again from behind his bench, he and his regalia were dripping with black splotches. So was half the room.

"Bailiff!" he shouted, rapping his gavel so ferociously it split in two. "Arrest these two women for contempt of court and assault."

"Contempt isn't the word for it, you murdering bloody bastard!" screamed Moira despite her lawyer's frantic efforts to keep her quiet. "It's you who ought to be hanged for what you just did to my husband! You dirty savage!"

Both women were wild, their hair flying every which way, their lovely faces distorted with rage. Jack Sanders cringed. He knew the judge and he was terrified for these two.

Maeve clung to Moira, her head spinning. She wanted to take a rifle and shoot the old scoundrel. She would have given anything to be able to kill this man who was legally murdering her father. How dare he?

Flushed with anger, His Lordship was intoning, ". . . you will both be transported to the prison camp for noncombatants in the East Transvaal. Take them away. Now!"

That was the last thing Maeve could ever remember about her brush with British justice, because before the soldiers could take hold of her, she turned to spit in the judge's face and was knocked to the floor unconscious. When she came to, she was handcuffed, sitting beside Moira in a prison train and on her way to her fate.

Before the women reached their destination, Pat Devereux's dead body was being collected by the same undertaker who had distributed the fans.

Unable to hide his tears, Jack Sanders paid for the burial and thought wretchedly of those two beautiful women headed for hell in the Transvaal. They wouldn't survive a week out there. It was judicial murder all over again, as if His Lordship wished to make damned certain he was safe from all Devereux everywhere.

"Ah, Maeve," he murmured to no one in particular. "It would kill your da all over again to know what that old bastard's done to you and Moira."

And there was not one damned thing anybody could do about it.

*

Led from the courtroom straight to a waiting train, Moira and her daughter were in a state of shock as much from their grief as from the sudden upheaval of their whole world. It was no longer Mrs. Patrick

Devereux, wife of the personable colonial administrator and British civil servant, with an attractive home and a clutch of African domestics—it was Moira Devereux, wife of the "traitor." Jesus! How could he have done this to her? And Maeve, too, poor thing! The man must have been daft! It was one thing to hate the Brits in Ireland and try to pry them loose, and quite another to go and wreck a perfectly happy life in the colonies and cause untold misery to your helpless wife and child as you did it. It wasn't fair, Moira lamented. It was a cruel fate for her— ruined along with him.

Maeve stood staring out between the bars of the prison train, tears coursing down her pale cheeks, seeing nothing of the landscape, the people, the color of the sky. All she could see was Papa under guard in that hot courtroom, a helpless prisoner sentenced to be hanged as a traitor to the Crown. It wasn't *his* country he was betraying, Maeve thought angrily. His country was far over the water. It wasn't her country either, as far as she was concerned, she had no country. She was Irish by blood, South African by a quirk of fate—and therefore a British subject by law. But it would take more than their law to ever make her *feel* British.

Remembering the home she would probably never see again, Maeve thought of all the happy times she and her family had had there— the musicales Moira used to give, with her at the piano and Maeve, in her pretty white muslin dresses, singing the latest songs from the London music halls or the songs her parents liked to a wildly admiring audience who spoke of "the child's gift." Nobody ever sang "Kathleen Mavourneen" the way Papa did, she thought, not even John McCormack on the Victor recordings. That voice of his could make you weep from the sheer beauty of it. . . .

Those *had* been happy times, the house full of guests, the servants bustling about, seeing to it that nobody went hungry, Moira presiding over the table in her lovely gowns. Maeve used to hear some of the grown-ups whisper about her mother when they thought she was out of earshot, but she was never able to piece together enough of their conversation to make sense of it. Some of it was probably jealousy, she thought. Moira was young and beautiful—and admired by nearly every man in the area.

There was one party in particular, when some man from way up north, a fellow who escorted rich British lords into the bush to hunt big game, caused quite a stir with his Christmas present to her mother—a superb tiger skin. Maeve could still remember the feel of its fur as she ran her hand over it while Moira and Pat looked on in amazement,

Moira all pink with excitement and Pat rather flushed too, but not looking terribly pleased, even though it was a fine present, fit for royalty.

That was an exciting night, she remembered, although the men got very drunk and the big-game hunter had to be carried home by several of his friends. How the ladies had carried on about that present! Moira was in her glory, looking lovely in a pink silk gown with flowers in her black hair and a string of pearls around her throat. Her enjoyment of the whole evening was so evident, so childlike in its intensity, that it made you happy for her that she could feel such pleasure.

Papa always wanted her to be happy. He adored her, thought Maeve, the tears coming faster. Now what would happen to her, thrown into a cattle train with a hundred others who had also displeased the Crown?

Papa, Maeve thought miserably, I wish we were still together. We need you. We need you so much. . . .

But Pat Devereux had vanished from their life just as surely as all those happy times had. The parties, Moira's piano, the tiger skin, the guests who used to attend their parties, Maeve's little pet monkey—all were gone now and, from the look of things, not likely to come again. At least not in this lifetime.

CHAPTER 2

*E*re, you women, keep in line if you wants to eat. No talking allowed in line. That's right." This was from their jailer, a fat blond thing, irritable and coarse.

Sergeant Davies liked things neat and orderly in Camp 3, East Transvaal. He was personally responsible for one hundred thirty-seven Boer women and children—and two Irishwomen who annoyed him more than all the Dutch put together. His prisoners were there because their men had had the temerity to oppose His Majesty's Army. Some had been hanged, some were in the field right now, creating destruction and devastation in their wake. Sergeant Davies hated rebellious civilians. They spoiled the army's leisure-time activities.

Standing hands on hips just to the left of the cook, he watched the shabby procession of bedraggled females shuffle toward the huge iron pots, tin bowls in hand to receive a helping of slop from the cook's two assistants. Two big, burly fellows from Manchester, they looked on impassively as the women paused to hold out their tins for a dollop of sticky, molten stuff that resembled oatmeal or thick pea soup but was, in fact, neither. There were rumors that the cook had mixed dead insects into it for spite, but this was merely a gloomy view of things. What insects there were had traveled in large bags of flour from England. The cook was far too lazy and unimaginative to add anything.

"Jesus, Mary, and Joseph!" muttered the red-haired girl as she glanced down into her bowl. "The slop's alive!" Maeve was on the verge of nausea.

Shrieks of disgust greeted that observation as several women in back of her crowded around, peering into the girl's tin, chattering a mile a minute among themselves in Afrikaans and accusing Sergeant Davies in English of trying to poison them.

"Go on with you! Move the line along! Whatever it is, it's more than you deserve," he shouted, waving his arms in the air and turning scarlet with indignation. "You with the red hair—what's the matter now?"

She was a tall girl, perhaps sixteen or seventeen, and pretty—for an Irish kid. But a born troublemaker. Davies did not like the Irish, any Irish. He especially did not like Maeve Devereux or her mother, Moira, who gave herself airs and spoke English like the Queen. They were his prisoners and they made him feel inferior. It was a serious error of tact.

"This food is disgusting," stated Maeve, holding out her battered tin. "It isn't fit for your dogs."

All eyes turned toward the girl—the cook, his two assistants, and every Boer prisoner in line. Nobody ever confronted Davies.

The silence was eerie, broken only by the buzzing of several flies flitting nervously over the steaming caldrons, everyone bathed in the sweat of a hot sun and agonizing tension.

"Well, well. Disgusting, is it?" the sergeant replied, grinning. "Listen to her lidyship."

Maeve felt the color drain from her face as Sergeant Davies raised his fat, hairy paw and knocked the tin from her hand. The contents splattered over the dry, dusty ground at their feet, drawing a cluster of curious flies. For a second the girl thought she saw another cruel smile flicker across Davies's fat face, the badly shaved stubble glistening a little in the sun. And then a bright red flush spread across his face as he reached out and struck her a tremendous blow to the jaw, sending her sprawling.

"Now," roared the sergeant, "lick it up! All of it. Maggots and all."

Reeling from the pain, Maeve raised herself to a shaky, half-seated position and tried to focus her blue eyes. All she could see were grayish blobs of steaming slop, the dusty brown ground, and the scuffed shoes of the crowd gathering around her. Right before her were a pair of large, gleaming boots. Huge boots. She stared in fascination. Until this moment, she had never noticed what enormous feet the sergeant had.

"Eat it, I said!"

The cook exchanged glance with his helpers. Davies was a right bastard when he wanted to be. Angrily, the Boer women looked around, holding their tins, muttering in Afrikaans, waiting to see what happened next.

To everyone's surprise, Maeve rose unsteadily to her feet and stood, swaying slightly in the heat. Locking eyes with the sergeant, she announced quite clearly, "No. I will not." She was gloriously defiant.

Astonished, Davies gaped at her, his face red and stupid in the scorching sun.

Taking advantage of his stupor, the girl turned around slowly and began walking away, deliberately, purposefully, a cold sweat pouring down her face, seeping into the rough calico of her dress, making tiny rivulets on her dust-coated, sunburned skin.

Not a sound except the buzzing of the flies disturbed the deadly quiet. She kept going, her steps stiff with fear, her heart pounding. But she felt strangely exhilarated.

And then, as Davies took a step in Maeve's direction, beet red with fury at the sight of her retreating back, the cluster of Boer women surged around the iron caldrons once more, distracting him enough to enable him to recover himself and expend his energy screaming at them and at the cook's assistants for allowing such disorder in the line.

*

That night Maeve sat quietly in the sick bay, keeping her mother company. Moira had the fever and Maeve was fearful for her life. Maeve kept swabbing Moira's forehead with wet compresses, but that was all she could do. There wasn't a drop of medicine in the whole camp, and the Dutch Red Cross doctor who kept tabs on the inmates wasn't allowed back for at least three more days. In the meanwhile, Maeve sat, waited, and despaired.

If her beautiful, black-haired mother were to die in this place—and it seemed a foregone conclusion—there was not a soul in the world who would know or care. These awful people. First they killed her father and now her mother. It was the worst nightmare possible.

The light of the kerosene lamp cast strange shadows on the bare wooden walls of the hut. Moira Devereux lay on a straw mattress, drenched in sweat, her eyes open but unfocused, her glossy hair splayed across the coarse pillow. Maeve gently held her hand and glanced at her mother. Finally she released the sobs that were nearly strangling her and ran to the open door, where she doubled over in pain and grief. Pounding with fury on the rough wall, she shrieked, "They're killing her just the way they killed my father! Murderers! Bloody murderers!"

The Boer women tried vainly to comfort her, but sobbing, Maeve fled into the darkness of the prison yard, wanting only to be alone with her despair.

Several yards from the sick bay and separated from it by empty space and a fence of barbed wire stood the British army barracks, brightly lit by kerosene lamps. Sergeant Davies and his men sat smoking cigarettes and playing cards, splitting the still night air from time to time with the sound of their raucous laughter.

"I hate you," Maeve said softly, fixing her eyes on the garish glare of their windows. Sergeant Davies's heavy profile was framed in one window, a perfect target if one only had a weapon.

Turning her back on the sight, Maeve sought out a spot on the steps of one of the two women's barracks—a primitive wooden affair— and clasped her hands around her knees. Staring into the darkness, she listened to the sounds of animals announcing themselves in the distance, the prolonged screech of hyenas sending chills down her spine. As often as she heard them, they always had this effect on her. They were wild and primitive, like the land they inhabited. Maeve wanted with all her heart to leave them far behind. In her dreams, she walked in lush green meadows, filled with wildflowers. The wildest creatures she ever wanted to see were tame deer. Or fluffy lap dogs like the ones the ladies carried in the *Illustrated London News*, live toys that could easily fit into a muff. Maeve had had her fill of exotic lands and half-naked savages. She longed for European vistas.

Resting her chin on her knees, she thought soberly of her plight, and she felt as if she were looking into an abyss. She was dispossessed, young and female, jailed in a British concentration camp through no fault of her own and probably about to be orphaned. If there was justice in this world, it would set her free. But, Maeve reflected bitterly, in this part of the world Justice wore British robes.

*

Next morning Maeve found Moira coherent for the first time in two days and asking for water. Maeve was thrilled, relieved that Moira could speak, but still worried about her temperature, for her skin was alarmingly hot. She fairly glowed with fever. Her porcelain complexion was flushed with scarlet patches now and her dark blue eyes glittered eerily.

"Maeve," she whispered, pulling her daughter's hand close to her hot cheek, "be an angel and get me some water. I'm parched. Will you do that for me?"

The girl hesitated. That meant going into the yard. Venturing into the yard meant the possibility of encountering Sergeant Davies. She trembled a little. But she must do this for her mother. Her mother must get better.

She glanced nervously at Moira as she started for the door, a thin, determined figure in a ragged brown dress and scuffed black ankle boots—ready to take on the enemy.

As Maeve headed for the communal well located dead center in the prison compound, she was startled to see a commotion at the entrance of the camp. Thank God! Sergeant Davies was standing in his favorite posture, hands on hips, flanked by his corporal, a skinny, ratlike fellow named Crane, and by another soldier, all three facing a tall man in a long black cassock and a broad-brimmed black hat.

Quickly drawing water at the well, Maeve kept her eyes on the tableau at the gate as she raised the bucket and filled her battered tin and Moira's. What a strange-looking man, the girl thought. His face was partially hidden by his odd headgear, and it wasn't until he turned in her direction that she realized he was a priest. A priest! What on earth was a priest doing here? Perhaps he wasn't really one. Perhaps he was some sort of itinerant Dutch preacher. That would make more sense. But what was he doing *here*?

Caught between her desire to know what was going on with the guards and their visitor and her duty to bring Moira the water, Maeve hesitated. And then as quickly as she could, she raced across the yard, being careful not to spill too much of her precious cargo.

"Mother," she exclaimed, spooning the water into her mother's lips, "I just spotted a priest at the gate. Sergeant Davies and Corporal Crane are talking to him. It looks as though they're arguing."

"Bring him here," Moira said softly. "I want to make my confession." She believed she was dying.

Maeve bit her lip.

"Bring him here," Moira repeated, entwining her fingers around Maeve's. "I think it's time."

Maeve felt a pang of fear in her stomach, and this time it had nothing to do with the sergeant. It was the first time Moira had let on that she knew she was in danger of dying.

"I don't know if they'll let him," Maeve replied, her eyes filling with tears of despair. She was afraid of the same thing as her mother, but terrified by this open admission of it. It was as if facing it squarely in the bright of day might make it real—not like her night fears, which always seemed to dissipate with the first rays of sun.

"Try," whispered Moira. "Please try." She wanted to confess her sins. She must.

Wiping her eyes, the girl stared in fright at her mother, turned quickly and ran out the door, flew down the stairs and across the yard, gasping. As Maeve halted, pausing to catch her breath at the barbed-wire fence that separated her from the soldiers and their visitor, she heard the sergeant say there were no Catholics among his prisoners, so his services wouldn't be needed. These Dutchmen liked only their own kind.

"What a black lie!" exclaimed Maeve, startling the men with the force of her anger. "I'm a Catholic, Father. My mother's a Catholic, and she's very ill. Will you come and hear her confession?"

"You see, Sergeant." The priest gestured toward the girl. "I am needed. And your own General Roberts has given me permission to visit your camp. Come now," the padre said with a mild and guileless smile. "I'm unarmed. I'm a man of the cloth. All I'm asking for is a chance to comfort my flock—with the blessing of your own military authorities. I'll do you no harm."

Davies and Corporal Crane looked at the priest, at the girl, and at each other.

"It's not proper to deny a dying woman the last rites," said Crane. "Even that one," he added under his breath.

"Well, at least it means we're going to be rid of her," Davies agreed. "All right, Padre. In you go. But don't take too long. The others won't even talk with you if you can't speak their lingo."

"Thank you, Sergeant. You'll get your reward in heaven, I'm sure."

I hope God Almighty isn't as soft as all that, Maeve thought as she escorted the man in the black cassock to the sick bay. Not that she ever expected anyone like the sergeant to make it to heaven. She imagined he'd be more at home in the other place.

As he walked quickly toward the wooden hut Maeve had indicated, the priest dropped his mild expression like a mask and asked her if she knew Caroline van der Veldt, one of the Boer women, a thin blond lady. He had come to speak with her.

"She's with my mother. But how do you know Mrs. van der Veldt, Father? She's not Catholic."

"Mutual friends," he replied brusquely.

Suddenly Maeve stared at this priest. When he had spoken with the soldiers he had used a brogue so thick she could have sworn he was a Corkman, born and bred. Now he was speaking with such a strange, rough accent she couldn't place it at all. It wasn't Irish or even English for that matter. And no Boer she had ever encountered could have managed it.

"Where are you from, Father?" she asked as she led him up the worn wooden steps of the hut.

"From a long way off," he answered. "From over the water."

Inside the barracks, Moira raised herself on an elbow as the man strode into the room, looking extremely tall silhouetted in the bright light beyond the open door. Caroline gave a sharp cry of astonishment and flung herself into his arms, weeping with joy.

Shocked by her behavior, Maeve could only gape. Imagine that! This tall foreigner was like no priest she had ever met in her life.

"Caroline," he said, addressing himself to Mrs. van der Veldt. "Is it all right to talk in front of these ladies?" he asked. When she nodded, he continued, "Your husband is four miles from here, gathering his men for a raid on the camp tomorrow night. He needs you women to create a diversion, some kind of ruckus that will keep the English so busy they won't be watching out for us. We'll need your help to pull it off."

Moira was fascinated by the tall figure talking to Caroline. He was a dark-haired man in his twenties with light blue eyes, broad shoulders, and a sunburned face. Irish. But with a bizarre accent. Australian? New Zealand? No. She was certain she had never heard it before. And it took some getting used to.

"What sort of father are you?" she asked weakly, staring at him with feverish eyes.

"No sort of father at all," he answered, to Moira's bewilderment. Then he explained. "This getup is the only way I could pay Caroline a visit. I used to be an altar boy, so it wasn't too difficult to mimic a priest."

Taking a closer look at the woman lying on the rough straw mattress, the stranger was moved by her beauty. It was so unexpected. Deathly ill, she was lovely in spite of it. With skin so white it was almost translucent, the flush on her cheeks highlighted her pallor and accented the deep, rich blue of her eyes, nearly indigo. He wondered what she had been like before.

"Caroline," he said, turning to the Boer woman, "are there any other women who need medical assistance?"

"Nellie van dem Bosch is eight months pregnant and Sarah van Kemp is seventy-three and sickly. Why?" she asked suddenly. "Surely you don't intend to leave anyone behind."

The man shook his head. "Not on your life. We're planning to empty the camp. I'll tell the men to make arrangements for evacuating the sick."

Glancing at the feverish woman before him, he asked Caroline quietly if she thought they could move her.

Moira raised her eyes to his. "If there's a chance of getting out of here, I won't be left behind. I'd rather die on the veldt than in a British prison."

Suddenly the visitor said, "You're not a Boer. What have you done to end up in here?"

"The British hanged my husband, and that was reason enough for them to put me here. They think all the Irish are dangerous. I only wish they were right."

The effort of speaking had made Moira hoarse and weakened her still further. Her head sank back onto the pillow as Maeve watched silently, praying her mother could survive an evacuation across this brutal landscape. But she was right. Better to die out there than this way, penned in like an animal.

"Who was your husband?" the stranger asked, one eye on the rapidly approaching figure of Sergeant Davies, who was heading toward the hut from across the yard.

"Pat Devereux," Moira replied with a weak smile. "He really *was* a terror."

Before their visitor could make a reply to that, there was a great crash of boots on the creaking stairs and Sergeant Davies was coming at them through the open door. As he entered the room, he could hear the sound of Latin prayers and caught *"et cum spiritu tuo"* as he saw the padre stand over Moira Devereux's bed, his right hand sketching a wide sign of the cross over her.

Clearing his throat, the sergeant said roughly, "All right, Padre, time's up."

Turning to the sergeant, the tall man in the cassock smiled. "If you don't mind, Sergeant," the women heard him say as Davies herded him out, "I'll make another trip in someday."

He received less than hearty encouragement.

*

After lights-out on the following night, the entire camp was in a subdued uproar. The soft murmuring of women's voices mingled with the cries of the night birds and the occasional prolonged yelping of a hyena off in the distance. In Camp 3 every woman and child was waiting for the signal to start the rebellion.

In sick bay, Caroline paced the floor with Maeve watching. Suddenly she stopped dead in front of her and said quietly, "Here we go."

As Moira looked on from her sickbed, Caroline lit the lamp in defiance of camp rules and began screaming at the red-haired girl, shouting anything that came to mind, making as much racket as she could. Maeve responded in kind, shrieking at the top of her lungs, pounding on the walls to make even more noise.

When the women and children in the other long hut heard the shouts, they took their cue and began to raise a din there, too, making such a commotion that they soon attracted the attention of the lone sentry on duty at the entrance to the camp.

"Hey, Sergeant!" they heard him shout. "There's a riot going on! Send in some men!"

The sound of English voices filled the air, and Maeve and Caroline ran to the fence to observe their captors' reaction. Sergeant Davies and Corporal Crane were already outside the barracks, shouting orders at their men and screaming at the women to cease and desist this uproar. They were angry and apparently bewildered as well. Nothing like this had ever happened before.

From the shadows cast by the wooden wall of their hut, the two women could see Sergeant Davies withdraw his revolver and gesture with it, indicating that his men should follow him into the prisoners' compound.

"Let's get Moira out of here," said Caroline, pulling Maeve along with her back inside the hut. "And then we'll show that fat pig what trouble looks like."

While the rest of the prisoners were shouting at their captors and hurling rocks at them as they attempted to enter the compound, Maeve and Caroline raced inside the sick bay and carried Moira out. And then, as the girl and her mother began making their way slowly toward the opposite side of the camp, Caroline seized the kerosene lamp in the hut and sent it crashing against the wall, pausing only long enough to see the flames lick at the dry wood and start to spread slowly across the floor and wall. Let Davies deal with this. The burning hut would make a perfect beacon for Marinus and his men.

Circumventing the building, Caroline took the long way around the camp to rejoin her friends, avoiding running into the English soldiers. They were wild with rage, screaming at the women, threatening them, even firing off their weapons into the air to try to restore order.

The noisier the soldiers became, the louder the women and children managed to shout. As Davies ordered his men to put out the fire in the sick bay, youngsters hurled stones at the soldiers, and were driven back only when the English began firing over their heads. In the confusion of the noise, the gunfire, and the flaming hut, Sergeant Davies didn't even hear the approach of the horses until it was too late. With all Davies's men but one inside the compound, distracted by the fire and the general commotion, Marinus van der Veldt and his men swooped down on them before they knew what was happening.

Infuriated by the surprise attack, the sergeant roared orders at his men, trying to regroup in the midst of this whirlwind attack, but the din of battle drowned out his voice. Not one to give up easily, Davies decided to take action by himself. If he was going to die, so would they.

As the Boers overran the compound, bullets whistling in the night air, horses and men outlined in the garish light of the flames, Davies recognized the "father" who had recently paid him a visit. "Bastard," he muttered, drawing a bead on him with his rifle.

"Look, Caroline," shouted Maeve as she saw him too. "It's our friend!"

Then she saw the sergeant. He would kill this man. Terrified, Maeve ran to where a fallen trooper lay and seized his rifle. With seconds to spare, the girl lifted the Lee-Enfield to her shoulder and fired three times. At the first shot, Davies's body jerked forward, his rifle falling slowly forward. At the second, he crashed to the ground, face in the dust. The third shot went wild.

Caroline stared in astonishment. Maeve was beginning to shake violently, overwhelmed by what she had just done. The dark-haired man cantered over to where she and Caroline were standing and dismounted, greeting them silently in the midst of all the uproar around them.

"Where did you learn to shoot like that?" he demanded, putting his arm around the trembling girl.

"In my own backyard," replied Maeve, still not really believing what she had done. Davies was not moving. He was dead, she thought, astonished that she was responsible. "It's the first time I've killed vermin with a rifle, though." She wasn't ashamed to say it.

As Caroline ran to her bearded, weary husband and ecstatically embraced him in the ghastly orange light of the burning camp, Maeve was staring, a little glassy-eyed at the "priest." All around them, women and children were shouting to husbands and fathers in the raiding party. And then suddenly he said with a quick smile, "I never got a chance to introduce myself yesterday. My name's Sean Farrell. Now," he added energetically, "where's your mother?" But his eyes were full of admiration for young Maeve.

*

When the Boers reached a safe area in the rear, the sick were met at a hospital by a Dutch doctor and nurses and given the first medicine they had had since capture by the British. After a few days of treatment, Moira began to make a slow recovery, her energy returning in small doses. It was still an effort to walk, but lying in a clean bed, she was able to talk for a little while, with Maeve sitting with her and sometimes reading to her from the few newspapers the doctor had in his possession. She was also able to have visitors, and Sean spent some time with her each day, making her laugh occasionally, which she hadn't done in a very long time. She enjoyed him. So did Maeve.

"What on earth ever made you come to South Africa?" demanded Moira one day shortly after they had been rescued. "It's not your fight. It seems a long way to go for a bit of a scrap."

Farrell laughed. "I came here to observe what was going on for a group of interested Europeans. You might say I'm a reporter."

That was stretching the truth well beyond its limits, but it was a plausible tale; he was, after all, sending back very detailed reports to some gentlemen in Berlin with an extremely keen interest in the fighting. One fellow in particular, a gentleman with a pointy mustache and blazing blue eyes, was his most assiduous reader. Hating the British despite his own family's many British relations, he was emphatically and emotionally on the side of the Boers.

Farrell smiled at Moira. "Well, I don't think it's so odd being here anyway. After all, your own husband opposed the British and he was no Boer."

That made Moira sigh. "No. He just hated the British. He used to say if we could kick them out of South Africa, maybe we can do it in Ireland one day. He was an optimist. His father was one of the Fenians who tried to start an uprising back home in '67. It failed, of course," she said wryly, "and the family scattered. He decided to try his luck here because it was so far from England."

It was a familiar tale, thought Sean Farrell. He knew it well. His mother's people could tell the same story. His father's people, however, came from a wild and mountainous place that could boast proudly of never having been conquered in six hundred years—while all their neighbors fell one after the other to the heathen Turks. Their peculiar christening rite of placing a pistol into the tiny hands of their male children spoke volumes about their attitude toward life.

Sean often wondered if his mother's people weren't lacking something in the way of spirit. In wild Montenegro, where his father was known as "the Warrior Bard," no Montenegrin would have dreamed of allowing foreigners to dominate them. Where Irish history was filled with depressing stories of Irish gullibility and British craftiness, the ballads of Montenegro celebrated native cunning at the expense of their enemies. One of their favorite folk dances involved the firing of weapons. Naturally, it was an all-male affair, a warrior's dance.

Reflecting on his compatriots' attitude toward women, Sean Farrell had to admit he was somewhat lacking in their eyes. He actually liked and admired certain ladies, not something a real Montenegrin would ever admit to. To most of them, women figured in importance after the oxen, and oxen were far behind the horse. If that pretty girl had saved his life in his father's country, her exploit would have been commemorated in a ballad mocking *him*. She would have been extolled as a heroine— before being sent back to her place in the kitchen.

Sean was grateful his upbringing had taken place away from Montenegro. If anything, it had taught him never to underestimate female capabilities. His own mother, Geraldine, was living proof of what a determined, crafty, ambitious woman could achieve with a will of iron and a sense of her own destiny.

Glancing at lovely Moira, Farrell suspected she might be much the same. She was certainly as beautiful as Geraldine, and if she was clever she might make just as big a fortune—if she could ever get herself out of this madhouse of a country. And the girl with her.

Brusquely he said to her, "I'm leaving with Caroline van der Veldt for Lourenço Marques in three days. I want you and Maeve to come with me. Your daughter saved my life. I want to return the favor."

Moira was startled. "But I've no money. I can't afford to go anyplace." What was this fellow thinking? Could she trust him?

"I have money. And I don't intend to leave you and Maeve in Lourenço Marques. I'm taking you to Europe. The gentlemen I'm working for would love to hear a firsthand account of British brutality from women and children who have been abused by them. You'll be treated like visiting royalty." He smiled. "You have nothing to lose."

Moira's lovely eyes flicked him a skeptical glance. As an innocent of sixteen she had listened to a smooth line of patter from Pat Devereux, had let him take her far from her native County Kildare to the strange place where he lived—halfway around the world and among savages— and then, after many years of uneventful domesticity, had the bad sense to get himself hanged. She wondered what this handsome fellow with the odd accent would do to her. Or what he might try.

"I don't know anyone in Europe."

"You know me. And Marinus van der Veldt would never entrust me with his wife and two sons if I were a rascal."

The idea that Caroline would be there altered things. Moira had to admit she couldn't imagine some solid, shrewd Dutchman allowing his wife and children to venture so far afield with any old adventurer. That he was sending them all the way to Europe was a little unsettling. It couldn't mean anything good for the struggle if he felt it necessary to shelter his most precious possessions in foreign lands.

From the expression on Moira's face, Farrell guessed what was going through her mind. "Mrs. van der Veldt and I are off on a sort of diplomatic mission. You and Maeve will be in good company, and you'll be company for Caroline and the children, too. She'll be pleading Kruger's cause to men who might be persuaded to send them weapons. A heartrending tale of woe from a beautiful woman would certainly never *harm* our chances."

"And afterward?"

"I won't leave you stranded and penniless," Sean said. "I have a wide variety of contacts who could be useful to you. Some are honorable, some not. You pick and choose."

Moira Devereux's eyes were the most beguiling and troubling shade of blue Sean had ever seen. One moment you could swear they were aquamarine, the next they seemed almost violet. It was the reflection of the light—or perhaps even of some inner turmoil. One thing was certain: once seen they were never forgotten. Her lovely face showed every bit of feeling that crossed her soul, but those eyes were worth all the rest. They would have turned a plain woman into a beauty, and Moira was exquisite to start with. Right now, she was pondering her future.

Married so young, taken far from a land of lush fields to a land of barren mountains and broad plateaus, Moira had loved Pat Devereux enough to adapt herself to provincial life in one of the Empire's outposts. A popular hostess in her own circle, she had danced at yearly balls at Government House, and with Pat had participated in the local musical society. Her daughter grew up with native nursemaids and strange pets, her gravest danger coming from the hot sun that had once left her milky skin covered with huge blisters the size of shillings. Maeve hated the African sun.

Moira had adapted to the life of a country lawyer's wife in the African backwater, but Maeve, born there, had never seemed to accept it. Now, with Pat gone, there was no need for either of them to stay. If the British didn't kill them with their concentration camps, poverty would, soon enough. Europe offered a second chance at life, perhaps Maeve's only escape. And Moira Devereux was not the sort of woman to discount the help of a charming adventurer—within limits.

"All right," she nodded after some hesitation. "Maeve and I will go with you. We'll tell the world how bad things are here and try to get the Europeans to open their purse strings to Kruger and his men."

"Splendid."

"But I warn you," added Moira, "if you try to play us dirty, there'll be hell to pay."

Nodding solemnly, Sean agreed. The concept of a blood vendetta over honor was not exactly unknown in Montenegro either. Perhaps he and Mrs. Devereux had a lot more in common than even he suspected.

"You have my word on it," he said simply. He was not about to harm them. If anything, he wanted to save them. Moira was worth it. And Maeve, that fascinating girl, deserved it. She was one of a kind.

When Sean Farrell left her that afternoon, Moira found herself in a state somewhere between elation and bewilderment. She wanted to find a way out of her predicament, and this stranger offered a better chance than she could ever have hoped for in her wildest dreams. Europe! It was incredible. But, she wondered, was it too good to be true?

Cautiously she recalled instances when other men had made promises to her—only to disappoint her in the end. Marriage was one of those instances. Life in the colonies hadn't been all that she had been led to believe, and although her life as Mrs. Patrick Devereux was infinitely better than it would have been had she not met him, Moira always thought she deserved more. More of everything. More of life in the great world. More excitement. This Sean Farrell certainly offered *that*.

But what sort of man was this good-looking fellow with the light blue eyes and the peculiar accent? She couldn't recall anyone else who had made such a strong impression on her since Pat had courted her. It wasn't even his good looks; it was something to do with his style. This was someone who was completely sure of himself, not a man who spent his time looking cautiously over his shoulder, waiting for a second opinion. She had known a few such men; they inevitably died young. It was a depressing thought, especially after her recent widowing.

When Maeve came to visit her that afternoon, Moira told her what she had decided, a little nervous about her daughter's reaction. To dream about getting out of South Africa was one thing—the announcement they were to leave within the week was bound to be a shock. She hoped Maeve didn't think she was too easily persuaded.

Sitting in the wicker armchair, staring out the window at the familiar landscape, watching two barely clad natives drive a water buffalo across a dusty path, Maeve didn't say anything at all. Moira thought at first she hadn't heard what she had said.

"I told him we'd go," she repeated, anxiously studying her daughter's face. "It's to be soon."

"All right," nodded the girl, absolutely solemn and seemingly turned to stone.

Exasperated, Moira demanded if it suited her.

"Oh, Mama," she replied, bursting into tears as she flung herself into Moira's arms. "I thought he'd leave without us! I was terrified he'd never ask!" Excitement and relief coursed through her veins. But there was an underlying sadness about leaving her papa behind.

As Maeve and her daughter held on to each other, laughing and crying at the same time, thrilled to be making their escape, grateful to be leaving behind a life that no longer had any meaning for them, Moira was struck by a sudden, uncanny suspicion.

"Maeve," she insisted, looking carefully at her child's tangled red hair and her dark blue eyes, "did you ever mention anything about leaving to Mr. Farrell?"

"From the first moment we arrived here. So did Caroline." Did her mother think she was stupid?

Moira burst out laughing. She had been afraid Maeve would think she was too susceptible, while all the time she was lagging far behind the girl. It amused her. And it worried her as well.

CHAPTER 3

*M*aeve thought the trip to Lourenço Marques in Portuguese East Africa was the most exciting journey she'd ever taken. With her mother and friends she traveled by oxcart through territory still in friendly hands, until they reached the border of the Portuguese colony, crossed it, and boarded the Delagoa Bay Railway for the trip to the coast.

As the train chugged through clearings hacked through parts of the jungle, gaily clad natives often came out to observe them, cautiously keeping their distance as the white men sped by in their steam-breathing machines. Every mile was taking her farther from her father—and farther from the people and land that murdered him.

From time to time, Maeve stood with Sean Farrell at the railed-in platform at the far end of their car, taking in the lush scenery, the distant green mountains, and the wild animals scattered grandly across the countryside. The frolicking gazelles were as numerous as the pigeons in Trafalgar Square in London, joked Farrell. And Maeve marveled at what that must be like. She wondered if she'd ever see it.

When their party reached the port city on the coast, an agent known to Caroline secured tickets for them on board a Dutch ship bound for Rotterdam. It was a three-day wait in Lourenço Marques for their departure, so the ladies sought out a local seamstress to run up a few dresses for them. They were nearly in rags from the privations of the prison camp and were ashamed to show themselves among the Europeans looking like beggars.

Sean Farrell didn't have that problem. He merely pulled several fine suits out of a huge leather satchel and took them to the nearest tailor for a good pressing.

When the ladies saw him strolling into the high-ceilinged lobby of the Hotel da Gama in cool white linen with a jaunty panama hat, they burst into spontaneous applause. The man looked just like one of the dashing explorers so often seen sipping gin on the veranda—in town between treks into the interior. There were lots of suntanned European faces on the wide veranda of the hotel, and inside the lobby, too, cooled by the constant slow twirling of fans high above the heads of the guests.

Ladies who waged never-ending battles to keep the sun from ruining their fair complexions sat languidly on the overstuffed white wicker furniture, fanning themselves with enervated, genteel gestures, gossiping softly as they whiled away the tropical days, leaden with ennui.

For all their heavy-lidded languor, Maeve noticed, the Portuguese and European women were not slow to notice Sean Farrell when he crossed the lobby with her or Moira on his arm. These ladies had a charming, rather sly way of taking in the sights, a little like cats, she thought. At the approach of the handsome blue-eyed Irishman, the dark-haired *latinas* would allow their eyes to roam, devouring all the details without resting too obviously on the object of their interest. What they made of his blonde, his brunette, and his young redhead, Maeve didn't know. But she enjoyed their curiosity. And she was very fond of this tall Irish-Montenegrin who was a friend of the van der Veldts.

Sean Farrell was as foreign to the girl as the Africans—or the British for that matter. He was impatient with rules if they made no sense and wasn't shy about saying so. There was none of the ridiculous worship of tradition Maeve had found so irritating among her parents' friends. If a thing was worthless, why not chuck it and start fresh? What did it matter if the old women and the preachers clucked their tongues and talked about disrespect for the past? Maeve couldn't see any use in respecting a past that had proved worthless.

And she loved to hear about one's "place in the sun," a German expression dear to their Kaiser, he told her. It was a fine image and it had a grand sound to it—like some splendid new opportunity. Maeve still wasn't quite sure what it meant to Sean, but she knew what it meant to her—the opening up of a new life in a new world. Perhaps she and her mother would be successful, perhaps not. But of one thing she was convinced: never again would she live like a dog with someone like

Sergeant Davies as her keeper. That life was gone forever.

The day Maeve and her party boarded the SS *Emma* and sailed for Europe was the happiest day she could remember. Wedged in at the railing between her mother and Caroline, trading jokes with young Jannie and Dirck van der Veldt, Maeve looked back at the waterfront filled with khaki-clad colonial troops, Portuguese ladies with parasols, and gleeful, waving black dockhands, all moving like dolls under the brilliant African sky, and she began to feel giddy with joy. She was leaving this place behind for good, and from now on, come what may, she would never be miserable again. She believed it with all her heart.

*

When Maeve and her party reached Amsterdam in December 1901, it was a snow-covered fairyland to her. She was entranced by the city, its frozen canals, its elegant houses with their zigzag and dancing facades, and especially by the magnificent Hotel Amstel, where she was staying in a suite fit for royalty. She was absolutely besotted by the luxury. Moira, who had spent her brief honeymoon at the Shelbourne in Dublin, was amused by the girl's carrying on. It reminds me of myself at the same age, she thought wistfully.

Standing in the lobby with her mother and Caroline, Maeve was fascinated to see the arrival of the famous English actress Lillie Langtry, stopping for a few days with "a gentleman admirer," according to gossip circulating in the dining room. The Jersey Lily was just as beautiful as all the photographs Maeve had seen, and the girl was awestruck to be in the same room as this ravishing creature, who seemed to exude an air of such opulence it made all the other ladies pale in comparison.

"I'd love to look like that someday," she declared to Moira and Caroline, who exchanged glances. The Jersey Lily looked like a plump kept woman. The fact that she and King Edward had been lovers did nothing to increase her prestige in Moira's eyes. But it all seemed incredibly glamorous to Maeve.

"She's an actress," Caroline declared in a low voice, which for her was the equivalent of being a public sinner.

"Oh, how marvelous," murmured Maeve, watching with fascination as Mrs. Langtry took in the adoring glances of her admirers and, with a gracious smile, practically floated across the lobby to where the brass elevator cage took the guests upstairs. Imagine! She plays out dramas onstage in front of crowds! Maeve caught a slight whiff of patchouli as the Jersey Lily swept past, resplendent in a sapphire-blue velvet *tailleur* trimmed with ermine beneath a gorgeous coat of some glossy brown fur,

couldn't envision any of them introducing a lion or a tiger into a home. Well, perhaps one of them. If he was a bit tight. Maybe.

"St. Petersburg must be a rare old place," Maeve murmured. She wondered if bringing bears to parties was the done thing.

"Oh, it's a beautiful city," he said warmly. "You see how lovely Amsterdam is, built on its canals? Well, Petersburg is set up in the same way, only the architecture is baroque and rococo French and Italian," he went on, regretting his choice of words. Maeve probably didn't know what that meant.

"Ah," she nodded. "You mean a bit like Versailles and the Belvedere Palace in Vienna."

He grinned. "Yes," he said, quite pleased. "Just that sort of thing." Strange little thing. Where did she ever pick up that information? It was delightful that she knew.

"Petersburg is gorgeous beyond belief, especially in the winter when the river Neva is frozen solid. People skate on it the way they do here. In the parks they build great ice mountains for sledding. Parties start early and last until dawn, with couples heading for the Gypsies out on the islands to end the evening. It's a marvelous place. The ladies never wear the same gowns twice. They order all their clothes from Paris and appear covered with jewels at all the great court receptions. Extraordinary atmosphere."

Maeve was enchanted. "Do they look as beautiful as Mrs. Langtry?"

"Oh, better." He smiled. "They're so loaded down with diamonds and pearls they glitter each time they move. It's an unforgettable sight to see the ceremonies at the Tsar's court. The Court of St. James's is nothing in comparison."

Moira's beautiful dark blue eyes were almost as round as her daughter's. She was delighted with his stories, though she didn't know whether or not to believe them. Caroline was not surprised by anything he said: her husband had told her Sean knew Kaiser Wilhelm personally.

"You said your sisters lived in St. Petersburg," Maeve persisted. "Do they have piles of diamonds?"

Moira thought that was a very impertinent question, and she said so. Sean wasn't at all offended. He replied that they did, declaring that they looked very fine in them, but that the Grand Duchess Vladimir had the biggest ones outside of the Tsar's mother's collection and she put everybody in the shade when she dressed for an event.

"And what of your mother?" Maeve asked, too curious to behave. "Does she have lovely diamonds too?"

"Enormous ones," he laughed. "When Mama appears dressed for

a party, my stepfather hires a private detective to guard her—from a discreet distance. She looks like a cross between the Queen of England and a heathen idol. Very nice effect."

"Ah," murmured Maeve, like Moira not really knowing whether to believe all this. If it was only a tall tale, she would feel foolish to put any faith in it. But if it was true, what kind of people were these?

All three ladies looked at Sean Farrell with new eyes. Either he was an outrageous liar—or he was one of the most exciting adventurers they had ever encountered.

Somehow, he didn't seem to be a liar. As Maeve sipped her tea from a dainty porcelain cup, she didn't see the restaurant with its polished wood paneling, its small waiters in neat white jackets, its amazing variety of Oriental foods—all she saw were diamonds glistening amid the snows of Petersburg, scattered far and wide. Piles of jewels.

It was a place she was determined to see. Perhaps Sean Farrell would take her there. He had brought them out of Africa, after all, and he was going to take them to Berlin. Why not to Petersburg? It must be grand, Maeve thought, with diamonds scattered about like pebbles on a beach and big bears careening through the streets. What fun! He probably even knew the Tsar himself.

Their stay in Amsterdam included several meetings with pro-Boer committees who were working hard to supply their overseas cousins with the wherewithal to keep up the struggle. Caroline was a surprisingly effective speaker with a genuine talent for loosening people's purse strings. Her accounts of British crimes against the civilian population were so moving, she succeeded in raising more money than anyone had expected. Maeve, Moira, and the two young van der Veldts were trotted out as victims of the British reign of terror and did their best to look appropriately solemn on cue.

While they were waiting for their German sponsors to arrive in the Dutch capital, Sean took the ladies shopping and outfitted them with warm winter coats purchased at a very elegant shop along one of the frozen canals, where highly polished wood gleamed on floors, doors, and walls. White-aproned servants fluttered about with trays of delicious cocoa for the ladies while models paraded the latest styles before them. The luxurious scent of exotic flowers filled the air.

Maeve was so impressed by the atmosphere, she never thought of the prices. She didn't have to since Sean was paying for everything, but the idea of the cost nearly staggered Moira and Caroline. When Maeve declared herself in love with a beautiful red woolen coat trimmed with ermine at the cuffs and collar—with a muff to match—her mother nearly said no.

Heart pounding, Maeve looked stricken. Farrell smiled and said he thought it was just the thing for her. Moira sighed and wondered what he was going to do next. But she was delighted all the same.

Facing herself in the triple mirror, so beautiful in her new coat with all that *fur*, Maeve was almost astonished by her own splendor. There she was in ermine, just like the Jersey Lily. Or at least in a bit of ermine. Her muff was wonderfully soft and rich, with little pockets inside for gloves and a few coins. It had several little tails like Mrs. Langtry's—so it must be the latest style—but it was quite a different affair. Still, it was *fur*, not velvet or any sort of cloth, and it was made from the same fur actresses would wear.

"In some circles ermine is considered appropriate only for royalty," the owner of the shop said to Moira, as if trying to warn her of some social gaffe. Moira looked unimpressed: Maeve wasn't likely to encounter any royalty, so therefore she wasn't worried.

"But royalty doesn't often look as fetching as this child does," Sean declared with a smile. "We think it's very becoming."

That ended the discussion. Maeve had her ermine-trimmed winter coat, and Moira and Caroline came away with collars, cuffs, and hats of fluffy fox on fine dark blue cashmere.

Caroline was amused by Farrell's generosity—and deeply grateful. Her husband, who was not a man given to overstatement, considered him a fine strategist and one of the boldest intriguers he had ever met. She wondered if he wasn't using some strategy here on Moira. Moira wondered the same thing and enjoyed it immensely.

What Mrs. Devereux found so delightful about Sean was his apparent disinclination to take things seriously. There was no sense of doom about him, even though he was deeply committed to the Boer cause. He was capable of creating a happy atmosphere she found intoxicating after the tragedy she had just left behind. Moira was still numb from what she had experienced in Africa and wanted to shut it out of her mind, to put it aside until she had recovered sufficiently to deal with it. He seemed to sense that. He was a godsend. And his good nature seemed genuine. If any man could make her want to pick up and go on with her life, she thought, it would have to be someone like Sean Farrell. Moira liked him very much. She also wondered just who on earth he was—and how he came to be that way.

That night, as Moira lay in bed, her mind racing with thoughts of the day, she heard a knock at the door and raced to open it, expecting Maeve.

Instead to her shock, it was Sean.

"Sean! What are you doing here?"

"Don't you know?" he asked, his look both pleading and passionate. "Weren't we thinking the same things today?" He closed the door.

Their lips met in a hungry kiss, their arms encircling each other as if they were the last two people on earth. Moira could not believe the emotions this young man was stirring deep within her as Sean swept her off her feet and carried her to her bed.

Sean gently removed her lace and satin nightgown, nuzzling her breasts, her belly, kissing her in her most private place. Moira was dazzled by Sean's wiry, muscular body, with its delicate dark curls circling his chest and leading down his stomach to his manhood, which was fully erect.

As he entered her, Moira gasped with the sensation she had not felt since Pat was arrested. She had thought she could never love a man in this way again after Pat was killed. As Sean deliberately, expertly led her to higher and higher plateaus of voluptuousness, she realized how wrong she had been.

*

One snowy afternoon, as Farrell and the ladies—minus Maeve and the two van der Veldt boys—were having tea in the elegant rotunda of the hotel, under a swirling art nouveau ceiling of stained glass, a tall gentleman in impeccable frock coat and striped trousers approached their table and bowed formally, clicking his heels together smartly. Farrell looked up and sprang to his feet, apparently delighted to see him. Moira and Caroline inclined their heads in subdued curiosity and smiled sweetly.

"Hubertus von Reuter," announced the stranger before Farrell could introduce him. "At your service."

Rising to the occasion, Moira gracefully extended her white hand and smiled graciously as Herr von Reuter kissed it. Caroline followed her example while she tried not to think what Marinus's reaction to this European habit would be. Boer burghers didn't go in for the "baise-mains."

Von Reuter was astonished by the women. From what he had heard, they were poor, haggard scarecrows, reduced to despair by the heartless and mindless brutality of the British. These two looked lovely, especially the black-haired woman with those extraordinary blue—or perhaps indigo—eyes. He hadn't expected the "poor unfortunate victims" to look so presentable. It was rather unsettling. He needed someone more pathetic.

Polite exchanges over, Sean Farrell explained to the ladies that Herr von Reuter was one of the German supporters of Kruger who were aiding their cause at the German court. The Kaiser was a friend of his. And a friend of theirs as well.

Von Reuter was avid for descriptions of any sort of depravity the ladies could document, he stated over coffee and cake. Were they beaten? Abused in any especially vicious way? Were they—please forgive his frankness, he added—subjected to immoral and sadistic behavior on the part of their captors?

At the last question, Moira and Caroline both lowered their eyes and gazed with great embarrassment at their hands. Moira thought this German had a great deal of cheek. What sort of report was he supposed to be preparing? He seemed awfully interested in "depravity." Wasn't being interned in the camp sufficiently horrific? she thought indignantly. Wasn't Pat's death enough? Caroline's thoughts were similar. Both women wondered about Herr von Reuter.

Sean Farrell coughed briefly, to break the silence that had descended upon the group. "You must understand, Herr von Reuter," he said at last, "that Mrs. Devereux and Mrs. van der Veldt have been put through hell. It is not easy for them to talk about their experiences with a stranger."

"I do understand, dear ladies," the tall German assured them with tender benevolence. "Perhaps I've been too frank. Just tell me what you can bear to talk about. I'll be happy to hear whatever you choose to reveal." His very pale blue eyes gleamed with concern. And expectation.

Settling back in the gilded plush chair, he looked a little like a child waiting for someone to read him a favorite fairy tale. Moira glanced at Caroline and decided she might as well begin. They hadn't crossed an ocean *not* to tell their story, after all.

Raising her head to bring her beautiful eyes level with von Reuter's, Moira was quite pleased she had his attention. He was admiring her fitted black silk bodice richly trimmed with jet beads. She hoped he wasn't too distracted to listen to her. If they had known he was going to appear today, she would have worn something more subdued. Her widow's weeds were just a wee bit too smart to arouse feelings of sorrow and pity. It was her own fault too, she told herself sternly.

". . . and then in the courtroom itself," she heard herself saying with a tremor in her voice, "rough soldiers actually ripped my arms from around my husband's neck before they led him off to be hanged. My daughter and I were manhandled and shipped off to the concentration camp without even a chance to appeal this unjust sentence."

With three pairs of eyes on her as she spoke—and a few others discreetly following her soft conversation from neighboring tables—Moira slowly took out a lace-trimmed linen handkerchief from her reticule and gently dabbed at her eyes. A large tear escaped anyway and rolled sadly down her cheek, landing with a tiny splatter on her black silk dress. Herr von Reuter was deeply moved. A Dutch lady at a table to their left was seen to take out her own handkerchief. The waiter hovering nearby blinked a few times.

"These people have no pity in their hearts for the feeble, the old, the helpless," Moira continued. "I nearly died of fever in that dreadful prison. They refused to let me have medical treatment. If it hadn't been for Sean Farrell and the German and Dutch doctors who took care of me once I had escaped, I wouldn't be here today."

From the expression on Hubertus von Reuter's handsome face, he was quite glad she *was*. "Thank God He saw fit to spare you, Frau Devereux," the German intoned with passion. "Thank God that you lived to testify against them."

To Caroline's mind, it was a bit excessive to invoke the Almighty so often. She wondered if Herr von Reuter was such a fervent Christian—or was he merely in raptures at meeting an angel like Moira? At any rate, the man was impressed, and that was all to the good. By the time she was able to tell him *her* story, he was taking notes in a small green morocco leather notebook with his monogram in tiny gold embossed letters, avid for further details.

Quietly sipping his coffee, Sean was pleased with the effect his ladies had made. Herr von Reuter, blond, blue-eyed, and Prussian to his heels, one of Berlin's biggest bankers and a sworn enemy of Britain, was stirred to the depths of his soul by what he was hearing. And seeing. That was a mixed blessing. He had known the man for several years and had never suspected he was so susceptible. He didn't know whether or not he was annoyed.

He certainly had no plans to share Moira Devereux with any Prussian banker.

*

Being in the thick of things was what Maeve loved best, and in Holland she was practically in the eye of the hurricane regarding the war. These Dutchmen were heart and soul for their cousins across the water, anti-British with a passion, and ready to shout themselves hoarse at rallies and even contribute money to the cause. It was heady stuff for a girl of seventeen to be called upon to sing the Boer anthem, the "Volkslied," at rallies of a thousand people and have the audience respond with such passion. It was even a bit unnerving. But then, as Sean remarked with admiration, it wasn't given to everyone to possess a voice like hers. Naturally it could move people.

Since her last experiences before an audience had been at Moira's prewar musicales in much more restrained circumstances, Maeve now found that she loved this particular gift of hers and was especially pleased that she could part men from their money because of it. It seemed a grand talent, and it was her contribution to the cause, which made her feel useful.

Her musical contribution to the Boer rallies had come about one night because young Dirck and Jannie had been called upon by some old preacher to sing the "Volkslied" and had been intimidated enough to request some help from her. Rising to the occasion, Maeve joined them and shortly afterward, her soaring, clear soprano was causing people to stop and stare at her as she gave a rendition of the Boer anthem that nobody had ever attempted before. It unleashed such an outpouring of coins and bank notes that she repeated her performance several times after that, to similar effect. Moira, rather pleased at this, fluffed up her curls and declared that the child had inherited all her talent from her mother. "Blood will tell," she said, smiling as she accepted the public's praise.

In between pleading the cause in private and in public, Maeve was learning more and more about her rescuer, Sean Farrell, and his odd family. His mother, Geraldine, was something of a character, she thought. Married to an elderly Prussian aristocrat, Graf Erich von Kleist—no relation to the poet, Sean said with a smile—this lady had been cold-shouldered by Berlin society until she captured the attention of the pious Empress by building a church for the notorious socialist workers of a Berlin district called Wedding—red Wedding. The church was such a success that the German Empress took a liking to the Gräfin von Kleist for her interest in good works and had her presented at court, which gave all of Berlin society fits and forced Geraldine down their throats.

"Is your mother pious?" Maeve asked innocently.

She didn't understand why he nearly choked on the wine he was drinking at the time, but she took it to mean "No."

Sean was such a dashing figure all the women adored him, especially Moira. This in turn excited the jealousy of Herr Hubertus von Reuter, who had his own ideas about the beautiful Mrs. Devereux. Maeve knew he admired her mother. He stared at Moira lustfully. When the girl mentioned this to Sean, he struggled to keep a straight face, but admitted Hubertus might be having something like an ecstatic seizure.

Now, this Herr von Reuter was one man Maeve liked to keep at as great a distance as possible, given his haughty tone and apparent disdain every time he glanced in her direction. Maeve didn't like him any better, either, after he once informed her that Sean's mother was "an adventuress" who owed her good fortune to the disgusting bad taste of barbaric royalty and a senile offshoot of a noble German family.

In South Africa this would have earned him a good punch in the jaw if any member of the lady's family had overheard him, and he would have received the same right there in Holland if Sean Farrell had been within earshot. But Maeve wasn't one to stir up trouble needlessly, and she noted his attitude and let it go at that. Still, she disliked him enough to avoid him whenever possible afterward, and she never forgot that nasty remark about the mother of the man who had freed her from Camp 3. It wasn't right and it wasn't gentlemanly, she thought. In fact, it was just the kind of thing one might expect from some blackguard of a stuck-up Prussian with hot eyes for *her* mother!

If von Reuter lacked a pleasant manner and what is commonly known as charm, he did have one useful asset—money—and he was generous in applying it to his enthusiasm for the Boer cause. On the day he, Sean, and their party departed for Germany and further outbursts of support, Hubertus arranged a send-off that pleased even Maeve.

Every pro-Boer citizen in Amsterdam seemed to be at the train station to bid farewell to his group of refugees as they departed to the accompaniment of brass bands. Apple-cheeked children sang the "Volks-lied" and threw bouquets of flowers as the train steamed out of the station, heading toward Germany. When the van der Veldts leaned from the window and responded with kisses, Maeve saw tears of gratitude in Caroline's eyes. Caroline was overwhelmed by the outpouring of sym-pathy and touched beyond words by the gesture, and she often spoke of it afterward.

Maeve settled in for the ride to Germany aboard a private railway car, the first trip she had ever taken in such grand style. This was Herr von Reuter's contribution too and she, Dirck, and Jannie thought he was a funny sort of man—not very kind, although he spoke long and loud about "paying back the British" and "advancing the cause of our noble Teutonic race." Maeve noticed that Sean Farrell didn't seem to be overly fond of him either, although he behaved with perfect manners. Herr von Reuter was so full of himself, he had no time for youngsters, she observed. It irritated Maeve that he seemed to have plenty of time for Moira. For some reason, *that* made her want to push him away whenever he approached her pretty mother. To Maeve's annoyance, Moira didn't appear to mind.

How can she bear to listen to him? Maeve wondered silently as she and twelve-year-old Dirck van der Veldt sipped tea and ate delicious spiced cookies in the parlor of the Pullman while their elders discussed their plans for Berlin. Ten-year-old Jannie sat at his mother's feet, his blond head resting against her knees—a little like a puppy, thought the girl. From the expression on Herr von Reuter's face, she could tell no child of *his* would ever be allowed to behave so informally.

Look at him, thought Maeve, so cold, so dried up. This German reminded her of a professor she had known back in South Africa, a solemn, self-important little man whose proudest boast was that he ran his family like a well-drilled army unit. How repulsive! She wouldn't be at all surprised if Herr von Reuter could make the same claim— although she couldn't imagine any woman being fool enough to marry him. Then again, the professor had had not one wife but two, the first unfortunate woman having died in childbirth.

Watching the two men—Sean Farrell and Hubertus von Reuter— Maeve knew they disliked each other. This was peculiar for two fellows who were supposed to be on the same side. Von Reuter's piercing blue eyes seemed to narrow every time Sean said something to Moira that made her laugh; it was as if he took any humor as a personal insult. Even his blond mustache seemed to quiver with annoyance when Farrell spoke. Maeve could tell that Caroline sensed it too. She looked at the German with a polite, guarded expression, whereas each time she looked at Sean, she seemed to glow. Sean had that effect on people, while von Reuter's personality withered all living things in his vicinity, decided Maeve. She hoped they would be well rid of him in Berlin.

Speeding through the Dutch countryside, the children waved at farmers driving sleds near the railroad tracks and at the occasional skaters on canals. Holland was as beautiful as that little crystal paperweight Farrell had bought her, Maeve thought. It was just like the pictures, so neat and orderly, so clean. The people were that way too. It was all so foreign to her after Africa, but it was wonderful. It was Europe! It was where she belonged.

As the landscape changed from Dutch to German, Maeve was scarcely aware of the difference until the train stopped and uniformed customs officers came on board. Their uniforms were different, and so was their manner. There was something very stiff about them, a little like Herr von Reuter. When they heard who he was and who their "illustrious passengers" were, they suddenly snapped to attention, clicking their heels—to Maeve's amusement—and declared their solidarity with the Boers. Passports were smartly stamped in no time at all, hands snapped to the brims of their caps, and with best wishes, they were out the door.

The ladies would have burst out laughing at such "Prussianism," but Herr von Reuter wouldn't have understood it. And they really wouldn't have been able to explain.

"Welcome to Germany," Sean said to Maeve, his eyes brimming with amusement. She noticed von Reuter wasn't at all amused.

The conductor announced, "Berlin, one hour!" "Will we meet your family in Berlin?" Maeve asked Sean.

"Oh, I would imagine," he replied with a laugh. "Mama will be there with every lady on her committees—all waving flags and creating quite a fuss. She'll have brass bands and God only knows what else. It will be a grand show."

"And what about your father? Will he be there too?"

For a second, Sean's expression changed. The girl thought he seemed faintly amused, but there was something else there too. Something mysterious.

Herr von Reuter gave a faintly veiled smirk. He knew something about Sean's father, apparently. Maeve was furious that she didn't. She decided to make it her business to find out as soon as possible.

"My father isn't likely to turn up at the station," he replied. "But I imagine my stepfather will be there—if he's up to it. He hasn't been in good health recently."

Sean's forecast about their reception was dead accurate. Not only did Geraldine have a brass band out to welcome them to Berlin—she had two, one a socialist group from Wedding. Huge banners were unfurled as the shiny black locomotive came chugging and steaming into the Anhalter Bahnhof. Both bandmasters struck up the "Volkslied" at the arrival of the "Boer victims," the enthusiasm marked by great cries of joy as the crowd caught sight of Sean and von Reuter waving to them from the windows of their Pullman car.

"Darling boy!" cried Geraldine as she spied Sean next to Hubertus, enjoying the frenzied reception. Snowflakes swirled as he waved to her. "Ah, look how brown he's become!" she exclaimed, delighted to see him looking so fit. Graf von Kleist was relieved the boy had returned in one piece. If anything had happened to him, his mother wouldn't be fit to live with. He waved to Sean, wondering where the poor, wretched victims were. This ought to be interesting.

A slim, blond young man stood next to Geraldine, looking curiously unmoved in the middle of the crowd of cheering, delighted Germans. He expressed appropriate relief that the gräfin's son was safe and ducked a few times so as not to get hit by the banners being unrolled all over the platform. People were really quite excited now, shouting all sorts of anti-British slogans and cheering the Boers. Even some of the fur-coated committeewomen were caught up in the excitement, pelting the Boers' Pullman car with a shower of flowers in the icy January air. Hundreds of marks' worth of roses fell on the tracks, leaving their fragrance behind amid the steam shooting from the train's iron wheels.

As the train came to a halt, Graf and Gräfin von Kleist ran to the steps of Sean's car, meeting him as he quickly descended. He enveloped Geraldine in his arms, kissing her on both cheeks, and she threw her arms around him and wept with happiness to see him alive and well. Geraldine always wept at train stations. In Petersburg, he had never met her or left her without a flood of tears.

"Mama," he said at last, as Geraldine pulled out a lacy white handkerchief and dried her eyes, "I wish to present our friends from South Africa—Frau van der Veldt, Frau Devereux, Fräulein Devereux and Dirck and Jannie van der Veldt. Ladies, Gräfin Geraldine von Kleist and Graf Erich von Kleist."

Maeve was slightly disoriented, surrounded by masses of cheering, friendly people who all seemed to be intent on wishing them well, pressing bouquets into their arms, or kissing them. Herr von Reuter might be lacking in personality, but his countrymen were certainly not shy about showing their feelings. She and the two young boys were a bit intimidated by all the attention. She held on to Dirck and Jannie so they wouldn't get swept away in the great, swirling crowd.

While Sean and the ladies waved to their well-wishers and he introduced Moira and Caroline to the committeewomen, Maeve and the boys were standing a little to the side, watching. To her surprise, she saw the handsome blond young man turn to Herr von Reuter and gracefully hand him a small bouquet of white roses. "Welcome home, Papa," he said. "Mission accomplished?"

Nodding curtly, von Reuter glanced briefly at the flowers, gave his son an icy look, and, to Maeve's astonishment, roughly pushed the bouquet at her. "Here," he snapped. "For you. My son ought to give these to a female."

Rude bastard, Maeve thought, shocked that he would be so nasty to her—and to his son. So there *had* been some poor, stupid woman. My God! It must have been a case of desperation to marry.

Seemingly unfazed by his father's behavior, the young man bowed cordially to the girl in the ermine-trimmed, red woolen coat and smiled politely. "Dietrich von Reuter," he said. He waited expectantly for some response.

Still amazed at the way Herr von Reuter had behaved, Maeve could only stare at this Dietrich, while awkwardly clutching the bouquet she had just received by default. He was so handsome. She had seen lots of good-looking blond boys back home, but this German was unlike any boy she had ever seen. He looked absolutely perfect. From his neatly clipped flaxen hair to his impeccably polished boots, he was so flawlessly beautiful she was staggered. No human being in her memory had ever had blue eyes like his. They were so light they seemed to have been painted with soft watercolors. The lashes and brows were dark brown. His face was a delicate oval, his nose small and straight, his mouth rather thin and very fine.

"I'm Maeve Devereux," she said at last. And then she smiled playfully. "Thank you for the flowers."

"You're most welcome." He smiled back, pleased to find his father's "Boer victims" less ragged than he had been led to expect. In fact, he thought, they were quite appealing.

When Maeve was presented to Geraldine and Erich von Kleist, the girl found herself looking into two more pairs of blue eyes, one pair curious, the other passionately concerned.

"This is the girl who saved your life," Geraldine murmured as her son introduced Maeve to his mother. "My God. Just a child. You brave, brave creature. I'm so grateful . . ."

The Gräfin Geraldine embraced Maeve ceremoniously, nearly smothering her in her deep, soft sables as the bands boomed out "Deutschland über Alles" and the happy onlookers cheered themselves hoarse with admiration for the "brave Boer girl." At that point, neither Maeve nor her mother felt it necessary to enlighten the population about their nationality.

*

That night, as Maeve lay curled up in a soft featherbed in the expensive Hotel Adlon, she thought she must have dreamed everything that had happened to her today: the journey to Berlin in the private Pullman, that ecstatic reception at the station, the ladies all in luxurious furs. That beautiful blond boy, Herr von Reuter's son. *His* son.

Maeve sighed and reached for the bouquet lying on the small table beside the carved Biedermeier bed in her elegant suite. The white roses gave off a sweet, subtle scent she found oddly exciting. The entire day had been overwhelming, she reflected. It was all so strange, as if she hadn't lived it but only dreamed it.

When she closed her eyes, she could picture herself back in the camp, dirty, despised, treated like a dog, forced to obey the orders of men who were scum in uniform. Forced to watch her beautiful mother sicken and come close to dying because of ill treatment. Utterly helpless. And then the courtroom again, and her darling father sentenced to die because he had the strength of his beliefs and the courage to act on them.

Frightened by the memory, Maeve sat up, clutching the bouquet, holding on to it as if it were a talisman. Her heart was beating so fast, she was frightened. Those were fantasies now; they were part of a life that was far away.

I'll never be that helpless again, she promised herself. That's over and done with. From now on, they'll have to work hard to humble *me*!

Maeve closed her eyes and once more found herself recalling the scene in the courtroom, the heat, the slowly swirling fans, the soldiers. There was Papa, surrounded by an armed escort, prevented from speaking to her as he was led off to be hanged.

"Maeve! . . . I" was all he managed to get out. What final words did he intend to say? What request would he have made? The girl sighed and buried her face in the pillow, fighting back tears.

What did you want me to know? she wondered, staring into the darkness, surrounded by the sweet scent of white roses. What was your message?

To her sadness, nothing answered her half-whispered queries, nothing but the soft, muffled, bittersweet sound of snow falling against the windowpane.

CHAPTER 4

*B*erlin was a revelation. It was the busiest city Maeve could ever imagine, having been exposed to only one European city in her life. It was also clean. And apparently it was heart and soul with the Boers. People cheered Caroline when she spoke—in German—at rallies, and Moira moved many an audience to tears—in English—at tea parties given by Sean's mother.

It was at one of these tea parties that a young officer, tall, slim, and sandy-haired, caused a visible stir by his presence, and proceeded to spend an inordinate amount of time talking to Moira Devereux, very appealing in her chic widow's weeds.

"Who is that fellow?" Maeve demanded as soon as she could reach Sean across a crowded room filled with Berlin matrons and their men.

"Crown Prince Friedrich Wilhelm," Sean responded glumly. He wasn't pleased.

"He seems to like Mama."

Farrell's blue eyes took on a threatening glare.

"I'm sure he does. In fact, I don't think the female has been born whom he *doesn't* like."

The girl nodded sagely, her thick auburn hair swaying slightly. "He's a bit of a skirt chaser, then?"

For a moment Sean almost laughed. Maeve sounded like a concerned mother anxious about her daughter's virtue.

"You might say so," he admitted.

"Then perhaps he can help us out. He's wearing a uniform. Maybe he can get us some soldiers."

"I wouldn't count on it. He's more of a decoration than a real soldier himself."

"But his father's the Kaiser," protested Maeve. "Surely if he were to ask, old Wilhelm wouldn't turn him down."

Smiling at this charming display of innocence—and ignorance of Hohenzollern family intricacies and the working of German diplomacy—Sean gave Maeve an affectionate pat on the head, ruffling her waves of glossy reddish hair.

"I must have you meet my sisters Militza and Stana one day," he murmured. "They have your love of the direct approach."

And he kept his wary eyes on Fritz and Moira—who seemed to be enjoying her tête-à-tête with Prussian royalty a little too much for his taste.

*

The day after Moira's encounter with Crown Prince Friedrich Wilhelm at Countess Geraldine's, Maeve noticed, to her astonishment, that her mother's sitting room at the Adlon was suddenly filled with baskets of fresh flowers. Roses, orchids, and gardenias—sent from God knows where in this freezing Berlin winter—were all over the place, on tables, next to chairs, on the mantel, underfoot. It was rather bizarre and altogether exotic.

"Read the cards," Moira directed as she saw Maeve's expression. "All courtesy of the same gentleman."

"Friedrich Wilhelm," Maeve read, picking up an embossed calling card from the nearest bouquet. Her head suddenly jerked up. "That's the prince," she exclaimed. "The Kaiser's son!"

"He was very interested in hearing about our troubles," said Moira. "He seems a nice young man."

Moira was lying. The young Hohenzollern struck her as a predatory male, somewhat along the lines of a fox after some chickens. He really did have a vulpine aspect too—long nose, narrow face, reddish blond hair. But the fact that he was Queen Victoria's great-grandson impressed Moira Devereux despite all the rest. Never in her life had she thought she'd be making small talk with royalty, let alone any member—however far removed—of Queen Victoria's family.

Like most British subjects born during the late queen's reign, Moira regarded Her Majesty with something akin to awe. Victoria was a semi-mythical old lady, embodying all the grandeur of the Empire in her own small, chubby person. In a way, she *was* the Empire. Even Irishmen cheered her when she visited Dublin, although they had been known to murder her emissaries.

Although Moira Devereux had no great love for the British, she had a respect for Queen Victoria that had survived even Pat's hanging and her stay in Camp 3.

"If Her Majesty were still alive," she had once commented, as she and Maeve stood watching Sergeant Davies across the dusty yard of the prison compound, "this never would have happened."

Maeve took that in stride and concluded that if fat Edward *had* allowed his judges to hang her father and throw her and Moira into prison, then he must be a dismal fellow indeed. She was ashamed to have any link to his Empire.

"Do you think the Crown Prince sent Mrs. van der Veldt flowers too?" Maeve asked, surveying the room. It really looked like a very elegant mortuary. That thought made her shudder involuntarily.

"I don't think so," Moira replied, with a peculiar flutter of her eyelashes. "These are all for my benefit."

"Do you think he wants to help us, then?"

Maeve saw the expression on her mother's face change. It was almost as if Moira was trying to conceal something from her, some grown-up business, probably boring.

"Umm," murmured her mother, "I think His Highness wants *something*."

And before Maeve could pursue it further, Moira turned and vanished into her bedroom to look through a pile of new clothes and decide what to wear.

*

"He filled up the whole room with flowers," Maeve declared to Sean as they sat in one of the beautiful ground-floor salons in Geraldine's palace. All around them were priceless objets d'art—Chinese and French porcelain, Fabergé boxes—and elaborate paintings in carved and gilded frames. The walls and furniture were sheathed in teal-blue silk, threaded lightly with gold. Very impressive.

"The whole room?" Sean demanded, getting back to the flowers.

"They were everywhere. You could scarcely move for fear of tripping over them."

Sean gave a disdainful little sniff, a mannerism Maeve found amusing—very *grand seigneur* she would have called it, if she had known what a *grand seigneur* was.

"I think he's trying to make an impression," Maeve confided with touching solemnity.

Sean glanced at her in that maddening way of grown-ups who don't want to share their superior wisdom with a child. "Umm," he murmured. He didn't look happy.

Any further discussion about Moira's new admirer was cut short when Geraldine sailed into the room. She was very elegant in a dark blue silk frock trimmed with fur at the neckline and sleeves and heavily encrusted with point lace. Several rows of large pearls rested on her lacy bosom, dazzling Maeve with their grandeur. Before meeting Geraldine she hadn't been aware that so many pearls actually existed.

"This is serious," announced the gräfin. "Her Majesty Kaiserin Augusta Viktoria has prevailed on the Emperor to receive you in a private audience. It's a tremendous honor."

"My God!" exclaimed the girl. "We're to meet the Kaiser!"

Geraldine nodded. "Yes, but you have to know how to behave properly. This is Germany."

Sean saw Maeve's bewilderment and hastened to explain. "Court etiquette is quite strict here. We'll have to teach you and the ladies how to conduct yourselves in the presence of His Majesty."

Geraldine smiled her encouragement. "It's all a bit like learning the rules of a game," she said. "The danger is in making a faux pas— a false step. Royalty is to be treated differently from the rest of humanity."

"Why?" Maeve inquired in surprise. She instantly regretted her ignorance, as her hostess raised her eyebrows in alarm at this lack of sophistication.

"Because royalty is used to being treated in certain ways, and *not* to do this is rude and ungracious. Do you want to offend our German Kaiser, for heaven's sake?"

"Oh no," she replied in alarm. "Never."

"Well then . . ."

And that began Maeve's introduction to the beau monde. Curtsying was the first lesson. With years of practice, the Gräfin von Kleist showed how one curtsied to various royal personages, emperors and empresses heading the list. These received an obeisance that nearly had one's head touching the floor. Lesser royalty received a modified version.

Moira was an apt pupil, having known ladies who had been received at the Court of St. James's. Maeve and Caroline seemed to regard the whole business as a necessary evil. It certainly wouldn't do to offend the Kaiser, but it all seemed so silly.

"Just look at it this way," Sean said as Maeve practiced curtsying before him for the tenth time. "If you were a princess, things would be a lot worse."

"How?" Maeve demanded, glancing at herself in one of the tall gilded mirrors of the salon. She looked ridiculous bowing and scraping in a white middy blouse and navy-blue serge skirt, showing black ankle boots and black stockings. If one had to curtsy, one ought to be in a gown.

"If you were a princess, your life would be an endless litany of rules with no allowances made for originality or creativity. Everything would have been laid down for you to follow, cradle to grave. Your whole existence would have been planned by others long ago. It's extremely boring."

"No!" Maeve exclaimed in disbelief. "Besides," she added, "how would you know? You're not a prince."

That provoked such a glare from Sean's blue eyes, it rattled the girl. It was a bit like the time she had asked him about his father, except then he had merely been amused. For a moment, she was afraid she had angered him. Frightened, she could only stare.

"True," he nodded, rather ironically Maeve thought. "But my father is a prince. A reigning prince. And my half brothers and sisters are princes and princesses. *That's* how I know."

He said it so simply Maeve knew instinctively he wasn't lying— although it seemed astonishing. Her large blue eyes got even bigger as she looked back at this tall, handsome fellow in the Savile Row suit, stiff collar, Lyons silk cravat, and diamond stickpin. Sean was almost royalty.

Maeve almost couldn't believe it. It wasn't as though he was ordinary—no ordinary man could have done what he'd done—but he was so easy to talk to. He put no distances between them, even though she was a mere girl from nowhere and he was—well, almost a prince, and a grown-up besides.

"He's not related to King Edward, is he?" she blurted out.

"Good God, no. He's Prince Nikolai of Montenegro, and his alliances are with the Russians, Italians, and Serbs. Two of my half sisters are Grand Duchesses of Russia, one is Queen of Italy."

"A queen!"

"Yes. A very lovely queen. Elena."

"Ah," Maeve reflected, still nearly in shock. "So you really do know about royalty."

"Oh yes." Sean smiled. "That I do."

"But why isn't your mother with your father?" she asked, puzzled.

This child had a tendency to tread on one's toes without realizing it, Sean reflected. He knew it was due to youthful ignorance, not malice, so he chose not to let it bother him. There were grown men in Paris and Petersburg who had ended up nursing sore jaws after similar questions.

But Maeve Devereux was just a curious young girl, so he could be tolerant. Besides, girl or not, she had saved his life, and that action had put her in a very special category. In a way, she reminded him of the plainspoken Montenegrins, who were direct and to the point—when they weren't being devious and cunning. He didn't suspect her of that.

"My parents were never married," he replied at last.

"Oh."

"It's rather a long story." He smiled at her crestfallen look. "Some day I must tell it to you."

Maeve didn't press him for details after that, but suddenly the whole world seemed turned on its head. If Sean's mother had given birth to him without a wedding ceremony back home, it would have been a tremendous scandal and she never would have been able to show her face again. It would have been the worst kind of disgrace. And yet here she was, clothed in silks, covered with jewels, and married to a man who had a palace. Countess Geraldine was certainly one in a million, Maeve thought.

And then, driven by her insatiable curiosity, Maeve hurried to an atlas at the first opportunity, to try to locate Montenegro.

*

Coached in curtsying by Geraldine, the "Boer victims" were ready to meet the Kaiser. Moira, as a recent widow, was decked out in the appropriate degree of mourning, which allowed for some decoration in the form of jet earrings and not much more. Caroline was elegantly but somberly attired in a tailored suit of deep cobalt blue with black soutache trim on the short jacket and at the hem of her skirt. And Maeve, a schoolgirl, was allowed to wear a black silk dress, recently run up by Geraldine's dressmaker.

Maeve was the difficulty. She had just turned seventeen, a sort of in-between age when a dark skirt and middy blouse were no longer really suitable, but she wasn't yet married, employed, or engaged, which would have qualified her for grown-up status.

"Any girl can use a good black silk dress," Sean had told his mother. "Besides, Maeve's too tall to wear short skirts any longer."

"I've never heard you so concerned about women's clothing. I thought it was the mother who had caught your eye." Her tone was icy.

"Mama! Maeve's hardly more than a child. Give me some credit for decency."

"I had already left home to make my way in the world by the time I was her age. Don't deceive yourself. She's not a baby," warned Geraldine.

"Sometimes you make me blush, you know. I happen to like grown women, in case you haven't noticed."

"Oh, I have," nodded Geraldine, as she ran her hand along her rows of pearls. "And I only wish you would marry one. Your father feels the same way."

At that point, Sean had gently kissed his mother goodbye and gone off for a drive. He hated the Marriage Question. It was getting to be Mama's goal in life—to see him paired off with some Teutonic heiress. Nikolai had a preference for a Russian fortune, but he was flexible. As long as the girl was rich and fertile, she was more than acceptable.

The only problem was, Sean preferred to indulge his own fancy, and he almost never fell in love with anyone remotely acceptable. In his heart, he admired women like Geraldine. Or Moira. He couldn't wait for the next time in bed with that beauty.

CHAPTER 5

O n the morning of the great day, Caroline, Moira, and Maeve assembled at Geraldine's palace and were put through their final curtsy drills. Jannie and Dirck had been left in the care of servants while Frau van der Veldt kept her appointment with the Kaiser.

"Now remember," Sean cautioned Maeve. "As soon as the footman opens the door, you step inside and make your curtsy. Don't hesitate. That's how it's done."

"And the Kaiser will speak first."

"Exactly."

"Just smile and don't say a word unless spoken to," Moira added, giving her daughter a tap on the shoulder. "You can be very indiscreet."

"Yes, Mama." Obviously Moira didn't trust her with royalty.

Maeve exchanged glances with Sean, who was wearing a very dashing military uniform—red tunic with gold frogging, a dazzling array of decorations splashed across his chest, and black trousers and gleaming black boots.

"I didn't know you were a soldier," Maeve declared, admiring him. "You certainly have a gorgeous uniform. Is it from . . . Montenegro?" she asked, hoping she was pronouncing it correctly.

"Yes." He grinned. "Second Montenegrin Light Infantry. Colonel."

Maeve was impressed. "You look grand enough to be a general," she said.

That made him smile too. "It is a bit overdone, but it's actually quite restrained by Russian or Austrian standards. You ought to see how the Chevalier Guards are outfitted in Petersburg. And by the way," he confided, "the Kaiser is second to no one in his love of uniforms. He has a collection of them from all over Europe. God only knows how he'll be dressed when we meet him."

"It should be a memorable event," murmured Moira, brushing past him on her way out the door. He caught a tantalizing scent of roses, reminding him of those stories of baskets of flowers in her suite at the Adlon. Damn!

*

Maeve's imagination ran wild as she was conveyed across Berlin to keep her appointment with Kaiser Wilhelm. What would he look like in person? she wondered. Would he be as fierce as he seemed in photographs? Would his mustaches really stand on end? Most of all, would he wear one of his beautiful plumed helmets?

"One final word, ladies," Sean confided to his charges as the coachman drove the shiny black berline with the golden crest through the wrought-iron entrance gates of the palace. "His Majesty has a withered arm due to the doctors' clumsiness at his birth. Pretend not to notice it."

Maeve was taken aback. "But his pictures don't show it," she protested. The Kaiser was one of her heroes; he was supposed to be perfect. Better, in fact.

"Royalty in the *Illustrated London News* and royalty in person are often two different things," Sean replied patiently. "Sometimes the photographs are a lot more impressive."

And at those words, their coach came to a splendid stop at the entrance to the palace and liveried servants came dashing out into the snow to hand down the passengers.

Wilhelm's palace, in the very heart of Prussia's capital, was more impressive for its size than its beauty. It was rather a plain building, with few flourishes on its facade other than a statue here and there. The Kaiser himself complained about it constantly, lamenting the fact that his subjects could stare right in his windows. He much preferred the new palace in Potsdam. But it did have a ceremonial purpose and a place of honor in Hohenzollern family tradition.

Once inside however, the visitors were dazzled by the grandeur of the furnishings. Helped out of their winter coats by waiting servants, the party was led by two footmen through endless corridors of polished parquet floors, gleaming with the wood of dozens of exotic trees, buffed by an army of servants till they shone. Tall vases of exquisite porcelain from Nymphenburg and Dresden stood like sentinels beside gilded mirrors in rococo frames. There seemed to be dozens of them, evenly stretched out along their path like signposts.

All along their route, Maeve saw more servants in livery than even Countess Geraldine employed. What was their function? she wondered. And didn't they feel foolish in those outfits? Imagine that—grown men wearing knee breeches and powdered wigs!

Moira was fascinated by the richness of the place. Never had she beheld entire miles of silken wall coverings, silken upholstery, tons of sparkling crystal chandeliers, and acres of oil paintings. It didn't seem possible that she had spent her life on the same planet as the people who lived in this great palace.

Is this what Buckingham Palace looked like? she mused. The life-size formal portrait of Queen Victoria on one of the landings could have been quite at home there. She thought it was a nice gesture that this German kaiser should have honored his grandmother in this way. It was really a very lovely painting, with Victoria presented as a slender young girl—probably before she had that tribe of children, Moira reflected. Maeve's arrival had meant the end of her own eighteen-inch waist. She could sympathize with a mother of nine.

"Almost there," Sean whispered to the ladies as their two escorts led them down yet another long gilded corridor.

And then, with a solemn flourish, the two servants came to an abrupt halt outside a large double door and rapped smartly twice.

Like clockwork it opened to reveal three gentlemen in uniform, one of them slim and sandy-haired with glorious upturned mustaches, but not quite as slender as the Crown Prince. His dark green uniform was laced with enough gold braid to enrapture even Maeve, and his medals gleamed almost as brightly as the parquet floors she had just traversed. The other two gentlemen, also in green, were obviously military men. They looked every inch the Prussian officers from lithographs of the Franco-Prussian War, stern, beefy, and bemedaled, with rolls of fat above tight collars.

"Once inside the door, curtsy," Geraldine had warned, so Maeve sank into a deep and reverent curtsy while Moira and Caroline followed suit. Beside them, Sean bowed formally, his brilliant scarlet tunic making a glorious contrast with the Prussian green.

"Welcome, dear ladies," Wilhelm said, indicating that they should rise. "I'm delighted to greet you in the name of the German people. We sympathize with your countrymen with all our hearts."

"Thank you, Your Majesty," murmured Caroline, a little over-come. "I'll repeat your kind words to our men when I return home."

While the grown-ups chatted and the Kaiser's two companions— German generals, both of them—asked questions about the weapons the British were using, Maeve let her eyes wander curiously around Wil-helm's beautifully paneled study. It was actually a fairly somber room, typically male in its decoration. None of the lavishness of the public rooms was visible here. This was evidently a real workplace for the Kaiser.

It was at that point Maeve noticed his desk, and when she did she had to force herself to restrain a giggle because it was certainly the oddest one she had ever seen. How bizarre! It was so tall it required a specially made seat that was a sort of saddle mounted upon what appeared to be an overgrown piano stool—only with the saddle in place of the traditional round seat. She could just picture the Kaiser seated on this contraption, galloping through his paperwork. Well, they surely did love horses, she thought, since she had seen countless statues of his ancestors perched upon them throughout the city. But in one's study! Fascinated, Maeve wished the Kaiser would take a seat there just so she could witness the effect. It must be highly original.

However, Maeve could tell that no one else seemed to find anything remotely comical about the desk and saddle, because all the grown-ups were solemnly discussing British beastliness, with Wilhelm speaking the loudest, his fierce mustaches quivering with passion as he gestured vi-olently, making quite a grand show, his blue eyes flashing with every other word.

Moira was now telling His Majesty about the brutal treatment she had endured in the camp, tears coming to her lovely eyes as she related her sad story. One of the beefy generals gallantly offered his handkerchief, his stern face showing his own emotion.

Maeve was only half listening. She was much more interested in the huge collection of photographs in the Kaiser's study—many of them of royalties she recognized from the pages of British periodicals. There was his grandmama, Queen Victoria, not young and pretty but ancient and bedecked with more diamonds than Maeve could even have imagined. The huge pear-shaped stones in her large earlobes must have been worth millions all by themselves. Odd how so much beautiful jewelry seemed to accumulate to ugly women. Then, next to Victoria, was the present Prince of Wales, formerly Duke of York, looking so much like his cousin the Tsar of Russia. Queen Alexandra of Great Britain came next, a radiant beauty, slim as a girl, followed by the Tsaritza of Russia, Grand Duchess Serge of Russia, and a very delicate blond beauty Maeve recognized as the Crown Princess of Romania. All members of the family. It was a little unreal.

Looking at this splendid collection of elegantly framed royalty, the girl wished she could have the frame from the Prince of Wales's picture. It was dark blue lapis, topped by a gilded ribbon. She had a favorite photograph of her father she'd like to put in its place.

Now Caroline was speaking in German and the generals, Maeve noticed, were bending forward to listen to every word, arms clasped in front of them, stern expressions on their faces.

Maeve's eyes were resting with admiration if not envy on Wilhelm's beautiful gold-embossed morocco leather desk appointments and their crystal accessories when the larger of the two generals turned to her unexpectedly and muttered, "Ach, Fräulein, he ordered you to eat maggots!"

Turning scarlet at the sudden attention, Maeve realized Caroline must have told them about Sergeant Davies.

"Yes sir." She nodded. "The dirty savage! And I was happy later on when I was finally able to shoot him."

Moira gave her such a look Maeve wished she had kept her mouth shut.

"You shot him?" demanded the Kaiser, instantly curious. Dumbfounded, in fact.

"Yes, Your Majesty. It was during our rescue. Sergeant Davies was about to shoot Sean, so I had to do it."

Maeve was now quite thoroughly mortified. Perhaps she shouldn't have mentioned it. She didn't want the Kaiser to think she was dangerous.

The generals seemed to approve. Moira did not. They'll think I raised a wild animal, was her exact thought.

"If Maeve hadn't done that, Your Majesty, I wouldn't be here today," Sean said loyally. "She is an amazing girl."

Nodding fiercely, Wilhelm said something to one of the generals and then went to one of the exquisite inlaid cabinets against the wall and withdrew something from a flat brown leather box.

"This is a very unusual honor for a woman," he declared solemnly, "but you deserve it, and I offer it with my sincere congratulations."

With that, he pinned the decoration onto Maeve's black silk dress and kissed her formally.

Prussia's Order of the Red Eagle, Third Class, never looked better, Sean thought.

Astonished, Maeve tried to think of the appropriate response. Geraldine's lessons hadn't included receiving imperial decorations, but good manners required something.

"Thank you, Your Majesty," Maeve murmured as she sank into the deepest curtsy she could manage. "I'll treasure it all my life."

That seemed to please everyone.

Wilhelm was then rash enough to inquire what Germany could offer the Boers in their hour of need and Maeve replied without hesitation, "Troops, Your Majesty."

With that, the bloom was definitely off the rose. The Kaiser hated being put on the spot and he equivocated, offering promises of more medical supplies—which Caroline was quick to thank him for.

The audience ended with Wilhelm presenting the ladies with beautifully framed photos of himself in full martial splendor—right hand clutching his field marshal's baton, face set in a severe expression, head covered with a gaudy hat dripping white plumes.

"You really have no sense," Moira lamented bitterly as the party was escorted back to their starting point. "You don't say such a thing to a man like that."

"What?" demanded Maeve, still embarrassed and defensive now.

"You don't ask royalty a point-blank question," Sean explained. But Maeve could see he was trying hard not to smile.

Caroline shook her blond head. "Don't be so hard on the girl. She did me a service by asking him that. Now I know what the answer to our hopes is."

"But he didn't say he'd send troops," Maeve said timidly. "He changed the subject."

"Exactly. Which means I can now go back home to Marinus. There will be no troops coming from Germany. This trip was a failure."

It was a waste of time despite all the fine words and the cheering European crowds. They were being left to their fate, thought Caroline. Well, it had all been a gamble anyway. Better to take the chance and lose than not to try.

"Caroline," said Sean, "even if worse comes to worst, European opinion will force the British to restrain themselves. Even the English people are making an outcry against the relocation policy and the camps."

"But we're going to lose the war," she said simply. "In spite of everything, in spite of all our suffering, we will lose. I'm going home."

Shortly afterward, she did just that, taking Dirck and Jannie with her. The farewells at Anhalter Station were quiet in comparison with the fanfare of their arrival. No brass bands and cheering crowds, just a slender woman and two little blond boys saying goodbye to a handful of friends. And it was cold, with a raw wind whipping at their coats.

"Goodbye, Sean." Caroline smiled, hugging him. "You were a good friend. God bless you for all you did."

"We'll meet again," he replied. "And it will be under better circumstances, I promise."

"Maeve," sighed Caroline. "Goodbye, darling. Don't ever become a diplomat." She smiled again as she fluffed up the girl's ermine collar with a maternal gesture. "And don't ever forget us."

"Never."

As Maeve and Sean said goodbye to the two boys, Maeve noticed Caroline whisper something to Moira as she embraced her. Moira shook her head and turned slightly pink in response.

And then came the time to board the train. After more kisses all around, the van der Veldts climbed on board and ran to the nearest window as baggage handlers attended to their luggage.

"Goodbye!" everyone shouted as the steam came whooshing out between the iron wheels of the shiny black locomotive. Dirck and Jannie waved their caps, the ladies their handkerchiefs.

"Until the next time!" Maeve cried, waving frantically, tears streaming down her cheeks. But with all the racket coming from the locomotive, she wasn't certain her friends even heard her.

"We will meet again," she said softly, brushing away the tears. "We have to."

But under the circumstances, she knew, it might be a very long time. No matter. They were friends and had shared both pain and adventure. They would never be forgotten.

On the way back to the Adlon, Maeve asked her mother what Caroline had said to her.

"Nothing," Moira retorted. "Nothing at all."

Grown-ups! Maeve thought. They always made such a secret of things. Why did they have to be so mysterious?

Moira, she observed, was a bit agitated. Wisely, she didn't ask the reason. But she knew Sean Farrell had noticed it too, and was trying to pretend he hadn't.

Staring out the glazed windows of the coach, Maeve wondered if she would ever reach their level of superior wisdom, or in fact any wisdom at all. There were days when she rather doubted it.

CHAPTER 6

After Caroline's departure for home, Maeve noticed a definite change in atmosphere. Moira was beginning to snap at her for any and all reasons, and Sean Farrell was not so much in evidence as he had been. Some business was taking him away to Paris for a visit to one of his sisters, the Grand Duchess Anastasia Nicolaievna—Stana. And now that banker, Herr von Reuter was prowling around. Maeve didn't like it. Moira, she noticed, didn't like it either, but she was allowing Herr von Reuter to call anyway.

And Crown Prince Friedrich Wilhelm was still in the picture, but now he was sending jewelry.

The best thing about Herr von Reuter, Maeve decided, was that beautiful son of his. Dietrich was a grown-up—twenty-four—but so much fun to be with, Maeve didn't care. He also had Moira's permission to call on her, which struck Maeve as odd since she didn't view herself as a "young lady"—but at least it gave her a chance to see the sights of Berlin with an exciting companion.

Dietrich was quite an assiduous host, taking Maeve for long sleigh rides through Berlin and its environs, bundled snugly under lap rugs of soft otter or fluffy fox while the little bells of the harness jangled merrily and chips of ice flew out from under the sharp hooves of the elegant trotters. Sometimes they stopped at the city's many frozen ponds to ice-skate, joining crowds of chic matrons, screeching children, and even the occasional officer. Maeve adored the snow. To her it was the most exotic phenomenon she had ever witnessed, and she loved playing in it. It seemed so European! And then, more than all the other things she discovered in Berlin, there was the opera.

It was a revelation to Maeve. *Roméo et Juliette* was the opera, and a slender, pretty American girl named Geraldine Farrar sang the female lead. Seated in Herr von Reuter's box with Dietrich, Hubertus, and Moira, Maeve fell in love with the whole atmosphere, the crowds of well-dressed people, the elegance of the theater itself, the glamour of the production. She identified with the heroine and was thrilled to see her so romantically in love. *There* was a woman with nobody to tell her how to behave, thought Maeve. It was heady stuff. She wept at the end and applauded like mad when Farrar, Berlin's newest darling, came out to take her curtain calls, dropping lovely curtsies to her frenzied admirers. People were shouting "Brava!" all over the hall.

"She curtsies very well," Maeve remarked to Moira, having recent experience in the art. The *other* Geraldine would certainly approve.

Dietrich burst out laughing. "And what about her singing?" he asked. "That's the main point."

"She's wonderful. I've never heard anything like it," said Maeve. "It's so exciting, all that running about, the fighting, the lovers . . ."

The red-haired girl smiled dreamily. She was a little overwhelmed by the whole experience. It seemed so much larger than life, almost like a fairy tale, with the crowds applauding, the singers presented with all those bouquets from well-wishers, the ritual of the curtain calls, where everybody had a turn to bask in the limelight and applause. It was better than any show she'd ever seen. It glittered. The audience glittered. It was life through a magic glass. I'd like to do that, Maeve thought. It would be grand.

The next day, when she and Dietrich went for a stroll on the busy Kurfürstendamm, Maeve was still thinking about the opera. They stopped for coffee at one of the glass-enclosed cafés, and she noticed there were postcards with Geraldine Farrar's picture on them for sale at the counter. Obligingly Dietrich bought her one. A nice souvenir, he said.

"Farrar is going to become a fantastic star," he said as the white-aproned waiter brought their coffee and pastry. "She has tremendous talent and great acting ability. And on top of it, she's beautiful. She has it all. Some singers have lovely voices but look like wood on stage. Some are lovely to look at and sound like reeds in the wind. She has everything."

Maeve was studying Dietrich's face. He was obviously enraptured with this pretty American girl; she wondered if he knew her personally.

She noticed what a fine complexion he had, fair as a girl's with just a slight flush of pink from the cold, like hers. The eyes were the only feature that looked as if it didn't quite belong. They were a sublime shade of light blue, which was fine, but they were somewhat spoiled by faint bluish circles underneath, as if Dietrich didn't get enough rest. Perhaps his father worked him too hard, Maeve speculated. That would be just like Herr von Reuter. Old slave driver.

"You remind me of the Lorelei," he told her quite unexpectedly, fixing those eyes on Maeve, who didn't know what he was talking about.

"You don't understand, do you?" he said, and smiled. "Well, the Lorelei is a very beautiful lady in German legends, a siren who tempts sailors to go off course and wreck their boats. There's a very lovely poem about her by one of our greatest poets."

Maeve didn't know whether to be flattered or not. Dietrich was obviously quite fond of this poem, but the girl couldn't easily picture herself as a siren, probably draped in flowing kelp and perched on a rock someplace, luring German sailors to destruction. How bizarre!

"She sounds dangerous," Maeve replied at last, making Dietrich smile again. She thought he had some very odd notions.

"Oh, she is," he assured Maeve. "Very beautiful and very dangerous."

And then he asked seriously, "How old are you?"

"I'll be eighteen next year." Why did that matter? she wondered.

Again he smiled, showing even white teeth. "Almost grown," he said.

"I don't really feel very grown-up," Maeve admitted. "I still feel the same as I was before they put us in that camp."

"Perhaps you don't wish to acknowledge everything that happened to you."

Maeve shook her head. "It's all past history now. If I think about it too much, I can't sleep. I don't want to dwell on it."

Dietrich reminded her a little of his father when he asked quietly, "Were they very brutal?"

"Dreadful." And she thought of her father torn from his family and condemned without mercy. She thought of the camp.

The young man was studying Maeve with the look a vet might give a prize horse. "I heard you shot one of the guards," he said, as if it were the most natural thing in the world.

At that, Maeve blushed and wanted to sink beneath the table. She had no regrets about shooting Sergeant Davies, but it just seemed glar-

ingly inappropriate as a topic of conversation now. It was embarrassing
to be identified as "the girl who shot the sergeant." She was afraid people
would be put off by it, that they would regard her as some sort of African
savage, uncivilized and barely housebroken.

"You see," Dietrich teased, "you *are* a dangerous girl."

"Not to you," Maeve replied, not wanting this Dietrich to be scared
off. "I wouldn't do you any harm."

"*Liebchen*, I wish that were true." He laughed, reaching across the
table to take Maeve's hand. "The trouble is, you don't really understand
just how dangerous you are. You're so adorable."

After that tête-à-tête in the café, Maeve noticed that Dietrich had
a tendency to nestle closer to her in the sleigh when they went driving.
It was very cozy, but unsettling at the same time.

His undoing came about a week after they saw the opera. He and
Maeve had taken a long ride out to the suburbs to go skating, and on
their return, Dietrich had stopped before the Hotel Adlon to let Maeve
out. There was nothing wrong with that except that as he kissed her
goodbye, Moira happened to glance out the window to see her daughter
and Hubertus's son in each other's arms for what seemed an indecently
long embrace in full view of the whole world. Gasping with indignation,
Moira waited for the shameless one to enter their suite, and when she
did, Maeve received such a fierce slap she nearly lost her balance.

"Little hussy!" raged her mother. "Are you trying to disgrace us?"

"What?" cried the girl, frightened and a little angry. "Mama!"

"Don't play the innocent with me, missy! What are you and that
boy doing?"

"Ice-skating mostly."

That sounded as flippant to Moira as it did to Maeve. She let fly
with another slap, determined to hurt her daughter.

"Mama, don't!"

"You're never to go out with him again. Never. He's too old for
you anyway. You're only a child. What a fool I was to think he was safe!
The devious little swine!"

"He isn't a swine, Mama. He's very nice."

"Don't be an idiot! Nobody's nice," Moira shouted. "Especially
where young girls are concerned. Men can never be trusted. Never! You
have to be aware of this." *She* was.

Despite all the fuss, Maeve didn't believe for one minute that
Dietrich was any sort of swine at all. She knew what a swine was, and
it wasn't Dietrich.

Then she began to wonder what Moira was doing with Herr von Reuter and the Crown Prince while she was out in the open air, driving through the suburbs.

*

Moira and her daughter were living in considerable luxury at the Adlon, thanks to Sean, but since his disappearance, Moira was becoming increasingly frantic about the whole thing. Had he vanished for good? Had he had his fill of them? Was there some woman in Paris other than his sister who was detaining him? She could only guess. And she missed him in another way as well. Meanwhile, Herr von Reuter and the Crown Prince were still paying calls. And they were hinting now that they couldn't wait forever.

It's preposterous, Moira reflected as Friedrich Wilhelm sat opposite her one evening in the chic dining room of the hotel, purring affectionate nonsense in English. This is a fellow whose sole interest in life seems to be women, thought Moira. He wasn't even put off by the fact that she was thirty-six and the mother of a grown daughter. All he saw was her lovely face, her curvy figure, her glistening mass of dark hair. She thought he was a bit daft. And there were rumors that the prince was soon to become engaged to the beautiful Duchess Cécilie, daughter of the Grand Duke and Duchess of Mecklenburg-Schwerin, wherever that was. She hoped the young lady had a tolerant nature. She would need it.

Friedrich Wilhelm smiled at the lovely Irishwoman from his side of the table and looked more like a fox than ever. Several diners from nearby tables were casting interested glances at the young prince in uniform. Three tables of his overdecorated aides-de-camp made certain His Highness's dinner was not disturbed by any citizen forward enough to attempt it.

"I would like to call on you tomorrow afternoon," Friedrich Wilhelm declared, his blue eyes resting lightly on Moira's shapely white shoulders. "In your suite."

Moira was no fool; she knew what the skinny little fox meant, and she inclined her head agreeably. Ridiculous as it was, she was terribly curious to find out how this Hohenzollern prince might be different from the rest of mankind. He was royalty; therefore there had to be *something* unique about him. The fact that he was Queen Victoria's great-grandson was also not lost upon Moira Devereux, one of the late Queen's lesser subjects. Nobody she knew had ever bedded royalty.

"In anticipation of seeing you tomorrow afternoon," continued the prince, "I would like to present you with something to wear."

Before Moira could reply, Friedrich Wilhelm produced a flat black leather envelope and graciously handed it to his lady.

"Please open it," he said, and smiled, sure of the effect.

Moira often wondered afterward if he'd arranged things that way, but at the very moment he was presenting her with his gift, the orchestra struck up "The Emperor Waltz," perhaps a hint for the future.

There in the box, on a background of white satin, was the most exquisite diamond bracelet Moira had ever seen.

Her eyelashes fluttered with desire—for the bracelet.

"Thank you, Your Highness," she murmured. "It's beautiful."

"May I put it on your wrist?"

"Please."

As she extended her right hand, Moira couldn't help but be aware of the interest this was causing. Waltzing couples were trying hard to see what he had given her. People at nearby tables were now gawking. Apparently the prince was used to being the center of attention and rather enjoyed it. He was beaming.

Moira wondered if anything in life really made sense. She was about to lose her virtue—after a fashion—to the Fox of Hohenzollern because she was desperate without news of Sean Farrell and was terrified of being abandoned in the middle of Europe with nobody to turn to.

Sitting in the Adlon's richly decorated dining room, under several huge crystal chandeliers, surrounded by ladies in elegant gowns, jewels, and feathers and men in white tie or military uniforms, Moira Devereux remembered what she had come from in Africa, and succumbing to the prince seemed a small inconvenience if it would prevent her and Maeve from ever having to go back there again.

At the same time, watching her lovely reflection in the mirror on the wall opposite their table, Moira looked at the woman in the black satin evening gown with its rich black lace frill at her décolletage, and she wondered if things here were so very different from back home. This young fool of a prince looked at her the same way as so many others . . .

"To our happiness tomorrow," Friedrich Wilhelm said tenderly, holding up his champagne glass.

Moira smiled sweetly and gracefully bowed her head. Well, if she was about to become a real courtesan, at least she was starting at the top.

Unfortunately for him, the prince was obliged to report for duty, giving his lady a twenty-four-hour reprieve from passion. But when he called upon her tomorrow, Fritz promised as he gently kissed her hand, love would be the only thing on his mind.

Moira's eyelashes fluttered a bit at that, while several dozen Germans in her vicinity tried to guess who she was and if she was going to be a fixture of Berlin night life in the near future.

Returning to her suite, Moira was overjoyed to discover Sean there, chatting with Maeve. They both noticed the diamonds at once.

"My God! I'm so happy to see you! Where have you been?" Moira wailed, throwing her arms around his neck. "I thought you had deserted us."

"Family business in Paris. My sister Stana's husband is a brute. I was sent by Papa to try to get him to change his ways."

"Were you successful?"

"Probably for the next few days." He shrugged. "And then His Highness will revert to being a brute. We've been through it all before."

Moira was stunning in this evening gown, he reflected. It left her exquisite shoulders bare and dipped down breathtakingly in the front to expose enough of her bosom to make him wonder how she managed to stay covered. Jet beads sparkled all over the bodice and whirled across the trumpet skirt to the hem, glittering with each step she took. It was Geraldine's, altered for Moira. It suited her admirably.

He would have been content just to stand there watching her if he hadn't seen that bracelet. Against the gleaming black satin of the gown, it flashed brilliant fires with each small gesture of her hand, a magnificent present.

"I see you've been attracting admirers," he said at last. He didn't look pleased.

"It's from the Crown Prince," Moira said, knowing he meant the bracelet.

"I might have guessed. He's probably exhausted the entire floral stock of Greater Berlin."

Maeve could sense the tension. Moira turned to her and suggested she go to her room. The grown-ups had something to discuss. Casting a long final glance at Sean, the girl left, bitterly regretting her banishment.

When she heard the sound of Maeve's door shutting, Moira turned to Farrell and said, "Why didn't you let us know you were coming back? I thought we had been abandoned."

"I'm sorry. It never occurred to me you'd think that."

She was exasperated. How could she not think that? Alone in Europe, living at someone else's expense in a grand hotel. If he were gone, she and Maeve would be out on the street.

"I don't think your royal admirer would allow that to happen," Sean said. "Those diamonds would keep you warm for a good long while."

Moira couldn't believe her ears. She went white, then red. Then she snaked out her right arm and caught Sean smartly on the cheek with a well-aimed slap.

"How dare you! You frighten me half to death and then accuse me of . . ." Moira reeled from the unfairness of it—as well as the truth.

"Moira," he cried, "calm yourself! For heaven's sake!"

She didn't answer. Instead she snatched a small porcelain statue from the table nearby. But before she could hurl it at him he neatly grabbed her arm, flipped her over onto the sofa, and pinned her arms to her sides.

"Stop this!" he ordered. "My God, what a temper you have. No wonder the British thought you were a danger to them!"

"I'll be a danger to you if you don't let go of me!"

"But why would you want to do that? I've come here to ask you if you want to get out of Berlin and see the world. That is"—he smiled—"if you can tear yourself away from young Fritz."

"Don't trifle with me," Moira cautioned, with murder in her eyes. They were dark indigo now, becoming darker with her anger.

"I'm sorry," he apologized. "I thought . . ."

"I know what you thought. It's not true," she lied. "Not true at all!"

"Ah. So perhaps you're not as enchanted with royalty as I imagined."

"Not with that speciman," Moira retorted, making Sean laugh so hard he let her go. "But he's coming round tomorrow to extract payment for the diamonds," she said. "And I don't want to be here when he arrives."

Moira was disheveled in a very alluring way, Sean thought—glossy black hair hanging halfway down her back, stray wisps delicately framing her heart-shaped face, black lace sinking lower around her lovely full bosom. The jet necklace she wore made a pattern like filigree against her creamy skin, emphasizing its beauty. Sean leaned closer and softly kissed her neck and shoulders.

"Where are you taking me now?" Moira demanded, not at all distracted.

"Belgrade," he murmured, stroking her lovely silken curves, making her shiver. "It's the capital of Serbia."

"Is it as grand as Berlin?" Moira asked. She put her arms around him and sank deeper into the sofa cushions.

"Not grand at all. Semibarbaric. But colorful," he hastened to add. "It will be an adventure."

"Do you think I ought to send back the bracelet?"

That made him smile. He sat up. "No," he said. "Keep it. Fritz may be put out, but it was a gift, freely given. Presents aren't supposed to be regarded as currency, after all."

"He'd probably only give it to another woman anyway," Moira agreed. "And it surely looks as fine on my wrist as it would on any other."

Exactly what his mother would have declared, Sean thought minutes later in the bedroom as he clasped his lips to Moira's and brought his long, slender fingers down her body to her most sensitive place.

They moved their bodies so that they were able to take each other in their mouths, ravenous for lovemaking after the separation. It was a night of ecstasy and abandon.

CHAPTER 7

*E*arly next morning, Maeve was startled awake by a swarthy fellow
who knocked at her door twice, then opened it to tell her to get
up and start packing. They were on their way to Serbia.

"Who are you?" she demanded, still half asleep.

"Kyril," came the reply. "I work for Ivan Petrovic. Get ready now,
little one."

"Ivan Petrovic?" Maeve muttered as she watched the stranger with
the funny accent close the door. Then she remembered it was the name
Sean used among his father's family. Was this a Montenegrin, then?

Thrilled at the idea of an adventure, she hopped out of bed, eager
to set out for this foreign kingdom.

After an early-morning departure from Berlin under a steady gray
drizzle, with a box of chocolates and a kind note from Geraldine, Maeve
settled in to watch the snow-draped European landscape fly by. Their
express train carried them across the Kaiser's empire into the Emperor
Franz Josef's domain, which Sean spoke of slightingly as a crazy quilt
coming apart at the seams. It looked solid enough from the train. And
the Austrian customs officers were a bit less pompous than the Germans,
greeting Moira with a charming kiss on the hand. Sean's papers produced
a sudden stiffening of the spine and a snappy salute, Maeve noticed.

Maeve reflected later that everything had got off to such a good
start for their trip *en famille* to the Balkans. Moira preened in her fine

feathers on board the Orient Express while Maeve studied their fellow passengers and listened in fascination to Kyril's descriptions of this gentleman or that lady seated in such splendor in the salon car. According to the swarthy Montenegrin, most of the men were no better than bandits in fine tailoring, and as for the women, he rolled his dark eyes expressively toward heaven and muttered, "Don't even ask, little one. The less said the better!" And his gold tooth gleamed wickedly beneath his drooping mustaches as he clicked his teeth in disgust.

No matter. Maeve luxuriated in the sybaritic atmosphere on board the Train of Kings, with its glittering crystal wall sconces, its inlaid paneling, its fine china, silver cutlery, and fresh flowers, and its contingent of waiters in black tie, who moved so noiselessly and carefully through the cars as they skillfully balanced huge silver platters of delicacies or popped champagne corks.

This was the epitome of luxury, finer than the train that had carried Maeve to Berlin. And best of all, she had Sean almost to herself—if one discounted the presence of Moira and Kyril. Maeve adored Sean Farrell. If only she weren't still just a child in his eyes!

Kyril, Sean's Montenegrin valet cum bodyguard, fascinated Maeve too. She had never in her life met anyone who carried so many weapons all at once. Proudly exhibiting his personal arsenal of two vicious-looking daggers, a Walther .38, and a Browning, which he concealed in the folds of a brightly colored sash wrapped around his waist, Kyril appeared to be ready for any contingency. "He would kill for me," Sean confided to Maeve, impressing her terribly. Looking at Kyril with his collection of weapons and his wolfish smile, Maeve didn't doubt it. What a treasure he would have been back in South Africa, she thought with a sigh.

Each time Maeve thought about Belgrade afterward, it all became a blur of oxcarts, ancient houses, and minarets—and mobs of Gypsies, all chattering at once, swarming around her with hands thrust out in her face, frightening her with their persistence, nearly toppling her into the street. And then came the tall Serb army officer, parting the Gypsies as a scythe parts a field of grain, commanding and frightening, a man who could inspire fear in the hardiest thug.

This man, Colonel Dragutin Dimitrievic, known as Colonel Apis, came to call on Sean in their hotel. Much later, Maeve learned that the fierce-looking colonel had come to plot with him against Serbia's King Alexander, an unlovable creature with an equally unlovable wife. The Montenegrins were backing the successor, their Prince's son-in-law.

This was the part of the Belgrade visit Maeve didn't understand at the time, since it was all very secret and was only explained to her afterward. But she recalled quite clearly what this clandestine business led to. She could never forget that part.

On their last day in Belgrade, she, Moira, and Sean went to dine in a charming place called the Tri Sesira. While Kyril stood guard, the three of them had just started selecting from the menu when a gang of ruffians burst into the dining room. To Maeve's horror, the band headed straight for their table, clearly intent on wreaking havoc.

Though Sean and Kyril put up a good fight, it was no contest. They were badly outnumbered. In desperation Sean managed to hold them off long enough for his bodyguard to bundle the two women out a rear exit with orders to get them back to Western Europe. Kyril was holding enough money—two thousand pounds sterling—to assure their comfort until Sean could rejoin them.

Weeping, Maeve had to be dragged off by Kyril as she begged to be allowed to stay and fight. It was like South Africa, she thought, half numb with fear and bewilderment. It was just like being torn from Papa. Only now she and Moira were running, stumbling, gasping for breath— hurling themselves along countless back alleys and up and down endless flights of stairs as Kyril rushed them to a safe house; there they hid until he could take them to the train station and see them off, dressed as peasant nuns on board the Belgrade-to-Vienna express. And then Kyril was gone, vanished into the back alleys to try to learn where those Serbs had taken Ivan Petrovic.

As the train pulled out of the station, Maeve and Moira sat with their heads down, disguised under a pile of clothes and rosary beads, surrounded by chattering peasants with live chickens and bags of turnips. But Maeve didn't fail to notice the Serb soldiers swarming all over the station platform, hunting for someone. And among them, tall and scowl- ing and obviously directing the whole operation, was Colonel Apis, the man who had had that secret meeting with Sean. The sight of him gave her a pang of fear which didn't leave her until she was safely out of Serbia and back in Austrian territory.

*

The scene at the main train station in Vienna was comical when the two supposed nuns stripped off their habits on the platform and handed them to the openmouthed porter. He gaped at them with huge eyes and an expression suggesting imminent paralysis. Never in his life had he seen such a thing. A couple of elderly ladies nearly fainted at the sacrilege.

Two gentlemen watching with great interest were disappointed to find the nuns fully clothed beneath their dark robes; they had been hoping for a scandal.

Giving all these observers a haughty flick of her eyelashes, Moira picked up her bundles, snatched Maeve away from the gentlemen who were saying all sorts of nonsense to her, and headed for the exit.

"Where to, Mama?"

"The nearest hotel. I'm exhausted."

Having no Austrian money, the ladies were forced to proceed on foot. Maeve managed to cadge the price of tram tickets from an elderly gentleman who looked sympathetic, by pretending her mother had had her purse snatched in a nearby park.

"Ach," said the fellow, clicking his tongue. "You really must be so careful these days. There are all kinds of rascals about now."

"It was a Gypsy," Maeve declared solemnly in German, recalling her experiences in Belgrade. "They're dreadful thieves."

That led to a great deal of indignation on the part of the gentleman about the vile ways of "those Romany scoundrels," the necessity for laws banning them from cities, and his contempt for their banditry in general. Then he got around to asking Maeve where she and her mother were staying, since their German marked them as foreigners. This was a bit tricky for Maeve, because she and Moira were wondering that very thing. Gamely she declared they were stopping at a very grand place in the center of the city. Father was there, waiting for them to return from their promenade.

"Very grand?" he murmured. "Chic clientele?"

"Oh yes," Maeve assured him. "Very aristocratic."

"Ah, that would be the Hotel Sacher on the Kärntnerstrasse. Well, it's only ten minutes by tram from here. Come. I'll help you get back to it."

"Thank you, sir," Maeve said with a smile, melting with gratitude.

Moira was watching the whole comedy with a mixture of amusement and concern. Maeve's skill as a confidence trickster was useful for the moment, but it was a side of the girl's character she had never before seen. All very well for getting them on the nearest tram, but unsettling if turned against her mother one day. That idea made Moira quite uneasy.

All the same, Moira thought as their good Samaritan bought them tickets and placed them on board a tram bound for the Kärntnerstrasse, she was lucky the girl had got them the name of a good hotel and the means to reach it. She was perishing with fatigue and wouldn't have been able to take a single step farther.

*

Once installed at the Hotel Sacher—along with an international clientele of aristocrats, bankers, and a handful of actresses—Maeve sent a letter to the Gräfin von Kleist, describing what had happened to them in Belgrade. Three days later, a telegram arrived thanking her and telling her the matter would be investigated.

That brief response concealed a fit of hysterics, frantic telegrams to Prince Nikolai in Cetinje, and a feverish conference with the Montenegrin ambassador. He was forced to read and reread Maeve's letter, pale with dread while Geraldine paced his study wailing like a banshee that her poor boy had probably been slaughtered by those damned Serbs, the dirty heathen swine. Balkan politics were a sewer of treachery.

The gräfin didn't realize her message was already old news in Cetinje. The faithful Kyril had dispatched a coded report via carrier pigeon to the Montenegrin capital within an hour of the attack at the Tri Sesira, and in return Colonel Apis had received a photograph and a letter, asking for a little restraint and cooperation. The letter announced the hour of execution of a Serb military attaché to Sofia, Bulgaria, if Ivan Petrovic was not released immediately. The accompanying photograph showed the unfortunate attaché bound hand and foot with a gag in his mouth and a Bulgarian newspaper, dated the previous day, covering his chest.

Since he was also one of Colonel Apis's closest friends, it gave Apis some food for thought. In the end, he had a discussion with the Montenegrin chargé d'affaires in Belgrade and admitted a frightening truth: he didn't have Ivan Petrovic. Apis claimed the attack was the work of King Alexander's men in the secret police, not his own operatives. An informant had apparently accused Nikolai Petrovic's son of trying to assassinate King Alexander, and Alexander—in his hysteria—had believed him.

Sweating profusely as he faced the skeptical Montenegrin chargé, Apis was telling the truth this time. He also knew he wasn't being believed. After a chilling silence, the Montenegrin demanded what the Serb intended to do to redeem himself. Apis set his face in a rigid grimace and replied that he would deal with his countrymen. But it would be difficult.

Well, difficult it might be, responded the Montenegrin, but it had better not be *too* difficult. They were, after all, holding his friend hostage to his actions. And from what he knew of Apis's reputation, the colonel didn't have many friends to spare.

With that, the Montenegrin turned abruptly and made his exit, leaving Apis to fume in silence. The arrogance of these people! He hated them. They were born troublemakers, rogues, and cutthroats. And they had him by the balls. That, more than all their other faults, was the worst crime of all.

In Vienna, Maeve and her mother were unaware of the uproar her letter had caused. The girl was convinced Sean was dead or dying, and she felt utterly helpless not being able to rescue him. Moira, she noticed, was not taking things so hard, and it infuriated her. For the first time in her life she viewed her mother as heartless.

"How can you not worry about him?" she cried angrily the afternoon they received Geraldine's reply. "It's so cruel!"

"My dear child," Moira retorted, "I suffered the greatest loss of my life when they hanged your father. I loved that man dearly. I used up all my tears on him."

"But you certainly had *something* left over for Sean Farrell, didn't you?" Maeve demanded, too furious to use her head. "You spent the night with him! And now you don't even care if he's dead or alive! How could you be so callous, Mama? How could you?"

Moira turned white and slapped her daughter so hard she was stunned herself.

"Don't you ever talk to me like that," she ordered in a cold, brittle voice. "I'm your mother, and whatever I've done, I've done for you, too. So don't take that high moral tone with me, missy. Not unless you want to find yourself out on the streets, starving. We're poor now, Maeveen. We must use whatever means we have to live."

She didn't love him, Maeve thought in shock. That was even harder to accept than the idea of Moira in his arms. Who wouldn't love Sean?

"And while we're on the subject," Moira added, determined to rub salt into the wound, "his mother is no better than she ought to be. That one's had a very checkered past."

That was cruel, Maeve thought. It wasn't necessary to say it. Geraldine had been kind to them.

"Well, I think she's wonderful."

Moira's eyelashes flickered with a faint trace of amusement. Her daughter was a stubborn thing, always had been. She could be contrary just for the pleasure of it sometimes.

"She's a great success. And she's no fool, that I'll admit. But what she has, she has from what you just objected to in your own mother. Think of that the next time you're tempted to criticize me."

And Moira left her daughter to contemplate the mysteries of human behavior.

Moira had given up Sean Farrell as a lost cause. For all his talk about taking care of them, he was gone—probably murdered—and not likely to make a reappearance in their lives. Well, there were others who were still very much alive and interested in her. There was Hubertus von Reuter.

While Maeve was sending her news to Geraldine, Moira was writing to Herr von Reuter, who made a trip to Vienna to see her and assure himself that she was all right. He was *very* pleased, and very anxious to ingratiate himself. He proved this by taking her to Vienna's most fashionable couturier to replace the wardrobe she had been obliged to leave behind in Belgrade. Moira sneaked Maeve in when Hubertus had left her to the fitters, and blandly ordered a few things for her daughter as well.

Serves him right, Maeve thought as the dressmakers showed her bolts of expensive fabric. She picked the finest and was told she had lovely taste. She also had no mercy on Herr von Reuter.

Hubertus persuaded Moira to come to Berlin as his guest after her wardrobe was replenished—along with her "charming daughter." Paris was out of the question, he said sternly after Moira had mentioned it. The French were swine. No pretty woman was safe with them.

"Mama," declared Maeve in Hubertus's hearing, "weren't you the one who was talking about swine a little while ago?"

The look Maeve received would have daunted a lesser soul. "Ah yes," Moira said grandly. "I was telling you how the Serb royalty was descended from pig farmers. It was a bit of history."

Hubertus nodded. "Exactly. One wonders what kind of people would make a swineherd their king. They are all barbarians east of Vienna, dear ladies. Take my word for it." And his tone hinted at depths of degradation unknown to Western man. After Belgrade, it seemed true.

Maeve took that to heart and kept quiet from then on, but she wondered what Moira's reaction would be when Dietrich—"that devious little swine"—was actually living under the same roof with them. It was something Maeve was looking forward to.

*

Unfortunately for Maeve—and for Dietrich, too—the younger von Reuter had been packed off to St. Petersburg for a stint in an allied bank. It was sincerely hoped by Hubertus that his old friend there would take his son under his wing and instruct him in the finer points of international finance. It was about time he was exposed to some responsibility.

Dietrich was his father's greatest worry. Already twenty-four, he showed no perceptible sign of taking a genuine interest in the family business. It embarrassed his father to know that the lowest clerk in his bank had more interest in the workings of the Von Reuter Bank than his only son, and Hubertus dreaded the day when it would all pass to Dietrich. That would prove a debacle, the destruction and disintegration of two generations of loving and intelligent labor.

What had he done to be stuck with a pleasure-crazed young fop like Dietrich? he often asked himself. Perhaps it was the fault of his late wife, God rest her soul. She had been artistically inclined, disposed to laugh easily; spent money without regard for common sense. The boy took after her, no doubt. There were even rumors of alien blood among her forebears—nothing that could be proved, of course, but still . . . For all his blue-eyed, blond good looks, just like all the von Reuters, there was something not quite right about the boy, some taint.

There were days when Hubertus wished he had merely had a daughter whose grateful husband could be molded into the proper Prussian style. It would have made his life so much easier.

*

Accepting Herr von Reuter's hospitality was made somewhat onerous to Moira by his passion for her. She found him attractive but unexciting, certainly not worth the effort to undress for. It rankled him, especially since he had spent a considerable amount of money trying to seduce her. And spending money on a woman was not his style.

Their parting of the ways came the night Hubertus tried to force his way into the guest bedroom, his intentions bolstered by an alarming amount of schnapps. At the sound of someone trying to unlock her door, Moira jumped out of bed and when she understood it was Hubertus yowling on her threshold, hastily constructed a makeshift barricade of chairs and a night table. She spent the next two hours in sullen fury, listening to an unimaginable litany of insults hurled at her in a thick, drunken tone from behind her locked door.

Maeve in the next bedroom opened her own door a crack, saw Herr von Reuter slobbering at Moira's door, and quickly ducked back inside her room. She was nearly hysterical with laughter, and practically choked trying not to make a sound: if Hubertus saw her laughing at him, there'd be no telling what he might do in a rage.

The uproar in the hallway seemed to go on for an eternity until Hubertus's servants carted him off to bed, dead drunk. It was not his finest hour.

After that shocking display of bad manners, Moira decamped for Paris, judging Berlin to be unsafe. She had in her possession the names of several gentlemen who might be able to help her—courtesy of Hubertus and Geraldine. She would certainly let them try.

Thanks to Hubertus, she also carried with her a very fine diamond and sapphire brooch, advance payment for services never rendered.

*

Maeve's stay in Berlin only depressed her. The gräfin had been distraught over the disappearance of her son, and beyond inviting the girl to her home once for tea—so she could hear firsthand the story of the attack in Belgrade—Geraldine was too upset to spare Maeve any time.

However, Maeve learned from Sean's mother that she had paid a furious visit to the Montenegrin ambassador after she learned of the kidnapping, and had demanded quick action from Nikolai. This was evidently delivered at the top of her lungs, with the gräfin screaming for retaliation and the nervous ambassador counseling patience, as far as Maeve could tell from Geraldine's account. It must have been a hair-raising moment in diplomacy.

After giving the girl her thoughts on the mediocrity of Prince Nikolai's man in Berlin, Geraldine proceeded to bewilder Maeve with a harangue about Balkan politics that left her head spinning. Not only were the Serbs not to be trusted, Geraldine swore, but the entire Balkan peninsula was a seething hotbed of treachery that pitted one kingdom against the other and all of them against the Turks—their former masters.

Montenegrins were distant kinsmen of the Serbs, but one would never know it, judging by their behavior. And Serbia itself was so shot through with corruption that this Colonel Apis Maeve had encountered was probably in the pay of several factions—with loyalty to none, including his own king.

"What about Prince Nikolai?" Maeve asked timidly.

"That old bandit!" Geraldine sputtered. "He's past master of the Balkan game. But he's my son's father and he won't throw Sean to the wolves. That's my only hope now," she muttered gloomily. "Nikolai will have to be clever and devious enough to thwart the Serbs' plans and get Sean back. The only problem is, we don't know exactly what Serbia wants."

After that afternoon of tea and politics, the gräfin seemed unable to decide how to behave toward the girl. On the one hand, she was grateful Maeve had saved Sean's life in Africa; on the other, she found her far too dangerous to allow her near her boy. Maeve was beautiful, young, and poor—an alarming combination. In some small way she even reminded Geraldine of herself thirty years earlier, when she was just a bit of a girl, fresh from the Liberties in Dublin, ready to conquer Paris.

Instead—by pure good luck—the blue-eyed blonde had conquered Prince Nikolai of Montenegro and had made her fortune by giving birth to his son.

With this in mind, Geraldine did not want to see Sean repeating his father's infatuation with a pretty nobody, or at least not before he was safely married to an impressive fortune. Whatever he did afterward was his own business.

Moira she found less troubling, for that one would be merely a passing fancy. Maeve was the danger, precisely because Sean was capable of loving her.

CHAPTER 8

When Maeve and her mother arrived in Paris in the early spring of 1902, they found a city full of life despite leaden skies and frequent showers. The classical beauty of the buildings, the wide boulevards lined with chestnut and sycamore trees, the elegance of the coaches, and, above all, the spirit of sparkling insouciance dazzled young Maeve.

She wasn't there very long before she realized this was a woman's city, a place where the population idolized certain ladies who were the uncrowned queens of Paris—Sarah Bernhardt, Réjane, La Belle Otero, Mata Hari. It was a revelation. Here women weren't criticized for thinking of nothing but their beauty, their sumptuous ensembles, their hair, their figures. It was almost a law that they should do so. The average Parisienne on the brand-new Métro exhibited more style than Maeve had witnessed among baronesses in Berlin. Geraldine had been educated here, she remembered. Well, it showed. And now Maeve was determined to take full advantage of it.

From the lowliest concierge to the aristocrat in his salon, each Parisian had his favorite *monstre sacré*. If the Divine Sarah appeared in a new play, it was an Event, worthy of serious discussion and febrile interest. If La Belle Otero—the Suicide's Siren—caused a new lover to go bankrupt and blow out his brains, it was yet another chapter in a fascinating saga. If the respected Musée Guimet, august bastion of Oriental scholarship, chose to present a nearly naked Mata Hari as a distinguished interpreter of sacred Javanese legends, it was an occasion as notable for the elegant gowns of the society women in the audience as for the lack of clothing on the star of the evening. The Parisienne might be flighty, fickle, or ever so slightly scandalous, but she was—thank God!—never dull. And La Belle Epoque was her finest hour.

Moira, practical as always, decided to put Sean's two thousand pounds sterling to good use by renting an apartment in a fashionable neighborhood and calling on her list of names furnished by the Gräfin Geraldine and Hubertus von Reuter. The Crown Prince's bracelet and Hubertus's brooch were impressive bits of window dressing, indicating a certain affluence on the part of the beautiful young widow.

Nothing put people off like poverty, Moira had once remarked to Maeve. If you wanted to get money from someone, you didn't dare look as if you needed it. The glitter of diamonds made a lovely camouflage.

Moira's calls brought her in contact with a varied circle of people, from Russian princes to French bankers. She received invitations to tea, to the theater, to the Chamber of Deputies—which she considered grand theater—and by the time society was looking forward to the races at Longchamps, Moira and her daughter were installed in a luxurious apartment on the avenue MacMahon, thanks to her friendship with Count André Viznitski, a dashing gentleman from St. Petersburg.

Count Viznitski was not on Moira's list, but a chance visit to the Louvre on a rainy afternoon had brought them together. The lady was so beautiful the count was fascinated and tried to strike up a conversation. This was unsuccessful due to Moira's imperfect command of French and her apparent hauteur.

Unimpressed, Moira had put her pretty nose in the air, giving the gentleman a look indicating she was not the sort of woman who deigned to speak to any old person off the street. Viznitski was amused and took her for an English lady, whereupon he switched to that language and introduced himself, producing his calling card emblazoned with the family crest and indicating an address near the Bois. Moira then perversely thought he might be some sort of gigolo and was even less willing to listen to him.

By dint of hard work and a great deal of charm, André Viznitski persuaded the lady to allow him to show her the magnificent eighteenth-century collections, and spoke so knowledgeably that Moira was willing to concede he must be a man of culture. When they had finished their promenade through the galleries, he insisted upon protecting her from the downpour, and to Moira's astonishment, he had a new motorcar waiting for him on the rue du Rivoli. He actually owned one! Her eyes widened.

Hesitating a split second, Moira accepted his invitation to take her home in this exotic vehicle, and for the first time in her life she experienced a ride in a horseless carriage. It was the strangest thing she could imagine. First the count handed her in, and while she settled into the luxurious interior of soft red leather seats, he went to the front of the thing and cranked something. It began to shudder and sputter as Moira looked on in delighted alarm. She clutched the brass door handle, fearful the contraption might take off, run down her new acquaintance, and go careening off into one of the shop windows of the arcade.

As the noise and the sputtering grew worse, Count Viznitski let out a cry of triumph, raced around to the driver's side of the motorcar, and jumped in.

"Will it explode?" Moira asked, still uncertain.

"Good Lord, no! It works like a charm."

And with that, he drove off down the rue du Rivoli, the proud master of a shiny black Panhard, the envy of all who saw him.

Moira thoroughly enjoyed her trip around Paris at the dizzy speed of twenty-five miles per hour, and she giggled like a girl when Viznitski honked at anybody who dared to get in his way. He was a man who considered the roads his own, apparently; he told Moira confidentially that in Russia he would simply have run over any peasant who failed to move fast enough.

"You must be very grand," she replied, eyeing the count with a certain skepticism.

"Oh, I am," he answered with a charming smile. "And I hope I'll have an opportunity to prove it to you."

André Viznitski was so sure of himself and so delightfully exotic that Moira decided to allow him to call on her—with his beautiful motorcar.

It was on his second visit to her apartment that André was able to lure the not unwilling Moira to her bedroom.

André's body was thin, almost emaciated compared to Pat's and Sean's wholesome masculinity. As he kissed her, he used his teeth to bite her lips. And instead of the delicate caresses she had felt with Sean, André seemed to like to pinch her nipples, bringing tears to her eyes.

As he slammed into her with fury, Moira felt a twinge of guilt for betraying Sean this soon. But then, as that familiar warmth started suffusing her body, she realized that a woman has to make her way in this world in order to get ahead.

*

That weekend, after their tryst, Moira and Maeve took up residence in a larger and more elegant apartment, paid for by Count Viznitski.

If there was a Countess Viznitski, he never mentioned it, although he spoke many times of his family—mother, brothers and sisters—in Russia. The count seemed to divide his time between several European and Russian residences, and he had the money to indulge any whim. He was a charming man, blond, not terribly tall, extremely slender, witty, very volatile, and incurably restless.

While André was in Paris, Moira accompanied him to parties, the theater, the races, the opera. And when he was gone, she spent the time amusing herself by taking piano and singing lessons.

As the wife of a colonial administrator in South Africa, Moira had been admired in her own circle for a lovely voice and a fine hand at the piano. She was the star of countless musicales and often whiled away hours at the piano. Now that she could do what she pleased, she wanted to resume that pleasant habit.

She also wanted a wider audience than darling Andrushka.

*

Maeve's fascination with Paris did not prevent her from mourning the loss of Sean Farrell. Since Geraldine had unaccountably stopped responding to her letters, she decided to search for information elsewhere. Sean had a sister, Stana the Duchess of Leuctenberg, whom he had recently visited in Paris. Perhaps Her Highness would know something of his whereabouts.

Undeterred by the fact that she didn't know the lady's address, Maeve asked Count Viznitski, a logical source of information. Viznitski laughed uneasily and said he certainly knew who the Duchess of Leuctenburg was, but he wasn't on intimate terms with the imperial family and their relatives.

"Well, do you know where her home is?" Maeve asked.

He did. But when Maeve ventured to pay the Duchess of Leuctenburg a visit, she was halted at the wrought-iron entrance gates of her imposing mansion and told brusquely by a sentry that Her Highness was in St. Petersburg. And no, she couldn't leave a message.

There seemed to be no way she could learn about Sean's fate. In despair, Maeve resolved to try one last, unlikely source. Buying very fine vellum writing paper at a stationer's shop in the rue Royale, she composed a neatly penned letter to Dietrich von Reuter asking for his help. Had he heard anything about Sean Farrell? Did he know anything about Sean's fate?

Dietrich was in St. Petersburg when the letter arrived, but he read it upon his return to Berlin, smiled, and quickly replied, regretting that he couldn't furnish any information. He was delighted Maeve hadn't forgotten him, he said. And he hoped to see her again.

Maeve sighed when she read that. She would have been happy to see him too, but Berlin was a long way from Paris, and old Hubertus wasn't likely to encourage their friendship—not after that embarrassing scene at Moira's door. She giggled even at the thought of it. Old fool.

Life was so unfair, Maeve thought. Dietrich was such a sweet boy and yet he had that awful father to contend with. She wished he lived in Paris and didn't have Hubertus hanging around his neck like a grim blond albatross. But there was no point in wishing for miracles. Life was not like the storybooks. There one could always slay the wicked dragon; in real life, one had to endure him.

*

While Moira had discovered the pleasures of the beau monde thanks to Count Viznitski, Maeve felt left out of things. She loved being in a glamorous city, she liked to see Moira enjoying herself after the horrors they had lived through, she even liked André Viznitski—even if she found him too mysterious at times—but she had nothing to do with herself except act as lady's maid to Moira. And that rankled.

On the night of her eighteenth birthday, Maeve, Moira, and Count Viznitski had a gala supper party at Maxim's where André had invited a lively crowd to wish the young beauty happy birthday and join in the celebration. The guest of honor was dazzling in the first grown-up gown of her life—a gift from Count Viznitski.

Over vehement protests by Moira, this elaborate cream satin and lace concoction by Paquin bared Maeve's lovely shoulders and so much of her bosom that there was a major battle over it before the party.

"It's all the style!" protested Maeve, eyeing herself proudly in the full-length mirror in her bedroom. "Do you want me to look like a ten-year-old with a collar up to my chin?"

"I don't want you to look like one of those whores at the Pré Catalan!" Moira retorted, yanking the lace higher over her daughter's plunging décolletage. "Now leave it like that. Jesus, Mary, and Joseph! You may as well be naked."

"But your neckline is just as low as mine," Maeve saw fit to point out. "And it doesn't seem to bother *you*!"

That was the limit. A sharp slap in the face put an end to all her attempts at logic. Moira glowered at her daughter and said forcefully, "Don't ever presume to correct your mother, missy. It's not your place."

With tears brimming in her own pretty eyes Maeve watched her exit. Then, as soon as Moira was out the door, the girl rearranged the delicate Brussels lace so that it fell the way Madame Paquin intended it—over a daringly low neckline that risked a scandal with each breath.

"Well," Maeve murmured to her own lovely image, *"C'est la mode,* after all!"

And she certainly didn't intend to be out of style on a night like this.

Madame Paquin had really outdone herself with this gown. It had been a pleasure to have such a lovely model—which wasn't always the case—so that alone made it enjoyable to create something memorable and chic. Undoubtedly it would rate a mention in the social columns, if she knew Count Viznitski. She hoped it would.

Since Maeve Devereux was not the daughter of some stuffy aristocrat who would be trying to marry her off while spending as little as possible on her clothes—after all, what were *husbands* for?—Madame Paquin had felt free to indulge her most extravagant fantasies.

This gown of cream duchesse satin fell from pearl-embroidered straps hanging off the shoulders. Its lace-drenched bodice, reembroidered with tiny seed pearls, dipped fashionably low over the V-shaped waist and hovered like a lacy cloud over an elegant trumpet skirt. The satin skirt was hidden under a gossamer overskirt of chiffon worked with a sunburst pattern of seed pearls swirling diagonally from the left hip in an ever-widening sweep of pearls and sparkling rhinestones right down to the hem. The petticoats were magnificent froths of fine Valenciennes lace, exquisitely visible when the train was held up for dancing. It cost a fortune and looked every bit of it.

Looking at herself in the mirror, Maeve could scarcely believe she was the same girl who had been knocked into the African dirt and ordered to eat maggots. Would she have believed it if anyone had told her she'd ever look like this in the same lifetime? Would *anyone* believe it?

Ah, Sean, she thought, you're missing a grand sight this evening. And with that, she slipped her velvet wrap over her shoulders and left for the party.

When Maeve and her mother entered the dining room at Maxim's where their guests were gathered, the girl experienced a rosy glow of admiration that was markedly different from the reception she had received as one of the "Boer victims" in Berlin. This was something on another level entirely, apart from politics or patriotism or anything one would wave a flag over. It was the triumph of a beautiful woman.

Viznitski enjoyed the moment, with Maeve in a delicate, cream-colored cloud of satin and lace on his right and Moira in deep sapphire blue on his left. On her wrist glittered Crown Prince Friedrich Wilhelm's gift.

Reflected in the curving etched mirrors of the dining room were a hundred revelers, the men in white tie or uniforms, the women in sumptuous gowns by the leading couturiers of Paris—a gorgeous tableau in constant movement, the women's jewels sparkling with each delicate movement of wrist or neck. Soft egret plumes crowned dozens of extravagant coiffures, held in place by jeweled hairpins. Wherever one glanced one could see the flash of diamonds, the gleam of expensive silks.

"What a glorious night," Maeve murmured to André Viznitski as he waltzed her around the room on a golden wave of Mumm champagne and soulful Gypsy music. "I don't think I've ever been so happy as I am right now. Thank you."

"It's my pleasure, *milochka*." André smiled, "I hope it's the first of many glorious evenings, don't you?"

And from the look in his eyes, Count Viznitski meant much more than Maeve had ever intended. Involuntarily, Maeve glanced over to where Moira was waltzing with some American millionaire. Her mother was glaring at the count with an expression that could only mean trouble.

*

There were two distinct results of the party at Maxim's: Maeve was sternly warned by her mother *never*, under any circumstances, to be alone with Count Viznitski, and more important, she happened to overhear some gossip that might prove useful.

Among the guests at the party had been a handful of theatrical people, mostly pretty actresses André had invited to dress up the room, and from their conversation Maeve had discovered that some fellow named Julien Roussel was nearly tearing his hair out trying to find a replacement for his pregnant wife in his music hall act. Desperate to escape from an unwanted career as Moira's chambermaid, Maeve inquired about this Monsieur Roussel and discovered he was auditioning girls in two days' time at the Théâtre des Variétés. The opportunity was too good to pass up, so, dressed in her most grown-up outfit, Maeve set off on the Métro for the theater. She had been thinking of just this kind of opportunity ever since she arrived in Paris.

Whatever glamor the Théâtre des Variétés possessed was not readily apparent during auditions. It looked as if it were a kind of warehouse for actors, with a bare stage except for a piano on one side and a cluster of nervous-looking girls on the other. A handsome couple—the Roussels—sat near the piano and looked dismal. Things were not going well at all, judging by the expression on their faces.

"Thank you, mademoiselle," Julien Roussel said politely to one downcast soul who had evidently just finished a song. The piano player silently rolled his eyes and shook his head in despair. One was worse than the next. It was as if all the pretty girls in Paris who knew how to sing and dance had suddenly departed for points unknown, and what was left was awful.

"Am I too late?" Maeve whispered to a tough-looking blonde who was regarding the scene with a bored eye.

"Not at all," she replied. "Julien will take a look at anything in skirts today. The more the merrier."

That didn't sound too encouraging to Maeve. As she glanced around at the competition she felt even worse. These girls all looked like what Moira called "professionals," which meant lots of makeup, piles of feathers on hats and boas, and a steely look that implied a lifetime of shoving people out of their way in streetcars and now on the new Métro. Some of them gave her a passing glance and dismissed her as no threat. She noticed that, too, and was annoyed.

They were all used to the auditioning process—except for Maeve—but she was quick enough to understand that she was supposed to get up there and sing something. The only thing was, she had no sheet music with her, not realizing that it was expected, and all the others did.

Well, she said to herself, then I'll have to sing something the piano player will know. The problem with that was, Maeve wasn't terribly au courant with French music, except for some of the arias from *Carmen* which she liked to listen to on the gramophone Count Viznitski had bought for Moira.

When her turn came, she smiled politely, announced her name—and had to pronounce it three times before anyone could understand it—and declared she would sing the seguidilla from *Carmen*. To the amusement of the piano player and the Roussels, she carried it off with a great deal of verve and even managed to throw in a few fancy dance steps. When she finished, Maeve looked flushed and delighted with herself, rather like a child who expects to be rewarded for its efforts.

"Very nice, mademoiselle," Julien announced with a nod. He glanced at his blond wife, who gave a brief shrug and rolled her eyes.

"Like Calvé," grinned the piano player, mentioning the name of one of France's best-known Carmens. He was charmed by this fresh-faced girl and thought she was a possibility. After all, Angélique Roussel had the same kind of glowing beauty, and Julien would be making a mistake to change style with her replacement. The girl had to look pretty above all else. The rest of her duties involved being an accessory to Julien.

"What do you think?" Roussel asked his wife.

"Passable," replied Angélique, looking carefully at the redhead. "She moves nicely. She's slim. Tall enough, too. The height's important. We can't have one too short."

All this made Maeve feel like a horse being inspected by the farmers back home. She almost expected them to ask to see her teeth. In fact, they did very soon afterward with a request to smile.

"Good strong teeth," noted Angélique. "That's a plus. We can't have one with gaps."

Maeve was also inspecting the Roussels and found them quite striking: Julien tall and slim with flashing dark eyes, black hair, and wonderful bearing, and Angélique blond and blue-eyed with a hint of gold in her complexion. Madame was also impressive for the stunning collection of stuffed birds on her large, overdecorated hat, a very chic touch. Where could she have got that hat? Maeve wondered, impressed. It was a masterpiece, loaded with ribbons, lace, plumes, and of course, the birds. So Parisian.

While Maeve was studying Angélique's headdress, Julien was looking at her carefully, and he was pleased by what he saw—a fresh young woman with magnificent coloring, lovely posture, and a certain refinement. She seemed to have no hard edges. And she would certainly look well in Angélique's stage costumes. God knew *somebody* had to be found for them, now that Angélique was in her fourth month of pregnancy and losing her ingenue appeal.

The pregnancy was a bitter point of contention between the Roussels. He was horrified that he was about to lose his partner just when they had arrived at the peak of their success. She was elated that she was going to be a mother—and have a good excuse to leave the stage forever. Let him support her, she declared. Other men supported their wives and didn't make them show their legs before audiences of old lechers and dissolute young men. It wasn't dignified. And Angélique had been brought up to respect the conventions—before eloping with Julien, whom her mother never ceased to refer to as "that oily seducer from Marseilles."

Poor Julien. He was exceptionally fastidious, not in the least oily, and spent large amounts of money on elegant eau de cologne. He didn't even come from Marseilles but from Grasse, where the fields were fragrant with the scent of lavender. This probably accounted for his passion for perfume. And right now he was desperate to find a good replacement for Angélique.

"Mademoiselle," he declared, taking Maeve's hand, "when can you begin to rehearse?"

Maeve looked up into his beautiful, velvety dark eyes and asked uncertainly, "Does that mean I've been hired?"

"Yes." He smiled. "I'd like to start training you right away. We open a new act in two weeks." And he hoped he knew what he was doing.

Two weeks, Maeve thought. Jesus!

"Well then," she replied, "I'll begin tomorrow." And she'd better be a quick study, she thought nervously.

*

Dietrich von Reuter had acquitted himself so well in St. Petersburg that Hubertus was willing to let him undertake a second foreign mission, either in London or in Paris. Herr von Reuter's hopes for a foreign branch of the bank had always lain dormant, and while he lacked the large family necessary to carry out his more grandiose plans, he did have Dietrich, who at least seemed willing to take up residence among aliens.

Hubertus had always appreciated the natural advantages of having one's own flesh and blood in key positions in a banking network. The Rothschilds in Germany and the Seligmans in America were skillful practitioners of this art. Now was the time for the von Reuters to expand. If Dietrich rose to the occasion, he would assure the future of their house. If he failed, Hubertus didn't want to live long enough to witness the family's disgrace.

There were two more reasons why Hubertus had decided to give his son additional responsibilities. At the New Year, Kaiser Wilhelm had graciously created Hubertus Baron von Reuter, enabling him to indulge his aristocratic fantasies. Now he was more determined than ever that the von Reuter dynasty—such as it was—should not be allowed to die out. This required grandchildren, but of course, he needed his son's cooperation there.

One would have thought that this would be an easy matter for a boy like his son, but just the opposite was true. Although Dietrich was young, handsome, and highly susceptible, his taste ran to the flashy, the foreign, and the scandalous. Not one decent German banker's daughter had ever found favor with him. He was almost temperamentally incapable of loving anyone worthy of his name.

The older Dietrich got, the more shallow his tastes became. He pursued chorus girls at the Winter Garden, Italian ballerinas, French singers, and most recently, a so-called Javanese dancer who wore more jewelry than clothing. Not one of these creatures could be considered a decent woman or looked upon as the mother of future von Reuters, yet Dietrich ran after them, adored them, squandered money on them. Hubertus was terrified that one of these leeches would one day show up on his doorstep, pregnant and demanding money to keep quiet. Or—God forbid—even pressing for marriage. It was a thought that made him break out in a cold sweat. He despised the mere idea of a mésalliance.

It was to ward off this possibility that the new baron decided to send Dietrich to London or Paris to work in the bank of a friend. Both men he selected had available daughters—pretty girls—who might possibly induce his boy to marry and do the right thing. He announced his plan at breakfast one morning. It was worth a try.

With almost palpable distaste, Dietrich looked at his father and pretended to be prepared to do his duty for the future of their house. He patiently listened to Hubertus cite his age—twenty-five now—as a reason for concern, and in disbelief Dietrich heard his parent offer him a shameless bribe. If Dietrich would pull himself together and act like a good Prussian banker, he, Hubertus, would offer him the deed to any mansion he wished. Naturally, this offer was good only if the proposed mistress of the house came up to the father's high standards.

Haughtily Dietrich stared at his father as if he were out of his mind, but he made an effort to placate him. He had spent his whole life humoring Hubertus, though it was beginning to exact its toll.

Dietrich loathed his father. He loathed the very sight of his elegantly trimmed Vandyke beard, the scent of his eau de cologne, the pompous way he had of rapping on a table to make a point. Hubertus was a soulless, selfish martinet who had tried unsuccessfully to mold him into his own image, puzzled that his only child was so different from himself.

It was a difference Hubertus ascribed to waywardness. To Dietrich it was more complicated. Deprived of his mother's company by her early death, the boy gravitated to any feminine presence that offered a promise of beauty, charm, and warmth—with just a touch of flamboyance. It was not a taste his father could understand. The baron's needs were more prosaic. Women, in his view, might be good or they might be bad, but they had better not call too much attention to themselves. That was vulgar. He despised that. Dietrich loved it. It was the great divide.

You want to ruin my life with your narrow-minded outlook, the boy thought as he stared fixedly at his father. You want to crush me with the burden of your own stupidity, but it's not going to work. Whatever he had to do, and no matter the price, he would never allow that to happen. Yes, he would go to Paris, but not to court the kind of girl Hubertus had in mind. He was going to Paris to hunt for Maeve Devereux.

*

The Gräfin Geraldine was frantic with uncertainty. It had been several months since Sean had vanished in Belgrade, and despite Nikolai's determination to bring back her son, he hadn't been able to do it.

The Montenegrins were furious with the Serbs, and Prince Nikolai was using every means he could to frighten them into complying with his demands. In St. Petersburg his daughters, the Grand Duchess Militza and Anastasia—Stana—Duchess of Leuctenberg were hard at work hammering away at their Romanov in-laws to intervene on Sean's behalf. Russian friendship was vitally important to King Alexander Obrenovic of Serbia, since he was despised by the rest of Europe. Alexander didn't dare offend his Russian patron, who was his only ally, especially since Peter Karageorgevic, the rival claimant to his throne, was alive and well and biding his time. There were only too many who wanted to see Peter installed in the palace in Belgrade.

Despite Russian approval, Alexander's attempts to make himself and his queen, Draga Mashin, beloved failed utterly, and slowly but surely St. Petersburg began to withdraw invitations, distancing themselves from the friendless young king whose army was already beginning to plot his murder—and Queen Draga's. He now saw enemies everywhere. When his secret police had informed him of Sean Farrell's presence in Belgrade, he had seen the hand of Montenegro plotting a coup against him. After all, Prince Nikolai was his rival's father-in-law.

Now Nikolai's son was in the Kalemegdan Fortress in Belgrade under heavy guard, under an assumed name, and Alexander was afraid either to let it be known he had captured him or to kill him. Indecision about this haunted his dreams, making him a wreck. If Nikolai *hadn't* plotted his death, killing his son would mean war with Montenegro. But now that he had him in prison, Nikolai might declare war on Serbia if he found out about it. So he didn't dare to do anything. Meanwhile the Russians were starting to make inquiries, prompted by the urging of Grand Duke Nicholas Nicolaievich, the Tsar's cousin.

In torment, Alexander didn't know what to do. And his own countrymen now seemed just as treacherous as his enemies.

Colonel Apis had discovered the identity of the prisoner two weeks after his incarceration, but he, too, had been reluctant to do anything. For one thing, the wild Montenegrins had kept their promise and sent him the head of his best friend, the attaché in Sofia, neatly wrapped in burlap, after their ultimatum had expired. He had nearly gone berserk at the sight, scaring his office staff half to death with his shrieks of rage.

Apis had been so outraged, his first reaction was to rush off to the Montenegrin Embassy to confront the ambassador, who was expecting him. He had prepared for the interview by concealing two revolvers on his person and ordering three large servants to stand by in his office. When the colonel came charging in, murder in his eyes, the ambassador needed two more men to protect him from Apis's wrath, and when it was all over, he sent Nikolai a cable stating he had nearly been torn limb from limb by this maniac. His office was utterly demolished.

"Well," declared Nikolai when he read the description of the scene, "at least it appears the colonel was telling the truth."

But it was small comfort to him. His boy was still missing and didn't seem likely to reappear. And Geraldine—his little Blondinka of years ago—would hold him personally responsible for her son's safety in the Balkans. No compromising with *her*.

"You're a ruling prince, a great warrior," Geraldine had recently written, "and yet you accept this insult from a people whose rulers are nothing more than pig farmers. Have you no shame, Nikolai Petrovic? I blush for you."

That was pretty raw provocation, which he wouldn't have tolerated from anyone else. Blondinka was a passionate woman who was hysterical over her boy's fate. Nikolai understood that. He had always loved her. It ripped him apart that he couldn't force those damned Serb bastards into obedience. His three other sons, Danilo, Mirko, and Peter, were already beginning to talk about "intervention," which meant an armed conflict to avenge Montenegrin honor. Blondinka had been in touch with them, too. And she was resurrecting the theme of a "Greater Montenegro," which called for the dismemberment of Serbia.

That was a weak point among the Montenegrins—expansion. Both countries desired it, but they would have to achieve it over the corpses of each other's armies. With King Alexander in such a weakened position vis-à-vis his own countrymen and young Ivan captured and maybe even killed by the Serbs, perhaps this was the opportunity Montenegro had been waiting for.

War was always the possibility of last resort, and Prince Nikolai was prepared to make the decision if he had to. His sons were eager for a fight, his daughters were trying to bring the Russians in on his side, and if he knew Blondinka, she was trying to recruit some Germans to help her rescue her boy.

Nikolai of Montenegro was not afraid of King Alexander Obrenovic. But Alexander would do well to fear *him*.

CHAPTER 9

*M*aeve had passed her training period as a music hall artiste with high honors. Despite their initial worries, the Roussels found themselves grateful to have discovered her. The pretty redhead was clever, graceful, and cheerful. She could learn the song-and-dance routines easily and had an instinct for the stage. The girl was a real find.

Not only did Maeve move like an angel but she had a surprisingly good voice as well. That was the bonus. She was able to contribute to the act in a way Angélique never could. Her only drawback was her tendency to turn her lines into comedy. Julien was adamant about that. This was a romantic duo, not a comic turn. And it was not about to change.

Actually Julien liked almost everything about Maeve but her name. It was so foreign, too foreign for the French public. And *she* hated the way the French pronounced it, mangling it by breaking it into two awkward syllables, Ma-eve. So they decided to compromise on this. Their billing read: Julien and Florine. Everybody liked that. Except for Moira.

"You were hired as a *what*?" Moira screeched the day Maeve came home with the good news. "Out of the question! It's not respectable."

"It's a lot more respectable than finding a Viznitski to keep me!" she had the bad taste to shout back.

That led to a fight that sent Maeve running for cover while Moira lashed out at her with every insult she could think of, and a few that were quite bizarre. She was slapped so many times she was nearly dizzy. And she had to lock herself in her room to protect herself while Moira calmed down. And all this because she wanted to get out of the house!

When her mother was more rational next morning, Maeve repeated her intention of beginning a stage career and was grateful to receive only a mild insult about probably being booed by the riffraff in the cheap seats. "You'll have to learn the hard way, I suppose," Moira sniffed.

"I'll take it in stride, Mama," Maeve replied.

André Viznitski was warmly encouraging and quite amused by the uproar. "You sound jealous," he said, smiling at Moira with such malice she was stunned. "Maeve is *une fille en fleur*. You're more like a lovely rose in the full afternoon of her bloom. There's a big difference."

To Maeve's intense embarrassment, she saw the color drain from Moira's lovely face as she stood up stiffly, fixed André with a truly awful glare, and exited in a flurry of silk and lace. The enchanting scent of Jasmine de Corse came wafting across the room in her wake—Moira's favorite new perfume. The room seemed to be floating in it.

"Your mother must have a headache," said Count Viznitski with another smile. "How unfortunate. Perhaps you would like to accompany me to that party tonight. We'll have a delightful time."

Maeve stared at him, unable to believe what she read in his eyes. He wanted *her* as a mistress too. Probably both at the same time!

"I don't feel well either, monsieur," Maeve said.

And she retreated to her bedroom and quietly locked the door behind her.

*

Moira *was* jealous. The idea of young Maeve up there on the stage of the Théâtre des Variétés was so unbelievable it had staggered her at first. Where had the girl got her talent from, after all, if not from her mother? And the notion that she, Moira, was somehow unsuitable came as a distinctly nasty shock.

Not that Moira had ever auditioned or had even asked to be considered for the job, but somehow she felt Roussel ought to have seen how much better she would have been. She knew she would. And no one had even thought to ask her. It was outrageous, humiliating.

Viznitski's barbed remark about her being a rose in the "afternoon of her bloom" was the final insult—especially now. Thanks to him, she was blooming in quite unexpected ways, and not all of them welcome. Moira had just learned she was pregnant.

Viznitski was not pleased. "Get rid of it" were his exact words.

Moira was stunned. She hadn't expected him to be elated, of course, but the idea of having to dispose of it was so ghastly she flinched. If she didn't find someone competent, she might very well be making a solo trip to the cemetery.

The whole episode rattled Moira. First, Maeve was growing up and appearing onstage—and doing quite well from the look of things—and here *she* was, pregnant. What a disgrace!

When she had been pregnant before, so many years ago, Pat had been so proud. So had she. Remembering that time, she was infuriated by Viznitski's reaction. It was as if the child wasn't good enough for him. *Her* child. Rubbish! At that moment she began to loathe André Viznitski. What a fool she was ever to have thought well of him. He was a barbarian if not a total degenerate. And he had made her his accomplice.

Maeve was unaware of her mother's worries. She was deliriously happy to be out of the house, away from Moira's orders and André's insinuations, but more than that, it was intoxicating to be greeted with delighted applause each night when she set foot onstage. It was a delicious sensation.

People loved her when she came strolling out dressed in her costume—a large picture hat trimmed with ruffles, a leg-baring pink, full-skirted tulle gown sewn with spangles, a low-cut bodice with yet more spangles, and long white kid gloves. A lacy parasol and a pair of neat kid dancing slippers completed her ensemble.

Maeve had very nice legs, which appealed to her audience, and although she wasn't as well endowed as Angélique in the upper part of her costume, what she had was set off to its best advantage. Nobody complained.

Julien Roussel was delighted things had worked out so well. He had been near despair when Angélique announced her news. It was the end of everything, he said grimly. All those years of working in hideous provincial towns, all those bad meals and low salaries . . . Now comes Paris and the Théâtre des Variétés and she does *this* to him!

Angélique had threatened to leave him at that point, and he had been intimidated enough to stop complaining. But the decision to hire the red-haired girl had been brilliant. She was a real crowd pleaser with a personality that seemed to seduce the audience. Florine was money in the bank, God bless her.

And Julien watched over her like a stern father.

On the day Moira was to go to a doctor to get rid of her problem, Julien and Maeve were presenting a new routine, and Maeve wanted her mother to see it.

"No, darling," Moira said firmly. "I don't feel well. I'm not going to go out this evening." She felt a sense of cold dread.

"But Mama, you may feel better later. Please come. It will be lovely."

"Darling, I know I won't be feeling any better," she replied with an edge to her voice. "I'll come see it when I'm able."

Maeve looked at her angrily this time, surprising her mother. "You don't care about me anymore," she said. "You just don't care." She wanted Moira to care more than anything.

"Don't be an idiot. I love you. But I'm ill. Do you expect me to sit through your show if I don't feel up to it? Be reasonable, Maeveen. I'll come as soon as possible."

*

The show went especially well that night, with Maeve and Julien singing and dancing their way through a new song that showed off Maeve's voice as well as her legs. The director of the theater paid a visit backstage to congratulate them, and for the first time Maeve found a large number of bouquets waiting for her.

"Well *chérie*," said Angélique with a smile, "I'd say you've arrived." She had been watching nervously from the wings.

A small crowd of well-wishers had gathered in the dressing room to offer congratulations and open a few bottles of Moët, mostly members of the other acts, the director, and an impresario who was interested in discussing another engagement with them. The dressing table mirror reflected a happy group, bubbling with enthusiasm—all except for the evening's star.

"It went well," Maeve sighed. "I'm happy for that."

Angélique noticed that she didn't look it. She looked quite downcast, in fact. What on earth could be bothering her? Julien had certainly not outshone her. Just the opposite. Perhaps it was some strange moodiness.

"I'm going to ask for a raise," Julien announced to his wife as soon as the director had departed. "It's about time."

"Let's have a drink to that," she replied. "Open up another bottle."

Maeve was delighted and miserable. Moira should have been here to witness her success, and she wasn't. And she hadn't even looked sick. It was a fake, a blatant fake. She simply hadn't wanted to be bothered.

"Are you all right?" Julien asked his new partner. "You look so sad."

"It's nothing." She smiled. "It's just that my feet hurt."

*

When Maeve returned home that night, she was angry to find Moira out. What a slap in the face! Not only was Moira not sick, she wasn't even pretending. Horribly disappointed, Maeve cried herself to sleep and wondered what had made her mother so callous. Perhaps it was jealousy, she thought miserably—though she had been angry at André Viznitski for suggesting that. If it was true, it made her think of Moira in a different way, and not an altogether flattering way at that. She didn't even want to acknowledge that possibility, it seemed so mean-spirited.

When Maeve awakened at nine in the morning and found herself alone in the apartment, she became uneasy. This was definitely odd, not at all her mother's way. Moira was a firm believer in the value of a good night's sleep.

Frightened by the idea that something had happened to her mother, Maeve rang up Count Viznitski. Was Moira with him? she asked nervously. She hated to have anything to do with him now, but Moira's welfare was more important than her own likes and dislikes.

"She's not home?" Viznitski purred, almost as if he had been waiting for her call. "How peculiar." He rather enjoyed this little game.

"Do you know where she might be?" Maeve persisted. It was ridiculous for him not to know. What sort of nonsense was he up to now?

The voice on the other end of the line hesitated. "Well," he temporized, "she said she wasn't feeling well. Perhaps she's in a clinic."

"A clinic?" Something in André's tone made the girl feel as if she'd been struck by a steel fist. Moira had complained of not feeling well, that was all. Why should she be in a clinic? It didn't make sense. He was leaving out something.

"What's happened to my mother?" Maeve suddenly demanded, her voice rising. "What have you done to her?"

He was behind it, whatever it was; Maeve knew that. It was all over his voice. His tone was oily with guilt.

Count Viznitski said nothing for a few seconds. Then, to Maeve's astonishment, he said, "She visited a doctor yesterday afternoon. And then a few hours later she began to hemorrhage. She's been in the clinic ever since."

The blood was pulsing so fiercely in her head, Maeve thought she would scream. She could only stare at the receiver in her hand. What was this monster hiding from her? And then she did scream.

"My mother is in some clinic and you don't even tell me? How could you? And why is she hemorrhaging? How did it happen?"

Viznitski tried to evade all Maeve's questions. "She didn't want you to worry," he said. "She made me promise not to tell you." He was sweating now.

"I don't believe you. Where is she? What have you done to her?"

"I'm sorry," he said. "I can't tell you."

"You mean you won't."

"I can't, believe me," he insisted, sweating more than ever now.

At that, Maeve slammed down the receiver with a bang and made an unholy racket. On his end, Count Viznitski jumped, startled by the noise.

"Damn," he muttered, slowly replacing his telephone. "The girl's a savage." And if he knew her type, she'd be on her way over to his apartment, thirsting for blood.

None of this should have happened. Yesterday he had taken his pregnant mistress to the office of a fashionable ladies' doctor on the boulevard des Italiens. There the doctor had injected a solution into her uterus to trigger a miscarriage. It had resulted in such an agony of pain and unchecked bleeding that the man had panicked, tried unsuccessfully to stop the hemorrhage himself, and then given up and decided to send her to a private clinic to let them take charge. By this time, she was unconscious and André was terrified.

After several hours of treatment—and a lot of unanswerable questions—Moira's life had been saved, but just barely. She was weak, feverish, and frightened, as much for Maeve as for herself. How could she have been so stupid and risked killing herself and leaving poor Maeve alone in a strange country with a scoundrel like André Viznitski nearby? That thought alone filled her with such determination to stay alive, she clung to it like a life raft, hating André with all the fury she could muster, determined not to let him kill her off so easily. If the British hadn't managed to murder her, weak as she was then, this damned Russian barbarian was surely not going to. Never!

She was ashamed she had agreed to do this. The baby was gone, and it had been hers as much as his. She didn't want it and, truthfully, she was glad it was gone, but it had been an evil thing to do, too terrible even to mention to the priest who had been called to give her the last rites. She had pretended she couldn't hear him, so he had given her a general absolution without bothering her for a confession. Nothing would make her confess it. People went to jail for these things. That would be the icing on the cake. She wasn't about to go through *that*. Not for a degenerate like Count Viznitski.

*

In their apartment, Maeve was in a state of near panic, scarcely able to see clearly. All she could picture was Moira in a coffin, being buried in foreign soil. Well, she wasn't going to let that happen. If Viznitski wouldn't tell her where her mother was, she would force it out of him.

Dressing as quickly as possible, the girl ran outside, hailed a cab, and leaped into it, telling the driver to head for Viznitski's address on the double.

Once there, she flung her coins at the cabbie and raced into the building, not even pausing at the concierge's loge.

That was a mistake. "Mademoiselle!" shouted the woman. "Come back here! Whom are you visiting?"

"Mind your own business!" Maeve shouted back. "I haven't got time for this blather!"

Who does she think she is? thought the concierge, thoroughly outraged. Nobody slights the concierge, not in this building!

By the time Maeve was in and out of the fancy wrought-iron elevator and alighting on the second floor—Viznitski's apartment—he was trying to leave. Startled, the count nearly collided with Maeve, a large Louis Vuitton bag in each hand. He was so pressed for time he hadn't even bothered to call his valet.

"Where are you going, Count Viznitski?" Maeve demanded, barring his way to the elevator. "You have company. Where are your manners?"

"Get out of my way. I don't wish to speak to you."

"Well, you'd better. Or else I'll call the nearest flic and accuse you of abducting my mother." Her face was set and hard, not like her.

"Don't be stupid! You don't want to bring the police into this, believe me."

He was pale. He looked dreadful, as if he hadn't slept all night. Maeve wondered what Moira looked like. She was almost afraid to know.

"I want to speak to my mother. Where is she?"

"She doesn't want to see you. She's very ill. I already told you this. You don't listen." Viznitski's face was as tense as hers.

"If she's so ill, all the more reason why I ought to see her. Where is she?"

Viznitski tried to push past her and she resolutely blocked his way. He would have to kill her; she wouldn't move any other way.

Now the fat concierge came puffing up the stairs in hot pursuit of the intruder. As she paused on the staircase, gasping for breath, she glanced first at Count Viznitski, then at the girl, not quite knowing what to think. Perhaps this was a friend of his.

"Monsieur," she managed at last, "shall I call the police?"

At the word "police" André turned a ghastly ashen color and nearly choked. "No!" he yelped. "Don't do that. I know the young lady. It's all right." Turning to Maeve, he gestured. "Come inside. We'll talk there."

Under the puzzled eyes of the old woman, André put down his two bags and guided or, more precisely, pushed Maeve into his apartment.

"Let go of me!" she shouted at him, pushing back furiously. "Don't you ever touch me!"

Viznitski closed the door on his curious audience and said to Maeve, "Your mother is resting at the Clinique St. Denis in Neuilly. She's all right now."

"What do you mean 'now'?" cried the girl. "She *was* in danger, then!"

"Yes," snapped André. "All right, if you must know. She nearly died yesterday afternoon."

The room seemed to swirl. All the luxurious décor—a masterpiece of art nouveau—spun past Maeve as she struggled to understand what André Viznitski was telling her. He had a part in it. She had somehow known it. The liar, the dirty liar.

"Don't be so upset," André said pettishly, witnessing an alarming surge of emotion in his visitor. "I told you she was all right. Calm yourself."

But Maeve showed no sign of calming down. If anything, she was even more agitated than before.

"What happened to her?" she demanded. "She told me she didn't feel well. How could she have come close to dying . . . ?"

Viznitski's expression changed subtly. The corners of his sensual mouth twitched ever so slightly, as if he were enjoying some private joke. "She was pregnant," he said at last. "Now she isn't. And that's why you can't go to the police, *milochka*. Accuse me and you force me to incriminate your lovely mother. Very nasty business."

As the realization hit Maeve, she was so disgusted she seized the nearest handy object and let fly with it—straight at André Viznitski's head.

He reacted swiftly. Hurling himself at the girl, he knocked her off balance and sent her sprawling onto the carpet. Maeve tried frantically to escape from his grasp as he pinned her to the floor with his weight, gloating at his easy victory. Little savage! He was getting an erection.

"Let go of me! Right now!"

"Not a chance," grunted Viznitski. "I've waited a long time for this moment. I'm going to enjoy it." How sweet it felt.

"Well, so am I!" replied Maeve, startling her attacker. And with that, she reached back over her head and got a firm grasp on the handle of a porcelain vase. Before the count could figure out what she meant, Maeve raised her right arm as high as she could and brought the vase—eighteenth-century Canton ware—down on his head with a great scream that shocked him almost as much as the impact itself.

Viznitski rolled off her, blood from his wound mingling with tiny chips of precious porcelain that flew around the room as the vase shattered under the tremendous blow.

Scrambling to safety, Maeve grabbed the nearest handy weapon—a pair of brass fire tongs—and stood over Count Viznitski, watching him the way a hunter might watch a dangerous beast he had managed to wound. She was struggling for breath, dead white and trembling with disgust. She saw him staring stupidly, his mouth open in bewilderment, looking like a drunkard in the middle of the beautiful blue and cream Aubusson carpet.

"Can you hear me, André Viznitski?" Maeve demanded, fixing him with a terrible expression in her beautiful eyes. "Are you conscious?"

"Yes," he muttered thickly, his eyes barely focused.

"Good," nodded Maeve. "Because I want you to hear me and understand every word I say. First, let me tell you I am driving directly to the Clinique St. Denis to see how Mama is. If she dies because of you, I will return and kill you. Second, you will never again set foot in our home or ever try to speak to me or Mama again. Do you understand?"

Half-conscious, André could only gape at the red-haired maniac who had nearly killed him and who was telling him she'd finish the job if Moira died. What kind of girl was this? He was used to excitable women, but no one had ever promised to murder him before, although one or two husbands had. What temperament! He swore she must have Tartar blood.

"Answer me," Maeve commanded. "I want to be absolutely sure you understand what I'm saying. I mean *every* word of it."

"Yes, yes," Viznitski agreed, groaning as he tried to rise from the carpet. Maeve pushed him back down with the aid of the tongs, keeping him off balance and still helpless. She didn't trust him.

"I hate you," the girl was saying to him as she looked straight through him, "but if Mama lives, you live. If she dies, you die. This I swear."

"Yes," groaned the count, still staggered by the outcome of his attempt to rape her. This was some sort of wild savage despite all appearances to the contrary. She was a danger to his very life—and after all the kindness he had shown her. The little ingrate! Savage!

"I'm leaving now," Maeve concluded, "and I'm going to the clinic. If you know any prayers, say them now."

CHAPTER 10

Colonel Apis—Dragutin Dimitrievic—the head of the Black Hand as well as of the Serb secret police, was caught in a predicament so maddening, so frustrating, even he would never have been able to devise it. He who had been receiving unofficial Russian subsidies to achieve the overthrow of Serbia's Russian-backed monarch had been summarily informed one afternoon that unless Sean Farrell, Nikolai Petrovic's son, was returned to Montenegro in good shape, the Russian ambassador would be forced to bring certain unpleasant facts to the attention of His Majesty, King Alexander. No need to specify. Apis knew, and it was enough to make him shudder. The blackmailing bastards! He didn't dare let Alexander know the extent of his disloyalty to him.

Reluctantly, Apis agreed to help. The plan was simple enough. Orders were to be presented for the transfer of prisoner number 47, signed by the commander of the Belgrade garrison and countersigned by the army's chief of staff. That these were both clever forgeries did not detract from their effectiveness.

In a very short time, prisoner number 47 was escorted up from his cell, looking pale from several months of confinement but cleanshaven and dressed in fairly decent fashion. Alexander—ever fearful of discovery by the Montenegrins and subsequent reprisals—had specified that he was not to be abused or maltreated in any way.

Led up from the depths, Sean sized up the men sent to escort him—where? he wondered—and was disappointed not to see a single familiar face. He had hoped Nikolai would engineer an escape, but this group contained not one Montenegrin. All were Serbs, wearing the uniform of the Serbian Army and looking as though they really were what they were supposed to be—worse luck.

When Sean's officer escort opened the door of the waiting black coach, he nearly flung him inside; he was that eager to get going. Waiting there was a solid-looking Serb officer wrapped in a gray army cloak and smoking a cigarette.

As the door slammed after him, Sean found himself facing his companion, Colonel Apis, who offered him a Turkish cigarette. Shaking his head, he declined. What was Apis here for? What kind of trick were they trying to play on him? Would he finally be murdered now?

The colonel hastened to assure him that King Alexander had been behind his abduction and imprisonment—just in case he might have the wrong idea. He, the colonel, had worked tirelessly to free him. The proof of that was his presence here right now.

Sean was unimpressed. The colonel had taken a very long time with his "tireless" efforts. He wasn't stupid. Still, Sean reasoned, Alexander was paranoid enough to have been behind this. After all, Sean had come to Belgrade to help plot his overthrow!

After expressing doubts about Apis's story, Sean demanded to know the whereabouts of the two women who were with him on the day he was abducted. Apis assured him that they and his man Kyril had vanished, Kyril probably to Montenegro, but as for the women, well, he really had no idea. Apis looked downcast enough for Sean to believe him. He hated to think of Moira or young Maeve at the mercy of some Serb brute. If they had come to grief because of him, he could never forgive himself.

At Apis's assurances that he had done his best to locate the women, to spare them the terrible fate of falling into the hands of Alexander's men, Sean merely smiled. The colonel would have been keen to have them to himself, he thought.

Still, it appeared the Devereux ladies had foiled everyone's plans that day, probably thanks to Kyril. The Montenegrin was an old campaigner, shrewd and tricky—more than a match for the Serbian secret police. With another smile Sean informed the glowering Apis that he was glad he hadn't harmed the women. Otherwise he'd feel duty bound to kill the colonel.

It wasn't the sort of sentiment Apis appreciated from a Montenegrin, and he made no reply except to chew on his impressive mustaches. He may have lost this battle; he was already planning the next round of the war.

CHAPTER 11

*D*ietrich von Reuter was full of hope when he arrived in Paris in that spring of 1902. The banker Hubertus had sent him to work with had a very attractive and musically gifted Belgian wife, Hélène, whom Dietrich liked at first glance. The two marriageable daughters, Charlotte and Gertrude—or, more informally, Lotte and Trudl—were plump, insipid, and pretty in an overblown fashion. They conjured up in Dietrich's mind horrible images of dumplings on legs, and their mother—a very elegant brunette beauty—arranged things so that the girls looked as lumpish as possible. Dietrich wondered if Hélène did this to nip any competition in the bud, or simply because she had decided not to waste money clothing them when it could be much better spent on her superb form. Their father adored them and lived for the day when he could see them decently united in marriage with good German bankers who would use the link to forge a dynasty that would spread across Europe. Unfortunately, he was as myopic regarding Dietrich as he was with his daughters, and he actually viewed young von Reuter as his man—a serious error of judgment.

Dietrich's father had arranged things so that his son would live at the imposing von Ebert residence on the boulevard Haussmann, the better to facilitate any budding romance and keep him under Herr von Ebert's fatherly eye at the same time. Hubertus insisted on *that*.

Romance was soon in bloom, but not the right kind. Frau von

Ebert was so taken with her handsome blond guest, she was soon spending hours with him, playing duets on the piano or singing her favorite Italian arias while he played for her. Since the lady had connections with many prominent men in the Parisian musical world, Dietrich encouraged this friendship, a little dazzled by Hélène's luscious figure and lavish hospitality. But his thoughts were elsewhere. He was still searching for the Lorelei.

*

Her brush with death and Count Viznitski's hasty departure for St. Petersburg had left Moira with scars that seemed beyond repair. She was profoundly ashamed of her relationship with a man who turned out to be as cold-blooded as a snake. She had been childishly naive and had ended up as badly as a seventeen-year-old country bumpkin adrift in the city for the first time. At thirty-seven she felt she should have known better. It was galling that she hadn't. It had shaken her self-confidence deeply.

To try to cheer Moira up, Maeve decided to send her and her maid to Nice to take the sun for a month. If nothing else, the Riviera sunshine would put some color back in her pale cheeks, and with Moira's flair for friendship, she would hardly lack for gentlemen anxious to amuse her. It would be a tonic. And Maeve could now afford to make a generous gesture, thanks to her success as Florine.

Maeve herself was happy. She and Julien Roussel had made the move to the Casino de Paris, where she was attracting very favorable notices. There were rumors in the press that the resident star was annoyed by Maeve's incursions into her territory, but the "offended one" herself laughed at them.

"Rumors like those are good for business," she confided one evening after she had reduced the audience to near frenzy. "People love to hear we're at each other's throats and would like to scratch each other's eyes out. The bastards will buy tickets just to be there in case it happens. It's the same reason some people love to attend public executions. Lust for blood, for excitement. They love you and yet they would gladly see you bleed for them. *Ce sont des salauds.*" She laughed gaily, uncorking a bottle of Moët. "So here's to us: may we outlast all our enemies!"

"But not our friends," Maeve replied, a shade too optimistically, as she and the blonde cheerfully clinked glasses with Julien, who was admiring all the feathers worn by the star attraction. God only knew how many birds had died for that display. Impressive. Maeve ought to consider more feathers, he reflected.

"Friends!" roared the blonde. "Little girl, you really are an innocent if you think you can count on friends. Roussel, teach this girl about life, will you? Or the bastards will eat her alive!"

Maeve hoped the tough French girl was only joking. The star, Yvette, wasn't that much older than she was—well, a few years—but she had all the cynicism of ten French concierges and twenty flics. "Get the money first—then talk about love" was one of her favorite maxims. Maeve wished Moira had had some of that attitude with Count Viznitski, but Moira wasn't as hard as this feisty girl from Enghien. Yvette would have reduced Viznitski to poverty, then abandoned him because he couldn't afford to amuse her any longer. That was the proper course to take with a Viznitski, but Moira had bungled her attempt at a career as a courtesan, and Maeve wished she would realize it. The only problem was, Moira seemed to harbor definite tendencies to waywardness.

The safe delivery of Angélique Roussel's son Hippolyte was cause for general rejoicing backstage at the Casino. It took place apparently while Julien and "Florine" were in the middle of a new act, requiring Maeve to swing back and forth on a flower-draped swing while Julien sang to her and then lifted her down onto the stage, where they began a sentimental duet.

The swing served an ulterior and strictly nonmusical purpose: it enabled Maeve to wear a frilly costume of the kind seen on circus performers, consisting of a spangled leotard with wispy cap sleeves, pink tights, and neat little kid boots. She looked like a delicious confection up there and as such was greatly admired by her public.

"*Oh, les jolies jambes!*" was the cry that greeted her descent from the perch. To her delight, she would see that in print in a glowing review of the act in the next day's *Petit Parisien*. Meanwhile, she was enjoying her triumph. She loved to move an audience.

There was to be a celebration at Fouquet's to fete Maeve's success and Julien Roussel's new son. Friends from the other acts were going to be there, and Yvette had graciously consented to show up with her latest admirer in tow. Since the owner of the restaurant was one of the Casino's star's greatest fans, there was expected to be a flow of champagne that would keep everyone floating in bubbles all night long.

Maeve was seated at the head of a big table with her Casino colleagues clustered around her, everyone toasting her success, when she suddenly felt her heart stop. Catching her breath, she rose from the table and dashed across the crowded room to where a young, blond man was standing, dressed in evening clothes, watching her, absolutely dumbfounded. He looked so adorable she felt like hugging him.

"Dietrich," she laughed, as he took both her hands and tenderly held them. "You look as if you've seen a ghost. Don't you recognize me?"

"My God!" he exclaimed. "Of course I do. I just couldn't believe my eyes. I thought I must be seeing things. *Liebchen,*" he murmured, kissing her softly on the cheek, "you've become so lovely, so grown-up. What's happened to you?" This was a different Maeve altogether, and he was delighted.

*

Dietrich's discovery of Maeve by chance at Fouquet's after he had been to the opera that evening was a gift from heaven as far as he was concerned. He had lost her address and spent several frustrating months trying to find her. Now he had the girl herself, his Lorelei, prettier than ever. That she was working at the Casino de Paris was astonishing, if not shocking. He didn't think it worthy of her.

Having invited Dietrich to see her perform, Maeve put all her vivacity into the next show, drawing waves of delighted applause. Julien was thrilled. "Florine" acted on the audience like catnip on cats. It drove them crazy.

"Yvette will be jealous," he teased her as she flounced backstage at the end of the act. "I think you're starting to make her nervous."

"Ha!" Maeve laughed. "I don't think the person's been born who could make that one nervous. She's got nerves of granite. Nothing rattles *her*." It was an amusing notion though.

Then she withdrew to her dressing room to change clothes, remove her makeup, and get ready to go out to dinner. Dietrich was right on time, punctual as a Swiss watch but oddly reticent, Maeve noticed.

"Don't you feel well?" she asked solicitously as they exited from the artists' entrance and climbed into a waiting horse cab. A few gentlemen at the stage door greeted her warmly, congratulating her on the evening's performance. Dietrich was startled that so many seemed to know her.

"Friends of friends," she said, smiling. "They're waiting for some of the chorus girls."

"Liebchen," he replied solemnly, taking her hand in both of his as the coach clattered off down the cobbled street. "I think you have a magnificent gift . . ."

"Thank you," Maeve replied cheerfully, still smiling at him in the semidarkness.

"But I also think you're wasting it—"

In the shadowed interior of the coach he couldn't really see the expression on her face, but he could guess at it from the way she pulled away from him. A wave of anger flowed through her entire body, as fiercely as if she had been hit by a jolt of electricity. She was furious; it was so unexpected. And so cruel!

"Then I won't invite you back to see me again. I'm sorry I bored you," she snapped, yanking her hand from his.

How dare he? The fellow hadn't seen her in months and he had the gall to criticize her! Everyone else loved her well enough!

"I'm sorry I made you angry," Dietrich said contritely. "Please forgive me. I phrased that so badly." Clumsy idiot. He had hurt her.

"That's the truth," Maeve retorted, glaring at him. "And it's also true that there are lots of people in this city who pay good money to see me waste my talents."

"I can understand why they adore you. Your audience applauded like mad. You're delightful," he said, trying to climb out of the hole he had just dug for himself.

"But none of that impresses *you*," she said coldly.

"Of course it does," Dietrich said emphatically. "It was wonderful to see how they loved you. It's just that with a voice like yours, it seems a crime against nature to subordinate it to a pair of tights. *That's* my sole objection. You are an adorable girl, Maeve. But you have a voice that deserves better from you. It needs a finer setting."

"Like Geraldine Farrar has?" Maeve threw back at him, much to his surprise. She had never forgotten seeing Farrar that night at the Berlin Opera. Or how Dietrich had admired the beautiful young American.

Startled, the young man paused, staring at Maeve in the shadows. He hadn't thought about comparing her to Farrar, a fairly recent arrival on the scene. Her voice reminded him of the quality possessed by Emma Calvé, a reigning star on two continents.

"Better than Farrar," he replied, "although you have in common with her a gorgeous middle register. But I think you may have more power than Farrar. And," he went on, impressed, "you can reach and hold a note higher and longer than she can. That is a superb gift. One day—with the proper training—you might resemble Melba there."

"Well, thank you very much, but I'm Maeve Devereux and I'm nobody but myself. And," she added with a touch of malice, "Nellie Melba is a ball of suet."

That broke the ice. Dietrich burst out laughing and Maeve laughed with him, her anger gone. She finally realized that Dietrich had been paying her a weighty compliment—even though German compliments often had the distinct sound of condemnation. Well, it was all right. She still loved his beautiful blond hair. And this time she felt free enough to run her fingers through it, caressing and ruffling it, making Dietrich protest. But she enjoyed doing it, a perverse kind of compliment of her own.

*

Frau Hélène von Ebert was consumed with passion for her husband's young associate, and although she was adept at concealing this from Karl and her daughters—who would have been horrified by it—Dietrich himself was constantly aware of the impact he had on her. And it had reached the point where he was living in fear of discovery by Karl.

Since Hélène's passion for Dietrich was second only to her passion for opera, she neatly combined the two by arranging for him to take her *to* the opera, a duty Karl found onerous. The boy enjoyed all that bellowing? Marvelous. Make use of him. Go. Have a good time.

Dietrich once inquired if Trudl and Lotte wouldn't like to see something—perhaps *Tannhäuser*, a good German opera—and as Karl was about to give his consent, Frau Hélène said with great conviction, "Let them wait until they can hear it at Bayreuth. These Frenchmen will only murder it, and the bad experience will turn them away from Wagner forever."

Herr von Ebert believed Richard Wagner was responsible for more bellowing than any ten Frenchmen combined, but the Kaiser thought highly of the fellow's work, so he assumed he must be worthy of respect. And Hélène knew her music, so what was he to do?

To the great disappointment of Lotte and Trudl, they would have to wait for Bayreuth.

This almost annoyed Dietrich, because if he had taken the girls to the opera he could have used it as proof that he was doing what he was supposed to be doing there. His father was not likely to be pleased knowing he and Frau von Ebert were becoming the most assiduous music lovers in Paris. If Herr von Ebert was complacent, Hubertus was not. He had never trusted his son.

Hélène von Ebert was jealous of her two daughters, and Dietrich could not fathom why. They were perfect examples of the round, milk-fed Teutonic beauty he found so repellent, while she was a slender, high-strung brunette with beautifully delineated features that would have done justice to an antique cameo. This was a woman born to stir men's blood, while Lotte and Trudl looked as if they had been created to churn butter in some alpine pasture. Unfortunate girls, he thought.

Maeve was the one girl on Dietrich's mind, and since their meeting at Fouquet's he had been calling on her as often as he could—whenever he could escape from his duties at the bank and from his hostess. He had annoyed Julien Roussel by taking Maeve to several vocal coaches, eliminating one after the other until she had found one she could tolerate—a German who adored the work of the Italian composer Puccini. Roussel thought this was an invasion of his territory. Dietrich considered it essential to Maeve's development as a singer.

Shortly after Maeve had introduced Dietrich to her partner, the Frenchman had taken her aside to warn her against him. The *boche* made him apprehensive; he was concerned for Maeve's well-being.

"He would like to own you," Roussel said seriously as he and "Florine" sat at the terrace of the Café de la Paix near the Opéra. "I can see it in his eyes. This is a dangerous, bad *boche*. They're all alike, all predators. His father probably helped Bismarck steal Alsace-Lorraine."

Julien's beautiful dark eyes were so full of foreboding, Maeve was astonished. He was a rather reticent man, not given to alarm unless something affected his work. She couldn't imagine him becoming so exercised over Dietrich.

Her blue eyes gave Julien a look indicating stark bewilderment. "I don't think Baron von Reuter helped the Iron Chancellor steal Alsace-Lorraine," she said.

"Then he helped finance his predatory impulses. It's all the same. He's a banker. He's a German. There you are."

Looking at Julien's solemn face over her cup of café au lait, Maeve nearly burst out laughing. Dietrich might be a man with conquest on his mind, but it wasn't the sort to imperil *la patrie*.

"I don't know why you find it so difficult to think of him being attracted to me," she said with just a shade of malice. "That's all there is to it, you know." *She* rather liked the idea.

"Maeve, there are hundreds of men who are attracted to you. That's evident each time you walk out onstage. But this *boche* wants to own you. He wants to carry you off and put you on some pretty pillow in his house and turn you into a sweet little pet. He's just too intense."

"You don't like him," she said flatly, her lovely eyes clouding over the way Moira's did when she was provoked. "You didn't like him when you met."

"Ah, *chérie*," smiled Julien. "I'm sorry if I hurt your feelings. I'm very fond of you. That's why this *boche* frightens me. He's thinking of himself, not you. He wants to use you for his own purposes."

That was a statement that could also apply to Julien, Maeve thought, not at all swayed by his concern. She liked the Frenchman. He had been very kind to her, and she liked Angélique, too, but their outlook was colored by their concern for their act. If Maeve were to leave, they would be forced to find another girl—who might not be so appealing. She had been a great discovery for them. They dreaded the idea of her departure.

"Julien," Maeve replied, shading her eyes against the summer sun, "don't worry so. You're popular enough to go it alone if you had to. The women are mad for you."

He nearly jumped in his seat. "See, you are thinking of leaving," he said in despair. "I knew it."

"I am *not*! I'm just stating a fact. I don't understand why you think I'm so important. Angélique quit and the earth didn't stop spinning, did it?"

Her partner chuckled. "Angélique didn't have your talent," he said. "She's my wife and I love her dearly, but I have to tell the truth. You're much better at this."

Surprised, she looked at him shyly, a little hesitant. "How good do you really think I am?" she asked.

"Good enough to put Yvette in the shade if you really wanted to. Audiences go crazy for you. That doesn't always happen. A girl can be beautiful, she can be charming, but unless she has that rare chemistry, she never quite catches on. You have that gift. I can't even describe it, Maeve, but I can recognize it."

Ah, thought the red-haired girl. Then so can Dietrich. And he was aiming a lot higher than the music hall. Well, why not? Was she inferior to Geraldine Farrar, whose career she was following through the newspapers? No, she was not. Farrar was the darling of the Royal Opera in Berlin and the special favorite of the Crown Prince, which made Maeve smile. She wondered if he had given Farrar beautiful diamond bracelets. Probably.

"Life is odd, Julien," she said. "You never know where it will lead you."

"Yes," he replied with a wary smile. "But don't forget that it sometimes leads beautiful young girls down the primrose path. Be careful," he warned her, playfully kissing her hand. Then he looked deep into her eyes with a warning that belied the smile.

*

Seeing Dietrich again was wonderful, Maeve thought. She was fond of the young German, though he occasionally reminded her of a drillmaster.

He had such faith in her it was touching, even if he was sometimes a bit too intense.

"Have you practiced your scales today, Maeve? Have you studied the score of that opera? Be careful in your German pronunciation. You sound too French . . ."

If she hadn't been swept away by her own desire to surpass Dietrich's hopes, she would have given up. But Maeve was stubborn. She hadn't survived Camp 3 and Sergeant Davies only to end up defeated by a lack of energy. If she had to cram thirty-six hours into twenty-four, so be it. If Dietrich said she needed a better German accent, she would work on it. If she had to make the transition from a pretty stage decoration in tights to Carmen at the Paris Opéra, she would do that, too. Maeve Devereux hadn't come halfway around the world to be a failure. Remembering where she had come from was a guarantee against laziness.

On some afternoons when she strolled down the boulevards, gazing into the shop windows and observing the passersby, Maeve found herself thinking of Caroline and Sean. When she did, it always made her sad, for they seemed to have vanished into the periphery of her life, not dead but beyond communication, somewhere out there, still remembering her—at least she hoped so—but so distant, so remote.

Both had disappeared into a whirlpool of violence, Caroline and her sons back into the war in South Africa and Sean into some sort of intrigue in the Balkans. Now the news from South Africa was of peace, so perhaps she might reestablish a link with Caroline after so many unanswered letters, but what of Sean?

In the back of her mind, Maeve wondered if perhaps Geraldine was deliberately withholding information from her. Despite the gräfin's warmth and friendliness when they first met, it was apparent to the girl that she had been deliberately brushed aside. She couldn't understand why.

Perhaps it was her behavior with the Kaiser. Had he complained to Geraldine after she asked him for troops? She had been gauche, of course, but she hadn't meant to offend him. If the gräfin had been put into that dreadful camp, she would have asked for the same thing.

Maeve didn't know what to think. She would never have imagined the gorgeously bejeweled Gräfin von Kleist afraid of a mere girl like herself. Maeve certainly meant her no harm. And she adored Sean, who was the light of his mother's life, so why had the friendship cooled so dramatically?

It was all beyond her. The only thing that was pellucidly clear was the feeling of having lost part of herself that terrible day in Belgrade when Sean Farrell was attacked by Serb ruffians and brutally torn from her life.

The nightly applause at the Casino, the lovely gowns she now wore, even Dietrich's infatuation, were nothing in comparison. Sean was quite simply the most attractive man she had ever met, and it seemed unnatural to Maeve that they would never meet again.

She had killed for him. Their friendship was sealed in something primitive and elemental, creating a deeper bond than all the champagne bubbling through her new life in Paris. The city was delightful but it held no emotional ties for Maeve, who would have felt utterly rootless there except for Moira's presence. Despite Maeve's progress in becoming a Parisienne, she was not "of the city" and she felt her foreignness in peculiar ways.

In a sense, Maeve felt a kindred spirit in Dietrich von Reuter, who was putting in his time at Herr von Ebert's bank. She enjoyed Dietrich's company, was flattered by his attention, and frequently used him to discourage the numerous gentlemen who were forever sending flowers to her dressing room. For this at least, Julien Roussel was grateful to the German.

It was Julien's persistent nightmare that one day Maeve might be seduced by some rich American or an English milord and run off with the fellow, leaving him stranded. He needed "Florine" just as she was. Actually the only real danger for him was that Maeve might be tempted to elope with this blond banker's son who seemed to view her as a successor to Calvé or Melba. For her, that was much more seductive than a pile of dollars or pounds, and therefore more dangerous.

Julien himself did not like opera, considering it pretentious and boring if it wasn't at least *French* opera, and he thought Maeve looked a damned sight better on the stage at the Casino than she'd ever look in Garnier's extravaganza. She wasn't beefy enough, Julien declared. Who ever heard of a slender soprano? It was all wrong for a girl like her. It was a silly notion, he swore, some overheated Teutonic fantasy.

He was terrified of losing her.

*

Maeve's music teacher, Herr Albrecht, was entranced with her. He told her she must practice her scales every day, but what she already possessed was so beautiful it must be treated with respect and never misused. He winced to think of her in a pair of pink tights traipsing around the stage of the Casino, singing banal music hall ditties and exposing her lovely limbs to the gaze of the vulgar-minded. It was most unseemly.

He was also sorely suspicious of the young banker who was paying for her music lessons, and one afternoon he declared solemnly that he had known young singers who had suffered devastating vocal setbacks with the loss of their virginity.

Maeve didn't know where to look or how she could manage to keep a straight face. She blushed bright pink and studied her fingernails. Dietrich coughed, went beet-red, then stared steadfastly at the keys of the piano as Herr Albrecht expounded his theories. The old fellow was as subtle as an ox—and built much the same way. What a lot of rubbish, Dietrich thought indignantly. Albrecht had very peculiar ideas. And a great deal of cheek. Dietrich was furious, and highly offended.

Later, as he and Maeve sat inside the Café de la Paix having coffee, von Reuter cleared his throat and offered the comment that perhaps Herr Albrecht wasn't the right teacher for her.

"Oh no!" Maeve protested vehemently. "I'm quite fond of him. He's taught me so many interesting things. Singing at half voice for rehearsals, for instance. All sorts of useful ways to protect your vocal power."

"Ah, yes. Well, of course he did spend twenty years at the Berlin Opera. But don't you think some of his ideas are a bit bizarre?" Dietrich's blue eyes looked carefully at Maeve from over the rim of his coffee cup. He was hoping she would take his meaning.

"No," she replied, shrugging lightly. "I think he's usually right on the money."

Gritting his teeth, Dietrich pursued the matter further: "I don't think *all* his ideas are quite normal."

This time Maeve had a hard time trying to pretend. "Which ones?" she asked innocently.

Her companion turned faintly pink with embarrassment, which annoyed him since he never blushed with any of the girls he usually chased. Hélène von Ebert made him turn colors occasionally but for other reasons. She could drain the blood out of a man.

Dietrich glanced down at his coffee cup and said, trying to sound nonchalant, "Well, I find it difficult to believe that losing one's virginity would ever affect the quality of one's voice."

A nosy lady at the next table turned sharply toward him in amazement and then struggled to keep a straight face. Dietrich looked quite icy. He was trying to appear dignified.

"Oh, *that*," nodded Maeve. "Well, it sounds logical to me."

"Don't be ridiculous!"

"It's not ridiculous at all," she replied, enjoying the chance to have some fun with Dietrich. He was so solemn at times. The man was adorable but so Teutonic. "Herr Albrecht explained it all to me, and he made me realize I have to be very careful about this. Many a soprano has become an alto or worse because she didn't watch herself."

"Oh for heaven's sake!"

"Please, Dietrich, people are staring," Maeve said, shushing him. He hated making scenes. That was undignified and common—unless one was berating foreigners for some failing. Then it was permitted.

"That is a very unhealthy and eccentric notion," he declared. "There is no scientific basis for it."

"Ah, but you're wrong about that. In fact, Herr Albrecht showed me an article about that very thing in a respected journal of medicine from Leipzig. They proved it at the university there."

"That is rubbish," he protested in an agitated whisper.

"Oh no. Eminent doctors verified its authenticity. There were interviews with singers, too."

"Which singers?" Dietrich demanded. "What were their names?"

"Oh, long German names. They slip my mind at the moment," said Maeve with a shrug, attacking the luscious éclair on her plate.

Dietrich's blue eyes swept over her face, searching for a trace of a sly smile at the corners of her mouth, but he failed to detect it. She seemed convinced of this damned silly nonsense. A very handy thing for her to believe when other men came knocking at her door, but entirely absurd as far as he was concerned. It could even be harmful, he reflected as he studied her lovely face beneath the large picture hat. It could be dreadful!

"I still think it's unnatural and irrational," he concluded.

"Doctors swear by it," Maeve replied. "And anyway, Dietrich, why would Herr Albrecht make up something like that if it wasn't true?"

She was watching him with a sort of feline glint in her beautiful blue eyes, admiring *his* beauty. And enjoying his inner turmoil.

"I can't imagine why anyone would make up such a story," he conceded. "There wouldn't be any reason."

"Well, then," Maeve said cheerfully, "there you are. It must be true."

"I didn't say that," Dietrich retorted. "I just said I can't understand why anyone would make it up. It strikes me as very strange."

He wanted to make love to Maeve. He was racking his brain to find the right place but wasn't able to, since she lived under Moira's watchful vigilance and he lived with the von Eberts. Finding a place to make love to Hélène was the simplest thing in the world, and it was in fact wearing him out. But he would have traded all those afternoons of steaming up the conservatory windows for a few hours alone with Maeve Devereux. Life was so cruel.

In the back of Dietrich's mind there was also a nagging fear that perhaps Maeve might reject him. She was a very capricious girl, stubborn and unpredictable. What if he failed to please her? Dietrich hated even to consider that remote possibility, but it could happen. She was inexperienced. What if she decided she never wanted to see him again after their first night together? The idea made him shudder.

That was one of the virtues of marriage, he reflected gloomily: you could be as inept as possible and the woman had to resign herself to her fate. If she wasn't married to you, she might simply throw you out of bed and send you packing. He could picture Maeve taking a high-handed attitude, after all, she had once *shot* an Englishman. She was a little spitfire, not the kind of girl to allow you any illusions.

"Do you think marriage would produce the same effect on the voice?" Dietrich asked timidly, after a lengthy pause over his café au lait.

The blue eyes across the table opened wider than usual. But only for a second.

"I don't know," the girl said lightly. "Perhaps there was something in the article we missed."

"Take another look," Dietrich advised. "Just for curiosity."

He was nearly dizzy with emotion. He had practically proposed to Maeve. How could he? Hubertus would never agree to such a marriage. He was in Paris to marry some little cow and produce offspring. Jesus!

He wanted Maeve Devereux more than anything. Those little actresses and singers he chased were nothing in comparison, just girls who could be bought and used to make him feel like a pasha among his harem. That was Dietrich's notion of utter bliss.

Dietrich had a very febrile imagination with a markedly bizarre cast of mind. He had once been to Constantinople with Hubertus as a ten-year-old and had been mistakenly allowed inside their host's harem. It had been so delightful being fussed over by a pack of overaffectionate, bejeweled, and gorgeously clothed women wearing too much makeup and heady Oriental perfume that the boy had been marked for life. His taste in women was focused on the exotic and the outré. He had been ruined.

Maeve was exotic in her own lovely way, which had nothing of the harem and everything of the *princesse lointaine*. She was his Lorelei, the far-off maiden who would bewitch a man from a distant, unassailable height. That Maeve exercised her charms from beyond the footlights was less romantic than inhabiting a misty mountaintop, but the effect was similar—infatuation and frenzy among her admirers. Dietrich ached to possess the Lorelei, and he knew he would never do it unless he did it in the way she wanted.

But he was powerless to marry her unless he became an orphan. And Hubertus was too damned healthy to do him that favor anytime soon. So there he was—pining to possess her, fated to gratify the indecent yearnings of Frau Hélène, and destined to marry a nice little cow.

The thought of it nearly made him weep with chagrin. But he managed to finish his coffee with dry eyes.

*

After their conversation at the Café de la Paix, Maeve and Dietrich never again mentioned Herr Albrecht's odd theory, but Maeve found Dietrich more determined than ever to transform her into a diva.

With typical patient application, Dietrich had persuaded Frau von Ebert that he had discovered the most marvelous new soprano. Wouldn't it be delightful to present this treasure at the von Eberts' traditional Christmas musicale? Knowing how Hélène loved to pose as a patroness of the arts, it was a shrewd move.

On a snowy Thursday in early December, Maeve put on her black silk dress from Berlin and her red wool coat from Amsterdam, and headed for the imposing von Ebert residence on the boulevard Haussmann. She had an impressive Paris wardrobe by now but regarded that coat and dress as lucky talismans. Their association with Sean was significant to her.

Maeve arrived by coach at the imposing von Ebert residence, presented herself to the old butler, and was ceremoniously ushered into the drawing room where Hélène sat waiting.

After the usual politenesses, Frau von Ebert offered her visitor tea, which Maeve took with lemon, avoiding milk, since it seemed to affect her voice badly before a performance. In the course of their conversation each woman studied the other with discreet curiosity. Maeve was impressed by Hélène's elegance. Her hostess was wearing a sapphire-blue afternoon frock from Worth trimmed by bands of black velvet at the high collar, cuffs, and hem. Around her neck was the longest strand of perfectly matched large pearls the girl had ever seen—and she had seen some fine examples in Berlin. Obviously, this woman was from a level of society Maeve had yet to encounter in Paris. She appeared to be a kind of human jewel. The final touches as far as Maeve was concerned were the tortoiseshell combs that held her glossy black coiffure in place. Scattered across the combs was a sprinkling of small diamonds, which most women would have found de trop, but on Hélène were casually elegant. Her finely tapered, beautifully manicured fingers had their own clusters of diamonds.

While Maeve was admiring the splendor of Frau von Ebert, her hostess was favorably impressed by the girl's own style. The dress was exquisite, thought Hélène, very refined. Not the sort of thing one might expect of an artiste. The delicate Lalique brooch of fine enamel with its small diamonds and opals—Dietrich's present—was very fine. And the pearl and diamond earrings—a gift to Moira from Count Viznitski— were superb. Evidently the creature was doing quite well. Or some gentleman was keeping her in high style. Hélène rather suspected the latter; Mademoiselle Devereux was beautiful. That kind of beauty did not go unnoticed—or unrewarded.

Well, thought Hélène, if this girl's singing is as impressive as her appearance, she'll be a great success. It annoyed her that Dietrich had been the one to discover her; he seemed too enthusiastic about her now.

The audition went splendidly, with Maeve singing Puccini's arias "O mia dimora umile" and "Mi chiamano Mimi" while Hélène accompanied her on the piano, a Bechstein. After the last note had died, Frau von Ebert looked up at the girl and nodded.

"The party is the next to the last Sunday of the month. Come at two o'clock. One of my friends could accompany you on the piano. Or you could bring your own accompanist. Let me know what you prefer."

"Monsieur von Reuter could accompany me," Maeve declared.

"Well, yes. I suppose he could." Hélène's dark eyes narrowed. The girl seemed so certain, it annoyed her. She added as an afterthought, "The fee will be five hundred francs. Is this suitable?"

To Hélène's astonishment, Maeve replied in tones of casual surprise, "My usual fee is seven hundred and fifty."

"Ah," murmured Frau von Ebert.

"If it doesn't suit you, perhaps you'd care to engage someone else." Maeve shrugged, indicating that she didn't care if her hostess did or did not. One had one's standards.

Those dark brown eyes fairly glittered. Hélène found this attitude irritating—but she recognized a gorgeously uncommon voice when she heard one, and she wanted to be the first to present this discovery to Paris before anyone else took her up.

Looking as if she had swallowed something distasteful, Hélène nodded. "Agreed. Now, *ma chère*, let's plan your recital."

When Maeve returned home to the pretty apartment she still shared with Moira, her mother was curious about the outcome of her interview and delighted when she heard the news.

"This is wonderful. The von Eberts are very well connected. And Dietrich tells me the wife knows everybody who counts in the musical establishment."

"You've been talking with Dietrich? The same Dietrich who was once 'that little swine'? Mama"—Maeve smiled—"how times have changed!"

"He's a nice young man. And he's mad about you. He told me so."

The girl smiled again, wryly. "He's under orders from Hubertus to marry and produce offspring. Poor boy. He feels like some sort of human sacrifice."

"But he's in love with you."

Yes, thought Maeve. He probably was. But that didn't alter anything. He had his destiny mapped out for him. She hoped *she* had a destiny. But not as the wife of some banker. Maeve enjoyed what she was doing and she hoped to continue it—on a new level very shortly. If Dietrich could help her achieve that, she would be grateful forever. But she was realistic enough not to see him as a husband. Not with Baron Hubertus in the picture. And she had no plans at all to become his mistress.

*

As final preparations for Maeve's recital got under way, Moira announced she would serve as her daughter's accompanist. It was logical, since she had ample time to rehearse with her, while Dietrich or Herr Albrecht did not. It was a good point, and Moira was capable of doing a splendid job. However, Maeve also knew her well enough to suspect an ulterior motive: she wanted to get a look inside the von Ebert mansion.

Dietrich was passionately concerned about Maeve's debut as a salon singer and he conferred with her and Moira every chance he could. Nervous about accompanying her himself at the piano under the jealous eye of Hélène von Ebert, he was also apprehensive about her choice of Moira. That fear subsided when he heard her play. Now his only concern was that her dazzling presence might detract attention from Maeve.

"See if you can get your mother to wear something simple," he advised her, as they sat at a café on the boulevard des Italiens. "Don't let her overshadow you. Remember—it's you the people want to see and hear."

Maeve laughed. "Am I so ugly?" she demanded.

"Good God," murmured Dietrich. "You're beautiful. It's your mother's tendency to seek the limelight that worries me. Forgive me for saying this, *Liebchen*, but she's a very vain woman. And she's jealous of you."

"Oh, don't be absurd. Why on earth would you even say such a thing?"

The young German grimaced. Moira wasn't the only woman he knew who was jealous of her daughter.

"Because she's a beautiful woman who wants to go on being beautiful, young, and admired—and now she finds people looking at you first. It's a blow to her pride, Maeve. Very understandable. If she had been born plain, the problem wouldn't exist."

Though Maeve hated to admit it, Dietrich wasn't far from the mark. Moira *was* peeved to be relegated to second place, and she did her best not to be outshone by a mere girl. The banker almost hated to think of how alluring she would be on the afternoon of the recital.

"I want all eyes to be on you," he said firmly as he gently kissed Maeve's hand. "When you walk into that room, I want the audience to respond to you in the same way they do at the Casino. Make sure you wear something very elegant. White or cream if possible. Those are good colors for you. Very striking."

Thinking of her Paquin gown, Maeve nodded. "All right. Cream it is."

"And I have a present for you," he added. "For good luck."

To Maeve's surprise, Dietrich picked up a long, rectangular package he had kept at his elbow and ceremoniously presented it to her. "Unwrap it," he said shyly. "I would like you to use it during your recital."

Tearing off the pale pink tissue paper wrapping and pink silk bows, Maeve discovered a magnificent peacock feather fan mounted on ivory, with end panels studded with tiny seed pearls.

"Dietrich," she marveled, "thank you. It's beautiful. Oh my, it's so elegant. I'm going to look very grand."

Smiling and kissing him quickly on the cheek, she made him turn pink with delight. That fan had cost a fortune at an expensive shop on the rue du Faubourg St. Honoré. In fact, it was outrageously pricey— no doubt created with the Russian trade in mind—but it was so exquisitely beautiful, Dietrich knew it would make a splendid accessory for Maeve— and help fix the audience's attention where it ought to be. On *her*.

There was one event, which took place two days before the musicale, that came as somewhat of a shock to Dietrich. Baron Hubertus von Reuter had arrived unexpectedly in Paris to stay with his son and friends for the holidays. When the young man returned to the house on the boulevard Haussmann and discovered his father standing before the drawing room fireplace that evening, he felt the bottom drop out of his stomach. "Hello, Papa," he managed. "How nice to see you."

Hubertus gave him a cool paternal glance and nodded grimly. Then he proceeded to complain about the unwholesome French climate and the arrogance of Parisian coachmen, all the while studying his son with the sort of look he usually reserved for clerks who were about to be sacked. It made Dietrich extremely nervous.

*

Dietrich was so flustered on the morning of Maeve's recital he found himself unable to eat. The women fussed over him, especially Lotte, the elder of the two daughters, who seemed to take it as a personal mission to make sure that he ate. This irritated Dietrich to such an extent he sullenly declined all nourishment and gave Lotte a glare so withering that she nearly burst into tears.

Hélène seemed extremely pleased with herself and ignored her lover's discomfort. She was apparently so excited over the recital she was oblivious to all minor distractions. Hubertus wasn't. After leaving the table, he sternly warned his son to watch his manners. Lotte was a very nice girl.

"Yes, Papa," he answered. But he was damned sulky about it, Hubertus thought. A very poor attitude. Young ruffian.

On the morning of her debut as a "serious" artist, Maeve let Moira and her maid, Arlette, fuss over her coiffure, allowing them the liberty to create a truly impressive confection with the masses of gleaming auburn waves. Remembering Hélène von Ebert's beautiful combs, Maeve had purchased several small, glittering ornaments herself, and now they were glinting nicely whenever she moved. Moira's finest earrings sparkled on her earlobes—real diamonds there.

"Wear this necklace," her mother insisted, placing a strand of pearls around her neck.

"Nothing around my throat," Maeve snapped unexpectedly. "I can't bear any pressure there."

Exchanging bemused glances with her maid, Moira was puzzled at Maeve's nervousness. She was used to an audience, so she shouldn't be rattled now, but she was. It was almost comical.

"Take deep breaths," Moira advised. "You'll feel better."

"I'm not nervous," Maeve insisted. "I feel fine. Really."

Arlette chuckled. "You remind me of a bride, mademoiselle. But don't worry. Those people will love you."

Maeve hoped so. They were certainly not her usual audience from the Casino. Half her appeal there was due to her legs, she told herself. It wasn't art that made them applaud; it was her pretty figure. What if that was really all she had? What if Herr Albrecht and Dietrich had no taste and were simply in love with her and too besotted to realize she was without talent? Men in love were daft!

Jesus, Mary, and Joseph! Maeve thought wildly. Those people at the von Eberts' mansion were connoisseurs who actually knew something about opera. Her heart began to beat faster. What if she disgraced herself and they laughed? It would be all over.

Worst of all, Julien would heave an immense sigh of relief to see her dream shattered. Oh, he would pretend to be sympathetic and would no doubt assure her that it didn't matter, that she was still the best partner he'd ever had . . . But she would have to settle for being Florine for the rest of her life! What a fate.

"Mama," she said suddenly to Moira, who was pinning a curl back, "can I sing?"

Her mother looked at her as if she had demanded to know what her name was. "Are you feeling all right, Maeveen?" Moira queried. "I think you're a bit overwrought."

"I'm not. I'm just worried. I don't want people to laugh," she said. She would die if anyone laughed.

"And what ever made you think of that eccentric notion? Nobody will laugh—unless you say something amusing or tell a joke. Those people will be very serious about their music and sit there like department store dummies, pretending to drink in every note—all the while thinking of their own problems and wondering if you're going to go on forever. Believe me, I know about these things. They're no different from the people who go to see you at the Casino. They're just filthy rich," she added as an afterthought.

"I have stage fright," Maeve declared solemnly.

"Well, no wonder, with Dietrich carrying on the way he has been. He's so nervous, he's got you worked up pretty well too. Don't fret, Maeve. It will all go well, you'll be seen by the people you want to notice you—and you'll be richer when you leave than when you arrived. Just think of that. And everyone will say how beautiful you are and how lovely you sounded. It will be a wonderful experience."

Maeve hoped so. Moira, she noticed, was like a rock. Well, Mama was used to playing the piano in public and being admired for it, while Maeve hadn't been in close proximity to an audience since her childhood musicales. Now she was used to having the footlights and orchestra act as a buffer between herself and the audience. This was much more intimate. Here the audience would be close enough to see every detail. Maeve didn't know how she would take to that now.

It was such a silly fear, even she was amused by it. But still it bothered her. She would be alone in that room, bearing the whole burden of singing before dozens of people who would be comparing her with every other soprano in Paris. It was a daunting thought.

Almost as if she had read her mind, Moira said, "Don't forget, I'll be there right behind you. You won't be in the lion's den all by yourself."

"Thank you, Mama," Maeve said gratefully. "I'm happy for that."

*

As the hour approached, Maeve was cold with nerves, dropping everything she touched, making Arlette shake her head in despair as she witnessed the most amazing display of stage fright she had ever seen. And this from a star of the Casino de Paris too!

"Du calme, mademoiselle," she counseled as she said farewell to the young mistress at the door of the apartment. *"Tout ira bien."*

Shivering inside her velvet-lined chinchilla cape in the hired coach, Maeve hummed the arias she would sing, closing her eyes to the passing urban landscape. The snow-covered streets of Paris rolled by, with pedestrians dodging horse cabs, elegant private coaches, and the very rare motorcar. Lavish Christmas displays enticed passersby in shop windows on the grand boulevards, while happy children frisked in the snow, pelting each other with snowballs in the gray light of a December afternoon, just as Maeve had once done in those far-off days in Amsterdam. That seemed like ancient history now.

Arriving at the mansion, Moira and Maeve were greeted effusively by Dietrich, who was even more nervous than Maeve. He was so grateful Moira appeared calm that he didn't even notice what she was wearing.

As it happened, she was quite elegant but subdued in a beautiful wine-colored velvet afternoon frock trimmed with rich Valenciennes lace at the relatively modest neckline and the sleeves. It would have got compliments from him on any other occasion. In order not to compete with Maeve, she had limited herself to simple jewelry—a single-strand pearl choker with matching bracelet, gifts from the detested Count Viznitski.

Maeve looked magnificent. Tall and slender in her pearl-embroidered duchesse satin Paquin gown with its deep décolleté, she left a trail of admirers in her wake as she took Dietrich's arm and proceeded into the swarm of guests to meet her hostess.

Gracefully fluttering her peacock fan, she murmured to her blond companion, "What do you think?"

"I think you're absolutely stunning," he whispered. "It's going to be a great success."

To assure that, he had made certain Hubertus would be out during the recital, visiting an old friend. Dietrich didn't know when he planned to return, but felt safe enough with him out of the house. His father was not interested in details and had simply been told Frau von Ebert had discovered a dazzling new soprano. He had looked bored and let it go at that.

Maeve found herself floating on a wave of nervous energy as she drifted through the grand formal rooms, seeing a swirl of elegant gowns and sumptuous jewels alongside gentlemen wearing all sorts of colored sashes and government decorations.

This was certainly the *gratin*, she thought. There was a sprinkling of artists, two music publishers—one French, one Italian—but most of the guests were wealthy businessmen, bankers, industrialists, and even a handful of aristocrats. All with their wives. A far cry from the company Moira had kept with Count Viznitski.

She was not so far gone, however, that she failed to notice two plump blond girls hovering near Dietrich at every opportunity. They were sisters from the look of them, and they seemed quite at home. Of course they would be, she thought, amused. They must be the von Ebert girls. Dietrich was so bad: they didn't seem nearly as dreadful as he made them out to be. Poor things. The one especially seemed quite taken with him, besotted in fact, while he obstinately ignored her. He had eyes only for Maeve.

Moira was impressed by the lavishness of the von Ebert residence. Wherever she looked, she saw oil paintings of immense size, rich paneling, exquisite furniture, Oriental carpets. It reminded her of the Kaiser's palace—or Geraldine's. The chandeliers were astonishing—huge clusters of sparkling crystal from the leading ateliers of Paris, Venice, and Prague. Frau von Ebert obviously enjoyed spending money. And her beefy husband, with his gray beard and muttonchops, looked as if he had bags of it.

When the time came for the recital, Moira whispered a few words of encouragement to Maeve, who was introduced to the company by her hostess. Everyone looked pleased with her, Moira noted, a good sign.

Herr von Ebert in particular was looking at the girl as if he was trying to place her. He seemed quite taken with her. The two plump blond daughters were still hovering near Dietrich, looking at him with great sheep's eyes while he gave Maeve all his attention—showing his feelings a bit too plainly, Moira thought. He looked like a young fellow hopelessly in love. The two blond bundles of satin and lace didn't like that. Their bad luck, Moira decided, not at all sympathetic.

Maeve looked out over her distinguished audience and smiled the way she did when she went out onstage with Julien—coquettishly, girlishly—and gently fluttered her beautiful feathers as Moira began her opening aria, "Mein Herr Marquis" from *Die Fledermaus,* her concession to the Germans in the room.

As Maeve's lovely voice gave a delightful lilt to the words, Dietrich was agonizing over each syllable, mentally guiding her over the pronunciation, almost afraid to look at her for fear his nervousness would throw her off. It was unnecessary. The red-haired girl finished with a graceful wave of her fan and a gracious nod to the ripple of applause and the beaming faces.

"She sings beautifully," Herr von Ebert whispered to Dietrich. "But I think I know her. I've heard her before. I'm sure of it. Wonderful figure. Very elegant."

"Yes," murmured the young man, his eyes on Maeve. He was pleased that he had bought that fan. It *did* make a splendid accessory. My God, how beautiful she was! Better than Farrar, better than anyone, unique.

Gathering confidence with each round of applause, Maeve began to relax. She and Moira had spent hours on these songs, so there were no surprises. Things flowed so smoothly it seemed as if they were weaving a melodious silken ribbon in Frau von Ebert's magnificent reception room, a little jewel of eighteenth-century gilt paneling and crystal chandeliers.

Maeve was so pleased with herself and her audience that toward the end of her program, when she had begun a bubbling rendition of Musetta's "Quando me'n vo' soletta per la via," she didn't see a bearded blond man enter the room through a side door and take a seat. To her bewilderment, Dietrich reacted as if he had been handed a death sentence.

Disconcerted, Maeve then saw the gentleman rise, fix her and Moira with a terrible stare, and depart, annoying several people in the vicinity as he made an indignant and noisy exit.

Jesus, Mary, and Joseph! she thought, fluttering her fan a little

more than usual. Hubertus! This was not a good sign. She turned back
to give Moira a quick glance. Thank God! No reaction. She hadn't seen
him.

As Maeve's lilting voice swirled around the room, caressing her
audience with Musetta's boast of how all the men adored her and loved
to see her go by, Herr von Ebert, who understood Italian, was thinking
how suitable the lyrics were. This was a stunner with exquisite shoulders,
a bewitching manner, and a tiny waist, wrapped in the prettiest cream
satin gown he had seen in ages. *Una bella ragazza* . . .

And then he turned unexpectedly to Dietrich and whispered, grinning from ear to ear, "It's Florine! My God! How extraordinary. Florine
in my home and I didn't realize it." He looked like a small boy who
had just won a prize at the fair.

When Maeve finished, the applause was more than polite—it was
enthusiastic, spontaneous. Dietrich was nearly exhausted from emotion;
he was applauding harder than anybody—except for Herr von Ebert,
who couldn't wait to congratulate Maeve.

Hélène, who ought to have been pleased with herself for giving
her guests the least boring singer in Paris, looked as if she wanted to
kill someone. Dietrich was in love with this girl. It was shamelessly
evident and a tremendous insult to *her*! How could he?

As the footmen made the rounds with trays of champagne flutes,
Maeve was so besieged by well-wishers, she didn't follow what was
happening at first. The music publisher from Milan was offering her
flowery compliments, and her head was spinning as she tried to understand
his heavily accented French. Dietrich was trying to make his way to her,
but was stopped in his tracks by his father, who was leading Lotte von
Ebert toward him like a donkey on a short rein.

As Maeve attempted to keep track of both the conversation and
Dietrich's progress, the room suddenly became quiet and Hélène von
Ebert materialized at Hubertus's side, took Dietrich's hand with steely
determination, and joined it forcibly to Lotte's—over his visible protest.

"Ladies and gentlemen," brayed Baron von Reuter in a voice that
could be heard all over the house, "I have just been given the honor by
my beautiful and charming hostess of announcing the news that has been
so dear to my heart. Her daughter Lotte has just become engaged to my
son, Dietrich. Please join with us in wishing them all the best!"

And he gave Dietrich a glare that said without equivocation: "Deny
this and I'll kill you."

As happy guests circled the newly betrothed couple, offering all
sorts of good wishes, Dietrich went dead white, staring in disbelief at

Maeve. She was as shocked as he was. In fact, she looked as if she had turned to stone.

"The devious little swine," hissed Moira. "I was right the first time!"

Without even replying, Maeve slammed shut her splendid fan, gave the treacherous boy a glare that made his heart stop, and strode straight toward the happy couple.

"All the best, Herr von Reuter," she said—just a shade too brightly as she took both his hands in hers. "I'm delighted to be present at such a *happy* occasion." Those blue eyes were ice-cold despite her smile.

"Please," he whispered. "This is not—"

Hubertus brushed him aside before he could say anything further.

Then Maeve turned to the ecstatic young fiancée and smiled as if she had just heard the most wonderful news in the world. "I wish you years of happiness, Fräulein. Long life with the man you love."

And then she returned to her circle of admirers and listened to Herr von Ebert extol her to the skies, insisting upon introducing her to Monsieur Carré, a friend of Hélène's who happened to be the director of the Opéra-Comique.

As Maeve stood smiling amid a crowd of delighted gentlemen, she saw Hubertus staring at her from the other side of the room, where he and Hélène had Dietrich cornered like a caged animal.

You bloody bastard, she thought, glaring back at him under her pretty smile. You're a cruel, vicious man. You think you've won, don't you? Well, I'm not half finished with you, boyo. Neither is Dietrich. You can force him to marry that girl, but you can't force him to stop loving me, you damned fool.

*

When Maeve made her exit, she had several promises of employment and her head held high. Moira thought it was the best performance she had ever seen.

CHAPTER 12

*D*ietrich's sudden betrothal was a tremendous shock to Maeve. It wasn't as if she felt jilted—she had never considered him a serious prospect—but the meanness and spitefulness on the part of his father was an insult she found hard to forgive.

It was the high-handedness that enraged Maeve—and this from a man she'd caught yowling like a banshee at Moira's door. The dirty hypocrite!

Why was chubby Lotte von Ebert a desirable wife? she wondered. If she had any attractions, they were surely well hidden. True, she did have a nice complexion, pretty eyes, and a big bosom, but even so she was nothing special. Girls like Lotte could be found in any shop in Berlin. Well, not quite, Maeve told herself sternly. There was something else—there was the money, great bags of it, that she would surely bring to her marriage. *That* was the attraction, at least for Hubertus.

Poor Dietrich, Maeve thought tenderly, sacrificed like a doomed little lamb on the altar of Hubertus's greed. She still had a soft spot for Dietrich, for his beauty, for his lovely eyes, for his faith in her. If she had never met Sean Farrell, it would have been Dietrich who occupied her secret dreams. As it was, she thought of him often enough anyway, and always with affection—even after her recital.

Hubertus had taken him by surprise as well as everyone else, and the poor boy had had the shocked expression of an animal caught between the steel jaws of a trap. He hadn't been responsible for it, so she could scarcely blame him. But she could blame Hubertus, and in fact she loathed him with a ferocity she hadn't felt since her last encounter with Count Viznitski. The man was a double-dyed scoundrel.

In the weeks that followed her recital, Maeve received many compliments and one genuine invitation to present herself for an audition. Still, considering that she was known only as a pretty stage ornament for the music hall, that one invitation meant quite a lot to her. She would have been heartbroken to know that she had just missed being invited to audition at La Scala because its director, Giulio Gatti-Casazza had recently engaged another soprano. Signor Riccordi, a friend of Hélène's and one of Italy's leading music publishers, had enjoyed her rendition of Musetta's aria so much he had asked Gatti-Casazza to consider giving her a hearing. But the other singer had already been hired, so that was that.

The gentleman who wanted Maeve to sing for him at his opera house was Raoul Gunsbourg of Monte Carlo. This was a better place to start than Italy, Moira advised. The climate was appealing, the clientele was *richissime*, and from what she'd seen of the place herself, the habitués were so addicted to gambling they would be a very distracted audience—easy on a pretty newcomer, unlike Paris or Milan. Especially Milan, where the spectators could turn savage at a moment's notice and pose a danger to life and limb. She'd heard this from Signor Riccordi himself at Maeve's recital. And he was an owner of opera houses.

"Have you no faith in me?" Maeve asked with a smile.

"I have lashings of faith in you," Moira replied. "It's the Italians I don't trust. Besides, the climate's very fine in Monte Carlo and it will be a lovely change from Paris. Think of the beautiful harbor and all those yachts. It will be marvelous."

Moira had already visited Monte Carlo once and was dying to return. It wasn't the gambling that attracted her—she disliked gambling—it was the international mixture of milords, grand dukes, plain millionaires, counts, and princes that made it so fascinating. It was Paris with semitropical vegetation and good weather. It was magnificent. It was *rich*.

"Well, of course I'll send Monsieur Gunsbourg a reply," Maeve promised, "but I wish the offer had come from Paris instead."

Moira's eyes got darker. Monte Carlo had millionaires, fine weather, and no lovesick German banker's son ready to throw himself across Maeve's path, making a nuisance of himself. Damned silly girl, wanting to be bothered with all that fuss when she didn't have to.

"Well, Mama," sighed Maeve, "I suppose it's Monte Carlo for us, then."

"Right." Moira nodded firmly. And she couldn't wait to get there.

*

Julien Roussel was not understanding. In fact, he showed all the bitterness of a jilted lover when "Florine" told him of her decision to quit the act to pursue a career as an opera singer. He was staggered.

"Those people will chew you up and spit out the pieces," he wailed. "The competition is tremendous. Think of all those treacherous Italians you'll be facing—on their own ground! Do you think a girl like you will ever be able to hold her own with them, *ma chère?* You'll be savaged! Trampled on! Destroyed!"

"Well, thank you so much for the vote of confidence," she exclaimed.

Julien sighed and ran his fingers through his thick, wavy hair, a sign of serious agitation with him. "I'm not trying to be harsh with you," he protested piously. "I'm just trying to let you know what you'll be in for."

"I know what I'm in for." Maeve nodded, making the ostrich plumes on her hat flutter. "And I know what I'm capable of. You don't have to worry about me, Julien. I'll take good care of myself."

"It's that damned German, von Reuter, isn't it? He planted this idea in your head. But I hear he's getting married. Is he going to keep you if you fall flat on your face as a diva?"

The shocked look Maeve darted at him told Julien he had gone way over the mark. She was wounded, deeply wounded, and she tried hard not to let it show. But she looked as if she could have killed him for saying it.

"I'm sorry," he apologized. "That was stupid of me. Please forgive me."

"Nobody is ever going to keep me," Maeve responded icily. "What's mine is mine and what isn't, I don't want. You've a hell of a nerve to throw that in my face, Julien. Especially since you know better."

And with that, Maeve swept out of her dressing room at the Casino de Paris and into the swirling snow flurries of a January afternoon. In a month she would be strolling among the palm trees and mimosas of the Côte d'Azur.

To Moira's satisfaction, Maeve had signed a contract with that ugly little man Raoul Gunsbourg to appear in Monte Carlo during the high season—February and March. She would sing Musetta in *La Bohème* and a few minor roles that could serve as her introduction to opera. It would showcase her talents, but spare her the burden of the whole production. Besides, Gunsbourg had signed Nellie Melba and she practically owned the role of Mimi in *La Bohème*, so there was no question of assigning that to the newcomer. Not if Gunsbourg wished to avoid bloodshed. Let the new girl start off gradually.

*

Monte Carlo in February 1903 was a gracious, sparkling jewel of a place, perched high above the beautiful blue waters of the Mediterranean. Maeve hadn't seen such lushness since Africa. Plants, flowers, shrubs, ran riot wherever the eye rested. Much of the vegetation was trimmed into decorative shapes in the splendid gardens of the pastel villas above the water, but wayward flowers and vines roamed at will, a gaudy blaze of colors winding along the Corniche. Maeve took in all this beauty and felt like a little animal waking up after its winter hibernation. Her senses were quivering.

The company Gunsbourg had assembled was first-rate: Nellie Melba, the darling of Covent Garden; Enrico Caruso, a young Italian tenor who was winning praise all over Italy and in South America; Antonio Scotti, a Neapolitan like Caruso; and from Russia of all places, a tall, handsome blond basso with a difficult name who greeted Maeve with a kiss and promptly nicknamed her Masha. His name was even more difficult than hers, she thought with amusement: Feodor Ivanovich Chaliapin. Fedya for short. Maeve didn't find it easy to warm to Nellie Melba, but she found the men charming.

Gunsbourg was almost endearingly ugly, a short, ebullient gentleman who had a million stories about his origins, and who adored his artists. He dressed with panache and loved recounting the exploits of his youth. He once startled Moira and Maeve by suddenly displaying a scar from "the Turkish wars" in the middle of a conversation on the terrace of the posh Hôtel de Paris, and was equally delighted to hear about their adventures in the Boer War. Gunsbourg was a character, Maeve decided, but she liked him.

On the night of her first performance as Musetta in *Bohème,* Maeve was even more nervous than she had been the afternoon of the recital. To distract herself as she sat alone in her dressing room waiting for her call, she picked up a Paris newspaper and began skimming it.

Idly passing over the international news—except for a brief item about South Africa, now at peace, which she read carefully—Maeve turned to the society columns, and went white.

"Damn!" she wailed. "He did it! Oh how awful! They won't be happy."

Shaking the newspaper with inexplicable fury, Maeve let out another cry of frustration and read on about the society wedding at the chapel of the German Embassy between Fräulein Charlotte Maria von Ebert of Paris and Herr Dietrich Franz von Reuter of Berlin. The bride was "exquisitely attired in a Worth creation of ivory duchesse satin trimmed with antique Brussels lace, and her veil of antique lace was adorned with a magnificent diamond tiara—a wedding gift from her parents—and a sprinkling of fresh orange blossoms, especially rushed in from Nice for the February nuptials." Three bridesmaids attended her, equally fetching in rich sapphire-blue velvet gowns edged with Valenciennes lace and little matching toques of velvet trimmed with lace and pearls. The bridegroom was a "distinguished young man-about-town whose family owns one of Berlin's most solid banks."

It was duly noted that his "fine complexion and pale blue eyes were well complemented by the somber elegance of his black morning coat." A sprig of lily of the valley, no doubt plucked from the bride's bouquet, adorned his lapel.

"I hate you!" wailed Maeve. "Why did you have to do it? Why didn't you stand up to the old bastard?"

She was beside herself, raging at the newspaper and creating a fine disturbance in her dressing room. Did she really expect Dietrich to say no to Hubertus and marry her? No, she did not. Did she expect him to elope with her or something equally romantic and daft? No, she did not. Well, then, said a stern voice, why was she so distraught?

Because it wasn't fair. And she was in love with him herself.

"My God!" Maeve exclaimed, throwing down the paper. The stage-hand outside in the hall had just given her the signal, three sharp raps on the door—no doubt wondering if Mademoiselle Devereux had gone mad.

"Time!" he shouted nervously. All these artists had their own peculiar ways of working up their nerve before a performance, but they didn't usually howl like wild animals.

"Anything wrong, Mademoiselle?" he inquired, looking genuinely concerned.

"Oh no, just my preperformance routine." Maeve laughed gaily, implying she always carried on like this by herself before going onstage.

Jesus, Mary, and Joseph, they'll throw a net over me! she thought in embarrassment.

"Everybody has her own little ways, and one is just as good as another," he replied with a grin, apparently not too scandalized. He had seen them all. *"In bocca al lupo,"* he added.

"Thanks," she nodded, cold and trembling as they arrived in the wings, just before her grand entrance.

Watching the merry scene at the Café Momus, where the Bohemians are celebrating with Mimi, Maeve received a kiss on the hand from Raoul Gunsbourg, who was standing by to offer moral support. Then it was time for Musetta to get into her carriage with her elderly lover and sweep grandly onto the stage, creating a hullabaloo as she brazenly flaunted herself before the eyes of her jealous former lover Marcello—using every possible means to make him aware of her dazzling charms.

"She's marvelous," said Gunsbourg to the stage manager as he followed Musetta's progress from the wings, and watched her tantalize Marcello, scandalize her old lover, and leave nobody in the dark as to her utter gorgeousness, displaying as much of her lovely form in the process as she could. Every man in the audience knew that Musetta was wearing pink garters with her black silk stockings that night.

Delighted with the newest addition to the house, the stagehand who had cued Maeve turned to Gunsbourg and laughed. "Look at that girl! She's driving the men crazy. And not just the ones onstage. Look at the audience."

It was true. Maeve, dazzling in a deep red velvet gown and blond curls, was practically seducing the whole theater. In her anger at Dietrich she wanted every man in the audience to fall in love with her, and she was relying on all those tricks she had learned as Florine. This Musetta was more music hall than grand opera, but her beautiful legs and fine figure earned their usual applause.

Old gentlemen who normally dozed through Nellie Melba's arias were sitting up and training opera glasses on the new girl. This one was a corker, and her antics certainly put Melba in the shade. At intermission it was being said with a chuckle that this Devereux creature was a real scene-stealer.

The newspaper reviewers didn't quite see it that way. Devoting most of their space to Nellie Melba, they lauded her sensitive portrayal of the "unfortunate little seamstress" and praised Caruso's passionate singing as Rodolfo. Maeve's Musetta was deemed "endearingly vulgar," and she was accused of relying on her splendid physical presence to make up for a shaky technique. "A spirited young animal with the possibility of a future in opera"—if she could only receive the necessary guidance.

Maeve and Moira were downcast at breakfast the next morning after Arlette handed them the morning papers.

"Damned prejudiced frogs" was Moira's verdict on them. "You put Nellie Melba in the shade and that's all there is to it."

"They're right," Maeve said, feeling miserable. "I do need work. It's a long way from the music hall to the opera. Perhaps Julien was right." Secretly she was afraid he was. How awful!

"Nonsense," snapped Moira. "I've got a good ear and so does Monsieur Gunsbourg. We're not mistaken about you. You're good. You just need more work, that's all. And don't you ever think that Melba herself didn't need to practice like mad before she became the great high muckety-muck she is today. That dreadful Russian friend of yours—the blond fellow with that tribe of children—he thinks you're good. And to listen to him, nobody besides himself is worth listening to. So take some encouragement from there."

Well, thought Maeve, that was all very fine for Mama to say. She had a very high-handed attitude because she wasn't the one they were criticizing in print. It was different if you were the target.

Thinking back on her performance, Maeve did have to agree that she spared no effort to entice all the males in her audience. She had felt so rejected at reading Dietrich's wedding announcement that she simply got carried away. But she really did have a good voice. Gunsbourg wouldn't have hired her if she hadn't. And both Caruso and Chaliapin liked her. She only wished more people would start sharing their opinion. She knew Nellie Melba never would, though. She could feel the ice in her look every time she came near Melba.

Maeve received a few lovely tributes after her performance in *La Bohème,* but the nicest one read simply: "To the most beautiful Musetta ever, DvR."

It had come with a gigantic basket of white orchids from the florist's shop near the Hôtel de Paris, and Maeve couldn't prevent herself from stopping by to inquire who had sent the flowers. Could he have come to see her? It didn't seem possible. But what if he had?

"The orchids were very fine," Maeve said to the florist, who had also witnessed her performance. "May I ask you to describe the person who sent them?"

"A handsome young blond gentleman," replied the florist. "Very fine complexion. German, I think, although he spoke our language quite fluently."

So he *had* come to see her. He had come to Monte Carlo to attend her opening night. Well, he had certainly contributed to her performance! If she hadn't read of his marriage ten minutes before going onstage, her Musetta wouldn't have been so wild. And it was because of Dietrich that she was there in the first place. Without him, she would probably still be displaying lots of leg at the Casino, playing trained poodle to Julien Roussel.

But Dietrich was on his honeymoon, Maeve remembered—in Italy, according to the newspaper. He must have made a special trip north just to see her. That was quite touching. Then Maeve wondered how Lotte had reacted to that. She could scarcely have been pleased.

*

Moira enjoyed being the mother of a budding artiste. Young and beautiful herself, she was often mistaken for Maeve's sister, which she enjoyed even more. Together they were admired and taken to parties all over the Côte. Things went swimmingly until one afternoon in the dining room of the Hôtel de Paris when they came face-to-face with a ghost from the past.

Maeve and Moira were having a light luncheon of lobster salad and Moët, enjoying the spectacle of millionaires at their leisure, when Moira looked up and saw a familiar figure strolling toward their table— André Viznitski, dressed in a cream-colored suit and wearing a white gardenia in his lapel with a large diamond stickpin in his figured silk cravat.

Moira nearly choked. Her face, half hidden under her lace-trimmed white picture hat, turned dead white. Maeve looked alarmed. But she hadn't yet spotted Viznitski.

"What is it, Mother? Are you all right?"

"It's him," Moira replied. "He's here!"

Half hoping to see Dietrich, Maeve looked up and flushed bright red at the sight of Count Viznitski, who looked right into her eyes and caught his breath in a mixture of shock and amazement.

"Say nothing to him," Maeve ordered. "We'll ignore the dirty beast."

Both ladies were nearly twitching with emotion by now. Viznitski hesitated for a fraction of a second. Then he followed the waiter to his table, uncomfortably close to theirs.

Taking the gilt-printed menu from the waiter's hand, he nodded curtly and pretended to study it, not listening to the list of house specialties the fellow felt obliged to rattle off. Viznitski felt as if his head were about to explode. Sweat was beading around his blond temples. Suddenly the airy dining room seemed uncomfortably hot and oppressive, as though someone had suddenly turned up the heat.

"Let's leave," Moira whispered. "I can't stand to be in the same room as that fiend."

"If we leave he'll like that. Why give him the satisfaction? Stay put, Mama. Maybe *he'll* leave. He looks nervous," she pointed out, grimly pleased. The damned Russian looked as if he were fighting off apoplexy.

"Maeveen!"

"Don't move a muscle, Mama. Here," she said sternly, refilling Moira's glass. "Take a good stiff drink. It will settle your nerves."

Moira promptly reached for the champagne flute and drained half the glass.

The dining room was very festively decorated with all sorts of spring flowers. A cascade of white and yellow roses blocked off part of Count Viznitski's table from Moira's view, so that helped. But it was a real effort for her to remain at the table. She wished herself a thousand miles away. And him dead.

Viznitski was struggling to stay put. He wanted to talk to Moira, but Maeve's presence put him off. He had scars from their last encounter and didn't want to risk more in the midst of this elegant crowd of diners. Maeve was a savage, despite the astonishing fact of her recent operatic career. Fascinating Musetta. He could really admire all that passion— if he weren't so afraid of her.

As Viznitski studied Moira from behind the roses, he noticed she was looking magnificent. No trace of dreadful aftereffects from her unfortunate experience in Paris. In fact, her eyes were a positively brilliant azure against that luminous pink and ivory Celtic complexion. Her white lace and muslin afternoon frock showed a couturier's touch, with exquisite embroidery and fine Brussels lace framing her neckline. Splendid creature.

Overcome with nostalgia for his beautiful mistress, Viznitski threw down his napkin, rose to his feet—as Moira went rigid—and strode purposefully to her table.

"Get out of here, you filthy, bloody swine," was the greeting he received from Moira, hissed through clenched teeth.

Viznitski was taken aback and his smile froze. He felt shocked, badly used, insulted. A few people at nearby tables glanced in his direction.

"I've nothing to say to you," Moira declared icily. "Go away."

Maeve's color rose as she glared at Count Viznitski. "Get out of my sight!" she commanded.

Now several pairs of curious eyes were turned in the direction of their table. A Romanian count whom Moira and Maeve had met at a party was watching from two tables over, mildly interested, suspecting some delicious scandal. He knew Count Viznitski from Petersburg, Paris, and Bucharest.

"Well," André said, trying to regain his composure in the face of such unrelenting hostility, "it's delightful to see you again."

Then, searching desperately for something cheerful to cover his retreat, he made his fatal error.

"I'm absolutely delighted to see that you still wear the earrings I bought you in Deauville. That was such a delightful time, don't you think?" Viznitski was babbling now, feeling his throat dry up as Moira and Maeve sat there, granite-faced, treating him with sullen contempt.

Suddenly, at the mention of those earrings, Moira reached up to her little pink earlobes, unfastened those diamond and pearl clusters with tense, jerky movements, and hurled first one, then the other straight at André Viznitski's head.

He caught one and saw the other sail past his left shoulder and land with a splash in the soup of a sandy-haired gentleman dining alone at a nearby table.

The startled gentleman fished it out with his spoon, looked curiously in the direction of the beautiful woman who had thrown it, and placed it beside his bowl of soup.

Horrified, the headwaiter came racing over to take away the soup as the gentleman rose, picked up the jewel, and crossed to where Moira and Maeve were confronting Viznitski. By now the entire dining room was gawking at the show.

"Excuse me, ma'am," he said with a smile, presenting her with the solitary earring. "I think you misplaced this."

In shock, Moira accepted the jewel, nodded grandly, and tossed it at Count Viznitski. "Take it," she said, "and be damned!"

Her head was spinning. She had almost forgotten André Viznitski in her stupefaction when she glanced up at the man who had handed her that earring. For a moment Moira thought she was hallucinating. There, standing before her, was a tall, fair, sandy-haired man who looked so much like Pat Devereux both ladies stared as if they had been turned to stone.

*

After the embarrassing spectacle in the hotel dining room, Moira's nerves were quivering for hours. The sight of Count Viznitski was so upsetting Maeve had had to call a doctor to give her mother something to calm her. But even that was nothing in comparison to the sight of the man who had given her back her earring.

At first glance, Moira had thought she was seeing a ghost. He had the same build, the same hair color, the same easy manner, even a certain facial resemblance to Pat. Maeve had been overwhelmed by the sight of him too. It was as if Pat, who had been brutally torn from their lives two years earlier, had come back.

But this time he was an American and his name was Charlie Lassiter.

Moira didn't exactly remember what he said after handing over her earring; all she remembered was Viznitski's departure. How she and Maeve got out of the dining room was a mystery. But she knew that Charlie Lassiter had gone with them to shield them from further encounters with Count Viznitski, whom he appraised as a scoundrel.

Maeve was as fascinated with the man as Moira was. His accent was so wonderful, so exotic. He was from New York in America, he said, and like them he had been through a war—fighting in Cuba with Teddy Roosevelt and the Rough Riders.

"But that's the president over there," she exclaimed, impressed. Teddy Roosevelt was the best-known American in the world. Everybody knew about him. And this Charlie Lassiter had been with him in Cuba! And he had wonderful stories to tell.

Moira didn't care one little bit about Teddy Roosevelt, America, or the Rough Riders, but when she saw Charlie she saw a bit of Pat— even if he had an American accent—and she was stirred by a lot of disturbing memories. It was maddening to think she might have fallen in love with this fellow, who was swimming in cash, and not poor Pat, who never had enough to satisfy her. It was her bad luck her family had never emigrated to America, the land of millionaires, instead of remaining in dismal Ireland, poor and downtrodden. Well, perhaps with Charlie Lassiter America was coming to her—and she wasn't about to waste her opportunity to enjoy its bounty.

Charlie was forty-one, tall, slim and sandy-haired, with the quick responses of an athlete, the deep lines around the eyes of an outdoorsman, and the spontaneous humor of his Irish mother. He was a widower, a war veteran, something of an adventurer in Latin America, and heir to a man who had been a business partner of Henry Flagler and John D. Rockefeller at the time they created Standard Oil.

Charlie's father had died leaving twenty million dollars in Standard Oil stock and thirty million more in mining shares, railroad stock, and real estate. Charlie himself had added several million more to this, married a South American beauty, and been widowed a few years later after building her a palace on Fifth Avenue.

His grief had known no bounds. Three months after he and Esmeralda had moved into the place, she was dead from influenza and Charlie called in a demolition company to level the house, not leaving one stone on top of another.

This was the most flamboyant testimony to grief New York had ever seen, and Carrère and Hastings, the celebrated architects who had built his house, were nearly as devastated as Charlie himself when they saw it come tumbling down one morning while the police cordoned off the block and a hundred curious spectators stood around wondering what was going on.

That had all happened five years before and the worst pain had finally subsided, but what was left was a restless ache and a sense of ennui Charlie just couldn't overcome. It had taken him to Europe, where he had hunted bison with Kaiser Wilhelm in the Imperial Hunting Preserve in East Prussia, shot grouse in the Highlands with various English lords, and even crossed the Russian Far East on the Trans-Siberian Express to hunt tigers on the frozen steppes, but nothing had really interested him for more than a brief time.

It startled him that Moira Devereux had caught his attention so quickly. Apparently she had a fine contempt for diamonds and Count Viznitski—at least when they came together. Most of the women he'd met lately would have begged to keep those earrings. Very fine large stones: money in the bank. Not Moira.

He admired her for that. He was no slavish admirer of money for money's sake either—although he had plenty of it. She might be hot-tempered, hasty, and proud as a demon but she was a beautiful woman without a mercenary bone in her body. That was a rare trait and getting rarer all the time.

Moira felt she had finally found the man who was going to do it for her. As she lay in bed with Charlie Lassiter, she thought that he combined the best aspects of Pat—his fair, handsome looks—and Sean—his passionate hunger and expert lovemaking. Charlie was bringing her to her second orgasm of the evening, and Moira hoped Charlie was enjoying it as much as she was. She didn't even mind taking Charlie's large penis in her mouth—although Viznitski's sadistic ministrations had almost ruined that for her forever.

Yes, Moira thought, her heart beating faster and faster, her breath quickening, this man might be the key to the golden kingdom.

*

Maeve's Monte Carlo debut had not been a resounding success, but a few good reviews appeared in newspapers as far afield as London, New York, and St. Petersburg, all very useful for the future. The experience had been invaluable to her.

Of her colleagues she liked the Italians, Caruso and Scotti, the best. Both men were artists whom the public already adored—especially Caruso, whose following seemed to increase with every performance—and they were not at all slow to congratulate a newcomer or offer good advice. Nellie Melba, on the other hand, seemed as remote as the late Queen Victoria. Compliments were definitely not her style.

The only male who could match Melba's penchant for self-aggrandizement was Feodor Chaliapin, the blond basso from Moscow with the lightest blue eyes in the world, a pretty Italian wife, and a flock of children.

Fedya had a truly magnificent voice and a total inability to take a backseat to anyone. That stupendous voice was enough to overwhelm any listener, but his tendency to change tempi when it suited him was a perpetual source of anxiety to his fellow singers. Maeve got on well enough with him by using what Moira called blarney. Women, she noticed, were usually more successful in dealing with him than his male colleagues, since he had a quick temper and wouldn't hesitate to throw a punch at another man. He was quite fond of women, and they returned the favor by pursuing him endlessly. Despite the wife and *bambini.*

He fascinated Maeve. For one thing, he had an astonishing amount of energy and could sculpt and draw like a professional as well as act and sing. There didn't seem to be anything Fedya couldn't do to perfection. As a token of admiration for Maeve, he had given her a delightful collection of sketches of her he had drawn without her being aware of it as she waited backstage for her cues. They were astonishingly good.

"Watch out for that one," Moira had commented sagely. "He's too damned clever by far." She had seen all the elegant, titled ladies who swarmed around the Russian, spoiling him like a pasha. He was too used to being adored in her opinion, a bad thing in a man. It made her a bit uneasy that he was casting fond eyes at Maeveen.

One afternoon, when Maeve was alone in her rented villa while Moira was exploring some charming Riviera village high above the Corniche with Charlie Lassiter, she received a liveried messenger bearing a very fine, gilt-embossed invitation to present herself at the villa of the Countess Lili Vorontzova to sing arias from *La Bohème, Carmen, Tosca,*

Don Giovanni, and *Le Nozze di Figaro.* Apparently Countess Lili had very definite tastes, Maeve thought upon reading this. The fee was quite generous. Why not? The name sounded Russian. Perhaps she might be useful in helping her track down the Duchess of Leuchtenberg.

"All right," she nodded to the footman who was awaiting her response. "Tell the countess I'll come." It was worth a try.

Chaliapin gave a shudder when Maeve told him the next day of her engagement as she strolled with him and three of his children along a path winding above the harbor. His "little imps," as he fondly called them, were beautifully dressed in white sailor outfits, looking like the little sprigs of nobility whose paths they crossed, promenading with their nannies.

Looking at Chaliapin and his family it was hard to believe he had once been a barefoot peasant child, raised by a drunken father in one of the worst slums of the Russian Empire. He had the bearing of a tsar. And a great distaste for private concerts for the aristocracy.

"I know Countess Vorontzova," he nodded glumly. "An old gossip. She is a dear friend of the Dowager Empress, our Tsar's mother. She once wished to hear me sing, so she sent a messenger to fetch me—on the spur of the moment. It was typical of them. No consideration. No thought for the wishes of the artist."

"You went?" Maeve marveled, startled beyond belief. She'd seen Fedya reduce presumptuous admirers to dumbstruck bewilderment with his hauteur when annoyed. She couldn't picture him meekly submitting to some countess's caprice—no matter whose mother she knew.

"You're surprised." He smiled.

"Astonished. You don't seem like a man who can be commanded so easily."

"Masha," he said, grinning now, "you're a sweet girl. But you don't understand the Romanovs."

"I've never met any."

"Count yourself lucky. They're a bunch of spoiled imperial parasites. To them Russia is a gigantic private estate that can be plundered at will. Anyone who resists them or their friends pays for it. You Europeans can't even begin to understand what life is like in Russia."

Maeve looked out over the brilliant blue harbor and wondered what kind of life Chaliapin really had there. She knew he was adored beyond belief at the Bolshoi in Moscow and the Maryinsky in St. Petersburg. She also knew he had the proud title of Imperial Soloist—grudgingly given to a man whose sympathies were with the left. She didn't know and couldn't even guess that his passport bore the notation "peasant" and that his children were categorized as peasants too.

"I once knew a man who told me there were only two real capitals in Europe—Paris and Petersburg," Maeve said lightly as she fixed the fluffy white bow in little Irina's hair. His two young sons were racing ahead of their sister, calling her to catch up with them.

Chaliapin gave a snort of disdain. "He must have been an aristocrat, then."

"He was," Maeve nodded. "And he was a fine man."

The Russian glanced down at her. Maeve was fairly tall for a woman but dainty in comparison with his height. "Masha," he said tenderly, "did he die?"

"I don't know. One minute we were eating lunch in Belgrade, the next minute he was being attacked by ruffians and his servant was dragging me and Mama out the door to save us. That was the last time I saw him. I think of him every day." She sighed.

"You're unusually faithful," Chaliapin remarked dryly. "I wish I could say the same of myself."

"I like what I like." Maeve shrugged. "And I liked him better than anyone. I only wish I knew what happened to him."

*

The recital at Countess Vorontzova's was a big success in that Maeve received her largest fee yet, graciously presented in a bouquet of white roses trailing silken streamers, but although she made an effort to learn what she could of the whereabouts of Sean's sister, Countess Vorontzova made it clear that she had no time for conversation. She was paying her to sing, not chat. And it occurred to Maeve that the countess viewed her as some sort of pretty performing toy, not as a guest. The performance over, she wasn't given so much as a glass of champagne before she was out the door and on her way home.

"Ah," nodded Fedya the next day when Maeve lunched with him and his pretty Italian wife, Iola, and two of their children at a small restaurant near the Prince's pink palace. "You see how they treat an artist. No finesse. No real appreciation. We're little more than trained bears for them."

Iola patted her husband's arm and assured him with a smile that he was her darling old bear. Chaliapin growled playfully and made everyone laugh with delight. He really did sound like a bear.

Maeve liked Iola. She had been a ballerina with an Italian troupe on tour in Moscow when Chaliapin had fallen head over heels in love with her, pursuing her relentlessly until she agreed to marry him.

The couple made a nice contrast, she with her small size, delicate features, and classic brunette coloring, Fedya with his height and fair Slavic complexion and light eyes. To Maeve they seemed to be a happily married couple—despite all the rumors about his women. Iola seemed to take it in stride as the price of marriage to a handsome man who was a popular idol. But it couldn't have been easy for her.

"You ought to ask your manager to bring you to Petersburg or Moscow next season," Madame Chaliapin said to Maeve. "It would be good exposure for you. The Russians are mad for European singers. And with your fine voice and good looks, you would be a wild success."

"Beware of grand dukes," warned Chaliapin as he watched his children crack the shells of their lobsters. "They might carry you off in a pile of sables and never let you out of Russia again."

"Fedya!" laughed his wife. "Don't frighten the girl."

"Oh, I'm not afraid of grand dukes," Maeve replied seriously as she dipped her spoon into a bowl of bouillabaisse. "In fact, I'm looking for them."

That sounded so businesslike that both Chaliapins burst out laughing. Lots of European women went looking for grand dukes. They were very generous to their mistresses.

"Well, be careful if you find any," Fedya said. "They can be very nasty when they don't get their own way. And I've heard their tastes are very odd."

Maeve blushed, taking the meaning of that laughter. It embarrassed her that they thought she was a gold digger. "It's information I'm looking for, not money," she protested. She wasn't Moira!

"Well," Iola replied. "That's definitely a novel approach. It may just work!"

And she gave her husband a bemused smile as she wondered what this lovely girl *really* was looking for. At least it didn't seem to be Fedya, and she liked her for that.

"I'm looking forward to the day when you play the Tsarevich to my Tsar in *Boris Godunov* at the Maryinsky," Chaliapin declared as he broke off a piece of crusty bread and handed it to little Irina on his right. "That should attract the attention of a whole pack of Romanovs. They're fond of our historical operas."

"But a tsarevich is a boy!" She was bewildered now.

"It's a female part like Cherubino." The Russian laughed. "It's meant to be sung by a woman—even though the character is a male."

"But it's in Russian," Maeve protested timidly. She could now sing in Italian, French, and German but Russian was daunting. She also felt unnerved at the thought of sharing the stage with Chaliapin as Tsar Boris. He'd chop off her head if she played it badly—a thought that gave her a chill.

"The Tsarevich is a small but important role," he persisted. "You sing very little and appear in only two scenes, including my death scene, where I hand the Empire over to you. But it would suit you. And it would be a nice way for you to expand your repertoire."

"Petersburg audiences would be enchanted," Iola declared. "You'd make a dashing Tsarevich. All red velvet and gold braid with a jaunty little cap and high, shiny boots. *Molto bello.*"

"Do you think the management would like to see an Irish girl play a Russian prince?" Maeve demurred. She could already see the critics complaining about a presumptuous foreigner depriving a native soprano of her rightful place.

"Don't worry about it, Masha." Chaliapin smiled, his light blue eyes sparkling at the prospect of Maeve as his Tsarevich. "I'll send you a copy of the score so you can study it. And I'll speak to the director of the Maryinsky, Prince Teliakovsky. Who knows? We may make a Russian of you yet."

*

All this was very nice, but there was one person who really did not like Maeve Devereux and expressed her opinion at every opportunity, resulting in the girl's removal from performances Gunsbourg had assigned her earlier. Nellie Melba's aversion to the redhead was such that she had given Gunsbourg an ultimatum the night after Maeve's appearance in *La Bohème*: if Devereux ever sets foot onstage with me again, then I go back to London and you can go to hell. Melba being Melba, it was a threat that worked. From that moment on, Maeve Devereux never again appeared on the same bill with Melba.

"Am I so bad, Fedya?" she asked Chaliapin in despair. "Is Gunsbourg regretting that he hired me, do you think?"

The Russian shook his head and gave her a wry smile. "Don't ever believe that," he replied. "He's scared to death of Madame Melba, who took fright herself the night you upstaged her in *Bohème*. This is a backhanded compliment actually. It means you're good enough to worry her."

"Then I'm good enough to sing more often."

"Oh yes, you certainly are. But not in Melba's vicinity."

"It's not fair," she said stubbornly, stamping her foot.

"Of course it's not fair. But how much in life is fair, *milochka?*"

he demanded with a sigh. "If you were Russian you'd probably be more accustomed to these stupid, arbitrary decisions. It's a way of life there."

They were strolling along a promenade above the bay, taking in the beauty of the sunlit water, the splendid yachts bobbing at anchor, the riotous cascade of flowers spilling down to the shore—a picture postcard of sunshine and spring in Monte Carlo. Suddenly Maeve looked up at the tall Russian and said firmly, "I'll succeed in spite of Nellie Melba, and she'll just have to learn to live with it."

Fedya smiled down at her. Melba was one of the greatest stars in the international firmament. This little girl had high hopes if she was even thinking of throwing down the gauntlet to *her*. Maeve still had a lot to learn.

"Be careful," he advised. "She has a lot of influence."

"Of course she has," Maeve agreed. "If she didn't have, then Gunsbourg wouldn't be so afraid to cross her. It's disgusting."

But as Maeve gazed thoughtfully at the gorgeous panorama stretched out beneath her, she was already planning her retaliation.

*

On the night of Melba's last *Bohème*, Maeve was standing in the wings with the stagehands, observing the prima donna as she did her star turn. Plump, double-chinned, and heavily corseted, Melba was not visually convincing as the fragile, consumptive little embroiderer Mimi, but that voice of hers was so beautiful nobody complained. Besides, Caruso, who was playing her lover Rodolfo, a starving poet, was no slimmer.

The first three acts went splendidly, and now it was time for the tragic fourth act, Mimi's death. As Madame Melba stood in the wings, observing the comic exchange between the four *bohémiens* just prior to her dramatic entrance, Maeve sidled over to the spot where Melba's maid waited with Mimi's handkerchief on a tray, ready for Melba to take onstage for her coughing fit.

As the women stood, eyes riveted on Caruso, Maeve stealthily removed the handkerchief from its tray and just as quickly replaced it with one of her own. With a nervous glance at the prima donna, she edged away and resumed watching the performance, heart pounding with excitement.

Now, as Musetta ran onstage to announce Mimi's desperate illness, Nellie Melba reached for the handkerchief she would cough into as she arrived in her lover's garret, a pitiable, dying wreck. Maeve gave a faint vindictive smile as she watched her disappear from sight, only to emerge onstage in Rodolfo's shabby room—sneezing. Racked with sneezes!

Musetta looked startled, Rodolfo and Marcello didn't know what to make of it—this was definitely not in Puccini's stage directions—and Nellie Melba was almost beside herself with outrage as she spotted traces of a fine gray powder in the creases of Mimi's handkerchief. This was sabotage. And one name sprang instantly to mind.

"I'll kill the little bitch!" she sputtered to Musetta, gasping for breath and doubled over with the force of her sneezing fit, while the audience appeared to find it all quite amusing. A clever new touch to liven up an old favorite, no doubt. And quite unlike Melba, who wasn't noted for her sense of humor onstage. Rather jolly.

After a heroic struggle to dominate her sneezing, Melba spent the last act trying desperately to appear frail and near death while inwardly wishing to dash offstage and strangle Maeve Devereux. As soon as Mimi had expired and the curtain had been rung down, Melba jumped off her deathbed, pushed aside her costars, and raced backstage, hunting for Maeve, who was leaning casually against a wooden crate, regarding her with brazen amusement.

"You little saboteur!" shrieked Melba as she slapped the girl smartly across the face. "You think you're so damned clever! Well, you're wrong. I knew it was you!"

Knocked off balance by the slap, Maeve feigned total innocence and outraged virtue, loudly protesting and threatening legal action.

"You must be mad!" she sputtered. "How dare you attack an innocent person! I'll send my lawyer after you. This is assault!"

Melba was having none of it. Surrounded by a growing crowd of stagehands and singers, she drew herself up to her full height and laced into Maeve Devereux so fiercely, one or two of the men were afraid for the girl. In fact, they placed themselves between the two women to protect the younger one.

"You listen to me, you little cipher!" shouted Madame Melba as she found Maeve just out of her reach, "I'll see to it that you never set foot onstage with me in any opera house in the world! And don't even think about appearing at Covent Garden! That's mine. That house belongs to Melba! You won't even get in there unless you can afford the price of a ticket—that I guarantee!"

And with that, she aimed another swat at Maeve, pushed aside two stagehands, and retreated to her dressing room to soothe her frazzled nerves, still sneezing a little, and quite furious.

"Did she hurt you, mademoiselle?" asked one of the crew, who found Melba's accusations unbelievable.

"Not as much as I hurt her," Maeve replied with a wink. "But I think I may be black-and-blue tomorrow."

*

Maeve had been so busy planning her revenge on Nellie Melba that she had failed to note the progress of Moira's affair with Charlie Lassiter. But when she and her mother were leaving for Paris after her last performance, he was the one who offered to drive them to the station. That was rather nice of him, Maeve thought, though it was apparent by his tone with Moira that more than kindness was involved. She was loaded down with packages from Monte Carlo's most expensive boutiques—and jewelers.

Jesus, Mary, and Joseph! Maeve thought with disgust, hadn't she learned her lesson after the experience with André Viznitski? Charlie seemed a fine fellow, but when it came right down to it, what was the difference between his relationship with Moira and Viznitski's? It was embarrassing to have a mother who was a tart, she reflected as she stood watching them on the station platform. There was Moira, looking girlish and pretty in a white linen shirtwaist trimmed lavishly with fine lace, a white lace parasol that cost a fortune, and an outrageously beribboned hat she never could have bought on her own either, and this rich American, elegantly turned out in a cream-colored suit, flowered silk tie, and diamond stickpin. She was the very image of a demimondaine.

Maeve almost hated to admit it, but they made a handsome couple. Still, it wasn't decent. Moira was apparently going to be a kept woman once more from the look of things. Those passionate, half-hidden glances and sweet little smiles meant just what Maeve thought they did. From a distance of several feet, she could hear enough of their conversation to know Moira would be meeting him in Paris to continue where they were leaving off in Monte Carlo.

And she once called Dietrich a little swine, Maeve remembered indignantly. That was the pot calling the kettle black! Poor Dietrich. For the first time, it occurred to Maeve that they *both* had quite a lot to put up with from their parents.

And that thought somehow comforted her on the train ride back to Paris.

*

When Maeve returned to Paris, she was startled to find several large bouquets awaiting her arrival. One was from Monsieur Carré of the

Opéra-Comique, who reminded her he wished to see her at her earliest possible convenience; the second was from Raoul Gunsbourg, who wished her a wonderful season in Paris; but the largest one was from DvR, welcoming her home.

"Dietrich," Maeve murmured, touched. He was so sweet; he couldn't get her out of his mind. And he really ought to. For a married man, this was a dangerous bit of foolishness.

"To my Lorelei," the card said, recalling a snowy morning in Berlin after he had taken her to see Geraldine Farrar in *Romeo et Juliette*. She could still remember how pink his complexion was from the cold.

Lorelei, Maeve reflected. That was a romantic notion he should have forgotten the day he married Lotte. And what did he call *her*? My dumpling? My angel cake? Somehow, culinary endearments seemed appropriate for that one.

Ah, you little cat, Maeve thought sternly. Was that a nice way to think of the poor girl just because she had married Dietrich? No, it was not. But it did seem fitting, she thought with a giggle as she glanced at her own twenty-inch waist. Lotte, on the other hand, had a big bosom, which was not the sort of thing to go unnoticed either. So in a way they were even. Well, everyone had *something* attractive about them—even a dumpling.

But it was all horribly comical. Poor Dietrich, who had such a preoccupation with the ethereal, married to someone as solidly terrestrial as Frau Lotte. She hoped the marriage would at least produce offspring and placate old Hubertus. Then perhaps the sacrifice wouldn't be totally in vain.

"Poor Dietrich," she murmured again. She was still very fond of him and that bothered her. It was a dangerous feeling, one she didn't wish to acknowledge right now.

Maeve didn't like to be that vulnerable.

*

Sean's escape from the Kalemegdan Fortress—arranged through St. Petersburg—had made a visit there a necessity, as much to thank his rescuers as to demonstrate his ties with Russia's imperial family—all for the benefit of those bastards in Belgrade. If the Serbs thought they would ever lord it over Nikolai Petrovic's family, they had a lot to learn.

St. Petersburg also provided Sean with other distractions, both pleasant and unpleasant. He took part as a foreign observer in the annual summer maneuvers of 1903 with the Imperial Guards Regiments at

Krasnoye Selo, where the hottest topic of conversation was the recent double murder in the Balkans in which King Alexander Obrenovic and his unpopular consort were reduced to chopped meat by *their* royal guards. Shocking, agreed Sean, shaking his head.

Apis was a bloody murderer—in every sense of the word. Though Sean had had no love for Alexander Obrenovic or for that greedy adventuress he had married, he found their slaughter by their own guards repulsive. Firing squads were one thing, but that crazed butchery was degenerate, worse than degenerate—stupid. It may have brought his brother-in-law Peter Karageorgevic to the throne, but it had alienated most of Europe.

Well, not all of Europe. Although several countries recalled their ambassadors in protest of the regicide, Montenegro's ambassador had been one of the first diplomats to pay a courtesy call on the new king, bringing along with him a very effusive letter of congratulations from Nikolai Petrovic. That bothered Sean almost as much as the massacre itself. It was shameless gloating, not worthy of his father. But very Montenegrin.

Sean still cherished memories of beautiful Moira Devereux and her pretty daughter, and he couldn't put them out of his mind. Whenever he spotted a tall, slender, black-haired woman in the salons of St. Petersburg or strolling on a fine day in the Summer Garden, he felt a catch at his heart. None of them could possibly be Moira, but the thought of her being alive somewhere, perhaps in the company of some other man, was enough to make him look. The idea that she might have forgotten him in some new and happy life almost guaranteed that he would look.

Geraldine had told him she had done her best to locate the women but had failed entirely. He'd accepted that with some reservations, not wishing to doubt his mother, but still uncertain how hard she had really tried. Half measures were not her style; if Geraldine had put her heart into it, she probably could have tracked down Dr. Livingstone before Stanley ever got to him. The trouble was, she had no incentive to locate the Devereux ladies and he knew it.

"Go to Paris," he'd said. Had they? In Paris, Moira would hardly have gone unnoticed. Even in Paris a woman that beautiful could turn heads. She had a naturalness that made her so delightfully accessible one could be beguiled by that beauty without being intimidated by it.

And what about young Maeve? he thought guiltily. She'd saved his life and he intended to repay that debt. Where was she now, so young and innocent and nearly alone in a strange land that devoured beautiful young girls? Thinking he was rescuing them, had he merely taken them from one jungle to another and left them there to fall prey to worse predators than the lions and hyenas back home?

Sean hated the uncertainty of it. He felt a responsibility for them, and although he had been separated from the women by sheer brute force, still thought that somehow he had let them down. Damn Colonel Apis! If it hadn't been for him and those Serb maniacs, Moira Devereux would be playing hostess at his Paris apartment, comfortable, protected, and cared for instead of contending with life on her own as a poor refugee struggling for her daily bread. That money he'd given Moira would only go so far, he knew. Then what? It depressed him even to think about it.

*

In November 1903, in Paris, Monsieur Carré, director of the Opéra-Comique, was in the position of a man who had an embarrassment of riches. His star Mary Garden, a small, slim Scotswoman with a knack for making scanty costumes "artistic," was annoyed with his newest discovery. The girl in question, a tall, slender redhead, had the effrontery to succeed in one of Garden's favorite roles—the one she had taken over during another singer's illness onstage, startling the audience by her triumph in it and thereby launching her career. Now that opera, *Louise*, was bringing good luck to another Celt, and Garden was piqued.

It was like poaching, she informed Carré in a fit of indignation. Maeve Devereux was no better than a thief. And who was she anyway? Nobody. All she ever did was rely on her legs, Garden screamed, making Carré smile. Mary Garden was famous for roles that exhibited precisely that portion of her anatomy. Very nice legs too.

"I'm sorry, Monsieur Carré," Maeve had replied with a shrug. "It's too bad the lady feels so strongly about her rights to *Louise*, since my contract calls for me to sing the role two more times this season. Besides," she added meaningfully, "Monsieur Charpentier told me himself how much he enjoys my interpretation. You *do* remember that?"

Carré did indeed. Charpentier had also told him privately how much he admired the way Maeve had sung the aria "Depuis le jour," the jewel of his opera. It had made him weep, he said emotionally. She was his Louise come to life.

That was Charpentier's view, and Carré hoped he never chose to enlighten Mary Garden with it. If he did, there would probably be bloodshed in the greenroom. Significantly, the public also seemed to share his view.

But Mary Garden and Carré had a relationship that was more than artistic, and he didn't want to have to listen to her complaints in their private hours. He was deeply chagrined. Composer and public adored Maeve; Mary resented her. He wanted to humor Mary, but Mademoiselle Devereux had a perfectly legitimate contract, signed and notarized, that said she was entitled to sing the role twice more this season. And she was not about to be shunted aside so easily.

"Over my dead body," retorted his mistress.

Mademoiselle Devereux then let it be known that she had just made the acquaintance of the most charming lawyer, whose specialty was—contracts! After her bad experience at Monte Carlo, she was prepared for war this time around.

The backstage intrigues of the Opéra-Comique were nothing compared with the turmoil of real life, Maeve thought. Moira, whose affair with Charlie Lassiter was still going strong, was becoming famous in sporting circles as a stunner whose good looks were equaled only by her dead aim with a rifle. This combination of *l'amour* and *la mort* was such an intoxicant to the international sporting set that the lovely widow was becoming almost as celebrated for her marksmanship as for her affair with Charlie. And she loved it.

Taken aback by Maeve's blossoming career as a singer, Moira had felt slighted at the unfairness of it all. Here was Maeve, a mere girl, a green little thing from nowhere, receiving applause for a talent she could only have got from her mother. It seemed an insult and it rankled. Moira was therefore determined to establish herself as a virtuoso in some other field, and during a weekend house party at a château in the Auvergne she got her chance in a totally unexpected way.

Invited by some duke to accompany Charlie to an exclusive shoot, Moira arrived with a tremendous amount of luggage but no guns. To the duke's amusement, she took him up on his offer to use his and proceeded to stun the company with the number of pheasants she bagged in two days' time. By the end of the weekend, Moira had established herself as a sportswoman and was trading hunting stories with French counts, British milords, and German Junkers, who had never met anyone quite like her.

It was not only her combination of stunning good looks and marksmanship that fascinated them but also her nonchalance. Without pausing for breath in her conversation, Moira could raise her rifle, sight her target, and blast it to kingdom come with her uncanny aim. Charlie had to work hard to keep up with her—and to keep the other men from monopolizing her.

"Where on earth did you ever learn to shoot like that?" he asked. "And why didn't you ever mention it to me?"

"South Africa," Moira replied, surprised. "And it never came up until now." Those big-game hunters had been useful for *something*!

"God Almighty," he marveled. "And I was afraid you might be the skittish type—you know, ready to run at the sound of gunfire."

That was such a novel idea it made Moira smile. If he only knew what she and Maeve had been through in that damned place. On reflection, she decided not to go into too many details for fear Maeve's bagging the sergeant might give her the edge, and she limited herself to descriptions of hunting parties on the veldt. She also neglected to mention several big-game hunters who had been a trifle more than friends. Some things were best left unsaid.

It was with a great smile of satisfaction that she received a gift of her own personal weapon from Charlie, who had ordered it from one of London's most exclusive sporting establishments. Other women might have been rewarded with diamonds from Charles Lassiter, but that meant nothing. This was a serious present, implying a mutual passion that was far more consuming than anything he had experienced in years. Moira had struck gold the day she devastated the aviaries of the Auvergne, and she intended to mine it for as long as she could.

With Moira's combination of natural beauty and startling aggressiveness regarding both man and beast, Charlie Lassiter was now well past the stage of mere infatuation. He couldn't get enough of her, and Maeve noticed that her mother's bills for outrageously expensive lingerie were keeping pace with her hunting parties. Mr. Lassiter's passion was beneficial to both gun shops and lingerie shops, it seemed. This said something about Moira's personality, but Maeve wasn't quite sure just what.

All the same, she wasn't at all surprised, merely horrified, when Moira appeared in her dressing room one night after a performance to tell her the latest news. She and Mr. Lassiter were sailing for America in two weeks.

"America," she repeated. "Whatever for?" This was dreadful. God only knew where that man might take her, once there. She'd heard stories about wild Indians—mostly by way of Karl May's novels—and she wasn't terribly pleased at the thought of her mother going among them.

Jesus! Maeve thought with a pang of fear. Moira had the most gorgeous long black hair. Indians spent all their time hunting for precisely her type of hair. She'd be a walking target the moment she set foot in that place. Her scalp would be hanging from a tepee on the Great Plains!

Was that in New York? Maeve wasn't quite sure. All she could think of were the bits about scalps.

"Don't look so alarmed, Maeveen," her mother said petulantly. "I'm coming back, for heaven's sake! It's not as if he was going to carry me away forever."

"But he's an American! He might want you to stay there with him."

This was even worse than she thought. She would be left an orphan in Paris, bereft of both father and mother, deserted, abandoned, cast off like some wretched stray kitten . . .

"Let's not have all this carrying-on," Moira said icily. "It's not called for. I'm a grown woman and I can travel anywhere I please. And right now it pleases me to visit New York."

She glanced around Maeve's small, rather untidy dressing room and sighed. "I think you're just upset because you've had to die again onstage. It's a pity there are so few happy endings in your line of work. It's making you morose."

"Mama," Maeve replied, "promise me you won't stay in America forever. Swear it."

"Cross my heart," Moira said lightly. "I'm not going to run off and leave my only child thousands of miles away by herself. What do you take me for?"

Maeve wasn't about to answer that. Looking at her beautiful mother, dressed by Paquin in a deep green velvet *tailleur* with her glossy black hair crowned by an elegant velvet and sable toque, Maeve could almost see her beginning to vanish right before her eyes—only to end up in a mansion on Fifth Avenue for the rest of her life.

"You said you're leaving in two weeks?" It seemed like a death sentence.

"Yes. We're sailing on the *Deutschland* from Hamburg. Charlie thinks very highly of German ships. He owns stock in the Hamburg-Amerika Linie."

"Then I expect you'll have a fine crossing."

"Yes." Those Germans would wait on him hand and foot. And on her, too, of course. How delightful.

Moira put her arm around her daughter, who seemed ready to cry. "I'll be back before you've had time to miss me, Maeveeen. And you won't be alone. Madame Blanchard will keep on running the house. And you'll have Arlette with you."

"It's still not the same. I'll miss you, Mama."

Moira was her best friend and the only person she could really trust. There were plenty of people she could spend time with—men who wanted to wine and dine her, prospective managers who wanted to take charge of her career, other artists who wanted information of one kind or another—but there was nobody Maeve could really feel at home or let down her guard with. For all Moira's faults, she had been there. And now she wasn't going to be. She was going to go traipsing off to America with some Yankee millionaire named Charlie Lassiter, and they were probably going to try to decimate the entire animal population east of the Mississippi.

Well, she thought reluctantly, Charlie was a decent fellow. But she resented the hold he had on her mother. She was jealous. And she was terrified of losing her.

The only other person Maeve would have turned to for comfort was Dietrich, but since his wedding she had put him beyond the pale. She was very fond of the boy, and she was secretly afraid she would make a fool of herself and end up in a disgraceful and unseemly love triangle if she ever let Dietrich back into her life.

Maeve did not want to be anyone's fluffy little toy—unlike some of her colleagues and others. But it was terribly lonely without a real friend. And to make matters worse, she was acquiring enemies without even trying. Mary Garden, the established star at the Opéra-Comique, loathed the very sight of her.

*

Maeve was in such low spirits the week after Moira's departure for America that she was looking forward to the end of her season and a vacation. La Garden's hostility had been offset by a growing number of fans who acted like an unpaid claque, applauding with abandon each time she set foot onstage, but despite such adulation, Maeve felt depressed.

She was feeling so blue one afternoon that when Dietrich tracked her down at the popular skating rink Le Palais des Glaces, she didn't even try to escape him.

Since her discovery of snow in Amsterdam upon her arrival in Europe, Maeve had been mad for it. Her happy days in Berlin had introduced her to ice-skating, and in the winter she spent hours with the fashionable crowd at Le Palais des Glaces, Paris's most chic rendezvous for the sporty set. Dietrich had heard this and had managed to locate her that afternoon while he was supposedly at lunch.

"You look even more beautiful than the night I saw you in Monte Carlo," he murmured, appearing at her side as she navigated the rink, using her little sable muff as a kind of counterbalance.

"Dietrich!" she exclaimed, nearly crashing into a gentleman who had just come out onto the ice. "What are you doing here?"

"Causing problems," he retorted, smiling as Maeve seemed unable to regain her composure. "Come, *Liebchen*. Let's go have a cup of cocoa before I cause you to have an unfortunate encounter with the ice. You're very excitable today."

Embarrassed because she was a pretty fair skater, Maeve decided that was a good idea. She didn't want to fall flat on her face in front of this crowd. But the shock of seeing him was still making her a little unsteady.

When they were safely seated at a small rinkside table, Dietrich called a waiter over and ordered two cups of cocoa, looking quite delighted to see her again.

"But how did you attend the performance in Monte Carlo?" she stammered. "You were on your honeymoon."

"I was in Italy. It was no trouble at all to take the train. Maeve, you were magnificent. I was so proud of you. All our hard work paid off splendidly."

Our hard work? she thought. Well, he *was* the one who had insisted she take lessons with Herr Albrecht and leave the Casino. Dietrich certainly took these things personally.

"Thank you for the gorgeous orchids. They were spectacular. I was so amazed you would take the time to come see me. I was thrilled when I found out that you really had been there."

"Do you imagine I would have missed it? My God, Maeve! It was everything we had been striving for. You put Nellie Melba in the shade with your high spirits and your acting. You were a Musetta who would drive a man crazy!"

Maeve was almost tempted to tell him the reason, but she kept still. She didn't want to encourage him. What was the point?

"How is your wife?" she asked politely.

His face took on a strained expression. The beautiful light blue eyes seemed actually to cloud over. "Very well, thank you."

"And your father?" She loathed old Hubertus but felt obliged to ask.

"As miserable as ever."

"Dietrich," she laughed. "That's not very filial!"

He shrugged. "One reaps what one sows." Then he added, "How's your mother? I always liked her."

Now it was Maeve's turn to look downcast. "She's in love with an American. He's taken her to New York."

"To live!" Dietrich exclaimed. "How could she run off and leave you here? A young girl needs her mother. Especially a girl like you."

He had visions of all sorts of roués pursuing this sweet child. Frenchmen were such filthy beasts.

"Are you suggesting I need a keeper?"

"Oh no." The young German shrugged again. "But a beautiful young girl should not be alone in Paris. It's too dangerous."

Maeve smiled. Dietrich was very sweet to be so concerned about her.

"I'll be fine. Really."

"I would like to take care of you, Maeve," he said quietly. "I love you. You know that."

"Nobody's ever going to keep me. I've seen what that can lead to. Don't ever insult me like that again."

He looked pained. "You always make things sound so dreadful. Just because things are the way they are now doesn't mean they will always be like that. What if I were free of Lotte? Would you marry me then?"

She stared at him. "That's a pretty big if."

"But what if I were? Would that change things for you?"

Maeve stared into his lovely light blue eyes, half mesmerized. He was not joking. For a moment she was almost frightened by this intensity. Dietrich, who was so refined and cultivated, was looking at her with such ruthlessness it wouldn't have been out of character in a cutthroat. She had never believed him capable of passionate feeling before.

Maeve trembled a little, blaming her nervousness on the cold air. "Ask me the question when it's a real possibility," she replied softly. "Then I'll be able to give you a real answer."

Dietrich nodded. "All right. But I warn you, I'm not saying this lightly. I've thought things out and I've decided I have to make some changes in my life. As it is now, it's unbearable."

Maeve's eyelashes flickered. "I'm sorry you're so unhappy. You were railroaded into this, so I'm not surprised it turned out badly."

"Yes," he agreed. "I was shanghaied. That's precisely what they did to me. Of course," he added, "the poor girl is no happier than I am. We're both suffering from our parents' pigheadedness."

Maeve didn't know what to say. She was very fond of Dietrich but she knew better than to say anything uncomplimentary about Lotte. She wondered if Frau von Reuter was about to produce offspring to further complicate matters. Dietrich hadn't mentioned it, so she supposed not; after all, it was the sort of thing he would have told her about, since it was the only reason for the marriage.

When she left him that day, she felt sad for him. Poor Dietrich seemed so utterly miserable.

As Maeve rode home in her elegant black coach, staring out the windows at the familiar Paris cityscape, she wondered what would happen if he were free to marry again after a divorce. He was a Protestant. They could divorce and remarry at will, unlike Catholics. What would she say if he asked her to marry him then? She liked Dietrich. Or she was in love with him? Sometimes she thought she was—for example, when she had read about his marriage just before going onstage in Monte Carlo. That aroused emotions she had never felt capable of. But was she really in love, or was she just imagining it because she wanted to be in love, and Dietrich was the most logical candidate? He was so beautiful. She certainly loved that.

"My God," Maeve murmured to herself. "How French!" Only the French would analyze something until they came to doubt their own feelings. Is that what she was learning in Paris? Marvelous.

Maeve wasn't terribly cerebral. She wasn't stupid either, just inclined to follow her feelings rather than her head. She was also usually right on target when it came to assessing people and their motives. There wasn't much that got past her. And she had the gift of cutting straight through to the heart of a matter, avoiding a lot of useless blather.

But she did not know what to do about Dietrich. And she wanted to do something.

In the tightly knit world of opera, there were fellow performers, allies, partners—and enemies—but very few friends and almost no one you could open your heart to.

One might expect rivalries from other sopranos, of course, but tenors, baritones, and bassos could be jealous too, although at the moment it was a soprano who was proving such a trial. One needed strong nerves to deal with her. Having a husband might help her to weather these storms, especially if he was as supportive and considerate as Dietrich.

What a pity he wasn't available, Maeve reflected, lost in gloom.

*

In the final week of her season at the Opéra-Comique, having sung her last performance as Louise to great acclaim, Maeve received a frantic telephone call from Monsieur Carré at six o'clock on a Saturday afternoon to come to the theater immediately. Mary Garden was desperately ill and unable to sing. Or even stand up. Could Maeve replace her in the final performance of the season?

"She won't like it" was Maeve's reaction. Also, there would be a society audience there, dressed to the nines and expecting Mary. On the other hand, the opera was *Tosca*, one she had been long prevented from doing because of Mary's implacable opposition. This would be a delightful revenge.

"Oh, you'll be marvelous," protested Carré, truly unstrung. "I know you've been rehearsing it with Marc Antoine. You can't fail."

"How do you know that?" she demanded in amazement. This was a secret; they certainly hadn't broadcast the news. In fact, they had done it with extreme discretion.

"Marc Antoine told me," replied Carré. "He said you were magnificent. He's quite excited about it. You'll be spectacular."

Carré was lying about his source. Marc Antoine had told him nothing. That bit of information had come from a furious Mary Garden, who had been told by someone that Marc Antoine, who was not overly fond of her, had been spending a remarkable amount of time with Maeve—studying the scores of Garden's favorite operas. Treacherous little backstabbing tenor!

Now Maeve's startled admission had confirmed the stories. She might be an untried Tosca, but she would have been well rehearsed by Marc Antoine de Marigny, who was a splendid Cavaradossi.

Marc Antoine was also the Opéra-Comique's reigning male idol, and lately he had been chafing at Mary's prima donna temperament. She had been getting very grand recently and had infuriated him several times onstage within the past two weeks. Carré was almost afraid of bloodshed between his male and female prima donnas.

"I'll do it," Maeve said at last. "But I want to wear my own costume."

"You can wear whatever you like!" exclaimed Carré. "Just be there."

"Fine."

Hanging up the telephone receiver, Maeve turned to her maid Arlette and smiled. "Garden's sick and I'm going to sing *Tosca*! Finally!"

"When?"

"In about two hours. Come on, Letty. Call the coachman and get my things ready. We're working tonight!"

*

Maeve's debut as Floria Tosca with Marc Antoine de Marigny as her stage lover Cavaradossi was one of those evenings in the theater when stars come into their own. Even the delight over Maeve's appearance as

Musetta in Monte Carlo was nothing compared with the frenzy she unleashed as Tosca.

In a supremely melodramatic role, Maeve simply ignited her audience. She took twelve curtain calls and was effusively embraced onstage at the end by Monsieur Carré, and by Marc Antoine in a state of near delirium. He was a happy man that night; he had just succeeded in staging an artistic coup d'état. From now on, Mary Garden was no longer the only female star in the house. She had just been dethroned.

The critics didn't know what to praise more, the singer's radiant beauty or her "soaring lyric soprano range with its beguiling dark color." This was a Tosca who could quite believably sweep a man off his feet or murder him—with equal passion. Someone even hinted that the sparks that passed between Tosca and Cavaradossi onstage might not be due entirely to illusion. Then the same critic noted acidly that Mary Garden had never seemed able to inspire the same kind of passion in Marigny when they had shared the stage.

"Not true," Marc Antoine laughed when he read that. "In fact, Mary's often inspired greater passion in me. On three different occasions I've had to restrain myself from killing her."

The lady was *not* amused.

She was also not amused when Marc Antoine was overheard to tell the company how refreshing it was to work with a leading lady who didn't trample her partner in order to hog the limelight. Generosity of spirit was not a well-known virtue among sopranos of his acquaintance.

"He has no loyalty," Mary raged to Carré. "He betrayed me. He's a loathsome little backstabber!"

Carré nodded his head solemnly and read between the lines. Marc Antoine had given a better performance with Maeve, and that was something Mary could not forgive.

"Well, *ma chère*," he replied, trying to be soothing. "Then perhaps you ought to develop a new partner. Someone who isn't so undependable."

And if he had things his way, Maeve and Marc Antoine were going to be inseparable!

There was a witness to Maeve's performance that night who was nearly as upset as her rival soprano. Dietrich had attended with his mother-in-law—Lotte now hated opera almost as much as she hated Dietrich—and he had been shocked to see the blatant sensuality Maeve had displayed. Worse than that, she and the tenor actually seemed unable to keep their hands off each other. That made him ill.

Maeve's triumph as Tosca at the Opéra-Comique had a counterpart later that night in the elegant von Reuter mansion. Driven to the verge of a breakdown by his reaction to the opera and by his determination to get rid of Lotte, break off with Hélène, and marry Maeve, Dietrich did the unthinkable. Alone with his mother-in-law at home while Lotte and her father and sister were attending a charity affair, Dietrich seized Hélène, carted her upstairs, and ravished her rather noisily—just in time to be discovered by all the returning von Eberts.

The hysteria that followed was so violent it looked for a while as if the young gentleman was going to be murdered by his wife, his father-in-law, or both. The evening ended with the master of the house hiding out in one of the darkened salons on the ground floor while his wife shrieked abuse at him as she hunted for him, calling him, among other things, "vermin," "Frenchified pervert," "*Schweinhund*," and "shame of the German race." The servants were so horrified they didn't know where to look.

In the days that followed, there was a stoic effort on the part of the von Eberts to act as if nothing out of the ordinary had taken place, but to the great surprise of their friends, Lotte moved out of her husband's house at the same time her mother departed for Belgium. Then came the revelation that both Lotte and her father were engaging lawyers to begin divorce proceedings.

The effect on society was absolutely sensational. With head held high, Lotte declined to say one single word about her divorce, neither blaming Dietrich nor even mentioning him. It was as if he had vanished from her world. And since she—the wronged? unhappy? dissatisfied one?—refused to bring up the subject, nobody else did. The scandal all Paris was lusting to hear in every juicy, intimate detail was no scandal after all. It was a nonevent. It was merely the civilized end of a marriage, with all the rules of decorum firmly intact. No matter what was whispered or suspected, Lotte von Reuter would rather die than admit the truth about "that dreadful night." Luckily for her husband. It was *his* social salvation too.

But Lotte didn't intend for him to escape quite so easily. To Trudl she made a solemn vow. No matter how long it took or how difficult it was to arrange, that *Schweinhund* would not cheat fate. He would suffer the consequences of his treachery one way or the other, so help her God!

And to prove the seriousness of her intent, Lotte solemnly put her hand on the family Bible to seal her oath.

CHAPTER 13

New York City was the busiest place Moira Devereux had ever seen. No European city could compare with it for sheer movement and energy. Even Berlin, packed with industrious Germans, couldn't match the uproar of its streets. In New York if you paused too long, you had a better than even chance of being trampled by pedestrians, run over by a trolley, or squashed by an automobile—all of which were more numerous on Fifth Avenue than they ever were on the Champs-Elysées.

Arriving on the SS *Deutschland*, Moira was politely interviewed by customs officers in her stateroom—as was the privilege of a lady traveling first class on an ocean liner. The steerage passengers received no such consideration and had already disembarked at Ellis Island to be herded like cattle and inspected for signs of degeneracy, disease, imbecility, and anarchy.

Moira's elegant Paris ensemble, her fine jewelry, and her association with Mr. Charles Lassiter favorably impressed the gentlemen from customs, and she was wished a pleasant stay in New York.

"That was it?" Moira asked in amazement. "I thought it would be quite a lengthy affair."

"Not likely. It's the steerage passengers who get the grilling. You ought to see what those poor buggers go through."

"I don't think I'd want to," she said warily.

New York was the Knickerbocker Hotel, Sherry's Restaurant, Millionaire's Row—where Vanderbilt after Vanderbilt had erected pseudo-French palaces—and Wall Street, where so much of Charlie's money seemed to be invested. There was also the Metropolitan Opera, where Maeve's friend Enrico Caruso was making his debut this season, eagerly awaited by society. Charlie escorted Moira to the gala event.

The Metropolitan was a huge theater compared with the opera houses Moira had seen in Europe. It had been recently redone in gleaming gilt and raspberry to satisfy the taste of its board of directors, one of whom was the much feared and respected J. P. Morgan, banker, devout Christian, and financial genius.

The Met's celebrated semicircle known as the Diamond Horseshoe offered the spectator a view of as much French couture and jewelry as any human could stand at one time. The overdressed women of the Vanderbilts, the Goulds, the Goelets, and the Astors displayed themselves in this raspberry-colored setting with as much sumptuousness as Moira had ever seen anywhere—including Berlin and Paris.

"Those boxes cost thirty thousand dollars apiece," Charlie informed his guest, who was wearing all the jewelry she had so painfully accumulated in Europe. Even with her ears, neck, and wrists covered with diamonds she felt poor compared with that lot in the Horseshoe. Theirs were bigger, much bigger. And more plentiful.

"You're beautiful without a single stone," Charlie whispered in her ear as he saw her trying to calculate all the carats on Mrs. Astor.

"Mm," murmured Moira. Jesus! The old woman had on more diamonds than Queen Victoria at her Jubilee! And she wasn't even royal. It was mind-boggling.

"Do diamonds fascinate you so, Moira?" he whispered. "You didn't seem to think so when you flung Viznitski's earrings in my soup in Monte Carlo."

She put her ostrich plume fan up to hide her smothered laughter. "Those diamonds were the devil's own," she whispered back. "I was just returning them to their source. I've nothing against them on principle."

Charlie raised her gloved hand to his lips as the houselights died and the audience settled in to view Enrico Caruso and Olive Fremstad in *Rigoletto*. "You're adorable," he said in amusement. "By the way, tomorrow I'm going to take you to meet some dear friends of mine."

Moira felt a sense of excitement, tinged with a thrill at the opening notes of the overture. Maeve ought to sing here one day, she thought. Paris and Berlin are nothing compared with it. There's more money per square inch of space in this opera house than in all of Paris.

"Your friends?" she whispered suddenly, drawing a sharp stare from a lady in the next seat.

"Yes," nodded Charlie. "They're dying to meet you."

"Oh, how nice," she murmured into her ostrich plumes.

This was getting to be interesting. She wondered if she would pass their inspection.

*

After Maeve's triumph in *Tosca*, Monsieur Carré knew he had a good thing in this red-haired girl with the figure of a sylph and the voice of a star. Marc Antoine was relentless in his praise, especially within earshot of Mary Garden, and relations between the ladies had become so strained they had begun to communicate through intermediaries. Maeve was relieved when the season was over, next year's contract had been signed— on much more advantageous terms—and she was on her way to St. Petersburg. At last!

Her maid, Arlette, was terrified. Having seen the usual Parisian behavior of Russian grand dukes, she was convinced Mademoiselle Devereux was risking her life, her health, and her virtue to go among them on their home ground.

Demimondaines in Paris who had loved them and left them told horrifying tales of Slavic passion that featured lots of biting, nipping, and bloodletting. Based on her own experience with Count Viznitski, Maeve was inclined to think there might be some truth to the stories. But she had spent time with Chaliapin and had come away unscathed, so she was skeptical of Arlette's rumors. Letty always believed any old thing she read in the cheap gutter press.

Then again, Maeve reflected as she and her maid boarded the Nord Express, Chaliapin had been surrounded by his wife and children when she had seen him offstage. He *did* have a formidable reputation for raising hell.

"I've brought along my rosary beads that were blessed at Lourdes and the dagger my father used against the Prussians in 1870," Arlette informed her young mistress. "I'm ready for the bears."

"Well," Maeve said with a smile, "I only hope they're ready for us."

In Maeve's compartment was a huge bouquet of expensive white roses from Dietrich, a typically sweet and considerate present she discovered only after saying goodbye to him: he had been concerned enough to get up at dawn to see her off at the station in freezing weather.

He was dreadfully upset she was going to Petersburg. He had been there himself and considered it unsafe for a single woman. He wasn't reassured either when she remarked that Chaliapin would be there and so would Marc Antoine. She and the tenor would be sharing top billing in *La Bohème*, *Tosca*, and *Carmen* at the Maryinsky.

"Be careful," he warned her, embracing her tenderly in the thirty-degree temperature. "Wear your furs all the time, keep your head and throat warm, and buy yourself a pair of *valenki* as soon as you arrive. Those are the felt boots all Russians possess. They'll keep your feet dry. The climate is abominable, the people are savages, and the men are drunken beasts."

"Well, with a recommendation like that I'm sure I'll have a marvelous time." Maeve laughed, hugging him.

"I love you, Maeve," Dietrich said as she started to pull free of him. "I want to marry you."

"I'll see you when I return," she replied. This was much too soon to talk of marriage. Really, he had no sense!

"I mean it," he persisted.

Mounting the steps of the carriage, Maeve pulled her fur coat around her and touched her fingertips to her lips. "Not while you're still married to Lotte," she said before she waved again and vanished into the compartment, where Arlette was already making herself comfortable. Although divorce proceedings had begun, he *was* still married.

Dietrich's beautiful eyes followed Maeve as she made her way through the corridors down to her compartment and finally to the window to wave to him once again. The train began to spit out steam, clanking its great iron wheels as it lurched forward, gathering steam for the long journey east.

She watched him wave back, very solemnly, standing there on the platform in his beautifully cut cashmere coat and his fur hat, looking like a young prince.

Dietrich was a very beautiful man; dirt didn't seem to touch him. He was so clean he was the only man Maeve knew whose nails were neater than hers. Most Frenchmen—including members of the upper classes—seemed to think of soap and water as something to be avoided at all costs. But in an age when most people smelled either ripe or downright revolting Dietrich trailed only a faint scent of expensive eau de cologne. Marc Antoine de Marigny and Enrico Caruso were the only tenors Maeve could recall with this pleasant trait. No wonder she enjoyed working with them both.

Watching her mistress closely as she waved goodbye to Monsieur le Baron, Arlette said quietly, "I hope all goes well with him, made-moiselle."

Maeve nodded as the figure on the railway platform grew smaller and smaller, finally vanishing altogether.

"Yes, Letty. I hope so too." She was very fond of this boy.

She knew this divorce of his was all for her benefit, and the idea of having caused it—even indirectly—was not the sort of thing she liked to think about. She was innocent of all evildoing yet somehow responsible. Love wasn't supposed to cause feelings of guilt, she thought, and yet here she was experiencing just that. It bothered her terribly.

"His troubles have nothing to do with you, mademoiselle," Arlette said loyally, as if she had just read her mind. "Don't blame yourself."

That made Maeve smile. Of course she was to blame. And that thought remained with her all the way to St. Petersburg, along with the roses.

*

Baron Hubertus von Reuter was the only person to whom Lotte revealed the truth about the divorce—in a letter in which she swore him to secrecy. White with fury, Hubertus had suffered such tremendous pains in his chest that his valet had been frightened into calling the doctor. Then, armed with a vial of pills, the baron had taken the first train to Paris to have it out with his son.

"Whoremongering pervert" was the most complimentary thing he called Dietrich when he swept into the mansion. To his astonishment, the boy didn't give a damn. He told his father the whole story of his marriage to Lotte—even gloating about his refusal to consummate their union just to cheat Hubertus of his grandchildren—and informed him that he had done it all to spite him.

"How could I have produced such a son? You're some sort of alien seed, nothing like my side of the family. You're contemptible!" screamed the banker while the servants ran for cover, not knowing what to do.

At that uncharacteristic outburst, Dietrich raised his head and stared his father coldly in the eye. "I hate you and your whole way of life, Papa," he replied, shocked at his own candor. "You don't give a damn about me or my happiness. All you ever cared about was the damned bank!"

Twenty-five years of dissembling, twenty-five years of docile hy-pocrisy were swept away in as many seconds. The dam had finally over-flowed its boundaries, leaving Dietrich awash with bitterness. Let the old man enjoy his bank, he thought. It would be the only comfort he'd have in his old age.

Now that he'd said the words, Dietrich felt his whole body relax, as if he'd just invoked the magic formula in some old fairy tale. But the dragon was still there, staring back at him in shock. He'd only wounded the beast, Dietrich thought bitterly; he hadn't killed him. What would that take? he wondered sullenly. How much longer would he have to endure him?

Hubertus was a tough old bastard. It was his pride and practically a point of honor with him to be impervious to human frailty. But even a dragon must have a weak spot somewhere, the son thought, studying his father with cold eyes. Nobody was invincible.

The father stared back, not quite ready to believe what he'd just heard. It bewildered him; it shook his faith in his own vaunted talents as a parent. It made him wonder about this boy and his ultimate fitness to succeed him, to assure the survival of the bank!

Look at him, the baron thought nervously—unshaven, disheveled, unkempt. This wasn't Dietrich. His boy was a fop. This bleary-eyed young ragamuffin was somebody else, a boy who'd lost his bearings—perhaps even his mental equilibrium. He'd read of things like that.

At the idea of budding insanity or even a lesser disorder, Baron Hubertus drew back in revulsion, horrified at the poor reflection on his house. If Dietrich was suffering from this kind of malady, he needed gentle handling right now. A boy who could involve himself in such a marital mess could be capable of further, possibly even more public stupidity. And that must be avoided at all costs. The bank couldn't afford it.

Visibly shaken, Hubertus cleared his throat and made an unaccustomed effort to strike what he hoped would be a paternal pose. He gingerly extended his hand in Dietrich's direction—making his son cringe as if he expected to be struck—and then thumped him awkwardly on the shoulder, almost the way one would pat a dog.

To Dietrich's amazement, he then announced that they would ride out the storm—thanks to Lotte's good sense. There would be no scandal. He must pull himself together and put all that behind him. Their future would depend on it. They would work together to overcome their problems.

Scornfully the boy flicked his father a glance of pure disgust. Then it occurred to him that if the old man was this worried, the time might be right to ask for some concessions. For some reason Hubertus had decided to tread softly and even though Dietrich couldn't imagine why, he wanted to take advantage of it. Boldly he asked for permission to keep his house in Paris. Incredibly his father nodded his assent. He was actually making a truce with the prodigal son!

Well, Dietrich thought, why not? Maybe Hubertus realized his worth after all. It seemed a lot to hope for from his father, but other people had a good opinion of Dietrich. He knew how to make friends. He had plenty of influential friends in Paris. People liked him—even if Hubertus did not. And by making good use of those contacts he might one day carve out an even greater career than Hubertus and leave his father in the dust. And the sooner the better.

Warily the two von Reuters looked at each other, two animals sizing up their opponents. A truce had gone into effect now, but both wondered how long it would last.

CHAPTER 14

Whon Maeve arrived in St. Petersburg, she was dazzled by all the snow. The Russian capital seemed to be an icy fairyland, just the sort of place one could see in old-fashioned paper-weights.

Little sleighs sped through the streets, the horses sleek and shiny as they pulled their gorgeously painted vehicles carrying lovely, fur-clad beauties or distinguished-looking gentlemen from the General Staff Building with their accompanying outriders.

The broad Nevsky Prospect with its imposing cathedrals, neoclassic government buildings, huge bazaars, and fashionable boutiques was swarming with life day and night in a constant parade of the famous and the notorious, the imperial and the destitute. Men and women in all the costumes of the huge Russian Empire thronged its sidewalks—Tartars, Kalmuks, Russian peasants, officers, Finnish milkmaids who hawked their dairy products in the capital, resident Europeans in elegantly tailored outfits with labels from Paris, Berlin, and London, and the housewives and students of the city, bundled up in colorful shawls or school uniforms. Somehow St. Petersburg looked like a gigantic opera set, complete with handsome Guards officers, humble priests, haughty grand duchesses, and a backdrop that was as grand as two centuries of imperial taste could make it. Maeve loved it.

She also loved to visit the noisy fairs held in the public parks and watch the bears—the real live Russian bears Sean had described, lumbering about on their hind legs, their powerful muscles rippling beneath shaggy coats. These muzzled creatures were the delight of the crowds who shrieked with laughter as their handlers put them through their paces, making them dance a clumsy jig or toss a ball with huge furry paws. Excited children, bundled into little balls of fur themselves, begged their parents for a kopek to throw to the handlers, then brought home little marzipan or gingerbread bears as souvenirs.

And Maeve noticed with a shock that the magnificent Paris gowns of the bejeweled and titled ladies who thronged the theaters often could have stood a cleaning. The Petersburg blend of glamour and filth sometimes rattled her, but it never failed to fascinate.

One aspect of Russian life never lost its charm, and that was their openhearted hospitality. While a Frenchman generally calculated down to the last sou what he would spend on guests, the Russians were unrestrained in their generosity, never seeming to care how much it cost to entertain friends. This appeared to be true at all levels of society, Maeve found, and stinginess was a trait that was despised above all others.

The imperial theaters in St. Petersburg and Moscow also benefited from this lavishness, and Maeve had never seen their equal in Europe. As servants of the imperial household in theory, the artists were provided with every imaginable costume and set with which to entertain the Tsar. The wealth of technical expertise at their disposal was staggering, and productions were notable for their sumptuousness. The imperial resources were fabulous, like something out of Ali Baba's cave, and it wasn't for nothing that the period was labeled the Silver Age of Russian art.

To a dazzled nineteen-year-old who had broken out of a British concentration camp in Africa not two years earlier, St. Petersburg seemed too exotic to be real. Standing in the swirling snow outside the ornate Maryinsky Theatre, Maeve stared at the poster announcing her name in Cyrillic letters and wondered if she was only imagining it. If she blinked, would it all suddenly vanish?

She smiled quietly, and silently promised herself she'd die rather than let go of what she'd gained.

*

The St. Petersburg season was in full swing in mid-January 1904, having officially begun with the Tsar's New Year's reception at the Winter Palace. There was some consternation over the unfortunate incident at the annual Blessing of the Waters: the gunners had bungled the salute and fired live ammunition in the direction of His Imperial Majesty as he and his retinue stood on the frozen Neva, but it was determined that the accident was due to incompetence, not some revolutionary spirit on the part of the troops.

Maeve, excited about her St. Petersburg debut, quickly became a sensation. Critics were almost unanimous in praising the newest European discovery for her "charm and distinction" as well as her superb diction and the vivid emotional nuances she brought to her roles.

The night she and Marc Antoine opened in *La Bohème*, she found herself nearly buried beneath an avalanche of floral tributes, and she was profoundly moved by the warmth of her reception. The second night, to her delight, she saw a banner unfurled in the balcony bearing the inscription in French, "We love you, Masha!"

"I love you too!" Maeve responded in Russian, which brought forth an ever greater round of applause. And with that, she plucked several flowers from her bouquets and flung them happily in the direction of her fans, causing a small uproar. Marc Antoine had his own success— each night, he was eagerly sought out by wealthy ladies who carried him off to parties all over the city. He was amassing an impressive list of invitations—and little baubles from Fabergé studded with diamonds and other precious jewels.

"If your voice ever fails you, you can go into the knickknack business," Maeve remarked one day. "You have enough to open a shop."

"Knickknacks! Use your eyes. These little *trucs* are loaded with diamonds. Nice party favors."

Very nice indeed. Marc Antoine always did have the gift for making friends, she thought. And he was especially popular with countesses who had husbands away from home.

All this was wonderful, but the best thing about performing at the Maryinsky was the opportunity it gave Maeve to observe Chaliapin at close range on his home ground.

From him she was learning more about acting and makeup than from anyone she had ever encountered in Paris. The man was a genius who could transform himself into a character so totally that Fedya Chaliapin vanished and in his place was a terrifyingly real Ivan the Terrible, Tsar Boris, highwayman, drunkard, or prince. So great was his talent that old friends swore he vanished at those times and actually became the characters he portrayed so convincingly. His was such a creative force that he could also bring out the best in his partners.

For all these reasons, the young singer from Paris was nearly dizzy with emotion the night she was at last to sing the role of the Tsarevich to Chaliapin's Boris Godunov. In the huge blue and gilt auditorium was a society audience that contained the flower of the aristocracy, the St. Petersburg diplomatic corps, dashing Guards officers and members of the imperial family. Tsar Nicholas II, the Tsaritza Alexandra Feodorovna and a cluster of grand dukes and duchesses sat in the huge imperial box, looking like every picture book photo of royalty Maeve had ever seen.

At Chaliapin's playful suggestion, Maeve took part in a number of crowd scenes—welcoming the new Tsar to Moscow, greeting the false Dimitri—looking very Slavic in a bright sarafan and richly embroidered shawl, getting a feel for the overall production, observing every aspect.

When it came time to do her scenes as the Tsarevich, she was like a racehorse straining at the bit, looking gorgeous in her red velvet tunic with rich gold froggings and soft high leather boots. If Maeve didn't look like a youth who could carry the future burdens of the Russian autocracy on his slender shoulders, she looked like the prettiest Tsarevich ever, and she drew delighted applause from the audience, who found no fault with her Russian diction—her chief worry.

Marc Antoine was watching her from the wings, having sent her off with the traditional *"In bocca al lupo."* He was to keep his eye on her and be aware of any faux pas. During the intermission he was pleased to report not one flaw, as Maeve sipped honeyed tea in her dressing room and received a brief visit from Fedya, still in character. Tsar Boris complimented her like a proud father and nodded, "A worthy Tsarevich. *Khorosho!*"

At the conclusion of the performance when Maeve was watching Chaliapin take more than twenty-five curtain calls and nearly vanish under the gifts of flowers littering the stage, she saw Prince Teliakovsky, the director of the theater, whisper to him and draw his attention to the box where Nicholas II sat applauding.

Within minutes, Tsar Boris, the Tsarevich, and the false Dimitri were on their way to the imperial box to be received by the Tsar of all the Russias.

"He wants to see *me!*" Maeve exclaimed. "Why?"

"Why not? It's an honor," muttered Chaliapin en route. "Use it in your future publicity." He didn't seem overwhelmed by it, though.

In the anteroom of the imperial box, servants were passing around trays of champagne when the artists were ceremoniously announced to the company. Several very tall Romanovs in splendid dress uniforms turned to observe Tsar Boris and his colleagues.

To Maeve's disillusionment, Nicholas was the shortest man present. The others—all uncles or cousins—stood head and shoulders above their Tsar, an unfortunate effect.

It had taken Maeve a few seconds to comprehend just what was causing the amazing light show in the room. Shafts of light bounced off all available surfaces, reflected off the mirrors, and glanced off the prisms of the chandelier: the accumulation of all those diamonds on the women.

Bedecked with diamonds, rubies, sapphires, and emeralds, the ladies were quite literally glittering. At least two of them were already familiar faces to Maeve. She had seen their pictures on the desk of Kaiser Wilhelm in Berlin—Alexandra Feodorovna and her sister, Grand Duchess Elizaveta, the wife of the Governor-General of Moscow.

Alexandra appeared to overshadow her husband, Maeve thought. She was a very tall woman, very stiff and unapproachable, looking as if she was bored to be there. Her good looks suffered from her tight expression and her obvious lack of enthusiasm. The grand duchess was more coolly regal, more gracious, and somehow more serene. She was also swimming with emeralds, gifts from her husband, the notorious Grand Duke Sergei. Her coloring was exquisite, Maeve noticed, porcelain skin, blue eyes, and auburn hair.

Glancing at Maeve and the grand duchess, Chaliapin was struck by their similarity. Little Masha could have passed for the daughter of the most beautiful woman in the imperial family.

To Maeve's horror, she realized she was still in costume. How was she going to curtsy? Geraldine's lessons hadn't been extended to cover *that* eventuality. Perspiring with nervousness, she hoped these Romanovs had a sense of humor, and followed Chaliapin's lead by bowing to the Tsar and Tsaritza, still in character. That produced an amused smile from Nicholas, who complimented her on her mastery of Russian and told her she made a very handsome Tsarevich.

As Maeve smiled with pleasure, Nicholas made a slight gesture which summoned a flunky bearing gifts. The Tsar then presented her with a beautiful gold cigarette case from Fabergé, bearing the imperial *chiffre* and the Tsar's portrait surrounded by diamonds. Chaliapin received a similar one in platinum, a useful item for him since he was a chain-smoker, a very Russian trait.

Clutching her imperial token of esteem, Maeve returned to her dressing room, half floating on air. She flung open the door and was proudly flourishing the gold case at her maid when suddenly Arlette interrupted her and gestured toward the back of the little room—where a uniformed gentleman was sitting on a little gilt chair, smiling at the sight of her, absolutely transfigured.

Maeve felt her legs go weak as she stared back, nearly frozen with shock. Then, dropping the Tsar's gift on the carpet in a daze, she threw herself into her admirer's arms, nearly knocking him off the chair with her emotion. She was hysterical with joy to see him alive. It seemed too good to be true—the answer to her prayers.

"Sean!" she gasped as Arlette wondered what was going on. Arlette had never seen the man in her life and couldn't imagine who could cause such a reaction in her young lady. All Monsieur von Reuter ever got was polite peck on the cheek. Now here was Mademoiselle kissing this fellow as if she never wanted to let go of him, holding him, hugging him, just going crazy with joy. It wasn't like her.

"Now," Maeve demanded in exasperation, "where on earth have you been for the past two years? And it had better be good!"

After Maeve changed herself from tsarevich to young lady again, Sean bundled her into her furs and into his sleigh for a ride through the snowy streets to a fashionable restaurant, the Medved, and one of its private dining rooms.

As they entered the restaurant, Maeve saw Chaliapin seated with some Russian friends, being lionized by a crowd of well-wishers. With a little cry of delight, she rushed to where he was seated and threw her arms around his neck, kissing him affectionately while Sean slapped him cheerfully on the back.

"Masha! I can see you've met my friend Ivan Petrovic," he said with a grin. "I knew you'd hit it off."

"Fedya! This is the man who was taken from me!" she exclaimed. "Don't you remember? The one I told you about in Monte Carlo!"

Startled, he burst out laughing. "Well, I guess you can credit me with reuniting you, *milochka*. I was the one who insisted that Ivan come to the theater tonight to see Boris. And my little Masha!"

"You darling! I'm in your debt forever."

After she and Sean had disappeared into one of the private dining rooms, Chaliapin was still smiling at the memory of the pretty girl by the harbor at Monte Carlo.

"I think of him every day," Maeve had declared. Now that she had found him again in St. Petersburg, he wondered what would happen.

"Let's drink to young love," he proposed with some irony. "It's such a brief and fleeting illusion."

In their private room, Maeve was so keyed up she barely glanced at her food. She was so happy to have Sean back, alive and well, she forgot everything else.

"What really happened to you?" she demanded once they were seated.

"Politics." He shrugged. "Alexander found out I was in Belgrade, had me kidnapped, and let me rot for months in prison. He was afraid to let me go once he'd captured me for fear it would lead to trouble with Montenegro. So the damned fool kept his mouth shut—and pretended not to know anything. I'm not going to say I was unhappy when I heard what happened to him. But I thought it could have been handled with more finesse."

"Well, how did you finally get out of there?" asked Maeve.

"Russian pressure on Serbia. My sister Stana kept at her brother-in-law to do something and he finally did. The Russian Embassy in Belgrade pulled it off. Through secret channels, of course."

"My God! Very cloak and dagger."

"Never underestimate Russian influence in the Balkans." He smiled. "By the way, I've waited a long time to thank you for letting my mother know what happened that day at the Tri Sesira. She told me about that."

"Did she also tell you that I kept writing to her to inquire about your whereabouts? I must have written for months."

Sean stared at her. "No," he said. "I tried to find out where you and Moira had gone but nobody knew. I was frantic to locate you as soon as I got out."

"Your mother knew we were in Paris," Maeve said firmly, looking him straight in the eye. "I kept after her for a long time."

The silence was embarrassing. Sean couldn't believe Maeve was lying. And he didn't want to admit to himself that it was a confirmation of his worst suspicions about his own mother. So Geraldine *had* lied. Damn!

Kyril, his loyal servant, had told him what a wildcat the girl had been, how he nearly had to strangle her to make her leave when she was so determined to stay and help him.

"The mother was smart enough to keep her mouth shut and follow me," Kyril had explained. "But the little one, she was crazy enough to want to take on those brutes. What a good time they would have had with her!"

Kyril had admired her nerve, but he hated to see a woman who didn't know her place. Fighting was definitely out of bounds, especially for such a soft little thing as Maeve. He solemnly predicted a bad end for her.

"Anyway," Maeve said, wanting to put an end to the awkwardness, "Mama isn't in St. Petersburg with me."

Sean's expression altered. He was horrified to think Moira would allow a young girl like Maeve to venture into Russia unchaperoned. She must be mad!

"Where is she, then? I hope she's well," he said uneasily.

" 'Well' isn't the word for it. She's absolutely enchanted with life at the moment. Mama's in America with Mr. Charles Lassiter, a millionaire from New York. And very big in sporting circles," she added with a sigh.

Poor Sean. Maeve had wanted him to know that Moira wasn't sitting around pining for him—while his mother was lying and pretending not to know where she was—but she hadn't expected this reaction. He looked quite stricken. Devastated. He even slumped a little in his chair, utterly crestfallen.

"We wanted to see you so badly," she added, trying to cheer him. "But you never found us. I tried to find you by going to call on your sister Stana in Paris, but her servants would never let me near her. They refused even to listen to me."

"Who the hell is this Lassiter?" he asked abruptly. "Is he rich?"

Maeve rolled her eyes. "As rich as Croesus," she replied. "His papa helped Mr. Rockefeller start Standard Oil. And he was a Rough Rider, too."

"A cowboy?" he exclaimed. My God! he thought.

"No," Maeve protested. "Well, at least he doesn't seem to be a cowboy. More of a sportsman. Lions, tigers, pheasants."

Now Sean rolled his eyes. What bad luck! "I hope she'll be happy," he managed. But it was an effort. Moira and some sort of rich cowboy! Damn!

As an afterthought, he said, "She must have believed I was dead. She knew how much I wanted to take you to Paris."

"We were both afraid you were dead, Sean. But somehow, in my mind, I refused to believe it. It just didn't seem possible that I would lose you forever after what we had been through."

"Thank God Fedya insisted I come to the Maryinsky this evening," he said, smiling. "You wouldn't believe how determined he was that I should see his little Masha. He's very fond of you."

"Have you known him for a long time?"

Sean laughed. "Do you remember that I once told you about going to a party with a bear?"

Maeve looked blank for a second. Then she recalled it. "Yes. You were telling us how wonderful Petersburg was. And how drunk you were."

"Well, who do you think that young singer was? It was Fedya. We became friends from that moment on. I think the world of him."

"Did he ever mention me?" she asked, curious.

"Yes. He came back from his Monte Carlo season delighted with his success and insisting that he was going to get the management of the Maryinsky to bring you to Petersburg. He was quite taken with you."

"But didn't he ever mention my name?" she demanded in exasperation.

"Frequently. Masha. All the time, Masha this, Masha that. If I had only known who this Masha was, don't you think I would have been in Paris on the first train? My God, you have no idea of the effect you had on me when you walked out on that stage. I thought I was imagining it. The Tsarevich looked so much like you. Then I borrowed a pair of opera glasses to get a better look at you and then I checked my program. Maeve Devereux! I even asked the old lady who opens the doors of the boxes who was playing the Tsarevich and she gave me your name too. I couldn't believe I had actually read it."

"Well, did you like what I did with the role?"

"I adored it." He laughed. "My God, Maeve, how did you ever get to the Maryinsky?"

Now it was Maeve's turn to laugh. "It's a long story," she said. "But I owe it all to von Reuter's son, Dietrich. He's very fond of me."

"He was in love with you in Berlin," Sean remembered.

Maeve glanced down. For some reason she didn't want to talk about Dietrich.

"He's an art lover," Maeve replied. "And I think he sometimes gets carried away with his enthusiasms."

Looking at Maeve with her beautiful auburn hair and her creamy skin, Sean could understand how the boy could very easily get carried away. This was not the ragged child he had met that day under a roasting sun in South Africa. This was an elegant young woman who had acquired a nice gloss of sophistication. Somehow those days seemed to belong to another epoch. It was as though they had never happened.

"Well." She smiled. "What brings you to St. Petersburg? Business?"

"In a way," he nodded. "I'm about to become engaged."

For a second she just went blank. This was not fair, she thought. Not fair at all.

"All the best," she said brightly. "Congratulations."

But she really wanted to scream.

How could he do this? she wondered in despair. How could he? She didn't care if he had been prevented by circumstances from joining them before now. This engagement was wrong. It ruined everything—everything that might have been—and that was the cruelest fate of all. It was South Africa all over again. *And* that day in Belgrade. It was sheer hell.

CHAPTER 15

C harlie's relatives notwithstanding, most of his friends in New York liked Moira Devereux for her bounce, her beauty, and her lilting Irish voice. It wasn't the brogue of everybody's housemaid and the corner policeman; it was something soft and polished, purring and whimsical, rather like Moira herself.

And if the lady had any doubts about Charlie's status, that was settled when the invitation to dine with "the Colonel" arrived. Teddy Roosevelt wished to see his old friend next Thursday for an informal dinner—and would he please bring Mrs. Devereux?

"How does he know about me?" gasped Moira, utterly astonished.

"Because I've written him to tell him about you. He's a wonderful man, great company. And he's interested in everything."

"I would imagine." The idea that he could be interested in meeting *her* made Moira's head spin. Well, she had once met Kaiser Wilhelm, so she ought to be used to the great of this world. But Colonel Roosevelt! He with the teeth and the big grin, and the Big Stick. He *was* America to the rest of the world. It was like meeting a hero of some old folk legend. Besides, the Kaiser hadn't invited her to dinner.

"What shall I wear, Charlie?" Moira asked, a little in awe at the idea.

"Well," he reflected, "he's very fond of his daughter, the one the press has labeled Princess Alice. And they've just named a shade of blue after her, so why not wear something in her color? You could hardly go wrong there."

Yes, Moira decided. That was very diplomatic. So off she went to make the rounds of the New York stores to hunt for The Dress. A private dressmaker was out of the question for this because it would take too long. She only hoped she could find what she needed, and on her second expedition she did. Saks had a very pretty dinner gown in Alice blue trimmed with Valenciennes lace at the neck and elbows. Their in-house dressmaker was able to fit Moira without too much trouble, since the gown needed only minor alterations, and two days later she had her dress, a slender column of blue satin with a froth of lace.

"Magnificent," Charlie declared when she modeled it for him. "And I have something from Tiffany's for you to go with it."

Handing her a small blue box, Charlie watched eagerly as Moira opened it to find a smaller velvet box inside. A ring box.

She glanced up at him, smiled shyly, and opened it to discover a three-carat diamond engagement ring.

Kissing him quickly, Moira wrapped her arms around his neck. "Is this to make a respectable woman of me?" she teased.

Charlie sighed and pulled her closer to him. "I love you," he said. "You're the first woman since Esmeralda I've said that to—and I mean it." He had said it so simply she almost missed it.

For a second, Moira thought she had imagined it. Men were notoriously reluctant to say those words—most seemed to view them as life-threatening. Those were words some men wouldn't utter even under torture. Yet here was Charlie Lassiter, millionaire, sportsman, and friend of presidents, saying them solemnly to her without a bit of prompting. It was such a triumph she almost wished she had an audience.

"I'm touched, Charlie," Moira replied as she ruffled his hair and left a trail of kisses down his neck.

"I don't want to hear that you're touched," he replied, seizing her roughly and pinning her down on the bed. "I want to hear you say the same thing to me! Moira, I'm crazy about you! I want to marry you!"

She didn't miss *that*. "Marry?" she asked in stunned surprise.

"Yes." He nodded fiercely. "Marry."

"When?" Moira asked, warming to the idea.

"Soon. Next week if you wish. In New York."

"What will I wear?" she murmured, mentally reviewing her wardrobe. "I'll need something suitable."

"I'd marry you in what you're wearing right now," he exclaimed. Why did a woman's first thought have to be for her wardrobe?

"But I don't know anyone in New York," she demurred. "And of course, I'd want Maeve to attend the ceremony."

"Darling," he whispered, "I know hundreds of people. We can fill up the church with them. And you can have a president of the United States at your wedding. How would you like that?"

This was all so astonishing to Moira she didn't know what to say. If he was playing some sort of practical joke on her, it wouldn't matter what she said. But if he was dead serious—and he seemed to be—she had better say the right thing.

Moira caressed him tenderly and kissed him several times for effect. "Charlie Lassiter," she murmured, "I love you dearly and I'd be flattered and honored to be your wife."

Since he didn't burst out laughing and declare the whole thing null and void, Moira decided he was serious. God Almighty! Mrs. Charles Lassiter! Mrs. Millionaire! Mrs. American Millionaire!

Contemplating the enormity of what she'd just done, Moira was nearly weak with awe. This was the end of worrying about money and the start of a gigantic spending spree. Every little thing she'd ever wanted was about to be hers. Nothing would be too good for her. Houses, gowns, jewels, horses, anything she wished for!

Becoming a bit more rational, Moira remembered to kiss Charlie several more times in a burst of passion as she reflected that it was a pity Maeve would have to miss the highlight of her mother's life. But one didn't dare hesitate at a time like this. Damn! It would have been nice to see Maeve in the audience watching *her* for a change.

But life was short and millionaires were capricious. And she didn't intend to allow anything to jeopardize her good fortune, especially not for a reason as sentimental as *that*. Maeve would get the news by telegram and have to be satisfied with that.

"I love you more than anything, Charlie," Moira whispered, wrapping her arms around him again in an embrace that had suddenly become possessive. "And I'm going to enjoy spending my life making you happy."

But as Charlie Lassiter buried his face in Moira's creamy bosom and ran his hands over her soft, velvety flesh, the future Mrs. Lassiter was already thinking of ways to make *her* life happy. His pleasure was incidental.

*

Maeve's success in the Russian capital brought her a great deal of satisfaction, but her reunion with Sean Farrell had been heartbreaking. He was to be engaged to some Montenegrin girl whose father was the leader of a clan that was important to Prince Nikolai. How medieval. Clans! My God! What sort of place was this Montenegro?

Marc Antoine was mildly sympathetic, but Maeve decided his heart was made of cast iron. Nothing seemed to upset him. He was French and practical. Women were always threatening to throw themselves in front of streetcars or some such nonsense if he didn't do this or that, he confided. And they never did. Broken hearts were the easiest thing in the world to mend. All one needed was practice.

Marc Antoine, with his wavy chestnut hair and lovely green eyes, got plenty of practice. He blamed Maeve's passionate devotion on her Celtic blood. Mary Garden was a Celt too, he pointed out with a shudder. Very temperamental. It must be something in the race. He himself was a *savoisien* and oblivious to inner turmoil, he maintained. He saved all that for the stage.

Sean Farrell was almost overwhelmed at discovering Maeve again. The little wild girl who had saved his life had developed into a beauty, and not just a beauty but a personality. Looking at her onstage at the Maryinsky, listening to her, he had found the transformation fascinating.

This elegant young Parisienne was the girl who had helped plan a jailbreak, faced a man down with a rifle, and shot him before he could shoot her rescuer. Sean would never forget that moment, the gunfire, the shouts of the Boers and the British soldiers, the hoofbeats on the dry, dusty ground as the men raced into the camp. But why had he been forced to miss her for so long? And Moira.

The day before Sean celebrated his engagement to Zofia Plamanac, he introduced Maeve to his sisters Stana and Militza at Militza's palace. Geraldine stayed away, citing her mourning as Graf von Kleist had just died. That was fine with Maeve; she had absolutely no wish to see the gräfin. She was afraid she'd slap her if she had to listen to any lies about not receiving her letters.

Small and lively, the Montenegrin princesses were delighted to meet the girl who had saved their brother's life. Standing next to Sean—whom they always called Ivan—they didn't seem part of the same family: they were as small and dark as he was tall and fair. But there was no doubt about their being a family. They wanted to hear the whole story of the escape from the camp and what happened to Maeve after she had to flee Belgrade.

Embarrassed to tell *all* the story to strangers, Maeve left out anything to do with Count Viznitski to protect Moira's reputation—no sense in letting people know that sort of thing. Besides, she didn't want Sean to know about Viznitski. The whole episode was too sordid.

Before Maeve left that afternoon, Sean promised to attend her performance of *Carmen* on the following Tuesday at the Bolshoi in Moscow. With Zofia Plamanac.

Driving Maeve back to the Astoria Hotel on St. Isaac's Square, he was aware of how unhappy she was. He was uneasy with Maeve. Two years ago there had been no barriers between them; now she was a grown-up and a beautiful woman.

"Did you ever love Mama?" Maeve asked unexpectedly as they drove furiously along Nevsky Prospect behind a handsome pair of Orlov trotters. Snow blew all around them, frosting the already icy street and the shops and churches along the route. The splendid colonnade of the Kazan Cathedral looked like a sculptor's creation in the gray January dusk.

"Yes," he replied. "I did. I thought Moira was the most beautiful woman I'd ever seen. I fell in love with her from the first moment I saw her."

"Then why did you not find us for all that time? I thought of you each day for two years, afraid you were dead, afraid you were suffering. My God! It looks as though you were having a wonderful old time in St. Petersburg! What a fool I was."

"Maeve! Don't ever say that!"

"Why? It seems to be the truth!"

"It's not the truth. I was locked up in a damned prison for months. You know that. I nearly went crazy worrying about you and Moira. As soon as I was released I demanded to know what had become of you. And Mama lied."

"She must be easily frightened," Maeve replied bitterly.

He smiled. "She has the nerve of a bandit."

"Then why did she have to tell you she had lost all trace of us?"

The snow was biting into their faces so fiercely Maeve pulled up her fur collar and turned hers to Sean's shoulder to try to shield herself from the sting. She was waiting for his answer.

She had to wait for a while. Finally he sighed. "Mama has lived all her life with only one love. Me. None of the men in her past—including my father—has ever managed to touch her heart. She can't bear the thought of losing me to another woman."

"But you're getting engaged tomorrow! And she's here to attend the ceremony. Is she jealous of your fiancée?"

He shook his head. "No."

"Well, then? Why would she be afraid of Mama?"

Sean pulled over to the side of the great boulevard. He couldn't believe this girl was so dense. It was almost endearing in a way.

"Maeve," he said, "it's not your mother she's afraid of."

Her head bobbed up. She stared straight into his blue eyes, the snow half blinding them both. The traffic on the Nevsky swirled around them, half a cavalry unit cantering by on patrol, heavy greatcoats hanging over the sides of their horses, the sound of the horses' hooves oddly muffled in the thick, packed snow.

Maeve didn't see or hear them. "It was me, then." Her heart was beating wildly.

"Yes."

She brushed a heavy frosting of snow off her eyelashes and asked, "Was there any reason for her to be afraid?"

Sean hesitated. He was getting engaged to Zofia Plamanac tomorrow, thereby firming up an important alliance for his father, since the wealthy Plamanacs were nearly undisputed lords of vast areas of western Montenegro—and their loyalty had been known to falter occasionally.

"There was plenty of reason. If I had spent the last two years close to you."

"But you didn't."

"I wanted to. I was in love with Moira and I loved you as if you were a sister. You are very dear to me. We have a blood tie after what happened in Africa. That's something that can't be broken."

"Well, I didn't love *you* like a brother," Maeve replied, unable to help herself.

Sean looked at her tenderly. He would have laughed at the way she said that if he hadn't known she would be mortally offended.

This girl fascinated him. To be brought back into her orbit after two years of worry and uncertainty was a blessing and a curse. Maeve had saved his life; there was absolutely no question of behaving dishonorably with her. She would never be a mistress. She would also never be his wife now, not with the Plamanacs arriving along with the Petrovici for the extravaganza tomorrow. There would be bloodshed and a return to the old vendettas if he jilted Zofia.

"Maeve," he said, "I wish things had worked out differently. I wish I had been able to take you to Paris."

"I went there anyway."

"And you've done well. You astonish me."

"Thank God someone took an interest in me," she retorted rather unkindly. She was sorry after she said it, but it had slipped out.

Sean almost missed the reference. Then he nodded. "Ah. Yes. The von Reuter boy."

"He loves me. And not like a sister."

"You really want to draw blood, don't you?" He smiled.

That made Maeve so angry, she reacted without thinking. If she had been inside somewhere she probably would have thrown something at him in rage. Here there was no possibility of that. Instead, she astonished Sean and several passersby flinging her arms around him and kissing him so ferociously he nearly lost control of the horses and both of them ended up on the sidewalk, dazed and gasping for breath.

"Goodbye!" she shouted over her shoulder to him as she sprinted down the street, elbowing her way through a flock of startled pedestrians in the swirling snow. *"Addio!"* she added with overtones of Tosca and Violetta. *"Addio a sempre!"*

That performance was so furious it made him hesitate to pursue her. Well, there was no point in it right now. She was angry and her feelings were hurt, but she was a beautiful young girl—with plenty of admirers. She wouldn't remain angry for long. There would always be someone to amuse her and take her mind off him.

By the time he ventured to Moscow to applaud her in *Carmen*, Maeve would probably find her stormy exit on the Nevsky hilarious. He hoped so. But after that scene, he couldn't wait to see what she was going to do onstage as the Gypsy spitfire. She certainly would have no problem with the part.

*

Two days before Maeve was to leave for Moscow, she woke up to hear a huge noise coming from the square outside her hotel. Jumping out of bed, she flung open the heavy drapes to look out on St. Isaac's Square, dense with people, all singing the imperial anthem, "God Save the Tsar." Her heart skipped a beat. There were many soldiers in that crowd, officers on horseback around the edges, and dozens of people carrying huge banners with inscriptions in Cyrillic letters. There were also large icons held aloft and portraits of the Tsar.

Desperate to know the worst, Maeve forced open the heavy window in the frigid air, wrapped her dressing gown around her, and shouted with all her strength to be heard over the uproar: "What is happening?" Then she tried to remember the Russian words and tried again. This time people waved up at her and cupped their hands around their mouths to shout back.

"Voina" was what they were calling out. War!

Stunned, Maeve felt her knees go weak. Sean would be in danger, she thought, grasping the frozen railing with both hands. No matter what she had said on Nevsky Prospect, she couldn't bear to think of that. She cared for him deeply, Dietrich or no Dietrich, Zofia or no Zofia, and she always would. "Oh God," she murmured. "Let Zofia have him. But send him home alive!" And she went back inside, weeping with fear for him.

*

When Dietrich von Reuter heard the news of the Russo-Japanese hostilities—followed by the shocking news of the destruction of all those Russian battleships at Port Arthur—he wired Hubertus in Berlin in their private code: "Have offer of share in underwriting of war loan with Seligman and Rothschild. Shall we proceed?"

Hubertus wired back: "Yes. Which side?" As if he had to ask!

Thanks to Dietrich, the von Reuter Bank was now in a consortium of leading European financial institutions preparing to underwrite the Japanese war effort.

It was all due to the boy's friendship with the famous British patroness of the arts, Sybil Seligman, that he had entered the great banking clan's orbit. Sybil, who was very fond of Dietrich, reminded her banker husband that the assets of the von Reuter Bank were highly stable—even if Dietrich wasn't. And Hubertus was flattered to have the bank's name on the same paper as Rothschild. It would be the first time the von Reuters had ever worked with them, and the prestige was enormous. Even if they were Jews.

Like many men of his time and his milieu, Baron Hubertus was vehemently anti-Semitic. He deplored insidious Jewish incursions into German cultural life, but he admitted that one dealt with "those people" if the money were right. With a Rothschild in the picture, it could hardly be wrong!

British financial institutions had taken the lead in the Japanese loans since Britain and Japan had had a friendship treaty dating back to 1902—putting Russian noses out of joint, but American bankers were not slow to respond either. Dietrich was sending wires to Hubertus claiming Jacob Schiff, the great Jewish philanthropist and banker from New York, was also backing the Japanese, and the American newspapers were full of admiration for the "plucky little Japs."

Maeve, sympathetic to the Russians since her triumph in St. Petersburg, joined with several artists to plan a benefit concert on her return to Paris, the proceeds of which were destined for the Russian Red Cross.

Deaf to Dietrich's insistence that it was sinfully wasteful to back the losers, Maeve had responded to the request of two very highly placed

Russian ladies and had agreed to perform without taking her usual fee. The Grand Duchess Militza and her sister Stana were delighted.

Moira and her new husband were lukewarm to the idea. It was the first thing Moira heard upon her return to Paris from her American idyll, and she was frankly uneasy about Maeveen being linked in any way with the Russians.

Moira's own experiences with Count Viznitski had made her a Russophobe, and months of reading pro-Japanese stories in the American press had convinced her the Tsar deserved to lose. What was Maeve thinking about, for heaven's sake?

"I was warmly received in St. Petersburg, Mama. Those people took me to their hearts and made me feel right at home. Now I just want to give them something in return."

"You shouldn't involve yourself. You're a singer. Stick to that."

"Well, that's precisely how I'm going to help."

"You're very stubborn, Maeve," Moira sighed. "Everyone else is hoping the Japanese boot the great bear so hard he'll never recover. Charlie says the Tsar's armies are taking a ferocious pounding."

Maeve knew that. The French newspapers were full of the most appalling stories of Russian hardships. Some French newspapers—supplied with money from St. Petersburg—were doing their best to win sympathy for the Tsar's troops. The Franco-Russian friendship had a base of solid gold, but the French were not any more willing to enter the fray on the Russian side than the British were on the side of the Mikado. One wasn't reckless—except with printer's ink.

*

While Maeve was beginning her second season with the Opéra-Comique, Moira was entering the beau monde on a wave of American dollars. She and Charlie had bought the Parisian town house of a debt-ridden count and had promptly spent a fortune renovating it. The elderly aristocrat was so distressed at seeing the wrecking crews demolish large chunks of his eighteenth-century interiors that he died soon after the sale and left his new fortune to a grateful cousin in Provence, who blessed the day Charlie Lassiter took a fancy to the dusty old pile.

"This is fit for royalty," Maeve declared, greatly impressed as Moira showed her around after her triumphant return from America as the newly married Mrs. Lassiter.

Bathrooms in gleaming Carrara marble were rising where salons and bedrooms had once stood. Americans were very keen on good plumbing, Moira explained proudly. The faucets and taps for these gorgeous bathrooms were gold and crystal. Charlie had a fine bathroom of his own off their bedroom suite with lots of black marble, ormolu, and malachite. And crystal lighting fixtures from Venice.

Thinking of the primitive plumbing back home in South Africa, Maeve smiled. She remembered how they had both gaped at the splendor of the bathrooms in that hotel in Amsterdam—two ladies fresh from the backwoods, mesmerized by a fancy porcelain tub. Now Moira would be lolling about in Italian marble.

"Are you happy, Mama?" Maeve asked suddenly, perched on the side of the new marble tub. At the end near the gold faucet was a mirror ornamented with frosted, etched glass, reflecting both women in silk afternoon frocks. Moira's was trimmed in dark fur, Maeve's in black velvet.

"Yes," Moira nodded. "I really do feel as if I belong with him. Charlie is very much his own man. Nobody owns him. He's passionate about what he likes—and what he hates. He's adventurous. He's honest. He doesn't have to bow his head to anybody, so he can be himself. I love him for that." She smiled. "Money is very liberating."

It was also a great bridge. Mrs. Charles Lassiter was considered suitable company in a way Moira Devereux never was. And if certain European collectors of millionaires wished to have Charlie at their parties, well, he could hardly leave his beautiful bride at home.

Moira had learned in America in unmistakable ways that money made the world go round. The newspapers were full of stories of self-made millionaires like Evelyn Walsh McLean's father, who had gone from dirt-poor prospector to millionaire and friend of the international set in a matter of years. His pretty daughter and her convivial spouse had run through millions on their honeymoon, and there were still millions to spare. It was intoxicating.

Charlie's old friend Henry Flagler, a handsome elderly gentleman who had been his father's business partner and who attended the wedding, had started out as a merchant, gone on to make a fortune in the boom years of the Civil War, helped take over the emerging oil industry, and was now enjoying the fruits of his long life in a white marble palace in Florida—a state he had practically created.

Moira was fascinated by these success stories. There was something exotic and swashbuckling about them. These American millionaires had worked themselves up from nothing to become so flamboyantly rich. It wasn't like European wealth, which descended from generation to generation in the same, predictable way. No. Americans were bored with old-fashioned ideas and tired old habits. Their enterprises were free-

spirited and freewheeling, as exciting as the men who created them—
and Moira considered any man who created millions a wonder of the
world.

"Maeve," she declared proudly, "Charlie and I are going to put in
a suite for you here. What colors would you like?"

Maeve hesitated, startled. "Well, Mama," she said, "I probably
won't need a suite, since I'm going to keep the apartment. But thank
you. How nice of Charlie to think of me."

Moira reacted visibly to that double-talk, her beautiful blue eyes
darkening, indicating shock, disbelief, bewilderment, pain.

"Whatever do you mean? Of course you'll live with your mother!"

"I don't want to crowd you, Mama."

"Don't worry about it. Not in this place! We've space for hundreds."

Maeve knew Moira was not about to let go easily. It wasn't her
nature.

"Oh, Mama, I know it's a huge place. That's not what I meant.
You and Charlie are newlyweds. You need time to be alone."

That wasn't working either. Maeve knew that Moira was probably
thinking it would be considered unseemly for her, a young unmarried
girl, to be on her own—now that Moira was suddenly so terribly respectable.

"It's not proper," Moira declared firmly. "Especially for a girl in
your position. A decent young woman needs her mother to stand between
her and the fast company she must keep in the theater. I've never failed
you before and I certainly don't intend to now!"

Fast company! As if anybody in the theater were comparable to
André Viznitski! Moira was apparently given to astonishing lapses of
memory these days. Had marriage turned her brain to mush? Or was
she creating a new persona as a virtuous wife and mother? That would
take some doing.

"Mama," she protested, "have them decorate a suite of rooms for
me in blue and gold if you wish, but I'm keeping the apartment."

Moira glared. "I'm hurt, Maeveen, well and truly hurt. Charlie
will be too. We want to offer you a grand home and you turn your back
on us. It's very upsetting." She paused and added with a touch of venom,
"When you marry and have children, I hope yours treat you in the same,
high-handed fashion one day—just so you learn what a mother's broken
heart feels like."

Well, thought Maeve, that was the bloody limit! All we need now
are the violins, she decided, turning pink with indignation.

Somehow she wasn't surprised by Moira's next question.

"Is this all because of the von Reuter boy? Is that the reason you've become so wayward and intractable?" Moira demanded sternly. "Have you been sleeping with him?"

That infuriated Maeve to such an extent she leaped to her feet, swirled around in a whoosh of silk petticoats, and informed her parent she was late for a rehearsal. If Moira weren't her mother Maeve would have slapped her for that. What a lot of bloody nerve! And from her, of all people!

"It's not a bad idea, Maeveen!" Moira called after her, making her even angrier. "You could do a lot worse. He's rich—"

"Damn it!" Maeve shouted back. "Is that the only thing that counts with you?"

"That's the only thing that counts with any sensible woman. And you'd better learn to accept it before it's too late!"

Pausing in her flight down the winding marble and wrought-iron staircase, Maeve stamped her foot and flung back at her mother, "Well, I don't accept it! I'll never accept it! I love Dietrich but I'll be damned if I'll ever be his mistress! It's Baroness von Reuter or nothing!"

Well, Moira reflected as she watched Maeve spin around and continue at top speed down the stairs, cross the marble foyer, and vanish out the ornate front door, at least she wasn't totally daft. If she was thinking of marrying the boy, at least she showed some residual good sense there. She might even be right to keep him at arm's length. Dietrich had a peculiar romantic temperament. A man like that didn't want a woman to be too willing. He'd worry about the competition. He'd make her life miserable questioning her about her past.

Smiling as she stood there thinking about Maeve and Dietrich, Moira felt pleased. Despite all the rumors surrounding him, she wasn't at all put off by the idea of a Baron von Reuter for a son-in-law. It would be a devastating blow for Hubertus. And it could only enhance her social standing: Mrs. Charles Lassiter, mother-in-law of the baron.

Good for you, Maeveen, she thought cheerfully. For once you're on the right track. Now just don't do anything to spoil it. You might never get a second chance.

CHAPTER 16

T he concert for the Russian Red Cross took place at the Théâtre du Châtelet in the presence of the French foreign minister, members of the beau monde, and an audience of well-dressed Russophiles who could afford the high price of tickets.

Le Figaro, which was regularly given infusions of Russian money by the Russian secret police, ran a full-page advertisement, extolling the artists who were graciously donating time and talent.

Enrico Caruso, fresh from his extravagant New York success, was given top billing, and Maeve was listed after Emma Calvé but before Mary Garden, which delighted her and made Mary scream. Marc Antoine was appearing too, singing an aria from *La Traviata* and a duet from the same opera with Maeve. He was fond of Russian countesses, he recalled, remembering all those adorable ladies in St. Petersburg. This was the least he could do.

To Maeve's annoyance, Moira and Charlie did not attend, although Charlie made a generous gift of three thousand francs to the Grand Duchess Militza for supplies for the wounded. He had been in the Spanish-American War and he knew what combat was.

After the concert, Maeve was invited several times to tea at Militza's Paris residence, where she met a strange assortment of psychics, faith healers, and fortune-tellers who were earnestly devoting themselves to the terrible problem of the hour. The Russo-Japanese War was not on the agenda—the problem was Stana's marriage, or more accurately its wreckage.

*

Since their stormy farewell on Nevsky Prospect, Maeve had learned that Sean had gone to the Far East as an observer, had been wounded in some remote part of Manchuria, and had been recalled to St. Petersburg, where he was nursed back to health by his new bride. This all came courtesy of Her Highness, the soon to be ex–Duchess of Leuchtenberg. And now he was in Paris on family business.

He was also anxious to see Maeve. And Moira.

To Maeve's annoyance, her mother was not at all opposed to the idea.

"But Mama," she protested, "how can you?"

Moira snapped back, "I can because I want to! I want Sean Farrell to see that I live in as grand a place as that tart of a gräfin!"

"You want to gloat."

"I want to enjoy my triumph."

"Well, you're one up on the gräfin, Mama. She's recently become a widow."

"My condolences to her," Moira replied, looking pleased.

Geraldine had wounded Moira's pride in Berlin on their return from Belgrade when she had done nothing to help them. At that point, fearful for the future, alone, and faced with supporting a daughter in foreign countries, Moira would have been grateful for her help. Instead, she had been forced to fend for herself as best she could. And she had ended up with André Viznitski.

Even with Charlie beside her, Moira still felt threatened by the mere thought of Count Viznitski. Her affair with him had been the nadir of her whole existence, a monumental error in judgment that had very nearly destroyed her—just when she thought she was finding her way.

Viznitski had forced her to risk her life through sheer callousness, then abandoned her to die by herself in that clinic—while he left town, the bastard! And the memory of that evil night returned frequently, far too frequently, leaving her shaken and terrified in the dark, her heart pounding, her arms thrashing the air—frantically trying to escape from a deathbed in a strange place, surrounded by frightening strangers.

If Geraldine had helped her in Berlin, none of that would ever have taken place. And she wouldn't be living in fear of Charlie finding out about that baby. The fact that Viznitski knew about the whole degrading mess and was vicious enough to reveal it to her new husband set her teeth on edge.

A little kindness from that bitch in Berlin could have prevented all of that.

*

Maeve's attitude had softened since she heard of Sean's being wounded in the Far East. Following the progress of the fighting through the newspapers, the girl was horrified at the suffering of the troops and by the plain incompetence of the high command.

French newspapers were printing fairly pro-Russian features, but even they were carrying stories of graft and corruption in the army that were enough to turn one's stomach. And the military tactics used by elderly Russian generals were not up to the standards set by the French-trained forces of the Japanese. Naval engagements were so one-sided that if the Tsar didn't do something soon, Japan would make the Pacific her very own lake.

*

Moira got her chance to flaunt her married splendor before Sean Farrell on the night Maeve sang her first Violetta at the Opéra-Comique.

Mrs. Lassiter was giving a huge party to celebrate the opening of her renovated mansion, and her guests were an eclectic mixture of rich Americans, international members of the sporty set, people from the arts, and even some French aristocrats, curious to see what the Americans had done to this venerable Parisian mansion. And Sean Farrell and his new wife.

Charlie and Moira had taken a whole parade of friends to see Maeve at the opera, and the resultant traffic jam of shiny new automobiles and sleek coaches had created quite a scene outside the theater.

Pedestrians stopped in their tracks to see Moira, dressed in a Paquin creation of palest pink silk trimmed with rows of exquisite Valenciennes lace and wearing her fabulous necklace of diamonds. This was set off by pale plumes of egret feathers in her black hair, held in place by diamond clips. They all stared at her as she descended from a brand-new Panhard automobile in a swish of silk and the glitter of diamonds and swept grandly into the foyer on Charlie's arm, looking like the patron saint of haute couture.

"*Ah, les beaux yeux,*" murmured someone in the crowd, almost overwhelmed by the splendor of Mrs. Lassiter and her entourage—all the women expensively gowned and loaded with jewels.

A few die-hard socialists shook their heads and muttered things about the jewelry on those painted parasites being able to feed a worker's family for years, but most of the onlookers merely blinked with amazement and wished they were wearing the same jewels.

It was a fine sight, they said. Very Parisian.

Once Violetta had expired in splendid voice in Alfredo's arms, Maeve and Marc Antoine took their curtain calls, received vast quantities of flowers, admitted their well-wishers backstage, changed clothes, and hurried off to Moira's party.

"This looks like the set for the first act," Marc Antoine whispered to Maeve as they entered the mansion, "only grander. My God! It's a real palace!"

"Charlie is rich," she whispered back. "Isn't it sumptuous?"

The tenor had been inside his share of palaces, but this one was truly dazzling. There was marble and gilding and magnificent painted ceilings wherever one glanced.

François Boucher had designed lavish pastoral scenes for the ceilings in the eighteenth century for an ancestor of the former owner, and Moira had liked them so much she had hired an expert from the Louvre to clean and restore them. Now they were glowing with life, revealing dozens of scantily clad shepherdesses being pursued across some idyllic Acadian landscape by a cluster of pink-cheeked cupids.

Below Boucher's extravaganza a swirl of partygoers in white tie and couture gowns, reflected in the huge gilded mirrors, floated through the marble columns and swept past bowers of flowers as musicians from the Paris Opéra played airs from Verdi and Puccini, the hostess's favorites.

When Maeve entered the reception room, she and Marc Antoine were announced by a gold-braided butler whose voice boomed out "Mademoiselle Maeve Devereux and Monsieur Marc Antoine de Marigny" loud enough to be heard in the suburbs. The guests, who were waiting impatiently for the star of the evening, turned in her direction and applauded delightedly, sweeping Maeve and her partner into the room on a cloud of approval.

Moira embraced her daughter in a shimmer of silk and laughed with her as, in the emotion of the moment, they got entangled. Marc Antoine very gently had to pry Moira's diamond bracelet loose from the lace cascading over Maeve's gown.

"*Voilà*, madame," he smiled, kissing her hand. "You won't have to be a Siamese twin tonight."

Sean Farrell was standing to the side, deep in discussion with a

French diplomat, when Maeve appeared in her cream-colored satin gown with a lace-drenched train and exquisite diamond ornaments in her up-swept auburn hair. She was even prettier now than she had been as Violetta. The tenor, he noticed, was preening like a peacock—probably his natural state.

Maeve seemed to float on a cloud of high spirits, soft light, and perfume. She was gracious, charming, delighted to be so admired and delightful to see. He remembered seeing her onstage at the Maryinsky, enchanting as the Tsarevich. And on the Nevsky Prospect that after-noon—furious, melodramatic, and still the prettiest girl on the boule-vard.

Later, when he had a chance to speak to her as they strolled in the lantern-lit gardens in the soft summer air, he congratulated her on her latest triumph and expressed his regrets for missing her Carmen in Moscow. Several months separation had restored her natural warmth, he was glad to observe.

Maeve smiled and half covered her face with her magnificent fan of peacock plumes. "I regretted that too," she admitted. "And I was a silly idiot that day on the Nevsky Prospect. I really do regret my hasty departure. I don't know what got into me."

Sean laughed. "After that, I was dying to see you in the opera. I couldn't imagine how your Carmen at the Bolshoi could be more pas-sionate than that little wildcat on the Nevsky. The Moscow audiences must have loved you."

Maeve laughed. "They did! I took twenty-one curtain calls that night. The governor-general sent me a huge basket of orchids and said I must come to Moscow again and give a recital at his residence."

Sean's expression turned grim. "Don't do that," he said quickly. "Don't ever go near Grand Duke Sergei. You can't imagine how vile he is."

Maeve was touched by his concern. She had already heard lurid tales about the grand duke; Sean's reaction made her realize they were not without foundation. She made a mental note to cross Sergei off her list of acceptable admirers.

Maeve fanned herself lightly with her peacock plumes—the fan Dietrich had given her as a good luck token for her first recital. She was attached to it and looked upon it as a sort of charm. "I was very sorry to learn you had been wounded," she said, changing the subject from dreadful grand dukes. "That put everything into perspective. I imagine your wife was frantic when she heard."

Sean glanced at her. "Yes," he nodded. "At that point Zofia was convinced she was about to lose me even before the wedding. We were married after I returned from the Far East."

"In St. Petersburg?"

"Oh no. In Cetinje," he replied. "My father insisted upon it. It was a national holiday. We received delegations from all over the country. Really, it was very touching."

Sean related this as if it were nothing out of the ordinary. It was almost like that day in Berlin when he told her his father was a prince of some far-off mountain country on the fringes of Europe. Very matter-of-fact. He was all the more charming for his lack of affectation, Maeve thought. And still the most handsome man she had ever seen. Well, Dietrich was very handsome too, perhaps even more handsome in some ways, but Sean was more exotic, which gave him that quality of a so-phisticated bandit she found so exciting. This beautiful man in flawless evening clothes had plotted a prison escape right under the noses of a well-armed enemy and had carried her and Moira out of Africa to a life she had only dreamed of. To the day she died, she would love him for that.

Maeve smiled into his beautiful blue eyes. "One day I would like to see Montenegro," she said. "Do they have an opera house there?"

"Good Lord, no!" He laughed. "We barely have a palace. Papa's palace is a fine two-story brick building with a balcony that any French banker would reject as not grand enough. We're very simple there. Any Montenegrin who saw this mansion would think the Tsar in St. Peters-burg must live in it."

"Is Montenegro that . . . plain?"

Sean laughed again. "The word is 'primitive.' We've spent our history fighting like hell against the Turks. We like to think of ourselves as the finest flower of Serbdom, preserved in our mountains after the lesser Serbs were defeated by the Turks at the Battle of Kossovo. This is our heritage and our honor."

Maeve thought about that. "And when did the Battle of Kossovo take place?" she inquired, thinking of recent history in the Balkans.

"In 1389," he replied.

"And they still talk about it?"

"They still live it. It's in the hearts and minds of every Serb in the world. And we Montenegrins are Serbs."

"They have long memories," she murmured in amazement.

"So do the Irish," he replied. "Who was Cromwell?"

"A bloody, murdering savage," Maeve replied without missing a beat.

"Well, then. Now I hope you understand."

Maeve smiled. "I've noticed that Montenegro exports her children."

Sean nodded. "Yes. My sisters have married well."

"And you don't spend much time in Montenegro either."

"Right again. I'm an auxiliary to diplomacy. As an unofficial but well-informed observer, I can often be useful to the Prince in ways an accredited diplomat could not. There are rules in official diplomacy that don't apply to the unofficial variety."

"Belgrade was unofficial, I take it."

"Belgrade"—he grinned—"was top secret and highly unofficial."

Maeve's large blue eyes widened a little as she looked at this handsome, black-haired Irishman who could be so strangely exotic.

"I think Colonel Apis was not your friend, no matter what he told you," she said, reflecting on their Balkan adventure.

"I think Colonel Apis tried to kill me," Sean replied. "I also think he would have killed you and Moira if he had been able."

He took her hand in its soft white kid glove and lightly kissed it. "Never, ever go to Belgrade," he warned. "Not that those maniacs will ever turn into opera lovers." He smiled. "But just stay away. It's a dangerous place."

"But you just told me Montenegrins and Serbians are all Serbs together. Surely it wouldn't be dangerous for *you*."

His eyes lit up with amusement. "My dear girl, there are Serbs and there are Serbs, just as there are Irish and Irish. It doesn't make us one big happy family."

"What *does* it make you, Sean?" she asked uncertainly, puzzled by Balkan politics.

He smiled again, with a wicked gleam in his eye. "It often makes us enemies," he answered.

Suddenly there was a burst of laughter from a group across the room and Maeve turned to see what was happening. She noticed Moira and another woman surrounded by a crowd of guests, all of them looking expectantly at their hostess, who was even more animated than usual. The other woman, a tall brunette beauty in a dazzling Worth gown of cream sewn with gold beads, appeared to be much younger and rather provocative. A complete stranger to Maeve, she seemed very much at ease. So did Moira, but to Maeve, who knew her mother's expression, that was deceptive. Moira was seething with hostility.

"Who is that girl?" she whispered to Sean, who appeared slightly uneasy all of a sudden.

"My wife," he replied. "And I think I'd better join her."

As Sean escorted Maeve to where the two ladies were standing, he gave Zofia a cool look, and saw her eyes sparkle with malice. Moira looked as if she was trying very hard to refrain from slapping her.

"Ivan," Zofia purred, slipping her arm through his, "Mrs. Lassiter and I were having a wonderful discussion. She claims she knew you before I did. Just how close were you?"

With Charlie Lassiter edging his way toward the circle of people who were hanging on to every word, Sean kissed Moira's hand and smiled.

"We were close enough for me to be in the rescue party that freed Mrs. Lassiter and her daughter from a British concentration camp in South Africa—and for them to save my life. I would say that's almost a blood tie, wouldn't you, my dear?"

Maeve's sharp eyes never left Zofia's face. She saw Zofia exhibit the merest glimmer of amusement as she gave her husband the point. The rest of the onlookers glanced at Moira in amazement and murmured appreciatively as she smiled with becoming modesty, her diamonds flashing eloquently.

"Madame, you are a genuine heroine," declared a gushy French count.

"So is Mademoiselle Devereux," Sean added hastily. "In fact she fired the bullet that did it." Why leave out the best part?

Moira and Zofia both turned to fix Maeve with tight little smiles, the one hating to share the credit, the other appraising a possible rival. The crowd clamored for more champagne and Charlie proposed a toast, which everyone thought a fine idea.

But it was clear to Maeve and even clearer to Sean that a declaration of war had been tendered under the glittering chandeliers of Moira Lassiter's ballroom, and it was going to be a long campaign.

*

Dietrich had been busy while the action was going on in the Far East, meeting with other European bankers and with representatives of the Japanese foreign ministry. His discussions had taken him to various European cities and even to New York, which he found stimulating.

The Americans had the German love of expansion, he told Maeve. He found them congenial enough. But their food was dreadful. Primitive, he shuddered.

"Poor Dietrich," she commiserated. "Didn't you find anyplace where you could enjoy a good meal?"

He thought hard. Then he nodded emphatically. "Yes, there was a good German restaurant called Luchow's. Wonderful place."

Maeve smiled. Did she really expect him to like anything else?

Dietrich reflected. "It's very popular with theatrical people," he added. "Victor Herbert's orchestra plays there. I spotted several well-known New York personalities having dinner on the night I dined there. It's all the rage."

"Well," said Maeve, "if I ever get to New York, I must eat there. Did I tell you that Fred Gaisberg asked me to make a recording for Victor Records?"

"That's wonderful!" Dietrich exclaimed. "When?"

"Next week. They'll set up the recording session in his suite at the Ritz. Mama will come with me to see what's going on, and I will sing several arias into a metal cone. It all sounds quite odd, but Caruso convinced me it was worth the effort. In fact," she added with a laugh, "Gaisberg got him to work on me at the time of the Red Cross concert."

"Well, that's splendid. That could mean an appearance in New York in a few months."

Maeve rolled her lovely blue eyes toward heaven. "It's a possibility," she said. "But certainly not this year. I'm to appear at the Maryinsky in December and January."

To her surprise, Dietrich said emphatically, "No!"

They were having a pleasant lunch in the dining room of a large and elegant hotel, surrounded by a clientele that included several cabinet ministers, a cluster of international aristocrats, and the French actors Lucien and Sacha Guitry. Several diners glanced in their direction after Dietrich's outburst.

"Don't make a scene," Maeve hissed, making the large ostrich plumes on her hat bob.

"Maeve," he said brusquely, "that is idiotic!" The color had drained from his handsome face, leaving a ghastly pallor. "Don't you ever read the newspapers?" he demanded. "They've had nothing but strikes and riots in Russia lately. The people are fed up with this damned war. Nicholas the Second is holed up in one of his suburban palaces and doesn't dare to venture into his own capital. His finance minister was blown up on the streets. Of course you're not going to St. Petersburg! I won't allow it!"

Maeve's blue eyes turned icy. "What?" she demanded in a tone so shrill it went clear through the entire dining room. Several diners turned around again. Two waiters looked nervous.

Dietrich's gaze was even icier. "I repeat what I just said. You will stay out of Russia until the trouble dies down. It's too dangerous for you."

At that, Maeve's expression softened. "You're very sweet to worry," she said. "You do have a kind heart."

"For heaven's sake! I love you. I want to marry you," he said fiercely, but quietly. "This isn't kindness. It's fear for you among those savages. *Liebchen*," he went on, "I'm a free man at last. You have always been so dear to me. And I know you return my feelings..."

At this point, Maeve's long lashes fluttered a bit from emotion as she nodded, encouraging Dietrich.

"It's true," she said softly. "Ever since those days in Berlin when you used to take me sleighing and Mama thought you were such a danger. I think I loved you from the moment you handed me that beautiful bouquet of white roses, two minutes after I arrived in Germany..."

"Then say you'll marry me," he prompted. "I love you dearly. If I didn't I would never have involved myself in that revolting divorce. I would have stayed married to that woman and taken a succession of mistresses," he said bitterly. "What I did, I did for you."

Maeve knew it was true and she felt utterly miserable because of it. She loved Dietrich, but she was uneasy to find herself the cause of such upheaval. It was not the way things ought to be. And yet was anything the way it ought to be? she wondered.

"Yes, I know it," she agreed. "It made me feel dreadful, knowing that I had caused all that unhappiness to poor Lotte, to you, to your families—"

"It was my father's doing," he said abruptly. "The blame is all his, not yours. I was the victim of a dreadful conspiracy. So were you," he added, recalling the night of Maeve's recital at the von Ebert mansion. "He tried to ruin my life. He must take the responsibility for it."

"Dietrich," she said tenderly, looking so beautiful in her blue silk afternoon frock and picture hat trimmed with ostrich plumes, "don't be so hateful toward him. I know it's hard, but you mustn't let it warp your emotions. You frighten me sometimes when you speak so hatefully. God knows Mama has given me some bad moments, but I allow for it. We sometimes fight, but I do love her very much..."

"Your mother is at least human," he replied. "My father left his humanity at the door when he became the head of the Von Reuter Bank. I don't want to do the same."

"You won't." She smiled. "I think you love life too much."

"I love you too much," he murmured, reaching for her hand. "Tell me you'll say yes."

At that, Maeve turned her face away, making Dietrich despair.

"Don't rush things," she said at last. "I do love you. But I'm not ready to marry. I want to do other things. I wouldn't be a good wife for you if my mind was on those things when it ought to be on you."

There was an awkward stone-cold silence. Maeve had never seen him look so hurt. She bit her lip and stared down at her hands, sorry to have hurt him so badly and unable to make him feel better.

"I love you and I don't understand you at all," he said at last. "You tell me you love me. Then in the next breath you say you can't marry me. Is this a game? What kind of woman treats a man like this?"

That question made Maeve so angry she flung her napkin down on the table and nearly rose from her seat. Two waiters came rushing up to assist her, then backed off awkwardly as she changed her mind and decided to stay put. Dietrich looked exasperated and flushed a deep shade of pink. This looked like the beginning of a scene.

"Dietrich," she said sharply, keeping her voice to a whisper, "I'm not Mama. She's decided to make a career out of keeping Charlie happy. Good for her. She'll be well rewarded for it. My career is different. I love it when I create a character onstage and make the audience care for her. I love it when they applaud and throw flowers and shout for me when I take curtain calls. It's like two or three glasses of the best champagne in the world—all at once! It makes me dizzy with excitement when they love me so much that they keep calling me back. I don't intend to give it up—or curtail my performances for anyone." She was flushed with emotion.

"That's what you're afraid of?" he exclaimed. "But that's foolish. I adore seeing you onstage. I'll do everything possible to help you succeed."

"Then don't tell me not to go to Russia," she replied, looking him directly in the eye. "If I must, I will."

Dietrich's light blue eyes looked for a second like an animal's.

"Do what you wish," he said quietly. But those eyes were full of fury.

*

By December 1904, Maeve had finished her season with the Opéra-Comique, had made a series of guest appearances in Berlin, Warsaw, and Vienna, and had received her first poor reviews since Monte Carlo. This rattled her, all the more so since it happened in Berlin, a city which held a sentimental place in her heart. She wasn't used to unkind words, and these were a nasty shock.

"Mademoiselle Devereux appeared as a rather distracted Juliette in Gounod's *Roméo et Juliette* last evening at the Theater des Westens," she translated from the newspaper to Arlette the morning after the disaster, "and the audience seemed to wonder why the French think so highly of her. She makes one long for Farrar, whose mastery of the role is sublime."

Maeve's cheeks were bright red with agitation. The newspaper was trembling in her hands as if she were reading in a stiff breeze. *"Merde!"*

"Oh, the swine!" Arlette exclaimed. "Don't listen to that rubbish, mademoiselle! Farrar is their favorite because she is under contract to the Royal Opera and the Kaiser loves her. So all the *boches* follow their leader."

Maeve loved Arlette for her loyalty. At times like these she appreciated her unshakable opinion that Mademoiselle Devereux was the best— and if anyone didn't agree with that, he could take a flying leap at himself.

Of course, she had to admit, Arlette was just a wee bit partisan.

"Farrar is a wonderful singer," Maeve conceded. "I've heard her and I find her much more appealing than—Mary Garden, for example."

Mary Garden was their favorite bête noire. Ever since the uproar over *Louise* at the Opéra-Comique, all she had to do was mention Mary Garden and Arlette's eyes would roll in her head, indicating sheer horror. Mary Garden was right after the Kaiser in Arlette's opinion.

"The *boches* are terribly prejudiced, mademoiselle. Farrar may be a fine singer but she's practically one of their own, so of course they would prefer her to anyone else. Especially someone from France," she added significantly.

"My throat was scratchy," Maeve reflected. "Caruso, my Neapolitan friend, always warned me to take good care of it, and I've been foolish lately. Now I'm paying for it. My top notes were shrill and reedy."

"Oh no!"

"Yes." Maeve nodded grimly. "I'm surprised the review wasn't worse."

It was awful to read a bad review. The shame of it mortified her— especially since it had appeared in Berlin's most widely read daily. Baron von Reuter might read it! Gräfin Geraldine might read it!

And they would sit back and gleefully lick their chops, assuring themselves that the presumptuous little nobody had got what she deserved.

The failure in *Roméo et Juliette* brought Maeve up short and made her wonder if she was merely deceiving herself. Perhaps Julien Roussel had been right. Perhaps Mary Garden had been right. Oh Lord! How revolting—to be a trained poodle at heart instead of a real singer!

"I *have* sounded much better, haven't I?" Maeve asked plaintively, looking crushed.

Arlette made an expressive gesture of commiseration. "Perhaps it was because of the sore throat, mademoiselle. You weren't quite yourself."

"Ah! I knew it!" Maeve wailed. My God, she must have been truly dreadful for Arlette to even hint at a fault. She was lost.

"It wasn't *that* apparent," the girl hastened to add. "Nobody should have noticed it. I'm so familiar with the sound of your voice that I was able to detect a little something different. But the *boches* shouldn't have. It was all dirty prejudice on their part," she insisted.

"My top notes were horrendous," Maeve said, as if she were atoning for a series of mortal sins.

"It was nothing to worry about, mademoiselle! Although," Arlette added, "I think you really ought to listen to Monsieur von Reuter. He always has sensible ideas about your health."

"Ha!" Maeve huffed. "He'd love to wrap me in cotton wool."

The dark-haired French girl smiled. "No, mademoiselle," she replied in amusement. "I think he'd like to wrap you in sables. And I also think you ought to give him a chance to try!"

*

Dietrich was hopelessly in love. Maeve knew it and didn't understand why it frightened her. She was in love with him and had even told him she loved him—but she couldn't bring herself to act on it.

It was as if that would ruin everything she had so painfully gained and would tie her down, making her dependent, and she dreaded that. The terrible specter of Moira being kept by André Viznitski seemed to loom over her head—when her thoughts didn't stray uncomfortably back to Camp 3 and Sergeant Davies. If she put Dietrich out of his misery and set a wedding date, Maeve had a vague but overwhelming fear of seeing herself imprisoned in a silken cage.

Even the fact that Moira seemed pleased by the idea of her becoming Baroness von Reuter was off-putting. My God, what a wonderful judge of men *she* was! The first thing she did in Paris was to become Viznitski's mistress! That was past history now, thank God. But it had happened and it had nearly killed her. Well, Moira seemed to have struck it rich this time, Maeve reflected. Charlie Lassiter was, much to her surprise, a very fine man. And he seemed to have good sense as well as bags of money. Moira needed that, she thought with a sigh. She needed both those qualities.

Maeve was still rather unsure of just what *she* needed. She knew she wasn't the sort of woman who wanted to wrap herself up in a husband's title and tie him to her with a tribe of little barons. Well, Dietrich didn't seem to want that either—or else he would have been content with Lotte. But would he really give her the support she needed to maintain a career that required a great deal of travel as well as constant concern over her voice, her health, and her physical well-being?

If she wanted a great international career, the diva would have to come first, not the baron. Would any man really put up with that? From what she knew about men, she wasn't about to put any money on it.

It was a peculiar thing about men that they took it for granted that a woman would sacrifice herself for them, follow them around like an adoring cocker spaniel, and be content to bask in their reflected glory. Well, that wasn't in her nature, Maeve decided. She wasn't meant to be in the audience. She was meant for center stage, right up there with Marc Antoine or Caruso or Chaliapin. And her husband would have to get used to it. Dietrich accepted that now. But what about in the future?

Then there was Baron Hubertus. Did she really want to go through life as his daughter-in-law? That was a daunting thought. God Almighty! No, it wasn't an easy choice, as much as Maeve cared for Dietrich. And it was complicated by so many things besides Dietrich himself. So many important things.

Yet she adored the man. She could close her eyes and recall every detail of that scene at the Anhalter Station in Berlin the day she and her party of Boer refugees had arrived to be greeted by those cheering crowds. There was Dietrich, the most beautiful young man she had ever seen, waiting with a bouquet of white roses. Of course, it was only by default she had received them, but he had been the first young man ever to give her flowers for any reason, and for that it was memorable. . . .

She had fallen in love with that blond beauty right then and there in the softly falling Berlin snow—a penniless refugee from the back of beyond and a fellow who looked like a prince.

A prince, Maeve thought with a dreamy smile. Well, she knew someone who really was a prince, even though he didn't have the title. Sean Farrell. And it wasn't even his good looks that came to mind whenever Maeve thought of him—it was that quality the French call *panache:* dash, spirit. Seeing Sean was an incitement to rebellion or to mad adventure, all the more so since he was clearly out of bounds for her.

She could accept that after having met his sisters. They were like characters from some fairy tale, surrounded by soothsayers, ladies-in-waiting, and strange customs. He had once told her the life of a princess was dreadful. After getting a glimpse of it, she was ready to admit he could have been right. They really were not like anyone else, and she had no wish to trade places with them. Still . . .

Besides, with his marriage he was now forever beyond her reach. There was romantic daydreaming, and there was common sense and plain decency, Maeve reminded herself sharply—almost as if she knew she had to stress the point for fear of straying, if only in her dreams. He had Zofia now; he wouldn't be thinking of anyone else.

Zofia. For a girl whose father was some sort of tribal chieftain, she looked quite a sophisticated lady. That gown and those jewels were worn with a sense of style not often associated with little nobodies from the backwoods. The girl had been educated in St. Petersburg and it showed, Maeve had to admit. There was the tinkle of gold rubles about her and the soft, bewitching feel of lush sable. The fact that she was a trouble-making bitch didn't detract from her dark good looks—unfortunately.

Maeve's one comforting thought about Zofia was her lifelong sentence to have Geraldine, Gräfin von Kleist, as her mother-in-law. Those two probably deserved each other—and if Geraldine ever thought the Montenegrin girl was causing Sean a moment's unhappiness, she'd make her life a living hell. That one was born to cause trouble!

It would be as dreadful as having old Hubertus as a father-in-law, Maeve decided with satisfaction.

"If only he could be removed from the picture," she had once told Dietrich only half in jest, "I'd marry you tomorrow."

But she hadn't been born that lucky.

CHAPTER 17

*D*ietrich was meeting with his father and some other bankers in Berlin when Maeve boarded the Nord Express in Paris for her trip to St. Petersburg. Hubertus was delighted with his son's connections and pleased to be receiving visits from emissaries of the Mikado, who were discussing the possibility of concessions to their European partners and dangling the tempting offer of a German-Japanese joint venture before Hubertus. The baron could almost envision a Von Reuter Bank rising in Tokyo.

It was a different matter entirely when Dietrich tried to broach the subject of a second marriage. If it concerned "that singer," Hubertus didn't want to hear a word of it. No more scandals, he insisted. They must find a decent girl he could love.

"I've found her, damn it!" Dietrich shouted at dinner one night. "And I tell you, she's going to be my wife!"

"Over my dead body," the baron retorted, looking glacial. "If you do this, I'll disinherit you, Dietrich. I'm telling you I'm fed up with your stupidity. You ran around like a satyr after that Belgian tart. Fine. Every young fellow has to sow his wild oats. This time, you will behave!" Hubertus roared, pounding his fist on the table. "Playtime is over for you!" His face twitched with the force of his fury.

Dietrich's face was pale with alarming red blotches now, a sure sign of strain. Hubertus had dismissed the servants as he and his son faced each other across the elegantly set table.

"Listen to me," the baron said angrily, "I'm stuck with you because you're my only son, but I don't have to leave you my fortune. I can give it to charity if I choose. And the way I feel right now, I'm considering it." A spasm in his chest hit him hard as he said this, making him stiffen suddenly. Then it passed as quickly as it had come.

The look of shock on his son's face let him know that the balance had shifted since their last confrontation, in Paris. Then Hubertus had been in such a state of bewilderment he hadn't been able to think clearly. Now he was himself again. And this time *he* was the one who didn't give a damn.

"I'm sorry you feel this way, Father. It pains me." That was a lie. Dietrich didn't care how Hubertus felt. But he was going to win this, no matter the price.

Hubertus rose and walked to where his son was seated. He put his arm around him in an unusual paternal gesture and patted his shoulder.

"It doesn't have to be this way, my boy. All I'm asking is a bit of common sense from you. You're not going to throw your life away for some little singer, are you? It's mad." He was forcing himself to be calm now, but at tremendous cost. He could feel the pain again, worse this time.

Dietrich suddenly noticed the strain in his father's face. There was a visible spasm of some sort. Breathing heavily now, the baron sank down on the chair next to Dietrich's and reached unsteadily for the bell to summon the servants.

"What is it, Father?"

"Chest pains. Don't be alarmed, my boy," he muttered. "It's nothing. I have medication for this."

As the butler entered the room, he saw the baron's condition, called for someone to fetch his pills, and tried to make him as comfortable as possible.

"Has this happened before?" Dietrich demanded later as he questioned his father's valet. "It's shocking to see him like this." The old bastard. He had hidden this from him. It was a secret, a carefully guarded secret at that!

"Baron von Reuter has been under a doctor's care for over a year." The man wanted to add, "Because of his wretched lout of a son," but he refrained. It didn't matter. Dietrich could almost read his mind.

"And does the doctor think it's serious?" Dietrich tried to sound concerned, like a dutiful Prussian son, but it rang false. He merely sounded hopeful.

"Serious enough, sir. He has to keep his medication handy at all times."

"Ach," murmured the son, "I really had no idea. How distressing." So the old man had a human frailty after all. He was no longer the invincible tyrant he once was. He had a weakness. He was vulnerable!

The valet looked Dietrich boldly in the eye and said, "Baron von Reuter needs absolute calm. When he is agitated he's very susceptible to these attacks. We must all try to make his life as peaceful as possible."

"I quite understand." Dietrich nodded thoughtfully. "I will, of course, try to ease my father's work load as much as possible in the future. It's the least I can do."

"I'm sure, sir," the servant replied, in a tone Dietrich found annoyingly ironic.

*

Maeve's journey to St. Petersburg had been enlivened by Sean's traveling on the same train with his wife, niece, and nephew. Nothing unusual about a family group taking a trip—but he had snatched the youngsters from their Paris home and smuggled them onto the Nord Express in two large Louis Vuitton trunks.

Once the train had crossed several borders and had arrived at the Warsaw station, the Duchess of Leuchtenberg boarded a private car that had been attached to the train and was reunited with her children. Maeve found the whole episode highly emotional and very satisfying. Sean always had been good at freeing people from prison!

The two children were obviously relieved to be returned to their mother's care. They were a bit bewildered by the whole thing, but glad to be free of their father, who had taken them from their divorcing mother.

It had taken a bit of doing. Sean had bribed the servants and on the night of the escape, Zofia entered the duke's mansion disguised as a nursemaid and, with Kyril and Sean waiting outside, succeeded in lowering the children out a ground-floor window and climbing out after them. The party was halfway across France before anyone even noticed their disappearance. By the time the runaways had arrived in Warsaw for their rendezvous with Stana, an article had appeared in *Le Figaro*, and the Quai d'Orsay was in an uproar over the embarrassing affair. The duke was in a rage.

Zofia, Maeve noticed, seemed to be in her element as a daring plotter and heroine of a real-life coup de theatre. She certainly had the nerve of a bandit, and Sean was delighted with her part in the whole affair.

Well, Maeve reflected after hearing the whole story, at least he hadn't married a Lotte. Zofia might be irritating, but she was no shrinking violet. And Maeve was embarrassed to find herself still jealous.

*

The St. Petersburg Maeve returned to was a far cry from the glittering capital she had seen the year before. Now it seemed oppressive and menacing, as grim as the icy blasts howling in from the Gulf of Finland. Pedestrians scurried down the wide boulevards like frightened sparrows, raked by the bitter winds and the sleet. Even the weather was depressing.

Soldiers on patrol now were different from the glamorous figures of last year. These men were either on their way to the Far East and the war or on the alert for trouble in the streets. After the assassination of the minister of finance on the Nevsky in broad daylight last summer, no government official was without his military escort. The soldiers suddenly bided their time as they patrolled the broad streets, waiting to go into action at a moment's notice—against the citizens.

"This is a frightening place, mademoiselle," Arlette whispered one afternoon as she and Maeve were returning to their hotel after a rehearsal. The sleigh in which they were traveling was being held up in traffic, along with a dozen others, while the police—backed up by cossacks— were checking the identities of the occupants.

"There's been trouble, miss," her driver informed her. "Terrorists again. The police are looking for them."

Shivering inside her chinchilla coat, Maeve pulled her collar higher and pushed her gloved hands deeper into her fur muff. The cold was making her shudder uncontrollably, nearly making her sick.

Watching the soldiers, she recoiled, remembering other soldiers in another place. The shouting, the rudeness, the brutal raw power, made her think for an instant she was back home in South Africa.

Don't be an idiot, she told herself. You're not there any longer. They aren't interested in you. Do you hear English? No. They won't bother a foreigner. They only treat their own like dirt here.

All the same she found it hard to control her trembling as an officer roughly pulled back the mesh netting from the sleigh to have a better view of the women. His cold face looked ugly. Brutal. Nasty fellow, she thought as he glanced quickly at her and Arlette, saw nothing to interest him, and walked on to the next sleigh.

It was several hours before Maeve found out what all the fuss was about. A bomb had gone off several blocks down the street and had narrowly escaped killing a general and his escort on their way to army headquarters.

"What a country," muttered Arlette.

For the first time, Maeve realized this foolish Japanese war was no longer confined to the Far East. It was being waged right in the heart of the Tsar's empire, on the very streets of his capital.

Dietrich had been right, she thought with a shudder as she looked out onto St. Isaac's Square from the window of her hotel suite, the same one as last year. Only now the citizens who gathered in the great square were no longer so carefree and keen on a great foreign adventure. They were worn down by humiliating defeats, hostile to the war, and ready to put an end to the madness at any price.

"I can't wait until my final performance," Maeve confided to her maid. "This place frightens me now. It's filled with such hatred it reminds me of the war in South Africa."

And if she hadn't been ashamed to look like a coward, she would have informed Prince Teliakovsky, the director of the Maryinsky, that she was leaving. It was only her reluctance to break her contract that was keeping her in St. Petersburg now.

Chaliapin was in a state of high excitement all through December, telling her his friends among the left were expecting a revolution that would rid Russia of her Tsar and all the rest of the Romanovs forever.

"It will be a fine thing, Masha," he declared, his light blue eyes glowing. "We'll be free of those bloodsuckers at last. We'll have a fresh start."

But from what Maeve could see of the increased military activity, the Romanovs were not to be dislodged so easily.

CHAPTER 18

New Year's Day came in drearily, as if it hadn't quite recovered from the halfhearted parties of the previous night. If the first of the year was any indication of what was to follow, then 1905 was not going to be a glorious example of peace, cheer, and goodwill.

The Tsar's annual New Year's Day reception at the Winter Palace was dismal as well, making veteran diplomats send home nervous reports on Nicholas's state of mind. The whole country seemed sunk in an atmosphere of unrelenting gloom. Memorial masses were being said in every church for the recent war dead, and the editorials of the *Novaya Vremya*, the capital's leading newspaper, were calling for a reevaluation of current government policy.

In the midst of all this despair, there was talk of a strike on the part of streetcar operators, almost guaranteeing chaos in the city. Life in St. Petersburg was becoming very turbulent.

Maeve's Russian had improved to the point where she understood most of the slang, and she often went shopping via streetcar so she could practice the language. The nobility spoke French and English, so the only way she could use her Russian was to mingle with ordinary people. The crowded Petersburg streetcars were wonderful places to do that.

Arlette thought she was mad to go among them, since the French girl suspected every other citizen of harboring a bomb under his coat. But there was no telling Mademoiselle anything. She was too stubborn for her own good. If she had any sense at all, both she and Arlette would be safe in Paris right now, not in the middle of God knows what foreign horror.

On the afternoon of Maeve's final performance at the Maryinsky, she was enjoying a pleasant luncheon at the elegant Medved Restaurant with Sean and Zofia when their waiter appeared and said there was a gentleman who was asking if he might join them. He was standing over there, explained the waiter, indicating a handsome, blond young man in a charcoal-gray Savile Row suit.

"Dietrich!" Maeve exclaimed. "Oh yes. Please!"

Sean was almost as glad to see von Reuter as Maeve was. He knew there was nobody more interested in a woman's safety than her lover, and if Dietrich wasn't that yet, then he was hoping to be. In any case, he would be extremely vigilant, and with all the rumors flying around, it wouldn't be long before everyone might need a protector.

Zofia was glad to see Dietrich too. The Russian capital was full of men like her brothers-in-law. She didn't like to think of this pretty girl fending for herself among all those predators. The German would keep them at a respectful distance. He was, she noticed, head over heels in love. It would be good for *her* if Maeve was so occupied.

*

That night Maeve sang a brilliant *Tosca*, even better than the first time at the Opéra-Comique, but there were empty seats in the theater despite her popularity. The box office reported a sold-out house, and she sighed, thinking of all those opera fans who were wasting their money tonight. The tickets were not refundable for any reason.

"It's all because of those rumors," Chaliapin had said as he sat with her in her dressing room before the performance. He wasn't singing this evening, but he had stopped by to see her in the role—and give her encouragement. She was, he noticed, very jumpy tonight.

Maeve appreciated his thoughtfulness. Iola and the children were at home in Moscow but Fedya was commuting between the two capitals these days. His wife was reporting all sorts of trouble in Moscow and pleading with him not to take part in any demonstrations for fear of running afoul of the police. They already considered him a "hooligan" and wouldn't hesitate to arrest him, she said. He must think of his children.

"Fedya," Maeve said as he finished fastening the gold cross around her neck, "do you think there will be a general uprising?"

Chaliapin centered the cross, his gift to her for her first Maryinsky

Tosca, and smiled at the effect. "This is so Italian, don't you think? The crucifix dangling above a pretty woman's décolletage. The flesh and the spirit nicely entwined."

"Fedya!"

The Russian smiled and kissed her playfully on the neck. "You look so lovely when you blush. It's not a common soprano trait."

"I'm not a common soprano." Maeve smiled back. "Now stop sidestepping and tell me—do you think there will be an uprising?"

He became serious. "An uprising? No. But I think there will be more demonstrations. I hear the factory workers are going to march to the Winter Palace tomorrow to present a petition to the Tsar. My servant told me the people are very excited about this. They actually believe they can make him listen to their problems. Poor things."

Maeve glanced up at her companion. "But Nicholas isn't there. Why doesn't anyone tell them they'd be wasting their time? He and his family are at Tsarskoye Selo. It's foolish."

Chaliapin sighed and raised his beautiful hands in a gesture of despair. "I don't know, Masha. Perhaps it's because there's no real communication between the throne and the rest of us. How is a factory worker to know the Tsar's schedule?"

Maeve thought the entire country was suffering from the same lack of organization. Life in St. Petersburg was becoming more precarious each day, with shortages in food and fuel and a steady overabundance of rumors. She was glad her season was over after this evening—for various reasons.

Dietrich wasn't able to attend her performance because he had some important business with somebody from the foreign ministry, but he had promised to fetch her after the show. Expecting him to be right on time—a nice Teutonic trait—Maeve had rejected Chaliapin's offer to escort her home and had sent him on his way to his friend Gorky's apartment, where he was probably going to stay up all night talking politics. To her bewilderment Dietrich was late. When he finally showed up, Maeve was greatly relieved.

As Maeve and Dietrich climbed into the sleigh that was waiting near the stage door, the driver gestured down the street. A few blocks away they saw a detachment of mounted cossacks making their way slowly toward them.

"Trouble tonight?" Maeve asked, settling into the seat beside Dietrich. She didn't protest as he pulled her close to him and wrapped the sleigh rug over their laps. The closer the better tonight.

Giving an expressive shrug, their driver chirruped to his horses and sped off, heading down the nearly deserted street for the Hotel Astoria halfway across town, where Dietrich was also staying.

"There's always trouble in this town lately," he replied. "The soldiers are worried about a big demonstration tomorrow. They're frightened by the people."

"Is the Tsar afraid of his people?"

The man guffawed. "The Tsar has no reason to be afraid. We love the Little Father. It's the Jews who are inciting the workers. Kick them out. All of them."

Dietrich murmured that the driver reminded him of his father. Maeve thought he was probably a member of the ultranationalist gang known as the Black Hundreds. These were reactionaries who loved their Tsar and hated Jews, blaming them for all of Russia's ills. Sean had told her about them. They were bad business, he had warned—and like dogs, they ran in packs. They were also the muscle behind most of the pogroms.

When Maeve and Dietrich reached the Astoria, they were startled to see more cossacks riding by, heading in the direction of the Winter Palace. Obviously, the regime had so little trust in its citizens that the government was taking every possible precaution to secure the palace, the General Staff Headquarters, and whatever else it deemed worthy of protection.

"Russia is a strange place," Maeve murmured, watching nervously as the cossacks, silent men in huge fur hats and long military greatcoats, rode by, lances held at the ready. For what? she wondered. "Sometimes it reminds me of home—during the war."

She and Dietrich got their keys and headed upstairs on the wrought-iron elevator. The lobby seemed unusually deserted to Maeve. It was well after midnight, but the Astoria's cosmopolitan guests were always coming and going at all hours. It was as if the tense mood outside was putting a damper on everyone this evening.

As Dietrich walked Maeve to her room, she slipped her fingers through his and lightly kissed him on the cheek. "I'm glad you came to Petersburg," she said, sighing, as she opened the door to her suite. "But why were you so late this evening after the opera?" she asked again.

"Troop movements. The damned soldiers had sealed off several main streets, and my driver and I were halted at four different checkpoints on the way to the theater. I don't know what they're expecting, but it's serious enough to disrupt traffic all over town. And I had a pass signed by the foreign minister himself," he added ruefully.

Maeve was distracted by heavy, muted sounds outside, unmistakably military sounds. She quickly entered the room and went to the window.

Suddenly she whirled around and gasped. "Look, Dietrich! That's an army out there!" Her heart was pounding now, fearful of what this might mean.

The young man went to her, and Maeve turned anxiously and nestled close to him, trembling as he put his arm around her. To Dietrich's surprise, he realized she wasn't wearing a corset. *That* was more unbelievable than the fact that half the Russian Army appeared to be passing before their hotel. Maeve always wore a corset; this was scandalous. He pressed gently against her, delighted to feel soft, warm flesh instead of hard steel ridges.

The girl clung to him, causing all sorts of havoc with his emotions. In Paris Dietrich had often spent hours plotting how to get Maeve alone and receptive to seduction. Now she was clinging to him like a lost child, frightened and looking to him for protection; he could scarcely take advantage of her. He also couldn't remain with her and keep his hands off her, he realized in embarrassment. My God, she had a lovely little body. Corseting something like that was a crime against nature, he thought as Maeve draped her arm around him, fascinated by the sight in the square below.

"Soldiers frighten me," she murmured. "In South Africa they took my father and hanged him. They put Mama and me in that dreadful jail."

"Shh," he whispered. "These soldiers won't harm you. But I'd advise you to stay indoors until the trouble passes. The word at the foreign ministry was 'Avoid the streets.'"

"My God," she said, her eyes growing wide as she watched them, "what are they afraid of? This doesn't make sense."

Dietrich sighed, gently nuzzling her cheek. Maeve smelled delicious, like summer flowers.

"They're afraid of a revolution," he said.

That was Chaliapin's hope, Maeve thought; Fedya was always praying for one. What if he was about to have his prayers answered?

Maeve had certainly heard gunfire in her life. She had shot game as a girl, she had even shot a human predator, but she found the muffled thud of horses' hooves out there far more threatening than any rifle shots. These mounted soldiers were terrifying in their slow, deliberate cadence. Riding in a nearly endless column, they had a frightening inevitability, as if they were harbingers of certain death.

"Dietrich," she whispered, burying her face in his shirt, "don't leave me. I can't bear to be alone here. I'm too frightened."

He tenderly stroked her hair as she nestled closer to him. "I don't ever want to leave you," he replied. "You should know that by now."

Maeve believed him. And although she felt a cold shudder of fear and excitement, it seemed perfectly natural to her when Dietrich started unbuttoning her blouse and carried her to the bed.

"I never want to hurt you either," he said.

Maeve lay there and let him do as he wished. Was she about to become a fallen woman? she wondered. She didn't want to go from man to man like Moira. But something told her that this was different: Dietrich loved her, she loved him, and there was absolutely nothing wrong with what they were doing.

Dietrich's body was smooth, but parts were covered with a fine layer of the purest golden hair. He was slender and looked like boys Maeve had seen swimming in South Africa. She couldn't keep her eyes off him. She was fascinated by his chest, by his slim hips and buttocks (square, unlike her curved form), and most of all his penis. She had never seen a man's penis, let alone an erect one, before. His skin was rosy—a deeper hue at the moment than usual—but his penis was a dark rose and looked like an exotic flower.

They kissed passionately, and Dietrich positioned his penis gently over her. He seemed to know what he was doing. As he entered her ever so slowly, it hurt, but not as badly as she had feared it would. She didn't feel the kind of passion she had hoped for, but she truly loved Dietrich and understood how much he longed for her. This seemed so unreal to Maeve that she felt almost like an onlooker, shocked by Dietrich's abandon, even a little in awe of it. She inspired all this, Maeve realized with a sense of alarm. These waves of hysterical affection washing over her body were her own creation. She had brought all this emotion into being, and she felt too inexperienced to savor it the way Moira—or Yvette— would. The thought saddened her as she caressed Dietrich.

Like a small animal, Maeve buried her face against her lover's chest and hoped she would learn quickly. She wanted to share his ecstasy soon.

*

Arlette knew something was wrong when she tried to bring Mademoiselle her breakfast the next morning and found the door locked. She knocked several times, gently at first and then more forcefully, and finally with such determination Mademoiselle Devereux awoke with a start.

"Arlette!" she called in embarrassment, "stop being so noisy! I hear you!"

She slid carefully out of bed, slipped into her robe, and looked back at Dietrich, who was curled up like a cat under her covers.

She couldn't very well allow her maid to see him there; that would be shameless. And she couldn't let her go running for the concierge to open the door either! That would be worse.

"Breakfast, mademoiselle," the maid explained with a stealthy glance as Maeve opened the door a little bit, enough to look at her, not far enough to pass a tray through.

"Thank you." Maeve nodded. Then she looked down and saw two of everything on her breakfast tray. She stiffened visibly.

Arlette's expression revealed nothing. "I thought you might be hungry this morning" was all she said.

Don't even ask, Maeve said sternly to herself. She must have been spying on me. How cheeky!

Dietrich was awake and quite pleased to be served breakfast in bed. Maeve placed the tray on her bedside table and pulled up a chair while he simply propped himself up against the pillows. He was irritatingly chipper, she noticed. He reminded her of a big, golden jungle cat lolling about as he waited for his mate to bring him the kill.

"Good morning," he said softly as Maeve silently poured him a cup of cocoa.

"Good morning yourself," she said shyly.

Maeve didn't know whether to be mortified or delighted as she sat there sipping her morning cocoa, as if it were the most natural thing in the world for Dietrich to be there in her bed, displaying a bare chest covered by a soft, golden down. Perhaps it wouldn't look so shocking if he were wearing a nightshirt, she thought. No, a nightshirt wouldn't help. Anyone who saw them like this would *know*.

Now she was in the same class as Violetta, Mimi, and Tosca—and Mama—Maeve decided solemnly as she handed Dietrich a plate containing a sweet roll, cheese, butter, and jam. She was a fallen woman.

Oh Lord! Moira would be pleased. Maeve wondered if people would be able to tell just by looking at her. Arlette obviously knew already. Little spy! Sean mustn't find out, she thought nervously. She would be too ashamed ever to look at him again if he knew. Then again, with a mother like his, perhaps he wouldn't consider it too shocking.

And while all this was going through her head, Maeve thought of that day in Herr Albrecht's studio when he had warned her of the dire consequences that befell sopranos who strayed. Oh Lord, no! He had only been trying to scare her. Well, it couldn't possibly be true, could it? she wondered. If Dietrich hadn't been sitting there, nibbling on a roll and serving as a witness to her actions, Maeve would have started on her scales right there. She was embarrassed to admit to herself that what she wanted to do was rush to the nearest piano and sing "Cara nome" with all its treacherous high notes—just to be sure.

She was still nervously pondering the ramifications of her new state when the telephone on her dressing table rang, startling her.

When she took the call and turned back to Dietrich, he noticed she had lost her color. She looked ill.

"What is it?" he asked.

"That was the Grand Duchess Stana. She said the army is ready to repel the mob if they try to surround the Winter Palace. She ordered me not to leave the hotel for any reason. The army will take any measures necessary to secure the city."

"My God! That sounds to me as if they're expecting an armed rebellion."

"But the people aren't planning anything like that, from what I've heard. The workers want to present a petition to Nicholas—who isn't here in town. It's all very mixed up."

Dietrich was thinking of Kaiser Wilhelm's fear of socialist mobs. He'd have the army out too, with orders to shoot to kill if he ever felt threatened by his subjects. From what he'd heard last night at that gathering of foreign ministry types, Nicholas would make the same decision.

"Maeve, get dressed," he said suddenly. "I'm going back to my room to change. I'll return in half an hour. You and Arlette stay put. And start packing."

Frightened by the implications of Stana's call, Maeve ran to the window and was appalled to find St. Isaac's Square dense with a slowly moving crowd of men, women, and children, many carrying icons and large portraits of the Tsar. They were remarkably quiet and self-controlled, pressing on with the force of a great dark river, heading in the direction of the Nevsky and the Winter Palace.

Fascinated by the size and the solemnity of the crowd, Maeve thought of that scene in *Boris Godunov* where the Tsar is received in Moscow by his people. These Russians below her window, trudging through the snow-covered square, were no more harmful than that. They were like a group of well-behaved schoolchildren on a pilgrimage. Stana had chattered hysterically about revolutionaries and regicides. That was nonsense.

Looking at them, she wondered how they would react if they ever had the chance to see their Tsar in person as she had. Would they be shocked at the emptiness of their consecrated ruler? Would they think one of those huge, pompous grand dukes was Nicholas II?

"God help you," Maeve murmured as she watched the spectacle, all those patient, orderly people wanting to see their Tsar to make things right. Somehow she didn't believe it was going to lead to any improvement.

*

Maeve bathed quickly, dressed in record time, and was helping Arlette pack when Dietrich returned, nervous and edgy.

"I've spoken with my acquaintance from the foreign ministry. He says the government's in a state of panic. Nobody knows what will happen, but he fears the worst. He also advises keeping indoors."

That warning proved useful a few hours later. Maeve and Dietrich were sitting in her room, talking quietly, when shots rang out in the square below. A cavalry detachment stationed near the Hôtel de France had fired on a group of workers, scattering them in a panic, wounding and trampling stragglers as the frightened civilians fled before the mounted soldiers.

"My God," Maeve whispered in shock, "they're murdering the people!"

Dietrich put his arm around Maeve as she began to sob, watching the fleeing civilians scatter in terror.

"Chaliapin was right about the Romanovs after all," she wept, mesmerized by the sheer horror of the scene. People were being cut down by a hail of bullets as Maeve and Dietrich looked on. It was even worse than what she remembered from South Africa, much worse. These people were unarmed and loyal to their government. They weren't revolutionaries, she thought in disgust. But after today, they damned well ought to be!

Dietrich was seeing the effect of gunfire on humans for the first time, and he was just as horrified as Maeve. Despite much talk by government functionaries about "Jewish revolutionary agitators," he didn't believe that line. These were Russian Orthodox factory workers with large banners asserting their love for the Little Father and dozens of holy icons held high above their heads. And this is how their Little Father reacted.

"If these people didn't hate Nicholas yesterday, they certainly will after today," he murmured, holding Maeve close to him, his eyes never leaving the horror on the square. "He really is a bloody tyrant."

Just then a stray bullet hit the side of the hotel, chipped off a piece of brick, and sent bits flying noisily against the window. Maeve threw herself on the floor, taking Dietrich with her. It was like the war all over again, she thought. How idiotic to be shot now by a stray bullet in this crazy country. At least the war had had a bitter logic. This massacre was sheer insanity.

People were being gunned down all over town—or at least in the central part of the city—by soldiers, some of whom had detrained from other cities just a few hours earlier.

At the Winter Palace, where the organizers of the demonstration had managed to lead their people, the Life Guards Regiment opened fire point-blank, killing dozens with the first volley and scattering the rest in a blind panic.

Sean Farrell and his servant, Kyril, had been standing near the palace behind the lines of mounted soldiers when the huge demonstration approached, icons and portraits of the Tsar at the head. Sean had escorted Zofia to Stana's home before dawn at his sister's urgent request, and he was now talking to an old friend from his Corps des Pages days, an officer in the Life Guards. As the brother-in-law of Grand Duke Nicholas and practically a Russian officer, Sean was more than welcome.

Sean would always remember the bright sunlight that morning, gleaming down on the gilded icon frames as the huge, dark mass of humanity surged forward, singing hymns, eager to meet their Tsar. Docile, respectful.

"This is a very orderly crowd," Sean remarked to his friend. "Obviously, the predictions were dead wrong." In his sisters' salons lately, all the talk was of regicide, murder, assassination. His Romanov in-laws were hysterical. He wished Stana were here to see these harmless peasants.

No sooner had the last word left his mouth than the officer in charge of the mounted troops drew his saber with a slow, practiced motion and barked, "Forward!" At that moment, the troops at the Narva Gate rode headlong into the demonstrators, signaling the beginning of the slaughter.

Sean was so stunned by the overreaction of the soldiers, he thought the officer in charge must have lost his mind. Even Kyril, who had never been known to shed a tear in pity, was visibly appalled.

These were old people and women with babies who were being trampled by the soldiers in plain view. The screams of the crowd mingled with the rifle shots of the infantry who had appeared behind the mounted troops, opening fire on the bewildered civilians in defiance of all common decency.

"This is murder!" Sean shouted at his friend. "They ought to shoot their commander!"

"Shut up, Ivan Petrovic!" the Russian replied, horrified. "Or they'll shoot *you*!"

And with that, he edged away from this lunatic who was probably going to be arrested for spreading revolutionary propaganda—Romanov relation or not.

*

The sunny morning vanished into a blur of snow and blood as the dead and wounded lay strewn across the city's broad streets and squares. The heavy tread of horses' hooves sounded on the Nevsky as cossack patrols made their rounds in the deepening twilight, warning anyone foolish enough to be out of doors to go home and stay there.

Maeve and Dietrich lay in each other's arms, horrified by the massacre. Putting down an armed insurrection was one thing; cold-blooded murder of defenseless people was another.

"During the war, I used to think there was nothing worse than what I was going through," Maeve murmured. "But I was wrong. My God, how could they do this?"

"Stupidity and inflexibility. The Tsar doesn't know any other way."

The girl nestled against Dietrich and buried her face against his chest. She didn't care if people clucked their tongues or called her a hussy now. Compared with the crimes of Nicholas II, her transgression was utterly trivial, modest in fact.

Maeve listened to Dietrich's heart beat faster as she moved closer, pulling the soft comforter tight around her, making a secure little nest for herself. She didn't *feel* like a sinner.

"Maeve," he whispered as he kissed her bare shoulder, "let's get married as soon as we can arrange it. We can have the civil ceremony when we get back to Paris."

She turned over and stared up at the plaster molding on the ceiling. "I think we ought to announce the engagement first," she said.

She was almost embarrassed to think of how happy Moira would be to hear the news. It would be the marital equivalent of bagging big game. She would announce the glad tidings to every one of those people she shot things with and she would speak grandly about "my future son-in-law, the baron." He would be Maeve's trophy, duly noted and recorded.

Almost cringing at the thought, Maeve nestled deeper into her covers and envisioned the cross-examination she would face upon her return. Moira would want to know all the details of just how she came to be engaged. What could Maeve say? That she had been seduced and that Dietrich was going to make an honest woman of her? That she had been carried away by passion? Moira would probably understand that.

Well, she could hardly claim to have been ravished—unless that involved clinging to a man and settling down gently onto a soft bed with him.

Really, it had all happened so quickly she was lying in his arms and kissing him before it dawned on her what was happening. But she didn't sit up at that point and say "Stop!" either. She remembered that especially well.

How ironic that she had once laughed at Moira's concern about her kissing Dietrich that time in Berlin. Then she had thought sleighing with him was much more dangerous. How times had changed!

Still, it was shocking how easily she had slid into sin—with help from him, of course—even though the actual act required some acrobatic skill. It was a good thing she was used to taking direction. Dietrich seemed quite accustomed to the whole thing, either a fortunate happenstance or a sign of widely scattered affections. It was not edifying to think of him doing all these intimate things with Frau Hélène, for instance. And God knows how many others! That could be an indication of rampant promiscuity, a dreadful thing. He could be another Marc Antoine.

Dietrich gently stroked Maeve's auburn hair and smiled. He loved her. She was as natural as a cat and endowed with an almost feline beauty. This was a wild little Lorelei, a siren whose song was an incitement to self-destruction. He loved her creamy skin, her russet hair, her long black eyelashes, the way she practically purred when she made love. This blend of startling sensuality and soft, dreamy innocence was intoxicating.

As he caressed Maeve he thought grimly of Hubertus and his threat of retaliation if he married her. That old hypocrite was not going to stand between him and his heart's desire. He loved a woman who was adored by hundreds of people, from Paris to St. Petersburg. Why couldn't that cold, rigid Prussian unbend and acknowledge her worth? How could he prefer a cow like Lotte to a queen like Maeve?

It was idiotic, especially now that Moira had married some rich American who was a friend of President Roosevelt. If that didn't almost guarantee respectability, he didn't know what did. Kaiser Wilhelm would have the Lassiters to dinner if they cared to come to Berlin. *There* was a man who adored millionaires. And since he also adored Theodore Roosevelt, they were almost assured a place at his table. Why couldn't Hubertus be more realistic? If Moira had married a friend of the American president, she ought to be acceptable to *him*. What the hell did his father want?

Dietrich knew exactly what he himself wanted. He wanted to marry this gorgeous creature and make her the most acclaimed singer of her generation. With him behind her, she would surpass everyone else. More than that, she would be everyone's secret desire and unavailable to anyone but him. Maeve would truly be a Lorelei, out of reach, beautiful, enchanting—and his and his alone.

Kissing Maeve's beautiful little ear, he pulled her closer to him, excited by her warmth, wanting all of her forever. Her budding sensuality aroused now, this time Maeve enjoyed their lovemaking much more. So much so that she and Dietrich made love three times that night.

*

Maeve and Dietrich left St. Petersburg in a state of numb horror. Chaliapin had telephoned to ask her if she wanted to accompany him and his friends to the mass funeral for the victims of the slaughter, but Dietrich had snatched the receiver from her hand at the mention of it to say he thought it was irresponsible of the Russian to expose her to any danger.

To Maeve's surprise, Fedya didn't lose control of his famous temper; he attributed the German's reaction to the concern of a nervous lover and simply wished them a safe journey home. He had been touched to learn that Maeve had made a generous contribution to the burial fund and thought she might want to join her Russian colleagues at the funeral.

"Don't do that again," Maeve said quietly to Dietrich. "It was rude."

"I'm sorry, *Liebchen*," he apologized. "Chaliapin wasn't thinking clearly if he wanted to put you in danger. It enraged me. After Sunday, how could he ask you to take part in any demonstration here?"

The incident was forgotten on the trip home, but Fedya remembered it for a long time to come, each time he saw the German afterward.

"She deserves better than that fellow," he remarked to Iola when he returned to Moscow. "I think she's being taken in by his good looks."

Iola wondered what sort of man little Masha was in love with to provoke that reaction from Fedya. He was very fond of her. Sometimes she was a bit afraid he was in love with her himself.

*

In Berlin the next day, the *Nord Allemeine Zeitung* was referring to "Bloody Sunday" in St. Petersburg, and newspaper readers around the world were awakening to more or less similar stories. Several international correspondents were able to spice up their accounts with stories of near annihilation at the hands of the cossacks, making their readers shudder in their armchairs over the utter beastliness of Russian rule.

Baron von Reuter was agitated to learn of the disorders in St. Petersburg, since Dietrich was visiting the Russian capital—although anything that weakened the Tsar in his war with Japan was welcome news. Hubertus was inspired to hope for a genuine revolution, overthrow of the dynasty, and utter ruin for Nicholas. It could only assure his Japanese investment.

He was relatively pleased when Dietrich arrived home—having sent Maeve on ahead to Paris, bearing an impressive diamond and emerald engagement ring—to report firsthand on the events in Petersburg.

Dietrich declined a predinner sherry and, pleading total exhaustion, retreated upstairs to bathe and nap before dinner. Most of the servants had the evening off, so the meal was to be simple, Hubertus said, strictly *en famille*.

Roast goose, one of his father's favorite dishes, was the main course—a trifle greasy, Dietrich felt. Heavy dumplings and sauerkraut complemented it, the former little balls of lead, the latter briny and tasting like vinegar. A plum pudding imported from Fortnum and Mason in London finished off the meal, also not to the son's taste. The Kaiser relished plum pudding, so Hubertus did likewise. The boy preferred anything French or Viennese in contrast.

Once Hubertus had consumed enough for several strong men, coffee was served and the footman sent away. Now was the time for serious business.

"So, my boy," said the baron, feeling pleasantly content with himself, "how was the situation in St. Petersburg? Is the government about to collapse in a pool of blood—or are they strong enough to weather these storms?"

"The people are disgusted with Nicholas and the dynasty. Their sons and brothers are being killed in the Far East, and their Tsar treats them like criminals when they try to speak to him. Meanwhile, some of his own relations are making fortunes as war profiteers and avoiding active service. It's a blueprint for revolution."

"The Kaiser wouldn't like to see his cousin lose his throne. He's genuinely fond of the Tsar," Hubertus declared. "Besides, Russian instability would have a detrimental effect on the balance of power in Europe. Her client states in the Balkans would run wild. They would threaten the Austrians with their expansionist Pan-Slav aggressions."

Dietrich smiled. "Right now anything might happen. When the Tsar has to murder his peaceful subjects out of pure cowardice, I'd say the time has come for him to step down from the throne."

"That sounds like some dangerous revolutionary nonsense. I believe in the sacred principle of monarchy. A king, a kaiser, a tsar—these men are consecrated by God to rule. They cannot step down. It can't be done."

"Then perhaps someone will throw them down," Dietrich replied blandly as he swirled a dark green liqueur in his glass. "In Nicholas's case, it would be a boon to mankind. I was almost hit by a stray bullet on Sunday. I have no sympathy for him."

Dietrich swept a lock of fair hair back from his eyes and fixed Hubertus with a steady, unswerving stare. Pausing for a split second, he said calmly, "I became engaged yesterday. You know the young lady, Papa. Are you going to wish me well?"

The baron put down his glass and rose slightly from the table, glaring at his son. He didn't like to be surprised in these matters.

"Who is she?" he demanded, fearing the worst in spite of all his warnings. "A German girl?" He was praying the boy would say yes.

Dietrich laughed his low, melodious laugh, a charming sound, very well bred and yet mischievous. It always irritated his father, as though the boy found something amusing that he, Hubertus, couldn't comprehend.

"No," he replied, looking Hubertus squarely in the eye. "Of course not. It's Maeve. Do you really think there could be anyone else?"

"No!" shouted the baron, turning red in the face. He banged his fist down hard on the table, knocking over his glass in the process. "It's out of the question!"

"Get used to it, Papa. Maeve will be my wife and eventually Baroness von Reuter. Don't you think that's a charming idea? She'll have all of Mama's jewelry. Only I'll have to have it reset for her, because you never did have any taste in ornaments. Luckily, the stones themselves are fine." He felt proud of his ability to stand up to the old man.

"You arrogant little worm! No taste! And you, the little snob, about to marry a singer! You're ridiculous. You have no sense of decorum!"

Hubertus was so violently red in the face he had begun to breathe heavily, pulling frantically at his stiff collar to make himself more comfortable. His heart was racing, making him feel sick. Those huge helpings of roast goose and dumplings were beginning to rise in his throat, causing painful indigestion.

"You filthy hypocrite!" Dietrich shouted, truly furious now, flinging the contents of his glass across the room, "I hate you now and I've always hated you! It gives me the greatest pleasure to make you miserable! Just think of it, Papa—your son happy at last with a girl he loves, and not some fat little cow either! A beautiful girl whom people admire! But not you. No, you're too stupid for that!"

Hubertus was feeling seriously ill now. He staggered a little as he reached the bellpull and tugged on it. To his distress, nobody came.

"Servants' night off," Dietrich said with a grim smile. His plan was coming true much sooner than expected.

"Get out of here!" Hubertus ordered with a furious gesture. "Go to hell! I disown you!"

The baron tried frantically once more to ring the bellpull, but the result was the same.

"I am leaving, Papa. I'll be at the Théâtre des Variétés if anyone needs me. Goodbye, old man." The hell with *you*, he thought grimly.

And he headed for the hallway to fetch his coat and hat.

*

Several hours later, a shocked and embarrassed servant had to ask the maître d' at a fashionable nightclub to call one of the patrons to the reception area.

"Is it important?" the man asked. "We're in the middle of our show. Can't it wait?"

The servant gave him a cold stare. "There's a man in there whose father has just passed away. He must come home at once."

"Oh." The maître d' lost a bit of his arrogance and nodded. "Of course. Well, just a minute. Point him out and I'll go speak to him myself."

Within minutes, Dietrich was standing before his father's mournful valet, looking puzzled and quite elegant in his evening clothes. Two young blondes at his table were glancing back at him, wondering what was going on. The maître d' stood there looking like a basset hound in white tie.

"What's the matter?" the young man demanded as he seized the valet's arm. "Is it Papa?"

The servant looked icy. "I regret to inform you, Herr von Reuter, that Baron Hubertus died at ten o'clock this evening. We tried for hours to locate you. I'm sorry," he added, almost as an afterthought. "I know you would have wished to be there."

"Papa!" Dietrich cried out. "Oh my God!"

He covered his face with his hands and nearly collapsed. "My God!" he cried. "How did it happen? Was anyone with him at the end?"

"Yes sir. His regular doctor. He apparently called him himself. There was nobody else around when he was stricken."

Dietrich thought the maître d' was looking at him as if he were nothing but a young wastrel. He knew the servant certainly was.

"Oh, Papa!" he said brokenly. "If I had only known!"

He was chauffeured back home to confront the remains and to hear the theories of Hubertus's doctor. Heart attack brought on by overindulgence in his favorite dishes. The sole footman had been questioned at length about the evening meal and had shown the doctor the remains of greasy goose and dumplings.

"A tragedy," the doctor commented sadly. "I've often warned my patients with heart trouble to eat lighter meals. But we Germans do love our national dishes."

Dietrich sighed as he raised his hand to his face, shaking his head in bewilderment. "Papa had pills for his illness," he said. "I wonder if he was able to take any."

The doctor pointed to an empty bottle on Hubertus's dresser. "Perhaps he did—too late. I found the empty bottle there when I entered the room."

Dietrich broke down and flung himself on Hubertus's rigid form, weeping for all he was worth as Dr. Hempel looked manfully away, wondering who this boy took after. Certainly the late baron was never known to carry on in such a startling way.

"Courage, young man," he said brusquely as he patted Dietrich on the shoulder. "You'll need all your strength to deal with what lies ahead."

Dietrich looked up, puzzled.

"The Von Reuter Bank, the funeral arrangements."

"Of course." Dietrich nodded. "Yes. That will require fortitude."

It was all his. Maeve was his, the Von Reuter Bank was his, all Hubertus's private fortune was his. The idea was almost humbling in its enormity. And all he had done was to flush eight pills down the toilet. It wasn't his fault that his father had a bad heart.

As he rose to his feet, Dietrich said solemnly, "With God as my witness, I'll do my best to live up to Papa's high opinion of me. This I swear."

CHAPTER 19

*D*ietrich placed a telephone call to Paris to wake Maeve from a sound sleep and tell her to go ahead with the most elaborate wedding plans possible.

His unexpected announcement shocked Maeve and led to her early-morning visit to Moira's mansion the following day. After struggling for several hours to find the right way to break the news of her engagement, Maeve decided to get it over with—even though it seemed almost indecently hasty to announce both the wedding plans and Hubertus's death together. She didn't want to give the impression of gloating over a fallen enemy.

By the time Maeve's smart black coach arrived in the courtyard of the Lassiter mansion, she was nervous but composed. Greeted by the French butler, Maurice, who expressed his delight to see her and hoped her trip to Russia had gone well, Maeve hurried inside, left her chinchilla coat in Maurice's care, and scampered up the marble staircase, past dozens of oil paintings, arriving breathless at her mother's suite.

A whole battery of maids and footmen were already at work in the huge house, carrying breakfast trays upstairs, polishing, sweeping, tending to the fireplaces. The mansion reminded Maeve of a hotel, a very grand hotel.

Moira was awake—sitting up in her gorgeous antique bed sipping her morning cocoa—and delighted to see her wandering child. Her lovely blue eyes came to rest at once on the emerald and diamond ring on her daughter's finger.

"You must be doing well to afford that bauble, Maeveen," she remarked. "The Russians are a generous people."

Maeve colored slightly. "I didn't buy it, Mama."

Her mother didn't think she had. Moira wasn't simple.

"Who did?" she demanded, putting down her cup and leaning forward among the pile of silken pink and white coverlets, ruffled pillows, and lace-trimmed sheets.

"Dietrich, of course," Maeve replied.

"Ah."

"We're engaged, Mama."

At those words, Moira gave a look of astonishment and held out her arms to bestow a hug on this child who had shown the first good sense of her life. "Well," she marveled, "the boy managed to win over Hubertus."

Maeve cleared her throat apprehensively as she settled down into a soft pink silk armchair. "Not exactly, Mama. The baron died last night of a heart attack. Dietrich called in the news at two this morning, all the way from Berlin."

Moira's head bobbed up in astonishment, her eyes round and shocked. "Dead!" she managed. "For a fact?"

"And about to be buried on Wednesday. I have to go. Will you and Charlie be coming with me?"

Moira was still digesting this startling bit of news. The old brute was dead and the son was now a baron, a fiancé, and probably rolling in money. It was a sobering thought.

"Of course we'll go." She nodded. "It wouldn't look right for the boy's future in-laws to miss that funeral. My God, what a stroke of luck for you, Maeveen! Charlie told me the Von Reuter Bank is as solid as the Rock of Gibraltar. You'll never have to fear the future now . . ."

"Mama," Maeve said quietly, "I'm going to marry Dietrich, not his bank. All that is his business, not mine."

"Don't be daft. If you have any sense, you'll make it your business. And don't be too harsh on the boy and expect the impossible from him. Of course he's wild about you now. But in a few years' time he'll start to stray the way they all do. Be prepared for it," warned Moira, wishing to erase any simpleminded illusions from the child's mind. "But make him pay for this," she added. "Let his little indiscretions add to your collection of jewels."

"Mama . . ."

"Don't think it won't happen. With all your pretty playacting, I sometimes think you spend half your time in the clouds. Marriage is an art form that demands relentless realism, Maeveen. Always keep that in mind."

Moira's lovely eyes rested in silent appraisal of that huge ring. "Gorgeous" was a mild term for it. It was breathtaking, splendid enough for a grand duke to bestow. Well, she thought, Dietrich did have an extravagant nature. She was pleased that her daughter was going to enjoy its largesse, even though she didn't want to be eclipsed by her.

It was all very well for Maeve to become a baroness, but she didn't want her to get any notions about outdoing her mother as an ornament of society. Let her stick to her singing and leave the entertaining and social climbing to Moira. Of course, acquiring a title did put her a bit ahead, but Moira wouldn't allow her to flaunt it in *her* face—even though it was all very well for her to do that to other people.

Suddenly Moira had an unpleasant thought about the reason for Maeve's startling announcement, and her eyes went narrow with suspicion.

"You're not in the family way, are you, Maeveen?" she demanded, as if she were presiding at the Inquisition.

"Mama! Of course not. What an idea!" But after St. Petersburg, she hoped she was telling the truth.

*

When Maeve and her mother and stepfather arrived at Berlin's Anhalter Station, they were met by Dietrich's servant, who had the von Reuter coach waiting to drive them straight to the house.

Maeve had insisted on seeing Dietrich immediately since she was concerned about his reaction to his father's death and wanted to be certain he was all right. The whole burden of the funeral arrangements had fallen on him and she feared he might be overwhelmed.

The minute she and her party entered the impressive marble foyer of the von Reuter mansion, Maeve realized Dietrich had everything well in hand. The whole place was draped in black crepe streamers, huge arrangements of flowers filled the rooms, a small chamber orchestra concealed behind a trellis of vines and smilax played selections from Bach and Wagner as Hubertus's mourners filed through the house to pay their last respects. When Maeve arrived they were undertaking Bach's First Violin Concerto in A Minor, a solemn and emotional piece. It was all very dignified and lavish, a tasteful farewell to a life marked by a certain earthly splendor.

*

To the consternation of the board of directors of the Von Reuter Bank, the new baron called a meeting the day after the funeral to inform them he was not returning to Berlin. They, the board, would take charge and he, the chairman, would resume residence in Paris, returning from time to time as business dictated.

"But sir," protested Herr von Richter, "your father would be a-ghast!"

Dietrich's icy blue eyes became even colder. "Gentlemen," he said quietly, "his wishes no longer carry any weight around here. He's dead, I'm alive, and I'm going back to Paris. I will handle international matters such as our Japanese loan. And for these affairs, a Paris base is a necessity. Any questions, gentlemen?"

The distinguished board members were too appalled to think straight, let alone pose questions. The boy might as well have said he was going off to be a Buddhist monk in Tibet. This was unthinkable. A von Reuter abandoning Berlin!

"Well, then, gentlemen," Dietrich announced, feeling relieved, "the only other thing I have to mention is my engagement to Fräulein Maeve Devereux."

By way of response he received a stricken silence—until Otto von Richter, more pragmatic than the rest, came forward to shake his hand and wish him well, causing the others to fall into step like elderly sheep. Champagne was sent for to toast the happy event, and the meeting ended on a tone of forced goodwill, even though some hidebound conservatives considered it scandalous to celebrate the day after Baron von Reuter had been buried.

"Gentlemen," von Richter declared to his colleagues after Dietrich had left, "a new day has dawned, and not necessarily one we can understand. But with God's help, we will persevere and try to steer this young man into the proper path."

That sounded dignified enough, but privately they were wondering if young Dietrich had just lost his mind.

"One thing I'll say for him," von Richter commented to one of his oldest friends later. "The boy has an eye for beauty. If that little singer doesn't ruin him, she might be the mother of a line of fine-looking children. Unlike that other one . . ."

"Ah, yes," murmured his friend. "Quite."

*

Maeve's sojourn in Berlin gave comfort to the newly bereaved Baron von Reuter—even if she was accompanied by Moira and Charlie. Plans were broached for an engagement party in Paris—a simple affair in keeping with Dietrich's mourning—and much grander expectations for the wedding as soon as decently possible.

The one snag was the divorce. As a divorced man, Dietrich could not possibly marry Maeve in a Catholic church—and even if he had been a genuine bachelor, a full-dress extravaganza was out of the question. That put a crimp in his plans, since he had been counting on marrying either in Notre Dame—like Napoleon—or in the Madeleine, the most fashionable church in society circles.

"It's the damned divorce," sighed Charlie. "We Protestants are all heretics anyway in the eyes of the priests, but the divorce makes it all the worse. Why don't you just marry in a civil ceremony? You'd have to do that anyway in France. It's their law."

True, thought Dietrich. One had to have one's marriage recorded at the *mairie* in order for it to count. The devout generally followed this up with a ceremony at the church, but with a church ceremony or without it, one would be legally married. And with the problems of Maeve's lack of real Catholic background—despite a baptism shortly after birth— and his divorce, which all the churchmen in Paris viewed with distaste, why not marry civilly? That way he'd gain his objective—Maeve—and be spared all sorts of ghastly lectures on marital good conduct.

Moira was the one to give him the ultimate seal of approval. "Priests are a meddlesome pack of hypocrites at best," she announced. "The fellow who marries you at the *mairie* will wish you well and tell you to be a good citizen. It's a lot easier to bear. And you're just as married."

"It's all right with me," sighed Maeve, regretting her chance to glide down a flower-drenched aisle to the strains of the wedding march from *Lohengrin*. "I'll marry you anywhere you wish." But she really would have preferred something more theatrical than standing before some fellow wearing a tricolor sash in a municipal office. Still, she loved Dietrich, and for him she'd make the sacrifice.

*

Before the young woman returned to Paris, she encountered by chance someone in Berlin who delighted her and gave her encouragement for her next German appearance.

It happened at the same café where she and Dietrich had gone the day after she had seen her first opera a few years earlier. Now Maeve was no longer an unknown visitor but an artist whom people recognized as she entered on her fiancé's arm. Apparently not all Berliners had shared the opinion of the critics. There were murmurs of appreciation.

Maeve and Dietrich were sitting quietly at a corner table, deep in conversation about their wedding, when a slim, curly-haired, blond gentleman with a wispy mustache and a receding hairline sauntered over to their table and extended his hand.

"Herr Strauss," Maeve purred, giving him a lovely smile before he could even introduce himself. "I'm honored. Please join us. This is my fiancé, Baron von Reuter."

Strauss laughed as he shook hands with Dietrich after kissing Maeve's hand. "How did you know who I was, Fräulein? We've never met," he said as a waiter came rushing up to pull out a chair for him.

"The whole world knows Richard Strauss. Your picture is as familiar to me as the Kaiser's," she said simply. Strauss, Dietrich noticed, was charmed. The musical director of the Berlin Royal Opera, the most famous conductor in Germany was also Germany's most celebrated living composer. This was wonderful!

As he took a cup of coffee with them, Strauss told Maeve not to mind the bad notices she had received for her Juliette. The man who wrote the worst one was a fool and a partisan of Farrar. He, Richard Strauss, who knew a thing or two about music, had found her to be a ravishing Juliette. In fact, he had liked her so much he wanted to know if her repertory extended to German works.

"I've never sung in a German opera yet," Maeve admitted. "I've always been intimidated by Wagner."

"You're too modest," Strauss replied with a smile. "I would like very much to see you in my operas. By the way," he said casually, "*Salome* is scheduled for its premiere in Dresden in December. Will you come? We've already signed the cast, but there will of course be other performances in other cities. Come and see if you can picture yourself as Salome. I can."

"Herr Strauss, I don't know what to say!"

"Say you'll come to Dresden," he replied. "I'll send you the tickets."

"Thank you!"

Dietrich was in a daze. He was so impressed by Strauss he hardly noticed that the composer had barely acknowledged his presence—something he wouldn't have tolerated from anyone else.

Maeve had noticed it and was annoyed with herself for not making more of an effort to include Dietrich in the conversation, but it was business and really had very little to do with him.

"Of course we'll go to Dresden," he said, nodding emphatically, after Strauss left. "This is a world premiere of an important work. They're talking about his production all over Europe. Everyone will want to be there."

Maeve looked at her fiancé and smiled. "Do you think I could ever attempt the German repertory?"

"I don't see why not. I can coach you in your diction. And you'd be an enchanting Elisabeth in *Tannhäuser*. Besides"—he smiled too—"if Herr Strauss can see you as one of his heroines, then it's settled. And by the way," he added, "Strauss writes magnificent roles for women. His male characters are much less interesting."

"I've heard this *Salome* is a bit daring," she reflected. "Several singers said no decent woman would attempt the role."

"All the better. The singer won't go unnoticed then if she raises a few eyebrows. What wonderful publicity."

Maeve took her fiancé's hand and enfolded it in her own.

"Let's get married in April," she suggested quietly. "That will give me a little time to arrange a proper trousseau. And it won't be so soon after the funeral."

"I'd marry you tomorrow," Dietrich replied. "If the Tsar of Russia could marry his fiancée immediately after burying his father, so can I. There's a precedent." And the Tsar loved his father, he thought.

Maeve laughed. "And they've called her the Funeral Bride ever since! To tell the truth, *Schatzi*, I've met her and they were right. What a gloomy thing she is!"

No. Despite imperial precedents, Maeve did not want to be a Funeral Bride. If Dietrich wanted a splendid wedding, he would have to let some time elapse between burying Hubertus and marrying Maeve. With the arrival of spring they could marry in the sunshine—if they were lucky, Paris weather being what it was.

*

Moira was full of plans for an extravagant engagement party which would allow her to preside over a society gathering and show off her home and her titled future son-in-law. The boy was in love with Maeve and that was all to the good. It ought to guarantee them at least a few happy years together—until boredom and restlessness set in and ruined it.

On the night of the engagement party—Valentine's Day, 1905—Moira's house was decorated as lavishly as three florists could manage. A private railway car was used to transport flowers from the Riviera for the occasion, and stairways, salons, and foyers were blossoming as if it were May instead of midwinter. Part of the orchestra of the Paris Opéra was engaged for the evening. Last-minute alterations had been completed on Maeve's gown, and everything was ready for a grand show.

Charlie Lassiter startled Maeve by saying—with some embarrassment—that if she had any misgivings about her future, nobody would think it strange, even if she were on the very threshold of the church, to call the whole thing off. He thought there was something a little *odd* about Dietrich.

His genuine concern touched her. It also amused her. "Charlie! I love Dietrich," she said with a laugh. "I couldn't do anything like that."

He kept quiet after that, but he felt he had done his duty and that gave him some satisfaction.

*

Maeve would always remember her engagement party, not for the beauty of her gown, the profusion of flowers, the eclectic mixture of guests, or the splendor of the music, but for the sudden appearance of a pretty brunette with a dark-eyed child.

Like the evil fairy in "Sleeping Beauty," she walked in uninvited and unannounced, wearing an expression of pure spitefulness.

The butler, Maurice, first spotted the intruder, tried to intercept her, and failed. She neatly sidestepped his grasp and headed straight toward the center of the room.

For a moment Maeve's heart nearly stopped. She glanced at Dietrich, afraid this had something to do with him, but the young baron looked completely blank. He didn't know the woman.

Then, as the music came to an abrupt halt, the woman strode right past Moira and stopped in front of Charlie Lassiter, holding the child out toward him. He went dead white and reacted as if the boy might bite him.

"Laura," he muttered, "what does this mean?"

"It means he belongs to you," she replied, her eyes large and gleaming with malice.

Maeve had never encountered such deadly silence. The entire crowd in the ballroom went still, nobody wishing to miss a word, all gawking at the brunette, at the child—a very handsome little boy—and at Charlie Lassiter, who looked as if he wished he were dead.

The next thing anybody heard was a sort of vocal explosion that sent Moira dashing across the floor in a fierce whirl of violet silk and amethysts.

"Get out of my house, you bloody little slut," she hissed, grabbing the woman with such force she nearly knocked her and the child to the floor. "Get out of here! Go and embarrass somebody else!" she ordered, as she propelled the intruder toward the foyer with the force of a hurricane. She kept her so off balance the woman couldn't properly cling to the child and counterattack with any hope of success.

Maeve stamped her foot and ordered the orchestra to start playing something, gave Charlie a look that could kill, and ran into the foyer after Moira. Dietrich, aghast at the wreckage of his second engagement party, ran after her.

"Who are you and where did you come from?" Moira was screaming at the now disheveled intruder, grabbing her by clumps of her long black hair, oblivious to the fact that the child was rolling on the carpet, wailing in fear.

"I'm Laura Milonari," yelped the brunette, "and you'd better ask Carlo where I come from."

"Carlo? Who is Carlo?"

"Charlie, Mama," said Maeve. "She must be Italian."

"Bloody dago whore!"

Moira's beautiful eyes were dark blue and absolutely wild. She looked ferocious enough to frighten Laura Milonari, who shrank back against the gilded paneling to try to escape her.

Laura's heart was pounding with fright. She had been prepared to cause a scandal, embarrass Charlie Lassiter—but being attacked by Mrs. Lassiter was not part of her plans. This woman was a virago, not the sweet, helpless little doll she thought she would encounter.

Moira picked up a walking stick that peeked out of a tall Chinese porcelain vase not far from the door and went after Laura Milonari with it, bringing it down on her back and shoulders at least a dozen times before the woman succeeded in reaching the door under a shower of invective. Moira was whacking her so hard she nearly broke the stick across her departing back as Laura scurried frantically out the door.

Then Mrs. Lassiter turned furiously toward the screaming child Signorina Milonari had abandoned in her desperation to flee.

"No, Mama!" shouted Maeve, quite terrified. She raced for the toddler, lifted him off the floor, and hustled him out the door to his sobbing mother as Dietrich tried to calm his future mother-in-law.

"Get out of here and don't ever come back or I'll have the police on you," Maeve threatened. "Get out! Get out!"

Laura, half dazed now and utterly bedraggled, looked at the red-haired girl. The pain from the beating was tremendous, making speech difficult.

"I don't have to come back," she gasped, trying hard to keep a grip on her screeching son. "I've done what I had to do. Now Carlo and that woman will have to live with it."

Her face was so full of hate Maeve felt the pit of her stomach turn cold. Without another word, she grabbed the heavy brass handle of the wrought-iron and glass door and slammed it shut in Laura Milonari's distorted face, putting a safe distance between the woman's hate and her mother. The noise of the door reverberated like thunder inside the foyer.

"Don't think that will be the end of her, Maeveen," Moira said warily. "Not that kind of little tart."

"It had better be," Maeve replied. "I wouldn't like to meet up with her again. What a horror!"

"And," Moira demanded acidly, "just what did you think I was about to do to the little bastard when you hit high C and ran out the door with it? Murder it?"

Maeve blushed. She wasn't exactly sure what Moira intended but it didn't look too good for the child.

"I wouldn't have harmed the brat," her mother stated flatly. "I was about to put it out on the steps."

Moira then turned to study herself in the nearest mirror and was pleased to see that her hair was fine. Only a few tangled strands had managed to work their way loose, while Laura's was a tangled mess— with a few clumps missing.

"Mama," Dietrich said, finally recovering his voice, "what a tigress you are!"

Moira glanced at him in amusement. "You haven't seen the half of it," she replied.

*

When Laura Milonari returned home that day, clutching her frightened son, bedraggled, insulted, and outraged, she lashed out angrily at the man who had put her up to her impromptu visit. He was a slender blond gentleman and her current lover—the man who had made it possible for her to come to Paris from Milan in order to wreck Moira Lassiter's peace of mind, and try to extract money from Charlie.

"That woman is an animal!" Laura shouted, gesticulating wildly. "She nearly ripped my head off! She's a savage! What kind of woman has he taken up with, for God's sake!"

The man smiled in his irritating way and replied that Moira Lassiter was a sensual witch with a murderous disposition, just the sort to appeal to a sportsman like Charlie.

Laura thought he deserved her—forgetting that she, not Charlie, had been the one to break off their affair in Italy so she could dally with a Milanese banker in her native city. Then she had been stuck with the boy, a nuisance until it had been suggested to her that he might finally prove useful now as bait in a blackmail scheme. But nobody had warned her about Moira.

André Viznitski, her visitor, smiled again, enjoying the idea of Moira's outrage. He'd have paid good money to see that cat fight. He wondered if the little red-haired spitfire had joined the fray. She was just as fiery as her mother—worse in some ways. He knew that from sad personal experience.

Well, Laura had proved a useful tool for his purposes. If her former lover decided to buy her off, fine for him. If not, at least he'd had his own fun. It frankly gave him great satisfaction to humiliate those Devereux witches in any way he could, and he looked forward to continuing the game.

*

The atmosphere at the Palais Lassiter was definitely charged with electricity for the rest of the evening. The idea that Charlie could have such a skeleton in his closet shocked Maeve deeply, but her mother's reaction to it unnerved her. Moira was never one to conceal her feelings unnecessarily, and tonight she had come close to going berserk. No matter what she'd told Maeve, Moira had had murder in her eyes when she started toward that child—and Maeve knew it. For the sake of everyone involved, she prayed with all her heart that her mother would never—under any circumstances—have to encounter that boy again. If she did, then Maeve feared for his safety.

*

Laura Milonari's appearance with that baby was a terrible scandal, spoiling what should have been a joyous family occasion. It made all the newspapers in Paris, and Charlie was mortified to receive a letter from his Aunt Ada a month later with a reference to it—as well as a clipping from the *New York Times*, which had carried the story.

Moira wasn't fit to live with for weeks afterward. As soon as her guests had left the party that night, she and Charlie had had a serious discussion at the top of their lungs, and the servants reported seeing Mrs. Lassiter fling some clothes into a trunk and dash wildly downstairs to summon the coachman to take her to the Ritz.

On her heels came Charlie, furious that she was leaving. He carried her, screaming, back upstairs and locked the door so she couldn't escape.

One of the housemaids swore later that Madame had used language to the master so shocking it was a miracle he hadn't killed her. She was a bold, impudent creature to carry on like that and threaten *him* with abandonment—as if she were the one with all the money! To get away with it, she had to have the poor man wrapped around her little finger!

Moira wasn't as sanguine as all that. Charlie had seen the dirty little brat and had suddenly discovered a paternal instinct. It was a bit late in the game as far as she was concerned—and now he actually was talking about having one with her!

She was nearly in despair over that and finally responded to Maeve's questions one day as they were having tea in her daughter's apartment.

Moira looked quite lovely as she sat in the cozy salon opposite Maeve, who had just spent the morning in rehearsals. Moira was wearing a beautiful deep blue silk and lace afternoon dress from Callot Soeurs. It was a wonderful choice, Maeve thought. It made Moira's eyes look even lovelier than usual.

"Do you think the girl was telling the truth?" her daughter asked. "She could have borrowed the child from a street beggar for all we know. The Gypsies on the boulevards do that all the time."

"Do you have eyes in your head, Maeveen? Of course the brat was his. The face was his even if the coloring was the mother's. That little bastard is Charlie's son and he knows it! I can't even pretend not to see the resemblance because it's so obvious. As much as I'd like not to see it," she added. "And now he wants one from me!"

Maeve was startled to hear Moira say this. She didn't generally speak so bluntly about her private matters. Just Maeve's.

"Well, why don't you have one?" she asked, slightly bewildered. "I wouldn't mind."

Moira rolled her eyes in sheer exasperation. The child was so obtuse.

"Don't you think I've tried? I wouldn't mind having one with him— even though it would be awful at my age. But it just hasn't happened!"

Maeve didn't know a lot about babies. She assumed that if Moira had given birth to her, there was always the possibility of her having another. Maeve wasn't about to mention it, but after all, wasn't that what had caused the near tragedy not terribly long ago? Moira had nearly become the mother of a Viznitski.

"I've made an appointment with a very famous doctor in Baden-Baden," she said. "He's supposed to be able to help women who have trouble conceiving. It's a secret," she added in embarrassment. "I told Charlie I had to take the cure because I'm fatigued. I'm going to spend a week there and see if this fellow can help me."

*

When Moira arrived in Baden Baden, she checked into Brenner's Park Hotel under an assumed name and kept her appointment with the famous German specialist. After a thorough and excruciatingly painful examination, the doctor asked point-blank, "When did you have the abortion, Frau Schmidt?"

"What are you talking about?" she asked him, stunned.

"Well, it's the only thing that would have left your insides so badly scarred. My God, whoever did it was a butcher. You're lucky you're alive today."

"I never had an abortion," Moira stated flatly. She didn't care that he could tell. She didn't care that he knew she was lying. Nothing would make her admit that.

"Well, Frau Schmidt, this abortion which you never had is preventing you from conceiving again. Do you have any children?"

"Yes," she said, staring at the man. "A daughter." What was he saying? No child with Charlie? Nothing to counterbalance that little dago brat?

"Not even the possibility?" Moira blurted out. "You can't be serious!"

"Gnädige Frau," the doctor replied gently, "I wish you could see what a mass of scar tissue you have. It's unbelievable. To the best of my knowledge, no woman with such extensive damage could ever conceive a child again."

Tears were welling in Moira's beautiful eyes. She looked so stricken the doctor felt sorry for her. He hated breaking bad news; it was so draining.

"I'm sorry, gnädige Frau," he murmured. "But I can't lie to you."

Moira's eyes were focused on a wall chart in his antiseptic-smelling examining room, a graph depicting the stages of pregnancy. She didn't notice it. She didn't see or hear the doctor either. She was too absorbed in the mad tangle of her own thoughts.

The clinic at St. Denis. The pain. The fear of dying and leaving Maeveen alone among foreigners. Viznitski. André Viznitski.

And that little brown-haired brat, yowling with fright in her foyer as she glared at him so full of fury. Charlie's only child.

My God, Moira thought, why had she been so stupid? Why couldn't she have met Charlie before she ever laid eyes on Viznitski? She had made the choice to be André's mistress thinking it would solve her problems. Now it turned out it had only created a hangman's noose for her new hopes.

Damn him! Moira thought later as she pounded her hotel bed with her fists. Why was she continuing to suffer from one stupid mistake? It wasn't fair!

There would never be any children for her and Charlie now. She wondered if he would hate her for this one day. Worse than that, would he find her less attractive now that she was sterile? That was a real possibility. Men were so egotistical. They all wanted little replicas of themselves, and if that was impossible, there was usually trouble. Damn!

And damn that Italian slut, Moira thought furiously, daring to bring that little bastard into her home! That was provocation. More, it was almost a declaration of war. The bitch! It was as if Laura Milonari had found the only weak spot in her defenses—before she herself had. It was eerie in its accuracy—and it was going to be a burden in the future.

*

Maeve noticed a change in Moira when she returned from Baden-Baden. She didn't look rested. If anything, she looked pale and drawn. She also refused to reveal what the doctor had told her, leading Maeve to conclude the trip had been a failure.

Despite that, she managed to regain her normal bounce after Charlie surprised her at breakfast one morning with a pair of diamond and sapphire earrings from Boucheron. They were an impressive example of the jeweler's art, being large enough to be highly visible across a crowded ballroom.

"Blue to match your beautiful eyes, Moira," he announced. "Do you like them?"

"I love them," she laughed. "You're too good to me, Charlie."

He looked abashed. "Not good enough at all. But I will be."

For starters, the earrings were certainly a step in the right direction.

*

The wedding took precedence over everything else on the ladies' agenda— except for Maeve's duties at the Opéra-Comique and a variety of guest appearances in Berlin, Warsaw, and Breslau, where she was singing in Puccini's operas. Her second Berlin appearance, as Mimi in *La Bohème* at the Royal Opera House, brought congratulations from Kaiser Wilhelm in the royal box.

Wilhelm burst out laughing as he recognized "the little Boer girl" who had asked for troops, and he complimented her on her singing and acting.

"If I hadn't been anointed by God to preside over the destiny of Germany," he confided, startling Maeve, "I would have been a great artist."

Not knowing how to respond to this amazing revelation, Maeve looked into the flashing imperial blue eyes and said with equal solemnity, "Your Majesty, it's our loss. You would probably have been one of the greatest actors of all time."

This bit of blarney went down quite well and earned Maeve an invitation to dinner, adding her to the list of various singers the Kaiser had honored at his table, including Geraldine Farrar, for whom all Berliners had a soft spot.

*

The night before the wedding, Maeve went to Moira's mansion for a last-minute conference of logistics and spent the night, since everything had been taken there for the occasion. Her trousseau, which had cost a fortune at the house of Paquin, was already packed in large Louis Vuitton trunks along with a dazzling assortment of lace-trimmed and embroidered lingerie from one of the fanciest convents in Paris.

This embroidery business was an interesting sideline to the nuns' other duties, and it brought in quite a bit of money by providing fine lingerie for aristocratic brides and babies. In Maeve's case there had been some question about accepting the order, but Moira's persistence won out and her daughter's nightgowns bore the same mark as those of several duchesses.

"How did you persuade them, Mama?" Maeve asked in surprise.

"Oh, I told them we were descended from Brian Boru, High King of Ireland. The head nun had a fine collection of copies of the *Almanach de Gotha* and *Burke's Peerage*, but I patiently explained that nobody had ever bothered to compile a listing for Celtic royalty."

Maeve laughed. "You told them that with a straight face?"

"Of course. And she then admitted defeat, took my word for it— and my money as well. If you offer them enough, it generally brings them around to your way of thinking."

Maeve wondered if Moira had ever told Dietrich this fable. He'd probably believe it and start figuring out a way to work it into a family crest. He was very keen on symbols.

CHAPTER 20

On the morning of her wedding, Maeve awakened to find a dismal gray sky and rain pouring down by the bucketful. She was so crestfallen she wanted to crawl back under the covers, but Arlette and Moira fed her, forced her into her bath, and kept chattering about "early-morning mists."

"If this is mist, I'm the Empress Alexandra," Maeve wailed as the pair, flanked by Madame Paquin herself and her chief assistant, dressed her in what had to be an outstanding specimen of the dressmaker's art.

No stage costume or evening gown Maeve had ever worn could compare with this. It was exquisite, and it should have been. Its creation had claimed the labor of a dozen seamstresses, embroiderers, and lace-makers.

As Maeve stood transfixed before the three-paneled mirror in Moira's dressing room, she saw the elegant satin train flare out in a burst of lace-trimmed splendor. Around her bodice and at the three-quarter sleeves, more lace—fine Carrickmacross from Ireland—showed off her creamy skin.

"Her small waist seems to belong to a doll," Madame Paquin remarked to Moira. Hardly any of her clients had one as tiny.

Satisfied that she had the costume right, Maeve held out her hand for the veil, a frothy confection of Carrickmacross lace worked with a delicate border of shamrocks and bees.

The headpiece had proved to be a bone of contention. Charlie wished her to wear the diamond tiara he and Moira had given her as a wedding present. It was only one of several generous gifts, including a fine pair of carriage horses from County Kildare. Maeve, on the other hand, preferred to wear a bridal wreath of fresh orange blossoms and gardenias.

Charlie had been quite forcefully in favor of the tiara, so to preserve peace in the family Maeve diplomatically opted for the diamonds. It was certainly no sacrifice; she was lucky she had them. But she did love fresh flowers.

"Well, I look a bit like Elisabeth in *Tannhäuser*," she murmured as she saw herself in the mirror. "It's a very nice effect."

It got even better as the sun came out unexpectedly an hour before she was to ride to the *mairie*. The alternate plans which called for a closed carriage were put aside, and Maeve was driven to her wedding in an open white landau, lavishly decorated with flowers, with Charlie sitting opposite her looking every inch the proud father.

Maeve's arrival at the *mairie* of the arrondissement seemed like opening night at the opera. At least two hundred uninvited spectators were straining against the velvet ropes Dietrich had ordered strung out on the sidewalk to clear the path of the guests into the city hall. Overhead a white canopy extended to the curb from the front portal, awaiting the entrance of the bride.

"My God!" Maeve exclaimed to Charlie as she reached her destination. "Who are all those people?"

"Your fans, I suppose. You're a very popular girl."

"Good Lord." She was used to a lot of fuss at the opera, but this was so unexpected. She couldn't imagine strangers milling around in the middle of the day to see her arrive at her wedding. Didn't they have anything better to do?

"Smile!" Charlie ordered. "Don't look so bewildered. They want to see a prima donna. Show them one so they can tell their grandchildren about this moment."

"Don't be daft!" Maeve laughed, quite pleased by all the fuss.

Since the people seemed so taken with her, Maeve decided she owed it to herself not to disappoint them. Turning on the kind of smile she usually reserved for curtain calls, she gamely descended from her carriage, took Charlie's arm, managed to maneuver both her train and her bouquet with her other hand, and swept grandly into the neoclassic building on a chorus of "Bravas!" It seemed to please everyone that she looked so fine. Several fans even applauded!

Once inside, she had to wait for her mother to loop up the long

train of her gown so as not to ruin it on the none-too-clean stairs up to
the office where the ceremony was to take place. Dietrich was there to
meet her and accompany her upstairs, with Moira, Charlie, Marc Antoine, and Arlette bringing up the rear. A few other specially invited
guests like Angélique and Julien Roussel were already in place, chatting
with the distinguished-looking representative of the Republic who was
to do the honors.

It wasn't the grand occasion Maeve had always pictured in her
mind—the solemn progress up the main aisle of some church, the gorgeous train of her splendid gown sweeping behind her, the scent of
hundreds of out-of-season flowers perfuming the air. It was a civil ceremony performed by some Frenchman with a red, white, and blue sash
over his business suit, his wing-tipped collar pinching his fat neck, his
spectacles glittering a little as he played his part in the business of uniting
Mademoiselle Maeve—he had a hard time with her first name—Devereux with Baron Dietrich von Reuter. Still, it was a real wedding and
that's what counted.

Moira, who had been escorted to her seat for the brief ceremony
by Charlie, was as happy as if she were sitting in a place of honor in
Notre Dame. This beauty in white silk and diamonds was the same girl
who had helped her raise hell in that kangaroo court and accompanied
her to jail. That bedraggled little ragamuffin who had plotted an uprising
was the same person standing so tall and straight beside Baron von Reuter,
looking as regal as Queen Victoria. And she was far more beautiful. In
fact, she was almost as beautiful as her own mother—Moira's supreme
compliment.

Mrs. Lassiter dabbed silently at her cheeks as a tear rolled down
one, then the other, splattering her five rows of pearls and the diamond
brooch adorning the bodice of her sea-green satin gown. Delicate lace
ruffles at her elbows fluttered as she discreetly applied her lace handkerchief to her tears of joy. The bobbing of soft ostrich plumes on her lace-
trimmed toque reflected her emotions; this was her ultimate triumph over
Hubertus and she was savoring it to her heart's delight.

Maeve's emotions were more complicated as she stood there covered
in fine lace and diamonds beside Dietrich. As she listened to the words
of the civil ceremony, she glanced shyly at her new husband and found
it difficult to believe this was actually happening. It all seemed a dream.

The fear and madness of South Africa, her father's terrible death,
Moira's escapades and her own ill-fated reunion with Sean Farrell—all
these memories swirled around her as she took her vows. The other
memories, the happy moments onstage, the wild success as Tosca that

night at the Opéra-Comique and her brilliant pairing with Marc Antoine came to mind too—all these events, both good and bad, so much a part of what she had been and what she had become.

Gazing tenderly at Dietrich through her misty bridal veil, Maeve vowed to make a success of her marriage and to make it a real marriage, not the kind of cynical arrangement Moira hinted at. She was La Devereux and that made her unique, but as Dietrich slipped the gold wedding band on her finger, Maeve promised herself that she would be a wonderful Baroness von Reuter and give the lie to all of Hubertus's dismal forebodings. She would make Dietrich proud of her. Better than that, she would make him happy.

"My God," he murmured as the final words of the ceremony faded away, "you're mine at last."

In response Maeve slipped her hand into his and whispered, "Forever."

*

To Maeve's surprise, there were even more people outside the *mairie* when she and Dietrich made their exit than there had been before. Two policemen were ordering the crowd back behind the velvet ropes to permit the departure of well-known Parisian figures ranging from Marc Antoine de Marigny to the millionaire Paris Singer.

"My God," murmured the bridegroom as he helped Maeve into the open carriage, "this is amazing. It's like a circus."

A few women in the crowd were practically jumping up and down with excitement at seeing Marc Antoine and Julien in the flesh. The star of the Casino had sent Angélique on ahead. His fans didn't want to see *her,* he maintained. They ought to savor their illusions. He and Marco certainly looked quite dashing in formal dress—a vision those girls in the crowd would lovingly describe to friends and family later. Marc Antoine was trying unsuccessfully to escape the clutches of an elderly female who was gushing over his green eyes. Julien was fending off a crazed trio of shopgirls who were shrieking in his ears.

As the carriage pulled away from the *mairie,* followed by a string of smart vehicles carrying Moira, Charlie, Angélique, and all the rest of the guests, Dietrich was startled to find himself pelted with flowers by Maeve's admirers. One bunch of daisies knocked his silk top hat off his head and onto the floor of the carriage.

Maeve was used to flying tributes and gaily laughed, blowing kisses to the crowd while her new husband tried his best to look composed.

"Never complain about flowers," she teased him. "It's the ripe tomatoes you have to watch out for!"

She gave her fans a gracious wave of her hand and indicated all was well.

The weather was now so splendid Moira's staff had been able to go along with the plans for extending the party outdoors. Gaily striped marquees decorated the elegant formal gardens as beautifully gowned ladies and their escorts in full morning dress sauntered among topiary trees. Waiters handed around flutes of Mumm's champagne and enticing little edibles, and a small orchestra played Mozart and Haydn in the background.

Japanese bankers, friends of the groom, mingled with the European guests, while Marc Antoine exercised his usual charm on susceptible ladies in couturier gowns.

The bride, everyone agreed, looked even more beautiful than she usually did, and it was hoped the bridegroom brought a more serious attitude to this marriage than he had to his first. Paris Singer commented to a male acquaintance that Moira ought to be careful with her new son-in-law. Look what had happened to Hélène von Ebert!

Charlie looked so wonderful beside Moira that for a second Maeve believed she was looking at Pat Devereux. He surely would be pleased for his daughter, she thought. It was a shame he wasn't there to see her now—a brand-new baroness in a sumptuous gown and diamonds in her hair.

The wedding gifts were on display in one of the salons—with three servants on duty to make certain none of them went missing. Moira wasn't so much in awe of her guests that she believed they were angels.

Two of the larger gifts—those chestnut carriage horses from Ireland—were in the stable at Dietrich's home, but there were plenty of things to stare at, including a fine Fabergé vodka set in enamel and gilt from Sean and Zofia Farrell, a splendid chased silver bowl from Fabergé's Moscow branch courtesy of Fedya and Iola Chaliapin, and a rather baroque silver tea service from Dietrich's nervous board of directors in Berlin. As a friendly gesture they had sent the bride a personal gift of sables which were very well received and locked away in the fur storage vault until next winter.

Marc Antoine had given his favorite soprano a set of pearl-handled silver fish knives and forks, and Julien and Angélique Roussel had contributed a lovely pair of fine Sèvres porcelain vases.

Other presents ranged from a magnificent long double strand of pearls from Dietrich's Japanese colleagues to a surprisingly nice set of monogrammed china from Charlie's two aunts in New York to a lovely crystal vase from President and Mrs. Roosevelt.

Monsieur Carré of the Opéra-Comique sent a set of Baccarat champagne flutes—to toast future successes—while Monsieur Gunsbourg of Monte Carlo dispatched four cases of Louis Roederer champagne, proving that the two directors had something in common.

The wedding was a great social occasion, and when the young couple finally left for the train station to pick up the Orient Express and depart for their honeymoon in Venice, the society reporter from *Le Figaro* was beginning his breathless account of La Devereux's wedding—complete with estimates of the money spent on flowers and gushing descriptions of the beauty of the bride and her mother, with the inevitable reminder to his readers that it was the handsome bridegroom's second trip to the altar, his first marriage having ended in divorce.

Maeve had already had a strained farewell with Moira, who had spent the better part of an hour trying to impart some final gems of maternal wisdom to her child. She was quite put out when Maeve declared she already had a fair idea of what transpired between spouses.

"So," Moira said with a gleam in her eye, "the little goose has already lost some of her feathers!"

"Jesus, Mama!"

Maeve turned pink and refused to divulge any information, except to say she had purchased a book in Berlin that explained everything Moira might have omitted, and no, she wasn't particularly horrified, numb with shock, or ill-disposed toward her wifely duties. Besides, associating with people like Marc Antoine, one heard lots of things about life, she declared ingenuously. And if Moira thought she was going to learn anything about those nights in St. Petersburg, she had come to the wrong girl, Maeve said to herself. That was off limits for discussion.

Giving Maeve a suspicious look that made her turn bright pink all over again, Moira gestured as if to pursue the topic, then shrugged, making all her diamonds sparkle. "All right," she nodded. "Perhaps that boy likes them innocent. Who can tell? Well, good luck to you, Maeveen. I do hope you and Dietrich will be happy."

"Thank you, Mama. We will."

Baron von Reuter kissed Moira affectionately, shook hands solemnly with Charlie, and impatiently whisked Maeve out of the house and into their waiting coach. After so many delays, he couldn't bear to be late for the train—and his honeymoon.

At the station the young couple were met by a porter who carted their trunks on board and congratulated them on their marriage—startling Maeve, who didn't expect all of Paris to know.

The Orient Express was the foremost luxury train in Europe and it lived up to its reputation. Its beautiful inlaid paneling caught the attention of the travelers as they entered and were conducted to their compartments by a multilingual employee who wished them a pleasant journey and deposited them into an elegantly designed enclosure fit for royalty. Everything about the train breathed luxury, comfort, and style.

Maeve remembered with a pang that the first time she had traveled on the train had been for that adventure in Belgrade with Sean Farrell.

Feeling guilty for dwelling on it, she tried to put that excursion out of her mind. Sean had been Moira's lover then and he had promised them a new life in Paris. At that time, Maeve had had no idea what went on between lovers. How far from those days she was now. A mere glance at Dietrich was enough to excite him, she reflected—not unhappily—and it seemed as if they had now made love in every available nook and cranny between Petersburg and Paris. The man was seemingly addicted to her, she thought, and he couldn't slake his desire if he made love to her a hundred times.

This passion made Dietrich so deliciously vulnerable, Maeve could never bring herself to refuse him even if she had wanted to—and of course she didn't. Her newly discovered pleasure was beginning to ensnare her as well. Never in her life had she been so sensitive to a touch or a silky caress. Maeve's responsiveness had reached the point where even Dietrich's whispered endearments were enough to arouse her. His way of murmuring into her ear and then punctuating his thoughts with a soft, explosive kiss on the same spot created a crescendo of startling desire that flowed from his lips through her whole body, finally reaching its peak in her delicate center, where it had the effect of a sensual tidal wave on her nervous system.

Even the thought of those kisses could send shivers through Maeve's body. But they were nothing compared with the violence he did to her emotions whenever Dietrich touched her breasts. The sensation was beyond belief. The slightest stroke of his fingers against her nipples wreaked the most delicious havoc on her senses. Whenever he kissed her breasts and tenderly took the hard, pink nipples into his mouth, Maeve thought she'd die—from pleasure. She had become a finely tuned instrument now, and all too willing to be played upon.

In their luxurious compartment on board the Orient Express, Maeve and Dietrich made love for the first time as man and wife, and nestled in soft linen sheets, lying warm and willing in Dietrich's arms,

Maeve experienced her first orgasm. The sensation was incredible, a stunning climax to everything she had felt until now. Suddenly Maeve seemed to be lighter than air, giddily lost in a paradise bounded only by her husband's arms. The emotional heights she scaled in those moments left her thrilled, exhausted and sated, limply clinging to Dietrich, too amazed to believe it was real—and greedily eager to recreate that passion again and again. He seemed as dazed as she was, Maeve noticed through her sensual afterglow. Their lovemaking had drained him as well.

She had a new life, Maeve thought with satisfaction, as she recalled her conversation with Sean on Nevsky Prospect. And now Dietrich was part of it. She smiled drowsily as she caressed his tousled hair, kissing him tenderly as he pulled her to him.

And Sean Farrell—or Ivan Petrovic—was with his pretty wife in faraway St. Petersburg, a princely Montenegrin in the midst of family intrigues. How strange life was, she reflected. The handsome adventurer who had freed her from a prison was near-royalty, and she herself was on her way to becoming as adored as some princesses.

*

The Grand Hôtel des Bains, one of Venice's showplaces, was located on the fashionable Lido, which meant that its guests had to board a gondola at the canal near the train station and settle in for the long ride to their destination, taking in a spectacular view of the city as they did.

"Wagner loved Venice," Dietrich said as he assisted his bride into the gleaming black gondola. He gave orders to the gondolier and sat back to observe the panorama, a scene out of a fairy tale.

"It's so exotic," Maeve said in delight. "I've never seen a city built on water like this."

"A thousand years ago it gave refuge to mainlanders fleeing the barbaric hordes from the north." Dietrich smiled. "Probably my ancestors. Now it welcomes artists and honeymoon couples. A nice change, don't you think?"

Their gondolier felt compelled to give his passengers a rundown of the local sights they were passing this morning, naming this church and that palazzo, reeling off associations with Lord Byron, Shelley, Napoleon, and of course, Richard Wagner.

Maeve smiled and nestled against Dietrich. She watched the Venetian's smooth movements as he guided their narrow craft down the Grand Canal carrying on a nonstop commentary, a fine-looking fellow in the usual blue-and-white-striped jersey and black-banded straw hat.

It all seemed magical, gliding almost noiselessly through watery boulevards past palaces of ocher, saffron, and rose with their striped poles and their private gondolas bobbing up and down before them. On second-floor terraces with Byzantine arches Maeve caught glimpses of maids shaking out comforters, gentlemen observing the passing traffic in the canal, ladies taking their morning coffee.

"What strange architecture," she mused. "I've never seen anything like it. It's so bizarre. But lovely. Like something out of the Arabian Nights."

"Venice has borrowed a little from everyone who ever came here, signora," their gondolier declared with a cheerful grin. "We're very international. If you would like a good look at our past, you and the signore ought to visit the Doges' Palace. Magnificent. Then go to St. Mark's Square and enjoy coffee and pastry while you listen to the music. Very nice."

As he said that, a line of black gondolas floated into sight, heading downstream—a funeral procession with several of the boats loaded with flowers, followed by the mourners who tailed the waterborne coffin. Maeve shuddered.

"They're going to our cemetery island," their gondolier explained. "With us, everything is done by water. Even the funerals."

Maeve burrowed close to Dietrich in the cushioned seat and slipped her fingers through his. She suddenly felt a coolness in the air.

"It's part of life too," he said with a shrug, putting his arm around her as he nodded in the direction of the procession. "But look over there, *Liebchen*—floating groceries."

To Maeve's surprise she saw a flotilla of gondolas piled high with baskets of bread, heaps of oranges, heads of lettuce, ice-packed scampi, eels, and octopus.

"They're making their rounds," the gondolier said. "They'll stop at several neighborhoods so the housewives can buy."

Venice seemed to Maeve like a giant stage set with water. She was pleased Dietrich had chosen it. She leaned cozily against him, smiling like a contented kitten as their boatman steered them out to the Lido, bellowing a decent enough rendition of "La donna è mobile" as he went.

*

The management of the Grand Hôtel des Bains was delighted to play host to such a distinguished and beautiful artist. The manager-director, Signor Belloti himself, greeted Maeve and Dietrich upon their arrival, presented her with a lovely bouquet of white roses, kissed her hand, and told her he had seen her in *La Bohème* in Monte Carlo, an unforgettable experience.

"We Venetians would like to see you at the Teatro La Fenice one day, Baronessa," he added as he conducted the couple to their suite, an airy place looking out over the Lido beach with a wide expanse of blue sky and water.

"I hope to accommodate the Venetians." Maeve smiled. "It would be my pleasure."

When their host took his leave, after supervising the arrival of their luggage and assuring them he was at their beck and call, Maeve and Dietrich sighed, gratefully closed the door, and rushed to the windows to take another look at the breathtaking view beyond their terrace.

"It's so beautiful," Maeve exclaimed, turning for a moment to stare at the bedroom.

From the floor to the ceiling, everything was exquisite, expensive, and dazzling. Fine mosaics in marble lay underfoot, while overhead a huge chandelier, laced with hundreds of glass flowers swirling in a maze of curved branches with whimsical touches of color, provided illumination. Dominating the room was a huge gilded bed, designed in a style that could only be called neo-Byzantine-Moorish-Venetian baroque. Various armoires, cabinets, dressing tables, and chairs echoed its fanciful lines, making the new baroness feel she had just stepped into some rich Middle Eastern fantasy. When she looked up, she saw there were dozens of plump nymphs pursued by satyrs scampering across the painted ceiling, reminding her of Moira's Parisian mansion.

"I think that looks like fun," Dietrich murmured as he, too, eyed the scene.

He slid his arm around Maeve and drew her closer to him, coming into conflict with her corset.

"Take off that dreadful thing," he whispered, kissing her little pink ear and sending a shock through her whole body. "It's like armor!"

"I thought we were going to see the sights," she said as she stroked his blond hair. "I can't be seen in public without my corset."

"I don't care if your public doesn't see you for a week." He smiled. "It's your husband who has precedence here."

Maeve laughed as Dietrich picked her up and carried her over to the bed. He was stronger than she had suspected; somehow she had never pictured him lifting anything heavier than a briefcase. This was exciting.

"Are you going to ravish me?" she asked cheerfully from among the pillows as she kicked off her shoes.

"Definitely. It's my barbaric blood. We Huns are known for that."

Dietrich undressed Maeve, marveling at the amount of under-clothing a lady wore. She seemed to have on every garment known to womankind. When she was finally down to her silk stockings, he sighed and didn't even bother to remove them. She looked rather sweet like that.

Maeve slid underneath the soft coverlet and smiled.

"You look very beautiful, Dietrich," she said as she observed him.

"You're not supposed to look," he replied, a bit rattled. "It's not ladylike."

"*You* can look."

"That's different."

"Well," Maeve retorted, "I've seen marble statues at the Louvre wearing just a little more than what you have on now."

Dietrich laughed, neatly folded his clothing over a chair, and slipped under the covers. "Well, *Liebchen,*" he murmured, "I don't mind you looking at antiquities in fig leaves, but since I've left mine home, it makes me shy to see you looking at me."

That wasn't a long-lasting affliction, Maeve found out, and it seemed to her afterward that when Moira asked her about the sights of Venice, all she could recall were painted ceilings of nymphs and the glisten of sunlight on the canals.

CHAPTER 21

The shock of seeing Laura Milonari and their son had been a lot more dangerous for Charlie than Moira ever suspected. Without telling his wife, he had begun sending money to Laura to use for little Gianni. He had almost no feeling for the mother, since she had jilted him for an Italian banker, but the thought of having a son who looked just like him thrilled Charlie. It was, in a way, compensation for a bad mistake in Italy several years ago—the only good thing to have survived his foolish affair with Laura. That had been stupidity compounded by lust in a strange city with too much romantic atmosphere and too much naïveté on his part. He was mourning Esmeralda and in need of affection. Meeting Laura seemed to guarantee a steady supply of that, but in fact it guaranteed only misery. She was a woman without softness. It had been a miserable period in his life, one best forgotten.

Charlie loved Moira; he loved her deeply. But he was fascinated by this small replica of himself and couldn't bear the thought of him growing up in poverty when it would be no sacrifice at all to provide him with a decent home, food, and clothing.

Therefore Charlie Lassiter sent a lawyer to visit Signorina Milonari in her small, cramped apartment in Clichy and proposed a contract: If she would swear never to come near him again, he would graciously provide a much better apartment for her and Gianni, a nurse to look after the child, and a monthly allowance to her and his son. If she ever showed up to confront him in person again, she would forfeit everything, and the contract would be rendered null and void.

Dazed by her good fortune, Laura agreed to it all and shortly afterward moved herself and her two-year-old son into a large, well-lit new apartment off the avenue MacMahon, a stylish Paris neighborhood.

*

Maeve and Dietrich had arrived in the Saxon capital of Dresden in December 1905, prepared for cold weather. Baroness von Reuter was nicely sheltered from the frigid temperatures by a sable muff, coat, and hat and fur-lined boots, but neither she nor her husband was prepared for the scene at their hotel. It seemed as if every music lover on the planet had taken it upon himself to head for Dresden and the world premiere of Richard Strauss's new opera *Salome*. And they all seemed to be descending on the same hotel.

"This is a madhouse," Dietrich muttered as he nearly collided with an English reporter upon entering. The entire lobby was filled with an excitable crowd who all seemed intent upon spotting celebrities. As Maeve stepped through the wrought-iron and glass doors and proceeded toward the front desk, three Italian ladies came scampering over to see if it was Luisa Tetrazzini under all that sable.

Jesus, Mary, and Joseph! Maeve thought in alarm. Was she putting on weight? Tetrazzini had a voice anyone would envy and a genuinely lovely personality—but she was the size of a house! Tetrazzini indeed!

"I'm Maeve Devereux," she said, removing her coat to reveal a slender figure in a tailored red wool suit.

"Ah, La Devereux!" exclaimed the leader of the pack. *"Che bella!"*

"And this is my husband," Maeve smiled, presenting a startled Dietrich to the three bejeweled strangers who were admiring her.

"Ah, Signor Devereux. *Piacere*," beamed the leader, loaded with diamonds, furs, egret plumes, and enough kohl on her eyes to make Cleopatra jealous.

"Baron von Reuter," Dietrich retorted, clicking his heels, not pleased at all. It wasn't the first time someone had called him Mr. Devereux, and it was beginning to gall him.

"You could have been friendlier to the old ladies," Maeve said later as they dressed for the opera. "It was a natural mistake on their part."

Dietrich looked annoyed. "I don't think it's natural at all. You are my wife, therefore you bear my name—not the other way round."

"But since they know about me and don't know you, of course they would think Devereux was my married name. It's nothing to grouse about, *Schatzi*. Sometimes you do have a very thin skin."

The baron whirled around to give his wife a sharp look, but she was busy fussing over her gown and chattering with Arlette, who was trying to straighten out the neckline.

"That's a trifle daring, isn't it?" he murmured. To his alarm, Maeve's creamy bosom seemed about to overflow its bodice. "I think you ought to raise it just a bit."

The women exchanged glances. Maeve nodded. Arlette obediently tugged it higher and fluffed up a border of lace to camouflage more of Maeve's cleavage.

"Happy?" she asked. "Now I look as if I'm dressed for a convent tea."

"Much better." He smiled.

Dietrich let his wife tie his white bow tie since she had the right touch, even better than any of his valets. He then lifted her magnificent diamond and sapphire necklace from its velvet box and fastened it around her neck.

"You look beautiful," he said. "Absolutely dazzling."

"And covered up to my neck."

"Modesty is a becoming trait," he said, smiling again. "Especially in a wife."

A moment later Dietrich turned away to let his valet help him into his tail coat and was surprised to hear a burst of smothered laughter from Arlette.

"What's the matter?" he inquired. "Does something amuse you?"

"No sir," the girl replied, digging her nails into the palms of her hands. "I just sneezed."

"Ah," he nodded. But Dietrich knew she was lying. He had caught a glimpse of Maeve in the mirror as she stuck her tongue out at him behind his back, and he was a bit shocked.

A married baroness ought to set a better example for the servants, he thought. These childish caprices were not seemly now, not even for an artiste, and certainly not in front of the help.

With a wrenching pang of guilt, Baron von Reuter recalled that Lotte would never have done such a thing—or at least not before that dreadful night. It was an unsettling recollection.

*

The world premiere of *Salome* was the biggest thing to happen to Dresden since anyone could remember. Although the city prided itself on being the royal capital of Saxony and had seen its share of artistic triumphs,

Strauss's latest work, based on the notorious play by Oscar Wilde, was being awaited with bated breath. The general feeling was that the elegantly decadent creation was destined for either a scandal of major proportions or frenzied acclaim. The audience crowding into the Court Opera House was hoping for a bit of both.

"The soprano singing the lead is as large as a beer barrel," Dietrich remarked as he and his beautiful wife were shown to their box. "I hope she doesn't attempt the Dance of the Seven Veils. Her usual specialty is chaste Rhine maidens." Speculation about the famous dance was a prime topic of conversation in the coffee houses.

"Then it ought to be an interesting evening." Maeve smiled. "I heard someone in the lobby betting twenty marks the police will raid the theater."

Glancing around the brightly lit auditorium with its gilt carvings and crystal chandeliers, Maeve recognized Richard Strauss and his formidable wife, Pauline, deep in conversation with a local music critic. Germany's leading composer and conductor was resting his baton tonight. Strauss was allowing Ernst von Schuch the honor of presiding over the first performance.

"Ah," Dietrich murmured, "look—Geraldine Farrar!"

Maeve took the mother-of-pearl opera glasses from her husband and trained them on her rival soprano. Farrar was lovely, a pretty brunette in an elegant Paris gown. Strauss had also invited her to the premiere and in fact had told her he was looking for a singer who could act and dance half-dressed while doing justice to his score.

The soprano had laughingly thanked him for the compliment but declined the opportunity. Her voice wasn't yet prepared for it, she said. Among Germany's fine collection of Wagnerian sopranos, the required combination of leather lungs and a shapely figure was even more elusive, a daunting obstacle to the proper staging of the masterpiece. For the time being, the sixteen-year-old siren of Judea would look depressingly matronly.

"Farrar looks quite nice this evening," Maeve commented as she handed the glasses back. "I always admired her voice."

"You're better on both counts," Dietrich replied, making his wife smile. Dietrich could be very sweet when he said things like that, she reflected. And behind her fan of large white ostrich plumes, Maeve tugged discreetly at her neckline, lowering it at least to the level of Geraldine Farrar's.

As the houselights finally dimmed and the cream of international society and the far-flung artistic community settled in for the one-act opera, a hush descended on the theater and the curtain rose on the banquet hall of the Tetrarch of Judea.

The opera began with a Guards officer praising the beauty of the Princess Salome and ended with the luscious and perverse heroine being crushed under the shields of the soldiers. In between, the aging Herod had lusted after his teenaged stepdaughter, begged Salome to dance, been repeatedly rebuffed, then granted his wish—only to have the vicious little vixen demand the head of Jokanaan—John the Baptist—as her reward.

When Salome took the severed head on its silver platter, an audible gasp rippled through the opera house. A few cries of "Disgusting!" accompanied it, but that was nothing compared with the reaction to the kiss Salome planted on Jokanaan's dead lips.

If they don't raid the place and stop the show now, it's a hit, Maeve thought, her eyes riveted to the scene. She listened for the sound of footsteps rushing up the aisle, but nothing happened. Not a single Saxon policeman appeared to cry "Stop!" Strauss's music, his gorgeous, revolutionary music, and the luscious decadence of the play had won the spectators' hearts.

A few diehards were revolted by the "lack of decency," but as Dietrich said, "He took his theme from the Bible, so who could really cast any stones?"

The applause at the end was violent, earsplitting, as people stood up and shouted, screamed, called for the composer. Herr Dr. Strauss, a blond, curly-haired Bavarian of mild appearance and peaceful manner, appeared onstage in evening dress to take the applause of his admirers. In his eyes was the look of a man who had just conquered the world.

Maeve was so keyed up by the disturbing beauty of the opera she insisted upon congratulating Herr Strauss as he was leaving the theater and telling him she was going to make Salome her finest role one day.

Frau Pauline Strauss looked coolly at the bejeweled, befurred young beauty and demanded an introduction. When she realized who Maeve was, she murmured nastily, "Ach, Juliette," recalling Maeve's Berlin disaster.

Strauss laughed and accepted Maeve's homage. He hoped, he said cheerfully, that it would be soon.

*

When Maeve and Dietrich were in their hotel bedroom that night, Baron von Reuter was bewildered to see his wife pile on half a dozen silk petticoats and dim the lights.

"What are you doing?" he inquired uncertainly as he stood watching her in his nightshirt, about to climb into bed.

"Shh. Just look," she ordered. "The soprano tonight, Marie Wittich, couldn't carry off the role, but I can. Oh, Dietrich, I could do it like no one else! I would be a gorgeous Salome!"

While he observed her from the large carved mahogany bed as a captive audience, Maeve floated around the room, imitating the ballet dancer who had actually performed the Dance of the Seven Veils.

She was alarmingly sensual, Dietrich noticed, dramatically flinging aside her silky coverings as she undulated in a controlled frenzy, hair and petticoats a swirl of color. He hadn't seen anyone move like that since he had visited Constantinople as a child and witnessed a Circassian girl entertain her harem colleagues with a belly dance. If he closed his eyes, he could almost picture it now, so many years later: the glossy black hair of the women, their jeweled hands, their slim feet painted with henna, the scent of rich Oriental perfume surrounding them . . .

Almost in a dream, he watched Maeve fling off the last "veil" but one, pause dramatically, and send her silky cover flying toward the ceiling before collapsing in a heap of exhausted passion in his arms, wearing nothing but her diamond and sapphire necklace.

Dietrich was so shocked by that performance he murmured, "My God, if you ever did that for anyone else, I think I'd kill you."

"Would you give me the head of John the Baptist?" she demanded, smiling triumphantly as she wrapped her arms around her husband.

"I'd give you John, the Twelve Apostles, and any other thing you chose to ask for," he replied, enfolding her in his embrace and dragging her under the down-filled comforter. "My God, if you had been onstage tonight, there would have been a scandal in Saxony!"

Dietrich was so aroused his heart was pounding as he kissed Maeve all over, unable to let her go. She was an intoxicant like champagne—or opium. When he made love to her he was embracing her, Salome, both of them together—wild, beautiful, sensual, and accessible only to him. She was unlike any of the other women he had had.

"I will kiss Jokanaan's lips," she murmured sleepily afterward. "And I will drive the people wild!"

As Dietrich cradled Maeve in his arms, he wondered uneasily if the beautiful woman he had married was beginning to crave strong sensations for their own sake, lured by the exotic and the bizarre.

As he kissed her ear and the back of her neck, Dietrich whispered, "Will you love me in ten years as much as you love me now?"

Maeve turned around in bewilderment and snuggled as close to him as possible. "What a silly question," she laughed. "In ten years, I imagine I'll love you even more. Why are you asking me such a foolish thing?"

He had to laugh too. He didn't really know, he admitted; he just wanted to be sure.

Maeve stroked his hair and kissed him very softly, treating him as sweetly as if he were a child. How could he ever doubt her? she wondered. What nonsense!

It was so silly. All the same, she was touched by his concern and even slightly amused by it. Infidelity was not a temptation. She was far too fond of him.

*

Maeve's wedding was the high point of 1905 in Moira's opinion, but there was actually something else to make it noteworthy for the Lassiters. Sergei Witte, Russia's minister of finance, met with a representative of Theodore Roosevelt and a representative of the Japanese emperor in Moira's yellow salon on a dreary day in June—quite soon after the Japanese Navy had annihilated the Russian fleet at the Battle of Tsushima.

Tsushima was the most spectacular naval confrontation since Trafalgar, and it had devastated Russian pride. In one afternoon, the Tsar's navy had been destroyed and Russian imperial prestige had suffered a tremendous blow.

With Charlie and Dietrich as low-level go-betweens, a series of secret conferences was arranged and terms discussed, leading ultimately to the Treaty of Portsmouth, New Hampshire, in August l905, with TR presiding as peacemaker.

To almost everyone's amazement, Witte carried the day and the Russians—pounded to a pulp by the Japanese in the war—emerged not too badly off. Charlie's role as nurturer of the peace gained him a good seat at the historic occasion and a visit to Roosevelt's home in Oyster Bay. TR gained the Nobel Peace Prize.

Dietrich, who had also gone to witness the event, was impressed by Theodore Roosevelt but still put off by American food. He found himself at a picnic at the President's home one day soon after the signing of the treaty and engaged in conversation by the imposing Witte, whose main topic of small talk at that moment was the horror of American cuisine. Potato salad, for instance. Or that horror, corn on the cob!

Dietrich commiserated with the statesman who had just pulled off the diplomatic coup of the decade. Witte couldn't wait to get home.

"Americans are not like us," the young baron declared solemnly.

"They're fine people, but it takes time to get accustomed to their ways. They do eat very strangely."

And both men cast dubious glances at the picnic table loaded with traditional delights which they deemed fit only for really hungry peasants.

For his great sacrifice on behalf of the motherland, Sergei Witte was created Count Witte on his return to St. Petersburg. When Dietrich read of it in *Le Figaro*, he thought it somehow appropriate.

*

At the New Year, 1906, Maeve had never felt better. She was a star of the Opéra-Comique, a welcome addition to various opera houses from Paris to St. Petersburg, and about to make her La Scala debut. It excited her almost as much as it terrified her, for she knew the reputation of the ferocious La Scala audience. If those people took a dislike to her, she was lost. If, on the other hand, they adored her, she would have the biggest triumph of her career.

"I want you to come to Milan with me," she said to Moira. "You and Charlie can take the train and be there in no time at all. I'm going to need all the support I can get."

"And where will your husband be?"

"With me, of course. But I need you, too. I'm frightened, Mama. These Milanese are bloodthirsty."

Moira nodded. "If Charlie says yes, we'll be there."

"If?"

"Well, I'll have to ask him first, of course." She smiled. "But I don't think he'll protest. He's very proud of you, Maeveen. He thinks you're wonderful."

He had also—under Moira's prodding—bestowed a hundred-thousand-dollar dowry on the girl, the European bride's ultimate insurance policy. Not quite having full confidence in her new son-in-law, Moira had waged an unrelenting campaign to assure her daughter's security in case her career collapsed, her marriage foundered, or both. Charlie, with a guilty conscience about his secret gifts to his child and its mother, readily acquiesced.

As he looked at it, it wouldn't harm him to be generous to his wife's child, and if his generosity to little Gianni was ever uncovered, it could be a good thing to fall back on. At least it could be used to silence Moira, who would be infuriated if she learned about the terms of his contract with Laura. Charlie Lassiter was a kind and generous man—but he wasn't a fool.

When the time approached for the departure for Milan, Maeve

and Moira, accompanied by their spouses, boarded a private Pullman in Paris and headed to Italy in grand style. After their detour to Milan, the Lassiters were going to Spain for shooting with the Duke of Alba, who was hosting King Manuel of Portugal among other notables at his castle. Moira was planning on making a few purchases in Milan for her hunting expedition. Her guns and Charlie's were British, from Purdy's, but she liked Italian leather bags.

Dietrich was consumed by a bad case of nerves, even worse than his wife's. He, too, knew of the La Scala audience, and he had firsthand memories of a conductor and a soprano physically carried out of the hall by a wildly disapproving mob. If that happened to Maeve, he would die. So, to prevent such a disgrace, he had engaged two large and burly bodyguards to remain in the wings and keep an eye on his beloved. At the slightest sign of a riot they were to carry her to safety straight out the stage door exit to a waiting coach. Maeve didn't have the smallest inkling of Dietrich's plans, and would have been astonished if she had.

Signor Giulio Gatti-Casazza, the black-bearded director of La Scala, was, with his chief conductor Arturo Toscanini, a partner in one of the finest duos in the world of opera. Conductor and director had restored an iron discipline to the house and raised the performance level to something bordering on the heavenly.

Although the "Maestro" sometimes drove his singers to distraction, he was as hard on himself as he was on them. One thing Maeve found difficult to get used to was Toscanini's insistence on full voice at rehearsals. She had been accustomed to mezza voce and she felt the strain.

"He's pleased with you," Dietrich observed. "That's a good sign."

They were sitting at a table in Milan's famous glass-enclosed Galleria, having coffee after a particularly grueling rehearsal of Puccini's *Manon Lescaut* when a well-dressed man approached them. He politely inquired if the lady was the "well-known soprano Maeve Devereux," and then promptly introduced himself as the head of the claque.

Maeve felt her heart freeze. She had heard terrible stories about these people; her worst nightmare was to have a confrontation with them. If one didn't buy them off, they would wreck a performance.

Dietrich, whose Italian was as fluent as hers, turned pale and assumed he was dealing with a thug. This gang was a sort of Mafia, and he knew damned well what the fellow was going to say, the dirty swine. He got the jump on him by announcing that he didn't deal with blackmailers.

Feigning distress, the music lover held out his hands in a gesture of wronged virtue. Maeve noticed half the habitués of the café observing the little show. Even if they couldn't hear the actual dialogue, these Milanese knew what was taking place. It was practically a tradition. Pay off the claque or suffer horrible consequences.

"How much will buy you off?" she demanded abruptly, shocking her husband, who protested audibly and angrily in German.

"Twenty thousand lire, signora." The Italian smiled, pleased at the lady's good sense.

"Twenty thousand! That's pretty cheap if you ask me. Dietrich, this blackguard must think I'm ending my career instead of enjoying my prime! It's an insult, twenty thousand. Demeaning! Absolutely unworthy as a bribe! So I think we'll just dispense with the idea altogether."

This was said in Maeve's best stage voice in clear, beautifully enunciated Italian designed to be heard by every Milanese artist, critic, and out-of-work tenor in her immediate vicinity. Since the Galleria was the office cum salon for all of musical Milan, the word spread like wildfire that the French soprano La Devereux had sent the leader of the claque packing and made him look damned foolish on top of it.

"Well, *Liebchen*," Dietrich sighed as he and La Devereux took a leisurely stroll back to their hotel. "You've certainly thrown down the gauntlet. They'll be out for blood now."

"You weren't about to pay their blackmail, were you?"

"No, I wouldn't have paid this thug, because I don't believe an artist of your caliber has to give in to blackmail."

"Right."

Dietrich's beautiful blue eyes looked grim. "But of course," he continued, "now we'll have to be prepared for the worst."

"I'm in great voice," Maeve replied, squeezing her husband's arm. "Don't worry about that."

"I'm not."

It was that damned claque that frightened him.

*

Charlie and Moira were seated with Dietrich in the director's box on the night of Maeve's debut at La Scala. The house had been sold out for weeks, the leaders of Milanese society were gathering in a blaze of family jewels and Paris gowns, and the notorious Marchesa Casati Stampi had appeared in a sable-trimmed orchid satin extravaganza, with a four-foot-long sautoir of pearls but minus the live snake she sometimes draped around her lovely neck. It was rumored that the poet Gabriele D'Annunzio had come down from his villa at Como to attend and to keep a rendezvous with his latest mistress.

To Dietrich's distress, the leader of the claque entered like a reigning star and sauntered to his seat in the parterre after giving a polite wave of his hand to the diva's husband.

"Who is that?" Moira demanded, regarding him through her opera glasses.

"A thug," replied the baron. "Nobody I'd care to associate with."

The director of La Scala thought it wise to refrain from adding anything to that description, and he assured Mrs. Lassiter the evening would be the highlight of her daughter's career.

Backstage in her dressing room, Maeve was frantic with nerves. She had already sent her husband out with the Lassiters and was now seated before her dressing table mirror with Arlette standing behind her, trying to fix her wig. It didn't look right, Maeve claimed. It was dreadful. The color was all wrong for her and the style was too modern.

"It's fine, madame. It looks perfectly eighteenth-century, really."

"My God! I must have been daft to think I could ever succeed here! Those Milanese will tear me to pieces. Did you see them? Did you see their eyes? Like cannibals!" She shuddered. "These are man-eaters."

Arlette went through this before almost every performance, so she was used to it by now. Madame always began by declaring she was doomed to failure; she, Arlette, had to reassure her; then Madame would take heart and declare she was ready to do her best. But tonight Maeve was stuck at the first stage of her preperformance routine, and Arlette was doing her best to persuade her she wouldn't fail. So far it wasn't working. This time, Madame was close to hysteria.

"*Manon* is a mistake," Maeve wept. "They'll compare me with all the others and say I was a disaster. Oh God! Don't even let me *see* a newspaper tomorrow morning. Swear you won't. Especially not the *Corriere della Sera*."

"Yes, madame. I promise."

"I'm feverish. My skin is practically on fire. And my costume feels tighter than usual. Everything is wrong!"

"Don't worry, madame. Please!"

Arlette had an inspiration. "Here, madame," she said. "Put on the cross Chaliapin gave you in St. Petersburg. It will be a good luck token. If it brought you good luck in the midst of their revolution, think of what it ought to do tonight."

"Ah," Maeve nodded. "You're right."

Arlette sighed with relief as Maeve fastened the gold cross around her neck. The mention of Chaliapin was an inspiration. Madame had such faith in his judgment he could calm her even without being there.

In fact, he was in the audience this evening, anxious to witness her first La Scala performance. This was not his first season and he was much less nervous than she was, having already conquered the Milanese several years earlier.

Maeve centered the cross, took a deep breath, and bowed her head. She was as ready as she'd ever be.

When she was waiting in the wings for her cue, she was surprised to see two very large men who had nothing to do with the show. Probably from the fire department, she thought vaguely, although they weren't wearing any sort of uniform. Safety regulations all over Europe required the presence of firemen backstage during a performance.

"*Buona sera, signora,*" they said pleasantly. "*In boca al lupo.*"

Maeve smiled pleasantly, heart pounding, hands trembling as she waited for the property master to help her into the coach in which she would make her entrance in the first scene. Dear God, what am I doing here? she thought. Then she suddenly recalled that day in Africa when she had been knocked to the ground by Sergeant Davies and ordered to eat dirt and maggots. Had she been scared then? Terrified, she remembered. And what had she done? She had refused to be intimidated. She had challenged him to do his worst by her act of defiance, and she had won. Now he was dead, and she was about to go onstage at La Scala.

Somehow, the thought of that bit of bravado at Camp 3 worked even better than Chaliapin's cross. *That* could have been fatal. Anything the Milanese could do to her would never even come close to the risk she took that day. The hell with the Milanese! Let them do their worst! Compared with Sergeant Davies, the harshest critic was just an inflated gasbag.

To Maeve's astonishment, she quickly felt comfortable enough to relax once she arrived onstage. Her knees stopped shaking, her animation returned, and she put on a bravura display of acting, delighting the audience which had greeted her coolly at first. By the time she and her partner had sung their first duet, the applause was so strong it drowned out the boos of the claque, who were striving manfully to turn the rest of the house against La Devereux. They gave up in defeat by the end of the second act and resigned themselves to enjoying the opera with the rest of the spectators, thereby infuriating their leader.

As Moira's party was having champagne with La Scala's director during the intermission, he declared the evening a wild success.

"It's a triumph, signora!" He beamed, thoughts of box office receipts dancing in his head. "She's won them over. The whole house will be in tears when she dies in the desert. *Ah, dio*! It will be marvelous!"

Moira was relieved. After all the horror stories, it was pleasant to experience this euphoria. She would have been wild with rage if anyone had spoiled Maeve's evening. After all, it was her evening too.

Charlie was pretty sanguine about the whole affair. Of course Maeve would be well received, he maintained. Why wouldn't she be? Dietrich admired his unswerving optimism. His father-in-law reminded him of Arlette.

For the occasion, Mrs. Lassiter had spared no effort to dazzle, and she was glittering with an elegant diamond tiara, diamond necklace, earrings, and various bracelets, all set off against a black silk and lace evening gown by Paquin, which plunged daringly low in the back to astonish those who hadn't already been overwhelmed by all those diamonds up front. She was a magnificent beauty with all the opulence of the era. Charlie hated to think of his Moira ever having to deal with simplicity; somehow it seemed inappropriate for her.

When the time came for curtain calls, Maeve received near hysterical enthusiasm. She took her reception with a becoming humility, sinking into a flawless curtsy to her admirers as they carried on like wild banshees. Alessandro Bonci, her partner of the evening, received a fair number of bravos himself, and the Milanese also insisted upon Toscanini showing himself to receive their cheers. It was a success on all fronts. Looking straight ahead into the black wall of the audience, Maeve plucked a white rose from one of her many bouquets and, kissing it, flung it gracefully in the direction of the director's box and Dietrich.

Maeve had disappeared behind the curtains for about the tenth time, when for no apparent reason she simply lurched forward and collapsed, mercifully spared an injury by the quick reflexes of one of her husband's strong-arm men. He managed to grab her before she hit the floor and carry her back to her dressing room, surrounded by a noisy following of artists and stagehands.

Fedya Chaliapin nearly collided with the group as he headed for Maeve's dressing room from the other direction, and he immediately took charge, calling for the house doctor, stretching Maeve out on the sofa, and ordering Arlette to fetch cold compresses. By the time Dietrich and the Lassiters got there, Maeve was sitting up, chattering about the performance, and having a glass of brandy, none the worse for wear.

"It must have been the excitement," she murmured. "I was so keyed up this evening, I'm not surprised I fainted."

Fedya had smiled like a Slavic Cheshire cat and taken her hand in his. "Masha," he inquired gently, "how long have you been married?"

"Since last year. Why?"

Chaliapin had five children, and right now he had his own suspicions about the cause of her sudden weakness.

"Oh, just curious," he replied. "I was thinking that perhaps this little fainting fit might be an indication that you and the baron may soon have company."

Maeve reflected afterward that Fedya must have thought her a very dense girl indeed when she inquired, puzzled, "Who might be coming?"

He loved to repeat that story later on. Masha was so sweet, so naive, he would say with a chuckle. It was part of her charm.

"Oh, I don't know." He grinned. "Can't *you* think of some little stranger who might be joining you?"

To Maeve's horror, the Italian doctor Dietrich called in to examine her at their hotel suite was of the same opinion as Fedya. After a very uncomfortable examination, with Arlette holding her hand to keep her calm, the elderly doctor sighed and confirmed that the baronessa was in good health and ought to have a fine, strong *bambino*.

The news came as a terrible jolt to Maeve. She looked stunned as the doctor announced it, too bewildered to comprehend the full implications of what he had just told her. Mechanically she accepted his congratulations while her mouth forced a strange, tight smile that seemed horribly false, even to her as she glimpsed herself in the mirror. How could such good news be so bad?

I'm going to have a baby now when I'm about to play Salome, she thought. That puts an end to it. It ruins my chances of a big premiere right now. Oh God, what bad timing! What a disaster.

The minute the doctor left the room, Maeve sank into a distraught little bundle, sobbing with disappointment. It wasn't the idea of the baby that appalled her—she'd certainly hoped to have a child with Dietrich. She loved him and would be proud to give him an heir—or heiress— eventually. It was just that now wasn't the right time to do it.

All her energies were directed toward Salome, not motherhood. Salome was a challenge she could look forward to. The idea of being somebody's mother frightened her. She wasn't certain she was cut out for that role yet. She'd had so little preparation.

Besides, Maeve thought nervously, babies were so demanding. Could she handle her responsibilities to a baby and fulfill her contracts? It was daunting even to think about. And she certainly wouldn't want to be a dreadful mother.

The whole idea was so frightening and so sudden it depressed her horribly. She felt stricken when she ought to have felt elated. Worse than that, she couldn't fake a joy she didn't feel, and for her husband's sake she really wished she could.

*

Dietrich was annoyed and even shocked at Maeve's unhappiness with her pregnancy. In his opinion, bringing a future Baron von Reuter into the world was at least equal to anything Maeve might do for the work of Richard Strauss. He was heart and soul for anything that would advance her career, but he was also her husband. And he thought she ought to be ecstatic about their child.

So did Moira. When she heard the news, she lost her color. "How wonderful," she managed in a strangely toneless voice. But she resented Maeve's predicament. Trust Maeveen to try to upstage her own mother.

Moira had no sympathy for Maeve's attitude. Her daughter was lamenting the very thing she herself would have paid a fortune for. And she hated to break the good news to Charlie, dreading his unspoken comparison with their bad luck. Maeveen was quite perverse to do this to her. It was cruel!

"Sometimes I don't understand her at all," Dietrich confided to his mother-in-law. "One would think she'd be thrilled. Instead, she seems bewildered."

"Maeveen has a very peculiar disposition," Moira replied. "She was always like that. But give her time. She might accept it after it arrives. If you're lucky," she added grimly. And that was the end of that.

*

On the following day, after Baron and Baroness von Reuter had seen her parents off at the train station, they had a terrible fight in the cab on the way back to the hotel. Maeve was to cancel her contract at La Scala and not even think about performing until after the birth of her child.

"Are you mad? I've worked hard enough to get where I am. How could I possibly cancel now? It would be insane. None of this will harm the baby."

"But you might faint again and injure yourself. Anything could happen."

"Dietrich," she snapped in exasperation, "Moira once crossed a desert while she was pregnant with me and I'm none the worse for it! Hearing good music won't harm this child."

"You are my wife!"

"Yes?"

He had angry red blotches spoiling his fine complexion now. He was furious, startling Maeve, who wasn't used to such passionate anger from him.

"As your husband I'm ordering you to leave the stage and rest for the duration of your pregnancy!"

"And I'm telling you I will not! I will complete my engagement here in Milan, come hell or high water!"

Dietrich's blond hair shook from the force of his anger as he shouted, "You are a selfish, egotistical prima donna!"

"Damned right I am! I'm an artist. I have to be!"

To her surprise, he burst out laughing. "You really are exasperating," he muttered, pulling away from her on the soft leather seat of the hackney cab.

"Dietrich," Maeve sighed, snuggling up against him and brushing his face with her fingertips. "I love you dearly. Never doubt that for a second. But it's hard for me to be happy about this! I am dying to sing Salome. Every soprano from Barcelona to Petersburg wants a go at it for a big premiere, and Strauss actually wants me to sing it. Now I won't be able to. By the time I get my figure back after the baby, it will probably be old-fashioned."

He sighed and kissed her tenderly on the ear. He couldn't imagine Strauss's music becoming old-fashioned quite that fast—my God, it was practically revolutionary!—but he understood Maeve's distress. "Should I apologize?" he asked, with just a slight edge to his voice.

"Don't be silly," she laughed. "It's nice that we're about to have offspring. We'll hire nannies and the baby will be well taken care of, but it will be a terrible strain on me for the next few months."

Dietrich pressed her hand and gently lifted it to his lips. "Well," he said, relenting, "perhaps it wouldn't hurt to finish your performances here at La Scala." He gritted his teeth and tried to be progressive about this, but it went against his better judgment.

"Of course it wouldn't harm the baby," she replied eagerly. "I'm scheduled for five more nights. That couldn't possibly be a problem at this stage."

"I'll have the bodyguards follow you around to protect you. And of course, Arlette will be within earshot at all times. It *could* be safe."

Maeve wondered if the pregnant women she had seen on the Métro in Paris and on trams in St. Petersburg had ever heard of such an arrangement. She had seen women with huge bellies trudging along the street, staggering beneath the burden of groceries or heavy laundry. They would have worshiped this fellow.

"But won't you be here too?" she asked suddenly, in surprise.

"No," he replied mournfully. "I have to go to New York and Chicago immediately on business because of our war loan. It's annoying, but it's an obligation I can't neglect."

"Ah," Maeve murmured. "Well, that's all right. As you said, I have plenty of company."

"I'm sorry, *Liebchen*," he said sadly. "I hate leaving you at a time like this."

"For heaven's sake, *Schatzi*, it's all right. Really. I'm not going to fall to pieces."

Maeve was already calculating that Dietrich's business ought to keep him occupied in America for at least a month—or even two. Wonderful! Then there wouldn't be any problem with Covent Garden.

Just before Maeve had left for Milan, Harry Higgens, the director, had sent her a cable asking her to replace another soprano—with profuse apologies for such short notice. He had heard the recordings she had done for Fred Gaisberg of Victor Records and seen her in person at the Opéra-Comique, and he wanted her to appear in London if at all possible.

The short notice would have annoyed Maeve under any other circumstances, but this was a special case for two reasons. First, she had always wanted to appear at Covent Garden—in brazen defiance of Nellie Melba's vows to ostracize her. And second, the soprano she was to replace was none other than Melba herself! The mere thought of her fury was enough to ensure Maeve's quick affirmative response. This would be revenge for all those slights at Monte Carlo—revenge made all the sweeter by her recent success in Milan. Now she would add a Covent Garden triumph to her roster. And Nellie Melba could go hang!

Maeve looked at her husband and smiled. He would be out of the country for a few months unable to prevent her from doing this. After all, she would only be singing in London for four performances in early June—the London season. Dietrich would be safely off in Chicago by then. Why not?

"I'll miss you," Maeve sighed. "I like to have you near me."

It was said with sincerity, but she didn't like to have him so near that he was able to put a stranglehold on her career. Some things were just none of his business.

And revenge for Monte Carlo was just too tempting to allow the opportunity to slip by.

CHAPTER 22

One of the first things Maeve did upon her return to Paris fresh from her La Scala triumph was to get in touch with Reutlinger's, one of the city's foremost theatrical photographers, and set up a photo session. Since she still looked good, she was going to take advantage of it while it lasted and have herself photographed in costume for her London publicity.

Arlette accompanied Maeve to the photographer's studio, carting along an armful of costumes, and La Devereux was properly photographed as Tosca in a magnificent velvet Empire gown and the tiara and necklace that were Maeve's wedding presents. There were half a dozen other pictures, all very nice but fairly ordinary until Maeve happened to notice a portrait of Sarah Bernhardt with La Grande Sarah posed as a sort of bohemian odalisque on a fine animal skin—draped sofa.

"That's it—the tiger skin! Do you still have it, monsieur?" she asked.

"Yes. Do you want me to lay it across the sofa?"

"Yes. We'll try that in my Thaïs costume."

Arlette muttered that she was pushing her luck there because it was as bare a piece of spangled tulle as she had in her wardrobe. And Madame had gained a little weight.

"Grand," Maeve replied, not at all put off. "Then I'll have a ripe, decadent look."

That wasn't the word for it when Maeve stepped from behind the door of the dressing room. Monsieur Reutlinger's assistant took one look at her and nearly dropped his master's most expensive camera lens.

"*Oh là là, madame,*" he gulped. "You look as if you've just come from the Garden of Eden!"

"Or Sodom and Gomorrah," muttered Arlette, clicking her teeth in stony disapproval.

Maeve's unwelcome condition had added a few pounds to her slim frame in places that had formerly been underpadded. Now she was bursting out of her beaded bodice, under what could only be described as a scanty breastplate of jewels and tassels. Thaïs, the courtesan of Alexandria, looked as if she were ready for business. Maeve twirled around in obvious delight and got Monsieur Reutlinger so excited he started to babble.

"This is unbelievable, madame! Oh yes, the tiger skin! Lie on it. Loll on it. Run your little fingers through his fur!"

Arlette declared that Madame looked indecent, as Maeve flung herself on the dead feline, stretching like a wild kitten.

"*Oh, les beaux yeux!*" murmured the assistant, a sturdy Norman farm boy. But he wasn't looking at her eyes.

"Arlette, fix my wig," Maeve commanded as she folded her arms over the tiger's head and embraced him. "Make it look disheveled, but in a nice way."

"If Monsieur le baron ever sees this, he'll murder you, madame," the girl whispered. "He's a jealous man. He won't stand for this display."

"Poof! He's on his way to New York."

Reutlinger was in heaven. When he was finished, he had a fine set of photos of La Devereux in all her splendor, exhibiting a sensual streak that nobody had yet suspected. Her last photos, taken with the baron and Herr Albrecht supervising the session, had been very pretty and charming, but there were no bare thighs peeking out from behind a beaded tunic. And certainly no swelling bosoms threatening to break loose from their fragile network of jewels!

"Oh God! These are marvelous," he crowed. "You'll be the talk of the town!"

"And the least clothed woman on the stage," Arlette sniffed. "This isn't right, madame. You'll see." The poor girl was truly horrified.

Maeve had to admit later that even she was shocked by Reutlinger's photos when he sent them to her a week later. She and the tiger both looked as if they were up to no good. But she was so voluptuous and so enticing in her pearls and bare feet it seemed a shame to put the photos away in a drawer and hide them just because they were—well—barely decent.

Reaching a compromise with Arlette, who was predicting a ban from the stage in London if she ever let those pictures reach England, Maeve had herself photographed in an elegant white satin gown stretched out on the same tiger. This time the effect was both decorous and oddly erotic—but tame enough to pass even the lord chamberlain's inspection.

Making that sacrifice to the public morals, Maeve then dispatched one of the "indecent" photos to Richard Strauss—just to remind him what a real Salome looked like. There were still premieres to do!

That done, Maeve was set to conquer England.

*

Taking the boat train to London by way of Calais and Dover, Maeve had a wicked attack of seasickness which she blamed on her condition. Arlette got just as sick and had no such excuse. The hairdresser and footman who accompanied them were both equally ill, and it was a groggy group that set foot on British soil. Harry Higgens himself, the director of Covent Garden, met his newest diva at Victoria Station with a huge bouquet of white roses and apologies for the weather. It was so foggy, visibility was limited to the space just before one's eyes.

"Welcome to London, Baroness," he smiled as he kissed her hand. "And we hope you'll be enjoying better weather soon. This is the sunny season."

Maeve thought his hopes were just a trifle exaggerated, judging by the look of things, but that wasn't important. Revenge on Melba was.

The social season was beginning as London was just starting to shake off its winter torpor. Society hostesses were vying with each other to provide rare entertainments for their guests, debutantes were being groomed for their presentations at court, and King Edward's horses were the odds-on favorites at Ascot.

Nellie Melba and Caruso were the favorite pair of songbirds at Covent Garden, and it was considered a near tragedy that Melba was too ill to perform her last several engagements. Everybody was praying for her swift recovery—and wondering how this pretty French soprano was ever going to be able to fill her shoes.

Caruso at least welcomed Maeve warmly and was glad to hear her news. One of his sons lived in London with his governess, and he introduced him proudly to "la baronessa." The child's mother, Ada Giachetti, was a soprano who was well known on the South American circuit. With her busy schedule and Caruso's, it was hard to provide stability for their sons, but August at Caruso's Villa Bellosguardo was sacred family time.

"It's not a good thing for the mama to travel so much," Enrico said sadly. "It makes the children so lonely." Maeve noticed that he found it perfectly fine in the papa though.

Maeve's schedule called for her to sing Tosca with Antonio Scotti as Scarpia and Caruso as Cavaradossi, Carmen with Alessandro Bonci as Don José, and Violetta in *La Traviata* with Caruso again as Alfredo. *Manon Lescaut*, her Milan triumph, would team her with an unknown.

To her delight, the Neapolitan regarded her as a cherished colleague, and told her she now sounded even better than that first time in Monte Carlo. Her middle register seemed to have grown more mellow, giving her a luscious, ripe quality. Very attractive. Just like her pose in white satin on that tiger skin.

"Ah, you've seen the photos," Maeve marveled. "That's quick."

"They're all over London," he laughed. "Everybody wants to buy them. Your manager has turned them into postcards."

Good for him, Maeve thought. One way or the other, we'll make some money here.

It was an odd thing, Maeve reflected as she prepared for her Covent Garden debut, but she was far less nervous than she had been for La Scala. With months to worry about that in advance, her first Milan appearance had seen her nearly hysterical with nerves, as if she had been about to face the lions at the Colosseum. London, even on such short notice, scarcely rattled her at all. And London was every bit as important as Milan—for reasons that were fiercely personal.

She had very little feeling for the London of King Edward VII. His name had been on her papa's death warrant, and that put him outside the pale as far as Maeve was concerned. She hoped Fat Teddy wouldn't show up at any of her performances either; she really wouldn't be able to bring herself to meet him.

Maeve had been lured by curiosity to the British capital. A German citizen through her marriage to Dietrich, she no longer feared British law. She had a German passport in her handbag and residences in Paris and Berlin. These people had no claim on her obedience. And Harry Higgens had only got her there because she had a score to settle.

Maeve Devereux was no longer a shabby little colonial for them to pack into prison this time but a diva, a baroness, and a one-woman display of Parisian haute couture at its zenith. She was ready for them. And more than ready to put Nellie Melba in the shade on her own turf.

London displeased Maeve because of its weather, its people, and its lack of cafés. The café depended on decent weather, and that was one item severely lacking in this city.

Maeve was staying at the Ritz with her entourage, and in between rehearsals she would display herself in all her glory on the carriage drive through the park that seemed to be de rigueur for a beauty like herself. With Arlette along for company, taking the part of a lady-in-waiting, Baroness von Reuter would make her promenade in an open landau behind a smart pair of black trotters.

To Maeve's outrage, she had encountered opposition to the presence of her carriage in that part of Hyde Park reserved for the gentry and had had to make the guardian of the gate aware of her aristocratic title before they allowed her in. Actresses were generally not considered sufficiently worthy to mingle with their "betters."

Maeve had done her best imitation of Dietrich—reacting with haughty Teutonic wrath, flinging her gilt-crested calling card in the face of the gatekeeper, and chattering nonstop in German about "idiotic mindless lackeys"—and the man had blinked, chewed his mustache thoughtfully, and allowed the German baroness to proceed.

"What does 'bitch' mean, madame?" Arlette inquired later as they were on their way home.

"Where did you hear that?"

"That's what the gatekeeper called you as we left."

Maeve burst out laughing. "I must remember that. Oh—it means *garce*," she informed her shocked maid.

"What a rotten thing to say. What a terrible lack of respect."

Maeve shrugged and twirled her lacy parasol as she acknowledged the greeting of a gentleman in a smart riding habit. Let the little man call her a bitch if he wished. She was promenading in a smart carriage and returning to the Ritz. He was a trained dog who probably lived in a hovel. All he had was his bark.

One of the best things about London—apart from the huge salary for her four performances—was the opportunity Maeve had to see the sights. She and Arlette took in the Changing of the Guard, sailed up the Thames to observe the bizarre ritual of swan-upping, shopped at Harrods and Liberty's, visited Oxford, Hampton Court, and Windsor, and saw a variety of famous people in carriages rolling through the streets.

There were almost as many uniforms, plumes, gold froggings, and sabers as in St. Petersburg, and the "professional beauties" of the King's elegant circle were spotted everywhere. It was a glorious time to be rich and titled—or merely rich. Love it or hate it, London was the capital of an empire, and it looked the part better than any stage designer could have wished.

The first three performances went well, with Maeve receiving fine reviews, invitations to dine with some of the city's leading patrons of the arts, and warm congratulations from Caruso and Scotti. Then came Tosca, her favorite and final role.

With her bags packed for an early-morning departure, Maeve felt relaxed and at ease as she made her entrance to greet her lover in the church, receiving the applause from the audience as a tonic.

She was enchanting, passionate, helpless, furious, and devious, a riveting Tosca. When Maeve sang "Vissi d'arte," the applause rolled in like thunder. She gave stiff competition to Caruso and Scotti in the field of acting that night and set off such pandemonium that the newspapers called it "Devereux-mania." Melba had a rival!

*

After Maeve's success at Covent Garden and the concomitant publicity, she was no longer an unknown quantity across the Channel. Harry Higgens indicated his wish for a second engagement the following year, and he and Maeve's manager were discussing terms.

Settled down into a peaceful routine, Maeve spent long hours walking in the park with Arlette in attendance or studying the scores of operas with Marc Antoine when he was available. She dabbled in watercolors. She knitted little sweaters that Arlette always ended up finishing. She enjoyed Dietrich's tender care and Sean's Petersburg gossip. But she was only biding her time, impatient for the day when she could return to the stage and attempt *Salome*.

The pregnancy was personally irritating to Moira, who put the best face on it that she could manage. The very word "baby" was a stab in the heart, given her terrible discovery in Baden-Baden. Maeve's vagabonding after Laura Milonari's dreadful revelation seemed an insult. The baby was a Devereux—even if it would be called Something von Reuter. It was theirs and that's what counted. She heartily disapproved of her daughter's London sojourn. Just like Dietrich.

The nuns at the convent that had provided Maeve's wedding lingerie under protest were much more gracious the second time around, raising no objection at all to working on a layette for the Baroness von Reuter's little bundle.

"Hypocritical old cows" was Maeve's opinion. But Moira considered it de rigueur for her grandchild.

The expectant parents knew things were getting out of hand when Mrs. Lassiter ordered a gilded cradle made for the baby in the same design that Napoleon had used for his son, the King of Rome. It was absolutely majestic, with a swarm of golden bees carved into the decoration and lovely lace hangings draped from the top of its stand, but it seemed overdone to Maeve—although Dietrich loved it. Sometimes she wondered if her husband was a frustrated artist like his Kaiser. He was very fond of décor and usually spent hours chatting with the stage designers in every opera house in which Maeve appeared.

Nothing was too extravagant for Dietrich when it came to Maeve's stage appearances. She had a vast personal wardrobe of costumes, enabling her to represent every heroine from Tosca to Thaïs to Violetta and many others in between. Incorporating the right to wear her own costumes into her contracts, Maeve was spared the indignity of making do with hand-me-downs from the wardrobe departments.

"You are a prima donna," Dietrich had informed her. "Therefore you must always appear as one. You will only wear costumes that have been created for you. Anything else would be unworthy of your talent."

In private life the Baroness von Reuter was beautifully dressed by Paquin, although she had a fondness for exquisitely tailored suits by Redfern, who knew how to style a *tailleur* better than anyone. Jewels—if they weren't part of the von Reuter family patrimony—generally came from Chaumet or Boucheron.

Accustomed to receiving compliments on her vast wardrobe, as well as her beauty and her voice, Maeve found this pregnancy a strange experience. It was eerie. This lump which had wrecked her fine figure was receiving all the attention, and Moira and Dietrich sat around discussing "his" future. She didn't seem to count.

"Don't get your hopes up," she retorted one evening, thoroughly exasperated. "He might turn out to be a she, and there go your plans for the future little baron. But you could do something very bold and train her to become Europe's first woman banker. If she doesn't follow her mother into the opera house."

"Don't listen to her," Moira said firmly. "Of course the baby will be a son." And she glared at Maeve for contradicting her.

"How can you be so sure, Mama?" Dietrich asked.

Moira looked embarrassed. "A very old woman who is supposed to know how to predict a child's sex told me."

"Some Gypsy in the Tuileries Garden!" Maeve hooted. "She said I'd have a fine son. How scientific! She probably tells every woman the same thing." It was amusing that Moira could be taken in by that.

Dietrich ignored the little mother's outburst and glanced back at Moira.

"Did she seem to know what she was saying?" he asked timidly.

"She was very sure of herself," Moira replied with a firm nod. "Some of them have second sight, you know. It's not for everyone to foretell these things." And she gave Maeve a withering glance.

"Oh Lord! Some old Romany hag who could barely speak French! She reminded me of those Gypsies in Belgrade who nearly knocked me to the ground and tried to rob me."

"They *are* known for their fortune-telling," Dietrich admitted to Moira.

Maeve shook her head. "It's all blather to get money from a gullible woman who wants to believe in them. I'm convinced I'm going to have a girl. And I've already chosen her name—Esmeralda."

Moira and her son-in-law exchanged glances. Then Moira made a small deprecating gesture as she silently shook her head. Pay her no mind, she seemed to say. Choose a nice masculine name. It will be all right.

*

The great event took place rather unexpectedly in the middle of the night in the midst of a late autumn snowstorm. Maeve woke up in pain, shook Dietrich awake, and demanded her doctor. A telephone call alerted him, and a coach was dispatched to bring him to the house.

"I don't like this," she said, beginning to pace the floor. "I can tell it's going to be long and painful."

"Don't get upset, *Liebchen*," Dietrich cautioned, throwing a woolen shawl around her shoulders as she walked up and down in her dressing gown. "You have to stay calm."

"Call my mother," Maeve replied. "I need her. I need her *now!*" She was so terrified her teeth were chattering. This was unnerving. And it was only the start.

Moira and Charlie arrived before the doctor, complaining of difficulties in traversing the snowy streets, and Charlie was instructed to stay with the baron and keep him out of the way. Moira didn't want him becoming hysterical and upsetting her daughter. He was a sensitive soul who was likely to go to pieces if he had to witness what was about to take place. Maeveen had no choice.

The snow was piling up so high in the streets that Dr. Christophe was also encountering serious difficulties in reaching his destination. At the same time, Maeve was becoming more and more agitated, especially since the pains had started to worsen. She had never experienced anything as frightening as this. Was this normal? she wondered.

"It will be hours for a first baby," Moira declared, not making her daughter feel any better. "The doctor will be here in plenty of time."

But each time Moira parted the lace curtains to peek outside into the black night, all she could see were snowflakes glittering against the pale glow of the streetlamps and not a sign of the coach.

When the pains began to get very bad, Maeve screamed for something to deaden them but there was nothing on hand.

"Then get some vodka! I've seen men lying half-numb in the streets from it. That's what I want now!" My God, this was torture! She was gasping for breath now, her face white with pain.

"You can't!" Moira protested. "The doctor will want to administer painkillers when he gets here. You can't mix these things."

"Where is he, then?" Maeve wailed, clutching Arlette's hand as she felt a tremendous spasm rip through her insides. "I hate people who have no regard for time! The baby will be here before he is!"

"It's the snow, madame," Arlette offered. "Nothing's moving out there."

That didn't placate Maeve, who doubled over and moaned like some species of coyote, nearly unnerving the two women with her. She didn't sound human. It was a combination of pain and overwhelming fear for her voice that was producing such strange sounds. Terrified to risk her vocal cords in high-pitched shrieks, the diva was relying on her lower register and her determination to control her breathing to help keep her cries as muted as she could manage. But the low, undulating moans were dreadful to hear. They sounded more animal than human.

"This is all Dietrich's fault," Maeve managed in between cries of pain. "I wish it were happening to him!"

"You were there at the start too, you know," Moira said wryly. "Don't put all the blame on the man."

"Ha! You ought to bring him in here so he can see what he's done to me," she retorted, gasping. And then she crumpled over again, unable to speak.

"Oh no, madame!" Arlette blurted out. "Monsieur would faint dead away, and then the doctor would have three patients to deal with. It would be too much!"

Maeve almost laughed at the thought of her husband facing her at this moment. Then an enormous wave of pain overwhelmed her, making her gasp for breath again, too far gone to scream.

"It's coming!" Moira shouted fifteen minutes later as Maeve clung to Arlette's hand and two other maids carried bowls of hot water and armloads of clean towels into the bedroom. "This child is in a devil of a hurry!"

As its mother let out a tremendous screech of pain, the baby's head emerged. Ten minutes later, Maeve was holding her freshly bathed son in her arms, aching, sobbing with relief, and begging Arlette and Moira to tell her if they thought she had harmed her voice.

Dr. Christophe was rushed up the stairs shortly thereafter. He did do a nice job of tending to the new mother and the baby, all the while apologizing for the inconvenience of his delay and his admiration for the job the ladies had done on their own. Maeve simply glared at him and declined to discuss it. Still half dazed from pain and sheer terror, she was not in a forgiving mood.

A few hours later, as Dietrich sat alone with Maeve and the baby, kissing her limp hand and gazing with almost unbearable tenderness and pride at their offspring, he heard her voice say clearly and forcefully, "Enjoy this one, *Schatzi*, and take good care of him. He's going to be our one and only."

Looking at the determined expression on Maeve's face, the baron didn't have the nerve to reply. He did, however, show his gratitude for his son by presenting her with a diamond necklace in the shape of rosettes of graduated size, a lovely thank-you.

Little Johannes Patrick had been in such a hurry to arrive that his mother had delivered him in less than two hours, which all the mothers of her acquaintance assured her was a great stroke of luck. Maeve felt she had survived Chinese torture and let everyone within earshot know how brave she had been to give birth without sleep-inducing drugs. Now that it was over with, she felt entitled to a medal for heroism, but privately she told her husband it was not something to be endured twice.

The one good thing about the delivery was the mother's quick recovery. Not at all groggy, Maeve had been tired but ambulatory only hours later, fussing over Baby in his ornate Napoleonic cradle and having a bowl of clear soup as Dietrich sat with her in her room, choosing a name for his heir.

"Anything but Hubertus," Maeve flatly declared. "Anything within reason, of course."

"I would like to name our son Johannes after my mother, Johanna," he said. "I was very fond of her."

"All right," Maeve nodded. "And Patrick for my father."

"Agreed."

Maeve leaned against her pillows and sighed. Johannes Patrick was really a beautiful little thing even if he was almost bald. The little bit of yellow down on his head made him look like a baby chick. And she would have been happier if he had been a redhead like herself—all she could see was blond fuzz, a tiny facsimile of Dietrich.

It wasn't fair, she thought; she had done all the work. She was entitled to someone who looked like her, even though Dietrich was a fine-looking fellow.

"You've made me so happy, Maeve," he said quietly. "This is what I've always wanted."

Maeve was pleased too. But somehow she found herself wondering what this beautiful, sleepy baby in the gilded cradle was going to do to her career. She had no intention of abandoning that for anything.

*

If the baby had come into the world in the midst of an unexpected snowstorm, he was christened on one of the very few sunny days in December of 1906.

Wrapped in layers of woolens over his lacy christening gown of Carrickmacross lace and swathed in an outer layer of ermine, the blond infant was carried to the baptismal font in the Madeleine Church in the rue Royale by his godmother, a colleague of Maeve's from the Opéra-Comique, and nervously eyed by his godfather, Marc Antoine de Marigny, who appeared nervous each time the baby made a sound.

Since Catholic custom forbade the mother to attend the baptism, his grandmother and father kept their eyes on little Johannes Patrick throughout the ceremony, and it was in Moira's arms that he rested on the return home, a rather puzzled infant who blinked and cried occasionally as he felt himself half smothered in an expensive pile of lace and fur on his first trip outside.

"He's going to be very intelligent," Dietrich declared as Johannes blinked his baby eyes at him and clung to his outstretched finger. "I think he ought to attend Heidelberg University and then perhaps one of the universities here in Paris. He'll be well equipped to take over after me if he has a varied experience."

Moira's blue eyes sparkled with amusement. "I think we'd better worry about nursemaids first," she said. "We can go on to higher education later."

"One can never start thinking too soon about these things, Mama," Dietrich replied. "We can't be complacent."

"Of course not, dear," Moira agreed as she removed a wayward strand of pearls from baby Johannes's grasp. But she did think her son-in-law was getting ahead of himself at this point.

"He's Hubertus's grandson," Maeve replied with a shrug when her mother told her later about Dietrich's plans for the child. "What would you expect for a future Baron von Reuter?"

She was grateful her father-in-law was no longer around to add his voice to the chorus of admirers who were now going to try to take over her son's life. The poor little lamb was too sweet to have to deal with *him*.

When Moira and the infant, flanked by Charlie and Dietrich, returned from the church after the baptism, Maeve was waiting to receive her son, worried about the effect of cold December air on such a little person.

If the cold air was bad for her vocal cords, what might it not do to little Hanno? A winter christening was a terrible idea, absolutely unhealthy. They should have waited for spring. Arlette nodded in perfect agreement and shook her head at the rashness of a trip outdoors in winter, annoying Moira.

The guest of honor was exhibited briefly to the assembled guests in his mother's arms, resplendent in a long, flowing lacy gown and bonnet, then removed to a cradle in one of the rooms in the suite reserved for Maeve on the first floor, overlooking the garden. His wet nurse, Marie Louise, fed him, changed him, and bundled him off to bed while she curled up in a cozy armchair to enjoy a tray of delicacies sent up from the feast downstairs.

For the christening, the parents and grandparents had invited an eclectic group of friends ranging from Marc Antoine, who was rehearsing Maeve for Verdi's *Rigoletto*, to Sean and Zofia Farrell, who were agitated over the constitution Prince Nikolai had recently been forced to grant his peasant subjects, to the Japanese diplomats who had worked with Dietrich on the war loan, to some rich Americans who knew Charlie from New York, to the lesser members of the Parisian upper crust, who never turned down invitations that assured them of good food and clever company.

On this happy occasion, Moira had worked her florist night and day to transform the Palais Lassiter into a spring garden. Roses and gardenias were blooming everywhere and the sweet scent made a heady contrast to the cold December weather outside. All the ladies were given nosegays of tiny roses, daisies, and baby's breath with silk pastel streamers bearing the name of the von Reuter heir in gold letters.

Servants in livery were busy passing around champagne flutes filled with Moët, as ladies in elegant gowns eyed Moira's luxurious decorations, her gown and jewels.

For the baptism at the Madeleine, Mrs. Lassiter had worn a chic blue *tailleur* edged with chinchilla under a chinchilla coat and hat, but to receive her guests at the reception she had changed into a superb afternoon gown by Worth—a voided velvet creation in deep green with fine black lace at the bosom and elbow-length sleeves. Her diamond and pearl choker and matching earrings completed the effect, drawing compliments from the most blasé guests.

With her slender figure and glowing complexion, Moira looked more like a sister than a mother—and certainly not like anybody's idea of a grandmother. Some Frenchman murmured something about Diane de Poitiers, the seemingly ageless mistress of Henri II, but Sean Farrell was recalling an evening in Berlin when a gorgeous woman in a jet-spangled black satin evening gown had taken his breath away.

Maeve was equally concerned about her first public appearance since the birth of her son, and she had chosen a royal-blue satin creation with a neckline whose lacy decoration did nothing to conceal her stunning décolletage. To her great satisfaction, Arlette had managed to lace her into the gown, which had been purchased the year before and never worn. Dietrich's new diamond necklace glittered on her bosom, sending forth rays of light with each breath and attracting a great deal of attention.

In the midst of the exquisite flowers, the fine food, and the general goodwill, a toast was proposed by a guest to the health of little Hanno, which then unleashed a wave of similar toasts with much champagne to wash them all down.

Charlie Lassiter, enjoying himself in conversation with some American friends who had hunted tigers with him in India, was carried away by the warm feeling and raised his glass to wish long life to Maeve's newborn son. Then, to the amazement of his listeners, Charlie confided that he had a son of his own and he was going to acknowledge him.

That piece of unsolicited information made the rounds faster than Marc Antoine's spiteful bit of gossip about Mary Garden and her spat with a famous English soprano in London. In no time at all, people were whispering about who the mother could be and casting nervous glances at beautiful Moira, wondering if she knew.

Dietrich was the first to hear the titillating bit of news from one of the Japanese, who innocently asked him if it was the custom in the West to consider all children equal under the law, even if they were illegitimate. When asked why that ever came up, he simply invoked Charlie's announcement of a few minutes earlier. Dietrich blanched.

Staring at his father-in-law, he wondered if the man had lost his mind. How could he even consider making that little bastard an acknowledged part of the family? How could he think of making him a sort of uncle to Johannes Patrick? It went against all notions of common sense and propriety. Against common decency! And to speak of it at the christening party!

Maeve was deep in conversation with Marc Antoine about her difficulties with the aria "Caro nome" when she noticed the shocked look on her husband's face as he spoke with the Japanese. What on earth could have prompted that stricken expression? Had someone just died?

Puzzled, she excused herself and went to Dietrich's side. He took her arm and tersely whispered the news. "No!" protested Maeve. "He couldn't! Mama would never stand for it!"

He laughed sourly. "I don't think she had much say in it."

As her guests were buzzing with the startling piece of news, Maeve decided she had better let her mother know before someone else did. There was such excitement in that ballroom it would be only minutes before Moira discovered what was causing the uproar anyway.

Maeve made a slight gesture in Moira's direction, indicating she wished to speak to her in private, but before she could, Hanno's godmother intercepted Mrs. Lassiter to ask naively if she had recently had a child.

The blue eyes turned glacial as Moira glared at the little fool.

"What on earth makes you think so?" she retorted.

Embarrassed, the woman looked slightly puzzled and responded, "Well, Monsieur was just toasting *his* son as well as Maeve's, so I naturally thought . . ."

Maeve saw the expression of sheer disbelief on her mother's face and groaned. The secret was out. So much for diplomacy and tact.

"Mama," she said, rushing to Moira's side, "don't get upset yet. First let's hear Charlie himself. Perhaps it's all a misunderstanding."

Dietrich had never seen a woman move as fast as Moira at that moment. Before Maeve could finish her sentence, she was across the room and demanding to know just what the devil her husband was telling people.

Caught unprepared for this confrontation, Charlie smiled guiltily, unable to think of a reply that wouldn't lead to out-and-out warfare. He glanced in embarrassment around the room, then at Moira.

"Oh, you fool!" she wailed. "How could you wreck a beautiful party like this with the mention of that scum?"

Even those who didn't speak English had no trouble understanding her. Moira was so outraged she didn't care who was there. She reached out and smacked her husband hard across the face with her ostrich fan, sending little bits of down flying high into the air, whirling around above everyone's head like dandelion fluff in a summer breeze.

"You are despicable!" she flung at him as she gathered up the magnificent lace-trimmed train of her gown and made an impassioned exit while the onlookers gasped and moved quickly aside before she trampled them on her way out of the room.

Charlie turned bright red and stood staring after his wife as if he couldn't believe his eyes. Then he headed for the door.

"No!" Dietrich shouted, throwing himself across his path. "Don't! It will only make things worse. Come. Let her cool off."

Lassiter hesitated, glanced in the direction of the white marble staircase to the first floor, then back at the room full of curious guests, and forced himself to make light of things. Slapping Dietrich on the shoulder, he smiled, gestured for the servants to pass around more champagne, and headed back into the center of things, claiming "a little family misunderstanding, nothing to worry about." But those with sharp eyes noted he was ashen.

Upstairs in Moira's gilt-and-white-paneled bedroom, with its pink silk coverlets and pillows, crystal chandelier, white and gold brocade drapes, and paintings by Winterhalter, Ingres, and Boucher, Moira was in a rage, flinging clothes into the middle of the bedroom and calling for her maid to pack them. Now!

Maeve had hurried upstairs to see what her mother was doing. Now she was appalled to find her ready to leave home.

"But Mama! You have a houseful of guests. You can't leave!"

"The devil I can't! If that whoremaster I married can make a public announcement of his shameful behavior, then I can do whatever I please."

Maeve's heart was racing. She was so upset at the idea of Moira rushing off to God knows where by herself that she could scarcely think straight. The whole thing was ridiculous.

"He had too much champagne, Mama. I'm sure he was caught up in the joy of the moment and didn't really mean to offend you."

Moira gave her child a steely-eyed glare. "Then you're saying he's a drunken sot who's too dense to know how to behave?"

"No!"

"Don't apologize. I'm in total agreement! He may be as rich as Croesus, but he has no manners. None at all."

With that, Moira ripped a drawer out of a jewel cabinet and flung it on the floor next to the clothes. Her frantic maid rushed around grabbing clothes, looking for a trunk, saying, "Yes, madame. Of course, madame," all the time thinking her mistress had gone mad.

Dietrich appeared in the doorway, pale and distracted as he rushed up to embrace Moira and offer his sympathy.

"Charlie was a *Schweinhund*," he declared with feeling. "It's unthinkable to do this to you and your family. Especially on this day."

"I'm leaving," Moira announced. "Let him enjoy his little bastard and its whorish mother if he wishes. Without me."

"Mama, where will you go?"

"I don't know. To the Ritz for tonight."

"Oh no. Come stay with us."

She shook her head. "No. It would be too easy for Charlie to find me there. Let him go wild searching for me."

"Then go to our house in Berlin," Dietrich suggested helpfully. "He wouldn't think of that right away."

Moira paused and glanced back at her son-in-law. "That's good, Dietrich. Very clever."

"It's shameful what he did. Humiliating." The young man shook his head in anger as he took Moira's hand and clasped it tenderly. "How could he even mention that trash in the same house where people are celebrating little Hanno's christening. It's beyond all taste and decency, Mama. And it's an insult to Maeve and our son as well."

Moira embraced him, touched by his loyalty. Then she asked, "When does the Nord Express leave for Berlin?"

"In a few hours. Come. We'll take you to our house, where you can wait until it's time to go to the station."

"Maeve," Moira ordered, "go back downstairs and show your face. Let Charlie think I'm still upstairs. He'll have the surprise of his life later."

"Mama, I think you're so angry, you don't know what you're doing. This is not a good idea."

Dietrich and Moira were outraged. The young banker asked in shocked tones, "Would you have your mother stay here to be insulted? Do you think she should let Charlie treat her like this?"

Maeve stared back at the two of them, absolutely beside herself.

"Well, it's *his* son, for heaven's sake. If he wants to acknowledge him, let him! Mama had nothing to do with that. Why should she even care? As long as she doesn't ever have to see him!"

"Oh my God!" Moira raged. "How can you be so dense? How would you like it if this boy suddenly announced he'd fathered a bastard on some little slut and was going to take care of him?"

Maeve laughed. "I'd say he was facing up to his responsibilities. Of course," she added, looking pointedly at Dietrich, "I'd want to kill him."

"Well, then?"

"But you knew about the child last year, Mama, when the mother wrecked my engagement party. It's old news."

"Not this part, Maeveen. This is the first time Charlie's ever mentioned him since that day. And what does he tell the world? That he wants to acknowledge him. Just the same as if he had been his wife's child. That's wrong, Maeveen! That's degrading."

Dietrich pushed his pale blond hair back with a nervous gesture. "This is just the thin tip of the wedge, Maeve," he added solemnly. "First he acknowledges the little bastard. Then the brat moves into the house to disgrace your mother. Next the little trash will be on an equal footing with you and our son. Charlie will make him his heir and leave you and Hanno out in the cold."

She stared at them in disbelief. "I don't care about inheriting anything from Charlie Lassiter. He's been generous beyond belief to me. He's already done more than enough for me. Don't be daft!"

"It's the principle of the thing," Dietrich replied coldly. "That little trash should not be considered our son's equal."

"You live in a fantasy world, Maeve," Moira said in disgust. "You can't be kind to this sort of aggressive scum. If you are, they'll have all of their rights and yours as well. If Charlie's talking about recognizing this child, it can only mean that Milonari woman has been seeing him and managing to twist him around her little finger. That kind of woman has to be fought with every weapon available. She's the lowest type of whore. If she can smell money, nothing will stop her from forcing that boy on us."

At that, Maeve held up her hands and accepted defeat. She thought they were both overreacting, but she also knew how Moira felt about this child. There was no reasoning with her.

"Mama," she said in resignation, "enjoy your trip to Berlin. I'll see you when you return."

She gave Dietrich a disgusted look as she swept out of the room and down the stairs. Maeve liked Charlie Lassiter. He had been stupid today and he had infuriated Moira because he let the whole world know he had something she couldn't give him. For all her beauty, she couldn't provide him with a son, and Laura Milonari could. That was his real sin.

Of course, the timing was dreadful. But Charlie didn't have a mean bone in his body, and if he was a shade too proud of being a father himself at the christening of his wife's grandson, well, that was forgivable. He wanted a child. He wanted one with Moira, and if not with her, then apparently with anyone.

"Poor Charlie," Maeve sighed as she reentered the room, wearing a gracious but forced smile. She felt sorry for the man. And she thought Moira was making a terrible mistake. On top of it, to hear her carrying on like an outraged duchess! One would think she had cornered the market on manners and morals!

It was all jealousy, and while Moira certainly had grounds for hurt feelings, she was simply not using her head. And that stiff-necked Prussian was no help at all, Maeve reflected angrily. He could be a proper fool when he got on his high horse.

*

Sean Farrell, who had witnessed the outburst in the ballroom, was so concerned for Moira that he waited until Dietrich and Maeve had both left her apartment and then knocked at the gilt-paneled doors to pay her a visit. With a temper like hers, she was bound to do some damned foolish thing—and God knows the von Reuter boy was just the sort of little snob to abet her in her silliness. If he was offering her advice, it could only be disastrous.

Moira opened the door at his knock and took a step back in surprise at finding Sean on her threshold. Then she tossed her head and declared grandly, "I'm leaving him! Let him have that brat and its whorish mother, too!"

Moira looked both beautiful and agitated. For a moment Sean remembered her as she was the night he returned to Berlin to find her wearing Friedrich Wilhelm's diamond bracelet. Then he put it out of his mind. That was another time. It was Mrs. Charlie Lassiter he was dealing with tonight.

Sitting down beside Moira on one of her silk sofas, Sean was a bit surprised to find himself in what seemed to be an enormous pile of clothing. There were pieces of clothing all over the room: gowns, bodices, petticoats, stockings. Either Moira's chambermaid had gone on strike or he had actually caught her in the middle of packing—a dangerous idea. Her lovely face, he noticed, was tearstained and tragic as she turned to him in anguish.

"He's a bastard!" she said angrily as she clutched one of her satin pillows. "I hate him."

Sean kissed her hand affectionately, then smiled. "No," he said quietly. "Charlie's just a bit drunk. *I'm* a bastard. And I imagine Princess Milena must have felt the way you do now when she found out about my mother and me."

Startled, Moira raised her head. This was the first time Sean had ever spoken like this about his birth. He had never before mentioned the pain it caused everyone. And despite her own troubles, Moira was fascinated to hear his revelation. She wanted to know more.

"What did the Princess do?" she asked, her eyes wide with expectation. She was hoping it was something similar to what she was planning. If it was good enough for royalty, it was good enough for her.

With a gleam in his eye, Sean said, "Her Highness tried to rid Montenegro of Mama by invoking witchcraft before I was born. When that didn't work, she saw to it that Mama and I were packed off to Europe after my birth. But she never raised her hand against me, and she always treated me kindly when I returned to visit my father. Her Highness is a wily woman, very crafty, very shrewd."

Moira laughed scornfully. "Fancy a princess putting up with that! No offense, Sean," she added quickly, "but it seems to me she accepted defeat."

He shook his head. "Wrong, Moira. Princess Milena scored a great victory. She retained the affection of Nikolai Petrovic, and she made him so grateful for her benevolence that she could have her way in anything anytime she pleased. What did it cost her? Nothing. And what did it give her? Power. Her children are princelings and Geraldine Farrell's son is not. So Her Highness preserved the status quo—and all the money Nikolai Petrovic spent on his bastard son never changed that. Think about it, Moira," he added significantly. "Put aside your feelings of wounded pride and ask yourself what it is you really want."

"I want to make that brat vanish from the face of the earth," she said passionately, with the gesture of an outraged prima donna.

She was so fierce about it Sean almost laughed. One thing about Moira, she wasn't reluctant to put her worst foot forward. She really needed to be stopped from making a hash of everything.

"Wrong," he replied solemnly as he took her jeweled hand and kissed it once again. "You want to make your very rich American husband so racked with guilt for offending you that he'll be eternally in your debt for remaining with him despite his shameful and dastardly behavior."

When she gave a disdainful toss of her head, Sean laughed in exasperation. "Moira! Your greatest asset—besides your beauty—is

Charlie's love for you! Look around you, woman. He's given you more luxury than you ever thought the world possessed! Stop being so damned bourgeois and become a real grande dame!"

"My God, you're cynical!" she exclaimed as she pulled her hand away.

"Damned right I am," he replied. "It's called survival. And you're not the woman I took you for if you don't play this card. Take my word for it—Charlie's feelings are in an uproar over this unexpected child of his. Use this to your advantage, Moira. But don't run off. That would be fatal. Stay home and let him expiate his guilt in a flow of precious stones."

Staring at Sean, Moira wavered. She was so angry right now she might not really be rational enough to make the right decision. This fellow was clever. Perhaps he was smarter than Dietrich about this. After all, he spoke from experience.

"Why are you telling me this?" she asked. "Why do you care?"

"For heaven's sake, Moira," Sean replied, "isn't it apparent? I do care for you. Life didn't work out for us the way I planned in Belgrade, but that didn't put an end to my feelings for you. I was more downcast than you'll ever know the day I found out about Charlie Lassiter. But I'd feel even worse if I had to see you throw away everything you've gained just to win an empty victory over Laura Milonari."

Moira rested her head on Sean's shoulder for a moment as she glanced at their reflection in one of her tall mirrors.

"Damn those Serb maniacs," she said, sighing briefly. "They caused me such a lot of trouble. More than you can imagine."

"Your own bad temper may cause you more," he replied with a smile. "Think about what I've said and don't be foolish."

*

After Sean returned to the party, Moira remained alone in her room. Sean *was* clever, no doubt about it. And he was objective enough to offer sensible advice. It was just that her feelings were hurt and she wanted revenge for that.

Still, if a real princess could choose to put up with her husband's bastard brat to win important concessions, there might be some merit in it. Glancing at herself in the mirror, Moira thought of the word "bourgeois" and frowned. She hated all the connotations of that word, recalling her priggish relatives back home in Ireland who were bourgeois to a man.

"Very well," she declared to her own reflection. "If a princess can live with such a thing—and profit from it—then so can I. But he'll pay for this, one way or another. I won't be made a fool of by anyone. And he'd better realize it!"

CHAPTER 23

Baron Dietrich von Reuter, international banker and man-about-town, was feeling very pleased with himself lately. Not only was he the husband of France's most beautiful diva—and proud father of a handsome heir—he was also important enough to be approached by the minions of Germany's foreign ministry to carry out a "patriotic mission" of the utmost secrecy. Assured that it was of particular concern to the All-Highest, Dietrich readily agreed.

At a meeting at the foreign ministry in Berlin, Dietrich was asked in the name of the Fatherland to go to Vienna and there arrange a transfer of funds from the Von Reuter Bank to the Viennese account of one Milan Jakopic—with the foreign minister depositing the money in Berlin in the name of Herr Jakopic to cover the whole affair. A simple matter for a banker.

Sensing something untoward, Dietrich asked curiously, "And what kind of sum are we speaking of, Herr Minister?"

The gentleman from the foreign ministry, a bull-necked Prussian type in a tight cutaway coat and starched wing collar, looked him in the eye and said casually, "Oh, about half a million marks, I should say. Yes, Herr Baron. Half a million."

At that point Dietrich looked startled and showed signs of asking embarrassing questions, but the foreign ministry gentleman abruptly held up his hands.

"A business matter our government is concerned with. A very private business, *ja?*" And his wink told the young man not to bother trying to meddle. Just take care of business and be a good German.

With the money safely deposited, Dietrich was satisfied he wasn't going to lose anything, so he found himself boarding the train to Vienna en route to his rendezvous with Herr Jakopic.

As Dietrich headed toward the Austrian capital on board his private Pullman, he poured himself a glass of champagne—Veuve Clicquot—and contemplated the Balkan situation. As usual, it was a hodgepodge of plots, schemes, diplomatic maneuvering, and seething restlessness that kept the gentlemen in various foreign offices constantly on their toes. That the Kaiser's men had asked him to help them he took as a great compliment. Perhaps this was a delayed reaction to his mission on behalf of Russo-Japanese relations? Who could tell? The important thing was, the All-Highest apparently approved of him. God, he almost wished that old bastard Hubertus were still alive to hear about this!

Lying on a polar bear rug stretched across a sofa in his bedroom, Dietrich reached for his glass and stared thoughtfully into the darkness as the train raced toward Vienna. What the hell was going on in the Balkans right now that the foreign ministry was about to further it with such a large infusion of cash? Jakopic was surely a Serb name, perhaps not the man's real name, but a Serb name nonetheless. Was this some dirty business directed against King Peter of Serbia, archenemy of the Hapsburgs? Relations between the two neighbors were generally dismal. And revolutions cost money. So did assassins. Could the sanctimonious old Emperor be considering this?

Or could this plot—if it was a plot—be directed against Prince Nikolai of Montenegro? Montenegrins were Serbs too. Perhaps Jakopic was a discontented subject of Nikolai Petrovic?

That thought made Dietrich take another sip of champagne. Maeve had been telling him all sorts of things about plots and conspiracies in Montenegro. So had the *Bourse Gazette*. Maeve's source was Zofia Farrell, that walking advertisement for marital uneasiness. With her links to the Montenegrin princely clan, she was certainly au courant.

Closing his eyes, Dietrich tried hard to shut out any unseemly thoughts about Zofia, but didn't succeed. What a gorgeous woman! Tall, slim, strikingly beautiful, she was temptation in a silk gown. A lot like Hélène von Ebert. Sultry and exotic. Probably very passionate. Jesus! Zofia was a splendid creature! Probably a little tiger in bed.

Pouring himself another glass of champagne, Dietrich felt ashamed that he was getting so carried away by the thought of Zofia's charms.

That was a dangerous interest. He was married to a beautiful woman of even greater attractions—and Zofia was the wife of a man who wouldn't hesitate to shoot someone who had dishonored him.

Stroking the fur of his ursine companion, Dietrich reflected on the fact that he had never really liked Sean Farrell, mostly because Maeve *did*. Hubertus had disliked both Sean and his mother, he remembered.

Well, he thought, Maeve had been overcome with gratitude at being rescued from that hellhole in Africa—so how could one fault her for that? Besides, her rescue had made it possible for her to become Baronness von Reuter, so of course one could understand her feelings. Still . . .

Dietrich tried not to think of Maeve near Sean Farrell. She had a romantic nature, very common in artistic people. She was susceptible to heroism and good looks. Well, she had married *him* after all, so that showed she was endowed with some residual good sense—even with all the rest.

But he didn't like to share her affection with anyone, especially someone like Sean Farrell. That could prove a risky attachment—too risky to endure.

As he stared into the darkness of the German countryside, Dietrich sipped his champagne and rather hoped this Herr Jakopic was a *Montenegrin* traitor.

*

Sean and his servant, Kyril, made the tiring journey to Cetinje via the Orient Express to Venice, steamboat from Venice to the Gulf of Kotor, then up the nearly impassable snow- and ice-clogged mountain trails by mule to reach Prince Nikolai and confer with him in his palace. There had been an attempt on the Prince's life and the Petrovici were plotting their retaliation.

Icy winds whipped the travelers as they arrived in the Montenegrin capital, so cold and snow-covered that the nearly deserted streets were rutted with the frozen grooves of carriage wheels.

Glimmers of light emanated from the various European legations that lined the main street, but for the most part, the town was dark, dreary, and sheathed in an icy fastness. The cry of an occasional hungry wolf broke the nighttime silence, blending in with the unending shriek of the wind as it whistled around roofs and tore at heavy shutters.

Sean, wrapped in a warm sealskin coat and hat, fur-lined boots and gloves, drove up to the entrance of the palace, past the ancient Orthodox cathedral where he had been christened on an icy morning so long ago, past the gloomy tower where Turkish heads used to be proudly displayed in Prince Nikolai's youth, and presented himself to the half-frozen sentry on duty.

"Welcome home, Ivan Petrovic. Good to have you back."

"Thank you, Milan. Good to see you."

Inside the two-story structure all was rich paneling and Venetian chandeliers, with attendants half in native dress and half in European-style uniforms. Kyril followed behind his master as they crossed to the billiard room to find the princes.

Danilo and Mirko were seated in deep leather armchairs having cigars when their brother entered. Both men wore elegant Savile Row suits in contrast to the elaborately gold-braided military uniforms they sported in their public appearances. They greeted each other warmly and got down to business, while Kyril stood guard outside the thick oak door, keeping away nosy intruders.

Sean and his brothers were deeply disturbed by the treachery so close to home, especially since the relatives of a member of the Montenegrin senate were involved. Nikolai was all the more incensed, since it was becoming clear a foreign power was involved, possibly Serbia or Turkey.

If this plot had originated in Serbia as a prelude to annexing Montenegro, it would be still more infuriating. Nikolai had sent Serbia's new king—his son-in-law—an effusive letter upon his accession to his blood-stained throne. Did he have so little regard for family ties that he could now countenance Nikolai's murder? All the Petrovici considered this a shocking lack of respect.

In the course of the conversation it was noted that Sean's father-in-law and brothers-in-law hadn't been seen in Cetinje lately. Where were the Plamanacs keeping themselves these days? Mirko inquired casually. Papa always enjoyed keeping his old friends about him in the winter. These gatherings of his chieftains helped pass many an hour reliving the old days and retelling the old ballads.

Sean was tempted to ask if their father was becoming sentimental but he stopped short. He knew Nikolai Petrovic well enough to answer that himself. The old man just liked to keep an eye on his vassals. It frustrated any attempts at rebellion.

Nikolai Petrovic was still a dominating personality at sixty-five, tall and broad with thick gray hair beneath his round, gold-embroidered traditional cap and the eyes and nose of a hawk. He somehow looked even bigger and more imposing in the Montenegrin national dress, and he wore it to full advantage. Of course, the fine cloth for his shirts and full trousers came from London or Milan, his gold-lavished vests were embroidered in St. Petersburg, and his tall boots were made to measure in Vienna, but Nikolai Petrovic was more than entitled to these little embellishments. It was not given to every man to be a prince. And princes were supposed to look different from the common herd.

Sean was announced by an old servant, and he stepped inside the Prince's private study to be enveloped in a hearty bear hug. The old man was as strong as ever, he noticed. Those arms were like iron.

"How was the journey, my boy? Rough going?"

"Only once I started Mount Lovćen. But I'm used to it. Father, it's good to see you," Sean said, smiling. "I'm glad to be back."

Nikolai patted him affectionately on the shoulder. "You've heard the news?" he asked abruptly.

"Yes. Do you suspect outsiders, Father?"

"Oh yes. But that's not as bad as the fact that we're also dealing with Montenegrin traitors. We have vipers in our midst, Ivan. And you know what we do with vipers."

Sean nodded as he and Nikolai looked each other in the eye. "Exterminate them," he said quietly.

*

Maeve was far from content with her new way of life in Paris. She loved little Hanno and even submitted to several sittings for a rather large portrait with the child to please Dietrich, but her days were devoted to reclaiming her figure and preparing for her return to the stage.

Marc Antoine was excited about seeing her as Gilda in *Rigoletto* with himself as the lecherous Duke of Mantua. They spent hours together discussing costumes and new ways of doing certain scenes, while Marie Louise placidly nursed the baby and occasionally carried him within earshot of his famous mother when she and her partner rehearsed.

Hanno was a baby with an admirably sunny disposition. Nothing seemed to upset him except wet diapers and the loss of his source of nourishment. As long as he was clean, warm, and nursing, he was content. Music soothed him, and he was known to smile beatifically at the sound of his mother's voice, prompting Maeve to comment that he obviously had a discerning ear.

Rigoletto was important because the role of Gilda was a new one that she had promised Monsieur Carré to do with Marc Antoine, but the role she was yearning for was still Salome. Her agent had told her there had been discreet inquiries from Heinrich Conreid of the Metropolitan Opera in New York, and Maeve's reply to that was, if they were planning on staging *Salome*, nobody could do it better than she could. And her price was high, just the same as Covent Garden.

The thought of dazzling audiences with a stunning performance as the vamp of Judea was the one thing that Maeve was focusing on these days. Life as a mama was limiting to a woman who was accustomed to performing and receiving mass hysteria as her reward. Though she loved her son, his father was getting on her nerves. And if she had to listen to the words "mother of my child" one more time, Maeve was convinced she'd scream.

Hanno was actually a delightful baby, a lively little fellow who seemed pleased with his lot in life and glad to be the center of attention— just like his mother. Maeve was fond of him but she felt very little desire to deprive him of his nursemaid's company. Hanno was not much of a conversationalist and his mother preferred to talk to her entourage rather than gurgle at them.

Moira was sporting a magnificent new sable coat and seemed re-signed to her role as grandmother, but she was not at all ready to accept her husband's paternity of a "little bastard." She didn't want to hear about him or see him, and if he ever ventured across her threshold, there'd be hell to pay.

Dietrich, who had been so ecstatic about the arrival of little Hanno, felt terrible for Moira. It was crude and disgraceful for Charlie to admit paternity, he maintained. He and Moira were both outraged and seemed to enjoy egging each other on to see who could summon up the most scornful terms in three languages to describe the situation. They were both pretty inventive, although Moira had the edge in English while Dietrich's command of gutter German could curl one's hair. Maeve disliked hearing that kind of language from him and curtly told him so. French was a draw.

"You know," Maeve said one evening as she and her husband dined alone, "for a loving father, you certainly don't have much compassion for other people's children."

Dietrich's beautiful blue eyes looked cold. "And what are you re-ferring to, *Liebchen*? Have I ever given you cause for worry?"

"No, you have not. But I do think it's excessive for you to encourage Mama in her hatred for the Milonari boy. It's not healthy. Charlie has a soft spot for the child, and her attitude is bound to provoke him. In fact," she said, "I'm surprised he's been so meek about it. Of course he feels guilty, so he's ashamed to say too much now, but if Mama doesn't stop dwelling on this, it will lead to trouble. I know you think very highly of my mother and I love you for that, but please don't encourage her obsession with this. It can only harm her marriage."

Dietrich eyed his wife with something bordering on frigid hauteur. Maeve had no business trying to tell him what to do. He was the head of the family, and he certainly knew how to treat a whore's bastard son.

"You're speaking to your husband," he said icily. "And I don't care to discuss this matter further."

Maeve's lovely head bobbed up rather sharply and her own blue eyes fixed his with an equally haughty stare. She hadn't incarnated royalty onstage for nothing.

"I don't recall asking what you cared to discuss," she retorted. "I'm trying to help my mother!"

"You'd do better to sympathize with her, then. I find your attitude quite puzzling."

"Oh, do you now? Well, I can return the favor. How is it any of your business what Charlie Lassiter cares to do with his son?"

"Don't provoke me, *Liebchen*. You have a sharp tongue at times."

"You haven't seen just how sharp it really is, *Schatzi*. I don't want Mama to say something foolish to Charlie over this and wreck a wonderful marriage. I want her to be happy. Stop inciting her to this stupidity!"

Dietrich glanced at his lovely wife, put down his silver knife and fork, and flung his damask napkin onto the table.

"You're spoiling my appetite with your lecture, you know. Are you going to continue?"

Glaring right back at Dietrich, Maeve flung down *her* napkin. As she suddenly rose, startling everyone, one of the footmen dashed across the room to pull back her chair.

"Don't make a scene," Dietrich ordered. "Sit down."

"This is not a scene. This is an *exit*. I'm surprised you can't tell the difference."

And with that, Maeve gathered up the train of her jet-beaded dinner gown and swept grandly out of the dining room, leaving Dietrich to continue his meal in solitary splendor beneath the massive crystal chandelier.

The two footmen glanced nervously at each other and awaited the master's orders.

"Clear away Madame's place. She is indisposed."

"Very good, sir."

But Madame didn't look indisposed to them. She looked thoroughly infuriated, and even though the couple had been speaking in German, their French servants could tell something was seriously amiss. La Devereux was practically sending out sparks.

Dietrich's obsession with Charlie's damned baby irritated Maeve. She had other things on her mind, and to that end she paid a visit to the leading character dancer of the Paris Opéra to ask her for help with Salome's Dance of the Seven Veils.

The statuesque dark-haired Dutchwoman gave her tea and listened politely. She seemed rather amused by the notion. But as she said grandly, she did not give lessons, although she was not unwilling to help a fellow artiste.

"I want to be able to sustain the entire role," Maeve explained as her hostess studied her carefully with her large, kohl-rimmed dark eyes. "All the other sopranos—so far—have had to have a stand-in. I want to play Salome as she ought to be played—wildly, sensuously, erotically. It will be a triumph if I can carry it off."

The dancer, who passed herself off as an exotic creature of the Indies although she was born and bred in Holland, smiled faintly. She could understand Maeve's determination. She herself had arrived in Paris with nothing more than a single franc in her purse and years of sordid domesticity behind her with a drunken Dutch colonial army officer—and an obsessive desire to conquer the French capital.

Margaretha Geertruida Zelle MacLeod succeeded beyond her wildest dreams and became the "Javanese" Mata Hari. Appearing half-naked in the prestigious halls of the Musée Guimet before audiences of the blasé Tout-Paris, the slender brunette enchanted French society with the erotic temple dances of the Indies and became the woman of the hour. Soon she was performing in all the European capitals, but she liked Berlin best because of the German viewpoint that accepted her as an artist of serious stature—an important distinction in her eyes.

Watching Mata Hari, Maeve was fascinated to observe her in repose. With her olive skin tones and gleaming black hair, she looked entirely believable as a Javanese. There was a trace of melancholy in her face that contrasted oddly with her well-established reputation as a *"femme légère,"* making the Irish girl recall stories she had heard about Mata Hari having lost a child to the wrath of vindictive natives. Whatever she was or whoever she was, Maeve had never met a woman who moved as beautifully as she did. She had the natural grace of a panther.

"I can't teach you to do overnight what I learned after years of study," the dancer said eventually. "But I can show you how to move."

"If you can show me how to move like Salome, I'll be in your debt," Maeve replied quickly. "Name your price."

The Dutchwoman smiled. "This is a very unusual situation. It's not really a performance. And I don't wish to let word get out that I give lessons or I'll be deluged with all sorts of requests. You can understand that, I think."

"Oh yes, madame," Maeve agreed.

Mata Hari smiled again. She had another motive. If this lovely girl had no sense of rhythm and rendered the Dance of the Seven Veils like a lumbering, flat-footed farm girl, she wanted no credit for her training. One had one's standards to maintain. On the other hand, this Baroness von Reuter had enough money to make her efforts worthwhile. And the Dutchwoman had heard her sing and had been impressed. It would be quite amusing to turn her into the sixteen-year-old vamp of the Bible.

With the large fee agreed upon, Maeve made the trip out to the dancer's elegant villa at Neuilly twice a week and immersed herself in the art of the dance. Mata Hari used an accompanist who rendered Strauss's score on the piano while she choreographed the dance with Maeve watching her closely, studying every gesture.

When the dancer decided to allow her pupil to attempt it, she was far from pleased. Her red-haired trainee didn't move badly, but she insisted on wearing far too many clothes.

"But I can't teach you to be Salome if you load yourself down with all this material. It's absurd," she protested.

Maeve was embarrassed to cavort around the large rehearsal hall in any less than what she was wearing, especially since there was the omnipresent accompanist observing them. Mata Hari had no such problem. She was used to appearing nude or nearly nude in her performances. It was her boast that she was the first woman to do so in Paris without a police raid.

"The body has to be free to show the rhythmic gestures. Without that, it's too silly. Remember, my dear, you have to fling off your garments along the way. Otherwise, what's the point? Salome wants to seduce a man, not rustle her draperies. There's a big difference."

"I feel awkward," Maeve admitted.

Despite her intentions, she felt ridiculous. Perhaps if she were in full rehearsal with costumes, props, and a full orchestra, things would be different. She simply felt silly now, especially with fat Monsieur Dufour sitting there, pounding away at the Bechstein and chain-smoking.

"I need atmosphere," she said lamely.

"All right. It may help. But you have to loosen up and free your body. Salome isn't a British governess, you know. She's a depraved little trollop."

"Madame is right, Baroness," the accompanist offered. "Think decadent thoughts. Picture yourself in your Thaïs costume back on that tiger skin. That's the right frame of mind."

Maeve blushed. "You saw those?"

"Oh yes." He grinned. "Very nice. That's the mood you need now. Try to re-create it."

That at least gave Maeve something to aim for, and the next time she returned to Neuilly she had a costume of various layers of diaphanous silk with silk tights that covered her entire body with pale flesh tones.

"Better," declared Mata Hari. "This is an improvement." She still thought it was too much, but she acknowledged the need for some covering. She herself had been forced to appear in a body stocking for performances in Monte Carlo, and she couldn't expect an artist of the opera to wear any less.

"Try this on," she said to Maeve. "Let's see how it looks."

She fastened a jeweled belt around the girl's hips and let the tassels hang down in front, swaying with each movement. It seemed a nice Salome-like touch, and Maeve decided to adopt it for the end of her performance so that she might be seen to be wearing *something*. It was even better than plain tights since it gave her a shockingly heathen aura.

For his part, Monsieur Dufour nodded his vigorous approval as Maeve flung aside her last veil and stood immobile, like a pagan statue, apparently clad only in her glittering jeweled belt.

"Pink lighting will make everything look deliciously naked, Baroness," he said. "The audience will think you haven't a stitch on except for your belt. Wonderfully erotic!"

"Will it look indecent?" she wondered nervously.

"Of course," he laughed. "But that's just the idea. No decent girl would carry on like that and ask for the head of John the Baptist, would she?"

Mata Hari took a cigarette from the accompanist and leaned against the upright piano, smiling at Maeve. She wasn't a bad pupil. She had a lovely, lithe little body that could suggest all sorts of depraved yearnings. She was a credit to her mentor.

"Will you have a private dress rehearsal for Monsieur le baron?" she asked, smiling as Maeve stood before the mirror, gracefully arranging her long cascade of auburn hair.

"Oh, I don't think so, madame," Maeve replied. "I intend to surprise him."

"Ah," murmured Mata Hari in amusement. "Well, good luck."

And as she watched the girl, she hoped Baron von Reuter had a liberal disposition or a disdain for convention. He would need both if he was to witness his wife performing *this* dance in public.

"And Baroness," whispered Monsieur Dufour rather wistfully, "see if you can get them to throw in a tiger skin. You really did look so deliciously depraved in those photographs. It was so sweet."

*

With all her preparation, Maeve was still waiting for something definite from the Metropolitan Opera. Her agent continued to haggle with Mr. Conreid over clauses and paragraphs, and Maeve was becoming more and more convinced she would never sing *Salome* in an important premiere—anywhere.

Dietrich was anxious about the Metropolitan as well. It attracted the elite of New York society, and even if they did choose to regard the opera as a display case for their gowns and jewels, they tended to be very partisan. If they liked a singer, a career was made. And Dietrich couldn't imagine them not liking Maeve.

After Paris, St. Petersburg, Monte Carlo, Milan, and London, Maeve's last important conquest ought to be New York. Aside from the publicity from a successful engagement there, New York hostesses loved to entertain their guests with performances by the stars of the Metropolitan Opera. Fees ran to the thousands of dollars for a few hours' work, and as Enrico Caruso once told Maeve, "It's so easy to become rich there because there are so many millionaires willing to spend their money on music. It's a very nice place."

With all that in mind, Maeve had sent Mr. Conreid every one of her Red Seal recordings for Victor Records, had asked Fred Gaisberg to use his gifts of persuasion, and had even charmed Conreid one day at tea in her Paris home. But there were still details to be worked out, and that irritated her no end.

CHAPTER 24

*M*ary Garden had added to her laurels by enjoying a successful season in New York as a highly touted foreign diva with Oscar Hammerstein's Manhattan Opera—a budding rival to Conreid's Metropolitan. With his generous contracts and aggressive publicity, Hammerstein posed a real threat to the Metropolitan, and there was a sort of battle of the divas raging in New York to see who could win the largest following. Mary Garden had done quite well. So had Luisa Tetrazzini, the chubby, ebullient Italian soprano who had conquered St. Petersburg several seasons earlier. But Conreid had scored the biggest coup by engaging lovely Geraldine Farrar, who simply seduced the audience on her opening night in November 1906 in the charming role of Juliette, Maeve's bête noire.

Dietrich, an admirer of Farrar despite his devotion to Maeve, had arranged for a friend in New York to send him clippings of her opening night reviews. Maeve had devoured the critics' comments and couldn't help comparing the hysterical praise heaped on Farrar with the "abuse" she had endured in Berlin for the same role.

"He sounds as if he's in love with her," Maeve sniffed. "My God! One would think he'd never seen a pretty girl before!"

Dietrich made a sort of noncommittal murmur as he scanned the article from the *New York Times*. Farrar had established herself in a single performance as New York's newest star, and the reporter for the

Times was making flattering comparisons with Emma Calvé's singing and Sarah Bernhardt's acting. He was apparently besotted with the slender, dark-haired girl from the Royal Berlin Opera.

"She's an American," Dietrich said. "It's natural for them to like one of their own."

"She's very good," Maeve retorted. "She'll be tough competition— if Mr. Conreid ever gets around to closing the deal. At the rate things are going, I'll never get to New York, so I won't have to worry about Farrar!"

"Don't be absurd. Of course Conreid will close the deal. But if he doesn't, remember that he has a rival—Hammerstein. The situation is in your favor, *Liebchen*. You're an established star, and they both want stars. Don't worry."

That was easy for Dietrich to say. He wasn't forced to listen to that damned Mary Garden in the corridors of the Opéra-Comique, regaling all and sundry with tales of "her adoring public in New York." It was sickening—at least to Maeve, Marc Antoine, and Arlette, who did a wickedly funny parody of the soprano in private.

Marc Antoine declared he found this self-praise highly distasteful and hinted at deep-seated insecurities. But Garden also had impressive clippings to back up her claims, and that irritated them all the more.

Maeve was going to conquer New York, she swore, and she was going to do it with *Salome*. Richard Strauss had given her his blessing and had even written to Conreid suggesting her for the role in the upcoming season. What more did the man need, for heaven's sake! Maeve was haunted by the specter of Mary Garden launching the role in New York, thus wrecking her own chances for a big premiere.

Monsieur Carré was delighted to welcome Maeve back for her third season. She had regained her figure thanks to her determination, and now she looked lovelier than ever. Marc Antoine was grateful to partner her once again, thereby saving himself from numerous, energy-draining fights with other unnamed sopranos of tyrannical disposition.

*

Trying to concentrate on her debut as Gilda in *Rigoletto*, Maeve spent hours with Herr Albrecht, her vocal coach, refining her phrasing and her gestures. With Marc Antoine as the corrupt and amoral Duke of Mantua, the production ought to fairly glitter with the beauty of its stars. The well-known Italian baritone singing the role of the hunchback Rigoletto looked like a caterpillar beside those two butterflies.

In her dressing room during intermission on the night of her first performance, Maeve was startled to hear a fierce pounding on the door. She had given orders not to be disturbed, and she glanced up sharply, making a little gesture of annoyance.

"Should I open it?" Arlette asked uncertainly.

Maeve nearly shook her head, but she was afraid it might be Monsieur Carré bearing a huge bouquet, and she wanted to hear his opinion of her performance so far. If that wild applause at the end of "Caro nome" was any indication, the audience was totally mad about her Gilda.

"Open it, Arlette," Maeve nodded as she quickly applied more lip rouge. "I think it must be Carré."

To her shock it was not. There, standing in the doorway of her little dressing room, was Laura Milonari, pale and nervous in the unflattering light of the corridor.

Staring at each other, Maeve and Laura seemed equally ill at ease. Arlette thought she'd seen everything now, with this trollop daring to call on Madame after all the trouble she'd caused.

"Baronessa," Laura began wretchedly, "may I speak to you? It's urgent. I have no one else to turn to."

Maeve looked appalled. "I have to go back onstage in four minutes," she declared, floundering for something to say to discourage this horrid woman. The nerve of her!

"Oh, please!" Laura wailed. "I must talk to you! I can't go to Carlo. He won't allow it. It's Gianni, my son! He's vanished. Please tell him, Baronessa. You have a son. You can imagine how I feel right now. I'm terrified for him."

Laura Milonari's eyes were bloodshot and swollen. She looked utterly devastated, her large, dark eyes ringed with circles, her cheeks dead white. Even her dress looked neglected, as if she had thrown on any old thing. The color was unflattering and made her look washed out and unappealing.

"Why don't you simply tell Charlie?" Maeve asked, puzzled.

"I can't. I can't go near him. I don't dare!"

That made no sense to Maeve. She was distracted, waiting for her call. She was certainly running a risk telling this creature to get in touch with Charlie. Moira would have had a fit. But she didn't know what else to say. If the boy was missing, it was serious business.

"Please tell him Gianni is gone. You'll see him. I can't," Laura wailed.

"When did he disappear?" Maeve asked nervously.

"Yesterday. He wandered off by himself and he never returned. His nurse shouldn't have allowed him out alone, but the foolish girl wasn't paying any attention. Now he's gone!" she sobbed. "Please make sure the father knows!"

"Does he know where you live?"

"Of course," replied Laura. "He's the one who pays for the apartment."

When she saw the shocked expression on Maeve Devereux's face, Laura bit her lip. She was an idiot to have let that out of the bag. That witch Charlie married would hear about their secret pact and raise hell. She could just imagine the lies he told that shrew to keep the peace.

"Charlie's been *maintaining* you?" Maeve exclaimed.

"Oh no! He's given me a place to live where I can raise his son decently. He made me promise never to come near him again. And I haven't! But *dio mio,* Baronessa, the child is missing! I must let him know."

Arlette was observing Laura like a cat. The maid's sharp eyes didn't miss much, and she was convinced the woman was genuinely distraught. She had seen her burst in upon Maeve's engagement party looking so beautiful and vindictive, but this was a different woman—racked with fear and terror for the fate of her child.

"Three minutes!" a stagehand called, rapping sharply on Maeve's door.

"I must go," Maeve said abruptly, hesitating between Laura and the door. In any case, she couldn't do anything until after the performance. Charlie wasn't nearby and she had to go back onstage. Damn!

"Please tell Carlo the first chance you get. Tonight!" Laura begged, catching hold of her arm as Maeve hurried out the door with Arlette in tow.

"Yes," Maeve called over her shoulder. "I'll tell him."

Nodding frantically, Laura put her hands over her face and crumpled against the dank stone wall of the corridor, a sobbing wreck in a plain brown dress, her hair falling in untidy waves and her pale face blotchy from weeping.

*

When Maeve took her curtain calls that evening, she received kisses on the hand from Monsieur Carré, Marc Antoine, and the conductor, all of whom were basking in the approval of a delirious public. It was a good performance. Gorgeous bouquets of roses and gardenias made their way to the star's dressing room, where bottles of Moët were uncorked to everyone's jubilation and the usual cluster of nosy reporters were poking around, asking questions about the offers from America.

"We're considering several," the diva replied. "We'll respond when we're ready. Enjoy yourselves, gentlemen."

They were showered with champagne and smiles but got no real answer to the questions that were intriguing musical circles. Was La Devereux about to follow Mary Garden's path across the wide Atlantic, and was she going to make even more money?

Ordinarily, Maeve would have been pleased to throw a few gossipy items at them, rather like tossing crumbs to pigeons, but tonight she had all she could do to stay there and listen to her guests. The idea of that child God knows where bothered her so much she couldn't wait to get away. The more she thought of it, the more she worried.

"Where are Mama and Charlie?" she whispered to Dietrich as he presented her with a lovely gold bracelet in the shape of a serpent, copied from the famous one Queen Alexandra often wore. Maeve's serpent had ruby eyes and tiny diamonds glistening on its fangs and caused a lot of admiring comments, but she didn't really care. She had to speak to her stepfather. Quickly. Where were they?

"Mama called before to say she was sorry, but she and Charlie decided to go to Paris Singer's party this evening. She said she'd be sure to hear you the next time you had to sing Gilda."

Damn! thought Maeve. Moira had wanted to show off her new jewels.

When Maeve and Dietrich returned home, Maeve reached the Palais Lassiter by telephone, but was told by the butler that Monsieur and Madame still hadn't returned from the party and weren't likely to come in before one o'clock.

Nothing was working out for her. Having given her word, Maeve felt obligated to reach Charlie one way or the other—but she hadn't counted on it being so difficult. And Dietrich was wondering why she wasn't coming to bed. She had left the opera house complaining she was exhausted, after all.

"I'm still excited about the performance," she told him. "You know how difficult it is to come back down to earth after a night like this."

"Yes, *Liebchen*." He smiled, kissing her neck. "You were wonderful. You were the greatest Gilda I've ever heard. You had the audience in the palm of your hand this evening."

It was true—even though she could barely concentrate during the last act. Something had got her through in spite of herself. Thank God for all those rehearsals with Marco. That's what had done it.

As Maeve glanced at the clock at her bedside, she wondered when Charlie was likely to get home. Settling into bed beside Dietrich, she tossed and turned, trying to imagine where a small child would have gone by himself. Perhaps he had been snatched by Gypsies. Oh Lord! What a thought. Little Gianni would be gone forever, probably raised as a beggar and a thief, trained to pick pockets and steal for a living.

Damn, she thought nervously, I wish Charlie and Moira had come to the opera. He could have had people out looking for the child by now.

Maeve sighed and curled up against Dietrich, who responded by kissing her neck and murmuring an endearment in her ear.

Stroking Dietrich's lovely hair, Maeve closed her eyes. She had to try again to reach Charlie. She couldn't just lie there, comfortable, soft, and warm in her silken bed while that pathetic little boy was wandering the streets of Paris, probably hungry, most likely frightened, and liable to be abducted by any sort of scoundrel. He was helpless, utterly dependent on a stranger's sense of decency, and vulnerable to predators of all kinds.

"Oh Jesus!" Maeve muttered, almost inaudibly. Moira would not be understanding. She would give her a severe tongue-lashing for siding with her worst enemy and call her a heartless monster who was betraying her own mother—she would certainly look upon this as a betrayal—and then she would carry on like a banshee. No good at all would come of this.

Maeve didn't want to hear any of it. She closed her eyes and sighed again. Then she flung off her covers and got out of bed, put on her negligee, and tiptoed out of the bedroom and headed downstairs to call her stepfather again.

A servant answered at Charlie's residence, informed her that it was too late to call the master to the telephone, and was told in no uncertain terms to haul him out of bed without alerting Madame because Baroness von Reuter had to speak to him without delay. It was urgent.

Within minutes Maeve heard Charlie's sleepy voice on the other end of the line.

"I hope the Baroness has a good reason for rousing me out of a sound sleep," he said in a bantering tone. "Are you all right? How did it go this evening?"

Maeve hesitated. No matter how gently she tried to break the news, it would be dreadful.

Trying hard to sound composed, Maeve apologized for calling at such a late hour and informed him of Laura Milonari's visit and the reason for it. Charlie was appalled, his thoughts racing, embarrassment over the woman's appearance mingled with genuine fear for the child. He was trying his best to do the decent thing, and the mother couldn't even be trusted to watch him. What kind of fool was she? he thought angrily. Here he was, risking Moira's anger by seeing to it that this son of his was well fed, well clothed, and well housed—and Laura Milonari loses him as if he were a stray dog! Jesus! All she cared for was the money. She couldn't give a damn about the child in spite of all her tears. She had been an actress when he met her in Milan—a bad actress. She still was.

Despite his anger at Laura for being so careless with the boy, Charlie knew he had to go to her and find out what he could do to help find him. It was his son and he would do all he could to bring him home.

Maeve returned to bed and found Dietrich half-asleep and wondering what had happened to her. Was she ill?

No, she wasn't ill, she told him, kissing him lightly on the cheek, just restless. She'd had a lot to think about this evening, and it was all due to overstimulation.

When she lay back on her pillow and closed her eyes this time, Maeve felt relieved. She had done the right thing. All hell would break loose when Moira and Dietrich found out, but she would have to endure it. If she hadn't done what she did, she would have been ashamed to look at herself in the mirror.

*

In Laura Milonari's apartment, she, the nursemaid, and her housekeeper were all weeping with fright, awaiting Charlie's arrival. He had telephoned her—to her relief—after speaking with Maeve, had thrown on some clothes, and had hurried over to question her about the boy's disappearance. As soon as he arrived, he brusquely demanded to know what the hell had happened.

All three women burst into tears all over again and had to be calmed before he could get the story out of them. The nursemaid admitted she had been negligent and begged forgiveness, literally on her knees. She was in such abject terror she was hardly able to speak. Laura was scarcely more rational. The housekeeper, an elderly Frenchwoman with a pince-nez and a pile of thick white hair, was the most levelheaded. She was fairly composed despite her tears and managed to give Charlie the details, which were very few.

Sometime after lunch Gianni had said something about wanting his favorite sweet, almond nougat, and while his nurse was carrying on a long and shameless flirtation with the porter of the apartment building, the housekeeper said acidly, he had wandered off. A search of the building and the neighborhood turned up nothing, but a neighboring concierge swore she had seen the child heading toward Monsieur Martin's confectionery shop. That was the last time anyone caught a glimpse of him. He apparently never reached the shop, and he seemed to have vanished into thin air.

"Did you keep searching?" Charlie demanded.

"Of course we did!" Laura replied, weeping. "No one can find him. That's why I called on your stepdaughter."

"You're lucky Maeve's a kindhearted girl. She relayed the message as soon as she could."

Laura nodded. "Well," she muttered, "at least one of them has a heart."

He let that slide. "You're a hell of a mother," he snapped. "You should have hired a competent person instead of this little fool. No wonder the child's gone missing." He was so full of contempt, Laura cringed.

"It's not my fault," Laura protested. "I hired someone to watch him. Who could tell that she was an idiot?"

The maligned nursemaid, a plump, dark-haired farm girl, covered her face with her hands and wept even louder at the prospect of losing her job now.

Charlie glanced around the apartment, a lovely place with large windows, fresh plants and flowers, and fine crystal electric light fixtures— a clean and modern home for the child, a decent place where Gianni could grow and flourish, safe from the hazards of the slums.

"If anything happens to my son," he said flatly, "you'll be out on the street. This is all for him, not for you, Laura. You live here only because of the boy. Remember that."

For a second, the woman felt as if someone had struck her. She had been so truly frightened by the child's disappearance she hadn't even thought of the consequences for herself if he didn't return. Carlo had just brought her back to reality.

"What do you mean?" she shrieked, "you'd really throw me out on the street?"

"That's exactly what I mean," he replied. "You're no better than a blackmailer. Gianni's mine and I won't abandon him even though his mother's a whore. But," he added angrily, "if anything has happened to my child because of your negligence, I'll evict you from here—that I promise!"

Shocked at the prospect of losing her beautiful home, Laura sobbed and flung herself at Charlie, flailing at him with both hands. He grabbed her and forcibly sat her down.

"Save your theatrics for the stage," he said coldly. "Worry about your son."

*

When Charlie returned home, he found Moira waiting up, concerned about his early-morning excursion. She looked quite fetching, her long black hair cascading over her shoulders and down the back of her lilac silk negligee, the black trim falling softly around her neck and bosom.

"What happened?" she asked. "Is there trouble?"

"Yes. My son's missing."

Moira had been about to put her arms around him. She stopped cold, unable even to make a reply. She was angry that there had been some communication from Laura. Otherwise how would he know?

"You could have the grace to say you're sorry to hear it," he snapped. "Even if it's a lie, it would be a kindness."

Moira wasn't a bit sorry. She wasn't even surprised. If appearances meant anything, that Milonari slut wasn't fit to raise sheep, let alone a child. She was just a selfish, careless little whore who would try to use the brat to extort money from Charlie, but wouldn't even give the boy the barest minimum of care. Moira could have told him that. But she wasn't about to now.

"Are you sure?" she asked, startling him by the mildness of her tone. She was thinking of Sean's advice. She would be very grand about this, she decided.

"Of course I'm sure. Laura and her whole household are in hysterics. The child gave them the slip and vanished into thin air."

"Call the police," she said flatly. "Get in touch with the prefect of police and tell him to get his men working on it. He was here at a party last month. He ought to be willing to help you with this."

At least Moira was practical. In all his excitement, Charlie hadn't even thought of calling the police prefect. His mind was in that much of a whirl.

"And offer a reward for the boy's return," she added. "That will encourage the coppers to do their best for you."

Moira didn't give a damn about little Gianni, but she didn't want Charlie to be able to hold it over her head in years to come that while his poor dear little bastard was lost and wandering the cold streets of Paris, she sat by and callously left him to his fate. Therefore she was giving him the benefit of her common sense. It changed nothing in her heart—and she was still going to raise hell if the brat ever crossed her threshold. Moira Lassiter was not about to go soppy with sweetness just because that whore couldn't keep track of her cub. But she could be practical.

Charlie's early-morning telephone call succeeded in rousing the prefect of police out of a sound sleep. Since this Monsieur Lassiter had enough money to buy half the town, he deigned to listen to him, and within hours the flics in Laura's part of town had been alerted to the fact that a three-year-old, dark-haired, dark-eyed male child was missing from his domicile. A reward of one thousand francs awaited the man who could return him to his mother. Police salaries being what they were, this was ample incentive to keep one's eyes peeled.

Maeve took time out later that morning to pay a call on Charlie and Moira to keep abreast of the family drama. Charlie was even more alarmed than he had been the previous night, and he looked wretched, with dark circles under his eyes and an unusually haggard air.

To avoid inflaming Moira, Maeve announced she had heard the news on the way in. She wasn't about to throw fat in the fire by admitting to having relayed the crucial message.

"The police are searching for him now, Maeve. No one's seen him yet."

"Arlette is praying to St. Anthony at a church around the corner. He's the saint who finds what's lost," she explained. "She tells me it's very effective."

"That's very sweet of her," Charlie nodded, touched. "Arlette's a good-hearted girl."

Moira sipped a cup of Chinese oolong tea and held her tongue. She and Maeve were wearing complementary shades of blue this morning and they looked very elegant.

Mrs. Lassiter presided over the silver tea service with studied hauteur. She resented the entire tawdry mess and wasn't entirely convinced the wretched brat was actually in any danger. The whole thing could be some sort of cheap hoax concocted by its mother to extort money out of softhearted Charlie, who was too sentimental for his own good. This combination of a charitable nature and piles of gold was a magnet for vermin of Milonari's type. Moira herself didn't believe the story and fully expected to see the woman on her doorstep once more, carting along the brat for a teary reunion with its foolish father.

*

Charlie felt so useless waiting at home while the police were out hunting for his son, he called his valet and chauffeur and left the house to conduct a search of his own. Years before, he and some cowboys had run a local bandit to ground in the wilds of North Dakota. He hoped he still had the right instincts. He had tracked enough game—of various kinds— in his lifetime.

Maeve departed for rehearsals, where Marc Antoine was waiting, leaving Moira alone at the Palais Lassiter. Half an hour after Maeve got into her black landau to head for the Opéra-Comique, another vehicle arrived, bearing a somber gentleman of distinguished mien and an aide. When the butler responded to the hallway bell, he was startled to find himself face-to-face with the prefect of police.

"Monsieur," he exclaimed, "what a surprise! Come in, please."

As the prefect handed his hat and rosewood walking stick to the butler and his assistant handed over his own hat, he gravely informed Maurice that he was on official business. He must speak to Monsieur Lassiter immediately.

"But that's impossible, monsieur. The master has gone out."

Sighing gloomily, the prefect appeared to gnaw on his thick, drooping mustache as he glanced at his aide.

"Then I will speak to Madame. Is she home?"

"Yes, monsieur. I'll announce you right away."

When Moira entered her salon, both men stood up, looking as solemn as crows. The prefect was not so overcome by the somberness of the occasion that he failed to notice his hostess's willowy figure encased in such an elegant frock. Or her magnificent pearl earrings.

"Gentlemen," she said, a bit uncertainly, "my husband isn't home yet. He's gone out searching with his men. Is there news?"

The two visitors looked so officially grim, Moira was fearful for a second. Had something happened to Charlie?

"Madame," the prefect informed her in tones of splendid doom, "the child has been found."

"Ah," she nodded, somewhat relieved. She had known all along this was a trick. He was probably going to tell her how overcome with joy the mother was now that she'd got him back. The cow!

"But," he continued, "we regret to inform you that he was discovered this morning at the foot of the Pont Alexandre Trois, tangled in a cluster of debris."

For an instant Moira didn't quite understand what he was saying.

"In the water?" she asked stupidly, shocked and not quite believing what she'd heard. If he was in the water, that could only mean . . .

"Yes, madame. Dead for at least a day."

To her own bewilderment she sank or rather collapsed into the nearest chair, not yet ready to comprehend the full ramifications of this. Charlie would be wild with grief. And she had nothing to offer him by way of compensation—no small, healthy Lassiter to replace little Gianni Milonari, who had taken such a hold on his heart.

"My God," she murmured. "I never thought it was anything but a hoax."

The prefect studied Madame Lassiter as she sat before him, stunned. She appeared disoriented, trying hard to comprehend this terrible fact.

"How do you think it happened?" Moira asked at last. "Could the boy have slipped on the riverbank and fallen in?"

"No, madame," her visitor replied. "This is murder."

"For heaven's sake, he was only three years old! How many enemies could he have had?"

The police prefect looked impassively at Madame Lassiter, with her beautiful blue eyes and her fine complexion. He had been in the ballroom on the night of Maeve's engagement party when Laura Milonari had burst in on them, carrying that child in her arms. He had watched as Moira attacked her. He had seen Maeve's look of fear as she snatched the child out of her mother's reach and spirited him out the door.

"I don't know, madame," he answered quietly. "But apparently he had one. You see, he didn't die from drowning. He was strangled before being thrown in the river."

"Good Lord," she murmured, appalled. "This will kill poor Charlie."

*

The sight of little Gianni Milonari lying stiff and cold on the marble slab in the morgue was an image Charlie Lassiter would never forget. Around the slender, childish neck was a rough, angry scar made by the length of cord his murderer had used on him. Bruises on the face and body had come from his final struggle, or more likely from the pounding he had taken as the river carried him along in its rush, only to trap him at the base of a bridge, caught up in a pile of branches, carriage wheels, and other flotsam. The handsome little boy was a horribly battered corpse.

"I'm sorry, monsieur," the attendant murmured as the tall American began to weep. "I'm so sorry."

Charlie tried hard to master his emotions, lost the struggle, and turned quickly away, his face contorted with grief and pain. "Thank you," he whispered.

When he returned to the Palais Lassiter, he found Maeve waiting there with her mother. The girl embraced him without a word as he broke down and sobbed, nearly strangled by his sorrow.

"He's dead, Maeve. The little boy. Who could do such a thing?"

"I'm sorry, Charlie," she said quietly. "It's a wicked thing. I hope they find the one who did it."

Moira stood slightly apart, at a loss for once. She was shocked by the murder, though she wasn't grief-stricken. The boy would have been trouble for her all his life, giving Laura Milonari an excuse to bleed her husband for years to come. Now he was gone—Laura's meal ticket—and Moira couldn't pretend to regret the loss. It was the method of his removal that stunned her. She wouldn't have wished it on him.

Though Charlie was so overwrought he was almost incapable of action, he knew he had a duty to fulfill and he wasn't about to shirk it. Laura Milonari may have been a whore and a fool, but she was still the boy's mother and she deserved to hear the news from him and not from some policeman.

"I'm going to the mother," he announced. "I have to break the news myself."

Moira stiffened. "As you wish," was all she said. But her expression was furious.

When Charlie arrived at Laura's apartment, he was startled to find a crowd of visitors filling the place, apparently keeping the woman company in her vigil. Most of them were women, obviously of a low type, with garishly made-up faces and cheap, gaudy clothing. The few males among them were of the struggling artist type—except for a bearded blond gentleman seated near Laura who seemed to exude affluence. He wore a beautifully tailored suit set off by a diamond stickpin in his silk cravat. Charlie paid no attention to him. He was too intent on having a word in private with the mother of his child.

When Signorina Milonari saw Charlie standing there in the middle of her salon, she stood up, went white, and let out a scream that froze everyone in the place.

"*Dio!* He's dead! That's why you've come." Her expression was tragic.

With a sea of curious eyes fixed on him, Charlie Lassiter went straight to Laura and said quietly, "I've come from the morgue. I identified the body an hour ago. I had to tell you in person." He paused. "Gianni was murdered."

With a wail, the woman threw herself on the floor, howling with grief. At least three of her women friends began to sob along with her while the rest crossed themselves and wept.

"*Ah, dio!*" screamed Laura. "My Gianni's gone! Murdered! I knew it. He was so good, so sweet. What a sin!"

The blatant hypocrisy of this woman who had thrown him over for a married Milanese banker and had only used little Gianni as a means of getting money from him sickened Charlie. The bitch hadn't even let him know of his son's existence until it was convenient for her. He felt a wave of nausea sweep over him, engulfing him.

Standing like a block of wood as he observed this staged emotional orgy, Charlie heard himself saying as if from a long way off, "If you had only taken care of my son, he'd be alive today, you damned fraud. The hell with your tears! The hell with you!"

Why hadn't she cared this much while the boy was alive? Hypocrite! Fraud! To everyone's shock, he shouted the words loud enough for even the neighbors to hear. Then he turned and made a furious exit from the room, leaving Laura sobbing on the floor among her friends, dismissed and hysterical.

Charlie was gripped by a rage so overwhelming he thought it would drive him mad. Slamming his way out of the crowded apartment, he descended the long, curving stairway on the double and shouted to his coachman, "Get me out of here!" as he climbed into the leather interior and banged the door shut.

He was nauseated, heartsick, and ashamed that he hadn't taken the child in. If he had, his only son wouldn't be lying on a marble slab in the morgue. He had failed that child, his child, and his grief fueled his rage at the mother.

Laura Milonari was no less furious than Charlie. Outraged by his behavior, she sat up drinking late into the night with her lover of the moment, André Viznitski.

Keeping Laura's glass well filled with Armagnac, Viznitski played on her loss, on her humiliation in her grief—and on the way Moira Lassiter had always hated the dear child and had once nearly harmed him.

"The woman's a devil," he said with loathing. "Proud as a queen and evil as sin. A wicked, manipulative creature."

"She wanted Gianni dead," Laura declared thickly. "She hated him. The bitch!"

"A woman like that always gets what she wants, *milochka*. She's sly and cunning. And rich. Nothing would be too much for her to pay to have some scoundrel get rid of whatever—or whoever—stands in her way."

Focusing bleary eyes on Viznitski, Laura felt the room swirl. She had drunk too much and it wasn't making her feel any better. On the contrary.

"What are you saying, André?" she asked dully.

"I'm saying, dear Laura, that I wouldn't be surprised if Mrs. Lassiter had someone kill your son. Who had the motive? Who had the money?" Viznitski persisted, his voice falling to a sinister whisper. "Think of it. It was Moira Lassiter. It had to be."

Drunk as she was, Laura heard that without any problem.

"She hated us. She would have killed poor Gianni the night I brought him to Carlo's home . . ." she muttered.

"You see? Who hates you enough to do this? It was Moira."

Half-sodden with drink, Laura fixed her bloodshot eyes on André and stared at him stupidly. It all made horrible sense. Carlo hadn't been swayed by her hate. He had acknowledged Gianni anyway and provided him with a home. Therefore, Moira had to take more drastic actions. She needed a permanent solution to her troubles. She wouldn't have done the murder herself. No, she was too grand for that. But she wouldn't have been too grand to hire someone to do it.

"I'll make her admit it," Laura said drunkenly. "I'll force her . . ."

Count Viznitski smiled benignly as he cradled Laura in his arms, stroking her tangled hair.

"Yes," he murmured. "That's what you must do—for the sake of justice for your little boy. He'll never rest while his murderer goes free, will he?"

Viznitski glanced down with distaste at the drunken sot in his arms. He disapproved of drunkenness in a woman. It recalled scenes out of *The Lower Depths*, a revolting if eerily accurate portrayal of seedy Moscow low life. But this stupid slut could be a priceless treasure if she could be molded into an instrument of retribution against Moira Devereux—and her daughter. She could be a real pearl beyond price.

CHAPTER 25

There had been a bitter quarrel between Charlie and Moira the night before the funeral. He had asked her to attend as a courtesy to him, and she had turned him down cold—precipitating a fierce outburst that was quite unusual for him. To make matters worse, he had asked Maeve to accompany him in her place, and to Dietrich's and Moira's horror she had agreed.

"It's déclassé," Dietrich snapped when they arrived home from the Lassiters'. "It's an enormous scandal for you to go to the little bastard's funeral. Why are you being so disloyal to Mama?"

Maeve fixed him with the coldest glare she could muster and turned on her heel. "Because it's the decent thing to do," she flung back over her shoulder. "You know damned well Charlie would come to Hanno's funeral—God forbid!"

"That's different!" Dietrich shouted, flushed with anger.

Maeve paused on the grand staircase and looked with amazement at her husband.

"How is it different?" she demanded. "A son's a son. It's the blood that counts."

"You're primitive! You've been too long in the tropics if you can't see the disgrace in this!"

That was so outrageous it made Maeve burst out laughing in his face. "Then I suppose I ought to get out my grass skirt and coconuts," she retorted as she headed upstairs past a long line of eighteenth-century oil paintings.

Dietrich couldn't come up with a logical reason for not attending the funeral, Maeve thought, and now he was resorting to insults. What a damned silly fool—and him with a doctor of law degree from Heidelberg University! She wondered what they taught those boys. Surely not rational thought. Any guttersnipe could have come up with his stupid reason for not going to the funeral. This lowered Dietrich in her eyes, just as if he had been expelled from his club for cheating at cards or had lost his business. It was very distasteful.

He doesn't even consider the poor child human, she thought. It was eerie. Somehow she wasn't surprised when her husband went out for the evening and spent the night at his club, avoiding all contact with her.

On the morning of the funeral, Charlie drove to Maeve's home in a closed carriage, looking absolutely grim. He and his coachman were both wearing black armbands and the horses were decked out with black ribbons in their manes. The air was fairly warm, and the prospect of a drive in a closed coach was daunting. Maeve would have much preferred an open landau.

When Maeve entered the church on Charlie's arm, she noticed a great many glances in her direction. That was nothing new; people did that whenever she appeared in public. But this time, there was no admiration in their faces. Laura Milonari's friends had cold hatred in their eyes.

Charlie, with his somber expression and his frosty demeanor, seemed impervious to anyone's disapproval. He escorted Maeve to the front of the church, near the small casket, and ignored the ripple of whispers behind him. He didn't speak Italian, but his stepdaughter did, and to her dismay she heard the word "*strega*"—witch—spat out with venom. These people were accusing Charlie's wife of being a witch who had turned his head and caused the death of his son. What's more, some of them were under the impression that Maeve was Moira. They were hurling the most obscene insults at her back.

This is an abomination, she thought. Here they were in a church, next to the child's little coffin, and these animals were indulging in the crudest obscenities. If she hadn't been concerned for the dignity of the occasion and the place, Maeve would have stood up and laced into them with all the fury she felt for their barbarism. As it was, at the tenth or twelfth mention of "*strega*," she turned her head sharply in the direction of the young girl who was hissing it at her back and froze her with a piercing stare. The offender looked startled and slunk into her seat, exchanging furtive glances with the two hags next to her.

"What are the bitches whispering?" Charlie asked, shocking Maeve. He was furious at the reception she was getting, and he wasn't so far gone in his grief that he missed any of it.

"They don't seem to like me," she said, understating the case rather lamely.

"Idiots!"

"It doesn't matter. Ignore them."

Laura arrived on the arm of a male friend—not Count Viznitski— and staggered, sobbing, into her seat. Immediately a cluster of black-clothed women swarmed all over her, offering whispered consolation or following her example by wailing at the top of their lungs. Charlie's face took on a hard, set grimace.

"They have no dignity," he muttered.

"It's their custom to mourn like this," Maeve whispered back. She was glad nobody in the crowd seemed to know English. Charlie's contempt for this lot was reaching its peak.

The beginning of the funeral Mass restored some semblance of decorum, with the mourners rattling their rosaries and responding with a vengeance to the priest's Latin. When Laura stood up, she fixed Maeve with a demented glare. If she hadn't been in a church, Maeve would have thought she was about to pronounce a curse on her.

Standing beside Charlie after the Mass, Maeve watched from beneath her mourning veil—the one she had purchased in Berlin—as the little coffin was placed inside the elegant hearse with its carved decorations and black-draped horses. She closed her eyes for a second to blink back tears. Gianni had been a handsome, healthy child. To think of him as a mangled corpse was sickening.

Laura Milonari had already been helped into her coach, and as Maeve and her stepfather waited to enter theirs, Charlie was surprised to see the prefect of police standing not far from the entrance to the church, observing things with a practiced eye. If Charlie hadn't been so preoccupied, he might have made more of the prefect's presence.

Maeve was silent nearly all the while it took to drive from the church to the Père Lachaise Cemetery. That crowd at the Mass had shaken her. It was the only time in her life she had seen people behave so badly in a place of worship, and she could only guess what would happen at the actual burial. They made the claque at La Scala appear warmly encouraging.

There was no mistaking their hostility. Maeve had heard enough of their insults to know they were holding her mother responsible for the boy's death. And on top of that, the fools took her for Moira! If Charlie had been able to understand even half of it, there would have been hell to pay.

When the funeral procession reached the cemetery, the priest seemed a bit nervous too, surrounded by such an incredibly angry crowd of mourners. He seemed to be making an effort to focus people's attention on the child looking down on them from a state of heavenly bliss, but all Maeve could see was a gang of crazed foreigners looking straight at her with murder in their eyes.

As the graveside service ended and the mourners stepped forward to take their final farewells, Laura Milonari flung herself sobbing on the small coffin, and then, as several friends clustered around her, she sank to her knees and began to tear her hair, wailing and weeping.

"She murdered my Gianni!" screamed Laura, beating her fists on the soft ground. "She murdered him because she hated him. She had everything and still she hated my poor little one! Oh my God! What a sin! What a heartless, evil bitch!"

With that, everyone in her entourage turned and seemed to take a step in Maeve's direction. Horrified, she stepped backward, fearful of being lynched on the spot.

The same thought had occurred to Charlie Lassiter. In fact, it looked perilously close to an incident he recalled from his days in North Dakota when he had witnessed an innocent man torn to pieces by a drunken mob, hell-bent on revenge.

"Paul!" he shouted to his driver. "Bring the coach! Now!"

While the large black vehicle came hurtling toward them—Paul had been as nervous as his master and had released the brake as soon as the Milonari woman started screeching—Charlie gripped Maeve's arm as tight as he could to prevent her from fleeing. In a remarkably controlled voice he ordered, "Keep calm and don't move till you can jump in the carriage. If you so much as turn your head, these bastards will be all over us."

Maeve could feel the perspiration dripping down the back of her black silk dress. It was the longest minute of her life as she faced down the crowd, taking in every detail—the black dresses on the women, black armbands on the men, two elderly Italian women in the front of the mob with holy medals shining on their shirtwaists, a couple of tough, low-class French girls in squashed straw hats with cheap ribbons and tattered silk flowers in the bands. She felt she was looking at a photograph that had captured a group of people in midstride and frozen them for eternity.

And then the eerie silence was shattered by the animal cries of Laura Milonari, who grabbed a clod of earth from the grave site and hurled it at Maeve, unleashing a torrent of vengeance. People plundered the ground for stones, earth, grave markers, anything to fling at the woman standing next to Charlie Lassiter.

The American seized his stepdaughter, shielding her with his body, as Paul came careening up to them in the coach. Tearing open the door, Charlie pushed Maeve inside, jumped in after her, and shouted at Paul to keep going at top speed.

The mourners swarmed around the coach like furious bees, and Paul used his whip to beat them off. The plate-glass windows shattered from the force of several well-aimed rocks as the coachman gained speed and sent the attackers racing out of his way, scattering in fright as the heavy black berline plowed through their midst, its driver not at all concerned if he ran them down.

"Are you all right?" Charlie asked anxiously. "Were you hit?" He gently helped Maeve up from the floor where he had thrown her and then flung himself over her to protect her from the worst of the attack. She was curled up like a small cat, afraid even to move while the stones clattered against the windows.

"I'm all right," she replied. "My God, you were the cool one back there," she said in admiration. "I was frantic to run, and they would have murdered me if I had."

"I know a lynch mob when I see one. You have a better chance by not making a move—until the right moment," he added grimly. "It's all in the timing."

Maeve raised her head tentatively and brought her eyes up to the level of the shattered window frame. They were out of the cemetery and racing down the boulevard. It was safe to sit after Charlie brushed the shreds of shattered glass off the leather seats.

"You know what they were saying!" Maeve declared in bewilderment. "They were accusing Mama of murder. The Milonari woman wants blood."

Charlie's face was unusually tight. She could see the vein standing out in his forehead. "If she ever dares to go near your mother—or you—it will be the last time she bothers anyone. I'll see to that."

That sounded reassuring. But Maeve knew Laura was probably smart enough not to come bounding up to the front door looking for a fight. The question was, what sort of underhanded scheme would she resort to to settle the score? And how wild and desperate to do it would she be?

When Moira caught sight of the battered black coach with the windows all shattered, she rushed outside to the courtyard to see if her daughter and husband had been killed. The idea of their having been attacked at the funeral had not even occurred to her. She assumed anarchists had thrown a bomb at Charlie's expensive berline.

"We're all right," Charlie assured her as she ran past the startled butler and threw open the coach door herself. "We were almost lynched at the cemetery, but we got away in one piece, thanks to our driver."

Moira stared at him as if he were speaking in a foreign language.

"The cemetery?" she asked in bewilderment. "What happened there?"

"Near murder," Maeve replied as Charlie helped her down from the coach, bits of glass still lodged in the folds of her black silk dress. "The people were crazed. They were making insane accusations about somebody murdering the child."

"But why attack you?"

"Well, Mama, this is hard for me to tell you, but they thought they had the suspect there at the funeral."

Moira stared at her daughter in disbelief. "They accused *you*?" she gasped. She couldn't even imagine such a thing. It was too bizarre.

Charlie shook his head slowly. "Not exactly, my dear. You see, they mistook Maeve for you."

For a second Moira didn't even react. She was so unprepared for that, it seemed to go right by her. She looked shaken as Maeve put her arm around her.

"But that's absurd," she protested. "How dare they?"

Charlie looked at his wife with dismal eyes. "Laura wants a scapegoat and she thinks she found one," he said. "It was the vilest thing I've ever seen. They started in the church itself, but I wasn't sharp enough to realize what was happening. Then after the burial, all hell broke loose. We were surrounded by a mob bent on murder. It was a miracle we escaped."

This was insane, Moira thought. How could anyone think she was capable of murder? With a shock she remembered the expression on the face of the prefect of police. Recalling that interview, she knew he had been studying her with unusual intensity. Had he thought she was a possible suspect? Good God!

"Charlie," she said, bewildered, "they actually accused me of murder?"

He nodded grimly. "They did. But I'm going to take precautions against any of those maniacs showing up here to cause an uproar. Anyone who says a word against you will have to answer to me. And I'll make them pay, believe me."

Charlie's words were reassuring, but not reassuring enough for Moira. She was a suspect in one of the nastiest murder cases of the year—and over a hundred people had once seen her attack the little victim and its mother in her home. No wonder those fools were saying she was the one who did it. Who hated the damned little brat as much as she did?

"It will be all right, Moira," Charlie said as he walked her into the house. "I love you and I know you're innocent."

But for Moira, somehow that wasn't enough. Could anyone in his right mind actually suspect her of this? The idea terrified her. If they did, that could jeopardize her place in society, perhaps make her unacceptable company. No! That was cruel! It wasn't fair. She had suffered so much to reach the status of Mrs. Charles Lassiter! Was some dead brat going to put all that at risk?

"I hope they find the killer," Moira said sincerely. "And I hope they don't waste any time, either."

Her life might depend on it—or at least that part of her life that was lived in the ballrooms and salons of international society. For Moira it was the only life that counted. And she wasn't about to relinquish it so easily.

*

The first indication Maeve had of just how ugly things could get was the shrill headline in one of the largest Paris dailies on the day after the funeral: MILLIONAIRE'S WIFE ACCUSED OF MURDER.

"God Almighty," she snapped. "What a lot of rubbish!"

"It's in all the papers, madame," Arlette said uneasily. "Monsieur le baron is so furious he's screaming about duels in the Bois and a libel suit."

"Oh, marvelous. Just what we need," muttered Maeve, picturing Dietrich with pistols at dawn, rather like the unfortunate Duc d'Enghien.

"It's a disgrace what they're saying about your *maman*. They ought to lock up that stupid slut instead of letting her sling mud at decent people."

"Too bad *she* wasn't the one they fished out of the Seine," Maeve said under her breath. "That would have solved a lot of problems."

At the Palais Lassiter there was even more of a shock. Because of the accusations of "that demented whore," as Moira called Laura Milonari, Mrs. Lassiter had to answer questions posed by a solemn police detective.

The idea that anyone could accuse her of murdering the child shook Moira so profoundly she didn't even go into a rage or indulge in any of her usual theatrics. She was truly stunned. Charlie was so incensed that, to the delight of newspaper editors all over Paris, he gave an interview accusing Laura of causing her son's death by negligence.

It was the major topic at society functions that spring and summer. At Longchamps, where Moira appeared in a succession of magnificent outfits by Worth, more people than usual stared in her direction and whispered excitedly behind her back. Mr. Lassiter, it was noted, had begun to show the first traces of gray in his sandy hair. And he had lost most of his normal ebullience.

Dietrich was his mother-in-law's staunchest defender and did actually challenge the editor of *Le Petit Parisien* to a duel in the Bois in mid-July. This in turn led to sensational stories in other papers based on alleged "eyewitness accounts." One had the baron shooting the editor with a hunting rifle, another had the editor skewering the baron with a rapier, still another had them firing pistols at ten paces, missing each other and wounding a passing pedestrian out for an early-morning promenade.

In fact, it was sabers, and Dietrich, a skillful duelist at Heidelberg, scored a direct hit on the newspaperman, slashing him neatly on the cheek from jaw to temple.

Maeve was in a panic that morning when she learned what her husband was up to. On his return from the undisclosed location of the *affaire d'honneur*, she raced to greet him at the front door in a state of nervous hysteria, fainting in his arms. The baron gallantly carried her upstairs, helped Arlette revive her, and curled up in bed with Maeve as he recounted his adventure.

"Oh, Dietrich, that was excessive," she murmured as she held him in her arms, stroking his beautiful hair. "You might have been killed."

"I'm a good duelist," he replied, kissing her neck. "I've bested better men than that many times. You shouldn't have worried."

"But *Schatzi*," she said, sighing tremulously, "you have to be careful. Think of me—and little Hanno."

"I do, *Liebchen*. I always do."

Maeve was so frankly excited by the idea of Dietrich carrying on like that, she began to kiss him all over, unbuttoning his silk shirt, sliding her hand over his chest, getting Dietrich so aroused he started to struggle out of his clothes and liberate Maeve from hers at top speed.

Shirt, trousers, drawers went flying across the room, joined by a shirtwaist, a skirt, petticoats, corset cover, corset, drawers, and stockings.

In all the rush to get undressed, they got tangled in the silk comforter and landed on the floor in a passionate embrace on the Aubusson carpet, out of breath and somewhat disoriented.

Arlette had the misfortune to open the door a few minutes later to inquire whether Madame was all right—only to find her employers wrapped in each other's arms on the carpet in what could only be described as a small bacchanale. Monsieur le baron was moaning in either great pain or tremendous pleasure as he clung to Maeve.

"I'm all right. Don't worry about me," Madame called out as the girl's mouth dropped open and she slammed the door in shock.

Arlette never said a word about that incident—and neither did Maeve—but it marked a turning point. From that moment on, the French girl considered La Devereux a creature of unbridled passion and unrestrained sensuality who could reduce a man to a quivering wreck. It was awe-inspiring, she declared to a friend afterward. Truly impressive.

Dietrich's reaction was more to the point. "You will knock upon entering Madame's bedroom," he said crisply to Arlette that afternoon. "Never deviate from that practice. Do you understand?"

"Yes, monsieur," she said, eyes downcast in perfect humility. But having seen Dietrich in that state, she would never again be awed by him—and he knew it.

CHAPTER 26

The only good thing to occur in Maeve's life in the summer of 1907 was the signing of the contract between Maeve Devereux, soprano, and Heinrich Conreid of the Metropolitan Opera in New York City. Conreid had come to Paris again and had met with Maeve at lunch at the Ritz to formalize the agreement which gave her a large portion of what she wanted—including the role of Salome at the Metropolitan's premiere of the work.

Maeve received a detailed list of performances in which she would appear and her fees for each, a clause freeing her from the grueling cross-country tour following the regular season, a guarantee of several performances with Enrico Caruso, the Met's top male star and her friend, and the right to wear her own costumes and have a private dressing room.

The last point was almost as difficult to guarantee as her exclusion from the cross-country tour. Apparently, space was at a premium back-stage and the established members of the company were often required to make do with woefully inadequate facilities. To favor a newcomer was not the way to keep peace among the troupe. Conreid sighed and agreed only when it was revealed that Oscar Hammerstein had offered a large, fully equipped, modern dressing room with electric lights all around the dressing table mirror—and a private bathroom.

Actually he hadn't, but Dietrich said it with such nonchalance that

Conreid felt compelled to win over the diva by trying to outdo his shrewd, cigar-chomping rival from the Manhattan Opera. If a dressing room was what La Devereux wanted, then a dressing room was what she'd get.

Maeve said, "Well, isn't that sweet?" and gave Dietrich a conspiratorial smile as she affixed her signature to the paper.

*

In early November, Moira and Charlie accompanied Maeve, Dietrich, Hanno, his nursemaid, Arlette, and Dietrich's valet to the train that would take them to Hamburg and the luxury liner awaiting them for their voyage across the Atlantic.

It was a sad parting. Moira was weary from the previous months of unrelenting slander, and Maeve was in unusually low spirits as well. At a concert she had given for the French Red Cross there had been empty seats for the first time in her career, and Monsieur Carré had blamed it on "the affair," his code word for the wretched mess involving Moira.

"Go to America and enjoy a new success there," he advised. "Paris audiences are fickle. By the time you return, they'll be obsessed with something else and they'll welcome you back with open arms."

Maeve hoped so, but the gutter press and even more respectable newspapers were still repeating Laura Milonari's accusations from time to time—with no leads in the search for the one who had killed little Gianni.

"Will you come to New York?" Maeve asked impulsively as Charlie kissed her goodbye. "Surely it would be a nice change from this."

"Maybe," he said. "We'll see."

Moira had always hoped to make a grand splash in New York society and was anxious to avoid America right now. There was no point in a visit when she was under such a cloud. Later would be a much better time—when people had forgotten about little Gianni.

In hardheaded opposition to Maeve's own suggestions, and in total agreement with Charlie, Dietrich had booked passage on the *Deutschland*, the pride and glory of the Hamburg-Amerika Linie.

This floating extravaganza of Teutonic luxury was so grandiose it seemed designed by descendants of those who had put together Germany's most flamboyant baroque castles. Restraint was not a German trait, and to Maeve, for whom it was the first transatlantic voyage, it was like Never-Never Land.

Everywhere one looked, there were acres of mirrors, huge bulbous chandeliers, carved turrets, Gothic arches, baroque curlicues, exotic carved statues of everybody from the former and present kaisers to American Indian chiefs—and an army of German crewmen who clicked heels as naturally as most people drew breath.

For Maeve and Dietrich there was a suite of masterfully overdecorated splendor featuring an attempt to re-create Mad King Ludwig's favorite style—overblown Wagnerian. Beds were suffocated beneath gold-braided and embroidered coverlets, pillows, and neck rolls while silken armchairs threatened to suck one into perilous depths of stuffing. Electric lights provided more than enough illumination and looked like great, shining clusters of bulrushes with silk shades.

The servants shared much simpler quarters, with Marie Louise and Arlette sharing space with little Hanno, and Dietrich's valet ensconced in a cubbyhole hardly larger than a broom closet. This ship was a sign of Germany's wealth and status, Dietrich proudly proclaimed, and he wasn't going to entrust the safety of his precious wife and child to anything less than the best.

"This is a little like the stage sets for Wagner's operas, madame," Arlette declared. "Any moment I expect the captain to burst into an aria from *Tannhäuser*."

Maeve laughed. She thought so too. But it was all very fine and grand, and the luxury of it soothed her.

Dietrich, she noticed, was warmly welcomed among the bankers and tycoons in the lounge, where he played poker with more or less success, and she received the usual admiring glances from his colleagues when she and her handsome husband descended the grand *escalier* into the dining room.

The baroness's diamond necklaces were favorably commented upon as they glittered like ice on her creamy bosom. Arlette noticed with amusement that Madame's décolletage was becoming more and more extravagant. That was the one are area Maeve had to thank little Hanno for, and she made the most of it, attributing its expansion to an act of God and considering it therefore, she said ingenuously, worthy of display.

*

The week-long party on board the *Deutschland* came to an abrupt end in New York with Maeve's introduction to members of the press. They were so eager to meet Conreid's latest European diva, they had themselves ferried out on a tender before the ship had even docked, and besieged Maeve on board as she graciously tried to be a good sport and give them the usual photos and small talk.

This crowd wanted a bit more than the routine. Apparently New

Yorkers, too, had heard about the Lassiter affair in all its gory details, and the ladies and gentlemen of the press were avid for scraps of scandal.

"Do you believe your mother murdered little Gianni, Maeve?" demanded one shameless hack right off the bat. Maeve burst out laughing, as much from surprise at his first-name coziness as from shock at the question.

"Would you believe *your* mother murdered anyone?" she shot back.

"Too bad she didn't!" Arlette muttered in French behind her, glowering at the man. *Quel cochon*!

"Is it true Moira Lassiter has been shunned by international society?" asked an excited lady with a pencil stuck in her upswept hair.

"Not lately." Maeve smiled. "Just last week she and my stepfather were guests of Sir Ernest Cassel at a shoot in Scotland. If that's being shunned, I wish them more of it." Sir Ernest, as even New York reporters knew, was one of Britain's wealthiest men and a personal friend of Edward VII.

Dietrich, who had been prepared for questions about Maeve's career, was furious. The audacity of this mob was grotesque. How dare they ask such things?

"My wife has arrived to be the ornament of the Metropolitan Opera," he snapped, sounding as pompous as the décor in the first-class lounge where Maeve was being grilled. "Why not ask something pertinent to her singing?"

They glanced briefly at the handsome blond baron in his Saville Row suit and then back to the beautiful auburn-haired baroness in her elegantly tailored royal-blue suit by Redfern, complete with matching chinchilla hat and muff. And her splendid pearls.

"Do you think Mr. Conreid was relying on the publicity value of the scandal when he engaged you, Madame Devereux?" persisted the woman with the pencil, a hard-faced harridan with beady eyes.

"I think Mr. Conreid is relying on my beautiful voice," Maeve pointed out, gaining a vigorous nod from Arlette, who was livid at the insolence of these foreigners.

At that moment, Dietrich was rising from his seat beside Maeve and signaling angrily to the ship's stewards to get rid of these people. Maeve took his free hand and slipped her fingers through his. She had seen Marie Louise approaching with Hanno, as planned, and she now rose in a cloud of Jasmine de Corse and hurried to fuss over her son and then present him to the waiting audience in her arms.

"Isn't he beautiful?" she cooed, hugging the handsome blond baby to her bosom as she smiled for the cameras. Hanno let out a wail of fright as photographers caught him playing with his mother's pearls, and he had to be calmed down, permitting Maeve to evade further questions about the scandal.

The noise level was now so great, all the press could hear was Maeve's smiling claim that she was a wicked woman only onstage, and if they wanted to see firsthand just how naughty she really was, then buy tickets to *Salome*'s premiere.

"It's a nice photograph of you and the little one," Arlette commented the next day as she opened the *New York Times* to see Maeve, Dietrich, Hanno, and herself looking like the happiest family group in the world.

"Umm," Maeve smiled. She had deliberately avoided the cameras until she had her son in her arms. If these parasites were going to try to depict her as Messalina's daughter, she wouldn't make it easy for them.

That picture of glowing maternal affection was really quite lovely, she reflected. It ought to make people think—or at least she hoped it would. But if that press reception was a foretaste of American hospitality, then she was ready to pack her bags right now. It was frightful.

"And the weather is dreadful on top of everything else, madame," Arlette sighed as she stared out the windows of their suite at the Astor Hotel, a favorite of the Metropolitan's stars. "You'll have to guard your throat especially well here. And little Hanno's, too."

"I'm tough," Maeve replied with a smile. "You don't have to worry about me."

But in her heart she wasn't too complacent about her chances in this aggressively forward town.

*

The Hotel Astor, on Broadway between Forty-fourth and Forty-fifth streets, was not terribly far from the opera, so it was more convenient than Moira's suggestion, the Plaza, and it was also a new hotel, full of modern utilities. Arlette was impressed. It seemed as grand as the *Deutschland* without all the pitching and rolling—and a lot less floridly decorated. The tone here was lavish but elegant, and the staff was noticeably friendlier. They all fussed over little Hanno and enjoyed his antics each time Arlette or Marie Louise paraded him in his pram.

Maeve was delighted to be reunited with Caruso and Chaliapin, but she noticed that while the chubby Neapolitan was a great favorite with cast and crew alike, the tall, blue-eyed Russian was given a wide berth, due to his brusque personality and towering ego. However, he was all smiles for his Masha, and regaled her and Arlette with sidesplitting stories of life in New York while he played with Hanno and told her how much he missed his own children.

Caruso, Maeve noticed, was the undisputed star of the Metropolitan Opera. When she sang with him in Monte Carlo and London she had been aware of his popularity, but New York had taken him to its heart in such ecstatic fashion she wouldn't have been surprised if they crowned him king one day.

His leading lady among leading ladies was beautiful Geraldine Farrar. If Caruso was the Met's king, then Farrar was surely its queen. Lovely, slender, and dark-haired, with a vivacity that charmed even people who didn't like opera, Farrar more than held her own against the Met's impressive list of resident sopranos—Louise Homer, Emma Eames, Olive Fremstad, Marcella Sembrich. She would be a hard act to follow, Maeve thought gloomily as she recalled every word of Farrar's delirious reviews.

On the night of Maeve's Metropolitan debut as Tosca with her London partners Caruso and Scotti, she was so nervous she ordered Marie Louise to keep Hanno away from her. He was in a bad mood with teething problems and was screeching like a little banshee. His distracted mother was frantically turning drawers upside down in her attempts to locate the gold cross and chain Chaliapin had given her in St. Petersburg. It was her good luck charm, and Maeve was not budging from her suite until she had it around her neck.

"Calm down, for heaven's sake!" Dietrich admonished, shocked at the sight in his wife's hotel dressing room. It looked as if a team of burglars had been at work. Clothes were dumped all over the place, with Maeve desperately pawing through piles of lingerie, flinging nightgowns left and right as she hunted for the blue velvet box containing the chain.

"Don't start up with me!" she warned. "I need Chaliapin's cross!"

Dietrich sighed patiently and tapped his fingers on the top of her dressing table. "Try your blue velvet evening bag," he ordered, eyeing the mess all around them.

Arlette went dashing to the armoire to locate the purse, opened it, and let out a cry of relief.

"It's here, madame!"

"Oh, Dietrich," Maeve gasped, "thank you! You darling! You knew!"

"Good memory." He smiled. "I recalled that you packed it away there to keep it safe."

"Oh, put it on," she said. "I don't know what I would have done if I hadn't found it."

"You would have given New Yorkers their newest star anyway," he answered, smiling again confidently. "You're beautiful and you're in magnificent voice. Your Tosca will be the one against which all the others will be measured."

Maeve flung her arms around him and sighed. "I love you, *Schatzi*," she whispered. "You know how to keep me on an even keel."

"I know an outstanding artist when I meet one," he replied. "I knew it from the first time I ever heard you sing at the Casino de Paris. Never be worried about other sopranos. There's no comparison," he said firmly as Maeve stroked his hair.

That was even better than Chaliapin's present for inspiring confidence, and that night when Maeve went on, she enraptured an audience that was prepared to resist the latest claimant to Farrar's crown.

A rare thing happened onstage that night. After Maeve had sung "Vissi d'arte," not a sound came from the huge auditorium. For long seconds Maeve and Antonio Scotti were plainly stunned. She had just created the kind of vocal fireworks that usually bring down the house. And then like thunder came the applause, rolling in from the jewel-drenched patrons of the Diamond Horseshoe to the cheapest seats of the balconies—mass hysteria on the part of an audience that had been too overwhelmed to move a muscle. Caruso's Italian fans were going mad, taking this "French girl" for one of their own.

Both the *New York Times* and the *Sun* lavished such praise on Maeve's Tosca that she and Dietrich were delirious the next morning over breakfast when Arlette presented them with copies of all the New York papers she could buy. Cheerfully translating her reviews into French for Arlette and Marie Louise, Maeve glowed with unabashed joy as she read the most gushing tributes she had received to date.

"Well," Dietrich said smiling proudly, "you see. Natural talent will prevail. They loved you."

That was good to know, thought Maeve. They'd better love her now because she was about to present them with a heroine so outrageous that not even a mother could love her—the Princess Salome.

*

While Maeve was performing at the Metropolitan Opera and keeping in touch with friends, humoring Fedya Chaliapin through a season that was less than receptive to his talents and trying to urge him toward a more tactful manner with his colleagues, Dietrich was making contacts with the established banking families of New York, including members of the German-Jewish community with whom he had worked on the Japanese war loan. He found their company congenial and their customs familiar.

The young baron's main complaint against America—aside from the food—was the tendency of the men to abdicate power to their women. The good German matrons of these families, on the other hand, appeared to adore their husbands and looked upon them with all the awe and respect due a paterfamilias—unlike the Yankee women who took over control of the home, hardly allowing the harried husband a word—unless it was to give them more money. This seemed to the baron to be a gross violation of the natural order.

As he discussed business with the Schiffs, Solomons, or Kahns, Dietrich felt a nostalgia for his orderly childhood, with a mother who ran the household with flair and adored Hubertus as though he were the rising sun. Not that Maeve was a bossy shrew, *Gott sei Dank*! But even though she adored him, he sometimes wondered if it was merely a physical attraction.

He couldn't imagine his mother—or Lotte—behaving with a husband the way Maeve behaved with him. The girl loved to caress him as if he were a cat. She could spend an outrageous amount of time lolling about in bed, with him cuddled up against her bosom as she lazily ran her fingers through his hair. Often she reminded him of those women in the harem in Constantinople—a beautiful, sensual thing, clad only in a pair of lacy drawers and a fortune in jewelry.

Dietrich occasionally wondered about his relationship to his beautiful wife. Somehow it didn't seem decent, as if Maeve were a mistress rather than a lawfully married woman. Lotte, his only experience with female Teutonic propriety, would never have allowed him to use her belly as a headrest or to nibble her toes. She would have thought him a dangerous pervert if he had tried to make love to her on the carpet.

Maeve treated him with a great deal of affection, Dietrich readily admitted, but there was no trace of awe. And with her extravagant dowry as well as the steep fees from her performances, La Devereux had a nice little nest egg—which freed her from financial dependence on him.

If Maeve stayed with him it was purely because she loved him. It was a situation that should have pleased Dietrich but didn't. A marriage based on something as fragile as affection was prone to shatter if the affection one day went elsewhere. It was a thought that haunted him—

especially when he saw Fedya Chaliapin watching Maeve with those cunning light eyes of his.

The Russian was a satyr, Dietrich thought primly. He was an uncivilized barbarian, prone to Asiatic displays of lustful drunkenness and generally low peasant behavior. Baron von Reuter was pleased that the New York public had labeled him barbaric for singing the role of Mefistofele half-naked. Maeve had teased her husband by claiming that Dietrich was merely jealous of Fedya's magnificent physique and fine legs—and that had irritated him even more.

"Never allow that peasant near you while you are unchaperoned," the baron had admonished her sternly. "He is uncouth."

"He's the greatest basso in the world," Maeve replied. "And he's my friend."

It was at moments like those that Dietrich would draw himself up to his full height and ask Maeve to check on their son. He heartily disliked Chaliapin, with his harem of women and his reputation as a drunken brawler. That Fedya had always treated Maeve with affection and respect was lost on Dietrich. He was constantly on the alert for the moment when the tall Russian would lose all control and indulge his wanton appetites with La Devereux.

In his heart, Baron von Reuter considered all Slavs even lower than the rest of Germany's European neighbors, and the time he had spent in St. Petersburg had done nothing to convince him he was wrong. Russian exuberance was so foreign to his whole upbringing that Dietrich viewed it as primitive, unstable, and treacherous. And the fact that the wildly extroverted Fedya was rumored to be in the process of divorcing his wife because of his love for another woman made him even more suspect now.

"Well, my virtue is safe." Maeve smiled at Dietrich's warning. "He's too taken with Maria Valentinova to be thinking of me."

"No woman is safe with a man like that," replied her husband, looking as prissy as a preacher.

"But *Schatzi*," Maeve retorted with a wicked glint in her blue eyes, "people once said the same about you. Don't you remember?"

That was too much. Baron von Reuter glared at his wife, turned sharply on his heel, and walked out the door. He didn't like her sense of humor. Or her taste for baiting her husband. She was becoming too damned American by far, and that was a dangerous sign. The sooner they returned to Europe the better!

*

Despite the strains of living among the natives, Dietrich had spent his time well, making profitable connections for the Von Reuter Bank, joining various German-American societies for businessmen and sportsmen, attending an endless number of sporting events and social occasions, and gaining regular mention in the society columns.

Baron and Baroness von Reuter participated in the German-American Ball at the Waldorf-Astoria, presented a large check to the German Ladies Charitable Society for Widows and Orphans, and joined with the wealthy German-Jewish banker James Speyer in inaugurating the Kaiser Wilhelm Visiting Professor Program at Columbia University.

The Kaiser Wilhelm Program was a master stroke of public relations whereby distinguished German and American academics would be exchanged—the German going to Columbia University and the American to the University of Berlin. The subject of their lectures was a theme dear to the heart of the Kaiser and his banking friends: high finance.

Columbia's resident German was Herr Hermann Schumacher, a noted professor of economics from Bonn University and the founder of the first University of Commerce at Cologne. Herr Schumacher had known Hubertus and was disposed to offer his son and successor volumes of free advice on the German and American financial scenes—something Dietrich regarded as worth any amount of money spent entertaining him.

Herr Schumacher was brilliant and gregarious. Over dinner at Luchow's, for example, he could offer a dozen different methods of floating bonds while pausing for breath between courses. The day he and the baron took in the automobile show at Madison Square Garden, Schumacher suggested ways of streamlining practices in the international department of the Von Reuter Bank that were positively revolutionary but brilliantly serviceable. The fact that he was a protégé of the Kaiser was also not lost upon the young man, for if the Kaiser liked anything it was a man who could help his emperor make money.

With such a respectable foothold on the international banking scene, Dietrich was more than pleased to be able to offer—at some difficulty even to him—tickets to the long-awaited premiere of *Salome* to those friends of his who had not been able to secure them.

It was the hottest item in New York. Scalpers were receiving outrageous prices for the hard-to-come-by tickets, and even the star herself had to beg and wheedle extra seats out of Heinrich Conreid, who was working himself into a state of nervous hysteria over *Salome*'s reception.

Strauss's opera had been a major triumph in Dresden and Milan, but how would the puritanical American audience react to this sort of thing? It was, after all, extremely decadent, not the sort of fluff loved by the bejeweled patrons of the Diamond Horseshoe. J. P. Morgan had glowered at the dress rehearsal and made disparaging comments over its sensual, provocative atmosphere—a bad sign. And Maeve hadn't done it in full costume either, leaving the final shock till the opening night.

On the evening of the premiere, Maeve was oddly calm, an unusual state for her. Arlette was the jittery one this time. The dark-haired French girl got nervous each time she thought of Madame onstage in her tights and jewels for the scene all New York was dying to see—the notorious Dance of the Seven Veils.

On Sunday the *New York Times* had run a very long article on *Salome*, with highlights of the score, a resumé of the story, and the unspoken message that this was an opera that would provide more titillation than a whole month of the French Follies. Anyone in search of depravity had better be at the Met on Tuesday night when Maeve Devereux was to incarnate Strauss's heroine. To make the point for those unfamiliar with Strauss, the *Times* reminded its readers that the libretto was Oscar Wilde's.

On the night of the big event, there were ten extra policemen outside the opera house, struggling to restrain hordes of would-be ticket seekers who had been foolish enough to wait till the last minute. Maeve and Arlette had left the Hotel Astor early in order to avoid the worst congestion and, upon arriving at the Met, had discovered that Herr Conreid was sick at home, completely enervated by all the hysteria and forced to miss the premiere he had struggled so hard to put on.

On the other hand, Giacomo Puccini, creator of such Met favorites as *Tosca*, *La Bohème*, and *Manon Lescaut*, was due to attend, adding to the list of celebrities in the theater on this historic occasion.

"Did you ever show Monsieur le baron what you're going to wear in the dance, madame?" Arlette inquired nervously as she massaged Maeve's back, relaxing the muscles before the show.

"No. He's seen the jewels I'm going to wear, of course. He gave them to me."

"But does he know that you're not going to be wearing much more than that at the end?"

Maeve forced herself to look innocent. "No. I don't think so. Of course," she added ingenuously, "I will be covered from my neck to my toes. There won't be any bare flesh showing."

Arlette rolled her eyes. No flesh showing! Madame would look as if she wasn't wearing a stitch except for the elaborate jewels Monsieur had had made for her. And on top of it, he was inviting every rich *boche* he knew in New York to come see his beautiful wife tonight. Very proper *boches* they were too.

"Couldn't you just wear a bit more, madame?" Arlette asked mildly.

"Don't be absurd. The whole point of the dance is to seduce Herod. How will Salome do that if she's too modest?"

"Well, it seems a bit too bare to me, madame. I have to tell you this because I'm very fond of you and I don't want to see you accused of causing heart attacks all over the Diamond Horseshoe."

Maeve turned around to stare at her maid. It wasn't like Arlette to be so concerned about her costumes—except for the tiger skin episode.

"You worry too much." She smiled. "Monsieur le baron knows I'm an artist about to launch a magnificent work. And I'm going to present my character as Herr Strauss conceived her."

"Well, I can't see why he didn't conceive her with more clothes on," Arlette retorted, unimpressed. "You're going to have all sorts of disgusting old men leering at you through their opera glasses."

Maeve hadn't thought of that. She shrugged. "Well, let them stare. I have nothing to hide."

That was certainly the truth, thought Arlette. And that was precisely the problem!

Since *Salome* took a mere hour and forty minutes, Conreid had arranged for a concert by the Met's brightest stars before the eagerly anticipated main event, and as Maeve and Arlette sat in her dressing room, Geraldine Farrar, Lina Cavalieri, Antonio Scotti, Enrico Caruso, and Marcella Sembrich were onstage, presenting favorite arias from some of the Met's most popular works.

Dietrich was seated in the director's box beside Conreid's assistant, who had to cover for his ailing boss. The baron had invited his distinguished colleague Herr Schumacher, whose brain was a constant source of valuable information and who was an aficionado of Strauss's music. In return for making it possible for Hermann to see the notorious work, the baron was hoping for useful inside information on Hessian railroad rates.

It was a bejeweled and befurred audience that packed the Metropolitan Opera that night. Leaders of New York society drew as much interest as the opera stars, and people were constantly craning their necks to see this or that socialite or tycoon. Baron von Reuter was pointed out several times as husband of the star, and ladies were quick to notice what a natty dresser he was, with his evening clothes cut in the latest style, featuring the slightly broader lapels and the longer-waisted jacket currently favored by men of fashion. Women considered Dietrich a blond Adonis; men tended to view him as a fop.

Maeve received a surprise visit backstage from Giacomo Puccini just before the curtain rose on *Salome*. The celebrated composer, who looked more like an impeccably dressed businessman than the popular idea of an artist, told her he had heard from Caruso what a superb interpreter of his work she was and he hoped to see her in *Tosca* one day. He didn't doubt that she would leave an unforgettable impression as Salome.

"I hope he enjoys Strauss," Arlette said after he departed and the stagehand outside the dressing room gave Maeve her call. What he was in for tonight was a far cry from the usual Puccini heroine.

Conductor Alfred Hertz had made his way to the podium and been warmly applauded, and had brought down his baton. Roman soldiers were in place, Jokanaan was in the cistern, and the Princess Salome was about to goad the Captain of the Guard, Narraboth, into disobeying her stepfather Herod and allowing her to see the dangerous, rabble-rousing prophet.

As the curtain went up on the scene of first-century Judea, Dietrich strained forward, anxious as a child at a Christmas pageant. This was Maeve's night to make history, he thought, almost giddy with anticipation. She was about to bring Richard Strauss's most exciting work to the New World.

Maeve was remarkably beautiful this evening. In her long black wig and exotic jewels, she looked seductive and youthful enough to impersonate the teenaged temptress. Like an exotic flower she fascinated Narroboth, enticing him, coquetting with him, cajoling him into disobeying the Tetrarch to humor a pretty girl's whim.

"Her German diction is superb," Herr Schumacher whispered to her proud husband. "She sounds like one of our own German sopranos."

"My contribution," Dietrich replied, delighted by the compliment. He had worked hard with Maeve on her pronunciation.

Things were going swimmingly. Carl Burrian, who had created the role of Herod in Dresden, was splendid as the neurotic Tetrarch, a man caught between his lust for his stepdaughter and his fear of divine displeasure. Herodias was a proper witch, a vicious consort for a depraved ruler. And the prophet Jokanaan was a tall, dark, foreboding masculine presence. But it was Salome who entranced the audience, a lovely, glittering, depraved and feline creature who was being transformed from a perverse innocent to the personification of sheer degeneracy.

Breaking with tradition established at the Dresden performance,

Maeve had absolutely refused to surrender the stage to a ballerina and had stipulated in her contract that she alone was to do the Dance of the Seven Veils.

As Herod begged her to dance for him—offering an assortment of bribes—Salome refused, working him into a frenzy of abject pleading. Finally, when she had reduced him to despair and desperation and he had sworn to grant whatever she asked of him, she agreed.

Dietrich was watching like a man possessed, observing Maeve's sinuous movements with increasing anxiety. He had attended the dress rehearsal at which members of the board of directors had been aghast at the realism of the play, and he thought that the question of the dance had been settled—a ballerina was to perform it after the first veil had dropped. But here was Maeve, acting like a refugee from a harem and showing no sign of stopping.

The music was almost as erotic and perverse as the character. Everyone in the audience craned their necks to see, barely breathing as La Devereux divested herself of one garment after the other in the most dazzling display of eroticism anybody could recall at the Met.

To Dietrich's embarrassment, Professor Schumacher seemed to be in the throes of apoplexy. His breathing was becoming more and more labored, and by the time Maeve was halfway through the dance, he was wheezing painfully. Herr Conreid's assistant sneaked a glance at the diva's husband. The baron looked appalled, staring straight ahead as if he had been frozen in his seat. He wanted to vanish from the face of the earth.

How dare she? Dietrich thought in bewilderment. This is indecent. Where is her shame? Hardly daring to look around, he could hear murmurings of shock everywhere.

"Depraved!" shrilled one lady nearby.

"She's better than Little Egypt," chuckled a gentleman.

"Shut up, you swine!" someone growled. "This is art!"

Herr Conreid's assistant was older than Dietrich but younger than the professor, and he thought Maeve Devereux looked just fine.

The diva whirled out of her last garment and flung it high in the air, coming to a graceful stop as the layer of chiffon fluttered slowly to the stage. Maeve appeared to be stark naked now, except for a sort of jeweled collar which fell low over her breasts and a jeweled belt which hung loosely around her hips. The soft pink lighting kissing the curves of her body completed the effect of sheer nudity—which made nearly all the gentlemen in the house grab opera glasses from their wives to study this phenomenon.

"*Wunderschön!*" roared Professor Schumacher, clapping as hard as he could. "Brava!"

"Filth!" shrilled a lady.

"Better than Ziegfeld!" someone else shouted.

Onstage Maeve heard an explosion of sound from the audience, and she wondered how Dietrich had liked her dance. Mata Hari would have been proud, she thought. Too bad she couldn't give her credit.

Then came the moment second only to the dance in audience anticipation. Having performed for Herod, Salome was now ready to exact her terrible price—and in due course, up from the cistern came the severed head of Jokanaan on a silver platter.

As Salome staggered slightly under her gruesome burden, several members of the audience in the front row leaped out of their seats and raced frantically for the exit. Up in the Diamond Horseshoe the doors of two boxes were flung open and two ladies, accompanied by two gentlemen, raced down a flight of stairs, calling for their carriages.

"Barbaric!" someone groaned.

"Depraved!"

"Indecent!"

Dietrich thought he was about to be sick as Maeve took the ghastly head and, with sensuous abandon, slowly kissed the lips. Herr Schumacher had his handkerchief pressed against his mouth, trying to stifle his queasiness.

"She's very good," Conreid's assistant whispered, trying to reassure the baron.

Dietrich nodded stiffly, eyes still straight ahead, face set. His heart was pounding with a ferocity that signaled nausea. How could Maeve act like that in full view of all New York? In full view of his German compatriots? He was humiliated, sick with humiliation. How could he ever face the colleagues who had seen his wife looking stark naked and depraved? She was supposed to have worn more of a costume—little chiffon pantaloons. *Mein Gott!* She was as bare as Mata Hari! A scandal!

When the Tetrarch Herod, outraged by Salome's blasphemous kiss, shouted to his soldiers to kill the woman, Dietrich was totally in agreement with him. He was already on his feet before the curtain fell, even before the first sounds of applause.

"Come," he said abruptly to the startled Herr Schumacher, who was still a little queasy from that final scene. "I'll take you home."

"But Herr Baron, aren't you going backstage to congratulate your wife?"

Dietrich shot him a look of pure venom.

"No wife of mine would carry on like that," he snapped. "Come. Let's get out of here."

"Baron," squeaked Conreid's assistant, "Madame will be shattered if you leave. It's unthinkable! She's just made history."

"Fine. You offer your congratulations. I will see her at home. Good night!"

As Dietrich and Herr Schumacher bundled themselves into overcoats, scarves, and top hats and descended the staircase to the exit, they were surrounded on all sides by operagoers who had very forceful ideas about the production. "Degenerate" seemed to be the favorite designation, right after "scandalous" and even "perverted."

Dietrich purposefully avoided anyone who might recognize him as he fled the theater, ashamed of Maeve's lack of decency. All he could recall was that performance she had put on for him in their hotel room in Dresden after *Salome*'s world premiere.

"I'll kill you if you ever do that for anyone else," he had gasped in astonishment.

And now she had laughed in his face by appearing nude before all of New York, including his friends and business associates. She was not worth his sacrifices, he thought bitterly. She was a disgrace.

CHAPTER 27

I waited for you in my dressing room until after everyone had left the theater," Maeve told Dietrich angrily the next morning. "You deserted me. Why did you do it?"

"Because you disgraced me, yourself, and our son! It was grotesque."

"The hell it was! I was wonderful," she replied. "It was the performance of a lifetime!"

The baron laughed sarcastically and ran his fingers nervously through his hair. "Well, I'll agree with *that*. I hear Conreid and the board of directors are going to remove *Salome* from the repertoire. She's a bit too wild for New York. Did you see the papers?"

"The *Times* said some very nice things."

"Nice? You're too optimistic by far. They were dwelling on its perversity, *Liebchen*. And how you did such a spectacular job as a degenerate!"

"Then," Maeve replied grandly as she made an exit stage left into her bedroom, fluttering her expensive lace peignoir in a swirl of injured feelings, "I've succeeded! The hell with the puritans. Strauss would have loved it!" She was defiant and proud despite her detractors.

Maeve couldn't fathom why Dietrich, who had been so eager for her to essay the role, should have turned on her now that she had given such a stunning performance. Apart from showing her figure, she had succeeded beyond belief in a role that was the most difficult she'd ever sung. Compared with her usual French and Italian repertoire with its lovely, soaring romantic arias, *Salome* posed a rugged obstacle course loaded with hazards from start to finish. It took nerve to attempt it and outstanding talent to carry it off. And she *had*!

"Dietrich!" Maeve shouted, rushing back into the salon before he could leave their suite, "you've no appreciation for art! You're a proper little bourgeois! You should have stayed married to the dumpling!"

The sound of the door slamming was all the response she got.

Arlette, who had come tiptoeing into the room, looked stricken. She had been right. Monsieur le baron hadn't taken it well at all.

"Oh, Letty!" Maeve wailed, bursting into tears. "Everything is rotten! He's furious and it's all because of the costume."

"You should have worn pantaloons," the maid sighed. "It wouldn't have looked so shocking then."

"Was I wrong?" Maeve asked in bewilderment.

"No, madame. You were right. But Monsieur just can't stand that much realism. Not for his wife."

"Oh, damn," Maeve replied. "I never thought the man who got divorced for bedding Hélène von Ebert would turn out to be a prude!"

"He wasn't married to Madame von Ebert," Arlette said grimly. "That's the difference."

*

Maeve received so much publicity over her performance as Salome that she was mobbed wherever she went. And it was pointed out to readers of the newspapers' society columns that she was less and less likely to be found in her husband's company. The implication of trouble in the marriage was a terrible humiliation, but the advice she got from Caruso and Chaliapin was to ignore the innuendos.

"Yes, Fedya," Maeve said bitterly as they chatted in her dressing room between acts of *La Traviata*, "but you're a man. It's easier for you."

"You think it's easy to read that I'm a drunken beast who acts like a savage? No, Masha, it infuriates me. My wife sees those trashy stories. My children see them. I hate the people who concoct them."

"But it's so hard to defend yourself. People who don't even know me would probably think I'm a girl who ought to be got rid of."

"Do strangers' opinions matter so much? Do they put bread on your table and clothe your son?" asked the Russian.

"No," she admitted.

"Then the hell with them. Keep your head high and keep looking like a grand duchess. Don't let the idiots get you down. It will all pass. And," he added with a wink, "get yourself photographed in all the most respectable places. And let people see you with Hanno. Motherhood is always very popular with the press."

Reaching over to her friend, Maeve gently kissed him on the cheek. Chaliapin's hand rested lightly around her waist for a moment. Then he slowly released her.

"You know, Masha," he said softly, "I've always been fond of you. The German doesn't like me because he's jealous of you, but I am a friend, a true friend. Never forget it."

She looked at Fedya, so tall and handsome in evening dress, and she smiled.

"I know," Maeve said quietly. "One of the few. And I'm so glad."

*

It was hinted about that Baron von Reuter was forced to return to Europe because of an emergency in the Berlin office, but the gossip columnists assured their readers that they doubted the truth of that. If there was trouble, it was of a much more intimate nature, they suggested, licking their chops with delight.

Dietrich's departure from New York on board the *Kronprinz* in late January 1908 caused as much of a mob scene as his arrival with Maeve a few months earlier.

His wife insisted upon seeing him off to try to quash rumors of marital problems, but she had no stomach for facing a brash crowd of newspaper people avid for scandal. Her face was hidden behind the dotted veil of her hat and her color was ashen.

Dietrich hesitated inside the comfortable interior of his new American automobile—a seven-thousand-dollar limousine, custom made with soft leather seats, crystal vases, and a glossy black finish his new chauffeur labored over each day. It was to remain in New York with Maeve until her departure in February, one of their nicer souvenirs.

"I don't want you to leave," she said, slipping her gloved fingers through his. "There's nothing in Berlin that needs you as much as I do."

"I don't think so. Old Richter is ailing and he runs the show there, so I have to know how sick he really is. This is my livelihood. I have a responsibility to the bank."

Maeve sank down in the cushions and smiled wanly. The beautiful blond Teutonic god she married was turning into a Prussian banker. She had even begun to notice a trace of Hubertus in him lately. What a fate!

"Before you go," Maeve said, "I want to tell you that I never meant to embarrass you. I love you and I love our son. Nothing will ever alter that."

There was a painful silence as Dietrich clasped his doeskin-gloved hands around his knees and stared straight ahead. He looked back at Maeve almost angrily, his face set in a hard mask.

"Well," he said finally, "you have a funny way of showing it."

"For heaven's sake, *Schatzi!*" she cried, "I'm offering an apology. What more can I do? Wear sackcloth and ashes? Commit suicide onstage at the Met? Would that satisfy you?"

"Don't be absurd. I'd hate to see you looking ugly—or dead. I love you too much."

"Well, then!" she exclaimed, relieved.

As the ship's smokestacks roared out the final boarding signal, Dietrich sighed and leaned over to embrace Maeve, resting his cheek against her soft sable coat. "I'm not going to Berlin to punish you," he said quietly. "Richter really is ill and I'm worried about him—and about what will happen if he dies. You're in fine shape. You don't need me nearly as much."

"Oh, Dietrich, you're wrong about that. I do need you. I'll miss you terribly."

He was touched, not enough to tell the chauffeur to turn the automobile around, but touched all the same.

"Come outside and put on a show for your damned public then." He smiled, delighting her.

So while the chauffeur kept the motor running, Baron and Baroness von Reuter bid each other an affectionate farewell under the eyes of several thousand people and—most important—the press.

Rising to the occasion, Maeve flung her arms around Dietrich, peeled back her veil, and kissed him while photographers popped away and the passengers lining the decks of the *Kronprinz* flung confetti and cheered. Farewells at dockside were notoriously emotional, and Maeve made certain this one would find her in her husband's arms before witnesses and on film.

"Bon voyage," she murmured as he held her close for the last time. "Cable me to let me know how things are in Berlin."

"I will," he promised, his expression softening. "My God, I'm sorry I'm leaving." He adored this woman, but he felt she had changed somehow.

"Then let's make sure the reunion is unforgettable. And I promise to play normal heroines from now on," she added.

"Goodbye, *Liebchen*. I'll count the days," he replied sadly.

It was a nice photograph that appeared in the papers, Maeve thought. Very sweet, very loving. That should help put an end to those stupid rumors. The only problem was, she wasn't so certain she shouldn't believe them herself.

It seemed an eternity until her last performance in late February, and by the time it arrived, she was packed, exhausted, and ready for the return voyage on the *Deutschland*.

It was a bad crossing with a maximum of stormy weather and queasy stomachs. Maeve felt dizzy most of the time and kept to her cabin, listening to Chaliapin's records, an unusual antidote to seasickness but one that seemed to work for her. Arlette stayed in bed, feeling like death. Only Hanno and Marie Louise remained impervious to the pitching and rolling of the ship, admired by the crew for their strong stomachs.

The arrival in Paris after docking at Cherbourg and taking the train was cheerful, even if Dietrich was still in Berlin. Moira and Charlie were there to welcome her back, and Moira was in splendid form, sporting sables head to toe, lashings of pearls, and a determination to look happy. Charlie, though, still appeared a bit subdued.

As soon as Moira had her daughter alone at the Palais Lassiter, she launched into her cross-examination.

"What on earth did you do in New York?" she demanded after they had dismissed the servants. "Your husband came here and sobbed his heart out as soon as he returned. He was talking about all sorts of bizarre things, poor boy."

"Oh, Mama! He was upset because of the mess after I sang *Salome*. The press called the opera depraved and decadent, and Dietrich was embarrassed because he'd invited so many prominent Germans to see it."

Moira looked stern. "Reports said you were stark naked," she replied. "I'd have been upset too!"

"I was covered from neck to toe!"

"Not the way we heard it."

"Well, your informants lied! I may have *looked* naked but I was certainly covered! It must have been the lighting."

Moira was unimpressed by her denials. "The poor boy actually sobbed, Maeveen. He said it broke his heart to have strangers gawking at what should have been his alone."

"Oh rubbish!" Maeve muttered indignantly. Why didn't he just get a set of diamond-studded golden shackles for her? "I'm not his personal property," she said finally. "He seems to have me confused with a pet poodle." Like Julien with his Florine.

"You won't be his *wife* if you don't keep your clothes on in public," Moira retorted. "Let that be a lesson to you. Stick to Puccini and Verdi heroines from now on. They wear real costumes!"

"Chaliapin loved me just the way I was," Maeve flung back defiantly.

"Oh, that one! Well, of course he would. He's a disgrace himself."

"Really, Mama," she said indignantly, "I don't care to discuss this further."

"Don't get too grand with me, missy. You're still my child. And my advice is still worth something."

Well, there was no winning this, Maeve thought wearily. Moira had become such a grande dame she was now an expert on everything and a copper-bottomed model of propriety.

"Oh, I know your advice is worth something, Mama," she replied as she took a cup of tea.

But silently she added as she smiled at Moira, But not for me!

*

André Viznitski had followed the newspaper coverage of the Lassiter affair, pleased that Moira's innocence had been put in doubt by nearly all the Paris dailies. He had even helped organize a boycott of Maeve's Red Cross concert, and he forced himself to listen to the increasingly incoherent ravings of Laura Milonari. But so far nothing much had come of it—except for casting aspersions on Moira's good name and giving the readers of the gutter press a thrill.

To Viznitski's extreme annoyance, the public prosecutor had not seen fit to accuse her of murder—and some hardy souls continued to invite her to parties, even though they were becoming fewer and fewer. Moira Lassiter was slowly being plunged into social oblivion, but not quickly enough for Viznitski. Charlie was taking it hard though, a good sign.

André had hoped Maeve's notoriety after *Salome* might cause her to lose some engagements over it, but producers were now trying to find out if she would repeat her performance in Europe! Still, Maeve might yet be the vehicle for causing distress to the Devereux if she could be properly exploited; at least André hoped so.

In the spring of 1908, shortly before the Paris season, Count Viznitski made the acquaintance of a young lady from the Opéra-Comique, a colleague of Maeve's. This took some doing because she considered herself very grand and didn't deign to see just anyone. But André was determined to question someone from the Opéra who could help him find a way to harm Maeve Devereux professionally or, at the very least, cause her a great deal of distress. A few dozen roses and a series of dinners at some of Paris's most celebrated restaurants proved useful.

Getting this Elise to talk about Maeve wasn't easy, since she clearly preferred to talk about herself, but she did have a lot to say about Marc Antoine de Marigny, Maeve's usual partner and her own bête noire. Her hatred for the tenor was truly all-encompassing. Wonderful!

"A handsome fellow," Viznitski declared, pouring his glamorous companion another glass of Moët as they sat at a good table at Maxim's. "A beautiful woman like you would look horribly mismatched with an ugly partner."

"Ha!" she sneered. "Let Devereux have him. I prefer almost anyone else."

"But dear lady, I've heard you sing with him. You were wonderful together."

"He doesn't suit me. It's a matter of taste, and," she added with a meaningful glance, "I don't mean artistically."

André moved closer to his companion and looked curious. "How is that?" he asked, studying Elise's lovely face.

She delicately fluttered her magnificent ostrich plume fan. "It's actually just a suspicion," she admitted, "but I've known enough artists to realize that things are not always what they seem onstage. A man may be the idol of silly shopgirls and yet leave a lot to be desired—as a man."

Viznitski saw the feline gleam in Elise's beautiful blue eyes and he felt as if he'd just struck gold.

"Excuse my naïveté," he said, trying to look puzzled, "but I don't quite follow you."

The blond soprano laughed and squeezed his hand. She was genuinely amused.

"Well, my dear Count." She smiled, with a sweetness that was truly endearing. "I'm telling you that despite all those countesses and well-publicized paper liaisons, Monsieur de Marigny seems to have a fondness for handsome young men. Of course," she added carefully as she saw Viznitski's jaw drop, "they may all be his relatives. Or old schoolmates. But they're all so *very* good-looking that it makes one wonder."

Viznitski's mind was already racing. If Maeve's favorite partner could be hounded off the stage in a sordid sex scandal, it would be marvelous! She and Marc Antoine were sensational together. Watching them in *La Bohème* or *Tosca*, it was hard to believe they weren't madly in love. Together they packed the house, creating long lines at the box office. What greater disaster could befall La Devereux than to lose her finest partner at the moment when her marriage to that German seemed so shaky?

"I'm shocked," André declared. "Truly shocked. It seems hard to credit."

"Would you like to see proof?" Elise smiled as she entwined her fingers in his.

"Yes," he replied, a little too quickly.

The lady was only too pleased to be able to offer him directions.

*

While rehearsals were starting for the season, Maeve was able to enjoy herself with her friends. Dietrich was spending an unusual amount of time in Berlin now, and she found herself occasionally keeping Zofia Farrell company as the Montenegrin girl awaited the birth of her first child.

Maeve wasn't all that fond of Zofia, but Sean had asked her to be kind, especially since his wife had miscarried last year and was nervous about her new pregnancy—and depressed by the intrigues in Montenegro. Zofia seemed to be taking things too much to heart.

"Ivan," his wife said quietly one evening, "have they been able to find the ringleaders of the plot against His Highness?"

"No. They're very clever. We've run down so many leads, only to have them vanish just as we were about to pounce. It's uncanny."

"But His Highness is safe?"

"Yes. He's surrounded by old friends in Cetinje—we hope. And he's anxious to see his grandson."

Zofia sighed and rested her head on his shoulder. "I hate these intrigues. It's so dangerous for you to deal with the people you have to associate with."

He smiled and stroked her dark hair. "I'm a match for any Montenegrin," he said. "They don't worry me. I know them all too well. I know how they think."

"Never turn your back on the Serbians," she warned. "Or on the Turks or Austrians either."

"Or on the Russians, Bulgarians, or Romanians for that matter." He smiled. "The world is not full of friends, my dear."

Ivan Petrovic and Kyril had traveled throughout Montenegro, the Prince's son ostensibly seeking to shore up ties with the various clan chieftains, but in reality searching for traitors. Hints of disloyalty on the part of various clans were whispered to him as he sat in tribal enclaves, listening to the bards chant the old ballads and drinking the cups of coffee offered as a sign of special distinction.

Of course it was always the clan across the valley or over the mountain that was doing the plotting, he noticed.

But one night, as he and Kyril had sat with a group of clansmen in western Montenegro, the country's most prosperous region, he heard the name Jordje Plamanac breathed ever so softly in his ear.

Startled, Ivan Petrovic revealed his shock with a glance, and his host replied with a subtle sign to silence his questions. The man was putting himself at risk by mentioning the Plamanac name, and if Ivan Petrovic was in on the plot, he had just signed his own death warrant. But the chieftain was an old man and a veteran of the Turkish Wars. His loyalty to Nikolai Petrovic made him trust this son of his—even if he *had* married a Plamanac bride.

The accusation of disloyalty on the part of Zofia's brother was a serious matter. It was also dangerous to Ivan Petrovic personally, since he had married into the family and could therefore be viewed as either a pawn or an active plotter. With a shock he now recalled his own brother's piercing look as he inquired whether Ivan had seen Milan or Jordje lately. Did his brothers already suspect Zofia's family?

Looking down at his wife as she lay cuddled by his side, he wondered if the accusations were true. God Almighty! It couldn't be possible that Zofia would ever raise a hand against his family, but what about old Milan her father, or young Jordje? Did they have plans to expand their holdings in Montenegro at Nikolai's expense? Greed was a powerful incentive, he knew, even for a man who was already one of the richest in the country. Perhaps even more so for such a man. But who could he be plotting with? Serbia? Austria? It was something that had to be discovered. Soon.

Maeve was disappointed that Sean had to leave Paris for business so soon after his arrival. Zofia was crushed. He was heartless to leave her alone in her condition, she declared—especially with all sorts of plots and intrigues against his family. God knows what might happen to a poor, defenseless mother-to-be under the circumstances. If he had a shred of decency in him, he would stay by her side.

*

The spring of 1908 was a particularly uneasy time in the Balkans. The Russian Tsar had been humiliated by the inept maneuvering of his foreign minister, Izvolsky, regarding Austria's annexation of Bosnia-

Herzogovina, and all Europe had witnessed the "Protectress of the Slavs" back off in alarm from a confrontation with Austria—and Germany.

Worse than revealing Russia's lack of military preparedness, the crisis had exposed the deviousness of her foreign policy. Izvolsky had given Austria his country's consent to the annexation of this small Slavic province in return for Russian access to the Bosporus—and had been duped. In deepest embarrassment, Russia found herself criticized for both her heartlessness in betraying her fellow Slavs and her stupidity in dealing with the Austrian foreign minister, Aehrenthal, a wily trickster.

With all this taking place, Kyril discovered a Serb from Belgrade who claimed to know who had organized the plot against Nikolai Petrovic. For money, he was willing to tell all.

This came as no great surprise to Sean—or Kyril. Colonel Apis of the Serbian secret police was the instigator. Greater Serbia was to be realized at the expense of its weaker neighbor—and without Prince Nikolai, Montenegro would be very weak indeed.

The really interesting part came a bit later when Sean and Kyril sequestered the Serb informant and offered him a choice between revealing the names of the Montenegrin traitors he worked with or having his brains splattered against the wall. The man watched as Sean loaded his revolver with cool deliberation. He hesitated, looked terrified, and finally blurted out the name—a senator close to the ruling family, Jordje Plamanac.

It was a bombshell. The shock of his brother-in-law's involvement staggered Sean. It sent Prince Nikolai into a rage. This dog of a traitor had links with his own family, and he had dared to do this? It violated all codes of loyalty. It was his death sentence.

Present at Jordje's interrogation, Sean felt sick with shame. This traitor had broken bread with him and he was the brother of Zofia, his wife. How could he stab them in the back? Sean demanded, nearly unhinged with his outrage over Jordje's treachery.

To his surprise, his brother-in-law just shook his head. It was politics, he assured Sean. Nothing personal. He would have had no pleasure in killing him.

The same could not be said for Prince Nikolai's attitude toward Jordje. After a brutal interrogation in the ruler's presence, the Plamanac traitor confessed his involvement in a plot to help Serbia's expansionist plans—while at the same time working covertly with Serbia's greatest enemy, Austria, to carve out a separate state in the western part of Montenegro, a Plamanac fief under Austrian protection. Both plans required the removal of Nikolai Petrovic.

This perfidy was almost too painful for Sean to deal with. Not only did it involve his brother-in-law—and naturally, his father-in-law, for whom an arrest warrant was quickly sworn out—but it also put Zofia's innocence into question.

Daughter of a traitor, sister of a traitor, only the fact that she had had no known recent contact with her family kept her off the list of suspects—that and the fact that her menfolk would have considered her, as a woman, too inconsequential to involve in such an important activity as plotting high treason.

Jordje went to his death invoking Zofia's loyalty to her husband and the Petrovici, and Sean wanted to believe it. His love for his father forced him to believe it. He couldn't stomach the thought of sleeping with a regicide.

In his mind's eye he recalled that distant day on the Nevsky Prospect with Maeve, remembering their bittersweet reunion in St. Petersburg— at precisely the moment he was to announce his engagement to Zofia Plamanac. His instincts had said, "Reconsider," but duty demanded compliance. How ironic that moment seemed now, viewed through the prism of today's betrayal.

The younger princes were disgusted, and Danilo, Mirko, and Peter were not slow to realize that in a subtle and painful way Ivan had been damaged by all this. He had married a Plamanac—on Nikolai's orders— and now his in-laws were traitors. They wondered if the old man would still favor him as much as he used to, and they were already silently speculating on the benefits they could obtain with Ivan reduced to disgrace and probably disinherited.

CHAPTER 28

Maeve's rehearsals in preparation for her return to the Paris stage were going well until the day Marc Antoine failed to show up for a scheduled practice session. Dismayed, she waited, finally rehearsed her role with a replacement, and remarked to Arlette afterward that it was very odd. Marc Antoine was always very punctilious about his opera duties. This wasn't like him at all and it worried her.

"Perhaps he's ill, madame," Arlette suggested nervously.

Considering that possibility, Maeve decided to pay him a visit. They were on pretty close terms, often rehearsing in each other's homes—with a houseful of servants around to eliminate any gossip of a romantic attachment. Sometimes Dietrich sat in on the rehearsals. Maeve thought about it and decided she and Arlette had better go visit Marco and find out what the matter was. And he'd better have a good excuse!

When the women arrived at the apartment building, a very elegant place, Maeve rang the concierge, announced that she was Monsieur de Marigny's partner, and asked to be announced.

"But madame," replied the woman, "I don't think he wants to be disturbed. He told me this morning that under no circumstances was I to let anyone in."

"That's rubbish. Monsieur de Marigny knew he had to be rehearsing *Tosca* with me this morning. He would never miss a rehearsal."

"Is he ill?" Arlette inquired.

"He looked fine to me." The concierge shrugged, bewildered.

"Then I'm going upstairs to find out just what's going on," Maeve declared. "Come on, Letty!"

What nerve! "Not to be disturbed!" Who did he think he was? Nobody had ever stood her up for a rehearsal. Was he curled up with some silly little countess? The dirty little lizard! The playboy!

Maeve was becoming more and more overheated as she and Arlette trooped up the stairs with the concierge right behind them, protesting that Monsieur wouldn't like this at all.

"Well, I didn't like being stood up," Maeve retorted. "And when I find him, he's going to learn the full extent of my displeasure!"

When the worried concierge indicated the correct door, Maeve took a deep breath and gave it three loud knocks, waited, then gave it three more, and finally looked at her companions. "He doesn't seem to be in there."

"He is, madame," nodded the concierge, whose nosy cat had followed them up the stairs and was now acting a little strange. The animal was so agitated it looked as if it was about to take some kind of fit.

Arlette, who adored animals, stared at the weird behavior and wondered what could be causing such distress. It seemed to be responding to something no one else could sense.

Suddenly she said to Maeve, "I smell something strange. Look at the cat. He must smell it too."

"My God!" exclaimed its horrified owner as she, too, caught the scent. "Gas!"

"Marc Antoine!"

"Open the door!"

"Oh hell," shouted Maeve, "get something heavy and we'll break it down!"

The concierge was no less frantic than Maeve. She saw visions of an explosion, the whole building going up in flames, dozens dead and herself out of a job. Maeve saw herself forced to make do with a replacement tenor, and whacked at the door like one possessed, desperate to get in.

With the combined efforts of the three women, who went at it with a chair, a doorstop, and a hammer, the lock shattered, and with a collective groan they found themselves inside and enveloped in a revolting odor of gas.

Maeve wrapped her handkerchief around her head, covering her nose and mouth, and Arlette did the same, while the concierge raced downstairs to call the fire brigade. Holding their breath, they flung open every window in the place as they ran from room to room, searching for Marc Antoine.

Suddenly opening the bedroom door, Arlette took Maeve's arm and pointed. He was slumped across his bed, unconscious. Beside him was a letter. Maeve snatched it up and grabbed hold of Marc Antoine's arms as Arlette helped lift him off the bed.

Together they dragged him—with considerable difficulty—across the salon, the foyer, and the corridor, where they stood doubled over and gasping for breath.

"Oh God!" Maeve wailed. "I think he's almost dead. How can we get him down the stairs and into the fresh air?"

As Maeve and Arlette were starting to stagger down the stairs with Marc Antoine, two members of the fire brigade met them, alerted by the concierge, and one man hoisted the tenor up onto his shoulder, while the other assisted the two women down the stairway, both ladies rather dizzy from the fumes.

In a few minutes the tenor was on his way to a private clinic, and Maeve and Arlette were following in Maeve's expensive American limousine, both still woozy and nearly hysterical with fear for Marc Antoine's life.

"Do you think it was an accident, madame?" Arlette asked, shaken. "The whole house might have blown up."

Maeve slowly shook her head. She had had time to read the note and hide it in her purse. "It's dreadful, Letty. It's just too awful to describe."

"He *wanted* to die?" the maid whispered in astonishment, trying hard to keep her voice down to prevent the chauffeur from overhearing. The glass panel with the speaking vent was closed between them, but Arlette was taking no chances. The man was a big gossip, and she didn't want this piece of news spread all over Paris.

*

When the tenor began to recover, he was violently sick but showed no sign of permanent damage. The doctor said he had apparently been overcome not too long before Maeve and Arlette had started banging on the door—fortunately for him.

"Monsieur de Marigny doesn't seem to recall anything," he said. "My guess is a defect in the stove."

"The concierge will have to get it checked," Maeve said, nodding.

"I once had trouble with something similar. These people never take proper care of the appliances."

While La Devereux was trying hard to sound like an outraged homemaker irritated over the laxness of concierges in general, the doctor was studying her lovely face, wondering just how much of it was acting.

"By the way," he said, "you don't think this could have been an attempted suicide, do you?"

Maeve's head jerked up and she burst out laughing, vastly amused. In her purse was a letter, written by the tenor minutes before he had closed all the windows and turned out the pilot light in the stove. It stated that he had taken this way out to avoid the ruin of his life and his career, with apologies to his friends, especially Maeve, who wouldn't be pleased with the sorry substitutes she would have to make do with. However, it couldn't be helped.

"Good Lord! Suicide!" she exclaimed. "Monsieur de Marigny is at the height of a brilliant career. He's enjoying himself too much to think of ending it all."

"Well, I know it sounded ridiculous, madame, but I am obliged to ask these things," he said.

"I quite understand, Doctor. In your position you'd be remiss if you didn't. But," she added, "I can assure you, in Monsieur de Marigny's case, it was just a faulty stove. He'll be beastly with his cook now, I'm afraid." She laughed again, showing pretty white teeth.

*

"I wish I were dead" was the first thing Marc Antoine said to his rescuer when he was able to speak.

"Don't be stupid. I read the letter and took it with me so nobody else could get hold of it. We're telling everyone it was a faulty stove, and you'd better do the same."

"Oh God! I can't even kill myself properly. What an embarrassment."

"Stop this!" she demanded, reaching down to shake him. "It's idiotic. No matter what happened, we can deal with it. Now tell me, just what the hell are you involved with?"

It was sordid. Marc Antoine had been friendly with several young men in a way that was more than the usual sort of male camaraderie, and one of them was blackmailing him. He was in despair. The more he paid, the more incessant the demands. It was bleeding him dry.

"My God, Marc Antoine," Maeve said at last. "What happened to all the countesses?"

He looked downcast. "I have an affectionate nature," he said at last, rather lamely. "It knows no bounds."

"You have no sense," she retorted. "You need a keeper!"

Maeve was shocked. It was the sort of thing she had heard of in laughing whispers, but here was Marc Antoine, the shopgirls' idol, entrapped by a blackmailer for serious moral lapses of an illegal and peculiar nature.

There was no question about helping him. Maeve was not about to risk losing the best Rodolfo this side of Caruso just because of that. Marco was her friend and she loved him. She would not abandon him. But getting him out of this mess would take some doing.

In the aftermath of the gas leak, Marc Antoine was inundated with flowers from admirers, expressing their gratitude that he hadn't been taken from them and offering prayers for his recovery. He was embarrassed but rather touched. Despite a few doubters, the public came to the conclusion that it was indeed an accident, and they reacted sympathetically.

"People are so careless with appliances" was Dietrich's comment. "He's lucky he's alive."

"Yes," Maeve replied with a smile. "So am I."

And now all they had to do was find the solution to his problems.

Dietrich, she noticed, was too preoccupied with his own affairs to spare much thought to the mysterious circumstances surrounding Marco's near asphyxiation. Well, that was all to the good. Her husband appeared to be the only person in Paris who wasn't trying to pry "the real story" out of her. It was as if he didn't care—and yet he had nothing against the tenor. In fact, they got on fairly well. Odd.

Dietrich had a lot on his mind lately, Maeve reflected, and all those trips to Berlin and Vienna seemed to be the cause of his present concerns. Whenever she asked about it, he would only shrug and sigh "Business," but it was causing him a lot of sleepless nights, and it was giving Maeve a great deal of concern.

*

Maeve's return to the stage of the Opéra-Comique was an event that Monsieur Carré looked forward to with both dread and anticipation. Her wildly provocative performance in New York had added a new sort of luster to her reputation and it was apparently going to entice an even larger audience than before to see her in *Tosca*. The only question was, would it be a favorable crowd?

Moira's unfortunate brush with scandal was still on people's minds, and Carré could even now recall those empty seats at the time of his star's Red Cross concert. However, Maeve's unusually large and loyal following, linked to Marc Antoine's, was almost a guarantee of success, and the opportunity to hear the two stars in *Tosca* would bring out a large house—as box office sales were already indicating. Those who might waver about hearing Maeve alone were not so particular that they would pass up the chance to hear the most glamorous couple on the operatic stage *together*. And to make things even more enticing, Carré had engaged Antonio Scotti for the villainous Scarpia, a role he had practically made his own. As Maeve's treacherous nemesis, he was almost terrifyingly superb, an unabashed, full-blooded terror.

On the evening of the performance, Arlette had dutifully dressed Madame in her first-act costume, made certain she had Chaliapin's gold cross around her neck for good luck, handed her the armful of flowers she was to carry into the church at her entrance, and said a prayer for success.

In the audience, sitting in the director's box with Carré, were the star's mother, stepfather, and husband, all hoping for a warm response from an audience that seemed unusually restless. Carré couldn't tell whether the people were simply uncomfortable from the heat or vaguely hostile. Mary Garden sat in a box not too far from her rival's family and noted with amusement that Moira Lassiter was wearing every diamond she possessed.

"She'd make La Belle Otero jealous with that parure," La Garden whispered to her companion, a Russian aristocrat of attractive appearance and solicitous manner.

"She seems to think they will ward off evil," he replied. "Perhaps that's the reason for their profusion."

If he had his way, Moira would need a lot more than a few million dollars' worth of brilliants to escape the fate she deserved.

Dietrich was nervous. Maeve was going to be facing an audience that still remembered all the ugly accusations of the past year—with the cause of all the rumors sitting right there in the theater. And with much of Parisian society still shunning Mrs. Lassiter, there were many people who secretly thought she was wicked enough to murder Laura Milonari's son. The scene at Maeve's engagement party had been described so many times to so many people that it had practically entered into the local folklore. Moira was a coldhearted bitch, they said. A horror.

Maeve's entrance was greeted with less than the usual outpouring of hysteria, Dietrich noticed—a bad sign. Perhaps to compensate for that, she seemed determined to win the audience over, throwing herself into the role with an energy that startled even Marc Antoine. This Tosca was both wildly flirtatious and insanely jealous, enough to drive a man crazy. Her mood swings seemed almost too real, and to compete with her, Marc Antoine found himself getting more and more physical, which seemed to please the audience—but not Baron von Reuter this evening.

"I wish he'd keep his hands off her," he hissed to Moira. "Damned lizard!"

"It's only acting," she hissed back. "You ought to be used to it by now!"

Perhaps, but after *Salome* he was becoming increasingly sensitive to Maeve's displays of sensuality onstage. She was showing signs of enjoying it, which was not the proper attitude for a Prussian wife and mother. Italians might be forgiven for this, but not Baroness von Reuter.

Carré noted with alarm that although Marc Antoine was receiving his usual rapturous applause, the audience appeared to be holding back where Maeve was concerned—and she was dazzling tonight. It was the best *Tosca* he could remember at the Opéra-Comique, and proof of that was the expression on Mary Garden's face. The woman was tortured with jealousy.

"They hate me!" Maeve was wailing to Arlette in her dressing room as her maid struggled to calm her and to lace her into the magnificent red velvet Empire gown she was to wear in Act Two—a copy of something the Empress Josephine had worn. Cut to display her cleavage, it was breathtaking, fully embroidered with gold from neckline to hem in a pattern of laurel leaves and roses, with a splendid train. A tiara of antique cameos and a matching necklace and bracelet completed her costume, the image of triumphant neoclassicism.

"They do seem a bit restrained," Arlette agreed, giving the final touches to Madame's ensemble. "But I think they're with you. Backstage everyone is crazy about your performance. The men think you're in top form."

"Ha!" she exclaimed. "Out there, the only one they're noticing is Marc Antoine!"

"The women just applaud louder than the men," Arlette said firmly. "He gets them so excited they become frenzied and they make a lot of noise. Remember all those little shopgirls outside the church at your wedding, madame? . . . Well, there. You see what I mean."

That was reasonable. Marc Antoine's fans were an especially hysterical lot, comparable only to that lynch mob at Père Lachaise. Of course they would carry on like lunatics for him and him alone, ignoring the magnificent performance of his partner. They would probably be jealous of her, a beauty whose allure they could never hope to surpass in a million years. Or even two million. Why be modest?

"I'm going to make such an impression in Act Two that even the people who love Marc Antoine and think Moira harmed that child won't be able to ignore me," she promised. "Wait!"

And with that, Maeve departed for Tosca's appointment at the Palazzo Farnese.

Antonio Scotti was a Scarpia so vicious that even the members of the audience who had been lukewarm to Maeve were beginning to feel pity for poor Tosca. Lecherous, vile, corrupt, and cruel, he tortured the heroine with fear for her lover while breaking down her will to resist his advances for fear of his spiteful wrath. Moira was dabbing at her eyes, and Charlie was clenching his fists. Dietrich noted with distaste that Scotti shared Marc Antoine's penchant for body contact, an irritating tendency.

"My God!" exclaimed Monsieur Carré. "These two are really turning up the temperature! It's fantastic!"

Then came the highlight of the second act, Tosca's great aria, "Vissi d'arte." As Tosca began the heartbreaking lament, wondering why she was being punished in such a way when she had tried all her life to live so decently, she finally struck sparks with this audience and brought them to feverish life, at the end applauding like mad.

As Scotti signaled his approval, Maeve lowered her head to catch her breath and enjoy the adulation before continuing the scene. What followed was open to dispute afterward, but according to Scotti, who was endowed with quick reflexes, the first sign of trouble was the sound that made him raise his eyes just as Maeve brought her head up to acknowledge the applause.

To his utter horror, he heard a whooshing noise and beheld something hurtling straight toward him and his partner from far up in the rafters. He stunned the audience by throwing himself at Maeve and knocking her down.

Before anyone could even realize what was happening, a large round weight came crashing down onto the stage just as Scotti shoved Maeve out of its way and sent her reeling to the ground, apparently struck by the missile. She collapsed in a tangle of red velvet, with her partner entrapped in the folds of her train.

Moira jumped to her feet as her daughter hit the stage. Her hands clenched the railing of the box and she screamed in sheer terror. Then, as Charlie leapt up, dead white, to assist her, Moira fainted, sinking to the floor of the box in a shining pile of silk and diamonds. Monsieur

Carré nearly fainted too, appalled by the sight of his brightest star killed by falling debris.

Arlette, who had witnessed the accident from the wings, wailed in terror and then raced out onto the stage along with two nearby stagehands to see if Maeve was still alive. At this point, no one actually knew if she had been struck by the falling object or simply pushed to the ground by her partner. But everyone in the house could see she was not getting to her feet, and a frantic Carré had stopped the show and ordered the houselights on while the audience was buzzing with alarm and speculating on Maeve's fate.

"Maëva!" the Neapolitan was shouting, "are you alive? Can you hear me?"

"Oh, madame," Arlette wailed. "Don't die!"

Dietrich had raced from his box to the orchestra pit at the first sign of trouble and startled the conductor by vaulting onto the stage, a feat he couldn't imagine duplicating under any other circumstances. As he threw himself over his wife, she opened her eyes, half-dazed, and blinked, surprised to see him there. None of this made sense.

"Why am I on the floor?" she asked, staring at Dietrich, Arlette, and Scotti. What had happened? she wondered groggily. "What are you and Arlette doing onstage? Get off! Are you mad?"

To the great relief of the house, they saw a handsome blond gentleman in evening dress pick La Devereux up and carry her toward center stage, her gorgeous red gown a bedraggled mess, its train lying ripped on the floor.

As they realized she was still alive and conscious, the audience let out a tremendous roar, reverberating throughout the entire house. Not even in Russia had Maeve ever heard such mad approval. Despite her shaky state, she waved to her admirers, kissed Dietrich, and wrapped her arms around his neck as he carried her offstage and headed for her dressing room, followed by the house physician.

Thrilled by the response to her accident, Maeve stunned her entourage by insisting she was going out there to finish her performance. With Moira, Arlette, and Dietrich all protesting her decision, she informed Carré that he could forget about an understudy. She was Tosca and she was going to continue.

"But madame!" he protested. "You've just suffered a tremendous shock. It isn't wise."

"Don't be silly. Those people just suffered a tremendous shock. They started off by being cold to me. Now they're worried about me. By the end of the evening I'll make them fans for life!" she declared, delighted. "They'll never forget what I did this night."

"Don't be ridiculous," snapped her husband. "Nobody would expect you to finish. That's why they have understudies."

"This is why they have *stars!*" Maeve retorted in an excess of panache. "Letty, get me the other gown. I'm going back onstage."

The applause that greeted her return to the stage was even wilder than when she had been carried off. Maeve was aching in every muscle and had to sit down to do the duet with Marc Antoine in the prison cell, but she forced herself to keep going, more from sheer stubbornness than anything else. If those people had had the gall to withhold their approval at the beginning of the opera, she'd make damned sure they'd never be tempted to do it again. She was Maeve Devereux and she was going to prove to them that she was indestructible. They could ignore her at their peril.

"Letty," Maeve announced after she had brought the opera to a rousing finale, "get a couple of strong men to carry me out to my automobile. I think I'm about to fall down."

*

It took two weeks in bed to compensate for her bravado that evening, but from that moment on, people began to look at Moira with different eyes. Her fainting at Maeve's accident convinced the populace that a woman with such strong maternal feelings could not connive at the murder of *anybody's* child. Those who had been heaping calumnies on her began to say they might have been mistaken. And if Moira was no murderess, then her daughter could hardly be censured for being her daughter. Things looked quite different now, everyone declared. Quite different.

The only person in Paris who remained unconvinced was Laura Milonari. "The little witch!" she shrieked, upon hearing the news of Maeve's triumph in *Tosca*. "Just because she gets knocked down onstage they feel sorry for her! Who cares? I wouldn't care if she had got killed!"

That was a very poor attitude, she was told, and even some of the harpies who had tried to stone Maeve at the funeral were beginning to say the mother showed a lot of feeling for her child when she fell down in a dead faint upon seeing her struck. At least she had a heart for her own, a great surprise to them all. Perhaps they had been mistaken . . .

"She doesn't have a heart for anyone!" Laura screamed. "She's a wicked, jealous bitch and she murdered my Gianni!"

But she was beginning to lose her audience.

*

The Paris public bestowed its wildest approval on Maeve Devereux the night she was almost splattered across the stage of the Opéra-Comique, due to poor maintenance of the scenery, and in the weeks that followed, Maeve received so many flowers, gifts, cards, and visits she was nearly overwhelmed. All this would have been marvelous except for one nagging problem. Marc Antoine, her adored Rodolfo, Alfredo, Mario, Don José, and Duke of Mantua, was being blackmailed, and despite her soothing words and efforts to make contact with the one man she knew who might be able to help him, the blackmail continued. Marc Antoine was in despair.

"It's no use," he said one night in her dressing room as they sat there between acts of *La Traviata*. "This creature will never let go and I can't keep on paying forever. If you can't get someone to help, I'm ready to take matters into my own hands."

Maeve's head bobbed up sharply, and she quickly put down her cup of honeyed tea. "What are you talking about?"

The Frenchman smiled grimly as he looked back at her. "I'm talking about putting an end to this mess—one way or the other. I was a fool to even think about allowing a woman to get involved in this. It's my problem and I'm the one who has to deal with it. It's not fair to you."

"Marc Antoine, don't be so foolish. The man I know isn't in Paris yet, but he will be. He's used to . . . unpleasant things. You're not."

"Oh, I don't know about that, *chérie*. My life has been a regular hell on earth these past few months."

Maeve reached out for her partner's hand and held it firmly in hers. "Marco," she said, using his pet name, "you mean the world to me. You're as dear to me as a member of my own family, and if you hadn't arranged for Mary Garden to get sick that afternoon"—she smiled wickedly—"we never would have had such success together. I'm sorry my man is so slow, but give him another week. He's an expert in these matters. He knows how to deal with scum."

She kissed his hand playfully. "One day I may ask you to help *me*," she said lightly. "So I need you alive and well for the future."

The tenor smiled. Maeve was one of the most resourceful women he knew. Sometimes he wondered if she needed anyone. He knew the German occasionally asked himself the same thing; Dietrich had told him so one night at a party when they were both drinking and observing Maeve, surrounded by a cluster of breathless admirers.

A knock on the door signaled the end to the intermission. "Madame!"

"Time to go back onstage and die," she said cheerfully as Marc Antoine kissed her softly on the cheek.

"It's a morbid way to make a living," he sighed, "all this dying. It takes its toll."

"Ah, well, it certainly beats the real thing." She smiled as Violetta headed upstairs to expire for the sixtieth time in her career. "In real life you don't get to take curtain calls afterward!"

*

It took another two days before Maeve had her chance to communicate with the gentleman she had in mind. He was a bit preoccupied with his own problems, and had no sympathy for actors, tenors, or perverts, as he said sternly, but he had always liked Maeve and he would try to help.

"Thank you, Kyril. I knew I could count on you," she said.

"This singer—is he the one who went to Petersburg with you a few years ago?"

"Yes. Do you remember him?"

"Sure," nodded the Montenegrin. "I saw a lot of women around him. I saw countesses elbowing each other out of the way just so they could get close to him. Damn silly cows. What a shock!"

"Apparently Marc Antoine has a lot of friends besides the ladies."

"He's a fool. He'll wind up dead one day under a park bench or floating in the river if he doesn't change his ways. If he's a man, let him act like a man—or let him kill himself. That's the way he should handle it." Kyril did not approve.

"Well, he's already tried to kill himself," she said, "and I stopped him. I want him alive and onstage with me. There's no better tenor around, and I'm not about to lose him because of this. He's too important to me."

The little one was very stubborn. Kyril had to admire her loyalty to this friend, and in a way he was glad Maeve wasn't in love with the man. He wouldn't have helped her if he thought she was cheating on her husband with him. He had his standards.

Abruptly Kyril asked, "How many people know about this?"

"Well, just me—and the blackmailer. At least I think so. I know Marc Antoine hasn't made this known to anyone else."

"Ah," nodded Kyril, his heavy-lidded brown eyes gleaming. "But what about the blackmailer?"

"He's an unknown quantity. But," she asked curiously, "do you think he would blab about it?"

"With scum like that, who can tell?" Kyril shrugged. "By the way, little one, what shall I do with the tenor's boyfriend when I find him?"

"Make him leave town and stop threatening Marco. Be firm," Maeve advised. "Be as forceful as you have to. Speak to him sternly and let him know he's going to be in serious trouble if he keeps this up."

The Montenegrin looked at Maeve and nodded reassuringly. He would set him straight, he promised. When he got done with him, the blackmailer would be looking for other pigeons to pluck.

Sean was back in Paris to guard Zofia in case Prince Nikolai and his brothers changed their minds about her innocence, and Kyril had come along with him. Besides his concern for Zofia, Sean was also worried about Moira and Maeve. Those accusations of murder were an atrocious insult, and he wanted to try to get to the bottom of this. Moira was hot-tempered, hasty, and reckless, but he didn't believe for a second that she had actually murdered Gianni Milonari. Kyril was conducting an investigation into it too. He was good at ferreting out information.

Besides, Kyril had had a soft spot for Maeve ever since that day long ago when she wanted to take on the Serbian secret police and fight for Ivan Petrovic. She wasn't too smart at times—but she had nerve. And she was loyal to her friends. It was just a pity that she was so damned loyal to this Marc Antoine. Her affection was sadly misplaced in his case. Back home he would have been quietly strangled by some outraged decent member of his own clan, and that would have been that. But Europeans were more tolerant. Kyril sighed.

Stalking the blackmailer wasn't that difficult because Marc Antoine knew several places where he could be found, and he even supplied a photograph. The Montenegrin located him on his third try and carefully trailed him back to his apartment in a seedy building up in Montmartre, not too far from the place du Tertre. Once there, he held a knife to his throat, pushed him through the door, and began the interrogation.

"Who are you?" stammered the Frenchman, a twenty-three-year-old with large dark eyes and a childish face.

"Nobody you want to know," replied Kyril in his rough accent as he tied the boy's wrists together and ordered him to sit on the floor— the better to keep him off balance. "Now tell me," he continued, "where the hell is the money you've been extorting from the singer?"

"What?" His head jerked up in astonishment, eyes wild with fear. "What are you talking about?"

"Don't play dumb. I've shot better men than you. Talk!"

"Did Marc Antoine send you?"

"Nobody sent me," retorted Kyril as he began to rifle all the drawers. Nothing in there. Damn!

The boy followed him with his eyes, frightened, nervous. When he saw the stranger hesitate near the bed, he glanced involuntarily at the mattress, more specifically at a slight bulge near the foot of the bed.

Kyril saw that look, grabbed the mattress, and began hacking away at it with a knife. In seconds he had a wad of bank notes in his hand and a very frightened boy trying to inch his way across the room like a terrified shellfish, frantic to escape.

Grabbing him by the collar, Kyril slammed his face against the wall and shoved his boot into his stomach.

"Now talk, damn you! Is this all the money you got from the singer?"

"Yes!"

"Liar!"

"No, no! I swear it," he said in terror. "Well, I spent five hundred francs, all right? But that's the rest."

"You're lying!"

"No!"

The Montenegrin continued to hold his wicked-looking knife, glancing from time to time at his host's throat. Suddenly he demanded, "Who put you up to this? Talk," he growled, approaching him with the knife.

"A Russian," the boy replied, surprising Kyril, who was just trying to intimidate him. This changed everything. Perhaps it was a bigger plot than Maeve realized. These Russians were devious as hell and not to be trusted. Now he was really intrigued.

"What Russian?" Kyril asked casually. "Paris is lousy with Russians."

"A count," retorted the blackmailer, one Jean-Yves Bourdonne. "A Russian count named André Viznitski."

"Why would a Russian care about a French pervert like the singer? Or you?" he asked contemptuously. "They have enough at home."

Jean-Yves tried his best to look ingratiating. "The Russian has a grudge against Marc Antoine's partner, the soprano Maeve Devereux. He's a little crazy, I think," confided the boy. "This is all directed against her. He thinks forcing Marc Antoine off the stage in a scandal or making him kill himself will hurt the woman. The tenor himself means nothing to him. He's just incidental."

Jean-Yves gulped as Kyril brought the blade of his knife dangerously close to his throat.

"This Viznitski thinks if he causes the tenor to crack under pressure he'll go berserk and kill himself. And then the woman will suffer. Ha! The dumb bastard doesn't know sopranos. She'll have a new partner ready to take over before Marc Antoine's body is even cold. This is his fantasy, monsieur. I'm doing this because I get to keep the money," the boy explained.

My God, thought Kyril. It made him furious to think Maeve was the real target of these degenerates. But it was a very Russian scheme, very devious and cunning, just the sort of thing you could expect from them. It was a shame their Tsar wasn't as clever as this Viznitski, Kyril reflected. That one was a poor, nervous specimen, not very cunning at all—rather stupid and henpecked, in fact.

"Show me where this Russian lives," Kyril ordered suddenly as he grabbed the bank notes and stuffed them into his pockets.

"Cut me loose," replied the boy.

"Not on your life!" The Montenegrin grinned, hoisting him to his feet.

"But I can take you there."

"Oh, you will." Kyril nodded. "Right now. Get moving."

There was an automobile downstairs, and as soon as Jean-Yves was shoved into the passenger seat, Kyril jumped in and, with a revolver in his hand, set off for Count Viznitski's.

"He lives on the third floor of that apartment," the boy informed Kyril. "You can go into the foyer and check the names. His is listed on a brass plate under apartment number six."

"Very good."

But to Jean-Yves's bewilderment, the stranger started the motor and drove off.

"What are you doing? I thought you wanted to find Viznitski."

"I forgot something," he replied. "Just a minor detour. It won't take long."

The French boy was sweating with fright. Viznitski would kill him if this foreigner burst in on him. He should have lied.

Kyril had tied his guest to the automobile's door handle, so there was no chance of his breaking away. The boy was very quiet, he noted as he headed toward the river.

"Were you friends with this tenor?" Kyril asked out of curiosity as the automobile rolled over cobblestones on the way to the quay.

"Sort of."

"Well, were you friends or not?" he persisted, annoyed with the evasive answer.

The boy shrugged. "He was nice to me. I liked him."

"So you showed your appreciation by trying to wreck his life—and help that Russian scum harm the woman."

Jean-Yves glanced at him petulantly, annoyed. "I needed money. He had it. What can I tell you, old man? Life is hard."

"Yes." Kyril nodded solemnly. "It is." Then he brought the automobile to a sudden stop at the edge of a deserted quay close to one of the Seine's bridges. Not a soul in sight.

Silently he shut off the motor, hopped out, went to the passenger side, slashed the cords that bound Jean-Yves to the handle of the door, and motioned to him to get out.

"What are we going to do?" the boy demanded, nervously looking around for any sign of life. "Where are we going? Let's go back to Viznitski's," he said, his voice rising. "I'll hand him over to you personally if you like. I promise! I'll tell the police everything. You can keep the money," he babbled, trying to break away and run, hands still tied in front of him.

Kyril looked at him with contempt, took out a revolver from inside his jacket, and aimed carefully at the fleeing boy. As Jean-Yves was lunging awkwardly along the quay, staggering like a drunken bear, the Montenegrin fired twice, shooting him in both legs.

"Oh God!" wailed the Frenchman. "Help! Help me!"

He crashed to the cobbled ground, one kneecap shattered, one shinbone splintered. Kyril approached, slowly and solemnly as death, observing his victim as he lay writhing in the pale glow of the moonlight.

"Oh, help me! Don't kill me! I'll go to the police with you. I'll turn myself in. I'll turn Viznitski in! Anything you want."

"Good," nodded Kyril as he lifted Jean-Yves, screaming in pain, to his feet. As the boy collapsed, he dragged him to the edge of the quay, gave him a swift kick, and sent him hurtling over the edge. He waited till he heard the splash before returning to the automobile. Then the Montenegrin made a slow semicircle with the Panhard and headed back across town to pay a midnight call on the Russian.

*

When André Viznitski was awakened from a sound sleep that night, he opened his eyes and froze at the sight of a revolver pointed straight at his head. The man holding the weapon was so frightening, he made André's flesh creep.

"You—Russian," the thug said, "why the hell are you trying to harm Maeve? Give me a good answer before I blow your brains out."

The question—the command—was so unexpected André could only stare, speechless from fright and bewilderment.

"Maeve? I don't know anyone by that name," he lied—not very well.

"Don't act stupid," Kyril ordered. "We both know you're responsible, and now you're going to pay for your sins."

Viznitski's mind was racing. How did this creature know what he'd done? Was he dreaming? Was he having a nightmare?

The thug was looking at him with such intensity André was terrified. It was almost as if he could see into his soul. He *knew*—but how could he? He had been so careful!

"Don't kill me," Count Viznitski pleaded. "I wanted revenge but then it got out of hand. I'm sorry," he added, almost as an afterthought. "I let myself get carried away. I never planned to kill the boy . . ."

"No," Kyril retorted. "You were going to let him do it to himself, poor bastard!"

Viznitski was disoriented, fearful, staring at the barrel of a gun. His mind was in a state of panic, his nerves shattered.

"Let me go," he begged. "I'll give you money if you let me go away. I'll never go near Moira again. Or her daughter either. Never . . ."

The thug with the drooping mustache kept studying him carefully, looking at him as if still undecided.

Abruptly the intruder said, "You will write a confession. Then, if I am satisfied, I'll let you leave town. Understand?"

"Yes," Viznitski nodded. "I'll leave Paris. I'll never return. Word of honor! I'll make it up to the women, I promise!"

Kyril kept watching him intently, disturbed by something. With Count Viznitski still under the barrel of his revolver, he allowed him to get out of bed and find paper and pen. He stood facing him, still holding the Browning as André scribbled away, hand trembling, face twitching with fright.

"This is my guarantee I'll never return to Paris," Viznitski babbled. "You can put me on the train yourself. It will be a solemn agreement between the two of us."

When André Viznitski handed his visitor the paper, Kyril glanced at it, then stared incredulously at the Russian.

"This has nothing to do with why I'm here," he declared, shocked. "You bastard . . ."

And with that he seized André by the lapels of his pajamas, caught him off balance, and sent him crashing headfirst through the windows and down to the sidewalk three stories below. It took less than four seconds.

Pocketing the letter Viznitski had just finished, Kyril quickly fled the apartment and was driving away before any curious neighbor even bothered to glance out the window into the darkened street.

Well, he had kept his word to the Russian, Kyril thought as he guided his motorcar through deserted streets. He *had* sent him out of town. Straight to hell.

Chewing the drooping end of his thick mustache, the Montenegrin shook his head in amazement at the confession he had badgered out of Viznitski. It wasn't the one he'd expected. But it was going to make Ivan Petrovic happy. Not to mention the women.

*

RUSSIAN SUICIDE CONFESSES TO MURDER was the headline *Le Figaro* carried two days later when it revealed to its readers that the notorious playboy Count André Viznitski had left behind a signed confession before hurling himself through his apartment window in a midnight fit of guilt. The letter had arrived anonymously and carried a Paris postmark.

"I lured Gianni Milonari into the street while his nursemaid was talking to an acquaintance. I then took him to a deserted stable, where I strangled him. The child fought for his life, but it was all over in a matter of minutes. I really had nothing against the child. I was even fond of him in my own way. It was all done to incriminate Moira Lassiter, who was well known for her hatred toward him. In this way I hoped to ruin her and her daughter. The boy was just the means to an end."

This was one of the biggest scandals of the year. People who had been shunning Moira suddenly came calling to offer their belated condolences to Charlie and to assure both Lassiters they had never really put any faith in those dreadful rumors.

Charlie was nearly numb with grief at the idea that anyone could have hated Moira enough to concoct such a demented revenge. He withdrew into himself for a time and worried his wife enough to make her take care he was never out of her sight. In a way it drew them even closer, since Charlie was now justified in his firm belief that his wife had been as much a victim as his poor child.

Moira's reaction to Viznitski's confession was so muted as to make those who knew her wonder. She had been vindicated and was so overwhelmed she couldn't trust herself to show her emotions. Gianni Milonari was no longer a threat, but she couldn't rejoice about it. As much as she'd hated the child, she was sorry he'd been removed from her life like this. How much better for everyone if he'd succumbed to influenza or diphtheria, she thought. It would have spared her untold anguish. And Charlie, too, of course. But she relished her role as a martyr.

Since she couldn't prove it, Maeve never told her mother that André had been helped into the next world by a shove from Kyril, but she said to Sean Farrell that whoever caused Viznitski to unburden himself deserved her gratitude. And Kyril *had* said Marco's troubles were over.

"Perhaps it was some latent desire to make amends," Sean said with a nod.

"Or perhaps he had help out the window," she replied, more to the point.

Sean never gave her an answer to that. Kyril feigned total ignorance.

Marc Antoine was unnerved a few days later to discover an article about the suicide of another Parisian, one Jean-Yves Bourdonne, found floating in the Seine.

"Maeve!" he shouted as he burst into her dressing room. "What have you done?" Poor Marco was so shocked he was shaking.

He never got a real answer to that question either, but to his surprise he received a small package in the mail containing most of the blackmail money that Jean-Yves left behind.

"Maeve," he asked nervously, "who took care of this? Does anyone know?" Marc Antoine had visions of the police paying them both a visit.

"Marco," she replied, "don't question your good luck. Just accept it. Believe me, it's the best way."

He never brought the subject up again.

*

Laura Milonari took the news somewhat differently, screaming that Moira Lassiter was behind this, too, accusing her of revenging herself on André for jilting her several years earlier, and raising such an uproar at Viznitski's funeral that a flic was called in to escort her out of the church.

"Mental problems" was the diagnosis of the examining physician at the clinic where they brought Laura that afternoon. "Delusions of persecution and advanced paranoia," he wrote on a small white file card. "The patient needs rest and complete isolation for the time being. The strain of losing her child has undermined her sanity and has made her incapable of conducting herself responsibly in society. Recommendation:

a stay of unspecified duration at the Charité Hospital where she can be treated and observed."

Laura was still screaming about Moira Lassiter when they wrapped her in a straitjacket and carted her off to the asylum.

CHAPTER 29

*M*aeve was delighted to be able to accompany Dietrich to Vienna on one of his trips when it turned out they both had business there. While her husband attended to banking matters, Baroness von Reuter would be listening to what the Director of the Court Opera might offer as an enticement to get La Devereux to perform there. That the Viennese wanted her to grace the Court Opera was a good indication they were also prepared to offer substantial financial compensation. Or at least Maeve hoped so.

Dietrich's business was not so straightforward, and he wasn't pleased at Maeve's insistence on accompanying him to Vienna. Charged with informing the mysterious Herr Jakopic that he could expect no further support from his European sponsors, Dietrich wasn't too sanguine about his reaction. The baron had read the newspapers and was therefore au courant with the volatile situation in Montenegro—and if this tall, craggy-faced, mustachioed Herr Jakopic wasn't one of the group that had tried to assassinate Prince Nikolai, then nobody was! The fellow had murder in his deep-set black eyes and practically oozing from his pores.

Dietrich was now quite anxious to put as much distance as possible between himself and these desperadoes. The thought of Sean Farrell ever finding out about his role in financing his father's would-be assassins was enough to make his flesh crawl. And at this point, he wasn't even certain that Farrell's friendship with Maeve would be enough to protect him from an untimely death if the truth ever came out. These damned Montenegrins were savages—and the Irish were nearly as bad! They both had such *severe* family feelings, a trait completely foreign to him.

The meeting with Herr Jakopic in the dining room of the Hotel Sacher was even uglier than Dietrich could have imagined. Incensed at his abandonment by his backers, the furious Herr Jakopic turned on the young banker, reviling him as a messenger boy and demanding to be put in touch with his masters. He wasn't finished with them, he announced arrogantly. But he had nothing further to say to Dietrich, whom he insulted lavishly in fluent gutter German.

Stunned by this public abuse from such vermin, the young baron departed the dining room with as much dignity as possible, but his heart was pounding with humiliation—and fear. These Serb maniacs were all dangerous, unstable madmen. For the first time it occurred to Dietrich that he was in over his head, playing at intrigues he had no right to attempt.

In his shame he found himself thinking Hubertus would never have allowed such scum to berate him in public. Hubertus would have made mincemeat of this Herr Jakopic. Why hadn't he been able to do something of the sort? Perhaps his father had been right about him. Perhaps he was not a real von Reuter but a fraud, a foolish, ungifted pawn who had allowed himself to be used by the bureaucrats only to be abused by this Jakopic trash. Dietrich's face was flushed with embarrassment as he made his way out of the Hotel Sacher, still reeling with indignation.

As he was walking distractedly along Kärntnerstrasse not far from St. Stephen's Cathedral, Dietrich was startled to feel a tap on his shoulder. Turning around in near fright, he found himself staring into the large brown eyes of Zofia Farrell, all alone and bundled into her sables on this frigid winter afternoon.

"Herr Baron." She smiled pleasantly. "What a nice surprise! And what brings you to Vienna? Where is your wife?"

"Conferring on musical matters," he replied, avoiding her first question. "And where is your husband?"

"On business," she said with another smile as she slipped her arm through his. "How nice to see you again. You're looking so well. Black always suited you," she declared, eyeing his fine cashmere coat and jaunty fur hat.

Dietrich felt the pressure of Zofia's arm as she leaned close to him. He could smell the scent of patchouli, warmed by her sables and perfuming the air around her—a rich, heady scent, very appropriate for this girl, he thought.

"Shall we walk together?" she suggested, smiling again into his eyes.

"Why not?" sighed Dietrich. It would be a pleasure after what he had just been subjected to, even though the idea now made him nervous.

Under any other circumstances, the baron would have been excited by the prospect of strolling arm in arm with the lovely Zofia; right now, the fact that she was Sean Farrell's wife made him uneasy. He had suddenly acquired a serious antipathy toward everything Montenegrin.

After strolling at length along the Ringstrasse, past an impressive collection of monuments to imperial Austria, Zofia complained of the cold and demanded to be taken back to her hotel. She was practically clinging to his arm, Dietrich now noticed with annoyance. That was how preoccupied he had become. He ought to have been more considerate of a woman in her condition. She was quite visibly pregnant.

After much wheedling on Zofia's part, she persuaded the baron to join her for tea in the hotel's pleasant *salon de thé*, an oasis of green palms and art nouveau stained-glass ceilings. Choosing a table sheltered by a small screen of potted palms and a trellis of white and pink roses, Zofia allowed Dietrich to help her out of her sables and flung them in a thick, glossy pile on the sofa beside her. On her head was a charming hat of the same rich fur, her delicate features framed by a fluff of soft dark sable and flushed by her promenade in the cold air. Even impending motherhood didn't detract from her good looks.

Dietrich, she noticed, was quite unlike himself. Well, why not? she thought cynically, after what had just happened to him. But even that was nothing compared with what he was about to experience. She would enjoy this.

"Herr Baron," Zofia declared after she and her guest had been served, "we Montenegrins are engaged in a struggle in which there can be only one winner . . ."

"I'm well aware of your connections, madame," Dietrich replied with a certain weariness.

"But you don't understand what I'm trying to say," Zofia snapped. "We who view things differently from Nikolai Petrovic need your help if we are going to win. We need money. So let's not have any more of these cheap excuses from our Western backers. Keep the money flowing! Now!"

For a second Dietrich only stared at her. Then he turned very pale and looked as if he was about to collapse from shock.

"You have no secrets from me, Herr Baron," she said. "You've been dealing with my father."

"What?" He suddenly felt as if he was strangling. The air had become suffocatingly close, with its blend of cigarette smoke, flowers, Zofia's patchouli scent, and the smell of his own fear. He was speechless before this woman who was smiling at him in a way that made him ache to slap her. He'd been had!

"Your contact is Milan Plamanac, not Jakopic," Zofia announced, enjoying Dietrich's sickly pallor. "And we aren't going to let you off so easily. Not you."

Dietrich saw himself plunging headlong into an abyss, bereft of all protection.

"What do you want from me?" he asked finally, his heart pounding.

"Money." Zofia shrugged.

"Out of the question. Your sponsors have lost patience with you. They won't send you any more!"

The Montenegrin girl laughed pleasantly, as if the baron had made an amusing little joke. "I'm talking about you," she informed him. "You're a banker. You have plenty of money."

"Impossible. I can't make you a loan to help finance a revolution!"

"I'm talking about a sum of money to prevent me from telling your wife and my husband what you've done. If either of them were to discover your part in the attempted coup, there'd be hell to pay."

Dietrich's hand tightened around the china cup he held, nearly spilling his tea all over the spotless linen cloth as he stared at this witch opposite him. This couldn't be happening, he thought in a panic. It had to be some sort of bad dream.

"You're out of your mind! I'd accuse *you*!" he stammered.

"No"—Zofia smiled—"you wouldn't. Ivan would kill you. He would never believe you—and he wouldn't harm the mother of his unborn child. So you see, Herr Baron, you really should just hand over the money and mind your business. Or are you so anxious to face Ivan Petrovic with pistols? He's a dead shot."

And with that Zofia rose and bade Dietrich a casual farewell—after stipulating her price for silence: one hundred thousand marks in bank notes.

"Think about it," she said. Then flinging her magnificent sables over her shoulders, she sauntered out to the general admiration of the entire room.

*

In despair Dietrich did think about it, and in the end he tried desperately to get hold of the fatso at the foreign ministry, but he couldn't even locate him. There is no one by that name in this department, came the answer from half a dozen secretaries. You are mistaken, *mein Herr*.

Abandoned by the double-dealing bureaucracy and faced with Zofia's threats, Dietrich was nearly unstrung. He didn't dare let Maeve find out about this for fear she would despise him—first as a backstabber, then as an embezzler. To his horror, he had actually become those things, and that made it all the worse. He had been undone by his vanity, and now he was prey for the vultures. In desperation he withdrew the money, terrified of being discovered, and delivered it to Madame Sean Farrell, who accepted it with all the graciousness a fox might bestow on a plump chicken.

The worst thing was that Dietrich was chronically short of cash, a condition aggravated by liberal overspending and recent losses in the stock market. He didn't have enough at his disposal to replace the money. Most of his fortune was presently in his Paris mansion, his Berlin residence, and Maeve's jewel case. If he was lucky, he would have a brief period of time before his secret was ferreted out. Then disgrace, the likes of which no von Reuter had ever been subjected to before, would engulf him, ruining him for all time.

If Dietrich was near hysteria over his actions, Zofia Farrell was as cool as steel. Back in Paris she welcomed Sean home with all the concern of a loving wife, forcefully disavowed any knowledge of her family's actions, pledged undying devotion to the Petrovic dynasty, and pointedly reminded her spouse that she was carrying his child, the grandchild of Nikolai Petrovic. How then could she raise a hand against them? It would be like disowning her own baby.

Taking Zofia at her word—if only to spare himself the anguish of doubting her—Sean accepted her story. But he had begun to sleep with a revolver hidden behind their bed.

*

Ten days after Zofia's return from Vienna, she and her husband were awakened in the middle of the night by a sudden burst of light flooding their bedroom and by the sound of a revolver being cocked. Before Sean could even reach for his weapon, he felt the cold barrel of his father-in-law's Browning pressed against his temple and heard a rough voice ordering him to keep still.

"Papa!" Zofia exclaimed, jostled out of a sound sleep. "What are you doing here?"

"Looking for my money," he replied. "Now hand it over before I splatter the wall with your brains—and his!"

"What are you talking about?" she demanded, frightened. "What money?"

"The money from our German contact. Don't play games with me, you devious little witch. I had someone watch you in Vienna. You're not as clever as you think!"

And as the young couple stared at him, a second man appeared behind Milan, a short, squat fellow with a full walrus mustache and a mane of black hair. And a large revolver.

"You, Marko, keep an eye on Ivan Petrovic," Milan ordered. "I'll deal with my daughter."

Seizing the girl by her long black hair, he flung her out of bed and onto the floor. Then he grabbed a crystal water carafe from her overdecorated dressing table and smashed it against the glass surface, producing a weapon with a vicious jagged edge.

"Now," he said as he held the razor-sharp glass against Zofia's cheek, "talk, or I'll cut your pretty face to ribbons."

"Leave her alone, you old bastard!" Sean roared. But Milan's henchman pressed the revolver to his head and prevented him from moving.

Eyeball to eyeball with her father as he threatened her with the broken carafe—two inches from her lovely face—Zofia suddenly burst into hysterical laughter. Then just as abruptly she stopped and said, as if it were the most normal thing in the world, "But Papa, don't you know when I'm only joking? I was keeping it safe for *you*."

Then to Sean's bewilderment she led Milan to the deep recesses of a hiding place in her dressing room and emerged with a leather satchel filled with German bank notes.

"You bitch!" said Sean. "I might have known."

"I hate you both!" Zofia said with feeling. "I would have loved to see you kill each other!"

"And what would you have got out of this, Zofia?" Sean demanded, furious enough to kill *her*.

"One hundred thousand marks' worth of freedom!" she replied, seizing the fox bedspread and flinging it in Milan's face. Temporarily blinded and trapped by the heavy fur, he tripped and discharged his revolver, staggering into the furniture.

At the first hint of commotion, the henchman spun around to protect his boss. Sean was out of bed in an instant, reaching for his hidden revolver and firing off two shots at Marko which struck the man in the arm and chest, felling him like an oak.

Now Zofia was screaming in terror as her husband lunged at her, grabbed her by the throat, and pinned her, shrieking, to the floor.

"You bitch! Tell me why I shouldn't kill you now!" he shouted. "You were part of the plot! You knew!"

Gasping for breath, Zofia flailed at him in a frenzy, panic-stricken and crazed with fright. Before Sean could strangle her in his outrage, Milan grabbed him by the hair and pulled him off her, holding him at bay with his Browning, forcing Sean to drop his own weapon.

"Ivan!" Zofia gasped, half dazed from the attack. "The baby! Kill me and you kill him!"

"You'd be well rid of her," Milan grunted. Then, standing over the little traitor, his wayward child, Milan Plamanac fired three bullets into her head and chest, splattering the valuable Aubusson carpet with scarlet.

As he raised his weapon to shoot his stunned son-in-law, Sean sprang at him, knocked him over the body, and crashed to the floor with him— sending them both sprawling over the carpet and causing Milan to drop the gun.

Milan bit Sean viciously as they struggled for the revolver, then suddenly gained a momentary advantage and kicked him violently in the groin. While his son-in-law writhed in agony on the floor, Milan freed himself from his grasp and rose unsteadily to his feet, seizing his Browning as he did.

"Die, Petrovic bastard," he murmured with satisfaction as he fired his remaining shots at Sean, somewhat shakily, nearly exhausted from such a fight at his age.

As the last bullet left the chamber, Milan realized there were sounds in the hall. The servants had probably been alerted to the disturbance by this time. Well, servants were useless creatures, no threat to a man like him. Then he suddenly prodded Marko with his boot and realized the man was dead. Damn. It was at that point he remembered Kyril. He must be in the house. Shit! That one was a savage. He'd be dead if Kyril ever found him!

But there was one last act of hatred Milan wanted to commit against the Petrovic dynasty, and he wanted it so much he was willing to risk an encounter with Kyril. Taking out a sharp Turkish stiletto, Milan Plamanac plunged it into Zofia's belly, slitting her like a pig and ripping out the baby. With a final loathsome gesture, he looked at his dead grandson and decapitated the tiny corpse, flinging it onto the carpet beside its mother.

*

When Ivan Petrovic awakened, he was lying in another room of his home with Kyril and his housekeeper standing at his bedside looking grim. The housekeeper, a Montenegrin, had obviously been weeping for a long time; her eyes were red and swollen. Kyril looked like a granite statue. Not a tear in his dark eyes, just tremendous, passionate hatred for Milan Plamanac and what he had done. Ivan noticed dully that Kyril's right arm was in a sling.

"Kyril," Sean whispered, trying to lift himself up and failing badly, "how is Zofia? Is she alive?" His worry was for his baby.

The Montenegrin blinked hard, pressed his lips together as if he was fighting to control himself, and slowly shook his head. "No. The old bastard killed her. He killed your son, too."

Before Sean could react to anything but the news of Zofia's death, a doctor appeared from behind Kyril and the woman and administered a painkiller, taking him by surprise. Before he could ask his servant how he knew the baby was a boy, he was lying back against the pillows once more, drifting into a soft, drugged sleep, his right shoulder shattered by a bullet and two other bullets lodged in his arm.

"We'll kill that old bastard," Kyril promised, speaking to an unconscious Ivan Petrovic. "I give you my word of honor. And if I have to do it myself, I promise that, too."

In all his life, Kyril had never seen anything like the nightmare he beheld in that room. Shot by Milan as he came rushing down the corridor, he had shot back, failed to bring down his target, and then staggered, wounded, toward the bedroom, where the stench of gunpowder lay heavily in the air. It hovered over the bodies like a shroud of gray mist.

There beside the bed was Zofia in a widening pool of blood, shot in the head and chest, her nightgown ripped to shreds, her belly torn open by a knife. The mutilated baby, a boy, lay close by his mother.

Horrified beyond belief, Kyril would have fled the room to vomit in the corridor but for his fear for Ivan Petrovic. He had to see if the young man had somehow survived the slaughter. When he emerged from that abattoir, dragging his master with him and shouting hoarsely for help, some of the servants who hadn't run off came scurrying out of their holes. The doctor and the police arrived at the same time, summoned by the frantic housekeeper, who had had the good sense to telephone for help at the first sound of gunfire.

*

Nothing so gruesome had happened in Western Europe in peacetime since the days of Jack the Ripper. The news of the attack on Sean and his wife was on the front page of every newspaper in Paris and mentioned in every paper from New York to St. Petersburg.

The day after the revolting murder, the Montenegrin ambassador to Paris paid a visit to Ivan Petrovic to verify his condition and question the servants. Prince Nikolai would want a full account.

Two days after the attack, the Gräfin Geraldine disembarked from the Nord Express and installed herself in her son's home to supervise his recovery. Her first task was to plan the funeral, which she did with great efficiency. Zofia and her son were buried side by side in the Orthodox cemetery in Paris, accompanied to their graves by representatives of the diplomatic community and members of society.

Despite his mother's furious opposition, Sean attended the service, wounded, in pain, and barely able to stand. He didn't care if it killed him, he told Geraldine. Zofia and that child were not going to be buried with him lying at home. Zofia was nothing to him, but the baby was his.

The grand duchesses Militza and Stana arrived too late for the ceremony, delayed by a snowstorm en route from St. Petersburg, but their presence did a lot to comfort their brother. They had never seen him so close to the edge, and they anxiously asked Kyril for information, horrified by the stories in the papers. Out of earshot of Ivan Petrovic, the Montenegrin informed them of the vendetta that now existed between the Petrovici and the Plamanacs, revealing the details of Jordje's death in Cetinje. And Zofia's shocking betrayal of both Ivan and Milan.

*

The attack on Sean and Zofia had been as much a shock to Maeve and Moira as it was to Geraldine, and they headed for the Farrell residence as soon as they heard the news, all of them alerted by Kyril, who dispatched a telegram as soon as his own wounds had been tended and he felt he could safely leave Ivan Petrovic's side for a few minutes to dictate the text to one of the French servants. They were there when Geraldine arrived in the foyer of the Farrell mansion, and the gräfin realized with a jolt that she was going to have to deal with Moira Lassiter.

The two women had stared at each other in stunned surprise, not having met since the last days of the Boer War and having no particular desire to meet again.

In an elegant gesture, Geraldine had divested herself of her magnificent sable coat, glided toward Moira—who was not looking all that welcoming—and held out both hands, gazing at her with the kind of expression people tend to adopt during moments of great personal crisis or tremendous natural disaster.

It had occurred to Moira to slap that pious expression from Geraldine Farrell's lovely face, but with Zofia lying in a coffin two rooms
away and Sean upstairs in bed with a fever from his wounds, she had
chosen to take the high ground and clasped the proffered hands, accepted
an airy kiss on the cheek, and had said, "It's good that you came as soon
as possible. Sean's wounds aren't life-threatening, but he's in a terrible
state. His father-in-law shot Zofia and ripped the baby out of the womb.
Then he decapitated the poor little mite. It was savage."

At that point, the gräfin had covered her mouth with her hands and
turned ashen, staring at Moira as if she was about to be sick.

"Your son swore he'd kill him and he's anxious to go after him.
Talk to him and tell him to wait until he's in better shape," Moira
suggested. "Otherwise, it will be plain suicide."

"The fool. He'll kill himself! No. He has to get better. Milan will
keep," Geraldine said, shaken. "But is he really out of danger?"

"According to his doctors, he is. But they're still struggling with
that fever."

There had been shock when Geraldine entered her son's room.
Maeve and Dietrich were keeping him company. The Devereux had
already established a beachhead, the gräfin thought. Perhaps the time
had come for a reunion.

"Mama," Sean said weakly. "Thank God. Did you hear?" he asked
abruptly.

"Yes. It's beyond belief," she said gently as she leaned over him to
kiss his forehead. "He'll die for it, don't worry."

"I hope he doesn't die until I'm ready to kill him," her son replied
weakly. "He's mine. And I won't relinquish the pleasure of killing him
to anyone."

The Petrovici were outraged over the Plamanacs' treachery. That
a member of the senate and a lifelong adviser could commit treason, plot
with the country's two worst enemies, and attempt to murder one of the
Prince's sons—and unborn grandson—made them wild for revenge.
Zofia's murder was looked upon as her just deserts and Milan's privilege.

Milan and his second son Stefan were listed as wanted men and
their possessions confiscated. Nikolai Petrovic was reported to be enlisting
the aid of the Tsar's secret police—one of the most corrupt but all-
encompassing spy agencies in existence, with its minions lurking in every
European capital. Wherever the Plamanacs had gone, they wouldn't
remain hidden long, Nikolai swore. And when he got his hands on them,
he was thinking of reestablishing the ancient custom of impaling traitors'
heads on the tower in the middle of his capital.

*

The horror of Zofia's murder affected all who knew her. The repulsive barbarism of it left people aghast, none more so than Dietrich, who was nearly unhinged by fear of her father. Moira was affected too, and her horror at the girl's mutilation was giving her nightmares. It was undermining her health.

As Moira lay in bed at night, she found herself going back to that hideous episode at the clinic in Neuilly, caught halfway between life and death through a quack doctor's error, with only her own stubbornness to keep her alive. And her nightmares now had a new theme. As she hovered just this side of death, calling frantically for Maeveen, Moira saw little Gianni appear at the far end of a long, dark corridor, running slowly toward her. When he had almost reached her, she would wake up, gasping for breath, shaken and terrified, frantic to flee.

After these nightmares had robbed her of sleep for three weeks in a row, she decided to consult a doctor. He told her the problem was due to strained nerves and suggested a cure in either Budapest or Karlsbad, where the waters were supposedly beneficial to ladies with nervous disorders. The cumulative effect of this past year had been deadly.

Since Charlie knew an Austrian archduke with a castle in the environs of Budapest and an estate stocked with every variety of wild game, it was off to the Hungarian capital with hopes that the famous waters would work their magic on Moira. If they didn't, at least the prospect of bagging hundreds of pheasants or deer would soothe Charlie. Paris Singer, heir to the sewing machine fortune and an old friend, was going to accompany them and help distract Moira.

CHAPTER 30

*D*ietrich's frequent trips to Berlin no longer bothered Maeve so much. Herr von Richter really was in poor health and she understood the need for Dietrich's presence there. But she couldn't help regretting the emptiness in her personal life. Her husband had changed this past year, and he was no longer as excited by her career as he had been.

"He's been called 'Monsieur Devereux' once too often," was how Arlette saw it, and she was as shrewd as they come.

The pleasure seemed to have gone out of it for him. It was as though Dietrich, having expended so much energy on steering Maeve to the top of her career, had suddenly lost interest in the game.

Her near death onstage had rekindled something of his former feeling but it was short-lived, with conflicts of scheduling putting an end to plans for a romantic second honeymoon in Venice. If it hadn't been for Hanno's presence, Maeve thought, Dietrich would probably never even bother coming back to their beautiful Paris home. As it was, his presence was becoming rarer and rarer. And she missed him. A lot.

"I feel so old, Letty," she said unexpectedly one day several months after Zofia's murder. "Do people reach a point in life when youth suddenly vanishes and everything turns stale—even if they're not really old?"

"I don't think so, madame," the French girl replied, startled by that plaintive tone. "I think people become discouraged from time to time and take things more seriously than they should. Everything passes. You should know that by now."

"Yes," Maeve sighed. "But it seems to be all the best things that pass!" She was secretly afraid she was losing her husband.

Arlette sat beside her and looked at her very candidly, her large dark eyes pensive. "I've been with you for a few years now, madame," she said, "and I've been very happy working for you. In that time I've seen lots of changes, and they've been for the better. You're now much more sure of yourself than you were at the start of your career, but this seems to worry Monsieur le baron. I think he liked it better when you brought every little problem to him and begged for his advice. It made him feel necessary."

"He's necessary to me *now!*" Maeve protested. "I love Dietrich. His opinion is important." And he had become so distant, so oddly remote. His eyes had a strange distracted look now.

"It wasn't with *Salome*," Arlette replied, rather daringly. "You knew what he would think of your costume, and you did it your way all the same. You were correct in your artistic judgment . . ."

Maeve smiled wryly. Arlette was not going to finish that thought by adding, "but very foolish as a wife." Well, it was true. It was the first major disagreement they'd had and she had prevailed—at the cost of seeing Dietrich leave New York.

What did he want from her? she wondered bitterly. He had encouraged her to become a prima donna, been pleased at first, and now seemed to prefer something else. If he had wanted a hausfrau, she thought, then why hadn't he stayed married to the dumpling?

*

Marc Antoine's explanation of the baron's behavior was jealousy—not jealousy of a particular man but of her career.

"Picture it, Maeve," he declared one afternoon as they sat at the Café de la Paix after rehearsals for Verdi's *Don Carlo* in which he was singing the title role and Maeve was singing Elisabeth. "Dietrich is a banker, born and bred to a job he finds stultifying. He has an artistic streak that seeks an outlet in his wife's career, but this never offers him real satisfaction. He watches you bloom as you create a role and have the chance to lose yourself in some other persona while he himself is stuck with being Baron von Reuter, banker and Prussian, till the day he dies. It must be hard on him," the tenor reflected sympathetically. "You have so many more lives than he can ever have."

Looking at things that way, Maeve thought Marc Antoine might be right. He was very good at unraveling motivation and he knew Dietrich by now. There was another reason. As a male he was probably closer to understanding another male than she was.

Before they left the café, Maeve asked her partner if he thought Dietrich still loved her. Her unhappiness was so transparent the tenor felt a catch at his heart.

Marc Antoine's green eyes looked down, an evasive gesture that made her despair. He seemed to be considering the question very carefully, almost too carefully.

Finally he said, "I think Dietrich is so confused in his own mind that he no longer knows what he feels. Be kind to him. Make him feel adored. Don't be contrary. And act more like a mistress than a wife," he added. "Cosset him."

That made sense, Maeve thought as she sat in her American limousine on the way home. But it also sounded as if Marc Antoine, too, saw her marriage as vulnerable and in need of buttressing, like a house that has been weakened by too many storms. It wasn't the sort of opinion that offered much comfort. It reminded her of a doctor advising the family of a dying man to keep the patient comfortable—and send for the priest as soon as possible.

Ah, Dietrich, *Schatzi*, she thought miserably, how did we ever end up like this? She could almost feel Hubertus's spiteful presence in the shadows delivering a pompous "I told you so."

*

Her mother was struggling with problems of another kind altogether. Moira had returned from Budapest with two secrets. The first was the discovery by a Hungarian doctor that her insides were not as badly mangled as her German specialist seemed to think, and in the opinion of this Dr. Ferenc, her sterility was caused by a simple polyp on the cervix, which he removed. He warned her, however, that as a woman in her mid-forties it might have made more sense for her to remain safely sterile, childbirth being so much more dangerous at her age.

The other secret was that she and Paris Singer had discovered an unbearable attraction for each other one afternoon while Charlie was out slaughtering game, and this had led to an abysmal loss of self-control in a hunting lodge deep in the forests of her host's estate.

It hadn't been premeditated, Moira told herself. She had been walking with Singer in the woods and they had taken shelter from the rain. Soaked and in need of dry clothing, they started a fire, hung their drenched outer clothing up to dry, and curled up on a sofa with a glass of schnapps. Moira put most of the blame on the schnapps for what happened afterward.

I was seduced, Moira rationalized. Paris Singer wasn't a man to be trusted with anything in skirts. He was a reprobate.

Singer, a tall blond fellow who reminded Maeve of the old Teutonic warriors from Wagner's operas, was very handsome, very rich, and highly susceptible to beauty in female form. The combination of setting, privacy, and proximity to Moira's half-dressed person was a heady temptation, and the schnapps took away the last lingering inhibitions the couple may have felt. Suddenly Moira found herself in Paris's arms, inciting him to venture well past the kissing stage.

"My God," he murmured as he caressed Mrs. Lassiter's full bosom, quivering above its rigid corset, "I want you. But I'm ashamed to do this to Charlie."

"So am I," she agreed, wrapping her arms around him. "It's not right."

There seemed to be mutual agreement about that. They both nodded seriously, looked decently embarrassed, and started kissing all over again, with Moira sliding farther and farther down under Paris Singer as she began to unfasten every lace, bow, and button in sight.

"This will be the first and last time," he declared to make himself feel better.

Moira nodded vigorously as he pulled off his trousers and silk drawers. Her clothes were already lying in a heap on the rough carpet, with the corset on top of the pile.

It was a long couch they were lying on, and Paris was thoughtful enough to see to it that Moira's pretty head was cushioned by a couple of throw pillows—embroidered with pious mottoes in Hungarian. The one directly beneath her glossy black tresses proclaimed: "A virtuous woman is a pearl beyond price."

As Moira buried her face against his neck, Singer ran his hand lightly over her soft curves, murmuring endearments as he explored her body. Then, as Moira wrapped her arms tighter around him and kissed his ear, he gently began to stroke her inner thigh, nibbling on her right nipple.

A little quiver of pleasure from Moira, followed by a series of ecstatic gasps and the unequivocal directive to keep going, roused Singer to greater efforts. Soon he was inside her, excited but anxious at the hysterical sounds the woman made.

"Am I hurting you?" he gasped as Moira seized his blond hair and sank her fingers into his curls.

"No," she murmured, eyes slightly glazed.

"Good."

He felt himself wheezing as she wrapped her legs around him and slid further into his embrace. Singer closed his eyes and moved deeper inside her, still gasping a little in bewilderment as she loosened her grip on his hair and dug her fingers into his back instead.

It was not a gentlemanly thought, he admitted to himself later as he and Moira lay limp and exhausted on the old couch, but how in the world did Charlie Lassiter survive living with this woman? He was surprised Charlie wasn't bald from having his hair ripped out.

After they had made love the first time, Moira then shocked him by climbing on top of him and ravishing *him*. That upset Singer. He knew it shouldn't have, since what they were doing was not condoned by either church or state, but the idea of a woman being so shameless, not to mention pleasure-crazed, disturbed him.

He liked taking the initiative in these matters. It was one of life's delights to make love to a beautiful woman and then share the warm afterglow—lying in her arms feeling sated, reading the weary satisfaction in her sleepy eyes. Having her pounce on him was just plain unseemly.

It didn't agree with Singer's ideas about feminine behavior and it made him think Charlie had bitten off a lot more than he could chew. Moira was oversexed, he decided. She'd kill poor Charlie if this was a sample of her normal bedroom style. He wondered how Charlie Lassiter could ever permit such blatant aggression from a wife. It just wasn't done.

Despite all those thoughts, Singer found Moira such a fascinating little vixen he couldn't even consider avoiding her. In fact, he was quivering with anticipation at the thought of what she might do next time.

*

Since Maeve's early disaster as Juliette in Berlin, she had mixed feelings about singing there. It was Dietrich's city and the gräfin's, and she still wanted to dazzle the populace, who were quite besotted with that *other* Geraldine and inclined to make comparisons.

In the spring of 1910, when Maeve was beginning a round of performances at Covent Garden, she was presented to Crown Prince Friedrich Wilhelm and Crown Princess Cécilie of Prussia. Young Fritz had a good memory for a pretty face, and he recalled meeting Maeve on her arrival in Germany all those years ago and seeing her more recently onstage at the Berlin Royal Opera. He even inquired about her dear mama, whom he had encountered on several occasions at hunts in East Prussia and Austria.

"Amazing woman, your mother," he enthused. "One of the best female shots I've ever met."

"Mama does lots of things well, Your Highness." Maeve smiled, recalling that avalanche of flowers years ago in Berlin. And the diamond bracelet.

"Yes," he nodded. "She certainly does."

Cécilie, an unusually beautiful princess whose mother was a Russian grand duchess, enjoyed opera and was looking for the right singer to use in one of her charity extravaganzas this winter.

Honoring Maeve with an invitation to tea at London's German Embassy, she explained that her Russian relatives had spoken highly of the diva's talent and her generosity at the time of the Russo-Japanese War. Apparently that Red Cross benefit had made a greater impression than Maeve realized.

"How can I help you, Your Highness?" Maeve asked, wondering what the princess was getting at.

Cécilie smiled and replied that she would like to ask Madame Devereux to appear in a charity performance of Franz Lehár's *The Merry Widow* to be given at Christmas at the Royal Opera to benefit the Berlin orphanages, one of her pet charities.

This means no fee, Maeve thought. They think everyone is as rich as they are.

"I'm honored, Your Highness," she said as the German footmen hovered over her, anxious to refill her teacup or offer another petit four. "But I'll have to consult my manager to see if it's possible. I'm scheduled for a series of performances this winter."

"Oh, I do hope you can help us, madame," said Cécilie. "My father-in-law enjoyed your last Berlin appearance so much. And so did we. It would be marvelous to see you in this role."

Thanking Her Highness for her flattering invitation, Maeve departed in a flurry of attention from the embassy staff, mulling over the offer.

Charity performances were done from time to time; in a way it was almost expected of an artist who had reached a certain level of success, but this would mean learning a new role in German. All that for one evening's work. It was daunting. On the other hand, the chance to shine in something lighthearted and lyrical before a Berlin society audience was tempting. It might even make Dietrich proud of her, and it wouldn't hurt him and the bank to buy lots of tickets to support the royal family's pet project.

After checking with her manager, Maeve telegraphed a yes to the Princess's secretary and was put in touch with the German stage director in charge of the production. Christmas was going to be spent in Berlin, she announced to Arlette and Marie Louise. Little Hanno was going to have his first German Christmas at Papa's Berlin mansion.

*

None of this interested Moira. In the fall of 1910 she had discovered she was pregnant, and what should have been a cause for rejoicing had become a curse. She didn't know if the baby was Charlie's or Paris Singer's.

In spite of Singer's shock at Moira's appetites, that afternoon at the hunting lodge had not been their last intimate encounter. There were several afternoons on board his yacht, not to mention at least two or three hurried outbursts of passion at house parties in the provinces. And now Moira was terrified that the baby she was carrying was going to resemble blond Paris and not sandy-haired Charlie.

If this child looked like the wrong man, she knew her marriage was finished. Charlie Lassiter might be charitable enough to acknowledge his own illegitimate offspring, but he'd probably kill her if she presented him with another man's bastard. Worst of all, there was no way of knowing whose baby it was until it was born. Moira was in torment.

The day she finally informed Charlie she was pregnant was probably the happiest day in his life since he lost Gianni. He embraced her tenderly and actually wept for joy, making Moira weep too—from sheer embarrassment. Then, to her utter mortification, he proceeded to tell all their friends the good news. It was not one of her better moments.

To Maeve's bewilderment, her mother was panic-stricken when she told her, almost in tears.

"But Mama," the girl laughed. "It's wonderful. It's just what you've been praying for ever since you married Charlie. And it will be a bond between you that will never be broken . . ."

"I'm too old for this, Maeveen," she replied. "It's not wise."

"Well, you're still young *enough*." Maeve laughed again. "Oh Mama, Hanno will be so thrilled to have a little playmate!"

"Then give him a brother," Moira snapped. "I shouldn't have to be bothered with such a nuisance right now."

Well, there was just no pleasing some people, Maeve thought in annoyance. Here was her mother, given just what she wanted, and now she didn't want it anymore.

"Mama," she said in puzzlement, "I don't understand you at times."

There was no response. Moira merely sat there, loaded with pearls, staring out the window and looking as if she had been given six months more to live.

"It will be over before you know it," Maeve said, trying to be optimistic. "And Charlie will be ecstatic when he's holding his child in his arms. Especially after the tragedy," she added quietly.

"Thank you very much for that little speech. I know exactly what it's like to suffer through a pregnancy. And I knew it a long time before *you* ever found out."

So there!

*

Maeve's partner in *The Merry Widow* was a popular German singer who welcomed her to Berlin with the remark that his name ought to go first on the program because he was an established star of the Royal Opera whereas she was a foreign guest artist.

"I'm a star wherever I sing," Maeve replied to that. "And since Devereux starts with a *D* and comes before your name in the alphabet, that's another good reason to put me first. And besides, the director *said* I was to be listed first, so that's all there is to it!"

And she flounced off to inspect her dressing room, leaving a gaggle of chorus girls clicking their tongues over "French impudence" and high-handed sopranos.

"Pompous pig!" was Maeve's estimate of the tenor's charms, and she and Arlette both lamented working with foreigners out of a misguided sense of charity.

In spite of that dismal first impression, things improved during rehearsals, and the tenor and the soprano declared themselves satisfied if both names were listed in large print on the same line of the program— above the name of the production. That done, everyone breathed a little easier and ruffled feathers were smoothed over to a general sigh of relief.

It seemed as if everyone in Berlin was excited about the operetta except for Baron von Reuter. Having lived through *Salome*, he was perhaps understandably nervous about his wife's latest German-language production in front of his associates, colleagues, and friends, but Maeve sensed it was more than that. He had seen a French version of Lehár's frothy confection and had enjoyed it greatly, so he wasn't worried about any surprises onstage. No. It was something private, something he was hiding. And that made his wife uneasy.

On Christmas Day, Dietrich went out unexpectedly while Maeve received her guests, embarrassed by her husband's disappearance. Hanno didn't make things any easier by repeatedly asking for Papa in front of everyone who came into the house.

When Baron von Reuter returned to the scene of the festivities, he found Maeve standing in front of the huge, gaily decorated Christmas tree, ceremoniously taking down several of the little satin baskets to present to the staff. They contained the names of each servant and concealed a surprise in cash, a yearly bonus, augmented by Maeve this year to the general delight of the parlormaids. The young baroness looked very lovely and very gracious surrounded by the maids in their best starched aprons and caps, all of them making a nice effect against the lavish Christmas decorations of fir and holly, ribbons and tinsel, a traditional German celebration.

Waiting until Maeve had finished dispensing the baskets, Dietrich turned to her with a flourish and bowed as he formally presented his Christmas gift in a large blue velvet box. Inside, his wife found a long sautoir of gold with pearls, emeralds, and diamonds in clusters every three inches.

"Oh, Dietrich!" she laughed, throwing her arms around his neck. "Thank you! You worried me. I didn't know what to think, *Schatzi*, when you left!"

"My jeweler didn't have it ready until an hour ago," he explained with a grin. "Believe me, I was a lot more nervous than you!"

That was no lie—at least the part about being nervous. Last night, when he dropped off what he thought was his gift to Fräulein Irma Schneider, a recent acquaintance of doubtful morals, he had made a horrifying error. Instead of leaving Irma with a pretty gold bracelet set with tiny diamonds, he had left the magnificent sautoir he'd purchased for Maeve.

Nearly hysterical at the magnitude of his mistake, Dietrich had called his chauffeur, been driven speedily across town, and ended up pleading with the tearful, angry Irma to relinquish her treasure for the much cheaper gold bracelet he was now offering. Since Irma knew the value of diamonds, pearls, and emeralds, that took some doing.

In the end, Dietrich added a check for five hundred marks to his gift and Irma shrugged petulantly, snatched the bracelet from his hands, and flung the velvet box containing the sautoir at her lover. She was still miffed, but her mood was improving. Baron von Reuter kissed her, put the box inside his overcoat pocket, and returned home in triumph.

*

Christmas Day was a pleasant interlude for his family; they hadn't been together in weeks. But there was something strained in the atmosphere, even after Dietrich presented his gift. Something lay simmering beneath the surface, unspoken and threatening.

That night, as Maeve slipped into bed, she kissed her husband affectionately, hoping for a loving response, and was stunned at his reaction—he immediately rolled over and curled into a ball, rather like an armadillo. It had been a long time since they had made love, but this was ridiculous!

Speechless, Maeve sat up, reached for the soft, thick gold tassel dangling from one of their electric light fixtures, pulled it sharply, and then yanked off Dietrich's covers.

"Aggh!" he exclaimed, just as startled. "What are you doing?"

"Demanding an explanation," she replied. "That was the rudest thing you've ever done to me. What on earth is wrong with you?"

He looked haggard. "I'm tired," he said. "I need my sleep just as much as you do. You've no idea of the troubles we're going through right now."

"Where?" she demanded in surprise, sensing his distress.

He sighed, hauled himself up on an elbow, and said, "At the bank, of course. Herr von Richter is now confined to his bed and his replacement isn't up to the demands of the job. We've discovered some tremendous irregularities lately," he added bitterly. "It's wearing me out."

Directing the fortunes of the Von Reuter Bank was never what Dietrich had aspired to. Otto von Richter's dedication had saved him from that. But now the old man was dying of cancer and the young baron found himself trapped in a web of deception—of his own creation—from which he could find no escape. He was almost overwhelmed with guilt, but he was driven by the determination not to live up to Hubertus's worst opinion of him, just to spite the old bastard. Still, the strain was tremendous. He was searching desperately for a miracle to save him.

"What can I do to help?" Maeve asked, fluffing up the pillows and leaning back against them.

"Nothing. It's a banking matter. I need to engage better people, that's all." He needed to be smarter, he thought. More serious.

He paused gloomily. "I may also close down our Paris branch. It's become too costly since we've made several bad loans, and we're in trouble there. If I cut my losses and retrench, the bank will be able to ride out the storm. If not, I don't know what I'll do."

Maeve stroked his blond hair, and Dietrich responded by nestling against her bosom as she wrapped an arm around him.

"I don't really want to move back to Berlin permanently," he said. "I'll miss you and Mama. And if she's having a baby, she'll need all the support she can get. It's a foolish thing to do at her age."

"She thinks so too," Maeve agreed with a sigh.

He glanced up at his wife. "Do you think you could move to Berlin?" He caught his breath, waiting for her answer. Hoping . . .

"No, not this year. I've signed a contract for the next season at the Opéra-Comique and I couldn't break it." She came quite close to saying, "Yes, I'll do it," but how could she? There would be a lawsuit and all sorts of unpleasantness. It was impossible.

There was a pause. Dietrich smiled bitterly as he stroked her arm. "You think like a prima donna now," he said reproachfully. "Not a wife."

"Perhaps that's because my husband has been away for so long." She said it almost wishing he would reveal the reason.

They left it at that. When Dietrich rolled over and closed his eyes again, Maeve said nothing. She simply turned out the light and did the same. He hadn't cared enough to explain, she thought sadly. He hadn't even bothered to reply. She had no way of knowing that Dietrich was afraid of breaking down if he did.

*

When Maeve returned to Paris after her acclaimed *Merry Widow*, she plunged into discussions of the next season's productions, tried to spend more time with four-year-old Hanno, and had to work hard to force herself to endure Moira's laments.

Moira was becoming so difficult she made Nellie Melba seem easy to please. None of it made any difference to Charlie. He was eager for the baby and he fussed over the little mother day and night, putting up with her bad temper, evil disposition, and black fits of despair.

"It's natural at her time of life," a doctor informed him. "It means nothing. Mrs. Lassiter will be herself again once the happy event takes place."

Charlie took his word for it, but Maeve wasn't so sure. Mama was really in despair over this pregnancy which had once been her dearest wish. Maeve couldn't understand her, but she helpfully redecorated a bedroom at the Palais Lassiter for the new arrival, shipped over Hanno's Napoleonic cradle, and began a hunt for nursemaids.

"She's concerned about her figure," Marc Antoine suggested. "It's only natural with such a splendid shape. And besides," he added, "there's always the fear of dying."

"Well, aren't you a crepehanger!" Maeve exclaimed. "Jesus! Thanks for the words of encouragement!"

Perhaps that was it, Maeve thought later. Perhaps Moira was afraid childbirth at her age would kill her. But she was in superb physical condition, and she was used to hunting—which Maeve loathed since it usually involved trekking great distances in the woods, getting rained on frequently, and carting around heavy weapons. If she could put up with all that and horses on top of it, she ought to be in good shape for the rigors of childbirth.

Besides, one would think that this would be her ultimate revenge on Laura Milonari and the high point of her existence. But Moira, apparently, did not.

*

Sean Farrell, recovering from his near assassination, paid Moira a visit to wish her well with her child. He had never forgotten Moira as she was in Berlin nine years ago, and he still had a tenderness for her. He was also grateful for the care she had given him after Milan's visit, even before Geraldine had arrived.

It had been Moira who stayed with him for the twenty-four hours immediately following the shooting to watch for the slightest change in his condition, and it had been Moira who changed the bandages and cleaned the hideous wounds. She had a strong stomach and a practicality he admired. It bothered him that she was so depressed right now at a time when she should have been delighted with herself.

Shocked by her attitude, Sean paid Maeve a call. She couldn't understand it either, she sighed. But she was going to keep an eye on her mother.

"That's good. She needs someone to do that." He nodded. "By the way," he said seriously, "do you know what my father received via the Serbian diplomatic pouch last week?"

The gleam in his eye made Maeve think of all sorts of lovely possibilities. "A present?" she asked. "A sort of peace offering?"

"A present. The head of Stefan Plamanac—courtesy of Colonel Apis of the Serbian secret police."

"Jesus!"

Maeve put down her teacup and shuddered. The papier-mâché head she had carted around in *Salome* had sent people rushing for the exits. She wondered what the real thing might do.

"My God!" she murmured. "What did your father say?"

"Well, I believe his first words were unmentionable, but there was a celebration in the palace that night. I also have it on good authority that Stefan's head occupied a prominent place." As Maeve blanched, he continued: "My family was quite pleased. Now all we have to do is locate Milan."

"You're not joking about this, are you?"

"Not at all. The vendetta is a tradition in Montenegro. We're committed to it."

"But a head! That's barbaric!" She stared at Sean, appalled. What kind of people were these?

Sean's expression turned bitter. "You think Milan's behavior was civilized? That savage murdered Zofia and our son. If I have the good luck to capture him, I'll make him wish he had fallen among the Turks."

It was hard to remember they were in the twentieth century, sitting in an elegant peach and white salon in Paris, surrounded by priceless objets d'art, in a home illuminated by electric lights. This discussion sounded more suitable for some primitive backwater in the Balkans where modern civilization hadn't yet managed to penetrate—Belgrade, for example, with its oxcarts, its brigands, and its bands of predatory Gypsies. Silently Maeve looked into Sean's blue eyes and slipped her fingers through his, an affectionate gesture. He tenderly raised her hand and kissed it, thinking of other days, other places.

"Maeve," he said at last, "if things had worked out differently in Belgrade, our lives would have turned out quite differently. And Zofia wouldn't be dead. Do you ever have any regrets?"

Maeve's eyes met his and held his gaze for a moment. "There's no going back in life," she said quietly. "You make your choice and live with it. That's the way it is in real life."

They both knew that—they were realists, wise in the ways of the world. But when Sean left that afternoon to begin his hunt for Milan Plamanac, Maeve took refuge in her bedroom, weeping uncontrollably.

The violence of her feelings made her ashamed. Here she was, a married woman who dearly loved Dietrich, carrying on like this because of her own sheer irrationality. What did she want, for heaven's sake? Did she want to stop being Dietrich's wife? No, she did not. Well, then, did she think Sean Farrell would just sweep her off to some wild place east of Vienna and live happily ever after with her, while Dietrich and her mother merrily forgot them and went about their own business with never a glance backward? Good Lord! If Maeve hadn't been weeping so hard, she would have laughed at the thought. She and Sean couldn't just go off on a swan boat as the lovers did in *Lohengrin* and forget about everybody else. Besides, they weren't even lovers! She adored him. He felt something for her—but nothing had ever happened between them that they would have been ashamed to tell either Moira or Dietrich.

Oh God, this was too ridiculous, Maeve thought miserably. What did she want from Sean Farrell? She couldn't really say. But when he even suggested she might have regrets about her life, he was able to reduce her to a weeping, silly ninny.

You know what your trouble is, she said to herself sternly in the mirror, looking with disgust at her red and swollen eyes. You want everything! Well, you can't have it. You just can't! So get used to that and pull yourself together, missy. *That's* what you have to do. She knew that. But she didn't feel any happier.

*

Baron von Reuter was growing more and more concerned about the stability of his bank. His bad judgment about loans had forced the liquidation of considerable assets in Paris, and rumors in financial circles were flying fast and furious about imminent disaster in the Berlin home office.

The most damaging bit of gossip hinted that Karl von Ebert, Dietrich's former father-in-law, was planning to buy out the Von Reuter Bank. It was a story that was causing the baron hysterical anxiety.

Trading on the Berlin bourse had been unusually light lately, with the notable exception of Russian and Romanian railroad shares—and the Von Reuter Bank. The railroad situation was understandable with both backward countries embarked on programs of desperate modernization, but why should the bank's shares suddenly become such a popular commodity?

To Dietrich's horror, he realized that if he couldn't keep a firm hold on the majority of his own bank's stock, he might lose control. Nervously he ordered his broker to try to corner the market. Buy every available share and seek out anyone who might wish to sell. Now!

Maeve first learned what was going on when she visited Berlin again in early January 1911 for several performances at the Royal Opera. During dinner one night, her husband gave her a quick rundown of the situation, offering to buy back all the shares of bank stock he had given her during their marriage. Hanno's, too.

Startled, Maeve asked, staring at him, "Are you still in trouble?" She thought whatever problems there were had been solved by now.

"The bank is facing a fight for control of its stock. We think my former father-in-law is behind it. He—or someone else—is trying to buy up all the available shares of our stock. To fight them off, I have to acquire even more. That's why I'm asking for yours."

"All right. I'll make them over to you as soon as I return home. You can't lose control of the bank. That would be dreadful!"

"Thank you," he replied, reaching for her hand. "You're an angel."

Maeve glanced around the dining room, with its formal portraits of deceased von Reuters, Dietrich's parents and grandparents, and she felt alien among these Prussian bankers. Dietrich always had too, but now he seemed more like them and much less the dilettante she had married.

He seemed to have aged since his wife had seen him a month earlier in Paris. He was now sporting a beard and mustache, rather like his father's, and the effect was depressing as far as Maeve was concerned.

Poor Dietrich, she thought. It was as if he was trying to look like Hubertus in order to fool people into believing he could think like him. It was a pathetic attempt to alter reality that fooled no one. The father, whose brusque personality always put people off, had been gifted with a real talent for banking. The son was not.

"How bad are things?" Maeve asked suddenly.

Dietrich sighed and leaned back in his carved Biedermeier chair, glancing nervously at the row of portraits opposite him. "Very bad," he admitted. "We're in desperate straits. If I can't keep the upper hand, the Von Reuter Bank will go out of existence and I'll bear the ignominy of being the one who lost it. I can't let that happen. I know it may sound odd coming from me," he said bitterly, "but I don't want to be unworthy of our name. I have to win this." If he didn't, he was finished. There would be no second chance for him now.

Dietrich was seated at the head of the damask-draped table with its magnificent gold epergne filled with hothouse flowers in the center, a large Venetian chandelier overhead, and gold service plates and vermeil cutlery before him and his wife. Around Maeve's neck was her diamond wedding necklace and on her wrists and ears more diamonds, all gifts from him. The sight depressed him now. All this show, all this ridiculous extravagance. For what, really?

"I've been a poor manager," he stated flatly. "I've been reckless when I thought I was being clever, and I overruled old Richter at times when I should have kept my mouth shut. Our son has a fool for a father—and no future. My God. I'm so ashamed!"

For a second, Dietrich looked as if he was about to break down; then he regained control of himself and sighed, looking away in embarrassment. He felt old before his time, used up, exhausted. He had reached the end Hubertus had always foreseen.

Maeve reached out and took his hand. "Don't be so hard on yourself. You weren't the only one running things. Otto von Richter has to share some of the blame too. After all, he's the one who had charge of the Berlin bank—with years of experience. Whatever happened was done with his consent, too." How could Dietrich think it was all his fault? Surely men like Richter had to bear part of the burden, she thought. It couldn't be *all* Dietrich's fault.

"Von Richter is a dying man. He's been ill for the past year, and he's been fighting it. All this has sapped his strength."

"Yes, and he kept the news of any trouble from you for as long as he could. It all started at the time of *Salome*," she said. "I can remember you being forced to return to Berlin because of Richter's first illness. He should have retired then and handed his post over to a younger man. He hasn't been entirely honest with you, *Schatzi*. It almost makes me wonder what else he's been hiding from you."

The thought of steady, reliable old Richter wheeling and dealing behind his back seemed absurd, especially since the old man was almost on his deathbed. But the idea was so shocking—coming from Maeve of all people—that it jolted Dietrich enough to make inquiries the next day. If he himself had embezzled money, what might Richter have done to him?

Meeting with Hermann Schumacher, former Kaiser Wilhelm Visiting Professor at Columbia and one of Germany's most respected financial thinkers, Dietrich discovered that Herr Schumacher was happy to see him to give him a warning similar to Maeve's.

Schumacher had been told by a colleague in strictest confidence that from what he had overheard at his club in Paris, it was Karl von Ebert who was behind the plan to take control of the Von Reuter Bank. Worse than that, Karl was trying hard to convince old Otto von Richter to sell his shares of the bank to him. Dietrich was stunned.

"Why would he do that?" he demanded, staring at his friend. "How could he bring himself to betray me? And Papa?"

"The word is that he's considering it," Schumacher replied. "I think you'd better act quickly if you want to win this battle."

The older man looked thoughtful. He liked young Dietrich—even if he wasn't up to the level of his father. At least he'd had the imagination to link up with the Schiffs, Rothschilds—and Maeve Devereux. In all his life, Hermann Schumacher had never seen anything like that girl's performance as Salome. She was magnificent. If Dietrich never did anything else in his life, he'd shown genius there, marrying her.

"I'll do my best to find out all I can," he promised. "I'm off to Frankfurt tomorrow and I may be able to pick up useful information there. Meanwhile, I'd advise you to get your hands on every available share of stock you can. And keep trying for more. This is war."

*

When Maeve left for her engagement in Vienna, she thought things were beginning to improve. Dietrich didn't seem as depressed as he had been when she'd arrived. They even went out to lunch at a restaurant on the outskirts of Berlin and watched the ice skaters from inside a cozy rustic lodge. Afterward, the baron bundled his wife into a sleigh and drove back to town, speeding along with some of his old flair. They got into a near accident on the Wilhelmstrasse with a furious army officer and left him cursing them from the sidewalk as they raced away, bells jingling like mad, Maeve laughing from sheer high spirits like a naughty schoolgirl.

"Mama used to think kissing you was dangerous," she laughed, clinging to Dietrich as they rounded a curve. "But I always said she was wrong. It was driving with you that put my life in danger!"

He chuckled at that, then, when they arrived home, lifted her out of the sleigh and carried her upstairs to the master bedroom while Hubertus's old servants stood around giving them dour looks for this display of impropriety.

Maeve and Dietrich reached the suite, slammed the doors shut, and flung off furs and boots. Then the baroness filled the large marble bathtub while wriggling out of her tailored suit, and her husband called downstairs for a bottle of Mumm and some caviar on toast.

When it arrived, carried in by one of the footmen, the fellow was scandalized to see that they intended to consume it in the bathtub, a unique custom in his view. Probably a French habit.

This had been Hubertus's suite, and Maeve took pleasure in lolling about in a warm, frothy bath with Dietrich, soaking off the afternoon chill and drinking Mumm champagne, all at the same time. It seemed sybaritic enough to make her old enemy spin in his grave.

Later, when they were lying in bed, warm and rosy from the bath and the champagne, Maeve nestled against Dietrich and murmured, "I love you, *Schatzi*. You were the one I picked out the first time I saw you, and you're still the one I love, come hell or high water."

He leaned on an elbow facing her and said, "What if I were to lose everything? What if I were to be disgraced before everyone?" His face was tense as he said it, betraying his inner turmoil.

"Even then."

"You don't mean that," he sighed. "You may say it now because you don't know how bad things can get. And if I were to fail, things would become catastrophic. You'd be ashamed of me." He couldn't face that and he knew it—even if she didn't.

"Dietrich," Maeve said firmly, wrapping her arms around him, "I'm not a quitter. I became successful because I worked hard and because I had talent. You saw what I had and you encouraged me to aim higher. And I'm telling you that you have enough brains to make a success of your life even if you lose the bank. There are other careers. Even other banks. And I have money," she added. "We'll never starve."

"*Liebchen*," he sighed, kissing her neck, "I'm a lot of things, but I'm not a leech. I couldn't live off my wife's earnings. They have a name for men like that." He fairly cringed at the thought of it. That would be the ultimate disgrace.

"Yes," she nodded. "A husband."

"A gigolo," he said in disgust.

Maeve burst out laughing. "Gigolos aren't married," she replied. "So don't even think like that."

"You're not taking this seriously enough."

"Yes I am. It's just that we're not looking at it in the same way. You know, *Schatzi*, I went through hell when I was a girl. The British hanged my father, threw Mama and me into a prison camp—from which we weren't supposed to emerge alive, let me tell you—and still I survived. And Dietrich, my darling, there's not anyone in the world of opera today who wouldn't say that not only have I survived but I have flourished!"

"*Liebling*, you're an artist, one of a kind. I'm not in the same category." He was merely a fraud, he thought bitterly, a self-deluding fool.

"*Schatzi*, I was a terrified seventeen-year-old who found herself facing the prospect of losing her mother in a remote jungle backwater prison. It was fight or die. Nothing less. When I left that place, I left my chief jailer dead on the ground and I swore that from that day on, nobody would ever make me feel that helpless or powerless again."

He smiled wryly. "Well, you certainly carried out your promise."

Maeve lay back on her pillows and stared up at the overdecorated chandelier of Austrian crystal. "I wish you had a bit of Irish blood in you, *Schatzi*. It might make all the difference. We're just too damned stubborn to admit defeat."

"I love you, Maeve," he said quietly. "I love you dearly. Maybe you'll give me some of your nerve." But he didn't believe it was possible anymore.

And Maeve was frightened by the sadness in his blue eyes.

CHAPTER 31

*T*he five performances at the Vienna Opera went smoothly enough. It was the first time Maeve had ever worked with Gustav Mahler, and she found him remarkably sensitive to soprano temperament. Apart from that, her suite at the Hotel Bristol close by the opera was a jewel of Austrian rococo and almost as cozy as her rooms at home. Nothing she could wish for had been forgotten. With Arlette relieved of most of the little errands she normally ran in foreign cities, it was a relaxing engagement for everyone.

*

After her Vienna engagement, Maeve decided to return to Berlin with Hanno to keep up Dietrich's spirits. Her last visit to Berlin had made her uneasy about him, and on the train ride across the border in a private Pullman car, she and Arlette discussed ways to cheer him up, talked about the prospects for that trip to Venice, and swore they would do all they could to make Monsieur le baron feel important.

"No talk about contracts or engagements," Maeve declared. "I'll make him the center of my world. He'll love it."

*

At about the same time Maeve's luggage was being loaded aboard the Berlin-bound express train, Baron von Reuter was alone in his bedroom at the von Reuter mansion, immaculately dressed and lying on his freshly made bed, his eyes closed, listening to one of his favorite recordings, Wagner's "Liebestod."

As the music soared with its legend of fatal love, Dietrich's thoughts struggled to keep pace. He was finished. This music, invoking its powerful theme of love and death, filled the room with all the passion he felt for Maeve, for life. Now it was a treacherously seductive reminder of his own mortality. On the table beside his bed lay a loaded Walther .38. Next to that was a letter from Otto von Richter, asking him to step aside for the good of the bank.

Dietrich still couldn't believe the gall of old Otto. It could only mean they knew—knew everything. They knew about the missing money and they knew who had taken it. He was sick with shame. Everything the von Reuters had worked for during two hundred years of patient, diligent expansion had been wrecked by his folly, his stupidity. He was damned forever in their eyes, and it was tearing him apart.

As the final, poignant notes of the "Liebestod" faded into the scratchiness of the record, Dietrich raised himself from his bed and removed the black disc from the phonograph. Then he reverently took another recording from its slipcase and placed it on the machine.

The baron smiled wanly as Maeve's voice filled the room with the opening notes of "Vissi d'arte," his favorite aria.

Dietrich closed his eyes, recalling Maeve as Tosca on so many nights. That passionate Tosca the night she scored her first success at the Opéra-Comique, the same night he wrecked his marriage to Lotte. That frantic New York Tosca when she was wild with fear of going onstage without Chaliapin's good luck charm. That near fatal Tosca when Scotti saved her life and restored her to the good graces of the Paris audience. God, how he loved Maeve! She was the dearest thing in his life. She had been the best thing, too.

As he listened to that voice, so thrilling in its emotion, so passionate in its pain, Dietrich felt tears come to his eyes. If it hadn't been for Maeve, he would have gone through life married to Lotte or someone like her, forced to take comfort in the arms of a series of forgettable little cocottes. Instead, he had loved and married a woman who was adored by thousands, a woman of beauty, grace, and style. And she had been his alone, a faithful, precious jewel in a world filled with fraud and flash.

Dietrich reached out and placed his hand on his bedside photograph of Maeve, his favorite, the one in white satin lying on that tiger skin. He reverently kissed it. Then, as Maeve's voice approached the end of the aria, Baron von Reuter took the revolver from beside the picture, placed the barrel of the weapon at his right temple and pulled the trigger at the last note. It was over in seconds.

*

Both women knew something terrible had happened when they arrived at the imposing von Reuter mansion. There was a black mourning wreath on the front door and a black band on the arm of the butler. He looked startled to see her, Maeve thought, as she glanced around nervously at the servants in the foyer. Something was wrong here. The atmosphere was eerie.

"Hans," she said uncertainly, "what's going on here? Did someone die?"

One of the parlormaids burst into tears and fled the foyer, weeping hysterically.

"Oh God!" Maeve whispered, staring at them all. "Where's my husband? Where is he?" she asked again, her voice rising in suspicion. "Is it the baron? Tell me! It is, isn't it?"

"My deepest regrets, Baroness," the butler replied, bowing stiffly. "We tried to telephone you in Vienna but the lines were down. We sent a telegram . . ."

"I never received word," she protested. "What on earth has happened here?" How could he be dead? she thought. No. Not possible.

Turning around in distraction, Maeve looked at Arlette, who spoke very little German, and announced in bewilderment, "He says Dietrich's dead!"

The French girl gasped and put her arms around Hanno, who raised his head and said, "He's lying. Papa's not dead. He's in Berlin."

With that, Maeve let out a cry and rushed upstairs, sobbing and calling for her husband, tearing open every door on her path, pushing the servants out of her way, refusing to believe this wicked lie.

Hanno followed, with Arlette close behind, the little boy frightened by his mother's behavior and Arlette feeling sick with fear for Maeve. She still couldn't believe it. Monsieur was so young. What could have carried him off so suddenly? Typhus? Scarlet fever? Influenza? Was there an epidemic she hadn't heard of in this city? She was half-stunned, nearly disoriented following Maeve's progress through the second floor, almost colliding with a German chambermaid as she came to an abrupt halt before the master bedroom door.

There, through the open door, she saw Maeve standing beside the bed on which Dietrich lay fully dressed in a morning coat and striped trousers. His eyes were closed, his arms folded on his breast. He didn't move.

Almost afraid to breathe, Arlette looked closer and saw to her horror that there was a blood-encrusted hole in his right temple, and some of the blood had stained the lacy pillowcase beneath his head.

Maeve seemed in shock, not making a sound, too numb with grief to move. Then, horrified by the sight of the wound, she turned, ashen-faced, to Arlette, as if she wanted further verification of what she saw yet didn't believe, and said in a hushed whisper, "How can it be, Letty? Do you see? Do you see?"

And then Maeve began to weep uncontrollably. Wailing, she threw herself on the bed, utterly crushed by this suicide she could not comprehend.

With Maeve speechless from sobbing and Hanno weeping in imitation of his mother, Arlette was thoroughly frightened for both of them. She scarcely left Maeve's side for fear she might be tempted to emulate Monsieur. Tosca was her favorite role, and as Arlette knew all too well, that ended with a pledge to meet before God and a death leap off the Castel Sant'Angelo. In the state Maeve was in, hysterical and incoherent with the pain of her loss, she might be thinking of it.

When Madame had collapsed onto a bed in one of the guest bedrooms and fallen asleep from exhaustion, Arlette took Hanno with her to talk to the butler and ask him to telephone the Gräfin Geraldine. The little boy spoke French, English, and German, and since Arlette spoke only French and some English, she desperately needed an interpreter.

It took some doing to get Geraldine to the telephone to talk to a *maid*, but when she heard what had happened, she said, "I'll be there as soon as I can. Go back upstairs, and don't leave her for a second. If the revolver is still around, hide it! Oh, the foolish boy! What a disaster!"

When Geraldine descended on the von Reuter mansion, she headed straight for Dietrich's room to view the corpse, crossed herself, and gently kissed his forehead. She had liked the poor boy. It was a ridiculous death for him. It marred his beauty, she thought, sighing tremulously. Nothing was so bad that it was worth a bullet in the head.

Then Geraldine noticed he had taken care with his clothing, as if he didn't trust his valet to choose the proper attire for the lying in state and wished to make certain he looked presentable. Everything was just so, very typical of Dietrich. There was even a gentleman's tortoiseshell brush on the night table, as if he had placed it there after smoothing down his beautiful pale blond hair for the last time before putting the gun to his head.

"Dear God!" sighed the gräfin. "What a waste!" Sean was made of sterner stuff. He'd be more inclined to send someone else to kingdom come than do such a daft thing to himself, thank the Lord for that! These Germans were altogether too fond of the concept of moral rehabilitation through suicide.

With Geraldine firmly in charge, Arlette felt relieved: Madame was inclined to listen to her. Since the gräfin spoke excellent French, the girl was soon able to learn the sequence of events that led up to Dietrich's shutting himself in his suite—Hubertus's old suite—and placing that .38 against his head.

It had happened after he tried unsuccessfully to place a telephone call, the butler said. Things frequently went wrong with the lines, but there had to be something besides that. The baron had returned to his suite, bathed, dressed himself, left word not to be disturbed, and then suddenly—a pistol shot. One of the chambermaids had discovered the body. The doctor had been called. The death certificate was signed an hour later.

That was all on the surface. Maeve had discovered a letter addressed to her lying on his night table and had read and reread it, weeping over each sentence.

"*Liebchen*," it began, "when you read this, I will no longer be among the living. I have no will to live, surrounded by treachery and responsible for the collapse of a great banking institution." The letter continued:

I love you dearly. Never doubt it. You were my beloved Lorelei, the single most beautiful thing I ever knew in life. Loving you was worth all I had to do to possess you—even hastening my own father's death. It was I who deliberately and out of malicious calculation provoked an argument the night of his fatal attack and destroyed his medication beforehand, knowing full well the effect it would have. None of this is your fault. I did what I had to do. Bring up our son differently from the way I was raised.

Today I suffered two blows which have left me without the will to go on. Old Richter, whom I have known and trusted since childhood, informed me of his decision to sell his bank stock to Karl von Ebert, thus speeding up our inevitable collapse. And then he asked me to abandon my position as head of our bank. It seems I have become a liability.

I love you, Maeve, but I cannot bear to live as a failure, an embarrassment to you and our dear son. I am a disgrace, even more than you can imagine. Forgive me for it, for my stupidity and my weakness, too. I wish I had been a stronger man, the man you deserved.

There is nothing more to say. God bless you. I will love you always. Dietrich.

Sobbing with grief, Maeve beat on the pillows, wailing like a wounded beast. It was insane. He loved her so much he had killed himself! That made a lot of sense. "Oh, you bloody idiot!" she screamed. "Why did you do it? I love you! I would have stood by you, but you didn't have enough faith in me to trust me! Oh, *Schatzi*, you didn't know me even after all this time."

Geraldine and Arlette had sent a telegram to the Lassiters after they had unsuccessfully tried the telephone. Geraldine was really afraid for the girl. This full-blown romantic hysteria was something unfamiliar to her—except as a recipient. Men had been known to do mad things over her, but she had never reciprocated. This was unknown territory. She had known a Saxon princess who had shot herself in despair over being denied permission to marry a Jewish banker, but that was not the normal course of events. One suffered in stoic silence and committed serial adultery.

"Does she always carry on like this?" Geraldine asked Arlette, who was weeping too.

"Madame has just suffered the greatest loss of her life," the girl replied. "I don't think 'carrying on' would be the proper way to describe it!" And she thought the gräfin was a very hard woman to say such a thing.

The very idea of Dietrich's suicide was an affront to Maeve. She had loved him, had made him proud of her, had given him little Hanno. What more could he want? The thought that he had been pushed over the edge by forces beyond her control embittered her and made her feel irrelevant in the end. He had succumbed to the shame of his failure while acknowledging his wife's dazzling success. For her this was a stab in the heart.

*

When the gleaming mahogany coffin was borne out of the church by six sturdy pallbearers and placed inside the sumptuous black and silver hearse, Maeve noted every detail of the ceremony. Her poor father had been cheated of all this formality, she remembered bitterly. At least Dietrich's exit from this life was being handled with the splendor due a Baron von Reuter.

Grief-stricken as she was, Maeve knew Dietrich would have appreciated the Wagnerian staging of his funeral. He loved a fine mise-en-scène and would have been pleased with this tribute.

The raw late January wind whipped the mourners unmercifully as they prepared to enter their coaches for the drive to the cemetery. Even though Maeve's long sable coat blocked some of the chill, it didn't prevent her from shivering violently as the gusts of wind tugged at her black mourning veil, threatening to rip it loose from its hairpins. Moira and Charlie hastily bundled her into the waiting coach, afraid she would catch cold in this frigid air. Hanno followed, weeping.

Moira pulled her daughter close to her once they were sealed inside and hoped the warmth from both fur coats would stop Maeve's shivering. Hanno buried his face in his mother's coat and sobbed as his grandmother tried to comfort him. Maeve leaned over silently and kissed her son repeatedly, too overcome to speak.

From inside the gleaming von Reuter coach, Maeve looked out to the gloomy splendor of the elaborate, black-draped hearse as it pulled away from the church and made its way to the cemetery.

The deceased lay in his magnificent glass-covered coffin, on display behind a panel of etched glass with Maeve's beautiful spray of white roses covering the casket. Above the glass panels rose a carved canopy painted in black with silver leaf, a glorious affair heavy with clusters of allegorical figures and masses of curlicues. All this was surmounted by thick black ostrich plumes at each corner, and on the top, as a final flourish, more plumes. Black swags draped the whole coach, and even the four horses that pulled the hearse were hung with black and silver covers, their black plumes bobbing with each heavy step, keeping time to their solemn pace.

Weeping beside Moira and Hanno, Maeve covered her face with her hands and sobbed, taking no comfort herself in any of this funereal splendor, deprived all too soon of a husband she loved.

The funeral was held in the same church from which Hubertus had been buried, and Dietrich was laid to rest in the family plot beside his father, despite Maeve's aversion to that after having read his suicide note. He had, for all practical purposes, killed Hubertus in order to marry her, and she would feel queasy every time she paid a visit to the cemetery. The thought of that on top of all the other daft things the poor boy had said in his letter left her in such a state, she was afraid for her sanity.

"Maeve," Marc Antoine had declared after paying his respects from Dresden, where he was appearing briefly at the opera, "Dietrich was not in his right mind, so you can't place any blame on yourself. You had nothing to do with it. It was his sickness that destroyed him, not you."

"He said he loved me, Marco. That's what makes it so stupid!" she sobbed. "I loved Dietrich too. You know I did! I was always loyal to him. I always would have been! No matter what happened to his damned bank!"

The tenor put his arm around her and sighed. "I never told you this before, but perhaps I should now—I always thought Dietrich was a typical Prussian about some things. A man like that couldn't bear the thought of a wife who was more successful than he was. It would drive him mad."

"Oh, Dietrich loathed the Prussian mentality," she protested. "He always hated his father's way of life, that rigidity, that lack of appreciation for anything that wasn't authoritarian."

"But you told me he killed himself over the ruin of his bank. That sounds very Prussian."

"Oh, Marc Antoine! Who knows? All I know is Dietrich is dead and I almost wish I were."

"No you don't," he said firmly. "That would solve nothing. Besides, you have a child to raise. Do you want him growing up without his mother as well as his father? It would be terrible."

At least she had something to anchor her to reality, Marc Antoine reflected as he took the train back to Dresden after the funeral. But he had never seen Maeve so dispirited and he wished he could do something to help her.

Poor Dietrich, he thought as he sat in his first-class compartment en route to Dresden. The playboy of Paris killing himself because he was a failure as a Prussian banker. Whoever would have thought it?

*

Two days after the funeral, Maeve received a cable from her old New York acquaintance, Herr Professor Schumacher. He apologized for intruding on her grief, but he had to speak to her. He had heard that the bank's board of directors were meeting in secret session to decide what to do about their problems. He strongly urged Maeve to attend.

Maeve talked it over with Moira and received an emphatic command to get herself to that meeting. The old bastards would devour her assets and her son's future if she didn't face up to them and fight.

"But Mama, I don't know anything about Dietrich's business!"

"Maeveen," she exclaimed, "don't be naive! If you have any concern for your son's future, you'll not only be there—you'll be there with counsel. They're so hopeless they may do anything. They may even approve the sale of the bank to von Ebert. Would you like that?"

"No," said Maeve, "I would not!"

She had watched in bewilderment as Lotte von Ebert, now the wife of a Berlin banker, walked into her salon, stood silently at Dietrich's casket, and smiled a vicious little smirk of satisfaction as she looked down on the face of the man who had humiliated her so shockingly in Paris. Then, with a hateful glance at Maeve, she swept out of the room, leaving everyone buzzing in her wake. Even Moira was rendered speechless by that display of arrogant gloating.

"Then you have to show up," her mother said firmly. "Remember how those British vultures disposed of your father? These old German bastards will do the same to you and your son if you don't fight. I'll go too."

"Well . . . thank you," Maeve replied, still bewildered.

"And we'll have Charlie with us. He'll get some lawyer to represent you. He's shrewd. You'll need someone like that to rely on now."

Well, thought Maeve, thank God for Herr Schumacher's concern. It was good to know her poor husband still had some people she could rely on. She only wished poor Dietrich had realized it.

When Maeve, Charlie, and her determined mother arrived at the marble-faced neoclassic granite building off the Wilhelmstrasse where the von Reuters had done business for nearly two hundred years, Maeve took in the high marble pillars, the brass tellers' cages, the neat and orderly arrangement of desks and carpets, and she sighed. It was the first time she had ever set foot in the place.

Guided down a long corridor by a flunky, Maeve's party finally arrived at the meeting room—a large, oak-paneled conference room with brocade drapes and a massive crystal chandelier above a long oval table of gleaming mahogany with matching leather-covered chairs down the length of it. Around the table sat the board of directors, a sad collection of aging, well-fed gentlemen with the look of men who had no pity on widows and orphans.

As Maeve's party entered, the bankers stood up, rather startled to see "the singer" and wondering why she was there. Several of them eyed the family group with blatant distrust. This wouldn't be easy.

"Good day, gentlemen. Please be seated," Maeve said graciously as she looked the room over—the mahogany, the chandelier, the men. "I was told you were having a discussion of our future. I thought I should join it."

Otto von Richter raised his white head and looked curiously at the young woman, a tall, slender figure in deepest mourning, wearing a magnificent sable coat over a black silk shirtwaist and skirt. Very appealing. Richter thought it was brazen of her to invade their meeting. She had no business here.

"Baroness," he said kindly, looking very old and frail, "we were planning to let you know what we decided *after* the meeting."

"I'm sure you were," Moira replied with undisguised sarcasm.

Von Richter and the others gave her a harsh stare. Busybody, they thought. She ought to leave well enough alone.

"As Baron von Reuter's widow, my stepdaughter naturally wishes to be present today. It would be unthinkable for her not to be privy to your discussions," declared the slim gentleman to her right.

The stepfather, they whispered. Thirty million in Standard Oil and railroad shares. Charlie was warmly greeted and offered a seat beside Maeve at the head of the table. Mrs. Lassiter, uninvited, took a seat next to him.

It was a hostile audience. Despite the courtesy and the polite words, Maeve knew that everyone in the room wanted to be rid of her, and that infuriated her. They were about to scramble to save themselves, leaving little Hanno alone and unprotected. The bastards!

"I look around this room and see no friendly faces," she said in sonorous German, surprising herself. Maeve hated speaking German on anything resembling a formal occasion, always afraid of mixing genders or using the wrong case and sounding semiliterate. Now here she was, facing these bankers and not giving a damn, allowing her heart to dictate her speech.

"I think that's a harsh view, Baroness," Herr von Richter said with a pained expression. He looked like an ancient drone. She could believe he was on his deathbed; his illness had left him shriveled and skeletal, a still-living mummy.

"Is it?" she replied. "I don't think so. You gentlemen were so kind at the funeral when we buried Dietrich, all of you offering me your deepest sympathy, your fondness for my dear husband, your concern for me and my son. But here you are today, ready to throw away my child's future—and you have no *right!*" she said, rising from her chair and pointing angrily at old Richter, who looked guilty and lowered his eyes in embarrassment.

Glancing up in shock at the tone of the woman's voice, the bankers were staring as if seeing her for the first time. The grief-stricken girl of three days ago was turning into a fury.

Still standing, Maeve looked directly at von Richter and said, "Old man, you are a scoundrel, hiding your wickedness behind your white hair! Do you know what drove my husband to take his own life, gentlemen?" Maeve asked breathlessly as she walked slowly around the table, stalking old Richter. "The betrayal, the wicked, shameless, spineless betrayal of his trusted adviser, Herr Otto von Richter. *That's* what killed my husband, just as surely as if Herr von Richter had pulled the trigger himself! *Betrayed!*" she repeated dramatically. "Betrayed by this scorpion, this evil heap of rotting flesh!"

This shocking declaration recalled Maeve as Salome, titillating New York with the vividness of her portrayal, delivering line after decadent line of Wilde's overblown text. She wished they had a musical accompaniment for this performance; she was that good. She had a real flair for abuse in German, she discovered, not without some pride.

"I protest!" shouted one of the stunned bankers. "This is outrageous!"

"So was Dietrich's death!" Maeve retorted. "So is this gathering without somebody to represent my son! You hyenas! You vampires! Are you going to batten on Dietrich's dead body, destroying two centuries of his family's work?"

"Baroness, you are overwrought!"

"Yes. I am! But I'm not stupid. You are, if you give up and hand this bank over to Karl von Ebert without a fight."

"This is really not within your province, Baroness," someone said, infuriating Maeve with his patronizing tone of voice.

"Oh, isn't it? Looking after her son's inheritance is every mother's duty," Charlie threw back at them in German, making all heads turn in his direction.

"Don't let yourselves be stampeded into throwing in the towel," he warned them. "I know the Paris branch of the bank is in the process of liquidation, but your Berlin branch was always strong. Entrench! Defend yourselves! Attack von Ebert if you have to."

"And for God's sake, don't make it easy for him!" Maeve exclaimed, looking straight at von Richter. "If you want to sell your shares, sell them to me!"

Otto looked mortally embarrassed. Maeve had rattled him when she accused him of causing Dietrich's death. He hadn't thought the boy cared that much one way or the other, really. All those years of Paris, traveling around with this girl, neglecting his duties . . .

"Gentlemen," Maeve said, "there is no reason except cowardice to let this bank go under. Two hundred years of Dietrich's family history and your own depositors are good reasons for fighting off von Ebert.

With good lawyers and a smart man like my stepfather to help, I'd be surprised if you can't create a brilliant defense. In fact," Maeve added, warming to her theme, "I'll make you a solemn promise. I will place my jewelry on the line if you need a few more million. This is my son's inheritance and his father's lifework. We must not fail." And with that she swept grandly out of the room.

To reinforce her promise, Maeve collected the splendid pile of jewelry she had accumulated during her marriage and ceremoniously carried it into the bank under guard, just to dazzle the troops.

The gentlemen were awed. Dietrich had given her a fortune, confirming all their worst suspicions about his legendary obsession for the singer. From her spectacular wedding necklace to that dazzling sautoir of last Christmas, it was all there now, securely behind the door of the vault. It could even be used to replace that vanished hundred thousand marks.

"You're not really going to let them get their paws on your jewelry!" exclaimed the gräfin. "That may be your old age insurance!"

"It may be Hanno's," Maeve said quietly.

Geraldine had been very kind lately. Feeling guilty over her shabby treatment of the girl years earlier, she had been a comforting presence throughout the days following Dietrich's death when Maeve had been too overwhelmed and distraught to think straight. She had even fussed over Moira, who had startled her with her pregnancy.

Moira, being more cynical than Maeve, had been polite but wary. She had a long memory. Her daughter felt so alone in Berlin that she welcomed the gräfin's help.

"All these maneuverings will take time," Geraldine pointed out. "I think we ought to take the offensive now and put von Ebert on notice that he can't just snap his fingers and acquire your bank. We'll hit him where it hurts. Now."

"What are you talking about? What can we do that the men can't?"

Geraldine smiled. She had a lovely smile. Now those well-tended white teeth were gleaming with anticipation.

"We can start a run on his bank," she replied. "I've seen it happen and it's a fearsome sight. One day a fellow banks his money, feeling secure in all that brass and marble around him, the next day he's in line with two hundred other frightened souls, screaming for his cash. Other people see the fuss and rush home for their bankbooks. Soon you have a mob out on the sidewalk, afraid they're going to lose their life's savings and screaming for someone's blood."

"My God, that's diabolical!" Maeve could just picture the scene—housewives wailing, men shouting, the police outside trying to control the crowd.

She had actually seen it happen in New York and had pitied those poor, frightened people. She had also rushed back to the Hotel Astor, shouting for Dietrich to ask him if they had any money in that bank. It had calmed her to learn they hadn't, but she could still recall the frenzy that gripped her at the time.

"I couldn't subject innocent people to that," Maeve said. "It would be too cruel."

The gräfin nodded, sighed, and sipped her tea. "You have a kind heart, my dear," she said. "You're too good for this bad world."

But Geraldine wasn't. Next morning, she and two strong men carrying a very large leather chest marched into the Von Ebert Bank with Geraldine in the lead. Looking very elegant in a sable coat and matching muff with little tails swinging with every movement, the gräfin strode up to the first desk in sight and grandly announced herself, declaring she was there to withdraw all her money.

Heads spun around as the gräfin said loudly in very aristocratic tones that she was closing her account in view of Herr von Ebert's recent financial difficulties.

A lady in a woolen coat with a thick fox collar and cuffs glanced at the person ahead of her in line and whispered excitedly, "That's the Gräfin von Kleist, the Kaiserin's friend. *Mein Gott*! If she's taking her money out of here they *must* be in trouble! She's as rich as Croesus!"

When the flustered bank employee went to get the manager, Geraldine gave the onlookers a gloomy look, and declared that if they had any concern for the welfare of their children, they ought to take their money and flee this place. The rumors she had heard at court were predicting nothing short of catastrophe, she said, stretching out the word "catastrophe" with a dramatic inflection that conveyed utter disaster.

"Rumors at court?" squeaked the lady.

"The Kaiser knows these things," a gentleman behind her muttered. "The rich tell each other."

By the time the bank manager came to speak to his distinguished client and try to assure her the bank was as solid as Krupp steel, tellers at the windows were starting to notice an unusual increase in withdrawals.

To the man's embarrassment, Geraldine refused to be placated and insisted upon closing out her account and carting it off in the chest. Nothing would convince her the money was safe, and she told him this in tones that carried throughout the whole room. People were peeking out from behind potted palms to get a look at this gräfin who was carrying away her money in a chest.

As Geraldine and her escorts left the bank with a pile of bank notes that didn't quite fill up the container—a mere twenty thousand marks—rumors were already starting to spread that the Kaiser himself had told her to save the family fortune. By afternoon, there were longer lines than usual at the bank, and at opening time the following day, more lines still. By the third day, there was an article in the Berlin *Börse Gazette* that the Von Ebert Bank, which had been rumored to be taking over another bank, was itself on very shaky ground.

"My God!" gasped Maeve when she read it. "I'll bet I know who started that rumor!" And she laughed nervously at the sheer gall of Geraldine Farrell.

*

"Von Ebert himself is meeting with your board of directors tomorrow," Charlie said about a week later. "He's beside himself. He's screaming about sabotage and every other damned thing. He wants to sell back the shares of stock he's recently acquired."

"His own bank's in trouble. People have no confidence in it," Maeve noted. "Have you seen the lines? Frightening."

"It is for *him*." Charlie smiled. "I must say, it took me by surprise. I thought they were rock-solid."

After some very serious discussions, Karl von Ebert withdrew his offer to take over the Von Reuter Bank, while the bank emerged stronger than ever through ridding itself of the Paris branch and pouring the money into more profitable enterprises closer to home. The one who ended up losing the most was von Ebert, who had a hell of a time convincing his depositors he was solvent. By the time he had to sell back the von Reuter stock to raise ready cash, he really wasn't—a fact the *Börse Gazette* kept hammering away at nearly every day, giving him problems with his digestion that led later to a quick departure for an Italian spa to rest and recoup his reserves of strength. He needed it badly.

*

While Maeve was savoring the victory, she received a letter written on fine vellum, sent from Lotte in Italy. "Baroness," it began, "I congratulate you. I hope you enjoy the fruits of your devotion to your late husband. Such fidelity is so rare, it is truly remarkable these days, especially since Dietrich hardly deserved it. If you go to 13 Beckstrasse, fourth floor, you might see what I mean. Her name is Irma Schneider and it was she, not the bank, that kept him in Berlin for all those extended trips. But you may already be aware of all this, since you yourself are a woman of the world and very *compréhensive*. Regards, Charlotte von Hoffmann, née von Ebert."

*

Maeve read the missive, dripping with venom, and ran to call downstairs for the chauffeur. Heartsick, she found the apartment building, walked slowly upstairs to the fourth floor, and located the notation "Fräulein Irma Schneider" on one of the doors. So, it was true, she thought, her head spinning.

Hesitating on the threshold, Maeve suddenly raised her gloved hand and knocked hard. Within minutes a young blond girl answered the door. "Yes, madame?"

"Are you Fräulein Schneider?" she asked, struck by the odor of cabbage, one of the world's least pleasant scents.

"No, madame. I'm the maid. If you wait a moment, I'll call her. Please come in."

Maeve did so, too unsure of what she wanted to have any other ideas. Looking around, she was disgusted to see a silver-framed photograph of Dietrich on a table. How could he? Repulsed by seeing it here, she reached for it and stared at it before smashing it on the floor.

"What's going on here? Who are you to destroy my property?" shouted a woman's voice.

Maeve looked up and saw Fräulein Irma Schneider, a slim blonde in an expensive peignoir. It was five in the afternoon. "Waiting for customers?" she asked rudely, incensed by the sight of her.

"Bitch! Get out of here, whoever you are! You must be drunk. Or crazy!"

Then, as Fräulein Schneider advanced on her unwanted guest, she stopped in her tracks, shocked. Baroness von Reuter!

"Frau Baroness," she murmured, stunned. "I wasn't expecting you."

Maeve said nothing. She was merely observing the girl, a pretty young blonde of fairly refined appearance with large blue eyes. For a moment Maeve stared, trying to place her. She had seen her somewhere before. Recently.

"I came to pay my respects, Frau Baroness," Irma said, guessing what was running through Maeve's mind. "That's where you saw me."

"Ah."

Irma looked at her awkwardly. "Would you like a drink?" she asked, trying to be polite. She really didn't know what to do, but she felt safe from physical abuse. The baroness was too stunned to do that.

"No—thank you," Maeve replied. "I don't want anything. I just had to know, that's all." She suddenly found herself struggling to breathe, her head in a whirl.

Irma sighed. "It was a way for him to escape his troubles and forget. It was rather an occasional thing. He just came here when he was in Berlin. He was very nice," she added. "But he had such problems . . ."

Maeve looked around the room, looked at Irma, the maid, the art nouveau decorations, and heard herself babble something that made no sense as she turned around and hurried down the stairs, not listening to anything else, not even seeing where she was going. Dietrich had been unfaithful. He had come here to be with another woman. Maeve couldn't get the horrible image out of her head. It tortured her, just as Lotte knew it would. Maeve recalled that smirk, that gloating . . .

"Ah, you bitch!" Maeve sobbed. "This was your revenge, wasn't it?"

Enclosed in the soft leather interior of a new Mercedes motorcar, Maeve buried her face in her sable muff and wept as if her heart would break. She was alone, totally alone, humiliated and absolutely unable to confront Dietrich, who had caused her this pain.

CHAPTER 32

*T*he encounter with Dietrich's mistress was such a shock it destroyed Maeve's equilibrium and left her in the grip of something akin to hysteria. Startling her parents and the gräfin, she announced the day after meeting Fräulein Schneider that the von Reuter mansion was going up for sale. She wanted nothing in Berlin to remind her of her unhappiness, she said flatly, and firmly rejected all Charlie's advice against acting hastily. The bank was Hanno's future, but the house was part of a past she suddenly had no wish to remember.

The discovery of Fräulein Schneider was such a wrenching experience for Maeve that she couldn't sleep for weeks afterward, tortured by thoughts of Dietrich with that woman—and with how many others?

The worst thing was that this woman who had ruined all her notions of a happy marriage hadn't even been in love with him! "An occasional thing" was her expression. As if Baron von Reuter was merely one name out of so many others on her list. What sort of slut had he been keeping company with, for heaven's sake?

No one could comfort Maeve. Moira was beginning to whisper about a nervous breakdown. Arlette kept a close watch on Madame, deliberately keeping sharp objects away from her.

Work was the only thing that still interested her, and while she was onstage she forgot her unhappiness and became whatever character the role called for. In her hotel room between performances misery reigned supreme.

She had been posthumously insulted by Dietrich, and no matter what he stated in that letter, she wanted to know just why he had found it necessary to chase other women when he had *her*. If he had helped ease old Hubertus out of this world because he was so mad for her, why did Fräulein Schneider have to figure in his life? It was unbelievably insulting and damned pointless as far as she was concerned.

*

In June, Moira was about to give birth to the Lassiter heir—or heiress— and the atmosphere in the house was so jumpy Maeve couldn't stand it. Stopping by to see her mother before leaving for an engagement at the Vienna Opera, she promised to have someone standing by at her hotel to relay the news so she would know if she had a brother or a sister. If the happy event still hadn't taken place by the time she was through, she'd be on the first train to Paris to assist at the birth. Otherwise, she'd have to welcome the new baby after she completed her stay in Vienna.

Moira hoped Maeve was still singing at the Vienna Opera when the time came. She had to cope with Charlie and his bad case of nerves; she didn't want Maeveen hanging about, probably sobbing and wailing at the foot of her bed, looking dismal. Hanno's birth had been hard enough on Moira. She didn't want to have to listen to Maeve carrying on through this one.

The one bright spot for Maeve at this time was her reunion with Sean in her dressing room after her performance in *Le Nozze di Figaro*, where she had sung the role of Cherubino. She had given a delightful characterization and was receiving a roomful of fawning admirers when Sean walked in with an armload of white roses.

"Oh my God! It's good to see you again," she sighed as she flung her arms around him, once Arlette had taken the roses. "I was beginning to be afraid for you."

"Not me, Maeve," he laughed. "I'm just about indestructible."

Well, thought Maeve as she buried her face against his chest, it was a good thing *somebody* was. Life was so precarious these days, it was one funeral after the other.

What Sean had to say to her when they were having a late supper at the Hotel Sacher was a lot less reassuring. He, Kyril, and Colonel Apis of the Serbian Secret Police were hunting Milan Plamanac as a joint venture, and they had tracked him to the suburbs of Vienna. The colonel was now an ally. This was a truly byzantine turn of events, Maeve thought.

"What!" she exclaimed, appalled. "Then you're in danger."

"Milan is in danger," Sean corrected her. "Please show some faith in my talents."

"Don't rely on Apis for anything," she warned him, suddenly losing all interest in the Wiener schnitzel before her. "He's so treacherous even he probably doesn't know whose side he's on."

"Well, he's on mine for the time being, and that's what counts now."

"He and your father-in-law are a perfect pair," she said gloomily. "Both double-dyed villains."

Sean glanced around the elegant dining room, with its large chandeliers, its damask, and its gleaming epergnes, and he noted the presence of several uniformed officers among the crowd. They had to be very high-ranking officers to afford this place, a magnet for the rich, the famous, and the notorious. He recognized an archduke with his current mistress and a well-known ballerina with her former lover. Both ladies were dripping with jewels, the preferred style for their type.

"People probably think I'm a kept woman," Maeve sighed, glancing at her resplendent reflection in one of the Sacher's gilded mirrors. She had got her jewelry back and was now loaded with diamonds in the manner of royalty—or courtesans. Both groups favored a lavish display.

"You're not observing the usual mourning period, I see."

"What's the point? Dietrich's dead and he never liked me to look ugly."

Sean laughed. "It's true. The boy was wild about you. I never met a man so mad about his own wife. I was sad to hear the news, Maeve. I couldn't understand it at all," he said quietly.

"Neither could I. Oh, Sean," she exclaimed, nearly bursting into tears, "he had a mistress! It was so dreadful! I wanted to die when I found out."

"What?"

"Yes. It's true! Lotte von Ebert made it her business to let me know. The cow!"

"The jealous bitch! Don't believe a word from her, Maeve."

"I met the mistress. I saw his picture on her table. She even admitted it."

Sean was shocked. Somehow he just couldn't picture Dietrich chasing other women. He was too obsessed with Maeve. But of course, he remembered there had been the recent financial difficulties.

After supper they took a drive to the Prater, Vienna's playground, and Sean offered to take her up in the Riesenrad, the huge ferris wheel, trying to amuse her. It was the biggest attraction there, on every tourist's itinerary, he said, smiling at her.

"All right," Maeve agreed, looking up at the huge contraption, a gigantic wheel with huge boxes attached to it, big as small rooms, where one stood or sat to view the panorama below.

Maeve had once been up in a gas balloon and had seen Paris and its environs from inside the clouds. Now she was going to see the lights of Vienna—and she wouldn't have to worry about landing in some angry farmer's field.

"Isn't this fantastic?" Sean enthused as Maeve edged closer to him for reassurance. Their box had a tendency to sway ever so slightly as they dangled above the city. A cluster of British milords and three ladies of unspecified nationality were sharing their compartment, everybody rendered a bit speechless by their ascent and by the dramatic view.

"It looks like a fairyland from up here," she murmured. "It reminds me of Luna Park in New York."

"Look," Sean murmured. "Can you see the lights of the Ringstrasse glowing like a diamond necklace around the city center?"

"Umm. Beautiful. It doesn't look real."

Vienna from so high in the air was a pageant of light, some of it brilliant, some muted, some moving, all so far below it looked like another world.

This is what the birds see, Maeve thought, resting her cheek against Sean's shoulder, moved by the fabulous light show on the ground.

When they arrived back on terra firma—greeted by Kyril, who was never far from his master—Maeve was quiet, almost regretting her return to the real world.

"That was so lovely." She smiled. "Thank you."

Sean looked at Maeve, glittering with her jewels, and he smiled back. "Would you like to go for a carriage drive?" he asked. "It's a lovely night. The air is mild and I know you don't have to sing tomorrow, so it can't harm you."

Maeve normally went to bed early and tried not to use her voice before a performance. She sometimes went so far as to stop speaking entirely for twenty-four hours before an important performance, and communicated by handwritten messages.

The temptation was there. She had had it drilled into her by old

Herr Albrecht that the night air was ruinous to the voice, but then again, he had told her many a tall tale. She still giggled every time she told anyone the story he concocted about sex and foolish sopranos.

"All right." Maeve smiled as she slipped her arm through Sean's. "Show me the sights."

Nestled beside Sean in the worn leather seat of a fiacre—with Kyril in the next vehicle—Maeve leaned her head on his shoulder, recalling that aborted sleigh ride on the Nevsky so many years ago.

"Sean . . . ?" she asked tentatively.

"Yes?"

"I—"

Whatever Maeve was about to say was cut short by something suddenly whizzing by close to her head. She gasped, bewildered, as a bullet tore clean through the elegantly braided hairpiece that augmented her fashionable coiffure.

"Down!" Sean yelled, pushing her to the floor. "Kyril!" he shouted, "someone's shooting!"

The driver of the fiacre let out a frantic curse and quickly whipped his horses, urging the poor beasts to outrun whoever was pursuing them.

Shots had been fired, but there was nobody in sight. Then suddenly, the driver of a dark Mercedes not two hundred feet away turned on his headlights, gunned his motor, and rode straight on toward the fiacre to take a second shot. The first had gone astray. Perhaps this would bring down the quarry.

"Keep down!" Sean shouted at Maeve as he felt her struggle to rise. He was holding a Walther .38 in his hand, waiting for the second volley.

The fiacre's coachman was in hysterics, praying, shouting, cursing all at the same time, whipping his horses into a lather in sheer terror.

"Here they come!"

In the light of the streetlamps on the nearly deserted stretch of the Ringstrasse, Sean saw the motorcar heading toward him, a chauffeur at the wheel, exposed in the open air, and a man hanging out of the enclosed compartment, trying to aim a weapon.

"Son of a dog!" he heard somebody shout in Serb—Kyril, still following in the second fiacre, threatening his driver with death or grave injury if he tried to change course, while the frightened Viennese shouted back, totally outraged and incoherent.

With Maeve flattened against the floorboards underfoot, Sean braced himself against the leather seat and fired, managing to hit the chauffeur. The man cried out and slumped over the wheel as the Mercedes began to veer off to the left despite the wild shouts and threats of its passenger, Milan Plamanac, who was cursing his driver, not realizing he had been killed.

As the car crashed into a lamppost, hurling the dead man out into the street with the force of the impact, Milan leaped out from the other side. Sean jumped down from the fiacre, revolver in hand, to pursue him.

Glad to be rid of *that* fare, the driver took off like a locomotive until Maeve popped up and pressed something into his back that felt like a gun. As he came to a grinding halt, she said, "Thanks!" handed him a few bills and hopped out, running down the Ringstrasse toward Sean and Kyril.

Milan Plamanac was furious. If that first shot hadn't gone wild, Ivan Petrovic would be dead and nobody the wiser. People in Cetinje would have known, of course, but nobody else. Now here he was, still in hot pursuit of his father-in-law, mad to kill him.

Milan felt two bullets whiz past his ear as he forced himself to go faster, the ground rising up under him, his breath coming in terrifying wheezes. Sean was younger and faster. He would kill him. He was already gaining on him.

As Kyril raced along in pursuit, he shouted back to Maeve to stay put, and saw her stop. Good. At least she had more sense than she had in Belgrade.

Milan was nearly at the end of his rope. As he put on a final, desperate burst of speed, he saw the headlights of a motorcar appear. Blinded, he stopped short and then felt the impact as the vehicle struck him, flipping him into the air like a puppet, flinging him facedown on the Ringstrasse, unconscious and harmless at last.

Colonel Apis got out of his motorcar and sauntered over to Sean and Kyril, who had come charging out of the shadows. The colonel seemed enormously pleased with himself, Maeve observed as she made her way cautiously toward the men, still uncertain whether Apis was friend or foe this evening.

When Apis spotted Maeve and recognized her, he was speechless. Baroness von Reuter! What irony. His dark eyes glittered as he surveyed her bedraggled gown and the quality of her diamonds. This was truly priceless.

With a dazed Milan Plamanac bundled into the colonel's automobile, Sean and Kyril tied him up and sat on him as they drove Maeve to the Hotel Bristol. Nobody said much during the drive through Vienna's dark streets. The men were already making plans for Milan's trip back home, disguised as part of Sean's baggage in a very secure container.

When Sean said goodbye to Maeve at the Bristol's elaborate front door, he kissed her tenderly and promised they would meet again soon. When? As soon as Milan Plamanac had faced Montenegrin justice.

Maeve put her arms around Sean and held him close for long seconds. All her affection for him had flared up once more with that near murder on the Ringstrasse. For the second time in as many months, Maeve had faced the loss of a man she loved. To lose Sean so soon after Dietrich would have sent her over the edge—and Maeve felt guilty at even admitting her own strong feelings for Sean Farrell. She had loved Dietrich. It didn't seem decent to feel this way now, but she couldn't help herself.

"You know where to find me," she said softly as they embraced. And she kissed him again so fiercely they both nearly lost their balance.

*

It was Colonel Apis who rather spoiled Sean's euphoria half an hour later, as they were ransacking Milan's lodgings and discovered the leather satchel he had stolen from Zofia on the night of her murder.

"Not much left of a hundred thousand marks," Kyril declared, badly disappointed. "The bastard must have had a good time."

"Oh yes," Apis agreed. "I wonder how Baron von Reuter would feel knowing the old bastard had squandered it so carelessly—"

Sean's head spun around. "What the hell are you talking about?" he demanded. "How would he have had any connection with this money?"

Apis smiled a loathsome, wolfish grin, showing strong white teeth. This was the moment he had been waiting for, a nice anticlimax to that touching scene at the hotel, much more to his cynical taste.

"Why, Ivan Petrovic," he said innocently, "Baron von Reuter was the source of the money. The Germans and Austrians were funding the Plamanacs through the Von Reuter Bank. Unfortunately for the baron, they withdrew their support before the Plamanacs were ready to be turned loose. Zofia blackmailed the young man for the money after the official sources dried up. It caused him great distress, as we all know. Such a sad fate . . ."

Seizing Apis by the collar, Sean flung him against the wall. "You're lying!" he shouted, half-demented with rage. "This can't be true! I don't believe you!"

Apis managed to free himself from Sean's grip and showed his fine teeth once more, relishing the moment despite the marks on his throat.

"I swear it on my honor as a Serb officer," he replied. "Von Reuter was a jealous man. This was all directed at you—the man he feared most. The only other man his wife could ever love. Touching, isn't it? These Europeans are so romantic, they're like children. Myself, I prefer other means of removing my rivals."

"Maeve couldn't know," Sean murmured almost to himself, forgetting Apis for a moment. "She couldn't know what he was doing . . ."

"God, no!" laughed Apis. "She would have abandoned him. That's what he couldn't live with, apparently. He knew he was lost if it ever came out. Poor fool. The Plamanacs had him by the balls. And Zofia was worse than the old man. She was a real witch—"

Apis never had a chance to finish his statement. Sean's fist caught him squarely on the chin and sent him crashing into the wall again.

"You Serb bastard!" he said, "don't you ever mention the name of my wife again. Or the name of Baroness von Reuter. Those names are forbidden for you! Do you understand?"

While Kyril stared in amazement, Colonel Apis nodded meekly, rubbing his sore chin. "Very well, Ivan Petrovic. As you wish."

It appeared to Apis that Ivan Petrovic shared at least one quality with the late Baron von Reuter: he was ridiculously attached to his women, a foolish attitude at best and a danger if carried to extremes. But after seeing Baroness von Reuter this evening, Colonel Apis could understand it. She was an exceptional woman in every way. And a danger to all who loved her!

*

Still dazed from her reunion with Sean and its shocking denouement on the Ringstrasse, Maeve didn't feel capable of answering any of Arlette's questions when she entered her hotel suite. She didn't care to explain why she, Vienna's newest and prettiest soprano, looked as bedraggled as if she had just been run over by a fiacre. And she didn't care to discuss Monsieur Farrell at all. Yes, they had spent an interesting evening. No, she wasn't injured. And Monsieur was *not* responsible for her unusual state. It was the Viennese traffic, Maeve maintained. There were some shockingly bad drivers in this city—make no mistake! And with that, she threw off her clothes and spent the next hour soaking in the marble bathtub, trying to recover her equilibrium.

Arlette was no fool. Maeve knew she didn't believe a word of what she said. She also knew the French girl was smart enough to know when to keep quiet and not pester her with questions. And truthfully, even Maeve herself didn't know what had happened to her on the Ringstrasse this evening, except that she hadn't felt so excited and so wild since those days in South Africa when, as a teenaged hellion, she had planned a jailbreak and shot old Sergeant Davies. It was almost embarrassing, she reflected, up to her neck in warm, perfumed bathwater, that she could now look upon that as a great adventure—and yearn for more of the same. Jesus! That wasn't normal. What kind of woman was she?

Maeve glanced at herself in the large, gilded bathroom mirror, framed by its contingent of little painted cupids, and she sighed. Perhaps that wild girl in South Africa was the real Maeve Devereux and this lovely lady, this Frau Baroness, this Madame Devereux, was the fraud, a beautiful, elegant creation she had concocted over the years to make the little wildcat acceptable to civilized society.

Well, she had succeeded. She was La Devereux and she had the bank account to prove it. But she was also Maeveen from the back of beyond—and of all the men she had met since those days, only Sean Farrell was capable of appreciating her true nature. Certainly poor Dietrich never had. He had an altogether different idea of her, something wrapped up in layers of Teutonic myth, lovesickness, and probably lots of champagne.

She was afraid to think of Dietrich now. Her thoughts were still such a tangle of anger, bewilderment, and sheer incomprehension that she usually started to weep each time she tried to sort out the mad puzzle of his suicide—and his fondness for Fräulein Schneider! Despite Fräulein Schneider, Maeve was still heartsick over his death and unable to come to terms with it. Only the idea of Sean back in her life gave her any relief from her misery—and yet it frightened her as well.

This semiroyal Montenegrin was no poseur. He was the genuine article, an adventurer, a man who took the kinds of risks that often led to an early death and a memorial service attended by dozens of lovely ladies weeping their eyes out. Life with this man wouldn't be easy. But it would never be dull.

Smiling sheepishly at her rosy, damp image in the mirror, Maeve closed her eyes and pictured Sean as she had first seen him, disguised as a priest and walking jauntily into the lion's den to plan a jailbreak right under the noses of her captors—and bringing it off with her help! After a start like that, one might say they were destined for each other.

Then, slowly coming back to reality, Maeve stopped smiling. She was becoming almost as romantic as poor Dietrich—and look what happened to him. What was wrong with her, for heaven's sake? Sean had a father who was a king. Kings' sons, even those born on the wrong side of the blanket, didn't marry women like her. It was taking too great a risk to defy someone like Nikolai Petrovic. It was almost like putting a curse on your marriage. That's what poor Dietrich had done. . . . She couldn't bear to let the same thing happen with Sean. She loved him too much.

Am I a bird of ill omen? she thought sadly. The reflection in the mirror gave no answer at all, merely showed a pretty girl up to her neck in soapsuds and looking pensive.

*

When Maeve awakened the next morning, Arlette had her breakfast tray ready: a pot of cocoa, delicious fresh rolls with Dundee's orange marmalade, and a telegram that had just arrived from Paris.

"Bonjour, madame," the maid said with a smile. "You have a message."

Maeve sank down a little farther in her heap of silken covers, enjoying their softness. Waking up was especially hard on some mornings, but when she finally sat up and read the telegram, she was ecstatic.

"A boy! Oh, Letty!" she exclaimed. "I have a brother! Good Lord! He's Hanno's uncle. Can you imagine? Little Hanno with a baby uncle!"

Both women were so excited they could hardly contain themselves, and Maeve and Arlette raced back to Paris as soon as possible to view the long-awaited heir to the Lassiter millions.

The atmosphere in the house was positively festive. Charlie himself greeted his stepdaughter at the door with a hug, and grinned broadly as she congratulated him on his son.

"Ah, Maeve, wait till you see the little fellow," he announced, practically dragging her up the grand white marble staircase. "He's got a fine pair of lungs and the thickest head of black hair I've ever seen on an infant. Looks just like his mother," he added proudly. "God, I'm thrilled to death with both of them!"

"Is Mama well?"

"Couldn't be better. She's one in a million, Maeve. She really is."

Moira was sitting up in a pink silk upholstered armchair having her hair done when Maeve and Charlie entered. She was wearing a spectacular pearl and diamond collar Maeve had never seen, probably a recent gift. This little bundle was going to be good for a whole avalanche of jewels.

"Mama! Congratulations! You look beautiful. How do you feel?"

"Absolutely tip-top." Moira smiled, embracing her wandering child. "Look," she pointed out, indicating her new collar. "Charlie's present after Desmond was born."

"Oh, how beautiful, Mama!" Maeve exclaimed. "I doubt if Queen Alexandra herself has one as fine."

Moira smiled complacently at that compliment. She loved being told her jewels were as fine as—or finer than—royalty's. In many cases, they actually were.

When Charlie left to meet some American friends for lunch and distribute specially imported Cuban cigars bearing the name, weight, and date of birth of the Lassiter heir, Moira sighed and said, "Maeveen, that nearly killed me. Do you know what that wild man did? He rushed me over to the American Embassy at the first sign of labor so I could give birth to the child on Yankee soil. Can you imagine? He and the ambassador had it all worked out in advance, you see. It was the only way to make sure the child would be able to become president one day— if it was a boy, of course."

Maeve was dumbfounded. She could just picture the scene—Moira screaming, Charlie hauling her off across town, the doctor racing after them, wondering if they'd gone mad. She was glad she had missed all that.

"Did he let you know about this plan in advance?" she asked curiously.

"No! I learned about it when I got my first pain. If I had been myself, I think I'd have killed him. As it was, I was in no condition to fight. Desmond was born five miserable hours after we crossed the embassy's threshold."

"And everything went well? No complications?"

"None. Apart from his father's mad decision to displace me from my own bed."

Maeve had to smile. Who could tell? She might one day be the half sister of an American president. She wondered if the Americans had a position comparable to that of Queen Mother. If not, Moira would surely be the first.

Suddenly she looked at her mother and said, "Desmond?" It had just sunk in.

"A fine name. Charlie's grandfather's name," her mother explained. "His father was Maurice and he was never fond of that one. Besides"— she shrugged—"people would reckon we'd named our baby after the butler and we'd never hear the end of it. Also," she added, "the *D* commemorates poor Dietrich, too."

Moira had been very fond of her handsome, titled son-in-law, and had actually wanted to name the baby after him. Desmond was the result of a coin toss—with a double-headed silver dollar Charlie carried around as a good luck charm.

"Well, that's sweet, Mama. I think that's very kind of you," Maeve declared, half touched, half embarrassed.

"Ah, the poor, dear lamb, Maeveen," Moira sighed, a tear beginning to well in her eye. "I still can't believe he's gone."

However, Moira could refresh her memory with a glance at the silver-framed mortuary photograph of Baron von Reuter she kept inside her large armoire, close to a small jewelry box. It was a kind of shrine to Dietrich, hidden away from prying eyes. She had adored the boy's blond good looks and had in fact ordered his valet to shave off that stupid beard before the formal lying in state, not wishing her handsome son-in-law to enter the pearly gates looking like a bad imitation of Hubertus.

When Maeve was ceremoniously escorted in to view young Desmond, a nursemaid and two assistants rose to greet her. The infant lay on display in Hanno's gilded cradle, a healthy-looking baby with a ruddy face, big blue eyes, and a mop of black hair.

"My God!" laughed Maeve as she stood gazing down on the sleepy-eyed baby. "He looks just like my old baby pictures! Nobody would ever deny he's yours, Mama!"

Thank God for a strong family resemblance, thought Moira for the hundredth time. Her imprint was so clear Des would probably turn out to look like a replica of his half sister, through and through. The Lassiters could claim he had their ruddy complexion and be satisfied with that. Nobody else was likely to look too hard for a family likeness, out of fear of finding one!

"I'm sure Hanno will be pleased with his new uncle—although he can't understand why *he's* the elder of the two. He thinks all uncles are grown-ups."

Moira smiled, pleased with her pretty baby—and her new jewels. The lavish diamond collar she was wearing, the pearl choker with a sapphire clasp, and spectacular emerald earrings in her jewel case were all recent acquisitions from Boucheron's, purchased by Charlie on the afternoon of Desmond's birth.

"We've just sent the happy announcement to New York," she gloated. "Now those two old biddies will really think I'm capable of anything. Well," she added reflectively, "I suppose I am, after all, *n'est-ce pas?*"

And she flashed a cheerful cat-that-ate-the-canary grin that spoke volumes. With this baby she had confounded her most severe detractors and replaced what Charlie thought was lost to him forever. He had his gorgeous Moira and now he had Desmond. The man was practically thumping his chest with pride.

"But between you and me, Maeveen," she said, "it's a hell of a way to get a few more baubles. I won't be trying this again anytime soon, that I can tell you!"

CHAPTER 33

*T*he summer of 1911 was one of those glorious moments that burst upon the world like shooting stars, only to vanish in a glimmer of iridescence, like stardust, leaving nothing but splendid memories behind.

In June, in Westminster Abbey, King George V and Queen Mary were crowned with all the glamour and pageantry Great Britain was capable of. The entire city, country, and empire were swept up in staging one gorgeous spectacle after the other to usher in the new reign.

Charlie Lassiter had received the most highly prized favor—outside of a seat in the abbey itself—that anyone could hope for, but due to the birth of his son, he wasn't going to be making the trip to London to enjoy it. A British friend had arranged for a hotel suite overlooking the parade route to be put at his disposal, and Charlie had thanked him and told him Maeve would be representing the family for the occasion.

Moira had been terribly disappointed. She wanted to be there herself—to upstage a whole clutch of duchesses with her jewels—and she wasn't afraid of the competition, either. Now Desmond's arrival had made that impossible. She was under doctor's order to rest for a month, so a trip across the Channel was impossible.

"Charlie was going to arrange to have me presented at court, too," she lamented as Maeve sat with her in her boudoir planning her own wardrobe. "I would have liked that." In fact, Moira had already planned her ensemble, right down to the ostrich plumes.

"I'm sure you'll have other opportunities, Mama. It's still early."

"No," Moira declared sadly. "I doubt it. Fat Teddy—the old bastard—liked rich Americans. They say this new one isn't the same sort."

"But Mama, you didn't want to be presented to Fat Teddy! He hanged Papa! You wouldn't have gone along with that, would you?"

Moira looked annoyed. "Of course not," she said loftily. "Don't be absurd."

But she wouldn't have balked at being presented informally to Queen Alexandra, whom she admired. She wondered about the new pair. This one didn't have his father's cosmopolitan tastes.

*

A glorious outpouring of sunshine greeted Maeve and her party—consisting of herself, Hanno, Arlette, Hanno's nurse, Maeve's footman, her hairdresser, her accompanist, and Marc Antoine—as they stepped off the train at Victoria Station.

Maeve and Marc Antoine were in London to sing at galas hosted by the Duchess of Marlborough and by Lady Warwick, a great patroness of the arts. They would be singing duets from Verdi and Puccini at two of the city's grandest palaces for an aristocratic audience including several royal dukes, duchesses, and princesses, but unlike her royal command performance in Berlin, these were going to cost her sponsors a fortune.

On the morning of the coronation, Maeve and her entourage ordered hampers of food from Fortnum and Mason along with bottles of Moët from the hotel and placed chairs on the balcony of their suite, the better to view the sights. Hanno was already shouting with delight each time he saw a mounted policeman canter down the street or heard a cheer arise from the multitude packing the sidewalks.

Despite the huge number of people, all seemed orderly and in fine spirits, some of them waving little Union Jacks even before the start of the parade.

Finally, after Hanno had begged the footman to run downstairs and buy him a Union Jack too, Maeve and Marc Antoine glanced outside and called to the rest of the group, "They're coming!" Everyone let out a shout and rushed to the balcony, champagne glasses in hand, to take a look at the royals.

It took some time before they actually got to see the coronation coaches bearing George V, Queen Mary, Queen Alexandra, and a host of lesser personages, but the sun shone brightly, the crowds cheered lustily, magnificent Guards regiments rode past on shiny mounts, thousands of colorfully garbed infantry from all corners of the Empire marched past in perfect unison, and foreign heads of state bowled along behind in open landaus, duly impressed with the extravaganza in which they were a footnote.

"Oh, look! The new Queen!" Maeve shouted, raising field glasses to get a closer view. "Mama would die to have those diamonds!" She laughed as she passed the glasses to Arlette, who had edged out Marc Antoine.

"Mon dieu, madame! I've never seen such jewels!" the girl exclaimed in awe, taking a good long look while the tenor nudged her impatiently, irked by this selfishness.

Poor Marc Antoine finally declared he'd miss everything if Arlette didn't stop hogging the field glasses, so she clicked her tongue in annoyance and handed them over, causing Maeve to wail a minute later that she wanted to see the King. Hurry up!

Despite the squabbles, everybody had a grand time and ended up toasting *"Le roi, la reine, et l'Empire Britannique!"* convinced that they had never seen such a spectacle in their lives and probably never would again. The fete lasted far into the night, with the London skyline red and gold from the barrage of fireworks rising high over the Thames and thousands of voices cheering the new monarchs, the new reign, and quite probably themselves into the bargain.

Coronation summer prompted such a dazzling display on the part of the aristocracy that even Maeve was impressed by the audiences she sang to. Duchesses, princesses, royal or gentry, these women had driven the great French fashion houses to work overtime to produce their splendid gowns. And their jewels were superb, as if the great families of England had cleaned out their vaults to adorn their women as lavishly as possible for the event.

"Makes me wish I were a jewel thief," Marc Antoine sighed after a performance at Lady Warwick's. "There must be enough diamonds on these ladies to cover the debt from the Franco-Prussian War and then some!"

"Even Mama would be impressed with that lot," Maeve said with a smile. "What a shame she's missing it."

It was a fabulous party, and afterward, in July, Maeve went to the stylish spa at Vichy by herself to recuperate. In practice, that meant Maeve was accompanied by Arlette while Hanno remained in Paris with his nurse and the new governess his mother had engaged to give him lessons. It was about time he had someone to teach him. He was a lively, intelligent child and he needed somebody to direct his curiosity into safe channels. If he was to go to Heidelberg University one day, Maeve declared, then he'd better get used to education now.

Maeve herself needed a vacation and a chance to recoup her strength: that was the reason for her trip to Vichy. She had felt her voice losing some of its quality lately—small imperfections of color and tone that worried her. When Arlette and Marc Antoine both remarked about her sounding "tired" in London, she had gone secretly to Berlin to visit a throat specialist, one recommended by Caruso.

Confirming her own worst fears, the doctor did in fact discover small nodes on her vocal cords, which he carefully removed, and he advised his famous patient to give up her engagements until the winter. Allow the throat to rest, he said, and it will heal as it should. This was simply a hazard of her profession, he assured her. A temporary nuisance, not a danger to her career. But it was also not something to neglect.

The mere thought of anything wrong with her vocal cords was so horrifying to Maeve that she had made arrangements for a vacation at once and ordered her manager not to accept any new bookings until January.

Pleading overwork and the stress of Dietrich's suicide, La Devereux boarded the train for the spa and arrived two days after Fedya Chaliapin, whom she discovered on crutches, returning from one of the bathing establishments.

Poor Fedya was suffering from the results of a bad fall onstage in Milan and from a fresh series of malicious attacks on the part of the Russian press. Maeve could tell which of the two bothered him more— he hadn't shut up about the "damned, hypocritical, ink-slinging hyenas" since her arrival, and she didn't imagine he would ever get it all out of his system. He was extremely touchy about this kind of thing, as she knew.

"Can you believe it, Masha?" he demanded in indignation as they sat beneath a shady tree having a picnic lunch on her second day. "The press accused me—*me*, for God's sake—of being just a poor simple-minded Tsar worshiper who flings himself onto the ground at first view of his emperor! It's embarrassing! Humiliating! As if I were some ig-noramus from the backwoods, overcome with awe to be in the presence of the Tsar! We once met Nicholas the Second, you and I. Do you remember?"

Nodding yes, Maeve didn't have to waste her voice on clarification because Fedya continued, never pausing for breath, "And did you see me fall to the floor on my face? Did you see me slobber over his hands? Did you see me grovel before any Romanov in that room?"

Maeve solemnly shook her head no.

"Well, there you are! And yet these hyenas have the gall to spread those lies about me in the press. I'm slandered before the entire nation!"

It took Maeve a while to learn all the details, but what happened stemmed from a poorly planned demonstration on the part of the Maryinsky chorus, who wanted to improve their working conditions.

Seizing upon the rare appearance of the Tsar in the theater one night, the badly paid chorus staged an impromptu plea to him during intermission, begging for higher salaries. Chaliapin, taken unawares, was startled to find himself in the midst of an emotional, keyed-up mob, all falling to their knees and singing the imperial anthem. A little dismayed and totally confused, he ended up kneeling too, not quite knowing what to do. Had something happened? Was the Tsar taken ill? Was a revolution about to begin?

At any rate, he was spotted with the chorus and this drew the scornful criticism of his leftist friends, who castigated him unmercifully for his "Tsar worship." He—infuriated by what he considered an unfair attack—was quarreling with everyone about it and absolutely incensed that he should be labeled a "Tsar-struck peasant."

Maeve suspected it was the peasant part that galled Fedya the most. Tall, handsome Fedya, as grand as any boyar, idolized at home and abroad, was always being taunted as a "peasant" by any number of hacks he had offended. And since he had a real talent for giving offense, he got it right back, often in print.

"It's jealousy," she said firmly. "You know how spiteful some people can be."

"Hyenas!" he declared with a growl, looking fierce. "Bloodsuckers!"

"Well, then, you know them for what they are. The Kaiser himself is proud to have you dine at his table. Fancy *him* wasting time on any old peasant." Maeve knew how much Fedya enjoyed the admiration of foreign royalty.

Fedya smiled, remembering that—and the imperial decoration that went with it. It was true. The Kaiser was mad about him, practically begging him to move to Berlin and make it his home.

"This is true, Masha," he agreed, stretching out under the tree and resting his head on her lap. "You understand me, I think."

Maeve was disconcerted to feel one of Fedya's beautiful hands suddenly slide down her thigh and stroke her as if she were a pet.

"I think I understand you better than you think I do," she replied, rising abruptly to dump him on the ground. "You lizard!"

*

To Arlette's dismay, she soon saw photographs of Maeve and Chaliapin in the local newspaper with captions suggesting a romance between the two idols. Was he leaving his second wife and tribe of children for La Devereux? Was she considering becoming the third Madame Chaliapin? Was she worried about the reaction of her fans?

After a few days of this nonsense, Maeve was echoing Chaliapin's cries of "ink-slinging hyenas," and dodging the reporters who dogged the couple wherever they showed their faces.

This farce went on until another gentleman arrived, settled in at the Grand Hotel, and soon replaced Chaliapin as Maeve's escort—although they occasionally lunched or dined *à trois*, which thoroughly rattled everyone interested in gawking at them. Now the "hyenas" were completely confused, which pleased Maeve enormously.

One pleasant evening, while she was strolling with Sean Farrell, he abruptly sat her down on a bench and said, "Maeve, I've fulfilled my duty to my son and to the Petrovic dynasty. Milan Plamanac is dead."

She glanced up sharply, knowing what that meant. Milan Plamanac was dead because Sean had killed him.

"Good," she nodded. "So there is justice in this world . . ."

"And I can get on with my life."

"Will you forget Zofia so easily?" she asked despite herself.

"Never. If there was ever a reason for disregarding paternal advice on marriage, that woman was it," he said bitterly.

Glancing at Sean, Maeve said quietly, "Don't let that bad experience ruin your life. Not all women are like that." She wasn't.

He nodded grimly. "I know that," he replied. "It was my bad luck to marry the one who was. But now I've wiped the slate clean, I hope."

But somehow he didn't look like a man who had wiped the slate clean. There was very little joy in his eyes. There was satisfaction, yes, but not joy. Maeve felt the same lack in herself. She slipped her arm through his and pressed gently against him.

"Maeve?" he said quietly as he stroked the cluster of auburn curls that had worked their way loose at the nape of her neck, "do you remember some months ago in Paris, when I asked you if you ever had regrets? About the ways things turned out in life?"

She looked at him carefully. "Yes," she nodded. "I remember."

"You said then that there was nothing one could do. Things were what they were—unchangeable."

Maeve acknowledged that, her diamonds sparkling in the moonlight as she nodded her head again. "That's what I said."

Sean asked abruptly, "Do you still feel that way?"

"No. That seems a million years ago now. I didn't know what lay ahead," she said sadly. "It's odd, isn't it, how one's whole life suddenly changes in so short a time? At that moment I felt as if I were chained to my fate."

"You had doubts, even then," he said gently. "I could tell it in your eyes."

"Was my misery so blatant?" she marveled.

"Not misery. Regret. You were still the same girl who hopped out of that sleigh on the Nevsky and caused such a scene. God, what a sight you were. I loved you." He could still picture that moment.

"Well, I always did have a dramatic flair," Maeve acknowledged with a smile. "But that day I was ripping mad. I nearly bowled over a dozen Russians just to get away from you. I wanted to kill you! And it took a long while to get over it."

Sean smiled too, looking at the expression in Maeve's eyes, exquisite deep blue eyes fringed with black lashes as long as any Italian's. Even Moira's lovely eyes didn't have the depth of expression hers did.

"I loved Dietrich," she said simply. "I fell in love with him the first time I saw him and resisted him all the time he was married to Lotte—just in case you had any ideas to the contrary. I am not a flighty girl."

"God Almighty," he murmured. "As if I ever thought you were!"

"But in the end, what did it matter? He had a mistress. He actually had another woman." She sighed, still miserable.

This was something she simply could not understand.

"Did you ever have a mistress? After marrying Zofia?" she asked.

"No."

"Truthfully."

"I'm not lying. I'll admit I was tempted a few times—especially in Petersburg." He smiled ruefully. "But in the Orthodox church the very act of adultery puts an end to a marriage. It would have been dishonorable for me to continue living with Zofia like that—and fool that I was, I behaved honorably with her."

"It reflected well on you." Maeve sighed. "I wish Dietrich had been as concerned with me . . ."

For a moment, she saw a strange expression cross Sean's face. Startled, Maeve raised her chin and looked him directly in the eye. "What is it?" she demanded. "You know something, don't you? Was I so stupid that I was the only person in Europe who didn't know about Fräulein Schneider?"

"Fräulein Schneider was nothing," he replied. "Your husband was involved in something far worse."

"What are you talking about?" she asked. "What do you know?"

"Maeve," he said, not knowing how to tell her, "Dietrich was being blackmailed. I'm convinced that this was the reason for his suicide."

"What?" Maeve suddenly lost her color as she stared at him, appalled. "Who would blackmail him? For what?"

Sean put his arm around her and pressed her close to him. Maeve was so agitated she was trembling, nearly too shocked for words. Dietrich blackmailed? It was crazy, she thought. Who would do it?

"It seems that the German foreign ministry was channeling funds to the Plamanacs via a well-known Berlin bank. Your husband was the courier. When the plot blew up in the Plamanacs' faces, the Germans withdrew their support. But my in-laws weren't ready to deal with that. Zofia took it upon herself to keep the money flowing by threatening to reveal your husband's part to you. And to me."

At this, Maeve looked so ill Sean was afraid she might faint.

"That witch!" Maeve shrieked, rallying. "Zofia sent that poor boy over the edge! Damn her! If she weren't already dead, I'd kill her myself!"

Out of breath with fury, she felt a pain in her chest that combined tight corseting with moral outrage. That Montenegrin bitch! Maeve had never liked her—never! Not even in the beginning! Now it turned out she had been right.

To appease Maeve, Sean quietly reminded her that old Milan had done what he did because Zofia had cheated and betrayed him as well as everyone else. That score, at least, was definitely settled.

"How did you find out?" she asked suddenly, still bewildered.

"Colonel Apis. He has a really loathsome knack for being au courant with many plots. He apparently informed Milan Plamanac that his daughter was cheating him by getting the money from Dietrich after your husband told him the funds had dried up."

"Well, then," said Maeve, puzzled, "where did Dietrich get the money to give her? He was hard-pressed for cash with all the problems the bank was having. It was driving him mad."

"Maeve," he replied gently, "he was being forced to dip into funds he didn't have. He was embezzling . . ."

Stunned by that, Maeve could only recall the pitiable suicide note he'd left: "I am a disgrace, even more than you can imagine." He had disgraced himself and Hubertus and all the other dead von Reuters whose stern portraits hung on the walls of that Berlin mansion. He had committed the ultimate sin for a von Reuter. And this was the only way to atone for it. "My God . . . !"

"When I went to search Milan's lodgings the night of the gunfight on the Ringstrasse, I found a satchel with the remains of the hundred thousand marks he stole from Zofia on the night he murdered her and our son."

"How much was left?" Maeve asked curiously, a bit dazed by all these ghastly revelations.

"Thirty thousand—which I'm returning to the bank. Your husband died in the middle of an investigation into the embezzlement. The bank never issued a statement on this matter, but there were rumors old Richter himself was a suspect. Ironically, they couldn't bring themselves to cast doubt on Baron von Reuter. It would have been too much for their sense of Prussian propriety."

At this, Maeve smiled wanly. "Poor Dietrich. If he hadn't cracked under the strain, he probably could have bluffed his way out of it. He wasn't tough enough for this bad world," she said quietly, her eyes overflowing with tears. "I would have helped him, you know. I was always ready for a fight—much more than he was . . ."

Losing all control, Maeve buried her face against Sean's chest and sobbed for poor Dietrich, so sweet and foolish. Such soft clay in that wicked woman's hands. Why hadn't he confided in her? Why had he been so frightened? My God! Of course he would have been afraid of Sean!

"Sean," Maeve said suddenly, "I want you to answer me, and I want you to tell me the truth. If you had known what my husband was involved in, would you have killed him?"

He shook his head. "No," he said. "That's probably what Zofia threatened him with, but I wouldn't have touched him. Maeve," he went on quietly, "I love you. I could never have harmed that boy, because of you—and Hanno. You once saved my life. There's no way on earth I could have taken away his. He was a pawn . . ."

A pawn. It was true, she thought sadly. Dietrich always had great ambitions that were a bit too much for his talents. And in the end he was a poor wretched suicide because he had finally gone too far. He had been trapped in a tangle of his own creation. My God, it was appalling.

After that, Maeve felt no desire for conversation. She sat with Sean for a long time on that bench in the middle of a pretty park, lost in memories—of the two of them in South Africa, of Dietrich the first time she had ever seen him, of the last time she saw him . . . She sat there for a long time, mute, nearly motionless, too worn out from emotion to put any of it into words.

With all her unhappiness Maeve looked so beautiful in the moonlight, with her hair in a cluster of curls, her diamonds glittering at throat and wrists, her white organza gown a little froth of semitransparency, that Sean would have liked to preserve this moment forever. Sometimes when he looked at Maeve he wondered if they had only imagined what had taken place in South Africa. How had that little ragamuffin rebel become La Devereux? How had she become Baroness von Reuter? That was his fault, he thought reproachfully, his alone. If things had only been different . . .

"Maeve," he said suddenly, "would you spend some time with me in the country? You've said you need rest. So do I."

Startled, she stared at him. "Which country?" she asked. "Where?"

"Any country you wish. Take your pick. We could stay at the seaside, in the Alps, in a dacha in the suburbs of St. Petersburg, in the Italian hill country. It doesn't matter. Very shortly all hell's going to break loose in the Balkans and I want to be with you in the time that remains. It's something we should have done years ago."

Maeve looked at him carefully. He was right. Nodding, she replied, "I would like to spend some time with you, Sean. I need to be with the people I love right now." Her heart was pounding.

"My time is yours," he answered.

*

Maeve was so enervated from the trauma of the past several months that she gratefully accepted the respite from stress and responded to her rare vacation the way a flower responds to sunlight. Being warned by her doctor not to exert herself, she was following his orders faithfully. There were no daily scales or vocalises, no new roles to study, nothing . . .

It surprised her that she could do without them. It surprised her even more how well suited she and Sean were. Their reunion in Vienna at the time of Milan's capture had been so strange that there hadn't been time for much besides a hurried farewell. Now there was time for all sorts of things, small pleasures both of them had neglected for too long. Still, it was a bittersweet experience.

The first night they made love had been in the Goldener Hirsch in Salzburg, the city's fanciest hotel—with Sean obliged to slink down the hall to her room in the best Feydeau farce manner and then sneak out before dawn or risk outraging the morals of Catholic Austria.

It had been quite exciting, as much from the naughty, childish thrill of breaking rules as from the act itself. She had been aroused in a way she'd almost forgotten and had been satisfied beyond all reasonable expectations. The effect was staggering.

The idea of making love with anyone but Dietrich was so novel to Maeve that no matter what happened, it would have been thrilling. Still, it had been a lovely thing, and not an experience to be ashamed of. There were worse things one could do, after all—steal sheep, burn villages, poison wells. But Maeve knew how people were. If word ever got out that Maeve Devereux had acquired a lover—when she ought to have been wrapped up in mourning for the baron—her life would be made miserable. Every self-proclaimed moralist in Europe, starting with Moira, would be prepared to castigate her from the coffee shop to the pulpit. And Fedya Chaliapin would be delighted, knowing that someone else was taking abuse for a change. How could they know how badly she needed comforting?

As Maeve lay cuddled beside Sean, affectionately stroking his hair, she nestled closer, pressed between him and the eiderdown. She was an artiste; therefore she was scandalous to begin with, she thought. Nellie Melba had caused an uproar in French monarchist circles years before when the Duke d'Orleans was flaunting their affair. Mathilde Kschessinska, prima ballerina of the Maryinsky, had provided gossip for the rumormongering set with her numerous affairs with the Romanovs and her illegitimate son by one of them. The American dancer Isadora Duncan, whose lovers included Ted Craig and more recently Paris Singer, had three illegitimate babies and zero husbands. And La Belle Otero was just so scandalous and wicked that decent ladies blushed at the mere mention of her name.

All in all, Maeve felt far removed from wickedness and not at all repentant. In her heart she was still angry with Dietrich and a bit inclined to put aside her normal caution with Sean. She loved him. She had loved him for years. She had loved him ever since he walked through that prison gate in Camp 3 and helped her escape from hell. This time, everything seemed possible, at least for a few weeks.

Having breakfast on a flower-draped balcony overlooking the mountains in the sunlit summer mornings, or wandering the woods as they scouted for a picnic spot at noon, even lolling at lakeside while Sean and Kyril tossed in fishing lines, Maeve felt utterly content. The fresh air, the flowers, the pleasant provincial life in Sean's company relaxed her and gave her a wonderful respite from several years of unending work, travel, and stress.

But at the back of her mind, there was a voice saying, "Enjoy it now, missy, for it won't last." And that voice had a distinctly Irish accent.

Maeve's holiday in Salzburg lengthened into a trip that took her down into Italy, where she and Sean stayed for a few days in a Venice filled with the latest news of Italy's war with Turkey over Tripoli, then boarded a steamer that carried them to the Bay of Kotor and Montenegro.

Just looking up at those stone mountains with their forbidding crags and barren slopes gave Maeve a better idea of Sean Farrell than anything he could have said.

"Mount Lovćen is our great monument," he informed her with a touch of pride. "It's one of nature's fortresses."

"I'd hate to have to climb it," Maeve murmured in awe.

"I have," he smiled. "It's not for the fainthearted."

"Neither is Montenegro, is it?"

"No. It's one of the most desolate places on earth. Only rocks and misery and not much more. But there's a power in those rocks that makes heroes." The pride in his voice was unmistakable now.

Fortunately for Maeve, Sean spared her a jaunt into the interior, but the recollection of that place never left her. She wondered how man could survive there, and she marveled at the fierce breed who called it home.

There was another reason to remember Mount Lovćen. They were looking at it in the distance from the deck of the steamer on their return to Italy when Sean suddenly turned to her and asked her to marry him.

"Don't be daft," Maeve replied, shading her eyes. "They'd never let you."

"I'm a grown man. I'll marry whom I please."

"Geraldine would make your life a misery if you even mentioned the idea! Then she'd start on me. No thank you!" She shuddered.

"Maeve, I love you! Besides," he added tenderly, "I've compromised you. I have to marry you."

"Have you become a Sicilian now?" she retorted. "That's how they do things."

"Maeve! Don't you love me?" he exclaimed, shocked.

She looked at this man with such venom it startled him. "Of course I love you," she replied. "What an idiotic question! But I'm not getting embroiled in some semiroyal scandal. And I'm not going to leap into a second marriage that would most likely end as badly as the first. I shouldn't marry anyone. I've no talent for it."

"I'm not Dietrich," Sean said, looking her straight in the eye. "I'm not likely to blow my brains out in a fit of nerves."

"No! You're more likely to have someone do it *to* you!" she replied, exasperated. "Colonel Apis or some other slimy toad. I couldn't bear to lose you like that!"

"There are no guarantees," he admitted. "This boat could sink in half an hour and we'd both be gone," he said as Maeve clutched the rail, looking around for life rafts. "You once had a close call onstage. Milan Plamanac shot me several times. We're still around."

"Marriage is different. It just is."

"Are you afraid of it?" he asked in surprise.

"Yes. I might be a bird of ill omen. I might be bad for you."

"Maeve!" he laughed. "Don't tell me you're superstitious!"

"I *am* about some things! I love you. I don't want to bring you bad luck." She had done that to Dietrich and she couldn't forget it.

Sean put his arm around her and felt her warmth against him. "We can still see each other in Paris, can't we?"

"Of course," Maeve agreed. "I'd be miserable if we didn't."

Well, he thought. That was fine with him. He planned on working on her hesitations just as long as it took. Then he wondered in alarm if there was anyone else who might be trying to do the same. He wasn't prepared to tolerate a rival for this woman. Maeve was his—whether she knew it or not. And anyone who didn't respect his claim was in for trouble.

*

Maeve's rest did her so much good she sounded better than ever. That was fine because in February she would need all her talent. She had agreed to sing *Salome* for an outlandish fee at a royal gathering in Sofia, Bulgaria. Marc Antoine was to be her Herod, with a Bulgarian tenor as Jokanaan.

The recently created Tsar Ferdinand had spared no expense to entertain his guests on the occasion of his son's coming of age. As Maeve's party rolled across Europe in a private Pullman, La Devereux was enthralled with the idea of performing before royalty in a city that had been until fairly recent times part of the exotic Ottoman Empire.

"I'm sure it's a vile place," muttered Marc Antoine, who had the privilege of traveling in Maeve's Pullman, along with Arlette. "I hear the people are peasants and savages, not much more than barbarians. I must be mad to do this."

"This Tsar has French blood, Marco. His mother was Princess Clementine of Orléans. He can't be a savage," Maeve pointed out. "And he's descended from Louis Quatorze."

That impressed Marc Antoine. Perhaps Bulgaria wouldn't be so bad after all.

Sean would be among the guests enjoying the festivities. He was to accompany his brother Danilo, since this was a gathering of the crown princes of Serbia, Greece, Montenegro, and Romania, all of them heading toward Sofia on board private Pullmans, ready to fete their Bulgarian colleague.

Actually, it was a political meeting meant to consolidate alliances, patch up old grievances, and plan a united strategy against the Turks. The latter, embroiled in a disastrous war with Italy over Tripoli and bogged down in an equally draining rebellion in Albania, were in no position to withstand a combined Balkan army bent on forcing them back to Asia Minor—or so it was earnestly hoped. If there was ever a time to realize the dream of centuries and plunder Turkish territories for the aggrandizement of the various Balkan States, now was that time. Ferdinand of Bulgaria intended to seize the initiative as soon as possible— hence the international gathering of future allies in his kingdom.

After an uneventful trip across the Balkans—with only minor problems caused by snow on the railroad tracks—Maeve and her party reached Sofia, were met at the station by a large gentleman in uniform bearing a bouquet for Madame Devereux, and were quickly escorted to their hotel, the Balkan, close by the Cathedral of St. Nedelja.

This was the main Orthodox church of Sofia, designed by Russian architects after the Turkish Wars of the 1870s, and it reminded Maeve of all those churches in St. Petersburg. It was to be the scene of the official Te Deum service for Bulgaria's young Crown Prince, attended by his family and all those other crown princes. Someone had arranged for Maeve's suite to have a good view of the avenue down which the royal party would ride in procession, and she already had her field glasses out.

Expecting to perform *Salome* in the royal palace, Maeve was disappointed to learn she would be singing it at the Military Club, one of Ferdinand's many recent contributions to his capital's architecture. He had also built an opera house and a new central market, added to the university, started an impressive spa, and extended somewhat primitive gardens into a real horticultural showcase. Busy fellow.

On Marc Antoine's first excursion around town he was decidedly unimpressed. The royal palace was drab, he said. The people were primitive, the streets were hopeless, and most of all, Sofia wasn't Paris. And the temperature was freezing.

Maeve kept her eyes open for Sean and managed to have tea with him under the crystal chandelier of the *salle de thé* of the hotel. As an unintended tribute to their visitor, the string quartet in the corner was playing "The Merry Widow Waltz," hardly Maeve's favorite under the circumstances. It tended to rekindle painful memories.

She looked radiant in a shimmer of sapphire satin, the bosom of her high-waisted afternoon gown a mass of lace with more lace revealed by a parting of the overlayer of satin at the side. Her Japanese pearls made a stunning impression, and so did her sables.

"How did the Te Deum go?" Maeve asked. She had watched the grand procession of royalty from her windows.

"Splendidly. Prince Boris is now officially an adult and he gets to wear a uniform even gaudier than mine." Sean looked very fine in his, which was loaded with gold braid and medals.

She laughed. "His father must have even more decorations than the Kaiser—and that's alarming."

"That's royalty. They collect uniforms, medals, and promises of friendship. Only the first two last. And none of them really means much."

"You're a cynic," she said, smiling at him.

"I'm a realist. By the way, I can't wait to hear your Salome tomorrow night. Following the performance you're to be presented to the Tsar and Tsaritza and attend a gala at the palace."

"Wonderful."

"You won't forget meeting Ferdinand." He smiled. "Nobody ever does."

Maeve wondered what he meant but didn't ask. She was too preoccupied with the preparations for the performance. As things worked out, she gave a magnificent portrayal of the depraved Salome and surprised Arlette by the modesty of her costume. In the Dance of the Seven Veils, Maeve whirled around in a glimmer of gold-embroidered chiffon—with little trousers—and managed to give the impression of bare skin without ever really baring it, much to her maid's astonishment and relief!

"Monsieur le baron would have been proud of you, madame," Arlette volunteered afterward. "You disappointed every dirty-minded old lecher in the room. They were all dying to see you in your skin."

"It wasn't Monsieur le baron I was thinking of!" Maeve retorted.

No matter what she told Sean on that boat in the Bay of Kotor, she was beginning to care very much about the opinion of Balkan royalty.

No crown prince was going to be able to boast he had seen La Devereux in nothing but baubles and bare skin. The other shocking part of the opera—lugging Jokanaan's severed head around—didn't make anybody turn a hair, severed heads being a sort of tradition in these parts.

Everybody understood Salome's lust for revenge and appreciated the method. There were no mad dashes for the exit in *that* room. Wild applause greeted the appearance of the prophet's detached head, and there were chuckles of amusement at Salome's kiss.

"Very nice," commented a Bulgarian general. "Very strong girl. We have girls like that in Macedonia, you know!"

And Maeve was left to wonder what would shock this lot. She was almost afraid to find out.

Later that evening, Madame Devereux was escorted to the palace by Monsieur de Marigny for the royal gala, and once inside they were dumbfounded by the contrast between the interior and exterior. It was sumptuous behind its plain facade.

Marc Antoine muttered under his breath that he hadn't seen so many toy soldiers in one place since last Bastille Day. There they were, lining the grand staircase, tall, enormous blond fellows in enough glitter and gold braid to rival even that other Tsar's troops. Drab on the outside, Ferdinand's palace was a living monument to opulence, with no expense spared to dazzle.

Amid a mob of brilliantly uniformed men, Maeve recognized Sean and Crown Prince Danilo, whose eyes lit up as he spotted her. There was also Crown Prince Alexander of Serbia, small, slim and somber, deep in discussion with the equally somber Crown Prince of Romania, a tall, spare fellow whose ears stuck out at a comic angle.

Maeve, in a gleaming white satin evening gown cut in the back to reveal a rich lace underskirt, was easily the most glamorous woman in the room. She shimmered with a radiance Sean hadn't seen since those days in Salzburg, her hair, skin, and jewels glowing in the light of the ballroom, her diamonds glittering with a brilliance that enhanced her delicate beauty. An exotic touch was the Prussian Order of the Red Eagle, which stood out impressively against all that whiteness. Marc Antoine looked like a handsome nonentity beside her, despite the red ribbon of the Legion d'honneur displayed rather conspicuously.

The ladies present were not an imposing collection, although Marc Antoine's expression changed when he was told the plainest lady in the room—the one with the biggest diamonds—was the Tsaritza Elenora. That produced a magnificent bow from Marc Antoine upon being presented, and the Tsaritza favored him with a few kind words about his performance. He truly loved royalty and gave the Tsaritza the sort of rapt attention she normally received only from her two beloved cairn terriers.

Other ladies were not slow to offer the male singers their own congratulations. The part most of them had liked best was Jokanaan's costume—a furry patchwork of pelts that displayed a great part of the tenor's physique. In this performance, Jokanaan showed more skin than Salome, and it set the ladies' pulses fluttering. If the men had been disappointed by Salome's modesty, the women were thrilled by Jokanaan's display of taut muscles and broad shoulders. For once in his career, Marco had been upstaged by a baritone, a humbling thought!

When Sean glanced in Maeve's direction to smile at her, he was amused to see only her back as she and Marc Antoine disappeared into another room, escorted by none other than their royal host.

"His Majesty likes the French," an equerry explained. "He says they are the only people who don't murder his native language."

Given a guided tour of the palace by the Tsar, Maeve was a little overwhelmed, but not so dazzled that she didn't realize he was really directing all his attention to her partner—most discreetly.

She found Ferdinand charming, with a sense of humor and irony not often found in kings. Tall and heavy with a superb bearing, the Tsar seemed more bon vivant than leader of a nation of peasants. As he was graciously showing his guests around his palace, he made a remark about beauty being a balm for the senses, which Maeve found quite flattering— until she realized in embarrassment that *she* was not the beauty he meant.

Somehow, Maeve could not picture Kaiser Wilhelm saying such a thing. Ferdinand, however, was not the usual sort of king. Invited to become Prince of Bulgaria by an assembly that had just lost its last European candidate, he had accepted despite the cold shoulder of most of the great European powers. Undaunted, this shrewd, ambitious grandson of Louis Philippe moved to Bulgaria, married a princess of Parma, fathered four children to create a royal family, overthrew the tough Bulgarian patriot who brought him to power, and ended up on friendly terms with Russia—which had originally so opposed his accession. A Catholic himself, he baptized his children in the Orthodox church of his new people and broke his wife's heart over this flagrant betrayal of her faith. She died young and unhappy, leaving Ferdinand with an heir, Russian goodwill, and nobody to interfere with his passion for handsome young men. The Tsaritza Elenora was a replacement for the Parma princess, but hardly a spouse. Her spurned affections went to her lively terriers and her four stepchildren.

*

When Maeve was preparing to leave Sofia, she noticed with annoyance that Marc Antoine had not yet started to pack.

"Come on, Marco," she said in exasperation. "You'll make us late."

"*Chérie*," he said diffidently, "I'm going to stay a bit longer."

"What?" Maeve stared at him, dumbstruck. "Whatever for?" she demanded, suddenly thinking he must be ill.

"Well, His Majesty has offered me a position here—a very nice position," he added. "Director of the Royal Opera."

"Is this a joke?"

"No! It's true. Tsar Ferdinand wants a French director of his new opera—and he wants me to put together a first-rate company. I agreed."

"For God's sake, Marco! He needs somebody like Carré, not you. This is ridiculous. Pack your bags and let's get going!"

"Maeve! I'm staying. It will be a challenge. I'm excited. I can't wait to start."

By this time, Maeve had heard all the stories about Ferdinand's harem of blond chauffeurs, not to mention military attachés, native and foreign, and she burst into tears.

"You're going to become some sort of Monsieur Pompadour!" she wailed. "You're a tart!" Hadn't he learned from past mistakes?

"Maeve, this is uncalled for! You're being unkind."

"Marco," she replied, "you really have no sense! You'll hate it here. You can't even speak the language. It's absurd!"

It didn't matter. Marc Antoine was so dazzled by the idea of becoming the Bulgarian Carré, he was adamant.

"Marc Antoine always was so very ambitious, madame," Arlette remarked as they waved goodbye from inside their Pullman car in the Sofia station. "But he won't last long here. He'll get bored and have one of his tantrums and then, pfft! back to Paris. Or," she sighed, "one of these big brutes will shoot him and that will be that."

Maeve struggled to hold back tears and failed, sobbing with misery as the train pulled slowly out of the station, leaving poor Marco behind in a land of peasants.

"They'll send him packing once he starts getting on his high horse," Arlette said, trying to cheer Maeve. "Nobody can stand him when he starts acting like the little dictator."

That was true. She just hoped they didn't shoot dictators here. Marc Antoine could be very irritating at times.

CHAPTER 34

On her return to Paris from the Balkans, Maeve found Moira taking to her role as mother of the Lassiter heir and the house loaded with presents for the baby. A gigantic teddy bear—a gift from President Roosevelt—occupied a place of honor near the cradle. Moira made certain nobody missed it.

Maeve smiled at that. "How is the little darling?" she asked her mother.

"Fine. He's become lively and quite greedy. All he wants to do is nurse. He drives that poor girl crazy." Moira was spared *that* bother.

"He sounds like Hanno. That's how he was."

Moira frowned. The child was lonely for his mother, especially since Dietrich's death. She didn't like Maeve being separated from him for so long. It wasn't good.

"You ought to stay closer to home," Moira advised. "Your son spends too much time with servants."

"I have to support myself and my son," Maeve replied, annoyed at this unwanted advice. She regretted these separations, but they were almost unavoidable. "Remember?"

Moira gave her a glare that would have frozen champagne. "We both know that's a lie. You spent most of July in bed with someone who wants to do just that!"

"Mama!" She hadn't thought Moira knew about that part of her summer. She certainly hadn't mentioned it.

Maeve turned bright red and gave Moira the satisfaction of knowing she had scored a direct hit. Well, she thought, at least the girl still has some shame. Moira had absolutely none, but thought Maeve ought to.

"People talk—even in the backwoods," Moira went on. "Geraldine Farrar happened to be visiting her old coach Lilli Lehmann, who has a villa in the area. Farrar heard about it from Lehmann and spread the news to friends in Paris. Now everyone in Paris thinks Sean Farrell is keeping you. Like it or not, there it is."

"Well, he's not keeping me. Nobody is."

"That's too bad," Moira retorted. "Sometimes I think you *need* a keeper. And Hanno needs a father. He had a fine one—until the poor dear went off his head."

"I love Sean Farrell but I can't marry him," Maeve replied. "Out of the question."

"Don't be absurd. He'd marry you in a minute. I know he would."

"Not in this lifetime. I'd have those wild Montenegrins out for my blood—as well as the gräfin. I couldn't face all that."

Moira looked at her lovely daughter and gave a scornful laugh. "Are you so weak and spineless all of a sudden that you'd let that blond tart in Berlin stand in your way? Remember who you are, Maeveen. You're a great star. People practically slobber over you wherever you go. You sparkle with all those diamonds. You have a fine home and money in the bank. You're the equal of any silly princess. Besides," she added, "Sean Farrell didn't marry a princess the first time around. He married that uppity bitch whose father was a fiend. None of your relatives is likely to go after him with a revolver."

Put that way, Maeve had to admit there was a lot of truth to Moira's argument. But that was only part of it. She was Maeve Devereux, the diva, the prima donna. If she married Sean, she might have trouble remaining one. She couldn't agree to stop singing. She also couldn't imagine a reigning monarch with a daughter-in-law who worked for a living. Not even a king of Montenegro, the wildest place in Europe.

Besides, she wondered deep down how Moira could ever countenance her marrying Sean. They had—at one time—been more than close.

"It wouldn't bother you, Mama?" she asked. The idea shocked *her*.

"No. Not now. I have what I want. Whatever happened between Sean Farrell and Moira Devereux doesn't affect Mrs. Charles Lassiter."

Well, Maeve thought, at least *that* wouldn't be a problem. If only she could be so certain about all those other things.

*

Sean had returned to Cetinje with Danilo after the festivities in Sofia and a few more meetings with potential allies. Several friendship treaties had been signed in preparation for the biggest all-out initiative against the Turks since the sixteenth century, and Montenegro intended to lead the fight. King Nikolai was already champing at the bit, ready for glory; Danilo, Mirko, and Peter were egging him on. Sean, on the other hand, had something else on his mind.

Just how difficult it was going to be to win Nikolai over became rudely apparent on the night he spoke to his father, declaring his intention to marry Maeve Devereux.

At first Nikolai didn't know who she was. She wasn't on the list of approved brides—he knew that. To Sean's fury he declared himself appalled when he was informed she was a singer. Out of the question!

Angered by this reaction from a man who hadn't been so scrupulous when he fathered *him*, Sean left Cetinje to consult with his sister Stana, his closest friend in the family. To his relief, she held out a slim hope. If they could get Queen Milena to speak up for him—stressing Maeve's banking fortune from her late husband, her connection to her stepfather's Standard Oil millions, and her own private fortune—they might make him reconsider his rejection. As far as she could see, Baroness von Reuter had all the necessary qualifications for a Petrovici spouse.

Sean hoped Stana was right. Maeve was the only woman he wanted—and now that she was free to marry him, he was afraid to lose her if he couldn't act soon. What kind of man was Nikolai Petrovic to deny him the solace of Maeve Devereux after inflicting Zofia on him? God, that was punishment! Was his father losing his grip on reality now that he had declared himself king after abandoning the traditional princely title? Nikolai was old, but Sean couldn't believe he was so old that he had forgotten what it meant to feel such passion for a woman. He had enjoyed enough of them in his own youth!

*

Maeve had been busy while Sean was racing around eastern Europe trying to arrange their marriage. Performances in London, Ostend, Berlin, and Dresden had taken much of her time, and there wasn't a bad review for any of them. In fact, the Germans called her voice "unrivaled in its lyric intensity" and enthused over her magnificent costumes. A command performance in Potsdam for the Crown Prince capped her Berlin triumph.

In the fall, when Maeve was thinking of her February performances in Monte Carlo, Sean arrived back in Paris bearing a sapphire and diamond engagement ring. He presented it to her in the midst of dinner at the Pré Catalan in late September.

"It's beautiful," she said, taken aback. "But how can I accept it?"

"Maeve! You can accept it as a token of my love and of my intention to marry you!"

"Your father still won't budge, will he? It's foolish to go ahead without his blessing."

"Why?" he asked. "You and I are the ones involved, not my father."

Looking at Sean from under her fringe of dark lashes, Maeve sighed. "Do you want to know the truth?"

"Of course!"

He thought he had never seen Maeve looking as lovely as she did at that moment—stunning in a deep violet gown, beautifully draped over her bosom in Grecian style and ornamented at each shoulder by a cluster of diamonds. Her diamond rosette necklace and diamond earrings sparkled magically in the subdued light, with more diamonds scattered in a delicate jeweled bandeau nestled among her curls.

Maeve sighed deeply, creating a light display as the stones rose and fell on her bosom.

"In Dietrich's suicide note he said he had killed his father in order to marry me." Her expression was desolate.

"Dietrich?" Sean exclaimed, then dropped his voice in embarrassment as Maeve looked stricken.

"Yes," she whispered. "He claimed he provoked Hubertus into a violent rage after he had disposed of his medication in advance. He deliberately caused the heart attack that killed him. All to marry me! I was an evil influence on him without even knowing it! I don't want to cause anyone such misfortune again."

That was truly Byzantine—Dietrich driven to murder in order to marry the woman he loved, then killing himself despite the love she had given him. . . .

"I'm so sorry," he said. "Maeve, it's horrible. But I swear to you my father's in no danger from me."

"I know that. But I'm still afraid. Perhaps it's not rational but I want his blessing. Otherwise it will never work out."

She sighed and reached for Sean's hand. "I know Dietrich wasn't in his right mind at the beginning and at the end of our marriage. Can you imagine how it feels to know this? Sometimes I can hardly stand thinking about it. I'm afraid of a second marriage, Sean. I do love you, but I want a semblance of goodwill from your family."

Spending time in Montenegro had given Sean insights into a variety of superstitions—fear of werewolves, fear of evil spirits, fear of witches and vampires—but he had never encountered this one. Maeve was afraid of parental malice. Dietrich had been driven to murder and suicide by it; she was afraid of what might happen to a new husband who defied his father to marry her. Considering the effect Hubertus's opposition had on Dietrich, he could hardly blame her for worrying. But *he* wasn't Dietrich.

"Maeve," he said hopefully, "would Charlie and Moira give you their blessing?"

"In a second."

"Well, then, you have half the battle won."

"I want your mother and father to approve as well. I doubt if either one would take me into the family without a fight."

Sean wished that damned German had never eased his conscience on his way out of this life. It was making things very difficult for him now.

"All right," he nodded. "I'll leave for Berlin tomorrow and tell Mama the news. I'll even have her give a party if you wish."

"Don't make things too difficult," she replied.

He smiled. "She'll welcome you with open arms."

*

Geraldine, no less than Nikolai, wanted a brilliant marriage for her son, but having lived through an attempt on his life by his late father-in-law, she was totally against allowing His Majesty from Montenegro a say in choosing the bride. With his luck he'd pick someone even worse the second time around! No. Geraldine was opposed to any intervention by Nikolai. If Sean wanted to marry Maeve Devereux, fine, she sighed, spreading her hands in a gesture of total acceptance.

In the back of her mind, Geraldine was already telling herself that if *that* didn't work out, there were several heiresses who might make quite acceptable *third* wives. One always had to keep one's eyes open and trust to fate. That was what had brought her to the heights she'd scaled. And that would see her through whatever lay ahead for her.

Besides, Maeve was rich and Sean was nearing forty, a mature man. It would be no disgrace to announce his engagement to the widowed Baroness von Reuter of Paris and Berlin, stepdaughter of Charles Lassiter of New York, Paris—and Standard Oil! Good God! He was lucky he didn't have to fight off a dozen rivals for her hand!

Geraldine's gracious letter welcoming Maeve into the family was a minor masterpiece of diplomacy. Forgotten were the bad old days. The gräfin was now looking forward to calling Maeve "daughter."

"She'd better not do it in *my* presence!" was Moira's response to that. "It's true she did you a great service when she started a run on that Berlin bank, but she only did it out of guilt. The woman simply likes to meddle—nothing more!"

"She also said she'd consider it a privilege to give us a party to announce the engagement."

"I'm sure she would," snapped Moira. "That's for the bride's. mother to do, not the groom's. Charlie and I will give you a party, don't worry. And she can come if she likes. We're not going to be traipsing over to Berlin just so *she* can show off."

This sounded rather contentious. Maeve hoped there would always be some space between Moira and Geraldine—say, the length of a country or even two.

The warmhearted welcome from the gräfin went a long way to alleviating Maeve's fear. Since she was no longer poor, unknown, and helpless, she was an acceptable daughter-in-law. A title and a pile of money could work wonders. And Geraldine was the more important parent in her son's life, the one whose name he bore. Whatever Sean was called informally in Montenegro, it had never been made official. He was Sean Farrell in western Europe.

"All right," Maeve said upon her return from a visit to Geraldine. "Let's have the wedding soon."

Sean barely had time to slip that large sapphire and diamond ring on her finger before he received a hand-delivered message from the Montenegrin ambassador to Paris.

"Come home at once," it read. "I want all my sons with me at this glorious moment of the reconquest. Leave at once. Nikolai."

"The reconquest?"

"The great crusade against the heathen Turks," the ambassador explained. "His Majesty has the honor of being the first to declare war."

"When?" Sean demanded, startled. He hadn't thought things would begin so quickly.

"As soon as possible. Take His Majesty at his word, Ivan Petrovic. Start packing!"

*

"It's all right," Maeve said stoically. "We're engaged. When the war is over, we'll be married."

"Maeve, I wish we could get married today."

She smiled wryly. "So do I," she admitted.

They were standing at the Gare de l'Est in a crowd of travelers, some of whom were Montenegrins from the embassy, en route home in preparation for the war. Two photographers were stalking Maeve, who looked stunning in a black velvet coat in the new kimono shape, edged with ermine and worn over a cream-colored afternoon frock. On her head was a velvet toque trimmed with jaunty ermine tails, reminding her of that muff of Lillie Langtry's so long ago. She looked lovely but felt desolate.

In keeping with the martial tone, Sean was dressed in a khaki service uniform. He was, after all, a soldier on his way to war.

"Don't be foolish and attempt anything Napoleonic," she warned him as the train's whistle shrieked twice, announcing its departure. "Remember, you have a lot to live for."

Pausing on the steps of the train as it began to gather up steam for the long trip east, Sean reached down and scooped her up in his arms. "I love you. I'll come back," he promised as he kissed her.

Maeve clung to him and the railing and tried to duck photographers, all at the same time. As she felt the train move, she kissed him again quickly and hopped back onto the platform, flinging a white rose at him from the bouquet the ambassador had just given her.

"A good luck charm!" he shouted back over the noise of the station. "I'll keep it with me during the campaign!"

"Be careful!" Maeve called out, running alongside as the long black train began to pull out of the station. She waved to Kyril, who appeared at a window, and shouted at him to take care of Ivan Petrovic. She was counting on him, she said, fighting back tears.

"Don't worry, little one," he called back. "It will be all right!"

It will be all right. So optimistic. So cheerful. Well, she had known war, and nothing about it had been all right. It had been full of senseless deaths, suffering, and starvation. She had been lucky to get out of it alive. Now Sean was heading into one that was going to be fought in a place even wilder than South Africa—and against heathens on top of it. She felt sick with fear for him.

*

With great determination, Sean and Kyril managed to reach Cetinje in time to rally around King Nikolai when he declared war on the Turks and sent his army of forty thousand streaming toward Albania and their objective—the fortress of Scutari.

The pretext for the war had been the Sultan's refusal to respond to the demands of the Balkan kings to improve the lot of their Christian subjects. With that out of the way, the attack was launched, with Serbia, Bulgaria, and Greece following Montenegro's lead at short intervals.

In the chancelleries of the great powers, statesmen and princes waited nervously for the outcome, concerned as always at the thought of territorial changes—with possible repercussions for themselves. Austria was already murmuring about the dangers of a Serbian rush for the Adriatic, and Italy was echoing her fears. The Kaiser, volatile as usual, displayed the attitude of a spectator at a brawl. Nobody talked about joining the Balkan kings, quite content to keep the fracas localized and far from themselves.

Everybody remembered all too well the tremors that had shaken European diplomacy in 1908 at the time of the annexation of Bosnia-Herzogovina, with Austria and Serbia nearly at each other's throats and Russia embarrassed to find herself outfoxed and unable to aid her client state in the face of Teutonic saber rattling. Nobody wanted a repetition of that now.

Sean and Kyril found themselves in a column heading south, their men wild with excitement at the prospect of loot. Discipline was not a notable characteristic of Montenegrins, and Sean was resigned to that fact—as long as they fought well. But as the product of a Russian military school, he had an appreciation for self-control. He was not tolerant of chaos.

One week into the war, the Montenegrins captured the fortress of Houms, one of the last great obstacles on the path to Scutari. As soon as he could find a working telegraph, Sean wired Maeve a message in Paris: "Great victory. Ten thousand Turks captured as well as heavy artillery. King Nikolai elated."

Nikolai was so delighted with this triumph he hosted a reception for the war correspondents from Britain, Austria, and Germany who were swarming around his headquarters. As he posed dramatically against the backdrop of the conquered fortress, he expressed his regrets over the loss of life but maintained that the present conflict would lead to a new and glorious era for the Balkans. And he, his sons, and his generals looked quite dramatic while the troops set about plundering whatever was available—a time-honored tradition.

To the annoyance of the League of Balkan Kings, Italy had just signed a peace treaty with the Ottoman Empire, ending the year-long war between them over Tripoli—and releasing the Turkish fleet for service against their new enemies. With considerable panache, the first thing the Turks did was to send a cruiser into the Black Sea to reduce Tsar Ferdinand's summer palace at Varna to a pile of rubble while he and his army were cutting a bloody path toward Salonika, on the Aegean.

Following the first victories, Montenegro felt invincible and plunged excitedly southward toward Scutari, halting at the next obstacle, the city of Berana, which had a strong garrison of Turks, supplemented by an Albanian contingent—who hated everything Montenegrin.

The five thousand Turks and four thousand Albanians in and around Berana were well armed with fourteen Krupp field guns and an adequate supply of rifles and ammunition, along with two months' provisions. This was not going to be an easy target, and King Nikolai was well aware of it, sending his best soldier, General Vokatitic, to plan the attack.

Crown Prince Danilo, Prince Peter, and Sean were in the thick of the fighting. With General Vokatitic planning an encircling movement from the east, the princes were to lead the first assault on Berana, softening up the Turks before Vokatitic and his division joined them for the final attack.

For nearly ten days the Montenegrins besieged the city, sending wave after wave against the Turkish outer positions, killing and being killed at an alarming rate. Sean distinguished himself early on by attacking a Turkish gun emplacement at the head of a small contingent and wiping out the Turks, seizing their Krupp field gun and turning it against the enemy. With bayonets and old Martini rifles, Nikolai's men decimated the Turks, mad for revenge for old, unforgotten feuds.

At a conference just behind the lines, Danilo, Peter, and Sean met with General Vokatitic to coordinate the final assault. They, the Petrovici, would lead the battle while the general would swing around to complete the encirclement, joining them for the entry into Berana at the head of the army. It was a highly optimistic conference, Sean thought wryly. Nothing was said about planning for a strategic withdrawal if things failed to go as planned. It was his experience that in battles, as in horse races, the final few minutes often produced surprising upsets.

*

Back in Paris, Maeve was frantic for news of the war, ordering Arlette to buy every English, French, and German newspaper she could get her hands on. All the European countries had war correspondents with the troops along the huge front, and one account claimed that this was the greatest concentration of fighting men massed on the continent since the days of Napoleon.

Maeve had just received a letter from Marc Antoine in Sofia—via the Bulgarian diplomatic pouch. He relayed news of the wildly enthusiastic send-off accorded Tsar Ferdinand at the head of his troops as they departed the capital for the distant front and "*la gloire*." Marc Antoine appeared to be in charge of "morale boosting," as he called it.

"What on earth do those Bulgarians have him doing?" Arlette wondered.

"I can't imagine," Maeve replied. "But he sounds happy."

Marc Antoine was in his glory. The Tsaritza Elenora, who had become almost as fond of him as she was of her cairn terriers, had taken him on as a sort of household pet cum equerry. As Bulgaria sent its sturdy warriors off to kill the Turks, blessed by the patriarch of Sofia and a clutch of his priests in splendid robes, Marc Antoine accompanied the Tsaritza and the royal children to the march-past and gave an impassioned rendition of the Bulgarian national anthem.

It was most impressive, all the more so since not all the warriors even knew they had a national anthem—one of the Tsar's new additions. With a gorgeous display of the national colors fluttering in the breeze behind him and the orchestra of the Royal Opera to back him up, Marc Antoine stood up there, wonderful to look at in his uniform, and sang this thing in Bulgarian as if it were the "Marseillaise," with all the audience-pleasing flourishes that used to annoy his colleagues at the Opéra-Comique.

Now he was put in charge of "patriotic assemblies" in Sofia's parks—outdoor concerts of patriotic airs to keep up the martial mood.

"I wonder if he has a uniform," Arlette mused. "If he does, it's probably fancier than the one the count wears in *The Merry Widow*."

It was, and whenever the short, dark, taciturn peasant population beheld this tall, light-haired, green-eyed apparition, they appeared awestruck, taking him for some sort of foreign general, weighed down by a ton of gold braid and epaulets.

Marc Antoine towered over most Bulgarians, and the women adored him, flinging flowers at him whenever he appeared onstage. There were rumors of affairs with the Tsar, the Tsaritza, three ladies-in-waiting, a rich banker's wife, and several foreign attachés. Nobody knew whether all or any of this was true, but Marc Antoine smiled charmingly, kept quiet, and had a fine time as the object of so much speculation.

*

While Maeve's former partner was helping boost Bulgarian morale, Sean was leading a detachment of Montenegrins in the final wave of assaults on Berana. Sean had suffered a wound during his capture of that field gun and it was Kyril who patched him up, using rakia—the regional liquor—as an antiseptic. While this produced unbelievable pain, it was commonly accepted as sensible procedure under the circumstances. After the wound had been washed out with rakia, Kyril applied a salve, the recipe for which had been given to him by a Franciscan monk who worked among the Albanian clans, a wild group long accustomed to gunshot wounds. Into it went extracts of pine resin, the green bark of elder twigs, white beeswax, and olive oil. Expecting it to come in handy, Kyril had prepared a large quantity before leaving for the front, and Sean was glad he had.

Despite the wound, Sean went back into action as soon as he could and led a daring night attack on the last Turkish positions before Berana. With heavy losses and crumbling morale, the Turks realized they were losing and had already started to flee the shell-scarred battle zone. The Montenegrins were almost ready to take the city. One last hard push and Berana would be theirs.

Sean had devised a strategy to wipe out the fiercest Turkish resistance at a point where a Montenegrin breakthrough would allow them to force their way inside the city itself, and to his surprise Prince Peter proposed replacing him in the attack. His half brother blandly explained that as a prince of the blood, it ought to fall to him or Danilo to lead what could be the decisive assault.

"The hell you will," Sean retorted. "This is mine. I've got the men ready to go. They know the plan. I'm the leader."

"I outrank you," Peter responded petulantly. "I can order you to hold back."

"You can damned well order anything you wish. But before you try leading an assault, you ought to practice getting your uniform dirty. This attack is going to depend on knowing what the hell you're doing out there in the dark. Rank doesn't mean a thing in this case."

Peter clenched his fists and glared as Sean turned on his heel and left the tent, roughly tearing aside the flap as he made his exit, furious with his brother. Little idiot! Who the hell was he to try to pull rank on him? Sean was hardly impressed with his skill in battle.

Sean's men overcame the final Turkish resistance and managed to cut a breach in their lines. Montenegrins poured into the city, and after a ferocious all-night battle Berana fell to King Nikolai's men just before noon, with the last pockets of Turkish and Albanian troops finally surrendering after a protracted defense that left large parts of the city in ruins. Both sides were exhausted, but the victors weren't so tired that they decided to forgo their reward.

In an outpouring of acclamation from the large Serb population of Berana, the conquerors staged a triumphal march through the heart of the town, leading to a Christian church where Danilo's chaplain celebrated a rousing Te Deum service with thousands of Serbs and Montenegrins waiting outside in the square, eager to participate but unable to cram themselves into the tiny building.

The Crown Prince was delighted. Cheered by the newly liberated Serbs of Berana, he had been mistaken for Nikolai during the victory parade and widely cheered by the onlookers, who flung flowers in his direction and wished him long life and greater victories. Sean and Peter, riding beside him, were cheered as well, both looking somewhat weary but elated. Only very sharp observers noted that they refused to look at each other, instead directing their gaze to the cheering populace.

General Vokatitic, riding beside Sean, was grimly appreciative of his men's work. Unsmiling and dour by nature, he was busy telling Sean that thanks to this victory, they had just acquired more than a dozen fine Krupp field guns and hundreds of rifles and ammunition. It would serve them well in the campaign.

That night when Nikolai Petrovic's telegram of congratulations arrived, Prince Peter was missing from the little family gathering that heard it read. He was looking for a functioning wireless so he could send his father his own news. And he was furious.

CHAPTER 35

While Sean was fighting his way toward Scutari with the Montenegrin forces, Marc Antoine's patron, Tsar Ferdinand, was experiencing the elation of victory farther east. Bulgaria's French-trained army was mauling her enemies and heading as fast as it could toward Salonika, collecting impressive victories at Kirk Kilissé and Adrianople.

Bulgaria had the Turks on the run, and Tsar Ferdinand was jubilantly sending home bulletins at frequent intervals, praising the bravery of his troops and asserting his country's claim to the Aegean port of Salonika—which made his Greek allies highly indignant, since it was also their claim.

*

Maeve had responded to an appeal from the Montenegrin princesses Militza and Stana to give charity concerts in Paris and St. Petersburg to raise money for the war wounded, and her Paris performance was a sold-out success. It was attended by the Tout-Paris, with Mrs. Charles Lassiter prominent among the ladies who contributed gifts to the raffle that concluded the show. Maeve got her old acquaintance Mata Hari to preside over the drawings, and her efforts raised hundreds of thousands of francs for medical supplies, blankets, and a first-aid station.

St. Petersburg was even more enthusiastic. Parisians had been gen-

erous, but St. Petersburg—home of militant pan-Slavism—was practically crazed in its response to charity appeals to help their Balkan
brothers. With none other than Grand Duke Nicholas Nicolaievich leading the way, Russians showered the fund-raisers with rubles, and so many
people had to be turned away from Maeve's concert that Stana coaxed
her into doing two others. The first was given in the elegant Hall of the
Nobility, the second in the Narodny Dom, and the third at the Maryinsky—with Fedya Chaliapin dropping by to join her in several Russian
folk songs at the last, which nearly caused a rather affectionate riot on
the part of his fans.

*

In the Balkans, far from the courts of Europe, the war was going brilliantly for the allies, who by November had racked up so many successes
that the Sultan's ambassadors in Europe were frantically trying to sue
for peace, terrified by the specter of Orthodox armies rampaging through
Constantinople. The Bulgarians were within reach of the capital, and
Ferdinand had astonished the Tsaritza Elenora by sending an officer
racing to Sofia to bring him his Byzantine robes. He was already planning
the Te Deum service in Santa Sophia.

Sean was in far less glamorous circumstances, settling in for a winter
siege of Scutari, Montenegro's main objective. Despite Nikolai's encouragement—sent from his headquarters in more comfortable areas—
his troops had been unable to seize the fortress, one of the strongest in
the Balkans.

Fierce fighting raged all around Scutari, with the Austrians and
other foreigners sending in emissaries under the white flag to escort their
own nationals out of the embattled city. But no matter how intolerable
life became inside Scutari, it held on, defiant and tempting, frustrating
the best efforts of its attackers to bring it to its knees.

In the atrocious winter conditions that were making life a misery
outside as well as inside, the besiegers were nearly as evil-tempered as
their quarry. In spite of all the money raised by their supporters, the
wounded were suffering bitterly from lack of medical supplies and even
the princes were feeling the effects of the brutal winter—although they
were fortunate enough to eat and sleep in better circumstances than their
men.

But all was not well among the Petrovici, and this showed itself in
big and small ways, undermining morale among those who knew it.
Ever since the battle of Berana, Prince Peter had developed a dislike
bordering on hatred for his half brother. That Ivan should have gone

ahead with his plan, succeeded brilliantly, and provided the long-awaited opening into Berana in defiance of *his* order to stand aside, had eaten at Peter. By now he loathed Ivan so much he no longer spoke to him and even pretended not to see him when the brothers attended strategy sessions.

Worse than that, Danilo, who ostensibly was trying to be even-handed, was secretly siding with Peter, damning Ivan with faint praise in his dispatches to Nikolai.

This rapid disintegration of family feeling worried the King. He loved Ivan and knew his worth. He also was shrewd enough to know Peter and Danilo and weigh the reports of General Vokatitic against theirs.

"My sons are as jealous as girls," he complained to one of his staff. "Let one distinguish himself and the others complain it was pure luck on his part and not due to any talent of his own. One would think I placed my daughters in command, not my boys!"

This was annoying to Nikolai, the more so when, for all their fighting, his men were still struggling in the environs of Scutari, mired in frozen muck and unable to capture the city.

On a visit to the Montenegrin lines in November 1912—a rough trip made more difficult by snow and ice—Nikolai harangued his generals, gave a stirring speech to his troops, and promoted Peter to captain in recognition of his valor in the campaign. Since Ivan was a colonel, Peter wanted to skip a few grades and become a general—to the utter horror of old Vokatitic—but Nikolai patiently explained that it would have a dismal effect on morale. It was enough that he was a prince, the King explained. That came from an accident of birth. As a soldier he would have to earn his rank, just like everyone else.

*

With the exception of the Montenegrins' siege of Scutari, the campaign was an unqualified success—for the kings. The Sultan was so fearful of losing everything, he begged for a truce, and with the Bulgarians overrunning Adrianople, not fifty miles from his capital, he was able to get his enemies to the conference table in London in December.

King Nikolai was in a vile humor. With Serbian and Bulgarian victories flung in his face, it was galling not to be able to claim the conquest of Scutari. He had also renounced his intentions of ruling Albania. These wild tribesmen would never tolerate a Montenegrin king, and, in fact, they were petitioning the great powers to recognize their independence from Turkey.

With the Turks in trouble, the Albanians were more than eager to

jump ship; moreover, they wanted nothing to do with Nikolai Petrovic
or any member of his family. Facing these hard facts, Nikolai's only
consolation was that the Albanians would also fight to the death to prevent
Serbia from annexing any part of their territory in her quest for access
to the Adriatic. Since Austria and Italy were just as opposed to Serbia's
plans as the Albanians were, Nikolai saw nothing good to be gained from
such a course and delighted in his neighbors' bad luck. Allies or not, he
had never really liked them.

Another more pressing problem was the division within the family.
That was a bad thing. So, to take some of the pressure off, he dispatched
a telegram to Ivan at winter headquarters, instructing him to get to
London as soon as possible—thereby removing him from the campaign
to allow Peter and Danilo a chance for glory, if there was any to be had.

Sean was stunned when he read the telegram. Here they were, dug
in before Scutari, waiting for a second go at it—for despite the peace
conference the Montenegrins were not budging—and Nikolai packs him
off to England as a "special envoy"! Damn.

"Ivan Petrovic," said Kyril, normally the most taciturn of men,
"this stinks."

"Damned right it does. And I know where the stink is coming
from."

But there was nothing he could do about it, so, accompanied by
Kyril, Ivan Petrovic packed his kit bag, made his way to the coast, and
started the trip west.

He had been sabotaged by Peter and Danilo, and Papa had sided
with them. He had beaten his brains out and received a small award
while Peter, the most incompetent of soldiers, had garnered a promotion!

"Ivan Petrovic, listen to me," Kyril said as they entrained at Venice,
bound for Paris where they would make connections for London, "Nikolai Petrovic knows his sons. He has to praise Danilo and Peter because
he can't say they're useless. But he knows what you did."

"This is a hell of a way to show it."

"Be glad you're out of that hellhole." Kyril smiled. "And picture
your brothers slogging through the frozen mud and wishing they were
on their way to a suite at Claridge's! They must envy you now."

Sean laughed. "They probably do," he admitted.

"Then look me in the eye and tell me your father has no regard
for what you did," Kyril said slyly. "Peter can have all the promotions
he wants. Right now he's up to his ass in frozen slush at Scutari, and
you're not."

Looking at things from that angle, Sean had to admit it was hardly a punishment. But he wanted to be the one who took the fortress, and now that opportunity might very well go to another. And with his luck, Prince Peter would become the hero of the campaign!

*

When Maeve received Sean's telegram from Venice telling her he would be in London for the conference, she made time to meet him there between performances in Berlin and Warsaw. Checking into Claridge's, she had a reunion with him and was shocked to see how thin he was. He had lost so much weight he seemed emaciated. No four-star chefs at the siege, he joked. He was lucky he hadn't always known what he was eating. The horses went from the front line to the spit. And so did lesser animals.

"My mother wrote me from Berlin that the Kaiser is furious with the Turks for their poor showing," Sean said. "Wilhelm says that they disgraced the German officers who trained them and that they are now unworthy of his friendship."

Maeve smiled. "He dearly loves a winner, doesn't he?"

"I think he's fond of the phrase, 'God is on the side of the heavy artillery'!"

They were dining in a private room at one of London's most elegant restaurants, Maeve looking regal in cream satin with heavy Brussels lace at the bodice and sleeves of her gown and displaying a glorious collection of diamonds at every available opportunity. She glittered when she moved, even at the merest turn of her head. She was breathtaking tonight.

Sean was quieter than usual. He was disgusted with the peace conference and the endless petty disputes about precedence and territory. With the tremendous loss of life back in the Balkans, all the delegates could think of was increasing their own prestige at the expense of their neighbors—and preventing anyone else from gaining what they couldn't have. Everything was so bloodless, so neat—in the conference room.

"Maeve," he said, reaching for her hand, "do you still want to get married?"

She burst out laughing. "What a question! Do birds fly? Do politicians steal? Of course I still want to. Let's set the date."

*

To avoid turning it into an extravaganza, Maeve and Sean decided on a quiet ceremony, attended only by Kyril, Arlette, and the immediate family—except for King Nikolai, who wasn't likely to show up anyway and in any case couldn't possibly leave Montenegro right now. Sean also mentioned the joyous news to the Montenegrin ambassador, who congratulated him warmly and wished him long life and happiness with his beautiful lady.

When Maeve and Sean drove to London's Orthodox cathedral a few days later where they intended to make the arrangements, they were kept waiting in the priest's study for half an hour while he disappeared inside for some sort of conversation. They could hear him. He sounded highly upset.

"What do you suppose is going on?" Maeve asked, puzzled.

"Probably some difficulty with a repairman or some such thing." Sean shrugged. "I wish he'd get on with it. It's cold in here."

"You should be used to that, coming from Scutari."

"After Scutari," he replied, "all I want is a good fire and a warm house."

When the gray-bearded priest in his black robes and splendid silver pectoral cross appeared at the door, he looked ashen.

"Father, are you all right?" Maeve asked. The poor man looked quite ill all of a sudden. Eerie transformation. Perhaps he had called his doctor while they were waiting.

"It's nothing, madame. Please come in and be seated."

When the couple sat down across from the father at his desk, they both noticed he was perspiring. And it was so cold they hadn't even removed their coats.

"We'll be brief." Sean smiled. "Baroness von Reuter and I would like to be married—as soon as possible. Small wedding. Just a few people. When can it be arranged?"

"Your name, sir."

"Sean Farrell."

Father Anastos looked even worse. He glanced at the couple, shook his head nervously, and replied, "No, I'm sorry. Out of the question."

"What?" Maeve exclaimed. "Why not, for heaven's sake?"

He groped, looking utterly wretched. "Ecclesiastical ruling," he said. "You are not a member of the Orthodox Church, are you, madame?"

"Well, no," Maeve admitted. "I'm not . . ."

"Ah, well, then," Father Anastos said, obviously relieved. "There you are. It's impossible. Both parties must be members of our faith."

"That's rubbish!" Sean replied. "Baroness von Reuter can be married to me in my church if she wishes. I don't know what kind of rules apply here."

Father Anastos was adamant. He seemed nervous, too, as if there was something he wasn't allowed to say. His eyes looked shifty.

Angry but undaunted, Maeve and Sean set out for the first Catholic church en route to the hotel. To their bewilderment, it was the same story there, except this time the impediment was the lack of an available baptismal certificate. Rules were rules, said the priest.

When the couple reached a civil bridal registry and heard a third version of official excuses, Sean was so furious he grabbed the clerk by his collar and lifted him off his feet as he bellowed, "What the hell is going on in this country? Why can't a man get married here?"

"Sir," whimpered the terrified little man, "the order came from the highest authority. If it were up to me, I'd perform the ceremony immediately. Indeed I would!"

Astonished, Sean dumped him on the floor, then picked him up and sat him down in a chair. "What are you talking about? What 'highest authority' are you referring to?"

"The foreign office, sir," he gulped nervously. "We received a memo two days ago absolutely forbidding us to perform a wedding for Sean Farrell and Baroness Maeve von Reuter. I'm sorry, sir, madam. But that's the problem."

This time it was Maeve who went wild. "It's your father and those bloody Montenegrins!" she yelled in full operatic splendor as she picked up a marble paperweight and sent it hurtling through the glass window into the next office, causing four secretaries to scream and duck down behind their desks in fright. "How dare he? Where does he get the gall to tell me who I can or can't marry?"

She was getting ready to wreck something else before the eyes of an astonished crowd when Sean hastily threw a couple of pound notes at the clerk for damages and bundled her out of the office in a fine rage and sounding remarkably like Geraldine!

*

To Maeve's disgust, Sean learned from Montenegro's ambassador to London that King Nikolai had requested the cooperation of the foreign offices of every country in Europe in blocking his son's marriage. The couple wouldn't find anyone to marry them, the ambassador said apologetically. His Majesty's wish.

"You can tell my father what I think of his meddling," Sean replied, letting loose with a string of phrases in Serb that left the gentleman wilting.

"I can't tell him that, Ivan Petrovic," he stammered. "He'd shoot me!"

"Well, I can," retorted Sean. "And I probably will."

The man was not exaggerating about the scope of the ban. When

Maeve reached Paris with Sean, it was the same there. Shocked at the extent of Nikolai's power, she told Moira she'd never been so miserable in her life or so dumbfounded. It was her first experience with any sort of embargo, and she declared it made her feel like a sheep with anthrax— too dangerous to admit to the fold.

Moira was aghast. She didn't care who Nikolai Petrovic was; he wasn't too grand for *her* daughter. Besides, from what she'd heard about Montenegro, it wasn't such a fancy place that it could afford to be so picky about who its king's bastard son married. After all, Nikolai himself hadn't bothered to marry Geraldine, had he?

When the Gräfin Geraldine heard about Nikolai's ban and the ready cooperation of the European powers, she was even angrier than Moira. She exploded in a rage that left precious Meissen shattered all over her breakfast room. If that old brigand thought he was going to wreck her boy's life by forbidding his marriage to the woman he loved—a woman with money of her own and a multimillionaire for a stepfather—he was off his trolley!

Money, as Nikolai was so fond of saying, made the world go 'round, and Maeve didn't lack it. Baroness von Reuter was perfectly acceptable to Geraldine, and that was that. Maeve had the Von Reuter Bank in good hands now—thanks to Dietrich's departure—and she had Charlie Lassiter in her pocket. What the hell did the old bandit want? Geraldine hated meddlers, she solemnly swore to her nervous maid. She hated people who didn't know how to leave well enough alone!

*

The only thing that was as dismal as Maeve's marriage prospects was the London peace conference. The Sultan's representative hemmed and hawed, trying to give his bedraggled army a chance to get its second wind. When it was all too apparent that the Ottoman Empire was not negotiating in good faith, the Balkan kings called home their representatives and resumed the war.

This time around, there was a definite feeling of mistrust among the allies. Montenegro was hysterically fearful of Serbia's intentions vis-à-vis Albania, and everybody harbored resentments and suspicions of Tsar Ferdinand's motives for *everything*. He had already proved somewhat less than forthright in his dealings with his Greek and Serbian allies, and now nobody trusted the Bulgarians, who were tough, dangerous fighters—eyeing some of the same territory Greece had staked out.

In the meantime, Sean was sent back to the battlefield at the Scutari front. The generals at field headquarters were glad to see him even if the princes were not. Peter was polite this time—which meant he was up to something—and Danilo was cordial but not really pleased. In addition, Prince Mirko had turned up in the area, resigned to losing his proposed kingdom but just as determined as the rest of the army to take Scutari.

Conditions behind the Montenegrin lines were not good, but what now prevailed in the besieged town was even worse, with people reduced to eating dogs, cats, and even more exotic beasts. The Sultan's men were despondent and took it as a gloomy sign of what was to come when the local pasha managed to escape under a white flag in a convoy of Christian monks.

The siege, never really called off, was renewed with a ferocity that surprised no one. For miles around, Albanian villages had been sacked and pillaged by the soldiers, and the villagers killed. When Sean protested the slaughter of women and children, his brothers shrugged. "They do the same to us," said Danilo and left it at that.

After several months of bitter fighting, the Montenegrins took Scutari and delighted their king, who called this the high point of his entire reign.

There was loot for the foot soldier and promotions for the officers. Peter became a major after Scutari and gained a chestful of medals, as did Danilo and Sean. The Te Deum that was celebrated in the city's largest Christian church was attended by every Montenegrin officer, and the captured Turkish commander, General Ali Reza, was treated with all military courtesy. But there was jubilation in the air, and no Montenegrin showed any restraint in celebrating the victory.

With an even greater string of victories now, the allies returned to the conference table in London and divided up the spoils. To the fury of all Montenegro, they saw Albania become independent, with hard-won Scutari slipping from their grasp. The Serbs, on the other hand, acquired large tracts of Macedonia, and the Bulgarians received Adrianople and a port on the Aegean, although they were forced to renounce Salonika in favor of Greece.

From hating the Turks, the allies now turned to hating each other in earnest. Things became so bad that only a month after the Treaty of London was signed, the former allies were at each other's throats, with Bulgaria launching an attack on Greece and Serbia on the last day of June 1913.

Tsar Ferdinand had been infuriated by the division of the spoils, and, having decided he was entitled to more, staged a surprise attack on his former allies, launching yet another conflict. However, he also found himself at war with Montenegro and Romania, who had jumped in at the last moment, and rather surprisingly with Turkey, who was now fighting alongside the Balkan kings against Tsar Ferdinand.

*

As Geraldine boarded the Orient Express to Venice for her journey to Cetinje, her son was traveling to Macedonia as an observer attached to the Serbian general staff, dispatched by King Nikolai to see how the fighting was going on that front, and, more important, to keep him out of the way of his brothers. If Ivan wanted to display his bravery, he could do it just as well in Macedonia and earn a few Serbian medals for his efforts.

While the battles were raging in the area of Stip, close to the Bulgarian border, Geraldine was making the arduous ascent up into the hills of Montenegro, accompanied by her nervous maid, two footmen, and a young man who was supposed to be a secretary but was actually a bodyguard.

The German legation in Cetinje had been alerted to expect her, and the head of the legation was already pacing the floor anxiously. He knew the gräfin's past history with King Nikolai and was eager to avoid any scandal that would reflect poorly on Germany. The woman was a terror. God only knew what she was up to now.

Geraldine, looking fit and youthful with her slim figure and leonine mane of blond hair, caused a sensation when her presence became known. Dressed by the finest couture houses of Paris, the gräfin was easily the most glamorous lady in all of Montenegro, and peasants stopped to stare at her in the street as she arrived at the legation with her staff and a number of trunks. Word went out that the Tsaritza of Russia had come to speak with the Petrovici. That vastly amused Geraldine, who was much more elegant than the Tsaritza—and twice as pretty.

Settling in, she sent word to the palace requesting an audience with Her Majesty, Queen Milena. Nikolai was away with his troops at Rieka, as she knew, and anyway, it was Milena she wished to see.

When the Queen received the request through her chief of protocol, she was startled. In her whole life she had barely spoken a dozen words to her husband's former mistress, but in view of what Stana had told her, the time for conversation had finally arrived. If Ivan's mother really wanted her boy married to a singer, a cipher in comparison with the royal and grand ducal spouses of her children, well, then—fine. She, Queen Milena, would be delighted to be her ally in this bizarre request.

CHAPTER 36

*I*n Paris, Maeve was returning home from a visit to her doctor, badly shaken by what he had just told her. She was pregnant—four months pregnant, to be exact—and the father of her child was at least a thousand miles away, fighting Bulgarians and unable to marry her even if he had been here in Paris! She looked so stricken that Arlette asked if she was all right, and was horrified to hear the news.

"Oh *mon dieu*, madame! This is awful. What will happen now?"

Maeve was at a loss to say. All she knew was that she wasn't about to give birth to anyone's bastard. She had to send Sean this information and pray that it might lead to a solution, but she wasn't even sure where he was, except that it was somewhere in Macedonia with a pack of wild Serbs. Marvelous. Meanwhile, she worried. And she wasn't going to tell Moira. She couldn't bear to listen to her.

"Oh, Letty," Maeve sighed. "What am I going to do? I can't give birth to this baby and I can't get rid of it. It's too dangerous. My God! What a scandal if anyone finds out about this! The public will disown me. They think I'm practically a saint!"

"Hmm," muttered Arlette, looking thoughtful. "Too bad Madame doesn't have a reputation like La Belle Otero. Nothing is too scandalous for her!"

Virtue, Maeve concluded, was a two-headed sword. And it looked as if she was going to get cut on it!

*

Sean was finding it tough going in Macedonia. The Bulgarians were ferocious fighters and inclined to keep fighting rather than retreat if there was the slightest chance of winning. Their French instructors had obviously drilled them well in the concept of élan, so dear to the hearts of all graduates of St.-Cyr. These soldiers had spirit and willpower to spare!

He and Kyril were attached to a Serbian position around Strumica when fighting erupted in their sector. Within hours their former allies, the Bulgarians, had achieved a stunning victory and had captured several thousand Serbs and a providential number of weapons. Along with dozens of weary Serb officers, Sean found himself forced to show his identity papers to their captors, who had lined up all the officers and were inspecting them as if searching for someone in particular.

"They're looking for Crown Prince Alexander," a nearby Serb muttered to Sean. "They think he's here."

That was their mistake. Alexander was in the field farther south, but the Bulgarians had heard from a spy that he was among the prisoners and they were trying hard to find him.

After the Bulgarian major took his papers and read them, he looked at Sean for a long time. The fact that his name was Sean Farrell was enough to make anyone wonder. It looked especially strange in Cyrillic letters. And nobody in the world would ever take it for Montenegrin. The sound was just too foreign and exotic here in the middle of Macedonia.

Nevertheless, the Bulgarian finally handed back the papers, glanced at him once more, and went on to the next prisoner. Sean felt relieved and even began to relax. That was when the Bulgarian returned with a general and a colonel and asked for his documents again, before bundling him off in an oxcart and taking him to their headquarters.

To Sean's regret, he found himself standing opposite a Bulgarian general whom he recognized from the London conference. Trying his best to keep his face in the shadows, he was roughly seized by an officer and pushed toward the brightly lit table where a group of Bulgarians was seated. They looked intently at the newcomer, and the general from the London conference took a better look at Sean and burst out laughing.

"Gentlemen!" he announced. "I don't know where Crown Prince Alexander is tonight, but we have a guest who ranks nearly as high in Montenegro! This is Nikolai Petrovic's son."

"The Crown Prince?" someone asked.

"No. The bastard," he replied. "Ivan Petrovic. Sean Farrell."

*

While Sean was being escorted under guard to Sofia, Maeve sent a wire to Marc Antoine from Budapest, where she was performing the role of Octavian in *Der Rosenkavalier*. "Florine expecting baby," it read. "Help if you can!"

That was such a shock to Marc Antoine that he left Sofia to join her as soon as possible and find out what was going on. When the tenor arrived in Budapest, he found Maeve and Arlette waiting for him, as arranged, at the Café New York, with its glittering bulbous chandeliers and acres of mirrors and marble-topped tables.

Before Marc Antoine could cross the crowded room and reach his partner, he was recognized by several ladies and besieged by a clutch of admirers as he made his way to her table. Maeve and Arlette watched impassively, waiting for one of those silly girls to swoon and fall at his feet, thereby making a complete spectacle of herself. It happened all the time with Marco. He had an unfortunate effect on women.

When the public realized who Maeve was, a buzz went around the café and the establishment's string quartet promptly switched to the lilting "Merry Widow Waltz" in irritating tribute to her Berlin success. Maeve was beginning to hate that music. She was still far from being a merry widow. In fact, she was as despondent as she'd ever been in her life!

Greeting Marco warmly, Maeve marveled at how quickly he had managed to reach Budapest. She didn't think the trains were still running from Sofia.

"For neutrals they are. If I were Bulgarian, I'd still be at the frontier."

"Strange way to run a war."

"Strange war." He smiled. "How are you?"

"Dreadful," she replied. "Absolutely dreadful." And her expression did nothing to deny it.

Maeve told him she was four months pregnant, unable to marry the baby's father, and didn't even know where he was. She was expecting this to wreck her career, disgrace Hanno, and lead to her being banned from Moira's house. And that was just the start.

"My God, Maeve," he declared in amazement, "you have to get married!"

Maeve and Arlette exchanged glances as if to say, "Isn't he the clever one?" Did Marc Antoine think he was telling them something they didn't know, for heaven's sake?

"Of course I do," she agreed. "The problem is I can't marry Sean."

For a second the tenor looked down at the cup of coffee in front of him, then raised his head, glanced at Maeve, and said simply, "Then marry me."

Maeve stared at him, stunned. She had never thought of *that*. Arlette looked even more startled.

"But Marco," Maeve babbled, "your fans would be so hurt . . ."

"Nonsense! They'd live with it. We'll get married in Sofia in a big wedding at the Orthodox cathedral. Gorgeous church. Maybe the Tsar and Tsaritza will attend. There'll be a large party. And about a year after the child is born, we'll just divorce. You can sue me for adultery or some such thing. Well"—he shrugged—"what else can we do? This way the baby will have a father and you won't be disgraced."

"Marco," she murmured, "you're a kind man."

He was embarrassed to see she was crying. He reached for his pocket handkerchief and handed it to her so she could dry her tears.

"You saved my life," he said. "Nobody would have done what you did for me. And don't think I've ever forgotten. I want to help you, Maeve. I love you."

Maeve and Marc Antoine were both a little overcome with emotion, and so was Arlette. To Maeve's surprise, her maid was dabbing at her eyes with a handkerchief and sniffing ever so quietly—Arlette who never cried. It was a bit unsettling for all of them.

Well, now at least she was going to have a name to put on the marriage certificate and a birth registry—even if it was the wrong one. This was dreadful. Sean's baby would have to go through life as de Marigny, but since she couldn't become Mrs. Farrell right now, it was the only option left to her. She was no Isadora Duncan. Besides, she thought with a shudder, Isadora wouldn't have to face Moira—that was reason enough to make a dash to the altar.

Despite the war, the Orient Express reached Sofia with few delays—even if the border guards were a bit overzealous in checking papers right now. Maeve hated to think what might happen to any Serb or Romanian the Bulgarians found. Neutrals were wished a pleasant journey and left unmolested.

*

Maeve and Arlette moved into the Balkan Hotel again on their arrival in Sofia, were warmly received by the manager, and found themselves waiting for Marc Antoine to make the wedding arrangements.

It was all a bit unreal. Sofia in July was hot and sultry, and Maeve was now five months into her pregnancy and feeling it. She was too enervated to do anything but rest, yet the baby prevented her from finding a comfortable position when she tried to stretch out.

"Damn!" she exclaimed. "It's like carting around a sack of potatoes—and it keeps shifting. I hate this! I wish the men were saddled with it!"

"Then the world's population would come to an end," replied Arlette, who was trying to make Madame more comfortable by unlacing her corset and rubbing her back. "You know how they are. They can't put up with the tiniest inconvenience."

Marc Antoine had already decided to make a personal plea to the Tsar in order to facilitate things. In Maeve's condition, the sooner she was married the better. She was starting to show all of a sudden, and although her stylish dresses were a good concealment, nobody was going to be fooled for much longer. She needed a husband *now*.

Taking advantage of Ferdinand's unexpected command to present himself at the palace, Marc Antoine arrived on time, cooled his heels in the anteroom for exactly five minutes, and saw the heavy gilded doors open to reveal a footman who announced, "You may enter, monsieur."

His Majesty was anxious to know whether or not his director of the Royal Opera had been successful in finding a French soprano, and was displeased by the negative answer.

"It's the war, Your Majesty. People are afraid to enter the country."

Ferdinand flicked him a disdainful glance with his small, close-set brown eyes and was startled to see Marc Antoine's expression suddenly change.

"Majesty?" he said timidly.

"Yes. What is it?"

"I have a great favor to ask. I want to marry and I need the wedding performed immediately. I will never trouble you again if you would grant me this request."

Ferdinand, for once in his life, was dumbfounded. Marco getting married? Was he hearing things?

"What did you say?"

"Majesty, I asked if you would authorize an immediate wedding."

"To whom, for God's sake?" the Tsar demanded, staring at him.

"To Maeve Devereux. Baroness von Reuter."

"Ah," smiled Ferdinand. "Our little Salome. Well, you certainly have fine taste in women. Is this some sort of joke? Why would she ever marry you? The gossip has it she's madly in love with Nikolai Petrovic's son. Permit me to observe that you're quite a different sort of person altogether."

"Majesty, the Baroness is expecting a child. Nikolai Petrovic has blocked their marriage in every country in Europe and she's desperate. If she gives birth to this child out of wedlock, the scandal will be enormous. It may wreck her career, and even if it doesn't do that, it would be a terrible embarrassment to her family. These are people with a position to maintain in society."

"She should have thought of that earlier," he replied, unimpressed.

Then suddenly Ferdinand glanced at Marc Antoine and nearly jumped from the shock of what had just occurred to him. This boy had given him his revenge on Nikolai Petrovic, handed it to him on a silver platter.

"That old bandit Nikolai has blocked their marriage?" he asked abruptly.

"Everywhere in Europe, Your Majesty. He's dead set against it."

"It would break his heart to see that girl become his daughter-in-law?" the Tsar asked, becoming quite pleased with himself. "It would crush him? Humiliate him? Infuriate him?"

Marc Antoine solemnly answered yes each time, wondering why Ferdinand was suddenly so cheerful. With all his worries about the war, he now looked absolutely radiant.

"We'll have the wedding," he announced grandly. "It will be a fantastic occasion. The entire court and diplomatic corps in full dress. The chorus of the Rilla monastery will chant the service. Flowers from the royal gardens will envelop the little bride. . . ."

The singer was thoroughly puzzled. Was Ferdinand talking about *his* wedding? He had to be, yet this didn't quite make sense. It was so far beyond what Marc Antoine had hoped for that he got carried away and kissed the Tsar's hand in gratitude several times.

"Thank you, Your Majesty," he babbled. "I'll be forever in your debt!"

"No you won't," Ferdinand replied coolly. "But Sean Farrell will be. He's here in Sofia now, in prison. We'll see just how much he wants to be a bridegroom. You may go," he added casually.

Marc Antoine was so astonished he almost forgot to bow as required on his way out the door. Sean in Sofia! God Almighty! That meant Maeve could marry him with Ferdinand staging a ceremony fit for a prince. This was unbelievable!

He couldn't wait to announce the news to the bride.

CHAPTER 37

"He's here!" Maeve exclaimed. "Oh, Marco, don't lie to me! Is he really here? In Sofia?"

"The Tsar says he is. He also says he'll let you and Sean marry. He was so kind. He took such a personal interest in it."

Maeve's expression changed. "Of course he would. He's fighting a war with Nikolai Petrovic. Why wouldn't he? If he's being kind and helpful, it only means he has his own reasons for it."

Marc Antoine looked crestfallen. "I thought you'd be delighted," he said. "It ought to make you happy."

She hugged him and made him sit down while Arlette ordered tea. "Darling boy." She smiled. "Doesn't it seem too good to be true, that Sean and I can marry here when no country in Europe will allow it? This isn't kindness. It's revenge!"

"Well, at least it's a wedding," he replied as he glanced at her middle. "And it's what you want." Right now she didn't dare dally.

"I hope it's what Sean wants," she said. "I know it will make his father furious." This could be a disaster!

*

The four Bulgarian officers who escorted Sean Farrell into the Balkan Hotel had to spirit him up the staff stairway because he looked awful and smelled worse. The manager refused to let the group use the fancy wrought-iron elevator for fear of scaring the guests.

When Maeve heard a knock at her door, she sent Arlette to answer it, thinking it was a visitor. No visitors, she said firmly. I'm going to try to rest.

To Arlette's amazement, she found herself confronting five men, four short, dark officers in Bulgarian uniform and one tall, bedraggled wreck who smelled worse than the Paris sewers. She let out a gasp and slammed the door shut in fright.

"Letty! For God's sake! It's me. Open up. I have to see Maeve. Don't you recognize me?"

Astonished, she opened the door a crack and peered out. That was Sean Farrell's voice, but where was he?

"Letty! I have to speak to Maeve," the dirty-looking one announced. "Don't be afraid. Come on, girl. Let me in."

Arlette gawked at Sean in stunned silence and stepped aside to allow him to enter, not knowing what to say.

He looked like a beggar. Unwashed, uncombed, dirty—he seemed the sort any honest person would avoid. And Monsieur le baron had always been so clean!

"Where's Maeve?" he asked eagerly.

"In there, monsieur. But please, don't go near her like that. You'll frighten her and she may lose the baby."

"Baby? What baby?"

Sean's face took on a strange expression. He let out a whoop, grabbed Arlette and embraced her—much to her horror—and went racing into the bedroom, eager to find Maeve and ask if what he had just heard was true.

Their reunion was marred by the distance he felt obliged to keep due to his filth. In desperation, the women made him remove every stitch of clothing and toss it down into the street, then soak himself in a warm bath, while Maeve telephoned Marc Antoine asking for fresh clothing from the skin up.

When the tenor arrived with an armload of clothes and two tailors, they managed to clothe Sean properly by letting out seams here and there and lengthening cuffs: he was slightly taller and more muscular than Marc Antoine. By the time the tailors were done with him, he was presentable and the Frenchman had lost two good summer suits.

Then Maeve explained what Marc Antoine had told her about Ferdinand's offer of a wedding in his capital. Sean was silent.

"I'm glad you're so wildly enthusiastic," she observed. "You make me feel as wanted as death!" She wanted to slap him.

"Don't be ridiculous. I love you. I want to marry you. But how can we do this? My father will consider it a betrayal—under these circumstances!"

"I'll consider it worse," she retorted. "Now, Sean my darling, I know how much you love your father, but he's not here to give you advice. I am. And I'm five months gone with your baby. Now, you listen to me and you make your decision. If you decide you can't bear to break your poor papa's heart, fine. But that means I'll marry Marc Antoine tomorrow morning—and your baby will go through life with another man's name. Think about it, boyo!" And she flounced out of the room in a fury.

Jesus! He was damned either way. If he married Maeve in Bulgaria as Ferdinand's guest, Nikolai might just shoot him. If he didn't, Maeve would marry the tenor and bring up his child under false pretenses. He loved that woman. He wanted his child. Maeve marry Marc Antoine! Never! What a ridiculous idea!

Damn, he thought as he looked at himself in the mirror. He had no choice. Maeve had to be a bride as soon as possible—even though she might end up a widow for the second time rather soon.

When Sean put his head around the door, he asked mildly, "Which church has the Tsar picked for the nuptials?"

Maeve looked up warily. "Is that a yes?"

"Damned right it is!" He grinned. "I'd never forgive myself if I didn't make an honest woman of you soon."

"Don't you wish!" she laughed. But her relief was evident.

Well, that at least was settled. Now there were the logistics for the ceremony. With the war drawing to a quick and unfavorable close for Bulgaria, Ferdinand wanted his revenge on at least one of his enemies fast. The details were left to Marc Antoine and the metropolitan of Sofia to work out.

With perfect cooperation the prelate declared the banns published and instructed the couple to present themselves at St. Nedelja's in three days. He then took Maeve on a tour of the cathedral and rehearsed her in the procedure of an Orthodox wedding.

"My God, madame!" Arlette exclaimed. "You'll need a gown. What will you wear?"

Maeve hadn't yet thought about it. Since this was a second marriage, bridal white hardly seemed appropriate—especially in her case!

"I'll use my pale blue gown," she decided. "It has a tunic and it ought to hide some of me. And I'll wear flowers in my hair. They have such lovely roses in this country."

By this time Sean had got Kyril, who had been captured with him, released from prison too, and cleaned up, and the Montenegrin was shocked at what he heard. Tsar Ferdinand was letting Ivan Petrovic marry Maeve in Sofia in defiance of King Nikolai! And Ivan was going to do it!

"There'll be hell to pay when your father hears this," he said solemnly. He could already picture Ivan Petrovic in Cetinje's new prison.

"There'd be worse if I didn't," Sean replied. "If I don't marry her, she's set to marry Marc Antoine de Marigny!"

That revelation left Kyril speechless. The little one must have lost her mind, he thought in shock. Then he saw Maeve's middle and he understood.

Ferdinand was so incensed over his beating at the hands of "these Balkan peasants" that he was staging a grandiose reception at the palace after the splendid wedding, to which all Sofia society was invited. Nikolai Petrovic might be part of the coalition that was bringing down Bulgaria's army, but the Tsar would deal him a blow from which he would never recover. His son would marry that singer, a girl unfit to be the mother of a semiroyal infant.

Marc Antoine was in heaven, planning the wedding. He and the head monk of the Rilla monastery had long discussions over the sacred music, and the Tsaritza Elenora, who had immersed herself in Red Cross work, took time out from visiting hospitals to pay an impromptu visit to Maeve's hotel suite to wish her good luck and inform her that the royal gardener was going to create her bridal bouquet.

"Her Majesty is such a lovely person," Marc Antoine said after Elenora had departed with her two yapping cairn terriers and a lady-in-waiting. "She's pretty much on her own here. She likes to take an interest in people."

"That was very gracious of her. She seems so *sympathique*."

"Oh, she is," Marc Antoine nodded. "She's almost like a mother to me."

Well, Maeve thought, obviously Marco was right at home in this place. And she had been so worried he'd never fit in!

The Bulgarians were being very gracious about the wedding—considering that the bridegroom was an official enemy. Sean was equally gracious in return, but he was not so grateful that he was about to cooperate with Ferdinand once the service was over and he and Maeve were legally married. No. He and Kyril were planning a surprise and not the sort that would be well received by his benefactors. Guarded by a quartet of soldiers, Sean and Kyril were already plotting their escape.

After the ceremony at St. Nedelja's, Maeve and Sean would be escorted back to the hotel, where they would change clothes and get ready to drive to the palace for the gala reception—which was to be filmed for distribution in every capital in Europe, thereby infuriating Nikolai Petrovic.

Ferdinand had already chosen the uniform he would wear for the cameras, a white one that permitted a maximum display of ribbons and medals. The Tsaritza would be quite plain beside him, but as he often remarked, speaking as an expert ornithologist, in the aviary the male often sports brighter plumage than its mate. Ferdinand was lucky he wasn't married to Moira!

On the day of the wedding Maeve spent two hours trying to find a corset that would pull her stomach in while allowing her to breathe, and when she descended to the lobby to be met by a cluster of excited guests, she was quite pale from the effects of tight lacing. She still managed to look lovely in her blue silk gown with its tunic floating around her like a cloud with each step she took. In her upswept hair was a garland of white roses and in her arms a magnificent bouquet of white and pink roses mixed with stephanotis and baby's breath, tied with silky white ribbons in a lovely cascade.

Merely walking across the street to the cathedral was "too banal," the French cinematographer declared, so La Devereux got into a flower-draped calèche with Marc Antoine opposite her and was driven around the block so she could be filmed arriving at the church in more elegant fashion. As a nice local touch, dozens of young girls flung rose petals around her in a fragrant blizzard of pink and white as she alighted on the church's threshold, smiling in delight at their spirited greeting. Some of them, she noticed in amusement, were shouting "Marco! Marco!" Even in the depths of Bulgaria she had to put up with his fans!

Inside the cathedral was a gathering of the elite of Sofia—a very small group, actually—and the diplomatic corps, plus anyone Marc Antoine had been able to round up from the Royal Opera. It was quite a respectable number and Ferdinand was pleased. He stood close by the altar with the Tsaritza and looked extremely impressive in his fine uniform and medals.

Despite the circumstances, Maeve felt very solemn as she stood beside Sean in the heart of this Orthodox cathedral. She had been married the first time in a simple civil ceremony in Paris. Now she was part of a glorious ritual with superb music that reminded her of a scene from the old Russian operas. If only Chaliapin could be here to enjoy it with her! He had once been a choir singer in the Russian church and would appreciate the sonorous, majestic beauty of the Bulgarian Mass.

As she stood beside Sean in her nuptial crown, holding a lit taper while the priest chanted the prayers and engulfed them in clouds of sweet, spicy incense, Maeve felt buoyed up by a sensation of warmth and well-being. In her heart at that moment she finally forgave Dietrich and put aside all thoughts of bitterness toward him. He had given her Hanno and he had released her for this new life. If he could see her now, he must wish her well. She only wished Moira and Charlie were present at this spectacular ceremony with the Tsar and Tsaritza of Bulgaria in the congregation and the masses of bright vestments and dress uniforms filling up the church.

Afterward, Ferdinand and Elenora signed the marriage registry as witnesses and the metropolitan of Sofia solemnly presented the marriage certificate to Maeve. She was now Mrs. Sean Farrell, and there was nothing Nikolai Petrovic or anyone else could do about it.

Arlette was so happy she couldn't stop weeping. And Kyril was pleased for Ivan Petrovic and his bride though privately dreading Nikolai's reaction.

Since the reception at the palace was to begin an hour after the wedding, there wasn't much time to lose, Sean decided. If he and Maeve were to get out of Sofia, it would have to be now. Unfortunately, he hadn't yet informed his new wife of his plans.

"What?" she gasped after they had returned under escort to the hotel. "Are you utterly mad? Foxy Ferdy will probably murder us if we try to run away!"

"Not if he doesn't catch us. I went through with the wedding because I wanted to marry you, but I'll be damned if I'll play trained poodle for him at this reception. The whole thing is just his way of insulting my father. I can't be a party to it."

"Well, how do we leave?" Maeve demanded in bewilderment. He had to be mad!

"We go out on the Orient Express which departs in half an hour. One of the few things one can count on in life is the punctuality of this train. It will get us out of Sofia. It's always on time."

"You're dreaming. There are four stout soldiers in the hallway who'll jump all over you if you go anyplace but the palace."

"Then we'll just have to divide and conquer," he replied with a wink.

Arlette was sent out to invite one of the soldiers in for champagne to celebrate the wedding, and he succumbed to her smiles and laughter and exotic foreign ways. As soon as he walked into the room, Kyril knocked him out with a doorstop and sent him crashing to the carpet.

The next three were not much more difficult, and soon the quartet was bound and gagged, with two of them stripped of their uniforms and papers and all four locked in different rooms.

Now Sean and Kyril had Bulgarian identification, uniforms, and a way to leave the hotel. After the women quickly packed a few things into traveling bags, Sean checked the corridors and, seeing nobody in the hall, hurried the party down the back staircase with Maeve and Arlette sandwiched in between the men.

At the rear of the hotel Sean found a coachman feeding his horses, and upon being offered a good price, he agreed to cart the group to the train station.

The fifteen minutes spent in the first-class lounge at the Sofia station were the most nerve-racking Maeve ever spent in her life. Each time she spotted soldiers outside, she was convinced that that foursome in the hotel had broken out and alerted the entire Bulgarian army. When she finally saw the train arrive and pull up to the platform, she was almost weak with relief.

As the Orient Express was steaming through the countryside bound for Bucharest, Sean and Kyril flung their Bulgarian uniforms out the window and changed into the suits Maeve had thrown into those bags on the way out the door. By the time the train arrived in Bucharest to be met by a detachment of Romanian soldiers looking for Bulgarians, all they could find were two French citizens and two Montenegrins. They wished them a good journey and Godspeed.

*

Things turned out less well for Marc Antoine. Waiting at the palace with the Tsar, the Tsaritza, the entire diplomatic corps, and the French cinematographer, he began to be nervous when the time for Maeve's entrance passed without any sign of her. She was never one to be late for a performance.

Ferdinand was beginning to be furious. With the diplomatic set murmuring in clusters beneath his dazzling chandeliers and the Tsaritza and her ladies looking apprehensive, he tried to be the agreeable host he normally was, but his anger was getting the better of him. This was unheard of—keeping a king waiting! Who the hell did they think they were?

Champagne was passed around the reception room, its sparkle doing a little to put people in a better mood but not enough to keep them from speculating about the reason for this shocking lack of good manners.

By the time the Tsar ordered the head of his household guard to rush over to the Balkan Hotel to hurry the newlyweds along, Maeve and Sean were heading for Romania, safely out of Ferdinand's jurisdiction. With the allied armies only fifty miles from Sofia, nobody farther out was paying any attention to orders issuing from the capital. It was simply a waste of time.

With perfect illogic, Ferdinand held Marc Antoine responsible for the debacle, stripped him of his post as director of the Royal Bulgarian Opera, and ordered him out of the country in twenty-four hours. He had failed him, Ferdinand said; therefore he had to go.

It was a sad farewell for Marc Antoine. The Tsaritza Elenora annoyed her husband by coming to the station to see him off, accompanied by her cairn terriers and ladies-in-waiting. She would miss him, she declared. He had been such a wonderful influence on Sofia's cultural life and such a dear, dear boy.

The tearful ladies-in-waiting expressed their disappointment at never again seeing him perform. The cairn terriers yapped in an agitated way and lifted their legs on the startled stationmaster, who was overwhelmed to greet the Tsaritza at his station and didn't know who the foreigner was but assumed he must be very important.

As Marc Antoine finally boarded the train, he rushed to find an open window so he could wave back to the ladies, who were now taking out lacy handkerchiefs to dry their tears. This was very touching. He had never had a tsaritza weeping over him before.

"Goodbye, Your Majesty," he called out, waving sadly as the huge black locomotive started up on its trip across Europe. "This has been one of the happiest times of my life. I'll always remember your country!"

By way of reply, a lovely white rose came sailing his way, thrown by one of the women on the platform. As the train gathered steam and began picking up speed, Marc Antoine caught the flower, kissed it, and held it aloft, as delighted as if he had received it onstage at the Opéra-Comique. He was leaving, but he was leaving in triumph.

And if he ever met up with Sean Farrell anytime soon, he'd kill him for wrecking what could have been a brilliant career as dictator of cultural life in one of the most flourishing capitals of southeastern Europe.

*

By the time Maeve and Sean reached Paris, the Second Balkan War was over and the peace treaty had been signed in Bucharest. Bulgaria was in mourning. She had gambled on expansion and had lost nearly everything she fought for. Serbia was not satisfied with her acquisitions in Macedonia. She wanted an outlet to the Adriatic as well, and with an independent Albania that was out of the question.

Nikolai Petrovic was in a jubilant mood. Montenegro had gained territory for its efforts and had seen Serbia kept off the coast. That pleased the Montenegrins enormously.

In the aftermath of victory, Sean made a trip to Cetinje to congratulate his father and announce his marriage. He knew Nikolai had been informed by now, but he felt obliged to tell him in person.

"What if he shoots you?" Maeve asked nervously. "Do you think he might?" After Zofia's murder, she feared the wrath of Montenegrin fathers.

"Not at all," he replied. "Father has probably reconciled himself to it by now." But he was going without her—accompanied by his bodyguard. He wouldn't risk Maeve on this trip.

Nikolai apparently had not reconciled himself sufficiently to the marriage, because he greeted his son with a slap that nearly made him reel.

"Disobedient young rascal!" he roared, once the doors were closed behind them. "You defied your father—your king! I should lock you up for this!"

Then, having got that off his chest, Nikolai shrugged. "But I don't care any longer," he declared. "You want a wife who sings? Fine. I was hoping to see you marry a princess."

"But Papa," he said, "Zofia wasn't a princess and you arranged *that* marriage." It still rankled.

"That was politics. I was misled into thinking the Plamanacs would be good for an alliance. It wasn't so." And he didn't care to discuss it.

Nikolai hated admitting he had made a mistake, so he continued in annoyance, "I was hoping to see you become a prince by way of a second marriage. I've wanted that for years."

When Sean looked blank, King Nikolai elaborated. "My boy," he sighed, settling into a large leather armchair, "when you were born, you caused a hell of a problem for me. I loved your mother and I was prepared to take responsibility for both of you—which I did. But Her Majesty hated you and Blondinka so much she made me swear a blood oath that I would never put you on an equal footing with her children. If I did, she swore she'd kill you."

"Queen Milena!" Sean exclaimed. "But she's been a second mother to me!"

Nikolai nodded as he gave a joyless laugh. "Of course! As long as she had her own way, she could be kind. You know, my boy, our

Montenegrin women aren't like those soft, sweet little Europeans. If I had ever shown any sign of giving you a title, you wouldn't have lasted long enough to enjoy it. With them, a promise made is a promise kept. So, to avoid losing you and suffering a tremendous scandal in my household, I decided I would try to arrange a title for you after Zofia died, but in a roundabout way. Germany is full of kings, princes, grand dukes. One of them ought to have a daughter he would part with for a good price. And *he* could make his new son-in-law a prince!"

Sean was dazed. All those years of affection from Queen Milena were nothing but a sham. And Nikolai's objection to Maeve was simply so he could put his Byzantine scheme into play, get his son ennobled and thwart Milena while still observing his solemnly sworn blood oath. No wonder European diplomats had a high regard for the King of Montenegro. The old man was as crafty and devious as any Jesuit!

"Well, then, Father," Sean said at last, "may I have your blessing?"

"Why not?" sighed Nikolai. "I can still do that for you—even though you wrecked my plans to do better."

But as Milena pointed out, the boy had pulled off a tremendous coup by letting Ferdinand release him from prison to marry the girl and then cheating him out of his propaganda effects and making a jackass of him in front of the entire Sofia diplomatic corps. That was such a brilliant stroke that all the diplomats present were still talking about it and sending amusing letters to their friends throughout Europe recounting how the Tsar turned purple with rage upon discovering the deception. It was the funniest story of the war, and everyone was saying how like Nikolai Sean was—cunning and daring. So how could he hold a grudge when his own flesh and blood had completely humiliated Ferdinand, whom he loathed? The boy was a real Petrovic, the King said privately. The royal blood showed.

Geraldine's reaction was surprisingly muted when her son told her what the King had told him. She had always hoped to see Sean given a title and had never been able to understand why Nikolai failed to do this—since his affection for his son was real.

"So the old she-devil would have killed you," she murmured. "That explains a lot now. The hypocrite! I hope she sees all her children come to a bad end! That's my curse on *her*!"

*

Maeve was relieved to welcome her husband home just in time to witness the birth of their child, a son they named Nicholas—a lively baby with his mother's auburn hair. Maeve considered that her personal triumph, a redhead at last! Everyone said he looked just like her.

Hanno was pleased with his new brother, liked his stepfather, and hoped this might be a sign that Mama was going to stay put for a while. He hated being left behind with tutors while she traipsed all over the Continent, singing for strangers. He loved his mama and missed her terribly.

Marc Antoine was persuaded with a great deal of tact to be one of Nick's godfathers. Despite his anger over the way he had to leave Bulgaria he adored Maeve, and he was somewhat pacified by the outpouring of affection that welcomed him home to Paris. His public was delighted to have him back and they begged him never to leave them again. He was a Frenchman and he belonged with them.

*

Europe had just come close to a general war and had drawn back in apprehension. Austria-Hungary was congratulating herself on keeping the treacherous Serbs and other pan-Slav crusaders out of her backyard with threats of war. Russia was reassessing her war preparedness. Germany was sure her Kaiser had saved her from a disastrous intervention in the Balkan scrap. And Tsar Ferdinand of Bulgaria was bitterly biding his time—and switching the emphasis in Bulgarian diplomacy from ties with Russia to a rapprochement with Germany.

*

By January 1914, Maeve was singing once more—Octavian in *Der Rosenkavalier* under the baton of its creator, Richard Strauss, at a glittering gala in Dresden, Tosca in Berlin for Kaiser Wilhelm, and Mimi in *La Bohème* at La Scala in Milan. Sean had no problem with that, he said. He admired a woman who could rouse an auditorium of strangers to wild adoration. That quality was usually found only in royalty and he was rather used to it.

Maeve loved her new husband for his easygoing ways and even made a sacrifice for him—she passed up the chance to perform on the lucrative North and South American circuits and concentrated on Europe and Russia. She wanted to be close to home these days, and while European opera houses were only a few days away by train, America was simply too far. And since she was in demand at outrageous salaries all over the Continent, this was hardly cause for tears.

Nikolai of Montenegro made a gracious gesture and appointed Sean his ambassador to France, a prestigious post that Sean had coveted for years. It was a reward for besting Tsar Ferdinand. Besides, the boy wouldn't do any worse than past ambassadors. He was trustworthy, loyal to his father, and intelligent enough not to be taken in by double-talk, although he could dissemble with the best of them if he had to. Most important, he was a Petrovic and not likely to be subverted by foreign interests.

When Pathé, the French film company, unexpectedly sent Maeve a copy of the film they had taken of her wedding she had been enchanted. Called *"Les Noces Balkaniques,"* it proved a major hit of 1913 at cinemas all over Europe, and two other film companies now approached her to inquire if La Devereux might possibly care to expand her repertoire by doing moving pictures during the interseason. Maeve was astonished.

"Why not try it?" Moira advised. "You looked very fine, and everybody on the Continent already knows you. Even Sarah Bernhardt does them. And nobody ever suggested it cheapened *her* art."

That was an idea, Maeve admitted. They also wanted to know if she could persuade that handsome fellow de Marigny to come along as well. The women just went mad for him. He'd be a major draw. And best of all, Pathé argued, none of this would harm a singer's voice. It was something to consider.

With all these plans bubbling away, 1914 seemed to offer nothing but joy. In the summer, shortly after Maeve's annual appearance at Covent Garden, she, Sean, the two boys, Arlette, Kyril, and a flock of servants boarded the Nord Express for a vacation in Russia as guests of Grand Duchess Stana and her imposing husband, Grand Duke Nicholas Nicolaievich.

Summer days playing tennis or croquet on the rolling expanse of green lawn surrounding Stana's estate in the environs of St. Petersburg gave way to summer nights bathed in the famous soft, pearly haze of the high northern latitudes. Maeve never forgot those wonderful evenings, enveloped in the magical glow of Petersburg's "white nights."

While Gypsies sang beneath milky midnight skies, parties of guests in elegant summer uniforms and delicate silk evening gowns clustered around their host and hostess on the lawn, drinking in the atmosphere and glass upon glass of Moët. Of course, some of the officers had other things on their minds besides Gypsy love songs in the midnight breeze.

"Are they preparing for a war?" Maeve asked her husband after a particularly boisterous evening of champagne toasts to "our Balkan brothers."

"They're always preparing for a war." He smiled as he wrapped his arms around her in the comfort of their bed. "They're officers. They get paid to prepare for war."

"But they sound as if they think there's going to be one soon!"

"There will be one someday. But let's hope it's in the very distant future. Go to sleep, darling. It's late."

Maeve still wasn't satisfied. The atmosphere was so martial she wondered if perhaps she had missed something. Was she so caught up in the make-believe world of opera that she'd been blind to real life?

Sean didn't seem worried, yet Stana and Grand Duke Nicholas were so keyed up—as if there was something in the air only they could sense, something exciting. Stana sometimes said she was blessed with second sight. Perhaps she was.

"What would start another war in the Balkans?" Maeve suddenly demanded.

At that, Sean blinked and sat up, looking serious. He didn't understand why his lovely wife was so concerned about the prospect of war on this magical, flower-scented summer evening, but he would try to be patient.

"A Serbian attack on Austria-Hungary," he replied. "Not likely in view of the size of each country, but not unlikely either in view of Serb megalomania. Our friend Colonel Apis told me just after the Peace of Bucharest was signed that Serbia was outraged at the Austrian maneuvering, which prevented her from gaining an outlet to the Adriatic. He promised he was going to set fire to the four corners of Europe in revenge."

Despite the mildness of the summer night, Maeve shuddered. "Slimy toad. He probably would!"

Sean laughed and put his arm around her. "Apis was downing his sixth glass of rakia in a café in Venice when he said this. It was the liquor and his wishful thinking. He probably hates Montenegro as much as he hates Austria. He hates everybody. He's a fanatic pan-Slav maniac who inspires silly little boys to dream about liberating every Slav in Franz Joseph's empire. That's all."

"That's enough! What if he actually starts a war?"

Sean smiled. "It would be a case of the lion versus the mouse. It would be Serbia's death knell and Apis knows it. He's a maniac but he's not a total fool."

"How can you tell the difference?" she replied.

After that, Maeve kept her ears attuned to military matters and became an attentive audience for Grand Duke Nicholas, who liked her to entertain him with the French music hall ditties she had sung so long ago as Florine. He had been one of her fans.

It was during one of those lighthearted family gatherings, with Stana and Nicholas and their friends sitting on the lawn in the pearly twilight and listening to "Florine" as she sang a charming, silly song about a girl named Lilli and her boyfriend Jojo, that His Highness was suddenly called to the telephone.

When he returned to the party he looked so strange, Maeve stopped in midperformance and stared. Stana took his hand, fearful of some family tragedy. Was it Papa? The Tsarevich? The Tsar?

"Ladies and gentlemen," Nicholas Nicolaievich announced in solemn tones, "this morning in Bosnia, the heir to the Austro-Hungarian Empire was assassinated by terrorists . . ."

A gasp of shock greeted the news. Officers glanced at the Grand Duke and at each other. Ladies murmured apprehensively. A few pious souls crossed themselves.

"Who were the terrorists?" Maeve asked suddenly, feeling her knees start to shake.

"Serbs—according to the Austrians," Nicholas replied. "We'll have to wait for the Ballplatz to confirm it, of course. I'm sure they will."

In her mind she could hear Sean relaying Colonel Apis's boast of setting fire to the four corners of Europe. Oh my God, she thought. Had he really done it?

With most of Europe, including its kings, on their summer vacations, war talk flared up, then died out except among the chancelleries and foreign offices. By July, when French president Poincaré arrived in St. Petersburg to pay an official visit, Sean noticed a hesitancy on the part of the Tsar to be drawn into talk of war. He also noticed how determined his sisters Militza and Stana were to talk of nothing else.

*

In the last days of July 1914, Sean received a telegram in St. Petersburg from Nikolai Petrovic in Cetinje. "Am prepared to declare war on Austria," it stated. "Return to Paris embassy and stay there. Royal order. Do not leave France. Need you as liaison to the French."

Maeve read the telegram, shook her head, and sank down on a nearby sofa. Her hands were shaking as she placed the message on the table at her elbow.

War mobilization notices appeared on public buildings the day after Maeve and Sean returned home to France. Paris awoke from its sleepy summer lull to become a capital again, decked out in tricolor bunting, with every café orator proclaiming it was France's sacred duty to fight the *boche* and liberate Alsace-Lorraine. Isolated pacifists were beaten up by cheering patriotic mobs, and men in uniform were suddenly everywhere.

In all her career Maeve had never heard the "Marseillaise" sung so often or so emotionally. At a diplomatic reception of allied ambassadors, she was startled to see two elderly gentlemen singing the national anthem with tears rolling down their cheeks.

"Alsatians," Sean told her afterward. "One of them told me he'd like to hear it sung once more in Strasbourg before he dies."

"This is going to be worse than that fracas in the Balkans, isn't it?" she asked. "It's going to suck in every country in Europe before it's over."

"It's already started to."

"Well, I suppose that puts an end to my German and Austrian tours this winter. The Kaiser will just have to do without me."

"And I'd suggest you put your Prussian Order of the Red Eagle in storage until this all blows over. I don't want you lynched by some crazed patriotic mob."

Maeve smiled ruefully. She was so proud of that decoration. It had been her first and was still her favorite. And it looked splendid against a white satin gown! She liked Wilhelm for giving it to her.

"Sean," she said seriously, "come what may, I'm staying here with you in Paris—even if the Germans besiege the city. Of course," she added, "if they show any sign of that, I'll pack Mama and the children off to a safe place. But I'm staying."

"Don't be absurd! I couldn't let you do that." He was appalled.

"Darling," she replied, "I'm telling, not asking."

There was no sense arguing with Maeve, he thought. If the Germans besieged Paris, of course he would send her to safety. But why quarrel about it now? They might as well just enjoy whatever remained of this peaceful summer day.

Maeve slipped her arm through his as they strolled down the Champs-Elysées, watching a troop column roll by bound for the Gare de l'Est, the boys all eager to shoot their *boche* and win a medal. "Darling," she announced, "I'll arrange Red Cross concerts. I'm good at raising money that way. Marc Antoine will help. We'll fund first-aid stations."

"What about the Opéra-Comique?"

"Don't worry. I'll fit it all in. Mama can play hostess at the embassy if she has to. She loves that. She'll be as patriotic as any born Montenegrin."

"Don't you think Charlie might want to return to America?"

"No. His home is here. I can't see him turning tail now. He'll organize American aid for France, if I know him. We'll all be in it together. Poor Hanno. We'll have to call him Jean for the duration!"

"You make it sound like a game. It isn't, you know. It's abominable."

"Then all the more reason to be together now," she replied quietly. "You, me, Mama, Charlie, the boys. We're family and that's going to be our strength and see us through."

"Even if they set fire to the four corners of Europe?" he asked bitterly, recalling Colonel Apis's words.

"Especially then." She would never leave him to take shelter by herself.

"It will be rough. You have no idea how bad it can get."

"It was rough in South Africa—and look what happened to us after that. We'll be all right, Sean. It's not our fate to go under so easily."

She looked up at him and gently kissed him in the late-afternoon sunlight while a truckload of soldiers waved at them and cheered, thinking he was also about to go off to the war.

"You know," Maeve said as they walked together, arm in arm, back to the embassy, "I knew the first time I met you that you were my fate. I really did."

"I wish I could make the same claim. It was the way you carried on that day on the Nevsky that convinced *me*. And I wasn't able to do a thing about it!" He smiled, still able to recall it so vividly. "What a wildcat! Do you think we'll grow old together?" he asked suddenly.

"We'd better," Maeve replied. "And although the outlook doesn't look too promising for a long life at the moment, I think we'll manage very well in the end, don't you?"

He paused in the middle of the crowded sidewalk and kissed her. "If I didn't believe that," he replied, "I wouldn't want to wake up in the morning."

And Sean Farrell and Maeve Devereux strolled calmly into the embassy to plan for the duration.